Nightschool

THE WEIRN BOOKS
Collector's Edition 1

SVETLANA CHMAKOVA

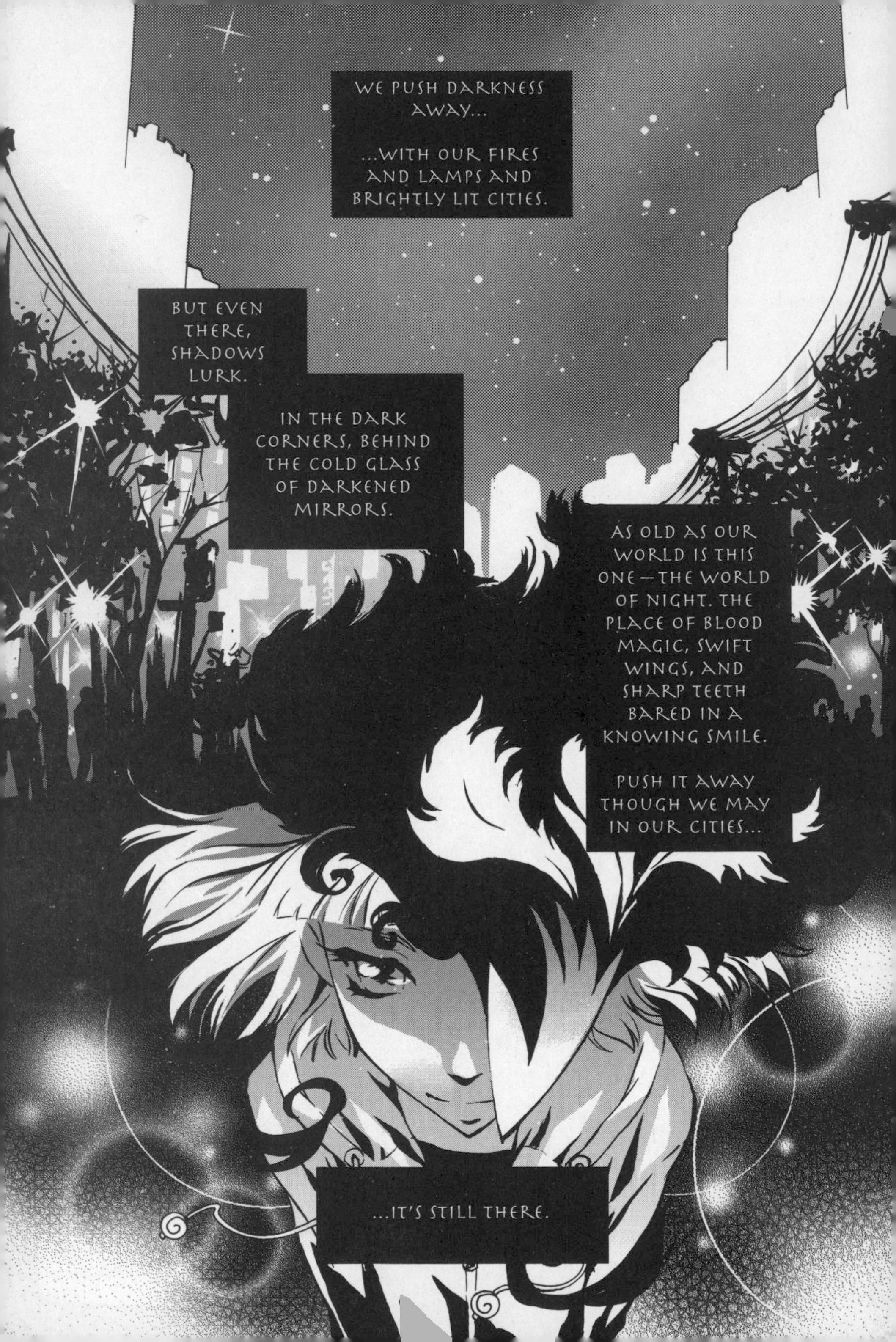
WE PUSH DARKNESS AWAY...
...WITH OUR FIRES AND LAMPS AND BRIGHTLY LIT CITIES.
BUT EVEN THERE, SHADOWS LURK.
IN THE DARK CORNERS, BEHIND THE COLD GLASS OF DARKENED MIRRORS.
AS OLD AS OUR WORLD IS THIS ONE—THE WORLD OF NIGHT. THE PLACE OF BLOOD MAGIC, SWIFT WINGS, AND SHARP TEETH BARED IN A KNOWING SMILE.
PUSH IT AWAY THOUGH WE MAY IN OUR CITIES...
...IT'S STILL THERE.

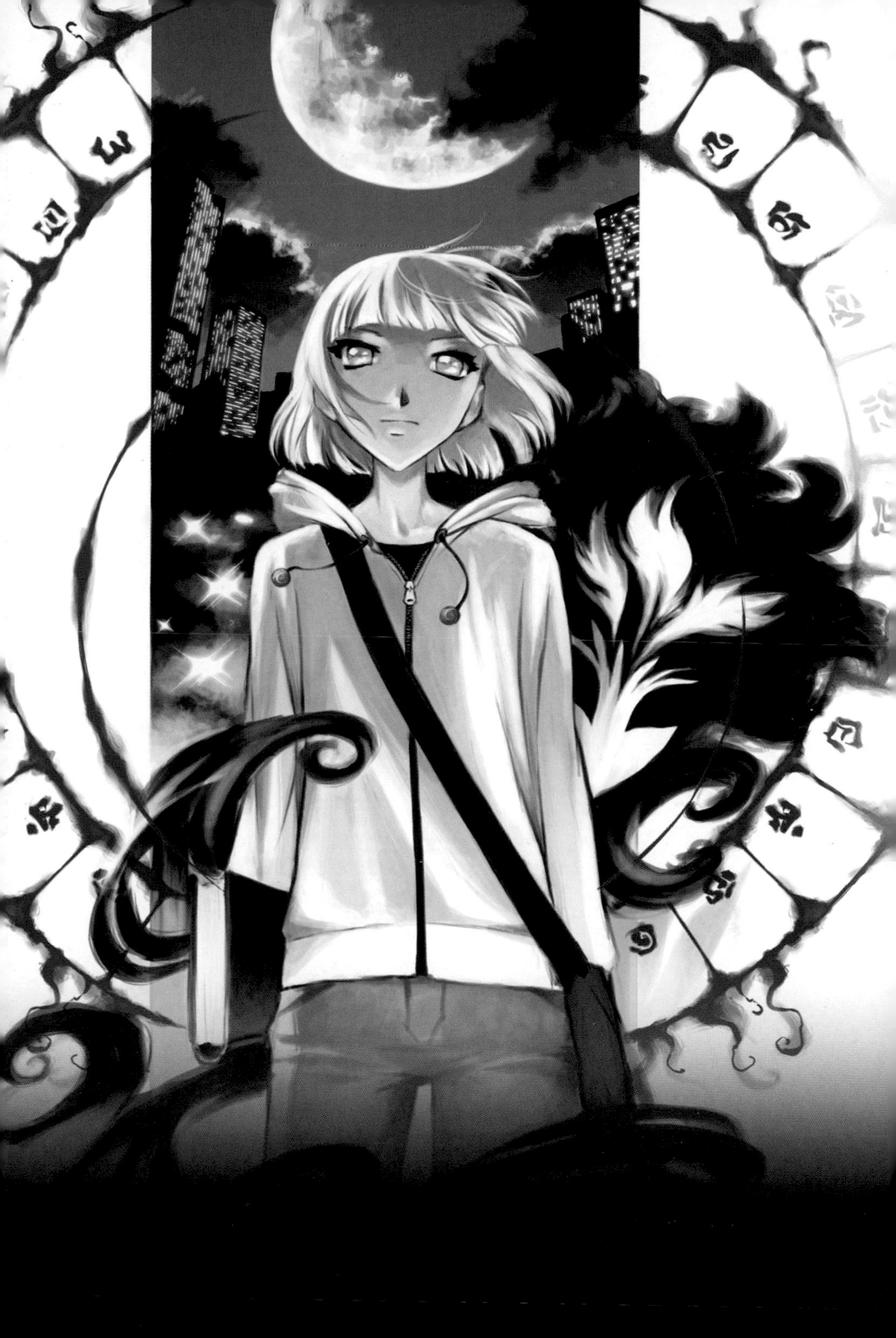

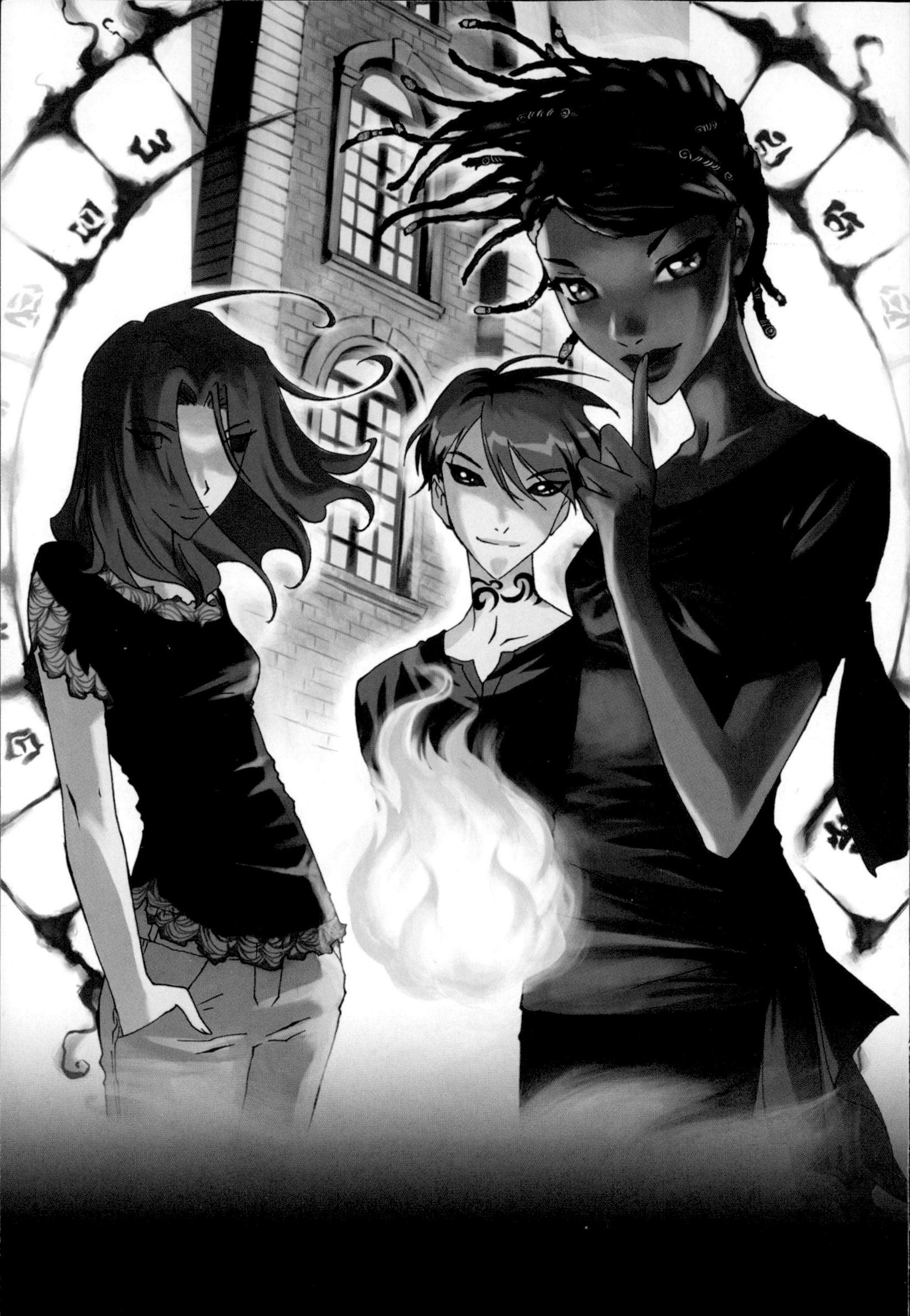

Dedicated to my parents

and

Barry McCarthy

Thank you ♡

Contents

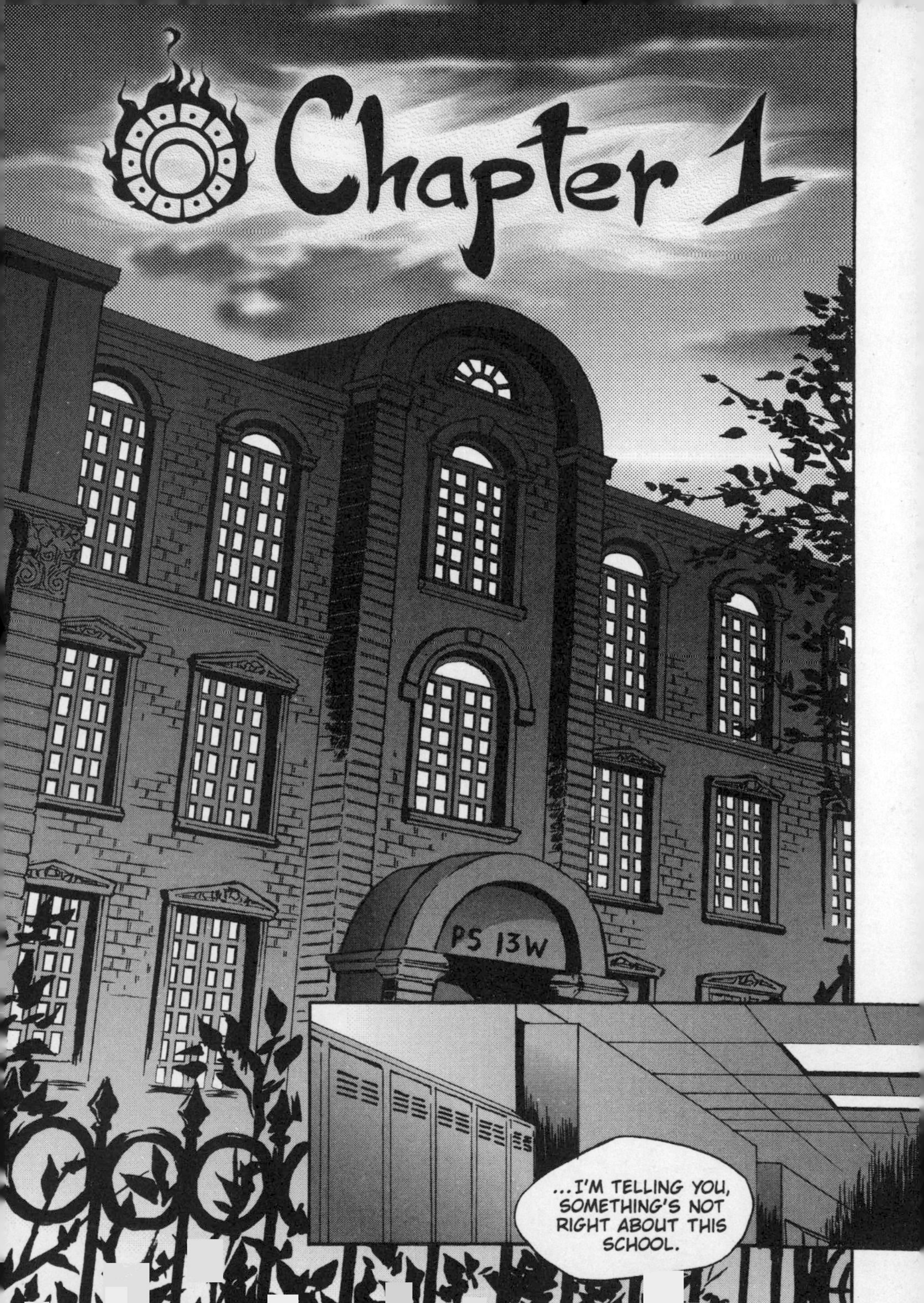
Chapter 1
PS 13W
...I'M TELLING YOU, SOMETHING'S NOT RIGHT ABOUT THIS SCHOOL.

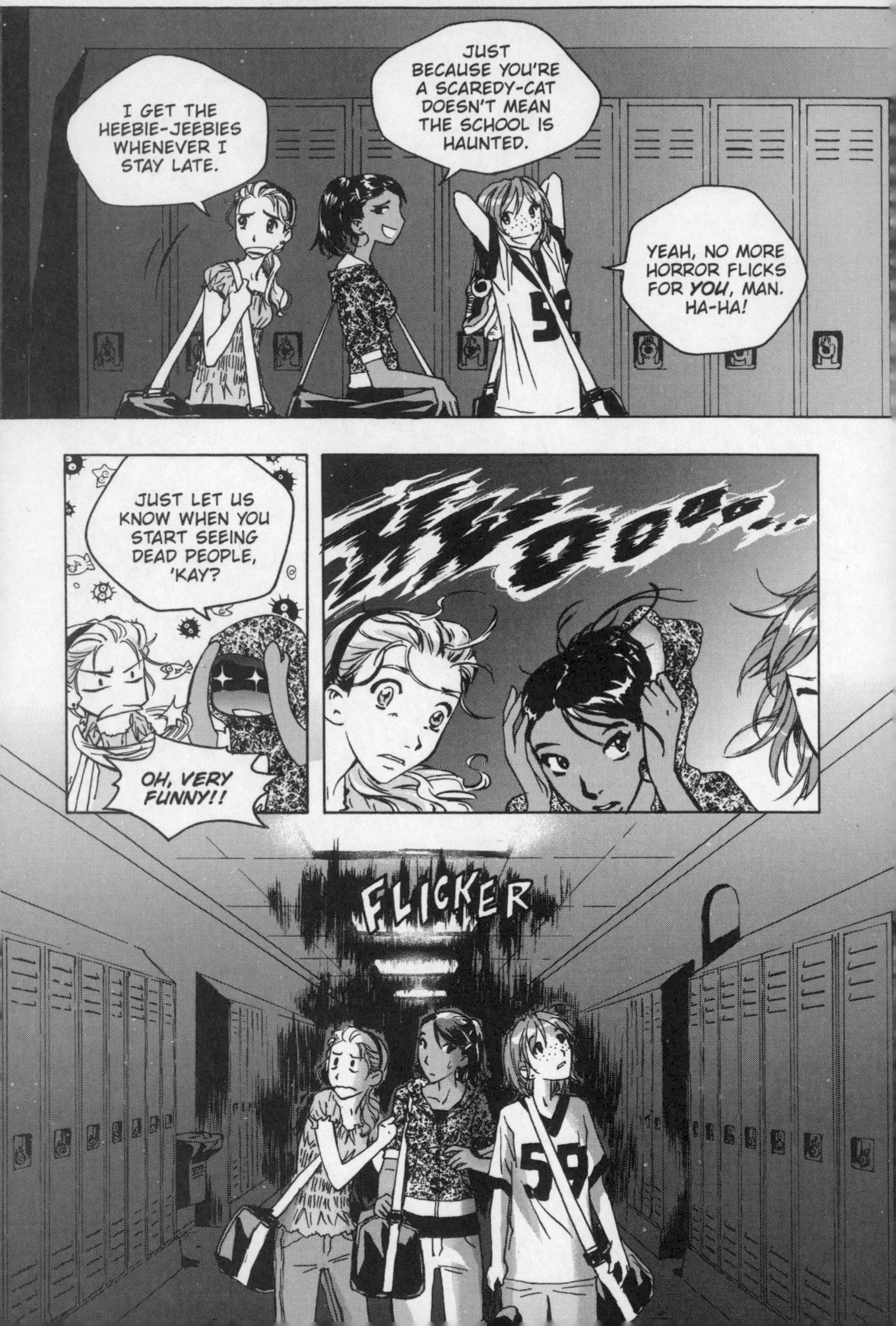
I GET THE HEEBIE-JEEBIES WHENEVER I STAY LATE.
JUST BECAUSE YOU'RE A SCAREDY-CAT DOESN'T MEAN THE SCHOOL IS HAUNTED.
YEAH, NO MORE HORROR FLICKS FOR *YOU*, MAN. HA-HA!
JUST LET US KNOW WHEN YOU START SEEING DEAD PEOPLE, 'KAY?
OH, VERY FUNNY!!
FWOOooo...
FLICKER

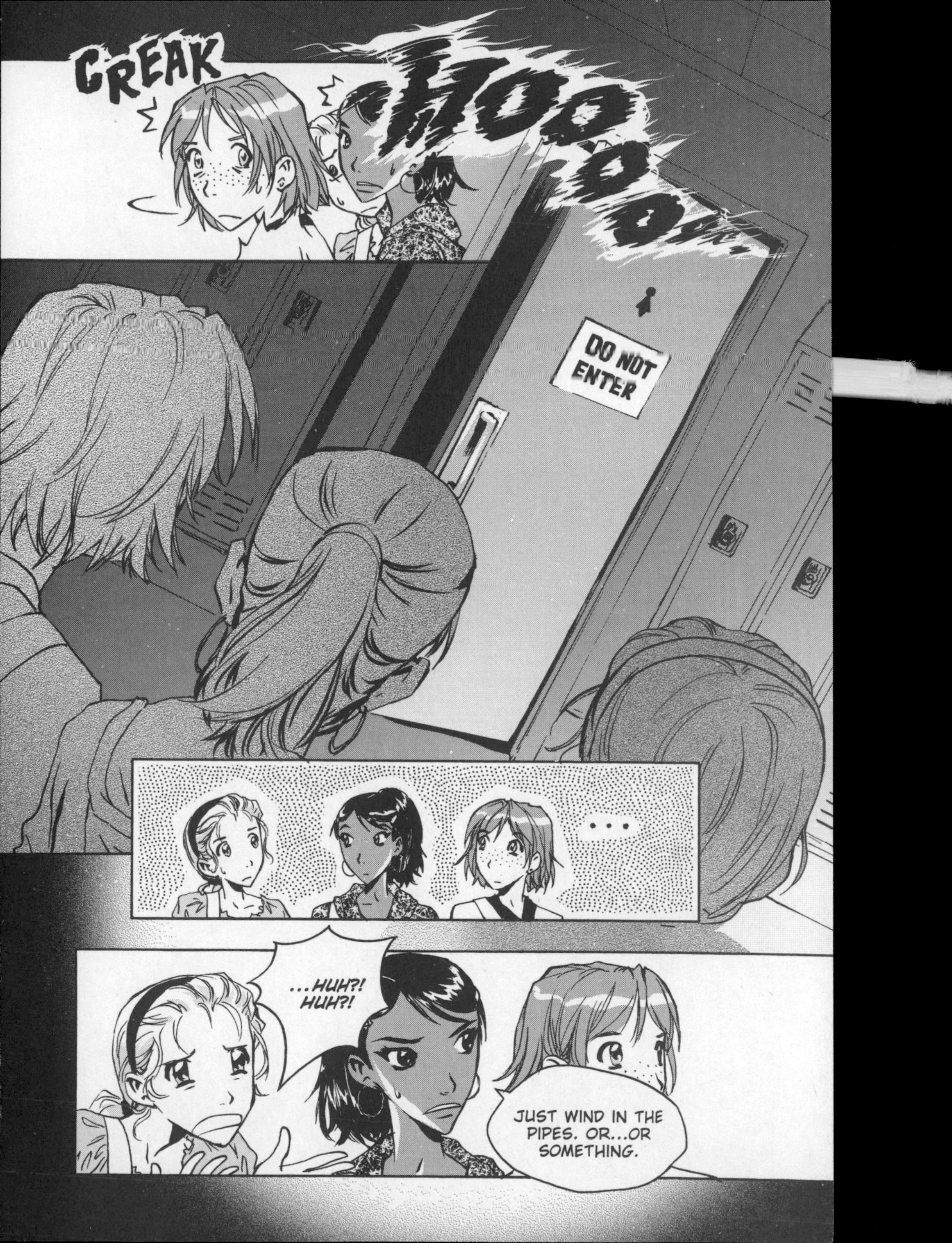
CREAK
WHOOOOO...
DO NOT ENTER
...
...HUH?! HUH?!
JUST WIND IN THE PIPES. OR...OR SOMETHING.

PEEK

ARGH, DON'T GO IN THERE!!

THIS ONE'S BEEN CLOSED SINCE LAST YEAR. AND TELL ME IT DOESN'T GIVE YOU THE CREEPS!

WELL, IT'S PRETTY DARK, BUT OTHER THAN THAT...

HEY, THE LIGHT SWITCH DOESN'T WORK.

WOW, THIS MIRROR'S HUGE.

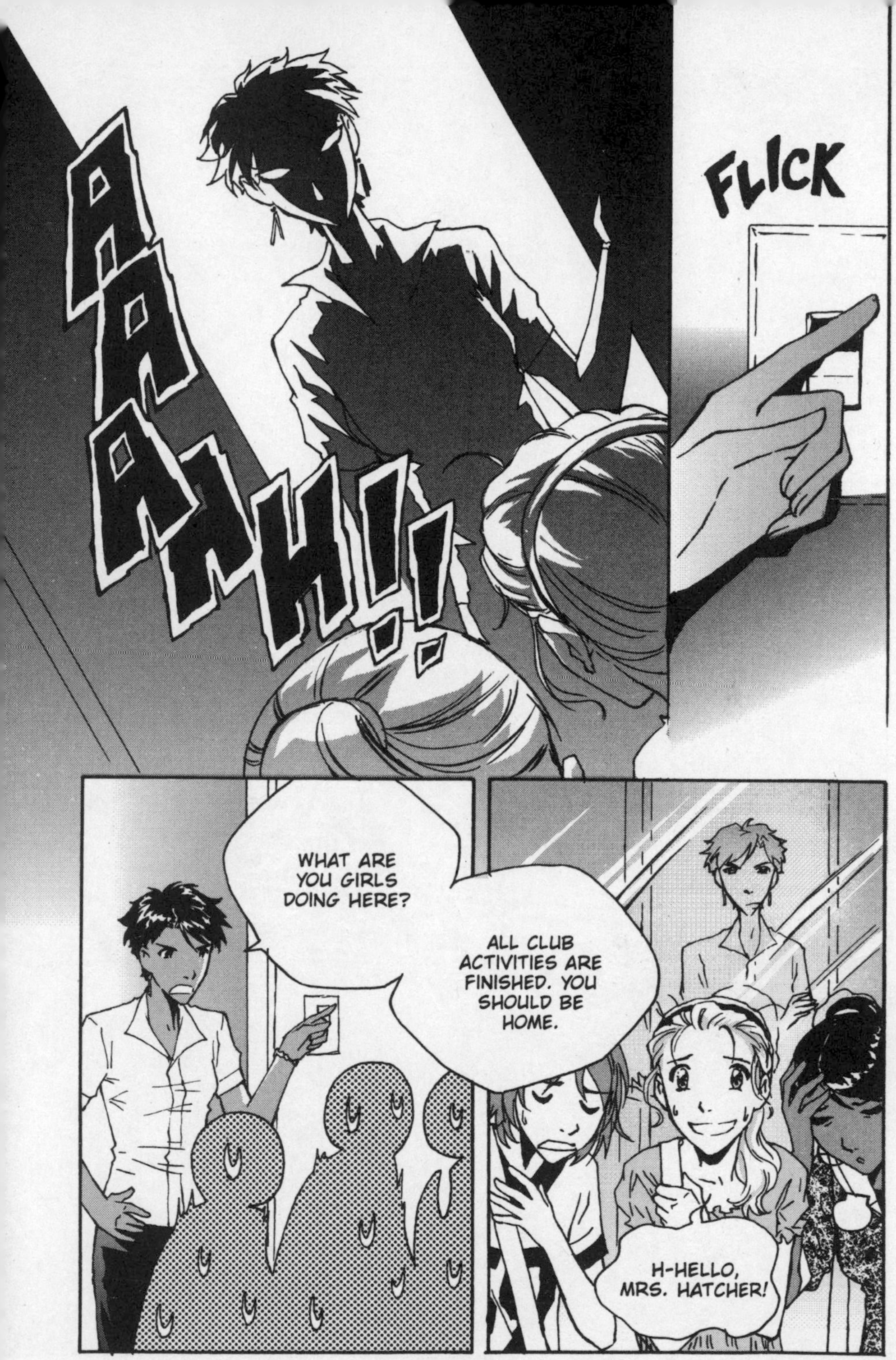
AAAAAH!!
FLICK
WHAT ARE YOU GIRLS DOING HERE?
ALL CLUB ACTIVITIES ARE FINISHED. YOU SHOULD BE HOME.
H-HELLO, MRS. HATCHER!

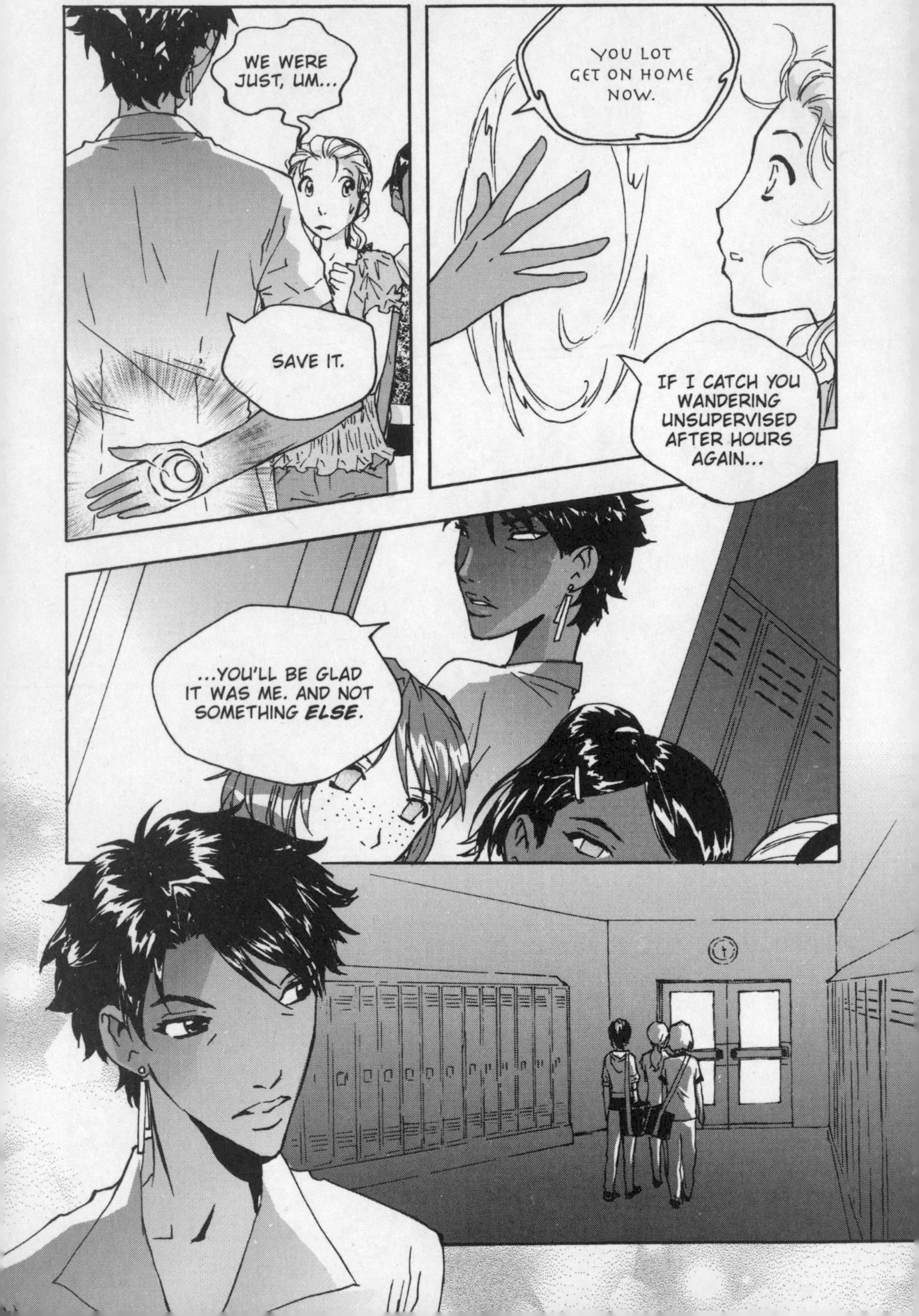
WE WERE JUST, UM...
SAVE IT.
YOU LOT GET ON HOME NOW.
IF I CATCH YOU WANDERING UNSUPERVISED AFTER HOURS AGAIN...
...YOU'LL BE GLAD IT WAS ME. AND NOT SOMETHING ELSE.

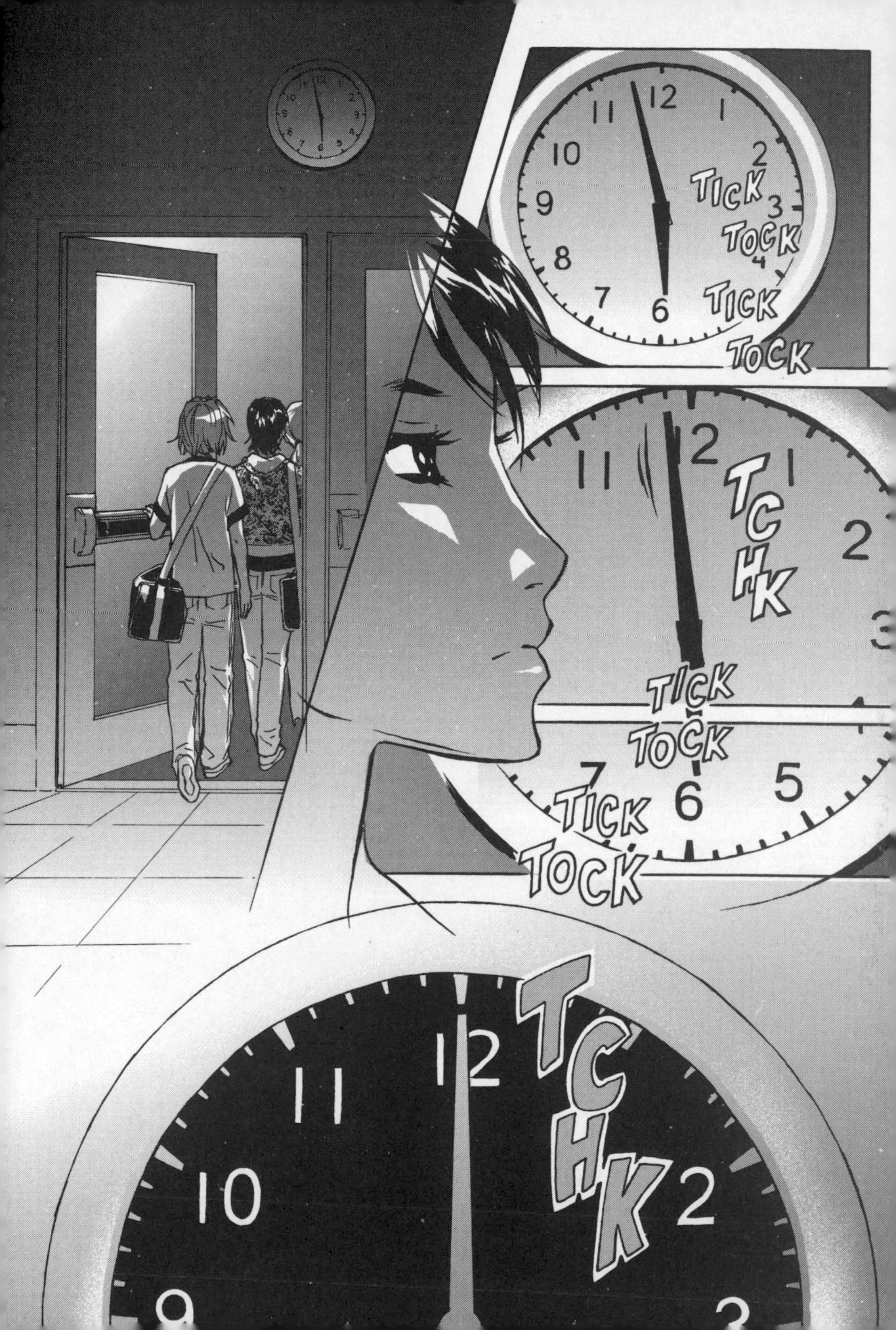
TICK
TOCK
TICK
TOCK
TCHK
TICK
TOCK
TICK
TOCK
TCHK

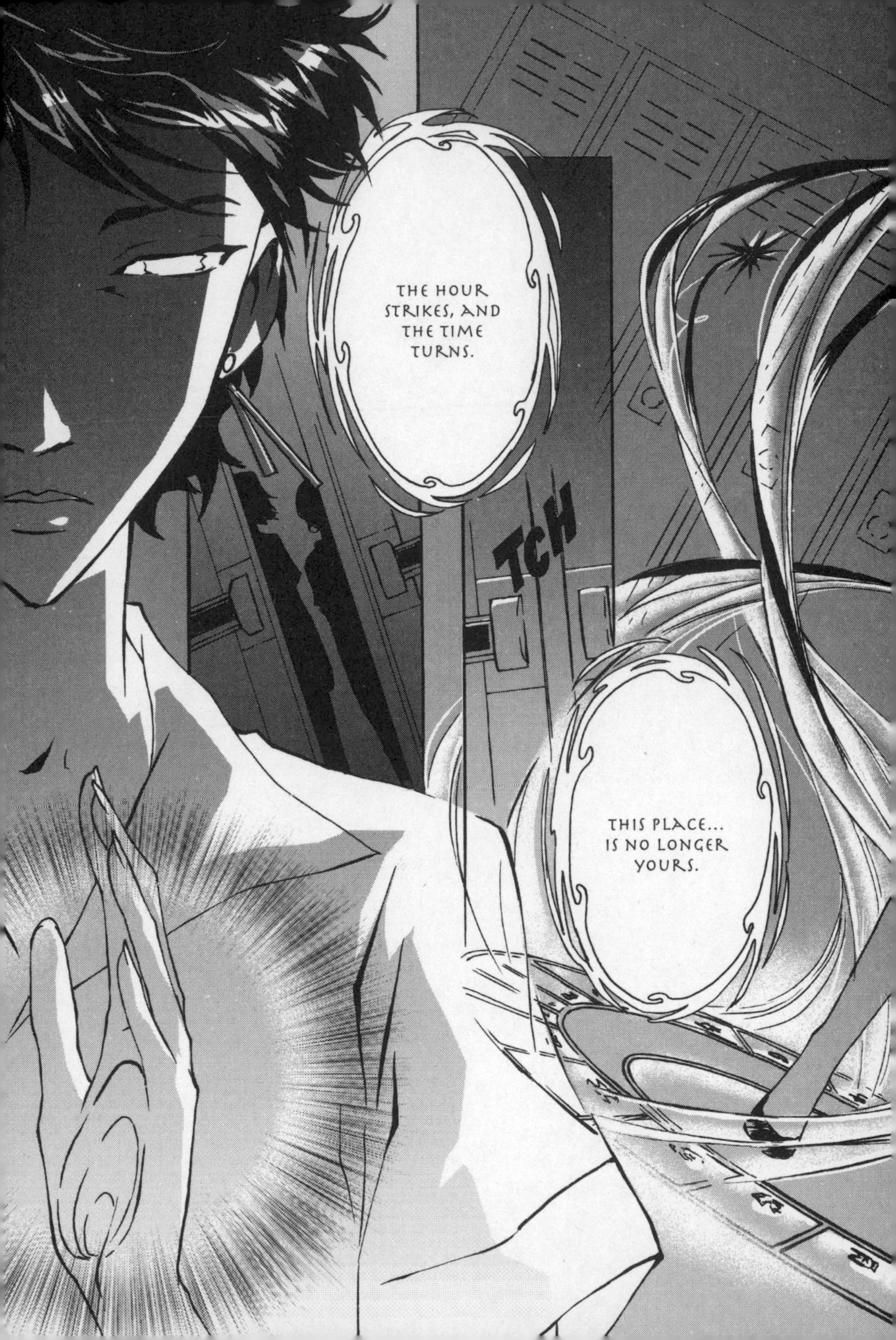
THE HOUR STRIKES, AND THE TIME TURNS.
TCH
THIS PLACE... IS NO LONGER YOURS.

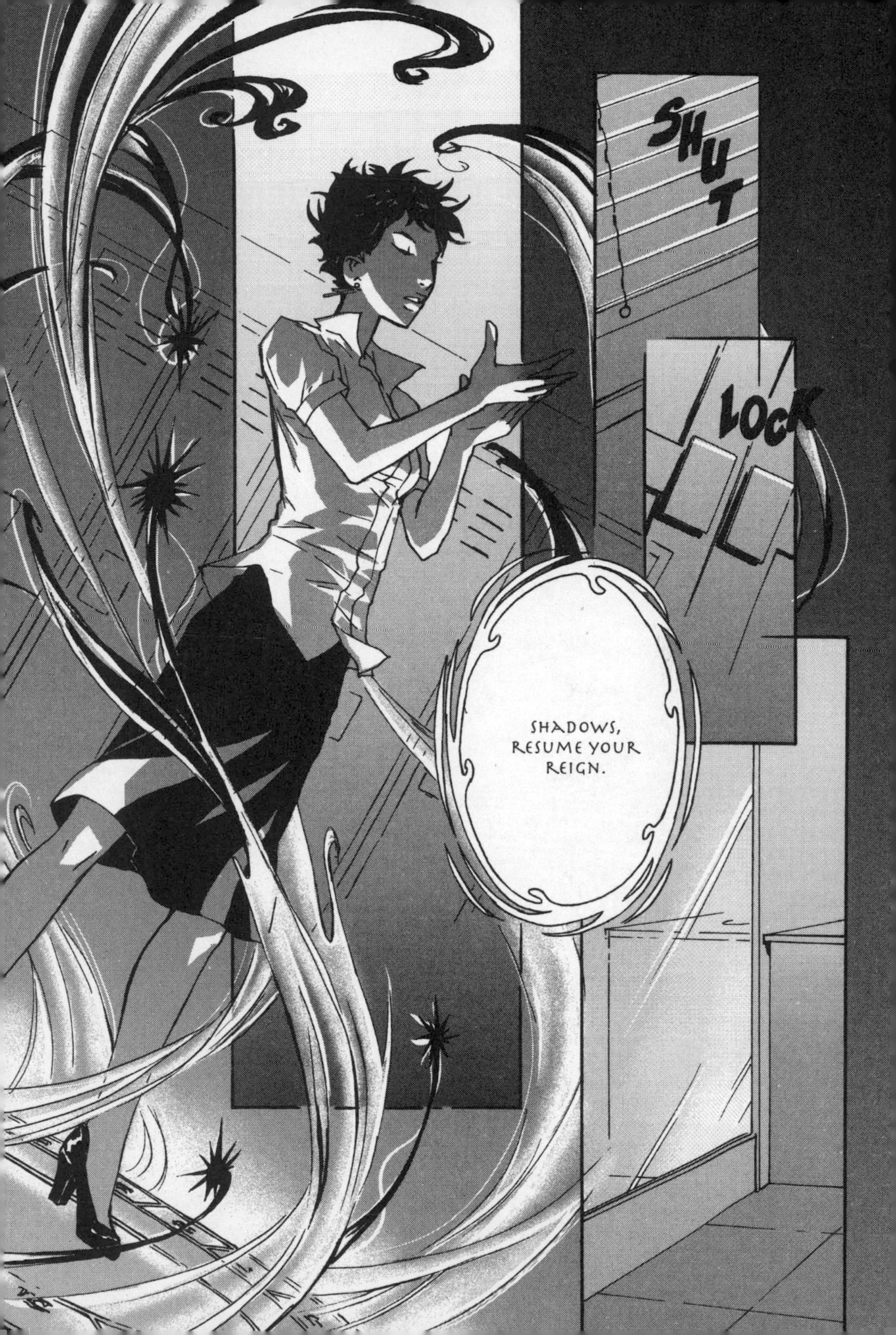
SHUT
LOCK
SHADOWS, RESUME YOUR REIGN.

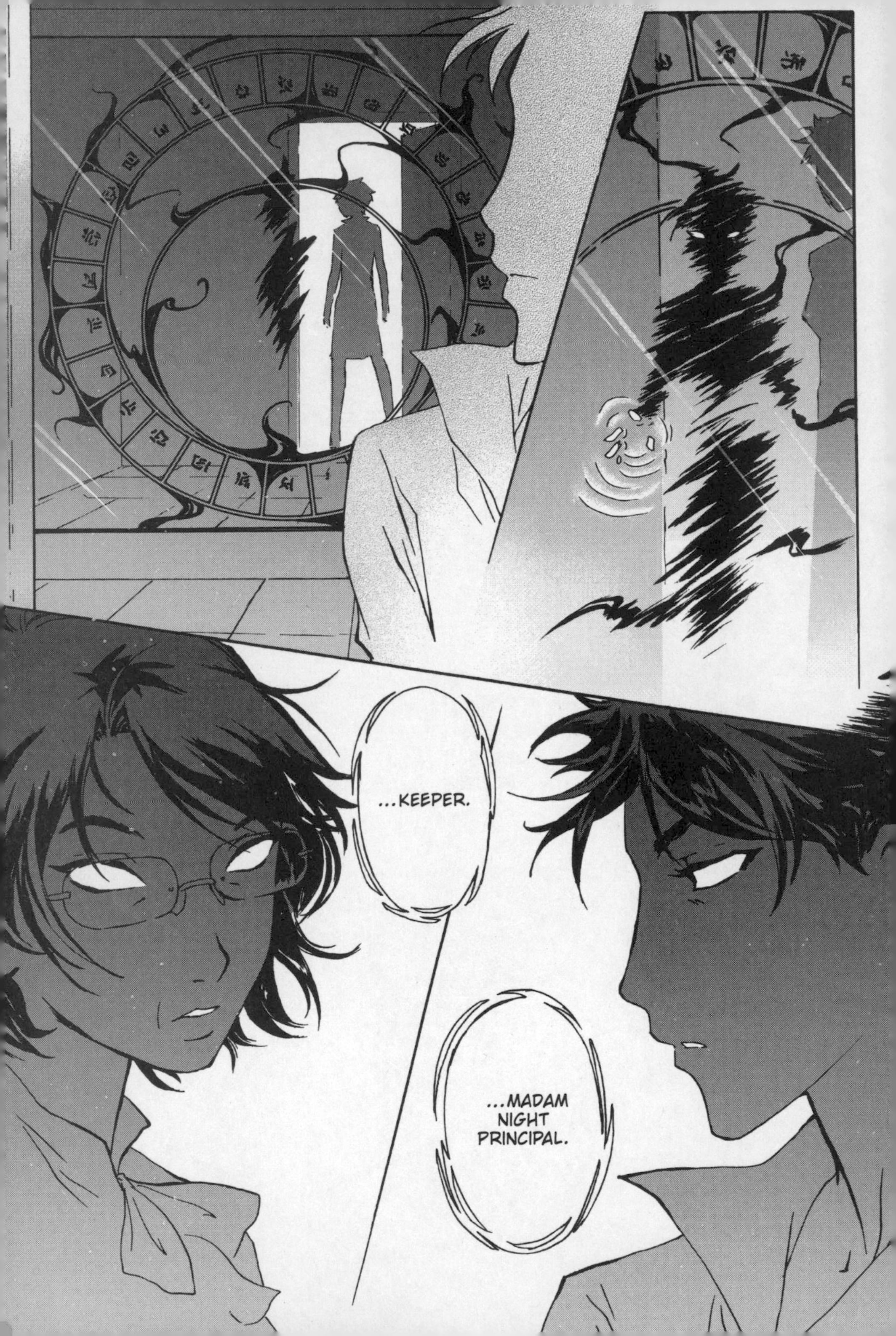
...KEEPER.
...MADAM NIGHT PRINCIPAL.

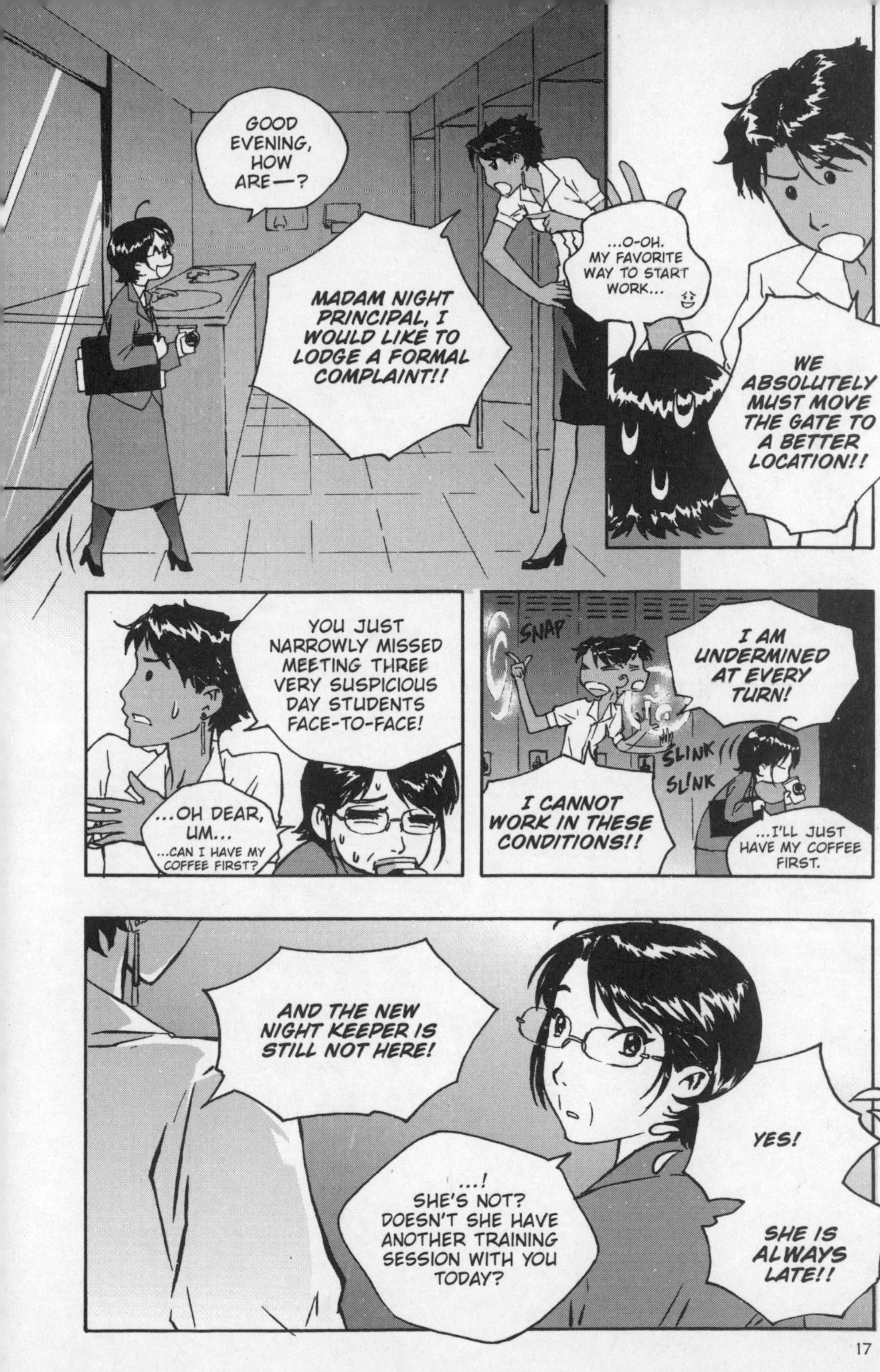
GOOD EVENING, HOW ARE—?
MADAM NIGHT PRINCIPAL, I WOULD LIKE TO LODGE A FORMAL COMPLAINT!!
...O-OH. MY FAVORITE WAY TO START WORK...
WE ABSOLUTELY MUST MOVE THE GATE TO A BETTER LOCATION!!
YOU JUST NARROWLY MISSED MEETING THREE VERY SUSPICIOUS DAY STUDENTS FACE-TO-FACE!
...OH DEAR, UM...
...CAN I HAVE MY COFFEE FIRST?
SNAP
I AM UNDERMINED AT EVERY TURN!
SLINK
SLINK
I CANNOT WORK IN THESE CONDITIONS!!
...I'LL JUST HAVE MY COFFEE FIRST.
AND THE NEW NIGHT KEEPER IS STILL NOT HERE!
...!
SHE'S NOT? DOESN'T SHE HAVE ANOTHER TRAINING SESSION WITH YOU TODAY?
YES!
SHE IS ALWAYS LATE!!

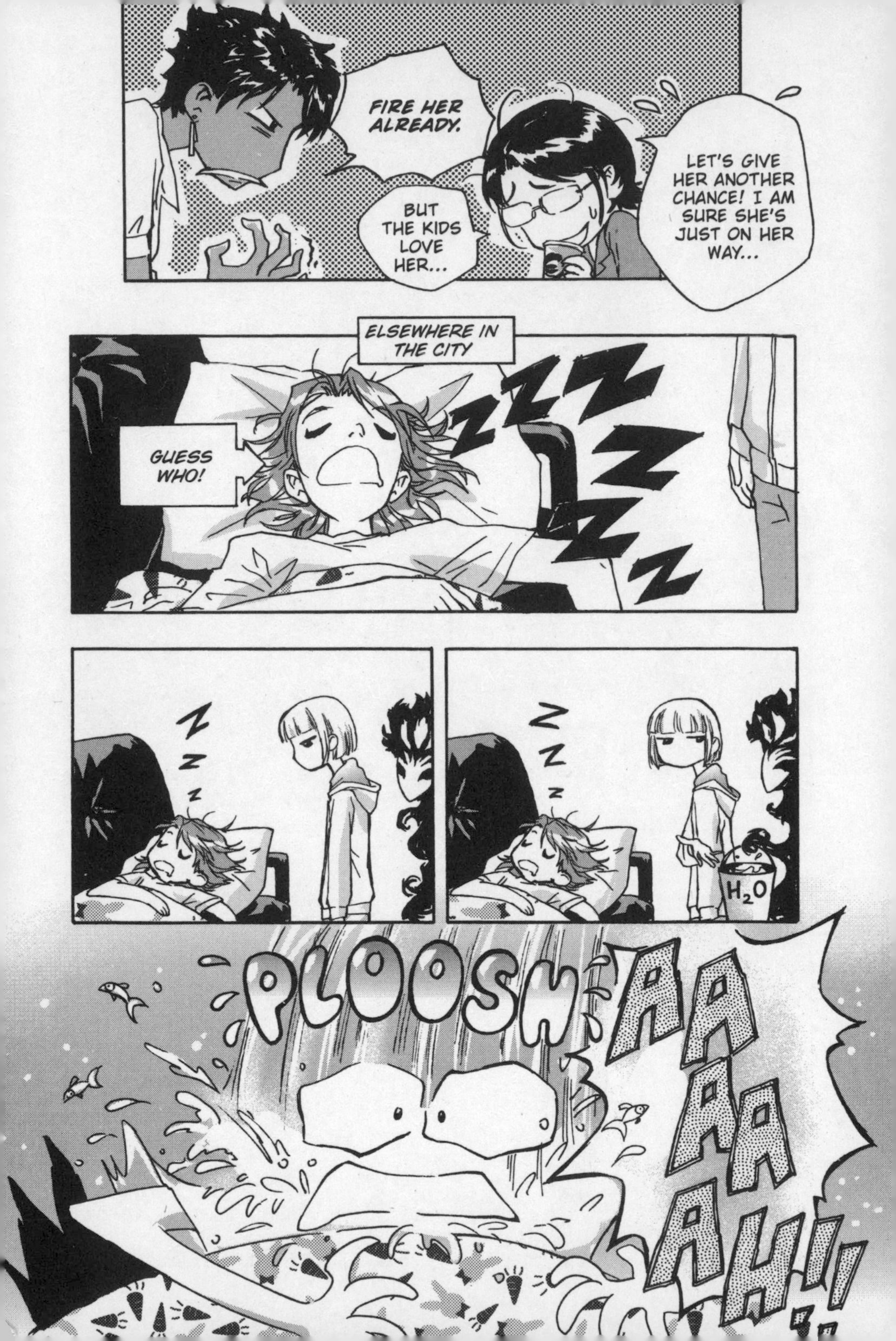
FIRE HER ALREADY.
BUT THE KIDS LOVE HER...
LET'S GIVE HER ANOTHER CHANCE! I AM SURE SHE'S JUST ON HER WAY...
ELSEWHERE IN THE CITY
GUESS WHO!
ZZZZZZ
ZZZ
ZZZ
H_2O
PLOOSH
AAAAAAHH!!

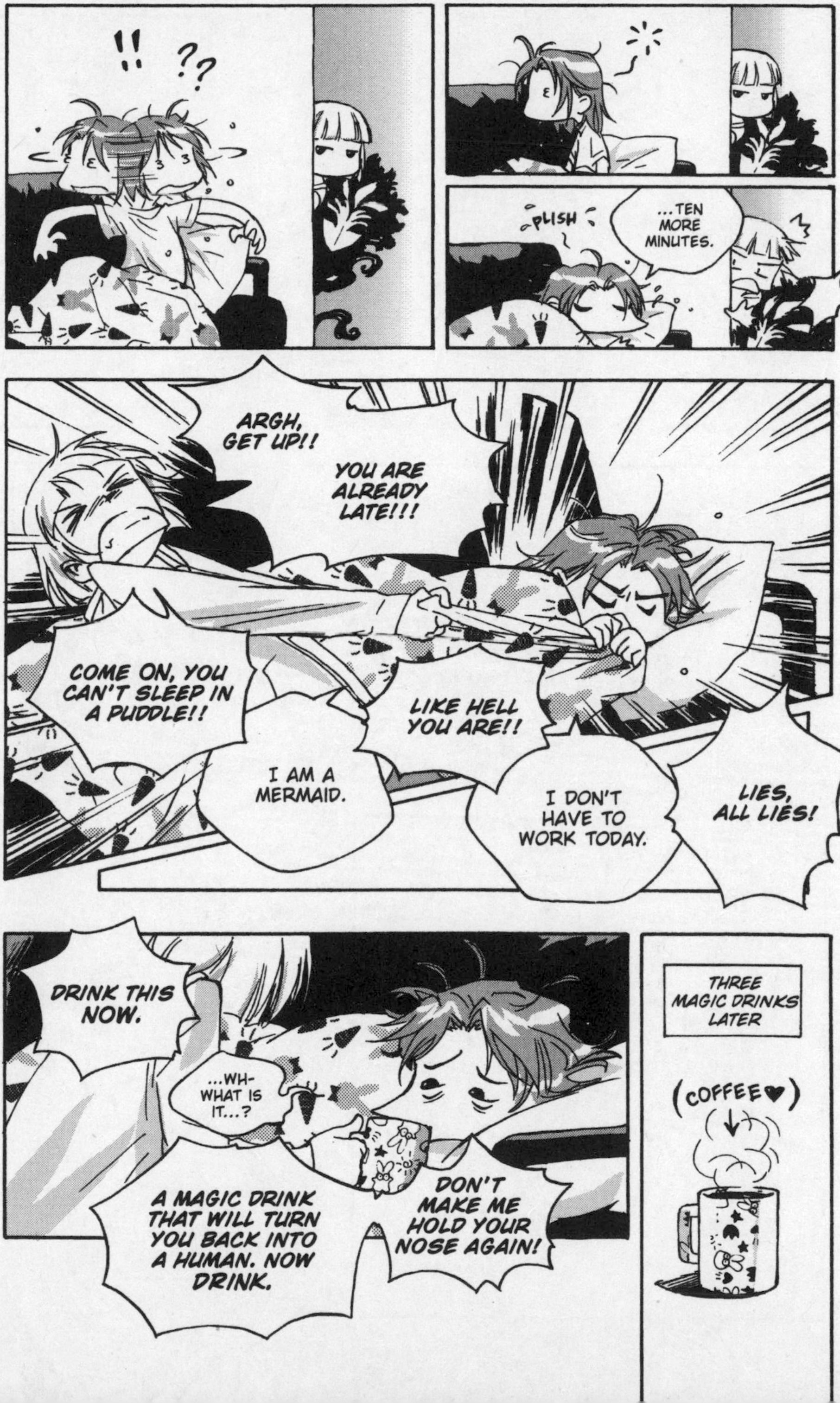
!!
??
PLISH
...TEN MORE MINUTES.
ARGH, GET UP!!
YOU ARE ALREADY LATE!!!
COME ON, YOU CAN'T SLEEP IN A PUDDLE!!
I AM A MERMAID.
LIKE HELL YOU ARE!!
I DON'T HAVE TO WORK TODAY.
LIES, ALL LIES!
DRINK THIS NOW.
...WH-WHAT IS IT...?
A MAGIC DRINK THAT WILL TURN YOU BACK INTO A HUMAN. NOW DRINK.
DON'T MAKE ME HOLD YOUR NOSE AGAIN!
THREE MAGIC DRINKS LATER
(COFFEE♥)

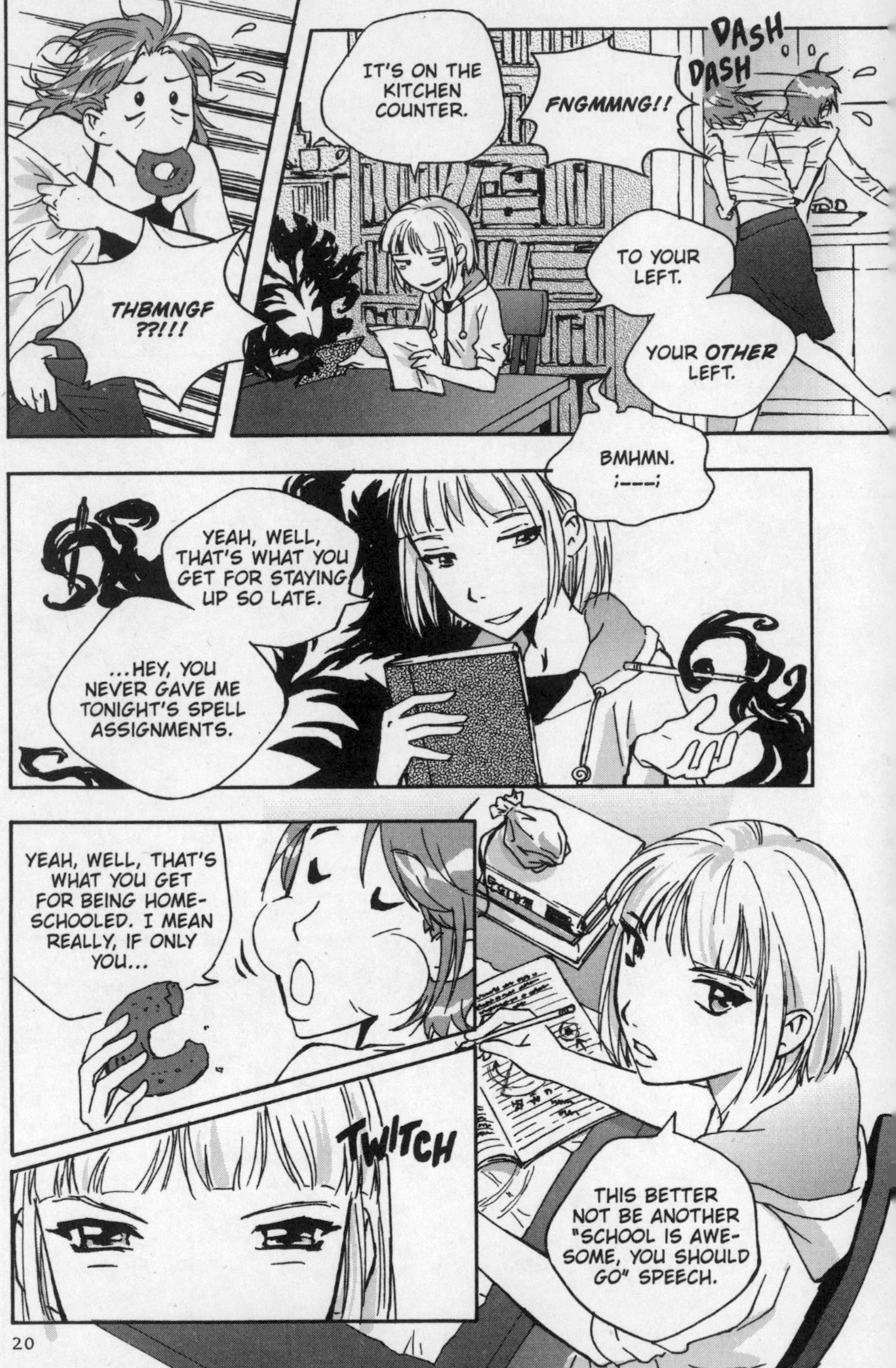
THBMNGF ??!!!
IT'S ON THE KITCHEN COUNTER.
FNGMMNG!!
DASH DASH
TO YOUR LEFT.
YOUR *OTHER* LEFT.
BMHMN. ;---;
YEAH, WELL, THAT'S WHAT YOU GET FOR STAYING UP SO LATE.
...HEY, YOU NEVER GAVE ME TONIGHT'S SPELL ASSIGNMENTS.
YEAH, WELL, THAT'S WHAT YOU GET FOR BEING HOME-SCHOOLED. I MEAN REALLY, IF ONLY YOU...
TWITCH
THIS BETTER NOT BE ANOTHER "SCHOOL IS AWE-SOME, YOU SHOULD GO" SPEECH.

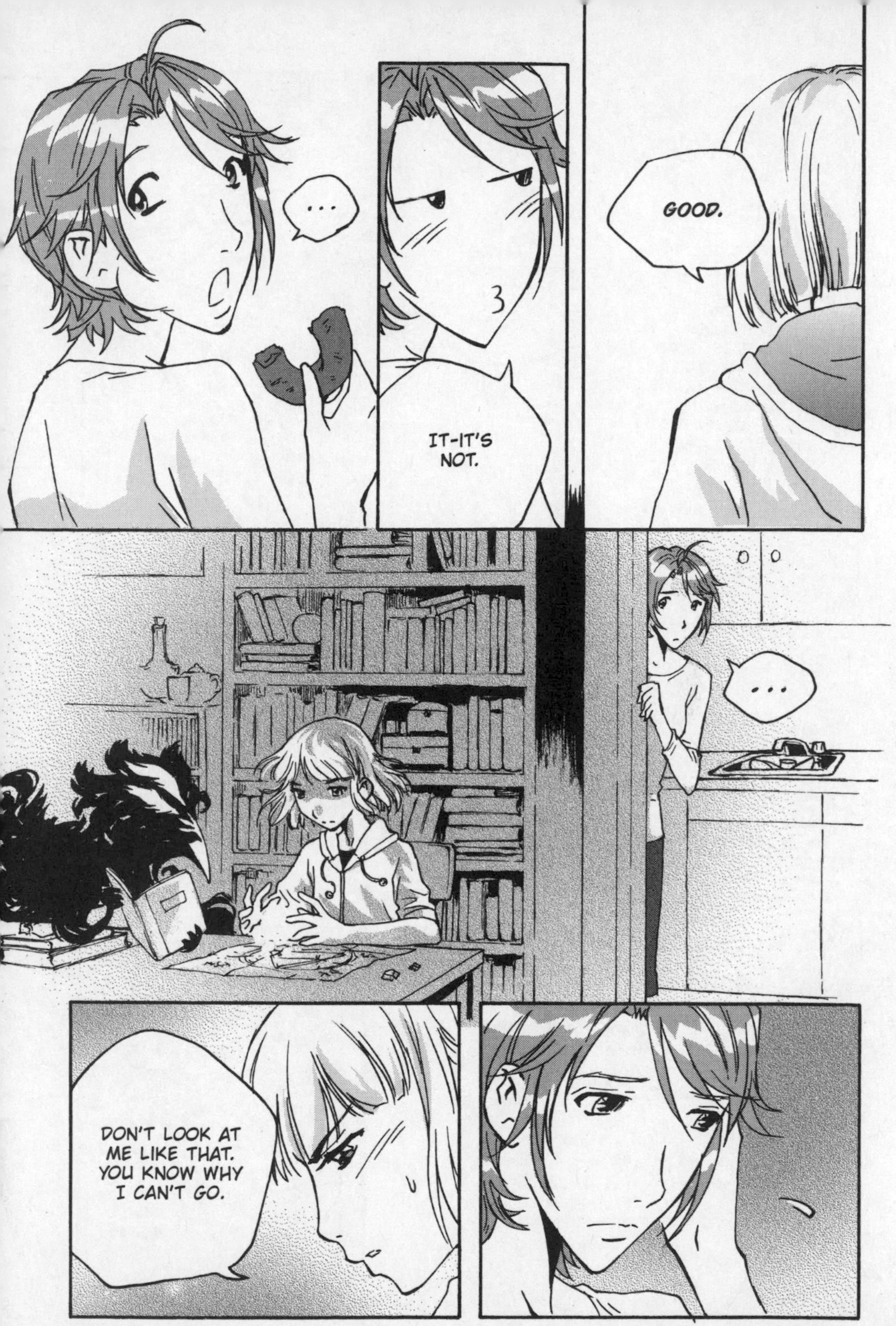
...
IT-IT'S NOT.
GOOD.
...
DON'T LOOK AT ME LIKE THAT. YOU KNOW WHY I CAN'T GO.

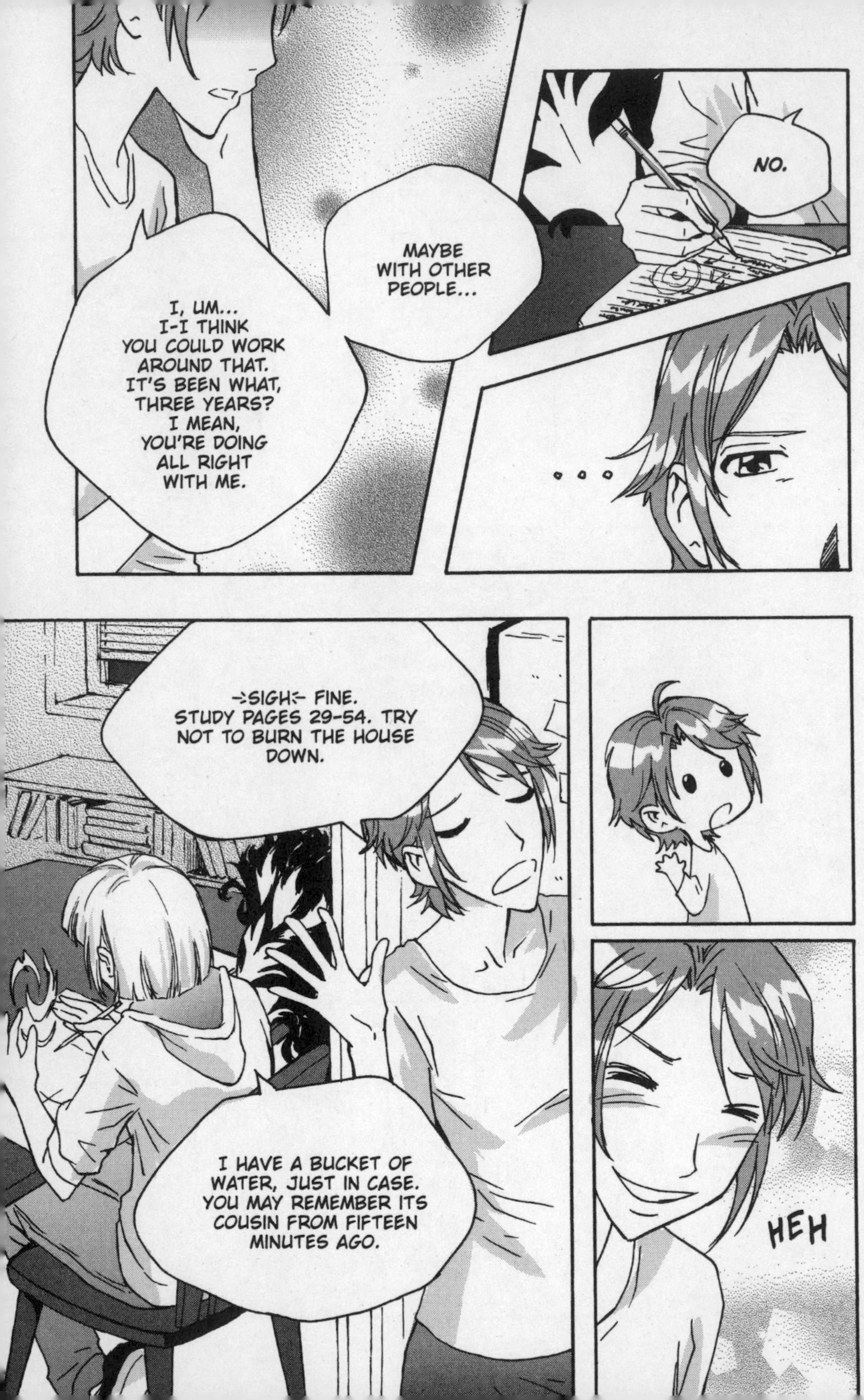
I, UM... I-I THINK YOU COULD WORK AROUND THAT. IT'S BEEN WHAT, THREE YEARS? I MEAN, YOU'RE DOING ALL RIGHT WITH ME.
MAYBE WITH OTHER PEOPLE...
NO.
...
⇾SIGH⇽ FINE. STUDY PAGES 29-54. TRY NOT TO BURN THE HOUSE DOWN.
I HAVE A BUCKET OF WATER, JUST IN CASE. YOU MAY REMEMBER ITS COUSIN FROM FIFTEEN MINUTES AGO.
HEH

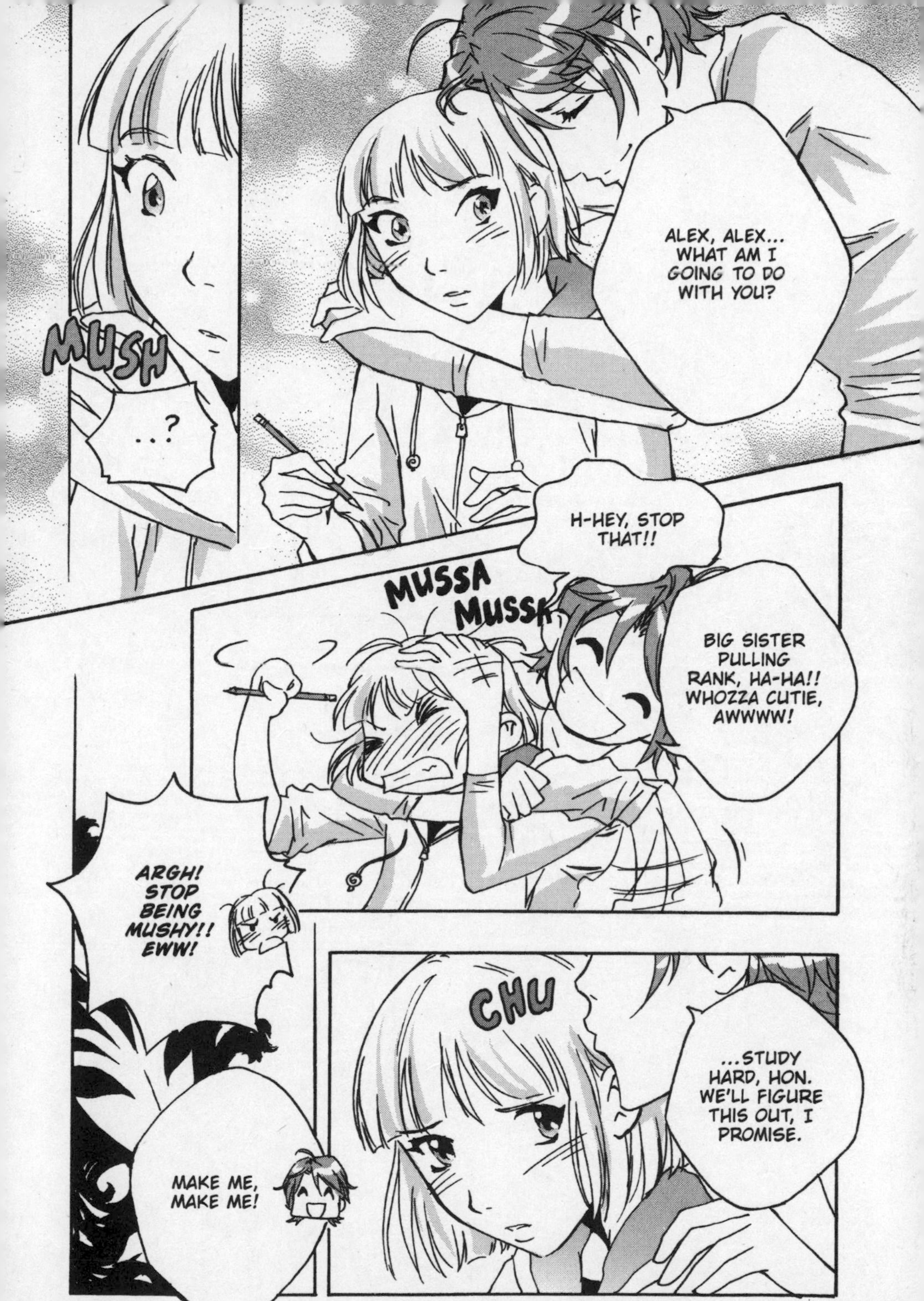
MUSH
...?
ALEX, ALEX... WHAT AM I GOING TO DO WITH YOU?
H-HEY, STOP THAT!!
MUSSA MUSSA
BIG SISTER PULLING RANK, HA-HA!! WHOZZA CUTIE, AWWWW!
ARGH! STOP BEING MUSHY!! EWW!
MAKE ME, MAKE ME!
CHU
...STUDY HARD, HON. WE'LL FIGURE THIS OUT, I PROMISE.

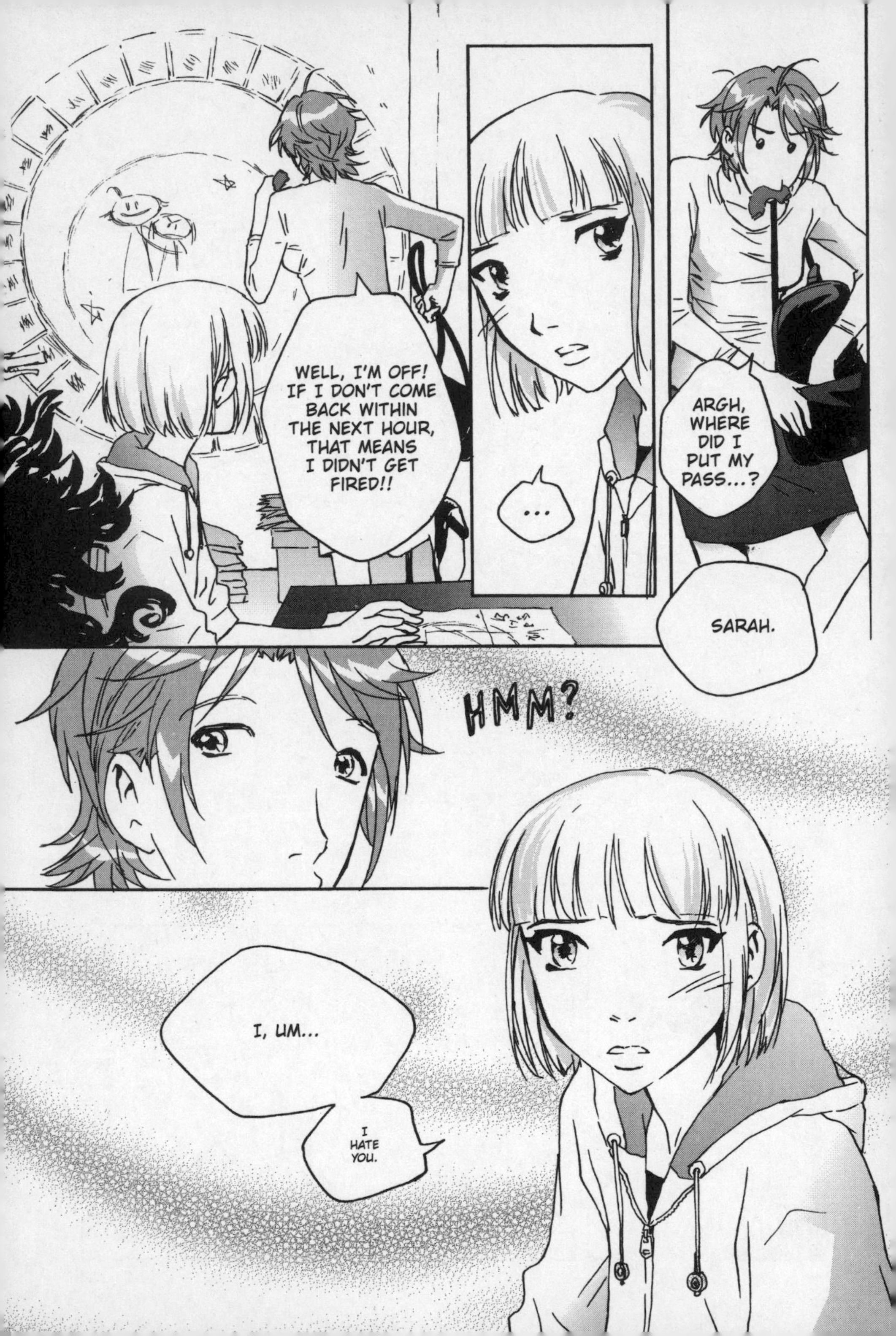
WELL, I'M OFF! IF I DON'T COME BACK WITHIN THE NEXT HOUR, THAT MEANS I DIDN'T GET FIRED!!
...
ARGH, WHERE DID I PUT MY PASS...?
SARAH.
HMM?
I, UM...
I HATE YOU.

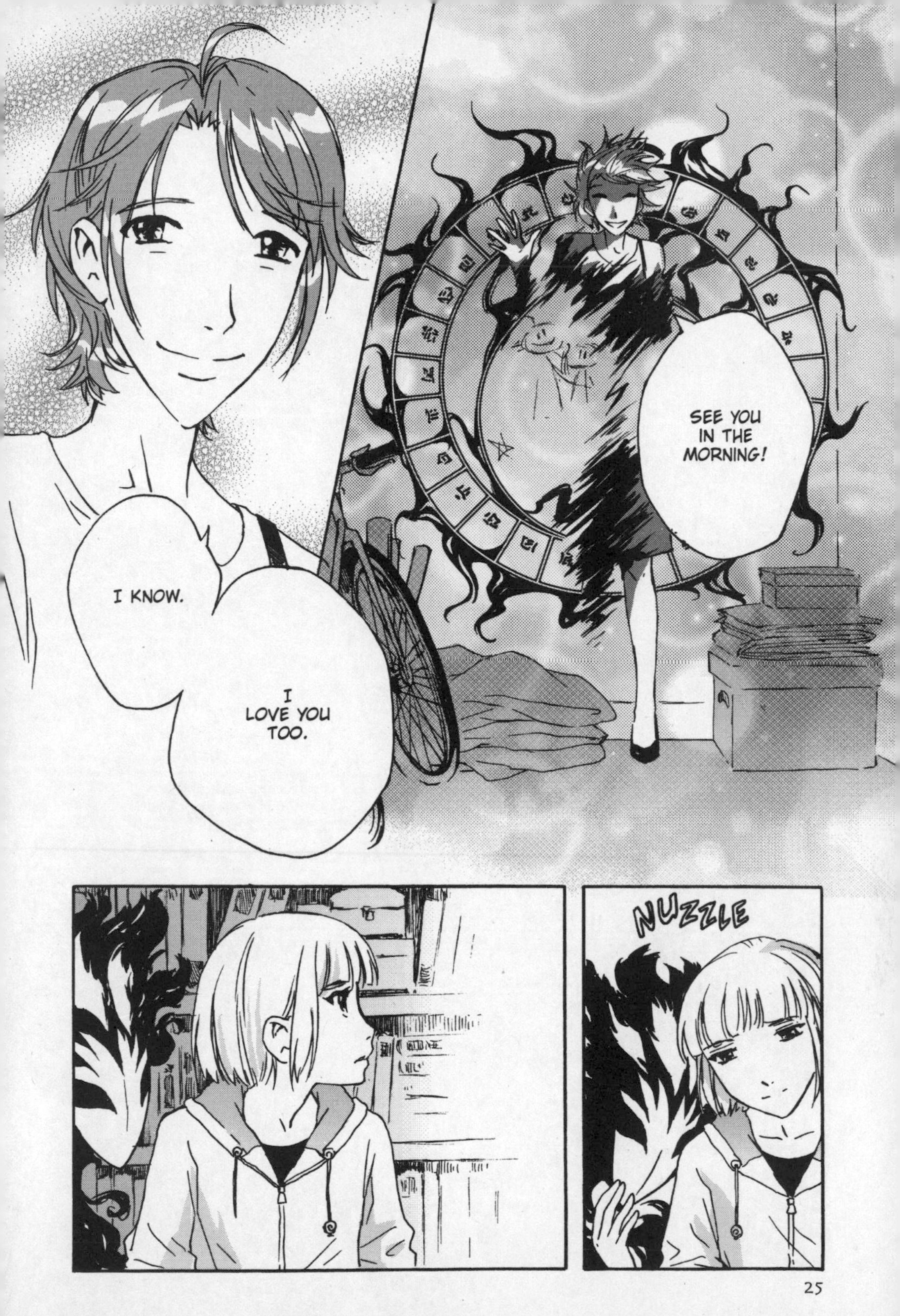
I KNOW.
I LOVE YOU TOO.
SEE YOU IN THE MORNING!
NUZZLE

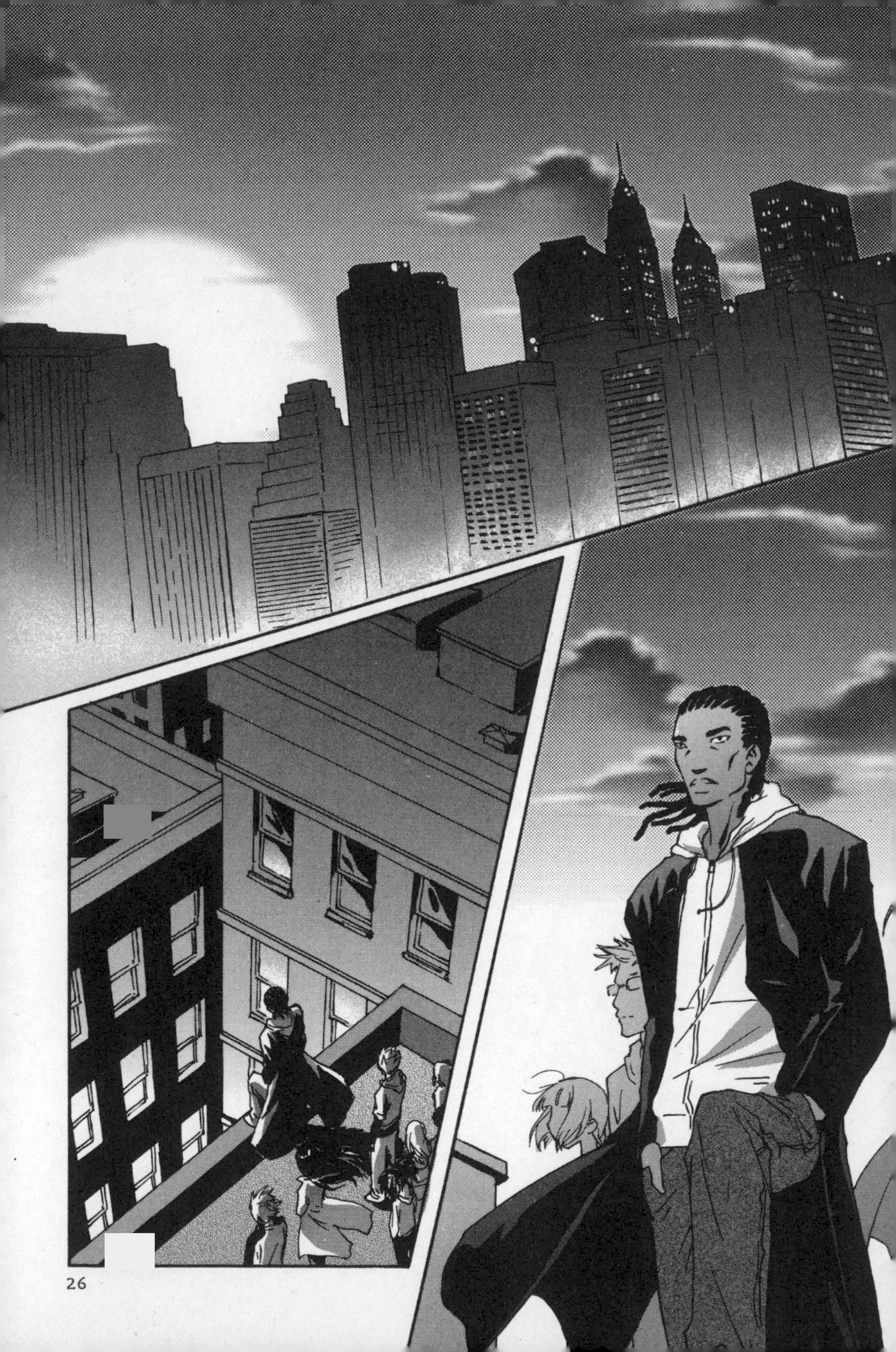

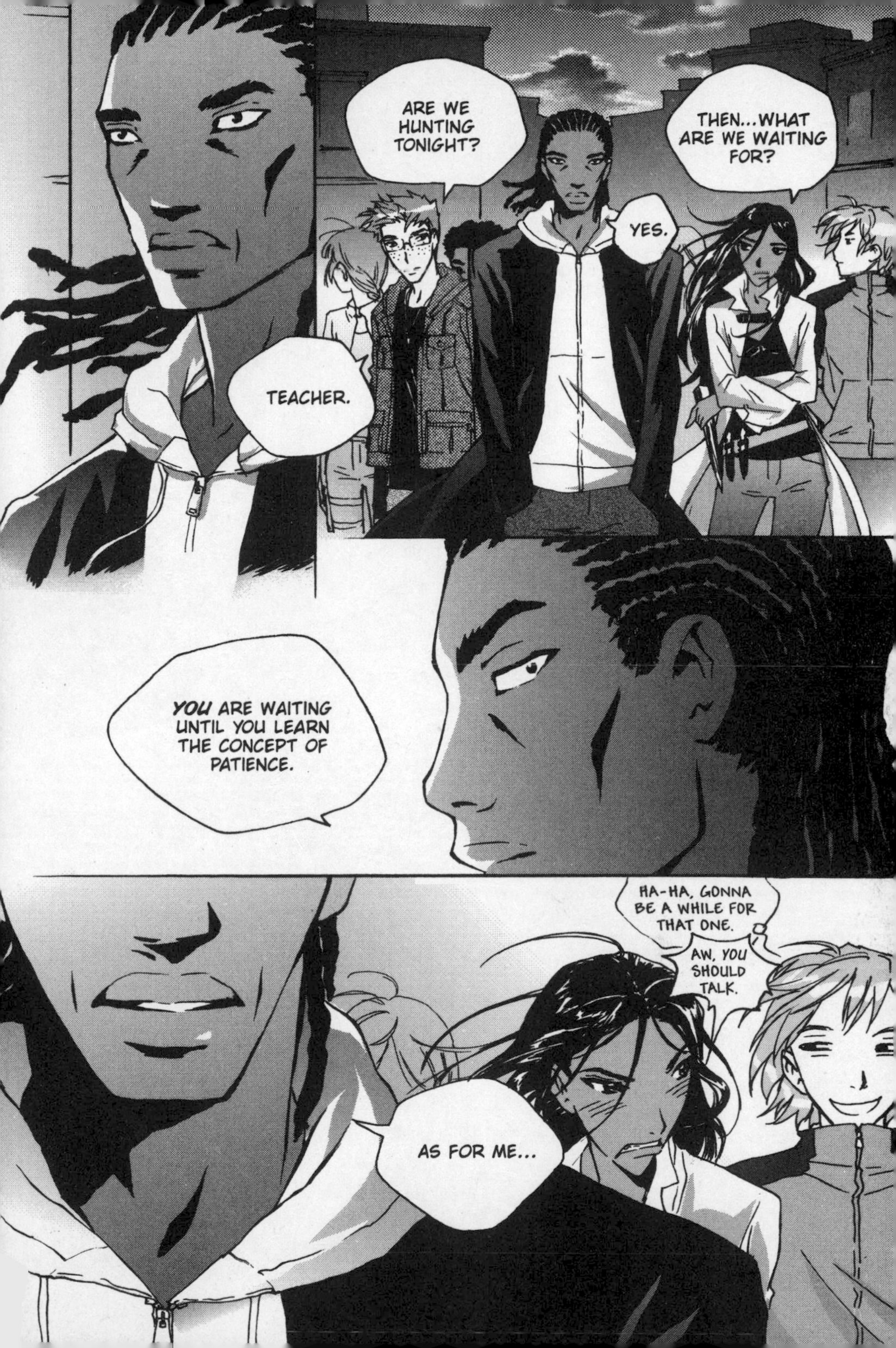
TEACHER.
ARE WE HUNTING TONIGHT?
YES.
THEN...WHAT ARE WE WAITING FOR?
YOU ARE WAITING UNTIL YOU LEARN THE CONCEPT OF PATIENCE.
HA-HA, GONNA BE A WHILE FOR THAT ONE.
AW, YOU SHOULD TALK.
AS FOR ME...

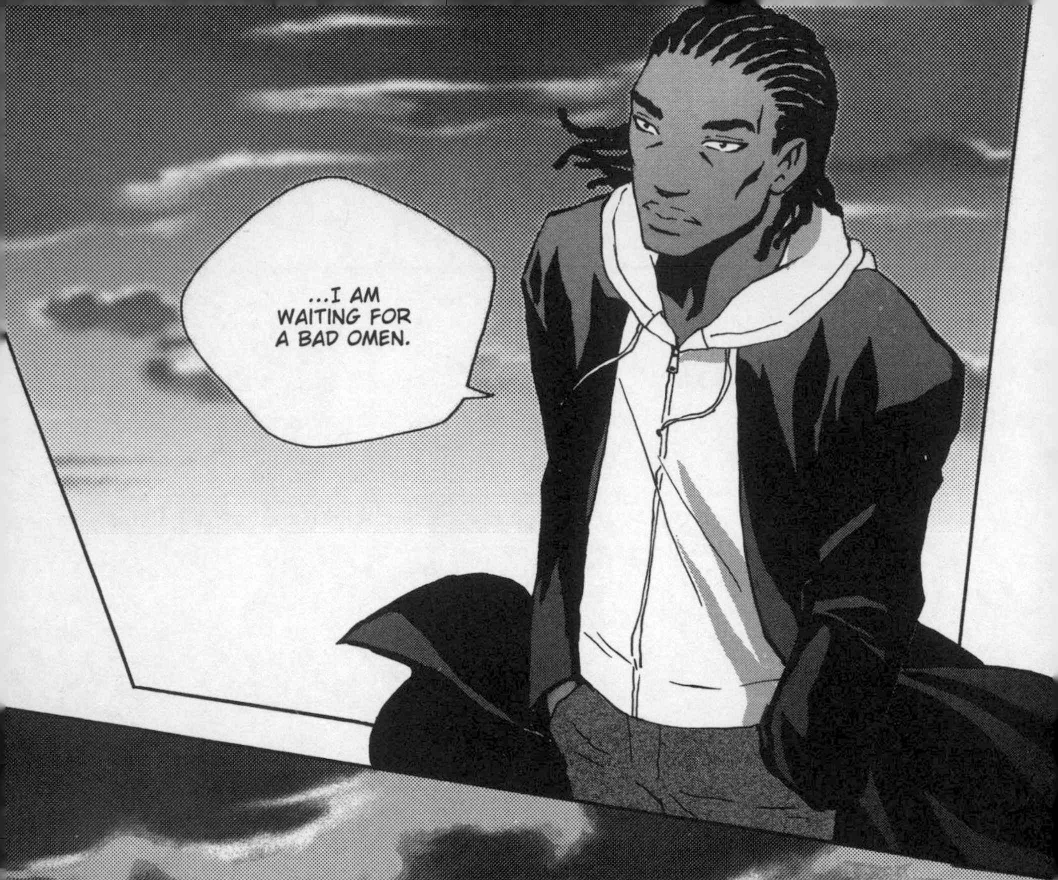
...I AM WAITING FOR A BAD OMEN.
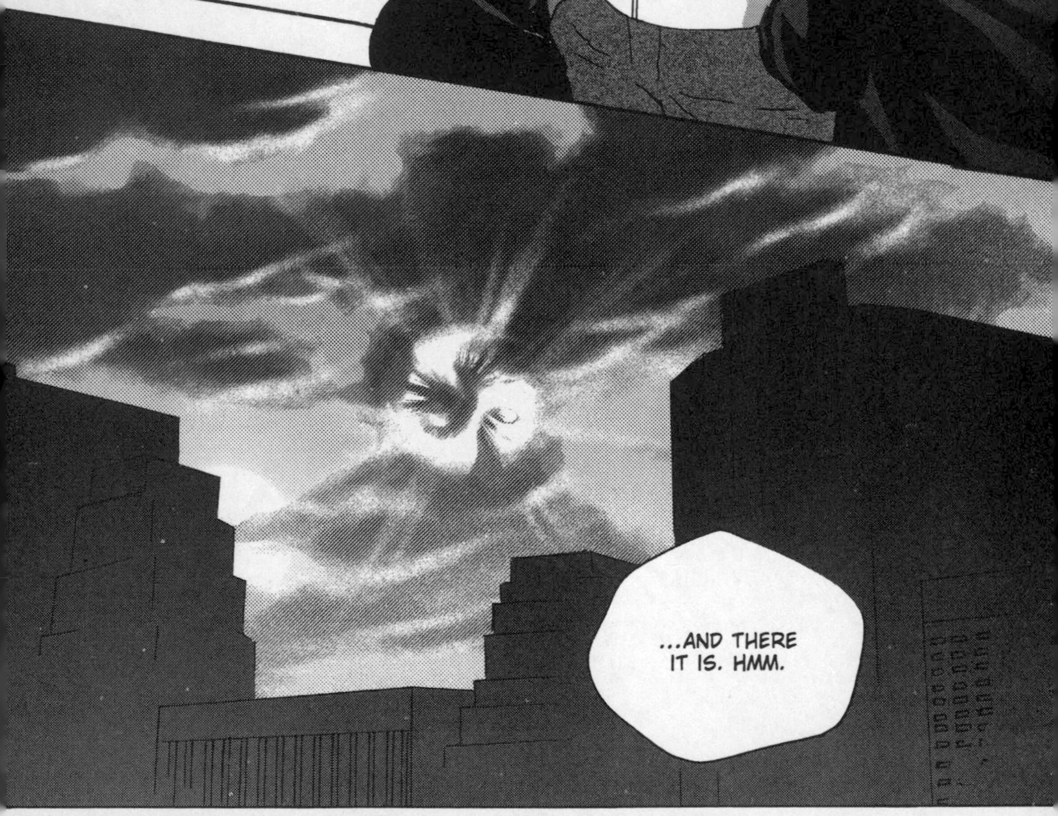
...AND THERE IT IS. HMM.

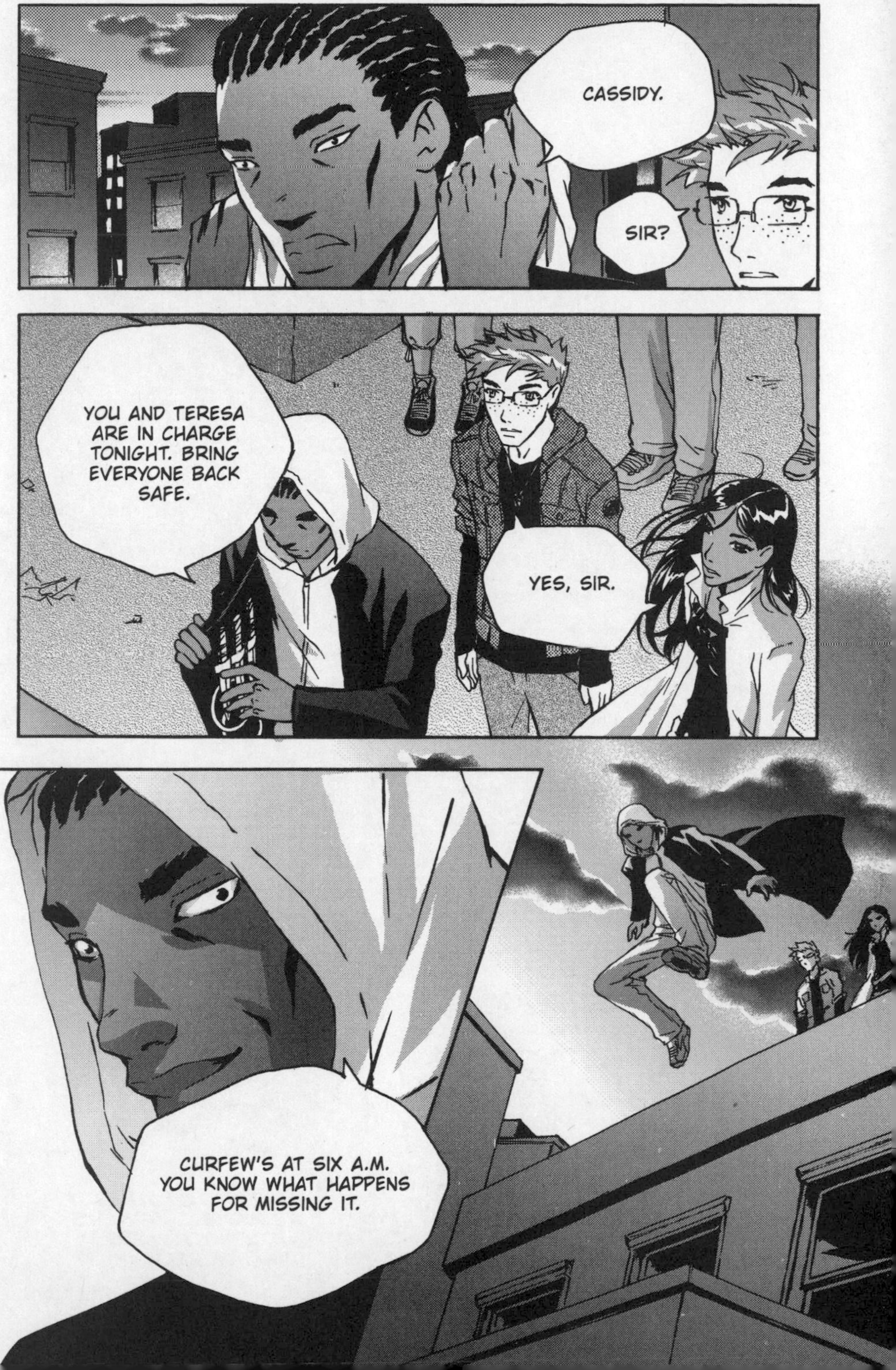
CASSIDY.
SIR?
YOU AND TERESA ARE IN CHARGE TONIGHT. BRING EVERYONE BACK SAFE.
YES, SIR.
CURFEW'S AT SIX A.M. YOU KNOW WHAT HAPPENS FOR MISSING IT.

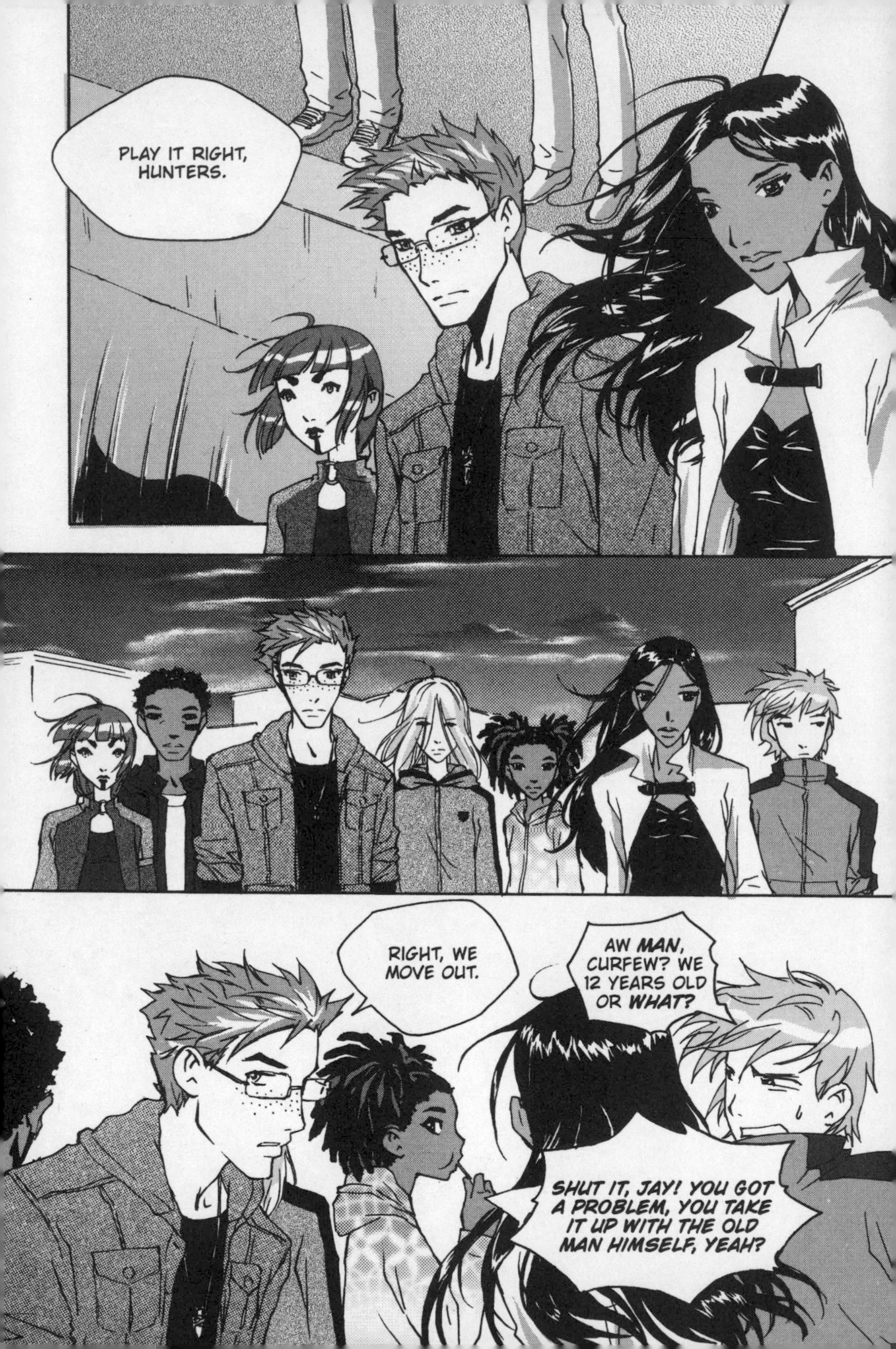
PLAY IT RIGHT, HUNTERS.
RIGHT, WE MOVE OUT.
AW *MAN*, CURFEW? WE 12 YEARS OLD OR *WHAT?*
SHUT IT, JAY! YOU GOT A PROBLEM, YOU TAKE IT UP WITH THE OLD MAN HIMSELF, YEAH?

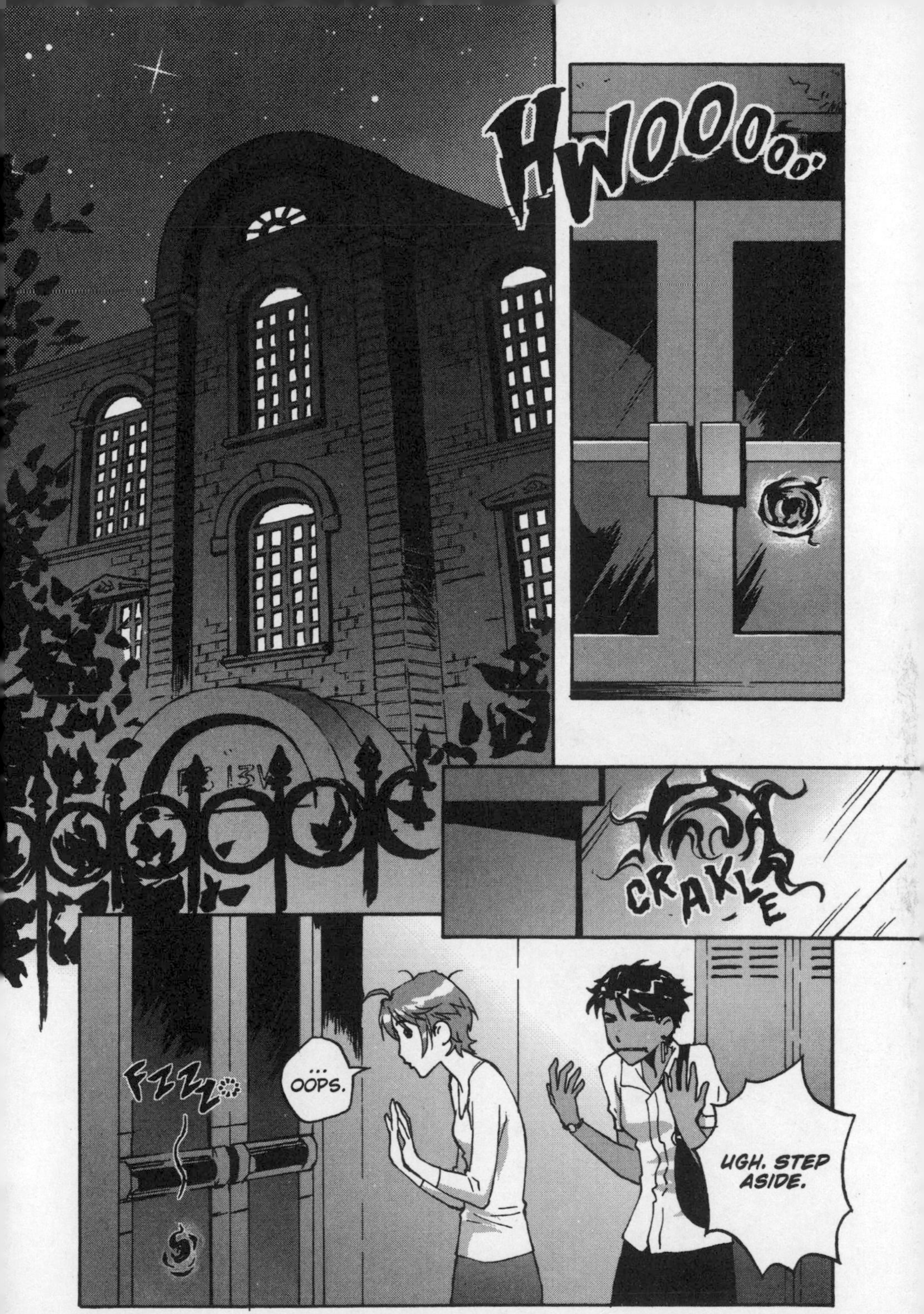
HWOOOo..
CRAKLE
FZZZ
... OOPS.
UGH. STEP ASIDE.

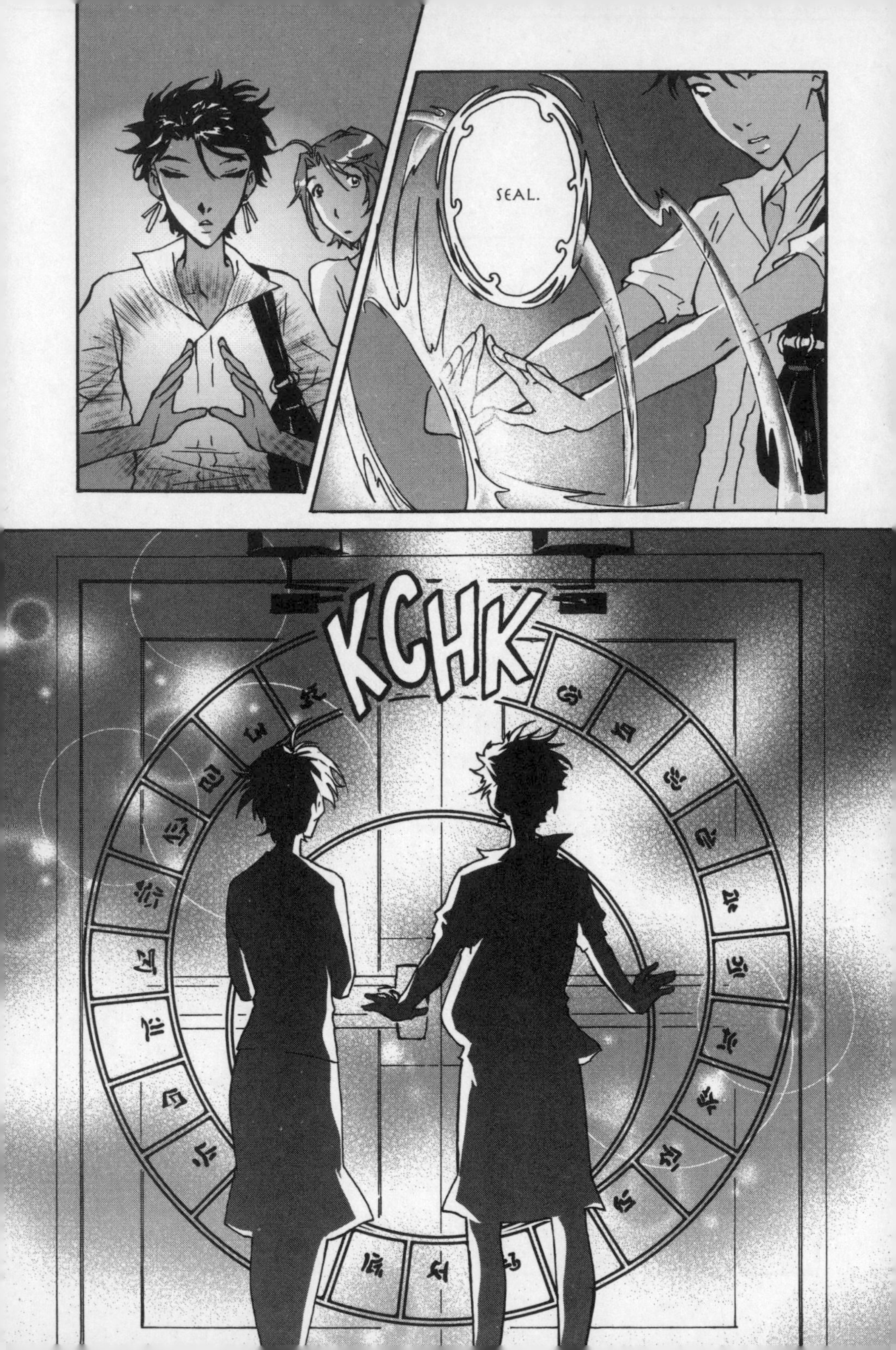
SEAL.
KCHK

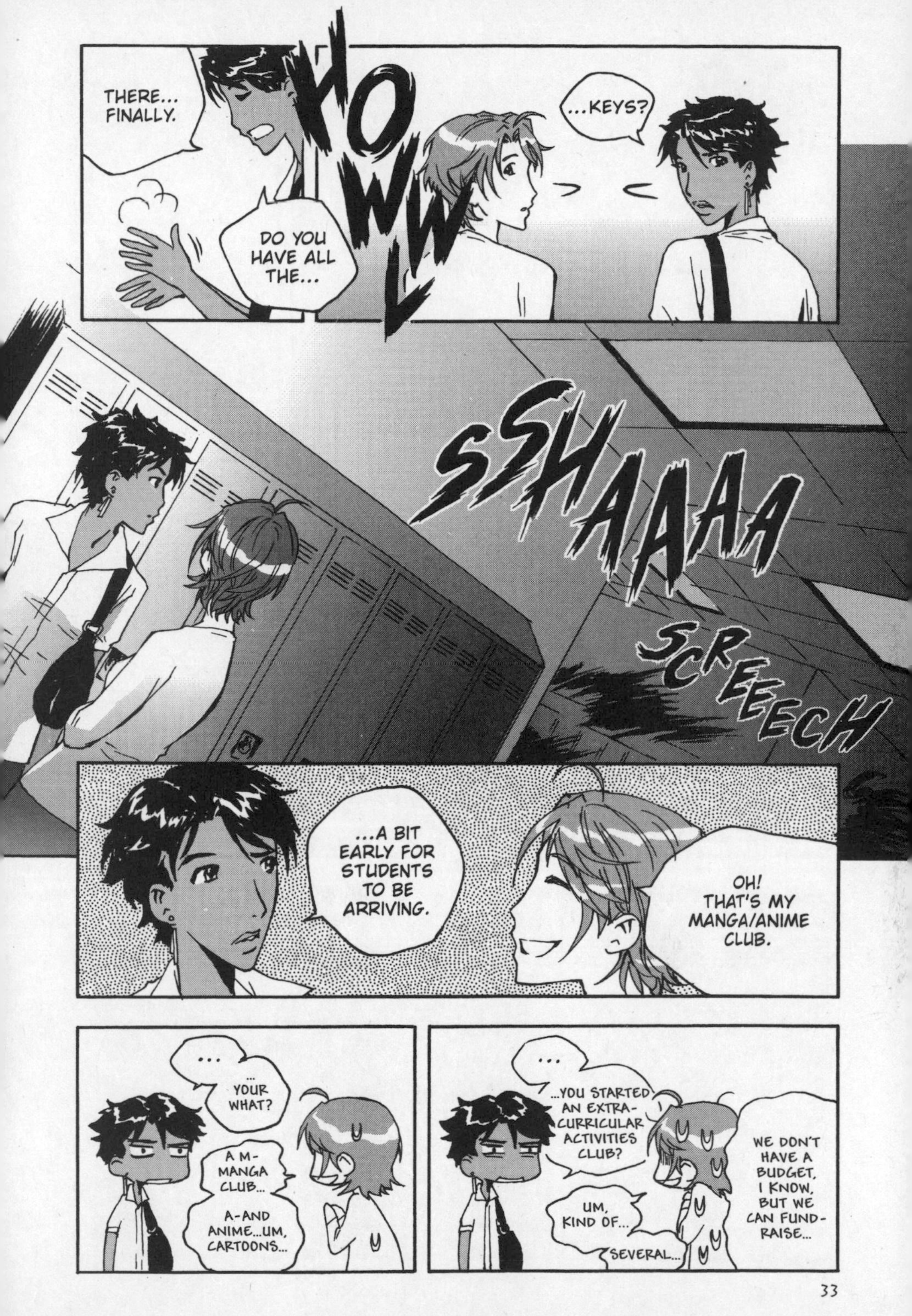
THERE... FINALLY.
HOWWWL
DO YOU HAVE ALL THE...
...KEYS?
sSHAAAA
SCREEECH
...A BIT EARLY FOR STUDENTS TO BE ARRIVING.
OH! THAT'S MY MANGA/ANIME CLUB.
...
... YOUR WHAT?
A M-MANGA CLUB...
A-AND ANIME...UM, CARTOONS...
...
...YOU STARTED AN EXTRA-CURRICULAR ACTIVITIES CLUB?
UM, KIND OF...
SEVERAL...
WE DON'T HAVE A BUDGET, I KNOW, BUT WE CAN FUND-RAISE...

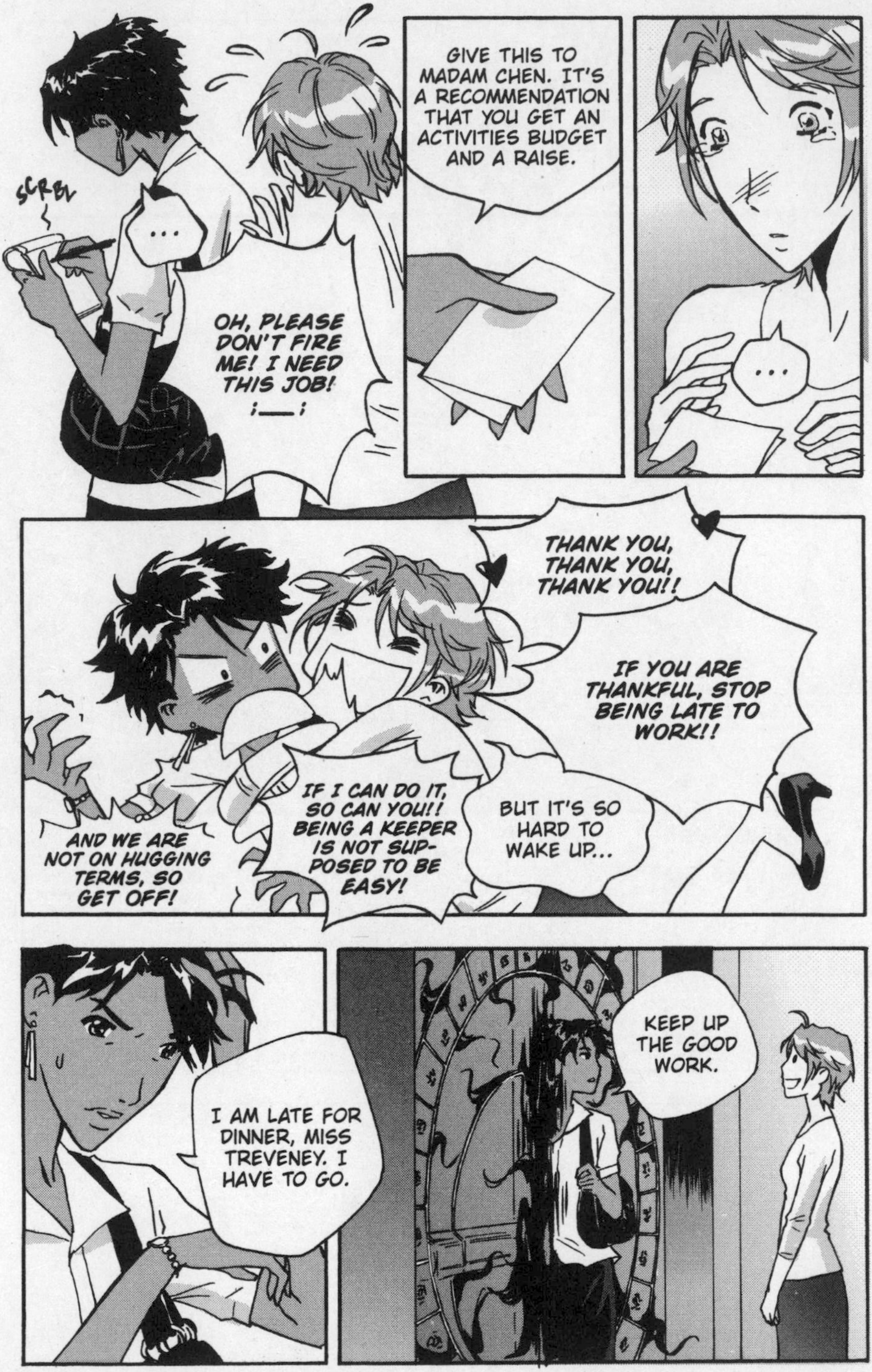
SCRBL
...
OH, PLEASE DON'T FIRE ME! I NEED THIS JOB! ;___;
GIVE THIS TO MADAM CHEN. IT'S A RECOMMENDATION THAT YOU GET AN ACTIVITIES BUDGET AND A RAISE.
...
THANK YOU, THANK YOU, THANK YOU!!
IF YOU ARE THANKFUL, STOP BEING LATE TO WORK!!
AND WE ARE NOT ON HUGGING TERMS, SO GET OFF!
IF I CAN DO IT, SO CAN YOU!! BEING A KEEPER IS NOT SUP-POSED TO BE EASY!
BUT IT'S SO HARD TO WAKE UP...
I AM LATE FOR DINNER, MISS TREVENEY. I HAVE TO GO.
KEEP UP THE GOOD WORK.

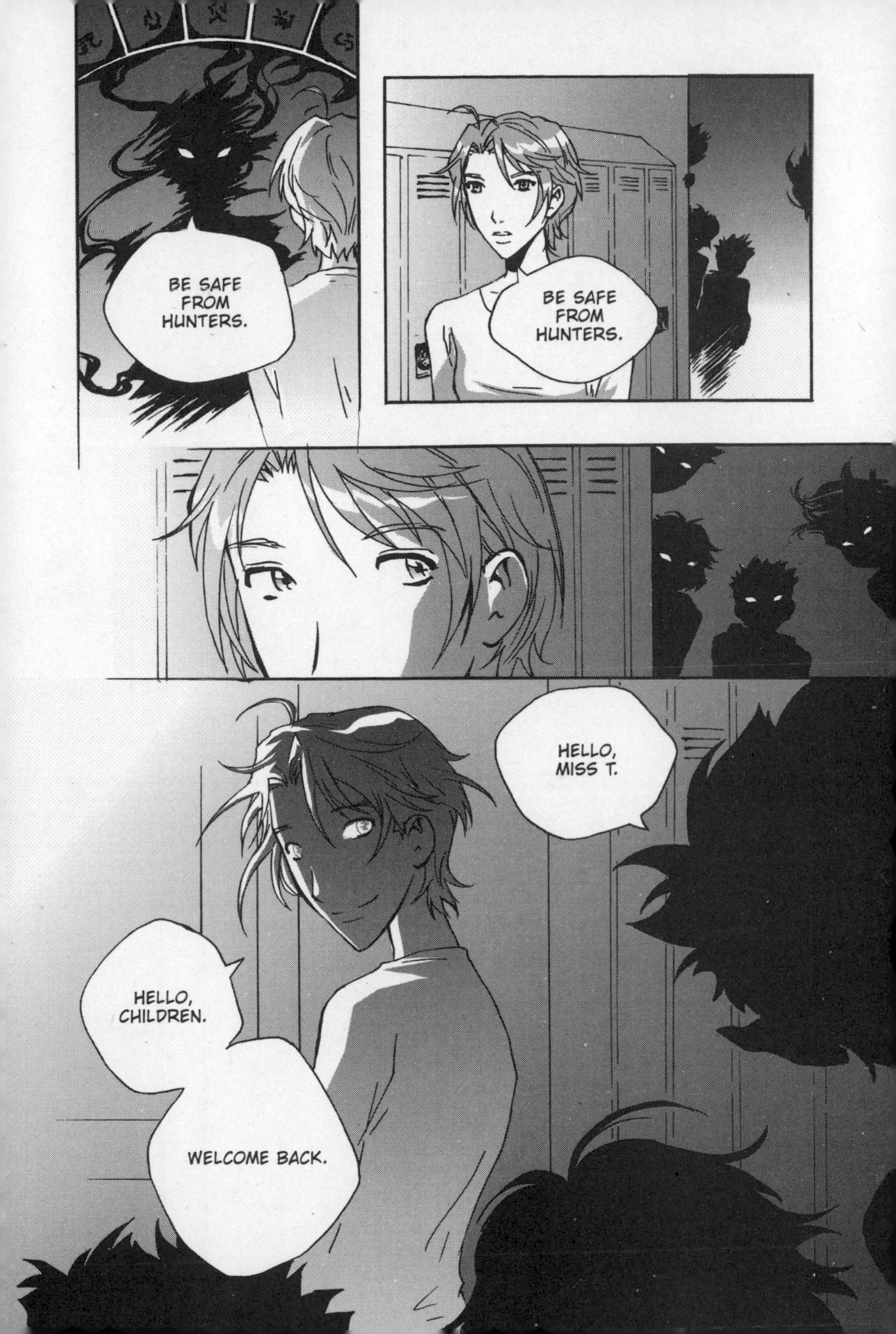
BE SAFE FROM HUNTERS.
BE SAFE FROM HUNTERS.
HELLO, MISS T.
HELLO, CHILDREN.
WELCOME BACK.

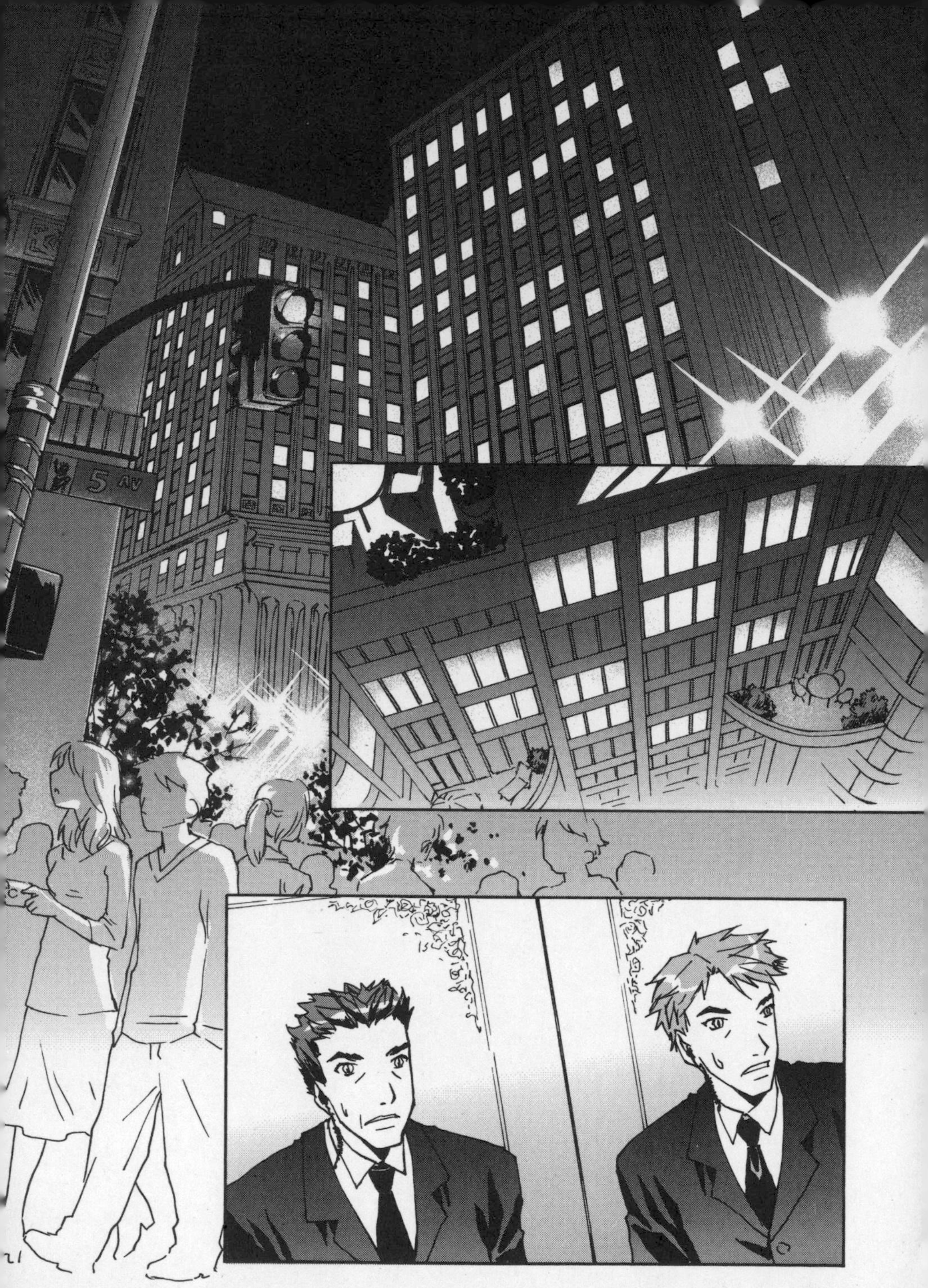
5 AV

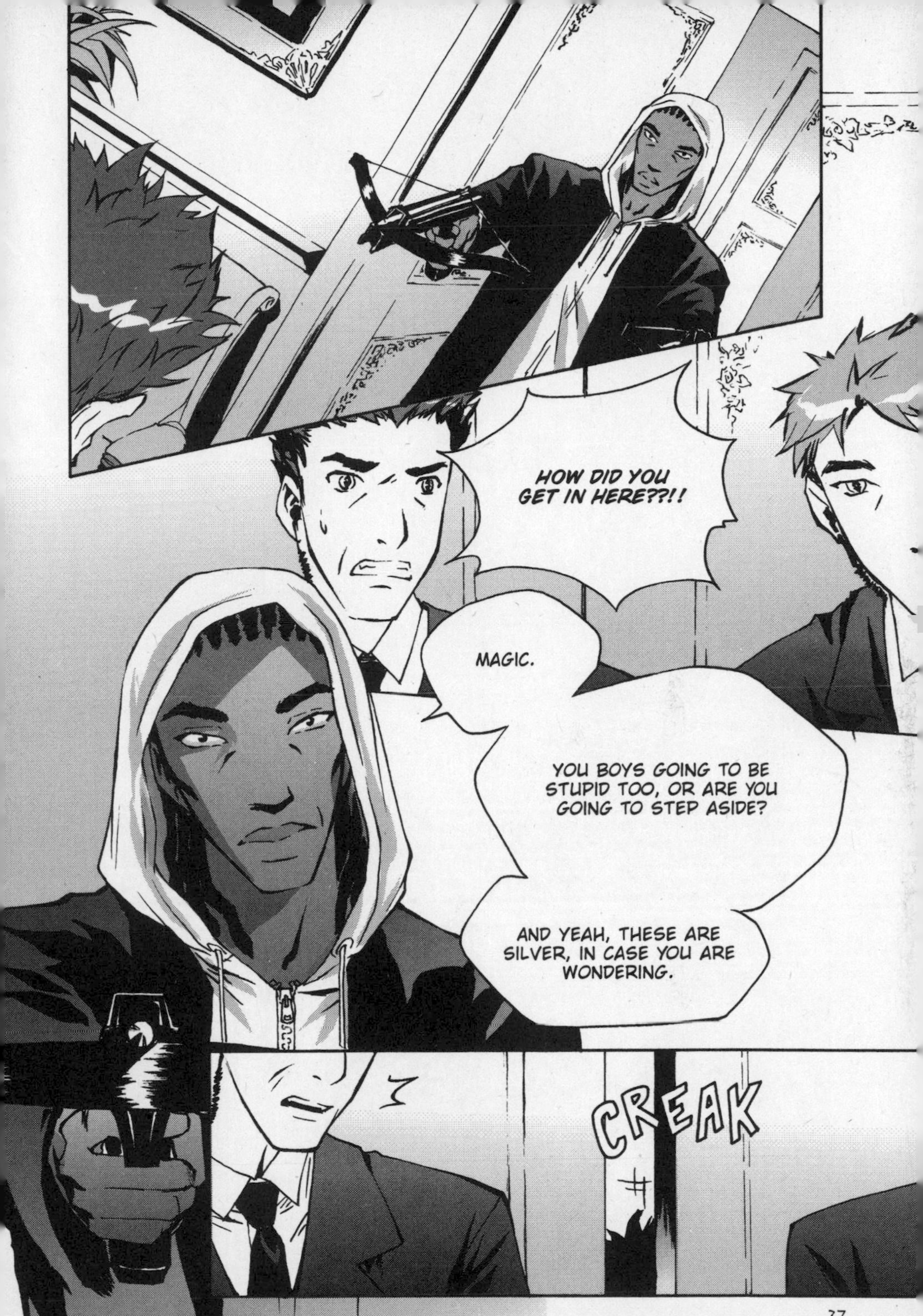
HOW DID YOU GET IN HERE??!!
MAGIC.
YOU BOYS GOING TO BE STUPID TOO, OR ARE YOU GOING TO STEP ASIDE?
AND YEAH, THESE ARE SILVER, IN CASE YOU ARE WONDERING.
CREAK

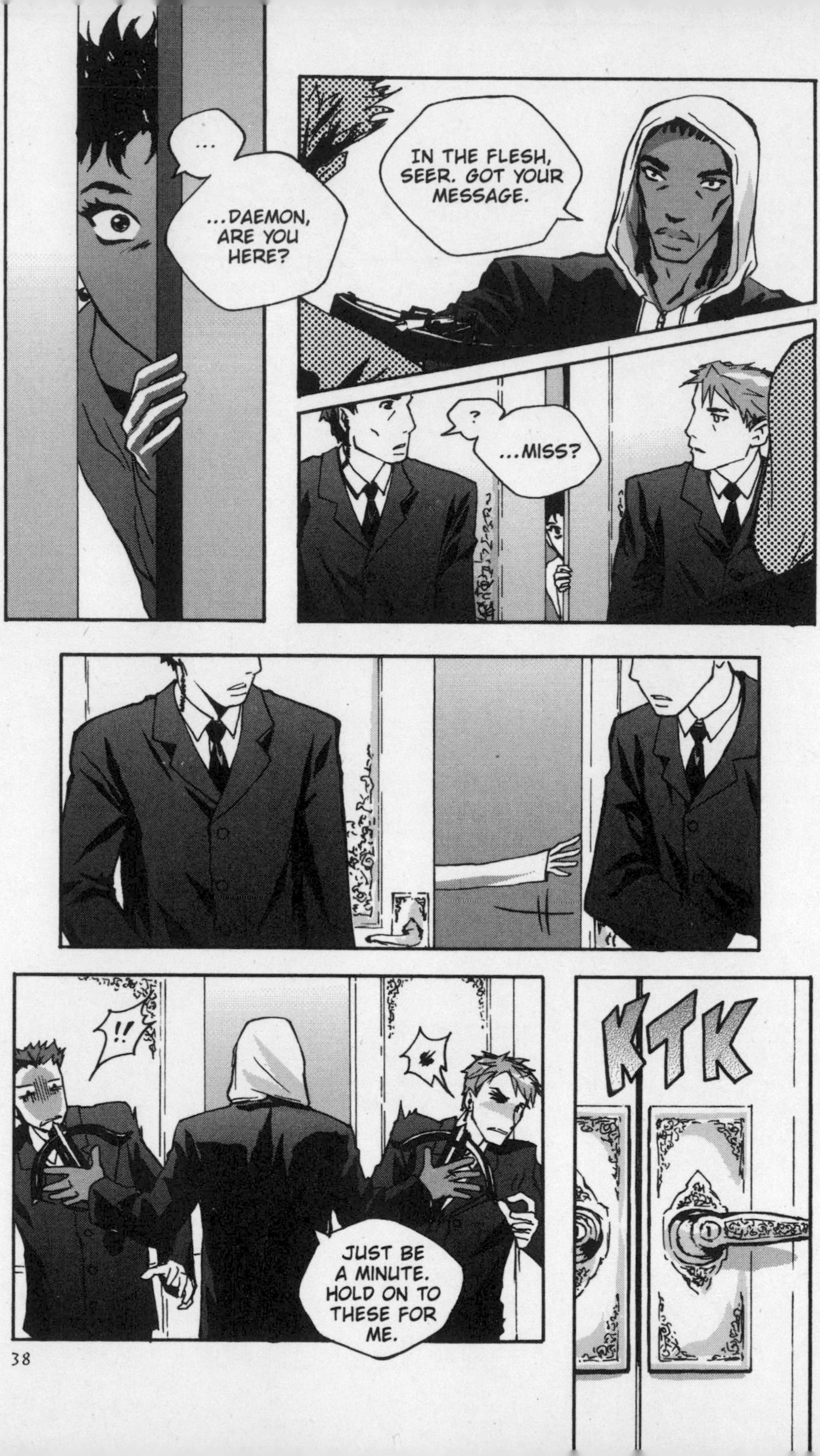
...
...DAEMON, ARE YOU HERE?
IN THE FLESH, SEER. GOT YOUR MESSAGE.
?
...MISS?
!!
JUST BE A MINUTE. HOLD ON TO THESE FOR ME.
KTK

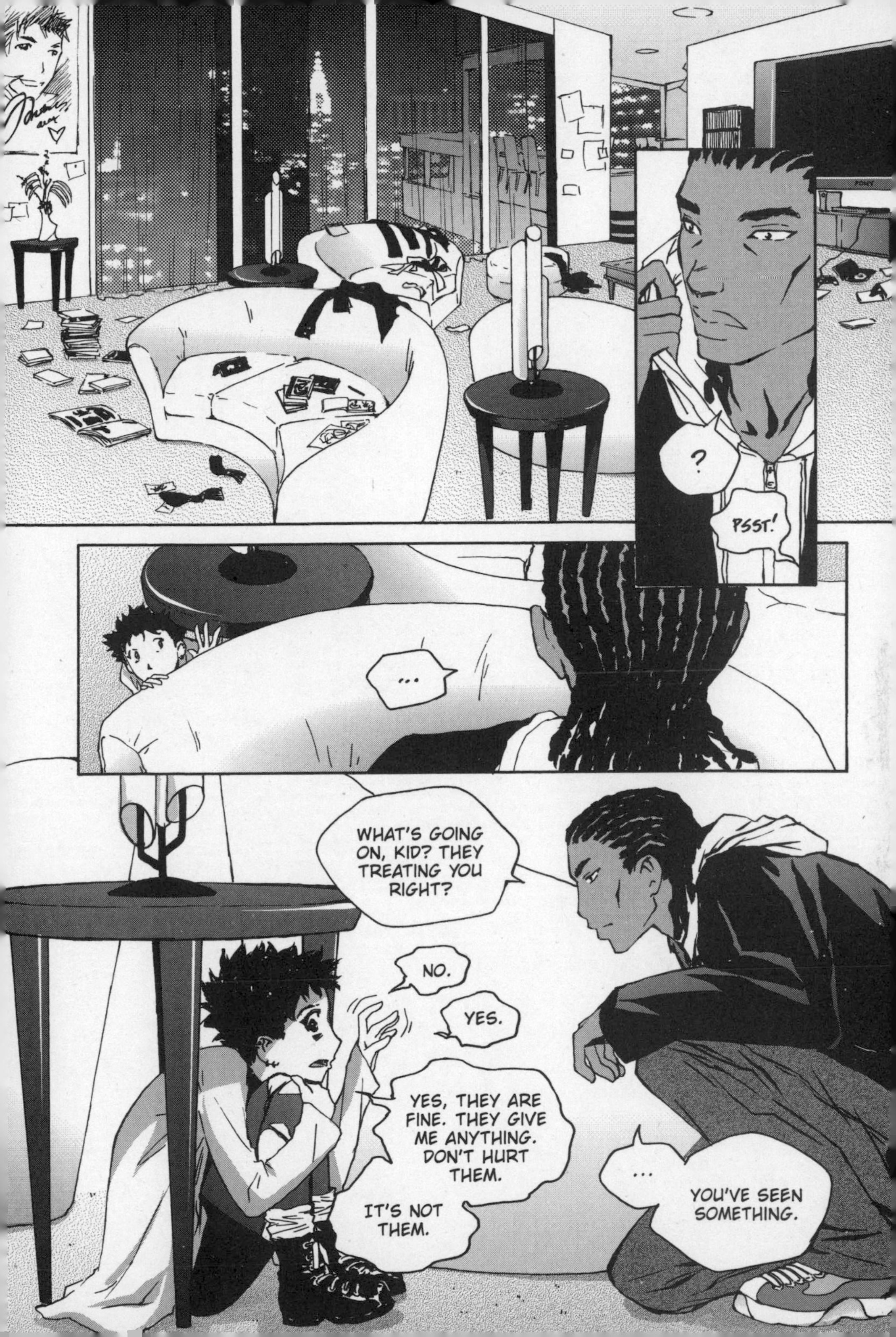
?
PSST!
...
WHAT'S GOING ON, KID? THEY TREATING YOU RIGHT?
NO.
YES.
YES, THEY ARE FINE. THEY GIVE ME ANYTHING. DON'T HURT THEM.
IT'S NOT THEM.
...
YOU'VE SEEN SOMETHING.

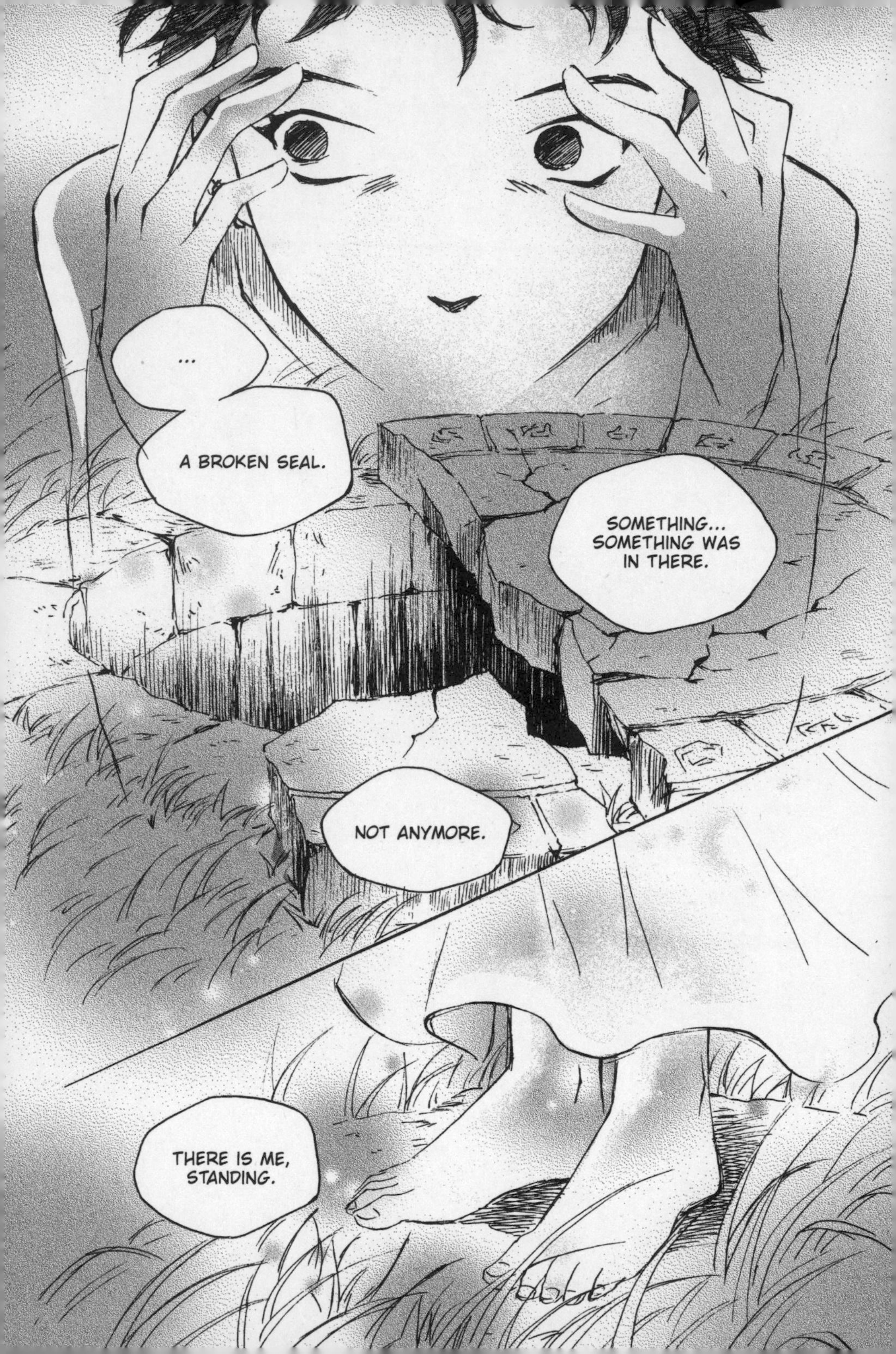
...
A BROKEN SEAL.
SOMETHING... SOMETHING WAS IN THERE.
NOT ANYMORE.
THERE IS ME, STANDING.

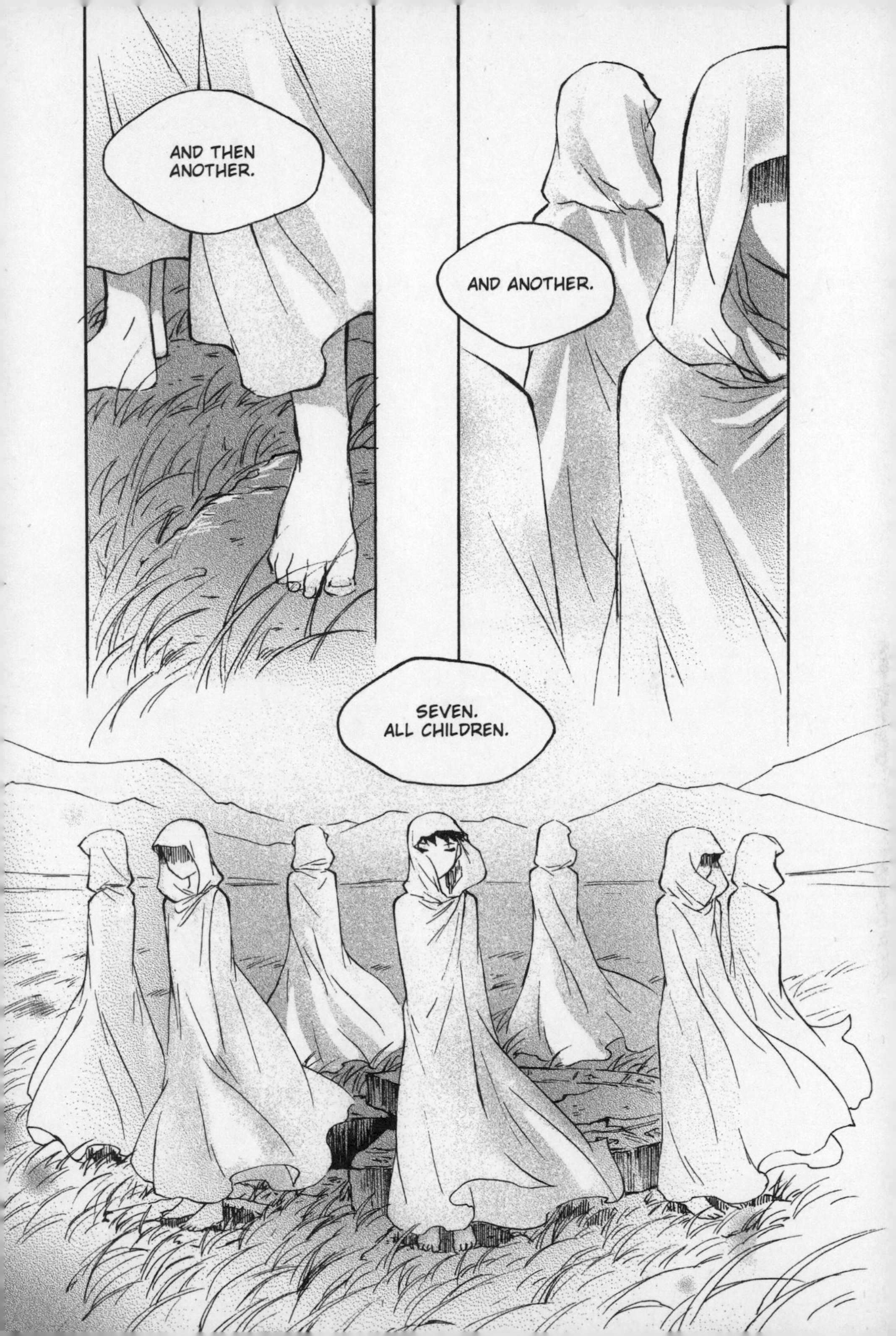
AND THEN ANOTHER.
AND ANOTHER.
SEVEN. ALL CHILDREN.

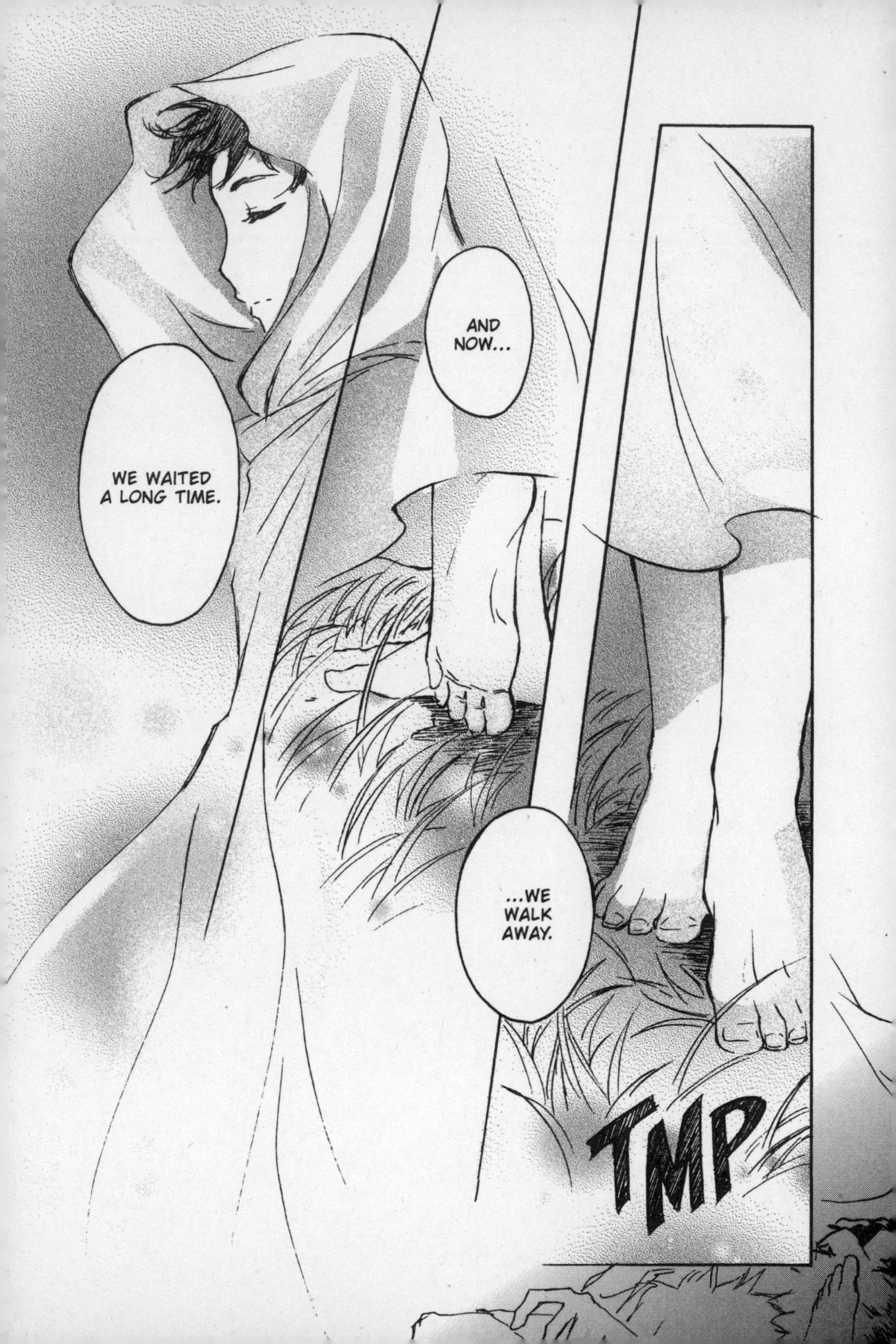
WE WAITED A LONG TIME.
AND NOW...
...WE WALK AWAY.
TMP

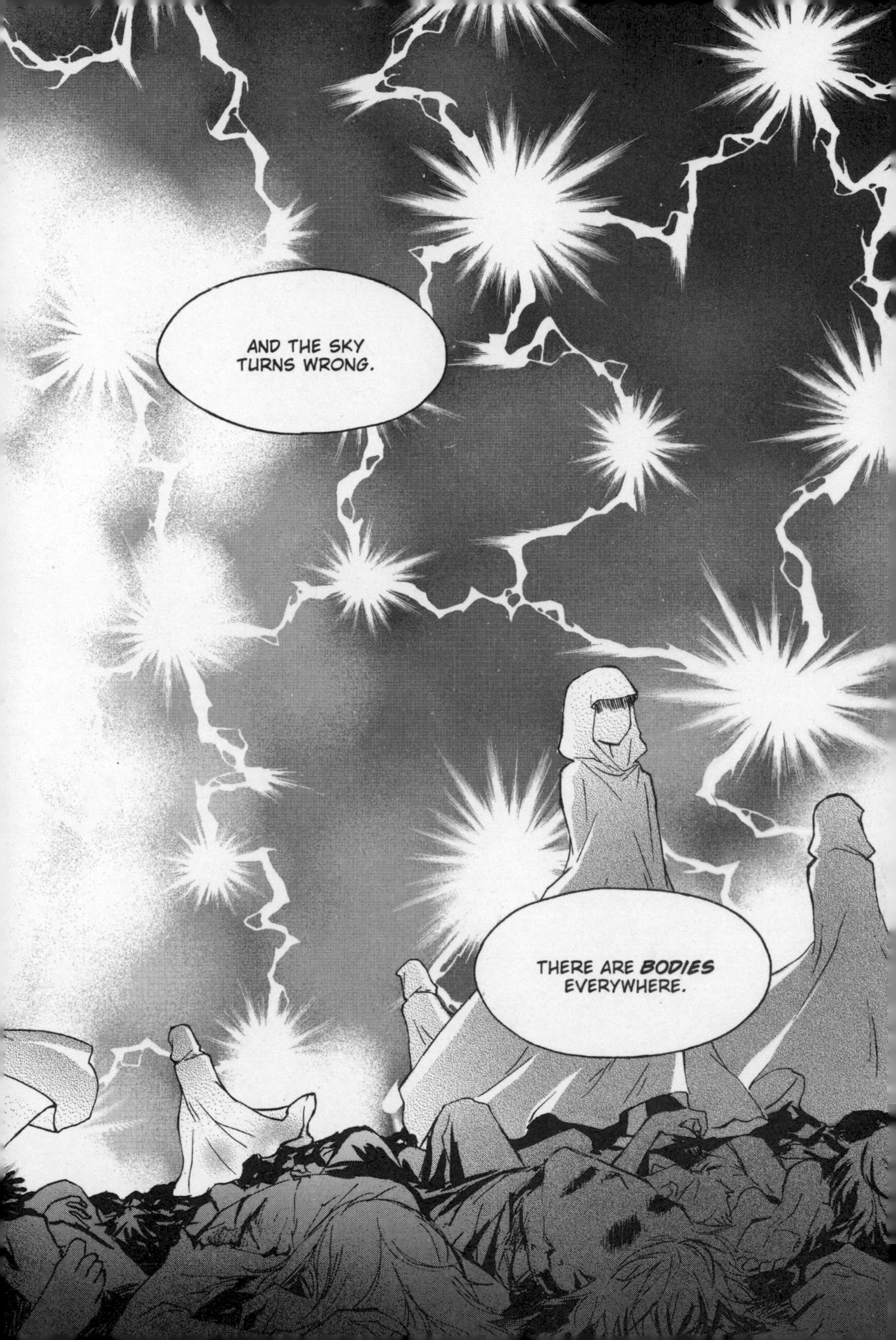
AND THE SKY TURNS WRONG.
THERE ARE *BODIES* EVERYWHERE.

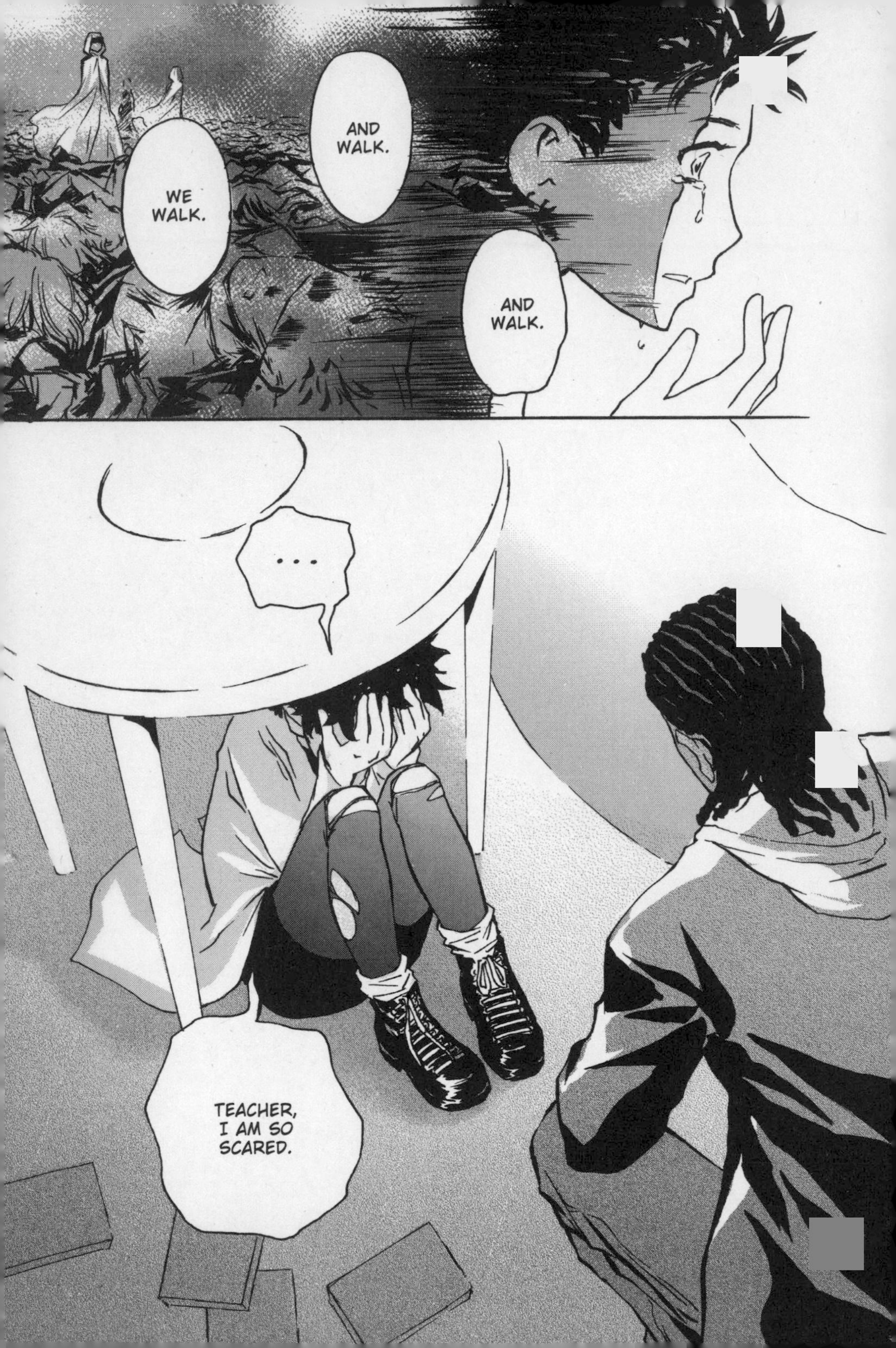
WE WALK.
AND WALK.
AND WALK.
...
TEACHER, I AM SO SCARED.

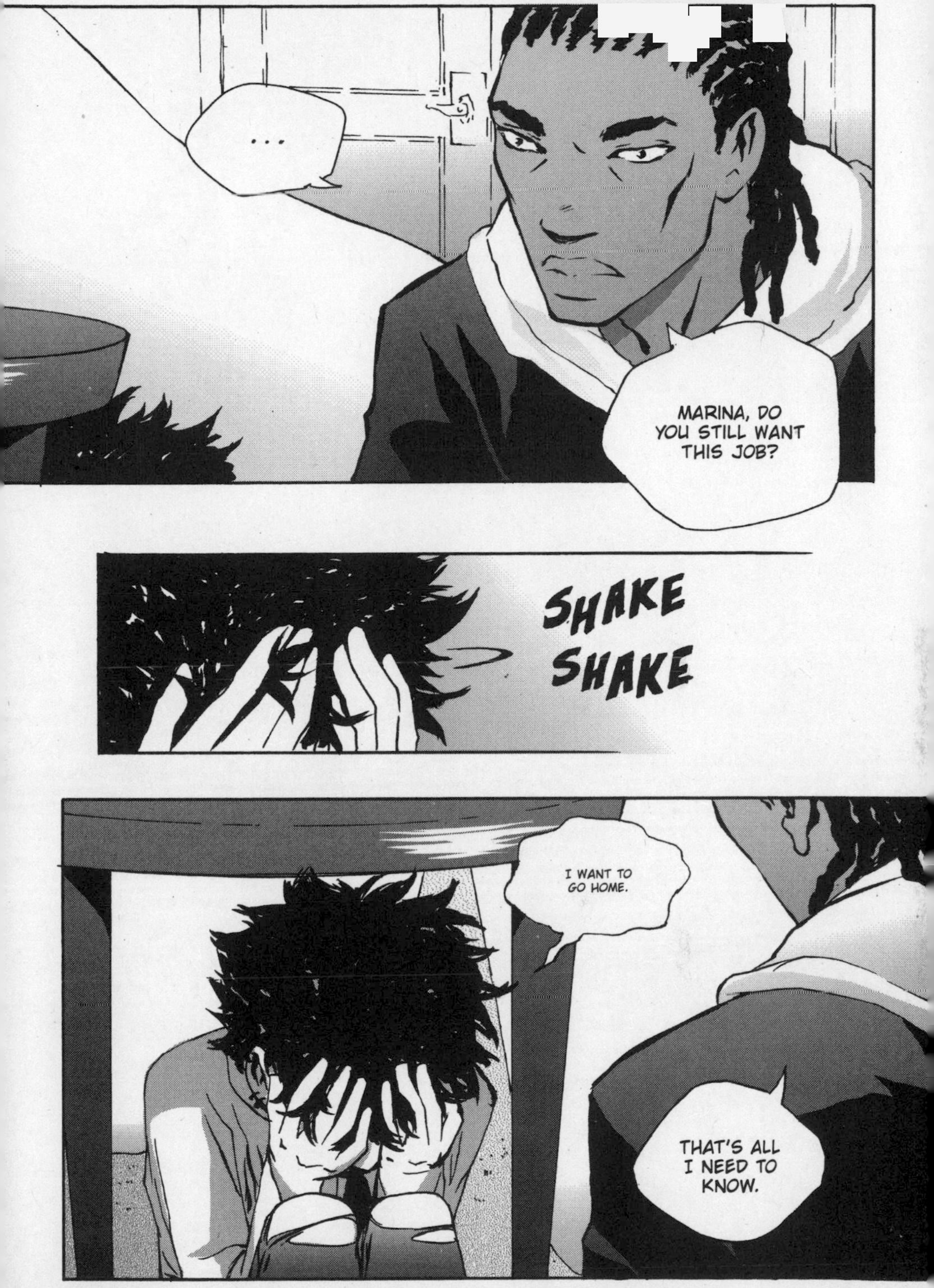
...
MARINA, DO YOU STILL WANT THIS JOB?
SHAKE SHAKE
I WANT TO GO HOME.
THAT'S ALL I NEED TO KNOW.

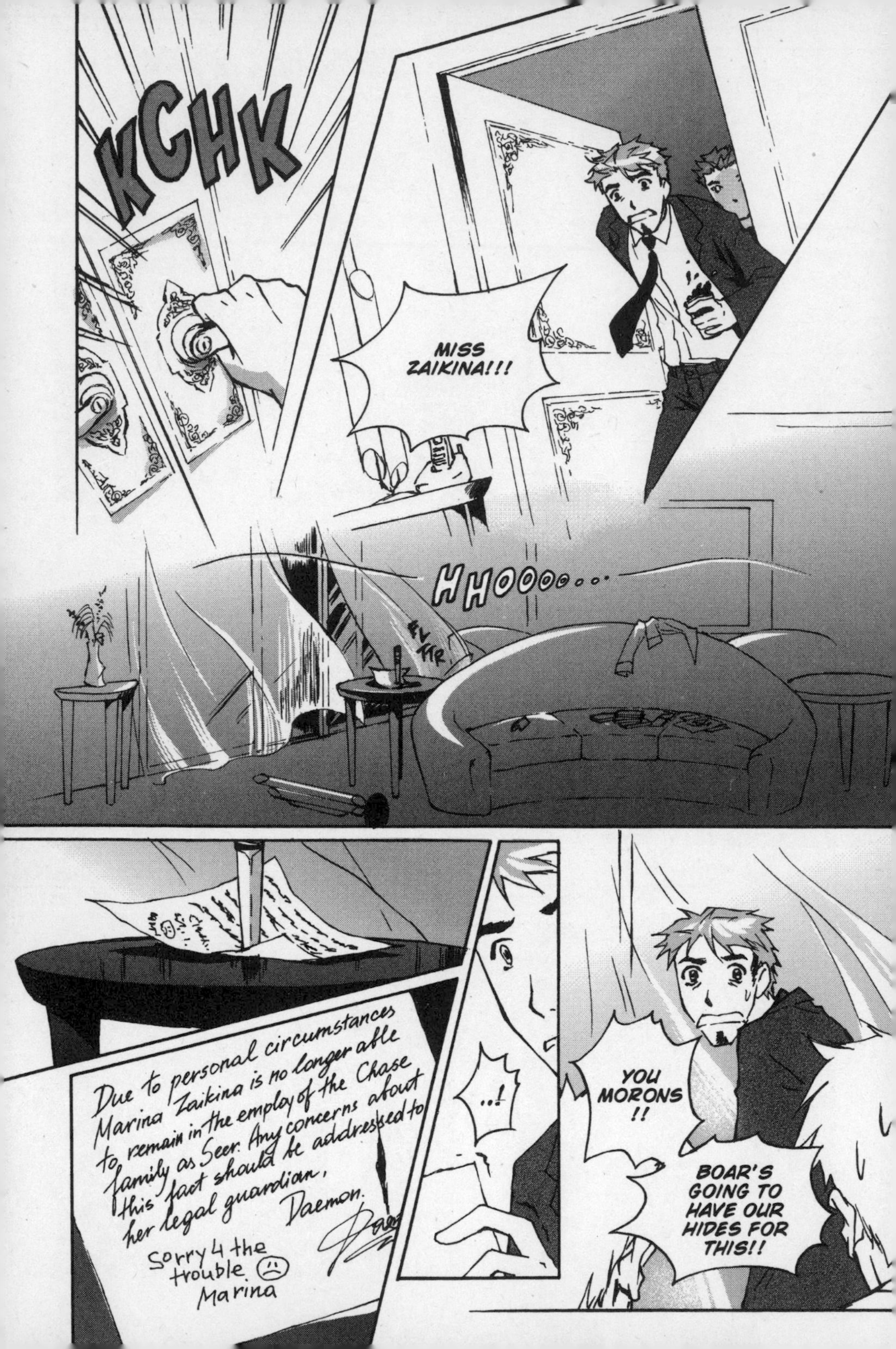
KCHK
MISS ZAIKINA!!!
HHOOooo...
Due to personal circumstances Marina Zaikina is no longer able to remain in the employ of the Chase family as Seer. Any concerns about this fact should be addressed to her legal guardian,
Daemon.
Sorry 4 the trouble. ☹
Marina
..!
YOU MORONS!!
BOAR'S GOING TO HAVE OUR HIDES FOR THIS!!

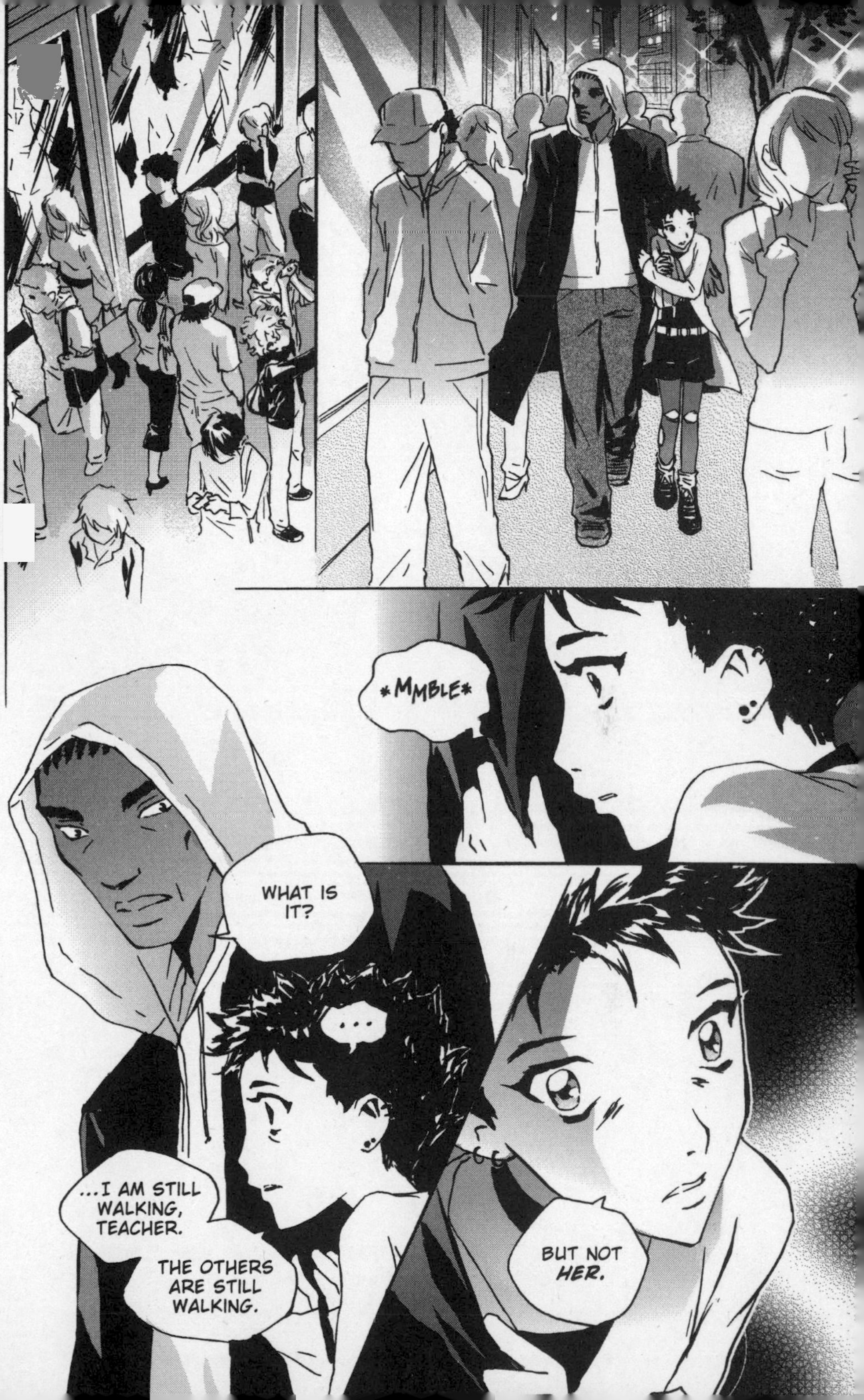
MMBLE
WHAT IS IT?
...
...I AM STILL WALKING, TEACHER.
THE OTHERS ARE STILL WALKING.
BUT NOT *HER.*

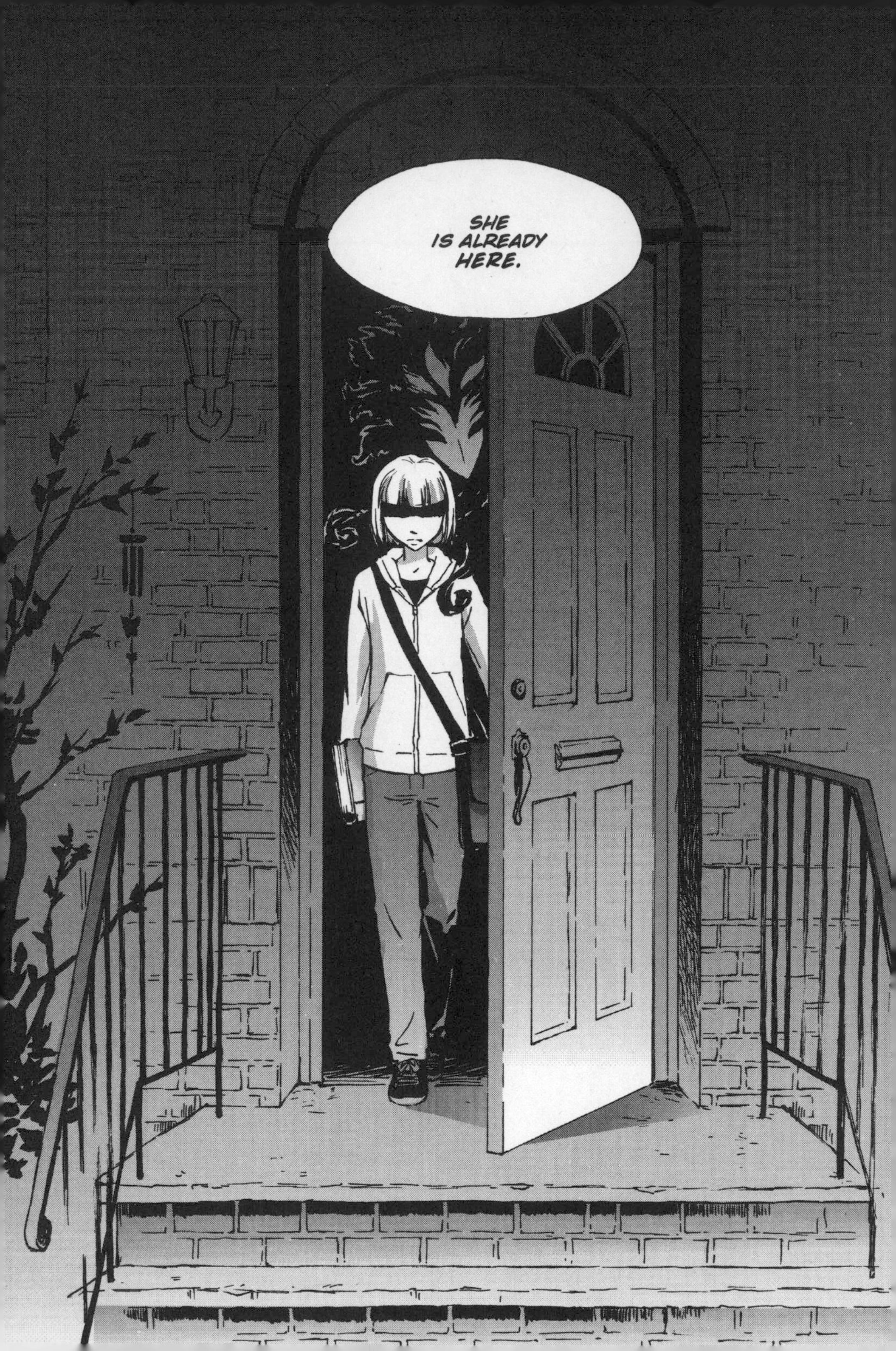
SHE IS ALREADY HERE.

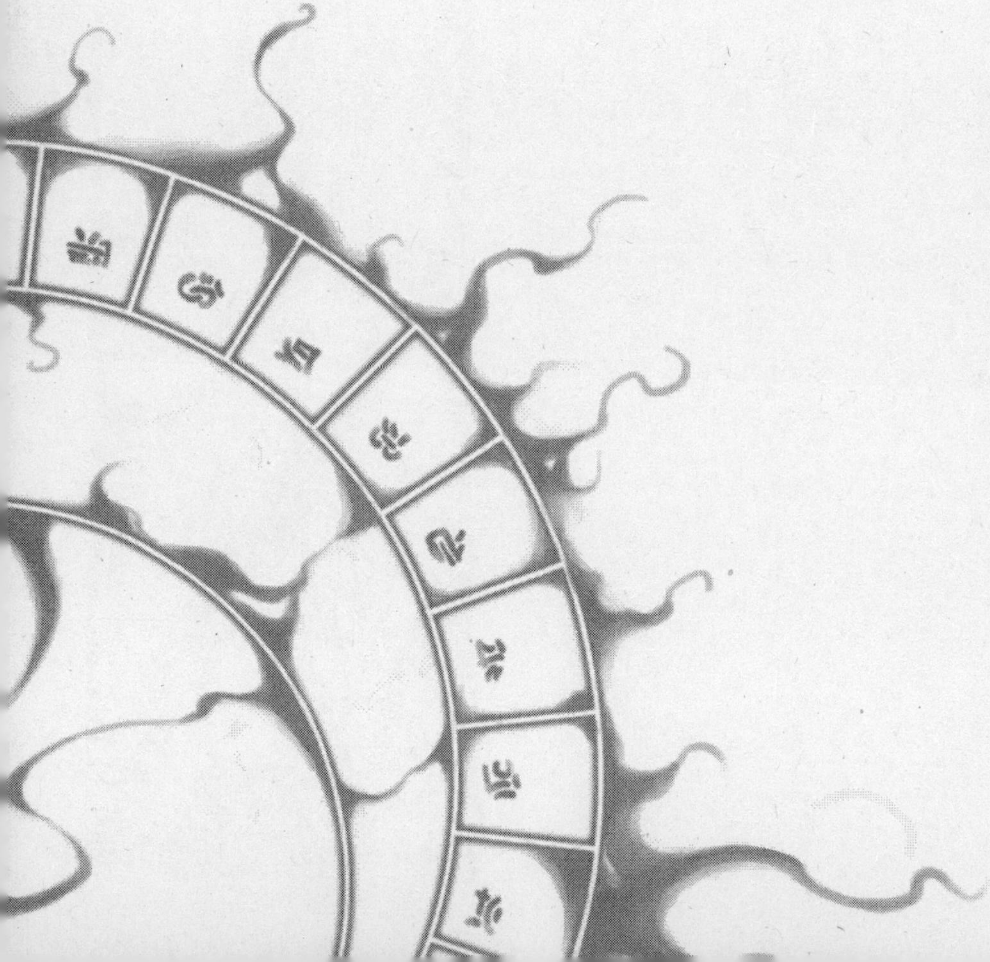

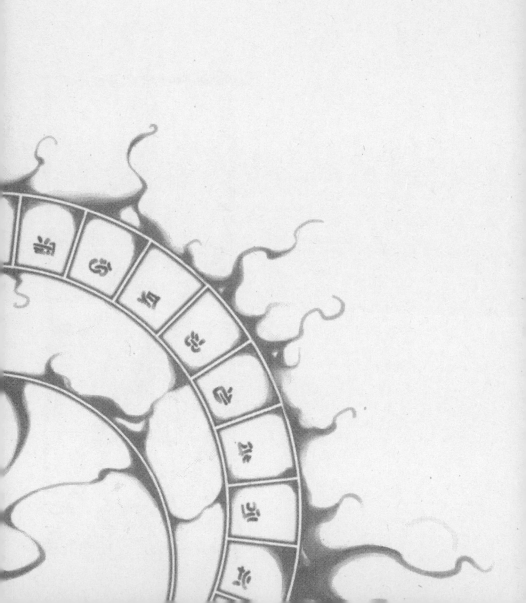

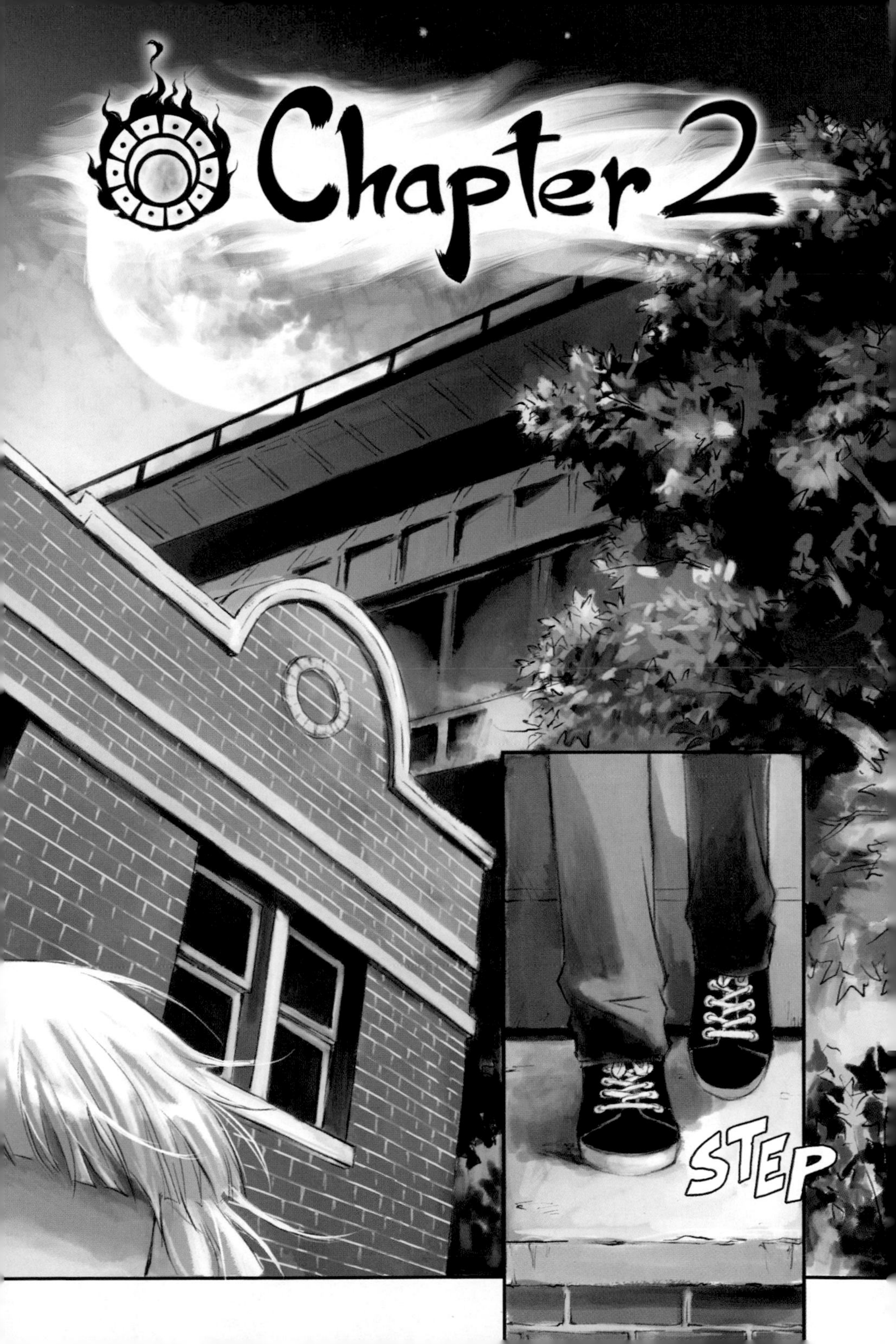
Chapter 2
STEP

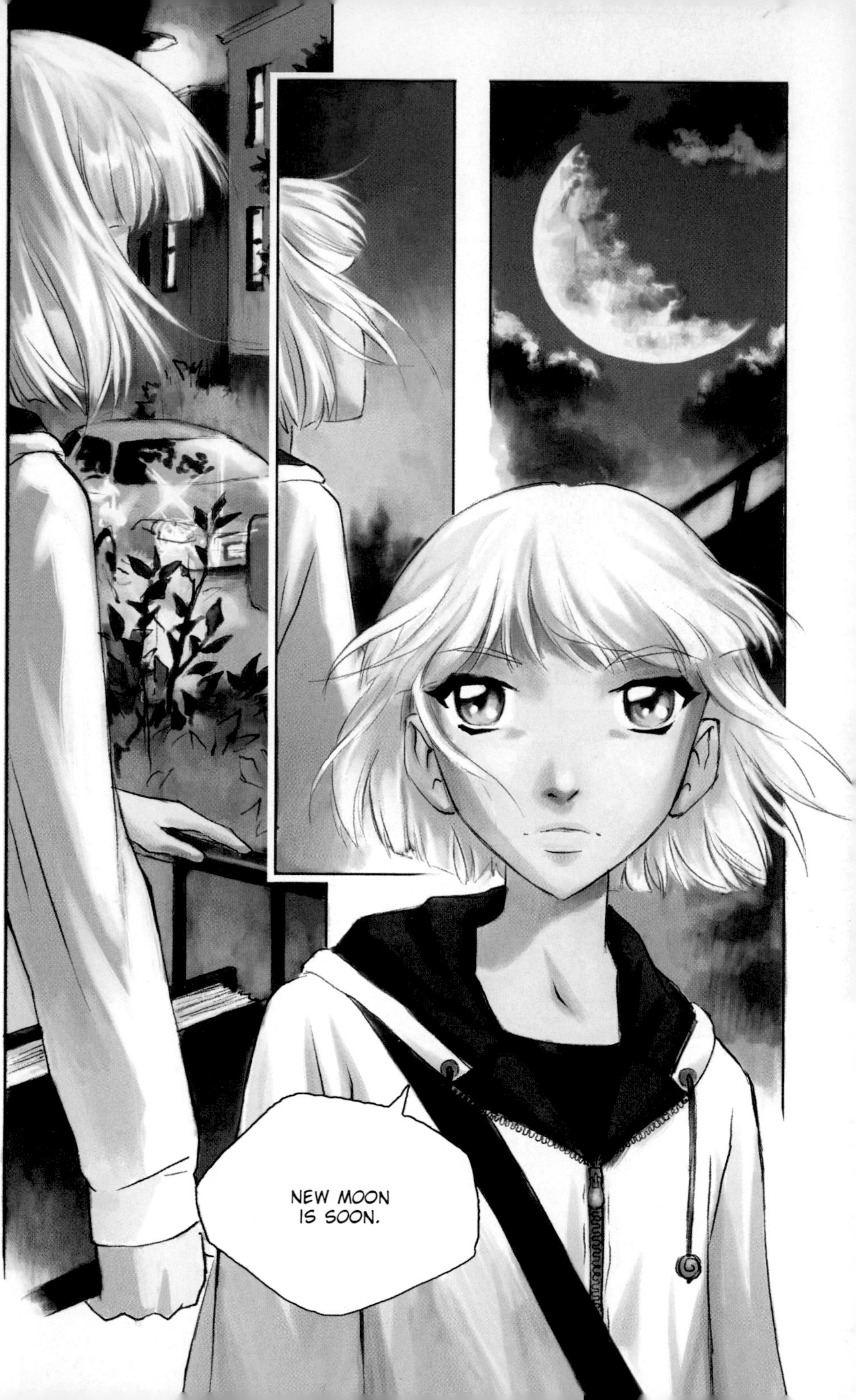
NEW MOON
IS SOON.

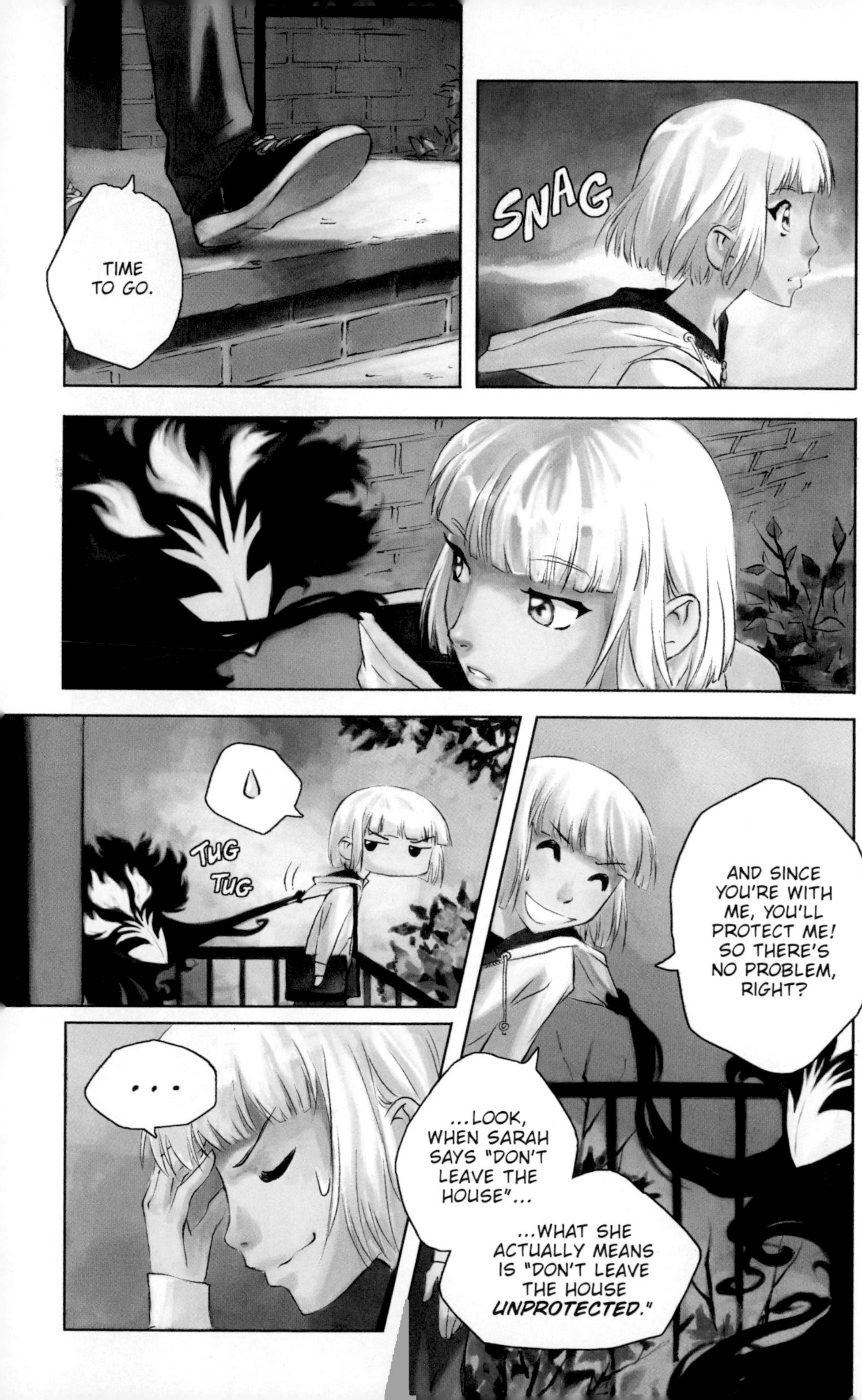
TIME TO GO.
SNAG
TUG TUG
AND SINCE YOU'RE WITH ME, YOU'LL PROTECT ME! SO THERE'S NO PROBLEM, RIGHT?
...
...LOOK, WHEN SARAH SAYS "DON'T LEAVE THE HOUSE"...
...WHAT SHE ACTUALLY MEANS IS "DON'T LEAVE THE HOUSE ***UNPROTECTED***."

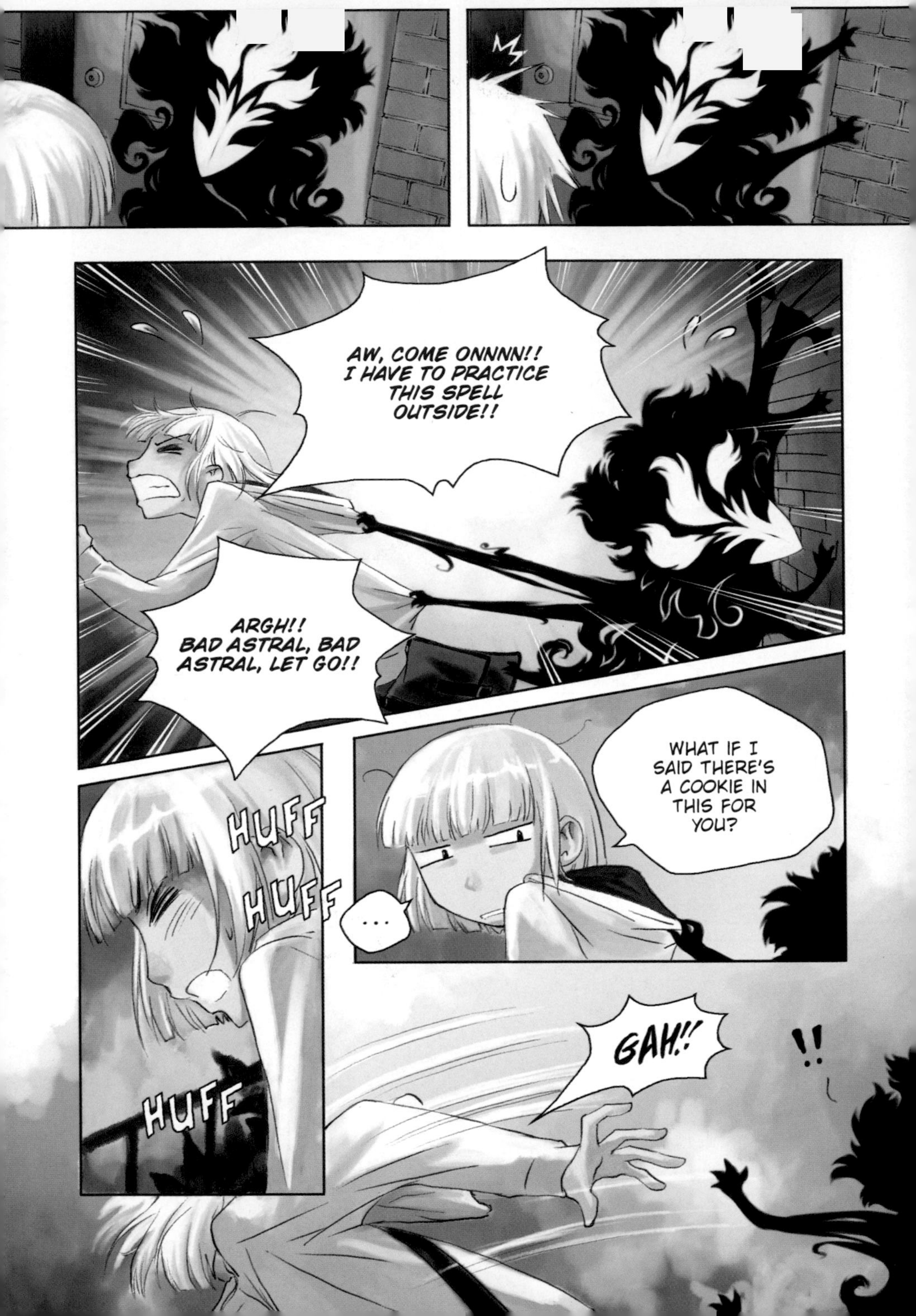
AW, COME ONNNN!! I HAVE TO PRACTICE THIS SPELL OUTSIDE!!
ARGH!! BAD ASTRAL, BAD ASTRAL, LET GO!!
HUFF
HUFF
HUFF
...
WHAT IF I SAID THERE'S A COOKIE IN THIS FOR YOU?
GAH!!
!!

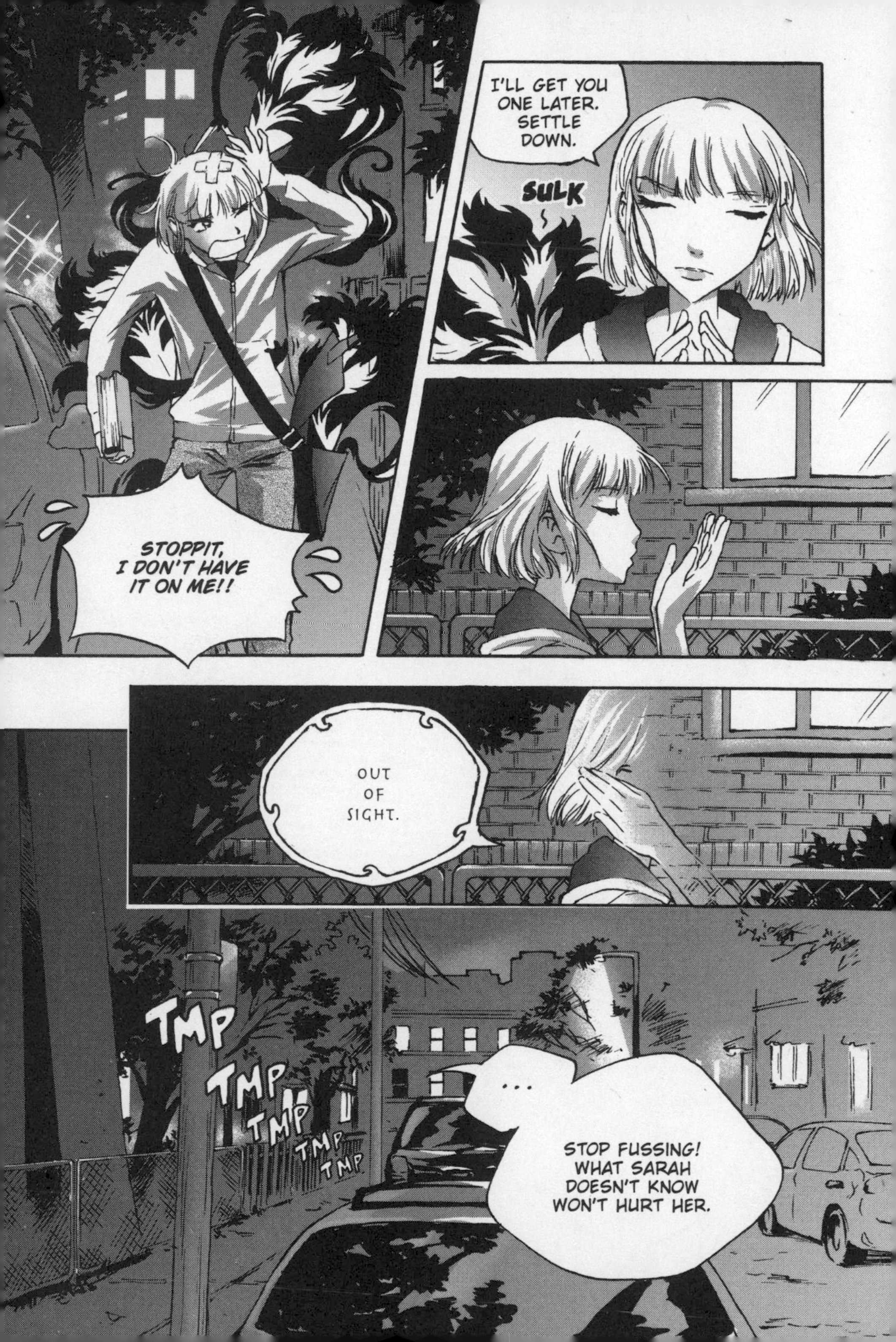
STOPPIT, I DON'T HAVE IT ON ME!!
I'LL GET YOU ONE LATER. SETTLE DOWN.
SULK
OUT OF SIGHT.
TMP TMP TMP TMP TMP
...
STOP FUSSING! WHAT SARAH DOESN'T KNOW WON'T HURT HER.

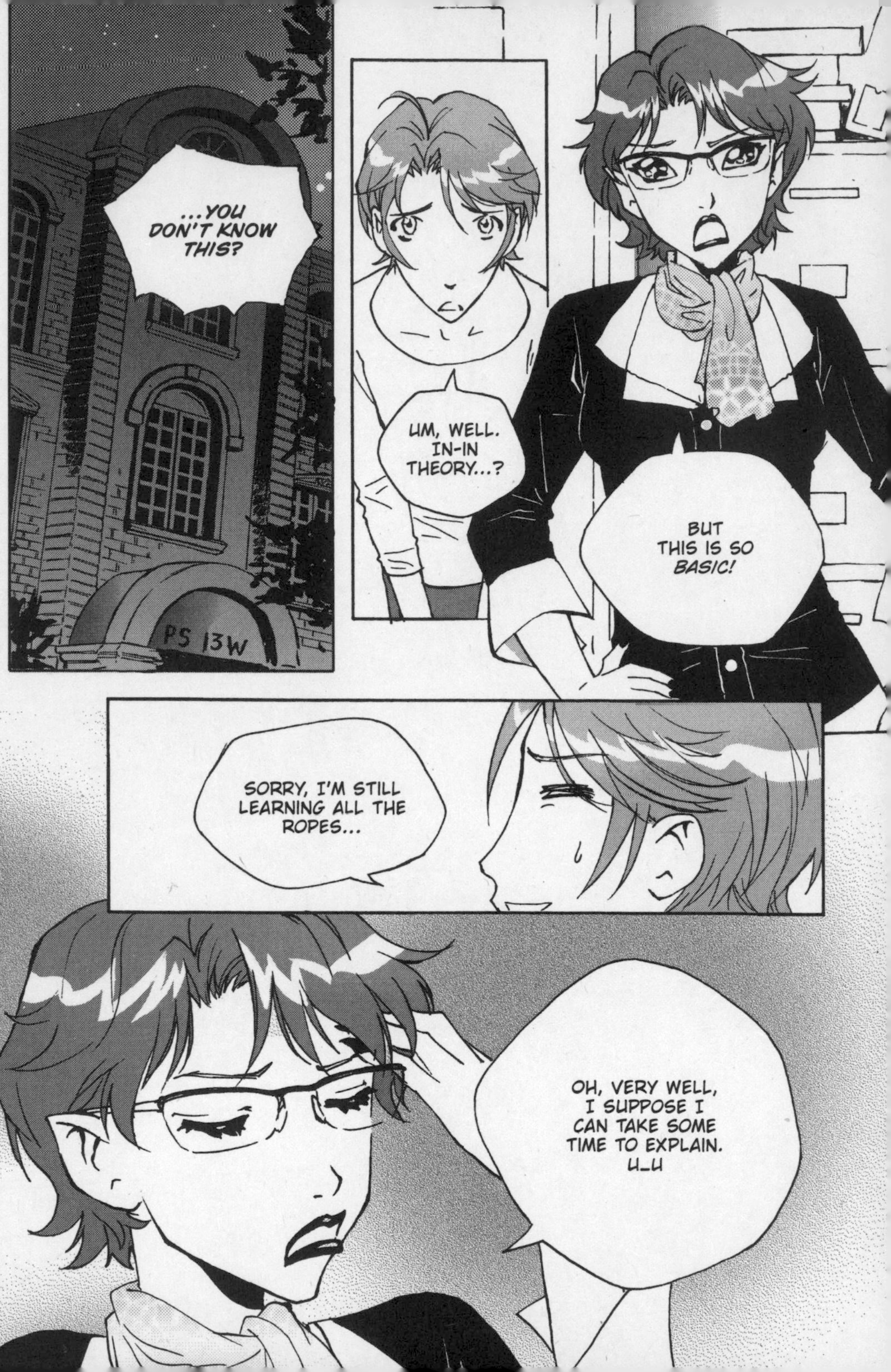
...YOU DON'T KNOW THIS?
UM, WELL. IN-IN THEORY...?
BUT THIS IS SO *BASIC!*
SORRY, I'M STILL LEARNING ALL THE ROPES...
OH, VERY WELL, I SUPPOSE I CAN TAKE SOME TIME TO EXPLAIN. u_u

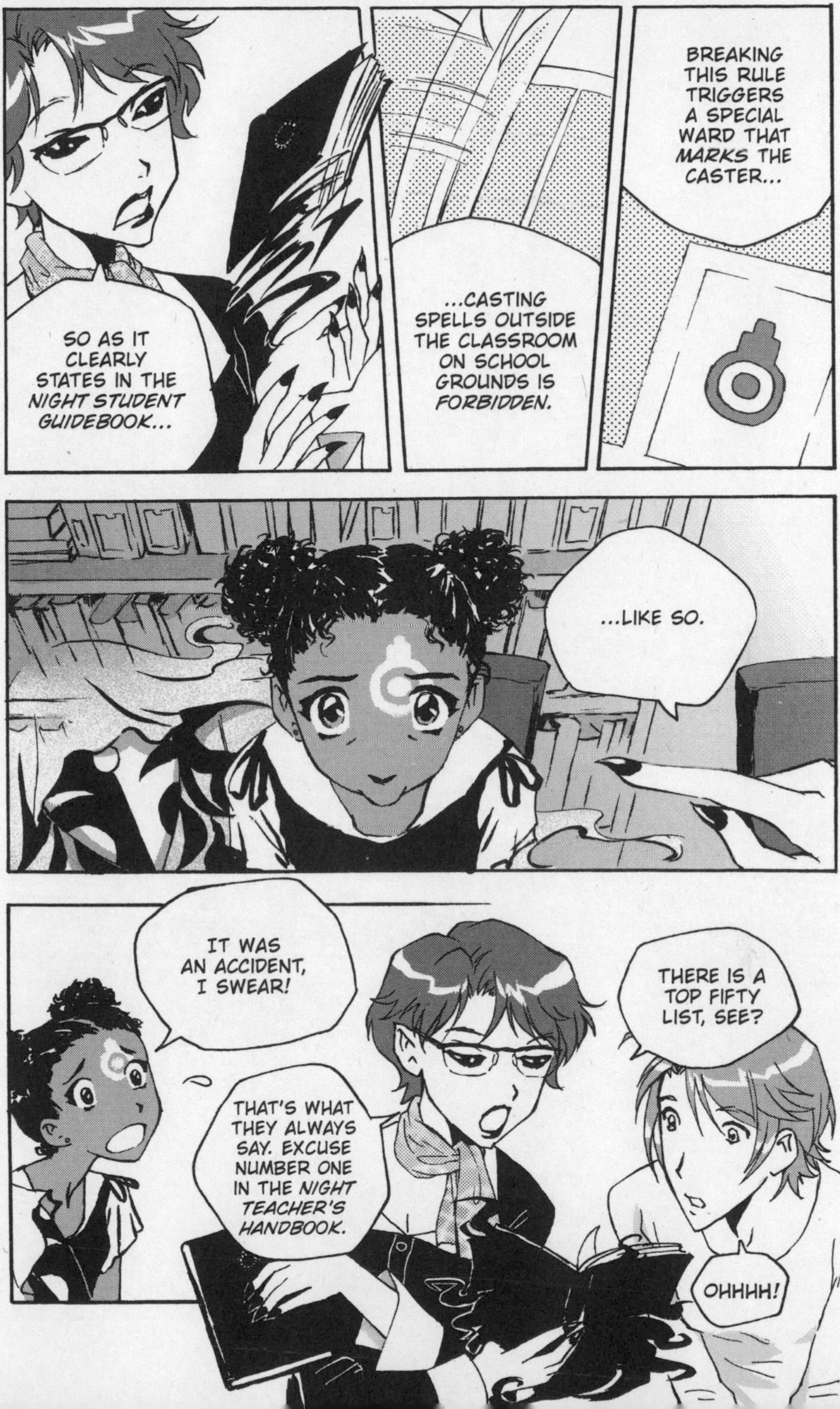
SO AS IT CLEARLY STATES IN THE *NIGHT STUDENT GUIDEBOOK*...
...CASTING SPELLS OUTSIDE THE CLASSROOM ON SCHOOL GROUNDS IS *FORBIDDEN*.
BREAKING THIS RULE TRIGGERS A SPECIAL WARD THAT *MARKS* THE CASTER...
...LIKE SO.
IT WAS AN ACCIDENT, I SWEAR!
THAT'S WHAT THEY ALWAYS SAY. EXCUSE NUMBER ONE IN THE *NIGHT TEACHER'S HANDBOOK*.
THERE IS A TOP FIFTY LIST, SEE?
OHHHH!

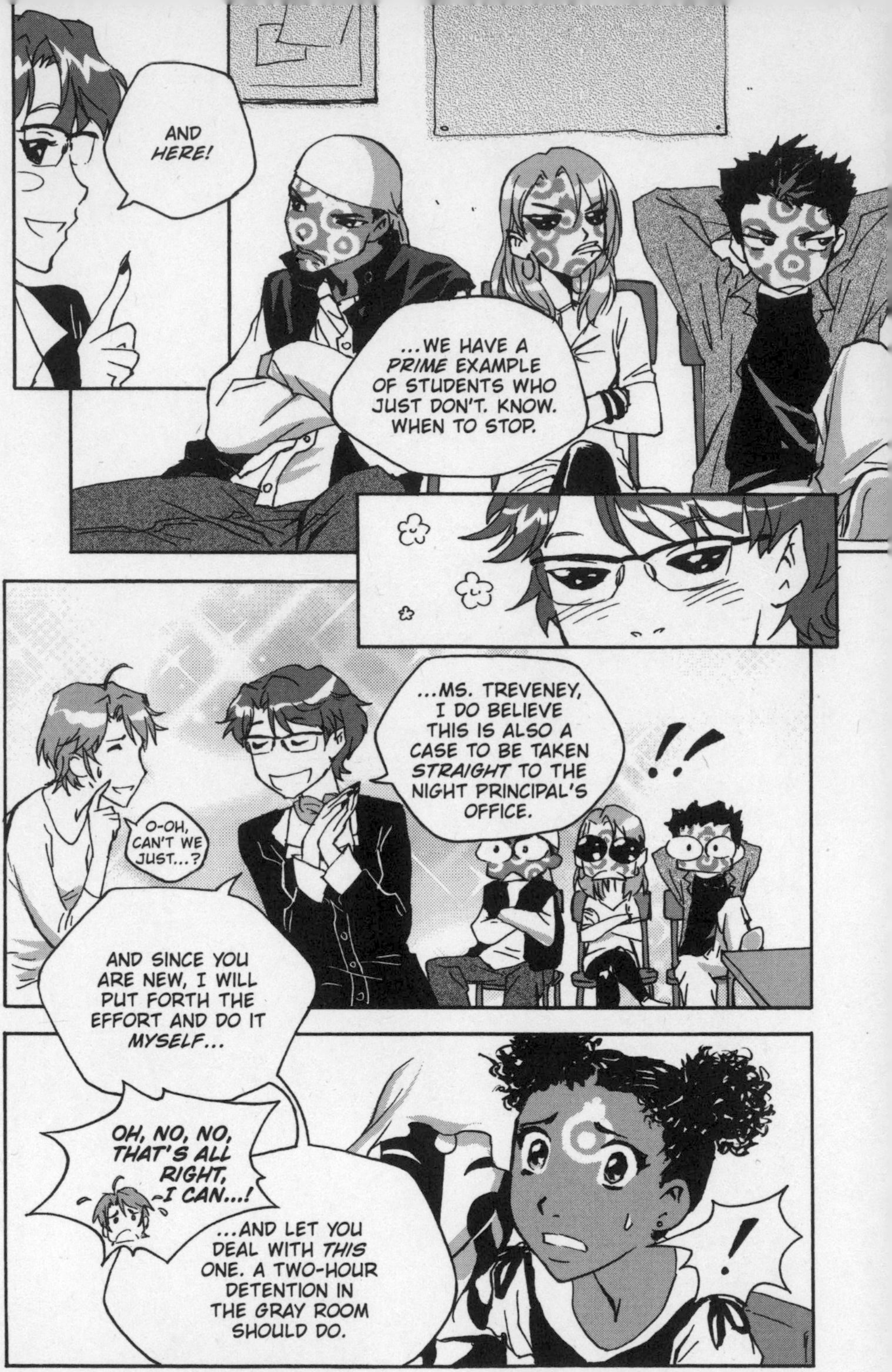
AND HERE!
...WE HAVE A PRIME EXAMPLE OF STUDENTS WHO JUST DON'T. KNOW. WHEN TO STOP.
...MS. TREVENEY, I DO BELIEVE THIS IS ALSO A CASE TO BE TAKEN STRAIGHT TO THE NIGHT PRINCIPAL'S OFFICE.
O-OH, CAN'T WE JUST...?
!!
AND SINCE YOU ARE NEW, I WILL PUT FORTH THE EFFORT AND DO IT MYSELF...
OH, NO, NO, THAT'S ALL RIGHT, I CAN...!
...AND LET YOU DEAL WITH THIS ONE. A TWO-HOUR DETENTION IN THE GRAY ROOM SHOULD DO.
!

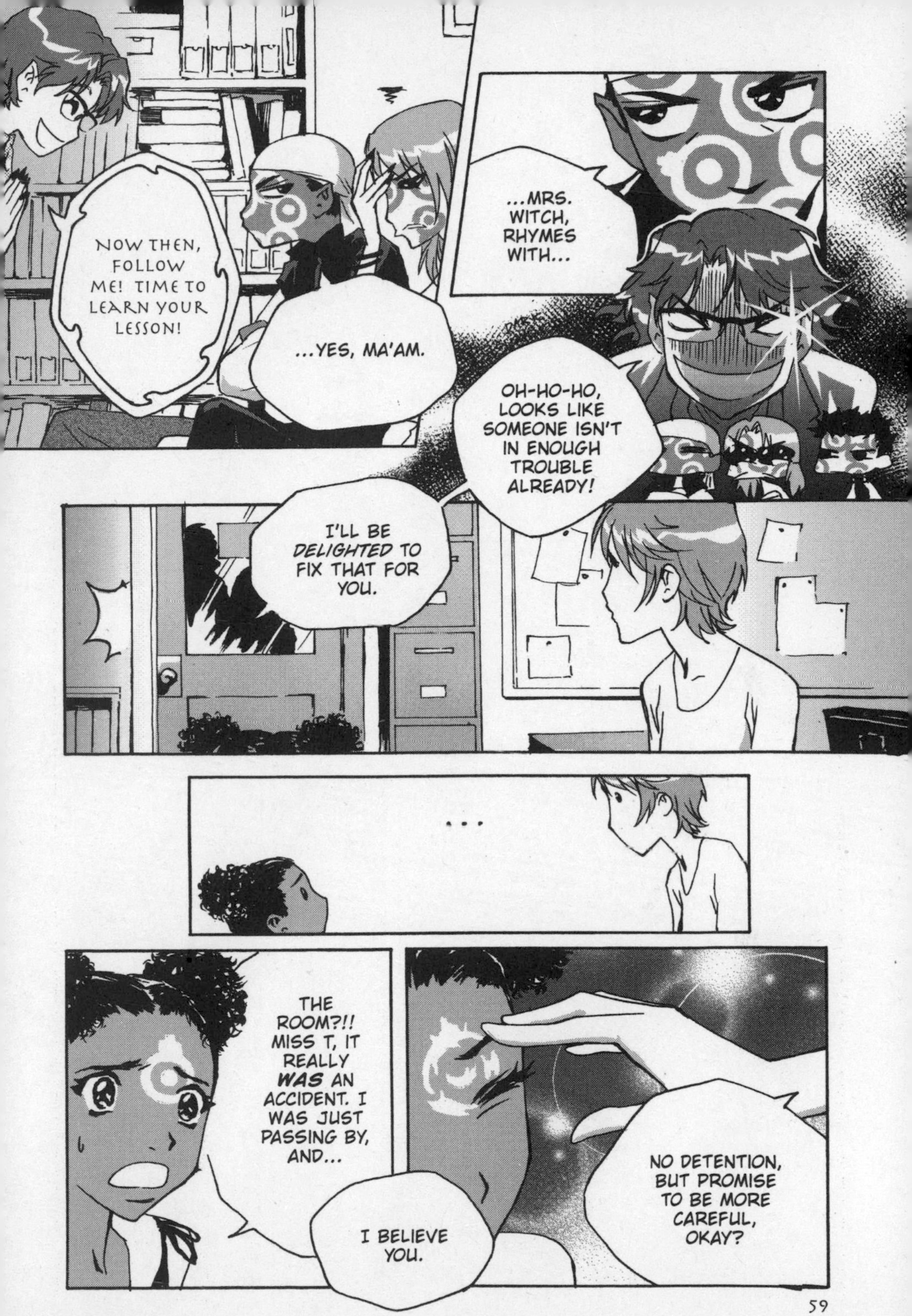
NOW THEN, FOLLOW ME! TIME TO LEARN YOUR LESSON!
...YES, MA'AM.
...MRS. WITCH, RHYMES WITH...
OH-HO-HO, LOOKS LIKE SOMEONE ISN'T IN ENOUGH TROUBLE ALREADY!
I'LL BE *DELIGHTED* TO FIX THAT FOR YOU.
...
THE ROOM?!! MISS T, IT REALLY ***WAS*** AN ACCIDENT. I WAS JUST PASSING BY, AND...
I BELIEVE YOU.
NO DETENTION, BUT PROMISE TO BE MORE CAREFUL, OKAY?

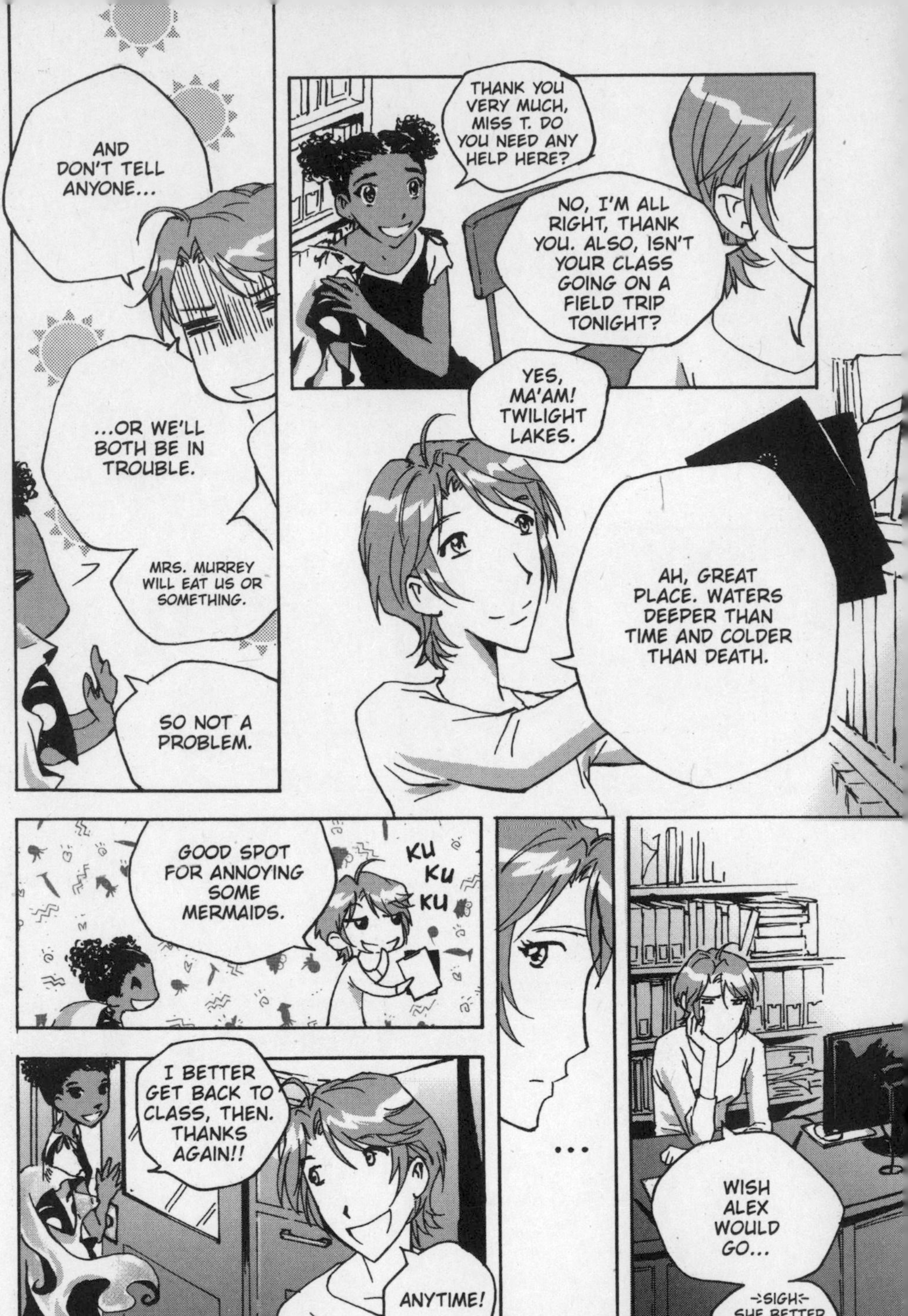
AND DON'T TELL ANYONE...
...OR WE'LL BOTH BE IN TROUBLE.
MRS. MURREY WILL EAT US OR SOMETHING.
SO NOT A PROBLEM.
THANK YOU VERY MUCH, MISS T. DO YOU NEED ANY HELP HERE?
NO, I'M ALL RIGHT, THANK YOU. ALSO, ISN'T YOUR CLASS GOING ON A FIELD TRIP TONIGHT?
YES, MA'AM! TWILIGHT LAKES.
AH, GREAT PLACE. WATERS DEEPER THAN TIME AND COLDER THAN DEATH.
GOOD SPOT FOR ANNOYING SOME MERMAIDS.
KU KU KU
I BETTER GET BACK TO CLASS, THEN. THANKS AGAIN!!
ANYTIME!
...
WISH ALEX WOULD GO...
SIGH
SHE BETTER BE STUDYING.

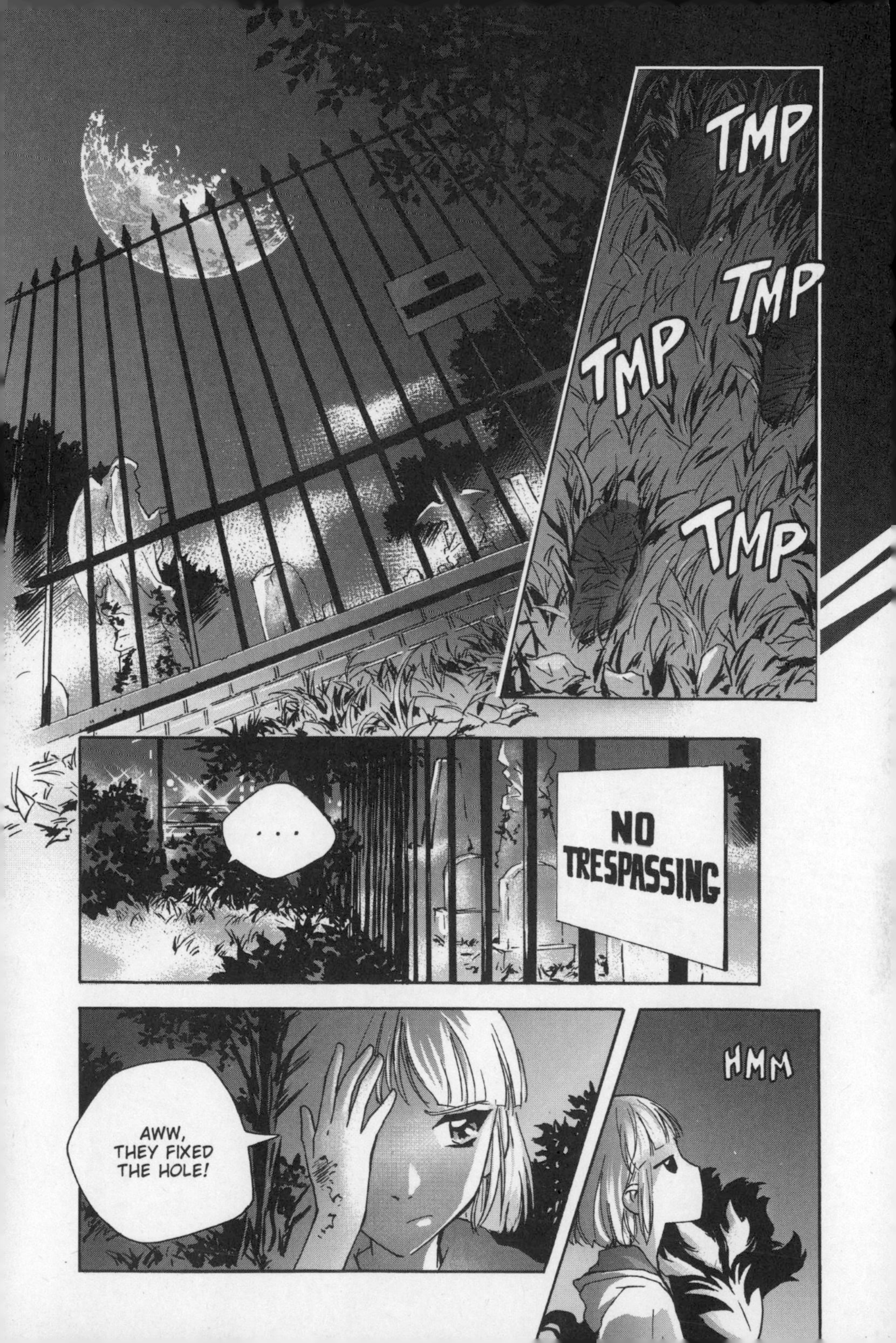
TMP
TMP
TMP
TMP
...
NO TRESPASSING
AWW, THEY FIXED THE HOLE!
HMM

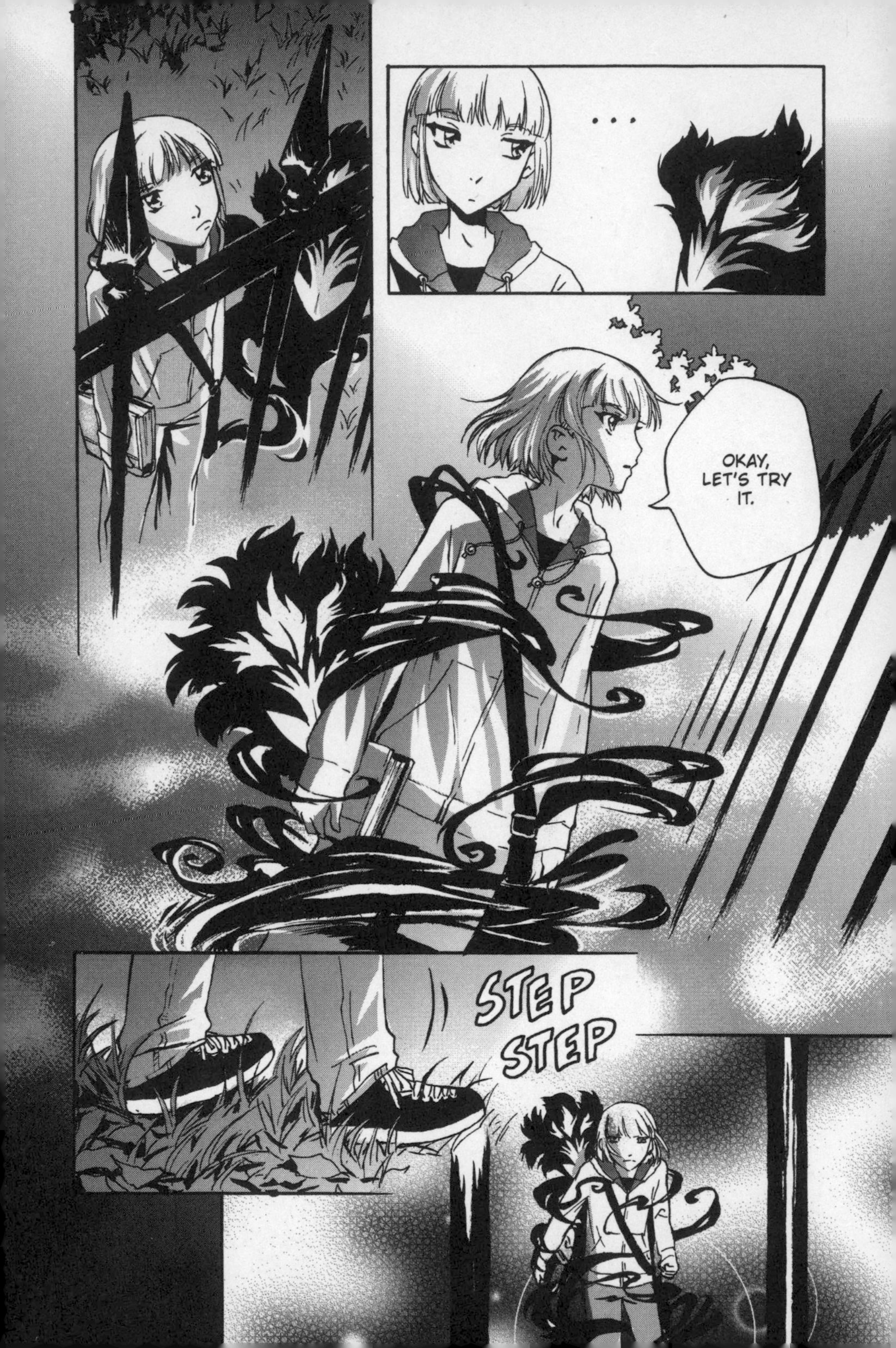
...
OKAY, LET'S TRY IT.
STEP STEP

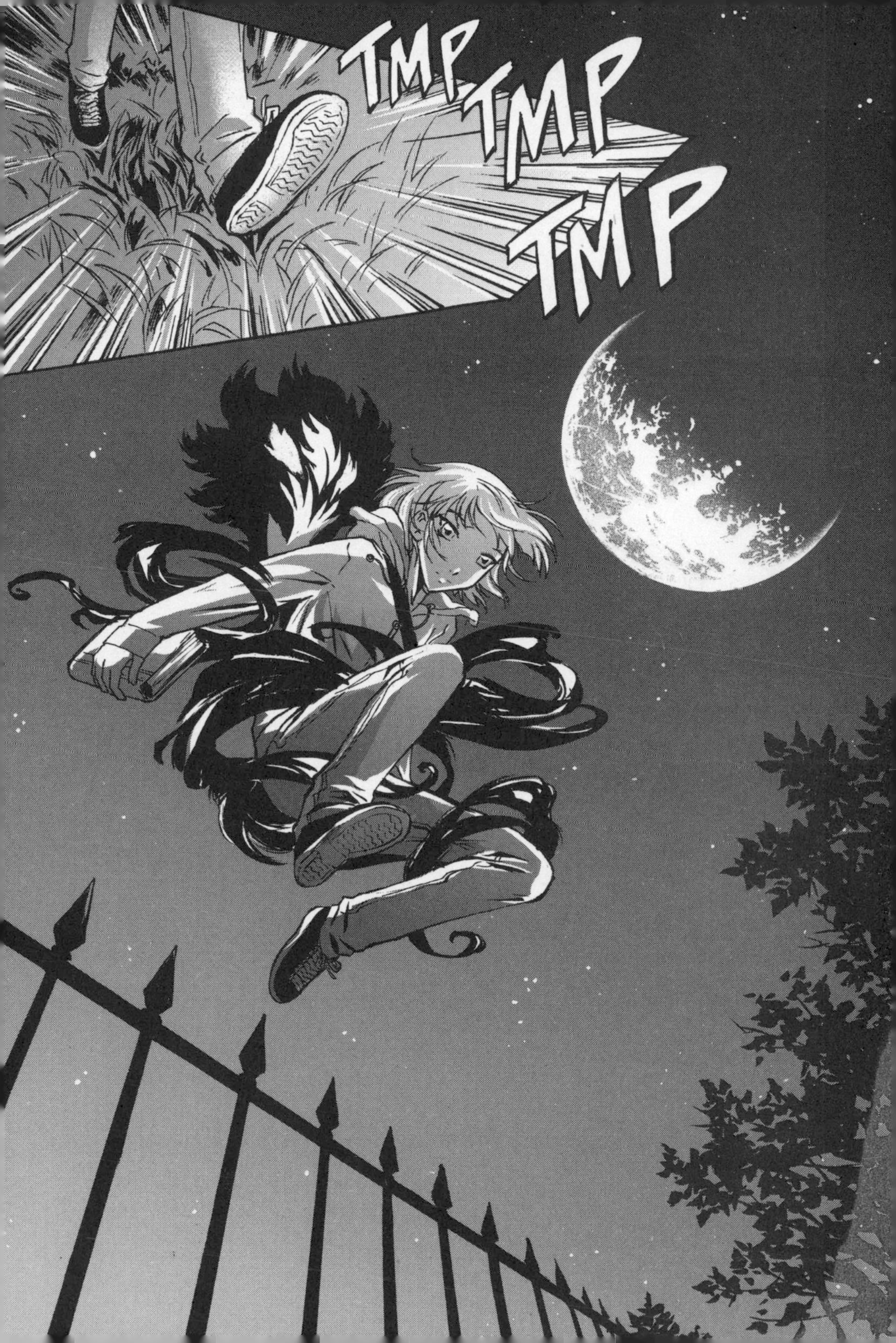
TMP TMP TMP

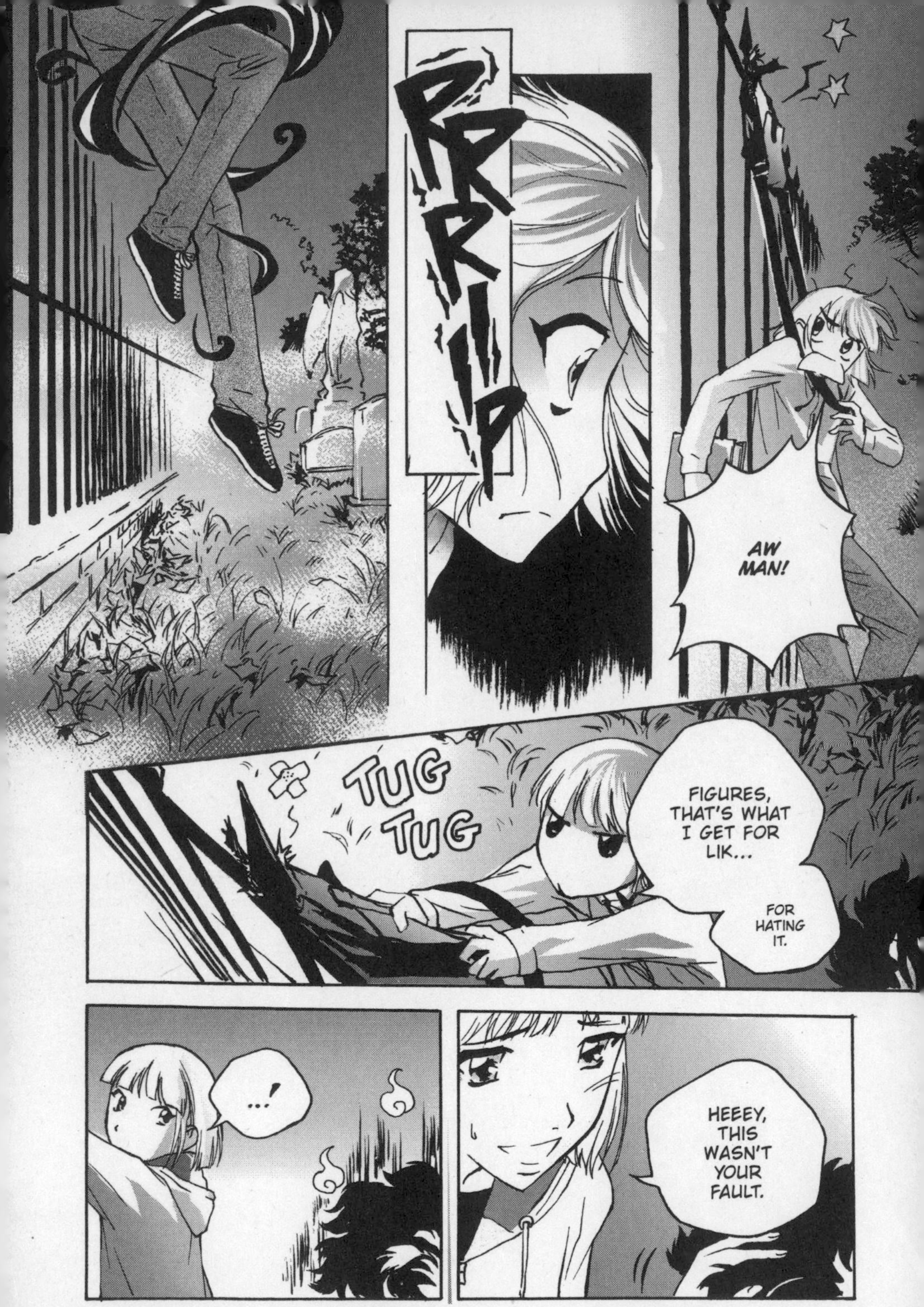
RRRIIP
AW MAN!
TUG TUG
FIGURES, THAT'S WHAT I GET FOR LIK...
FOR HATING IT.
...!
HEEEY, THIS WASN'T YOUR FAULT.

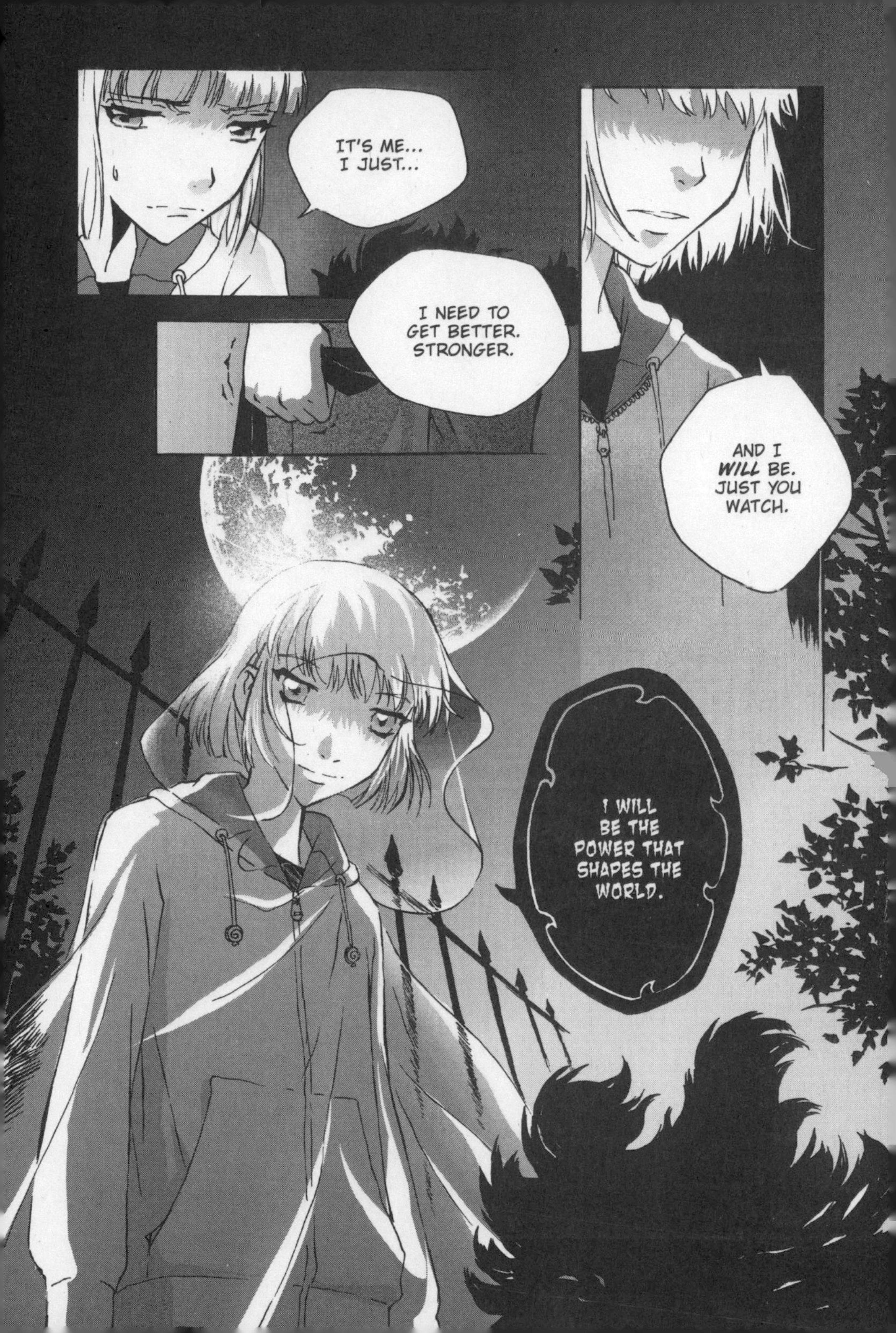
IT'S ME... I JUST...
I NEED TO GET BETTER. STRONGER.
AND I WILL BE. JUST YOU WATCH.
I WILL BE THE POWER THAT SHAPES THE WORLD.

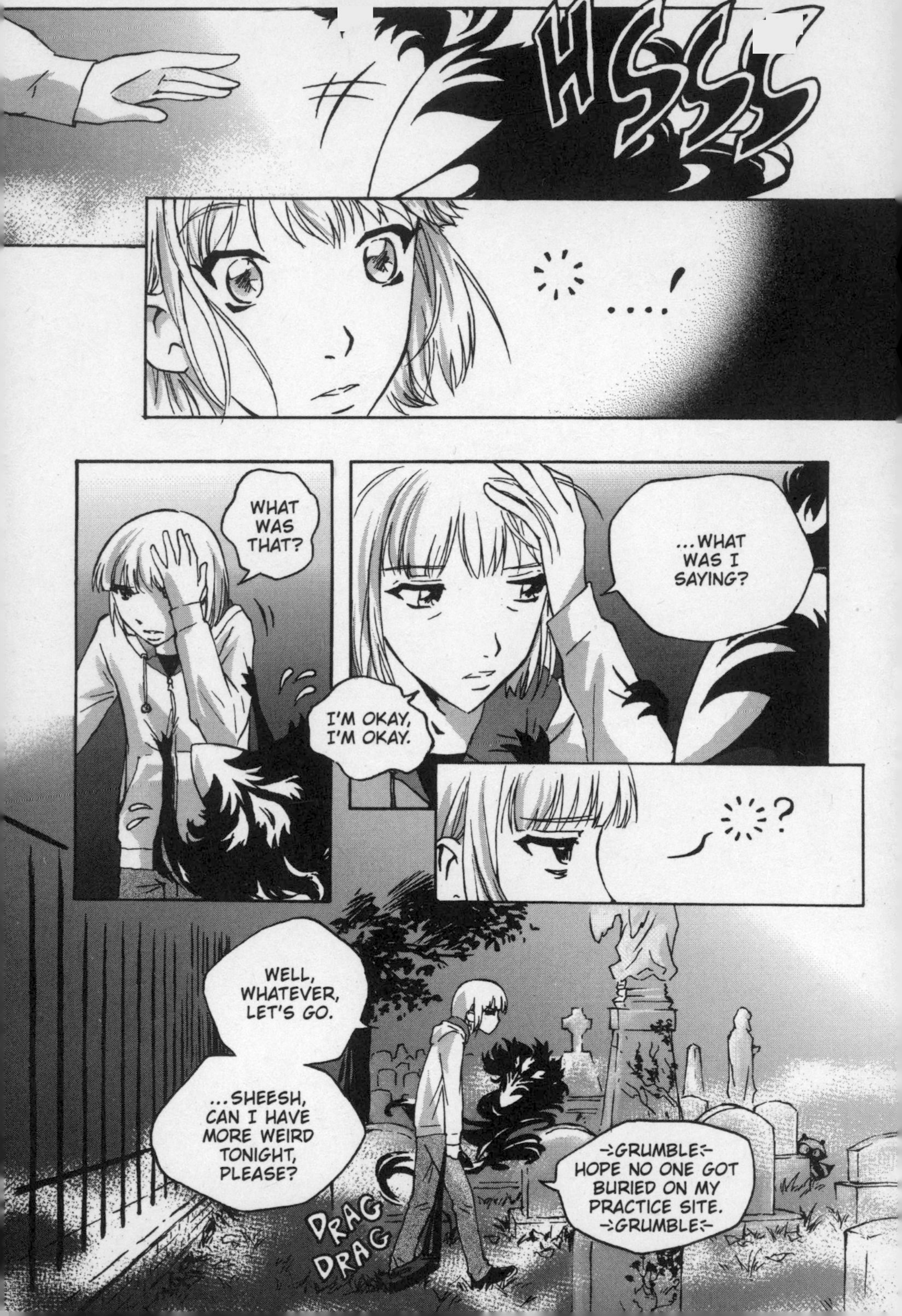
HSSS
....!
WHAT WAS THAT?
I'M OKAY, I'M OKAY.
...WHAT WAS I SAYING?
?
WELL, WHATEVER, LET'S GO.
...SHEESH, CAN I HAVE MORE WEIRD TONIGHT, PLEASE?
DRAG DRAG
-GRUMBLE- HOPE NO ONE GOT BURIED ON MY PRACTICE SITE. -GRUMBLE-

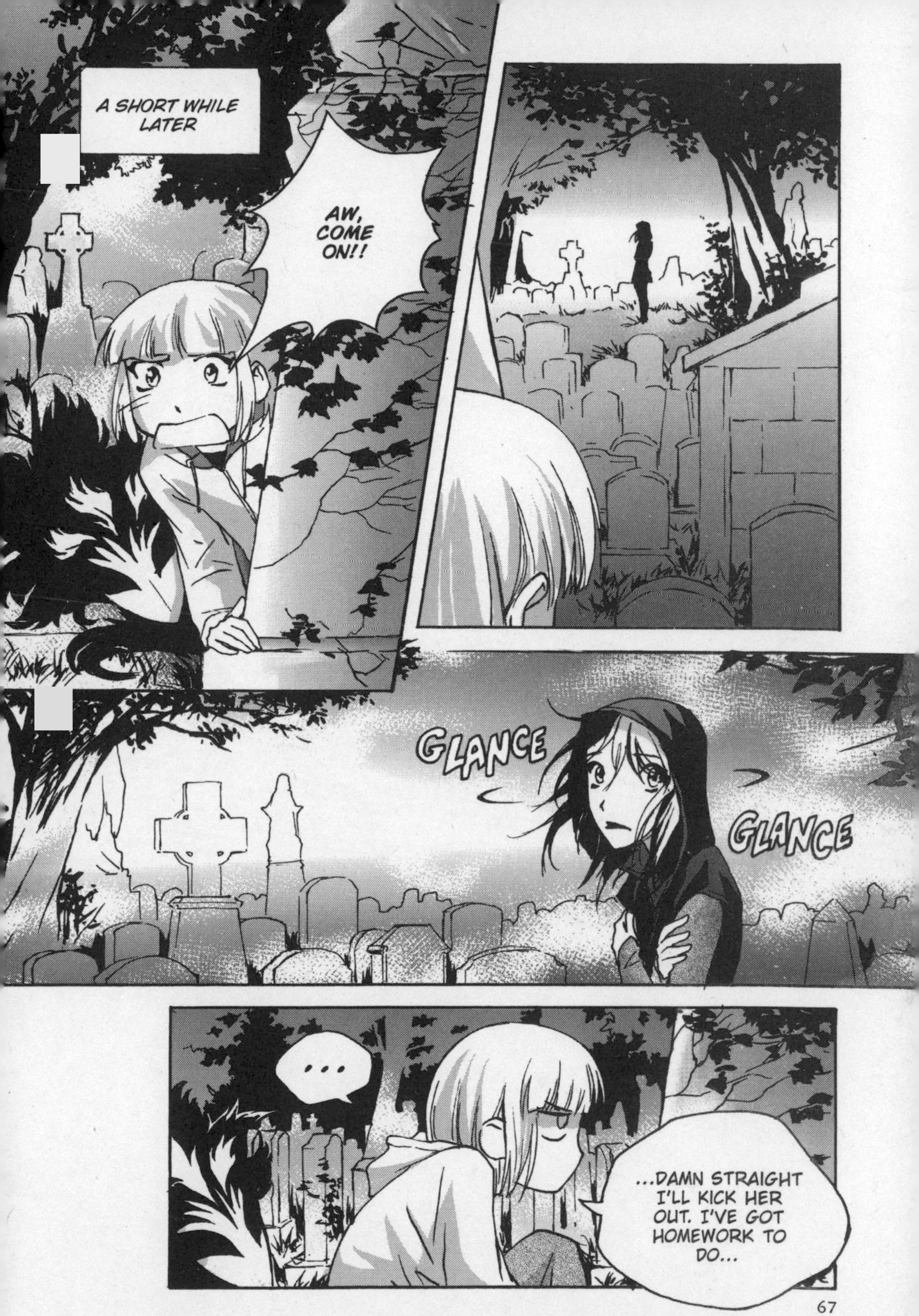
A SHORT WHILE LATER
AW, COME ON!!
GLANCE
GLANCE
...
...DAMN STRAIGHT I'LL KICK HER OUT. I'VE GOT HOMEWORK TO DO...

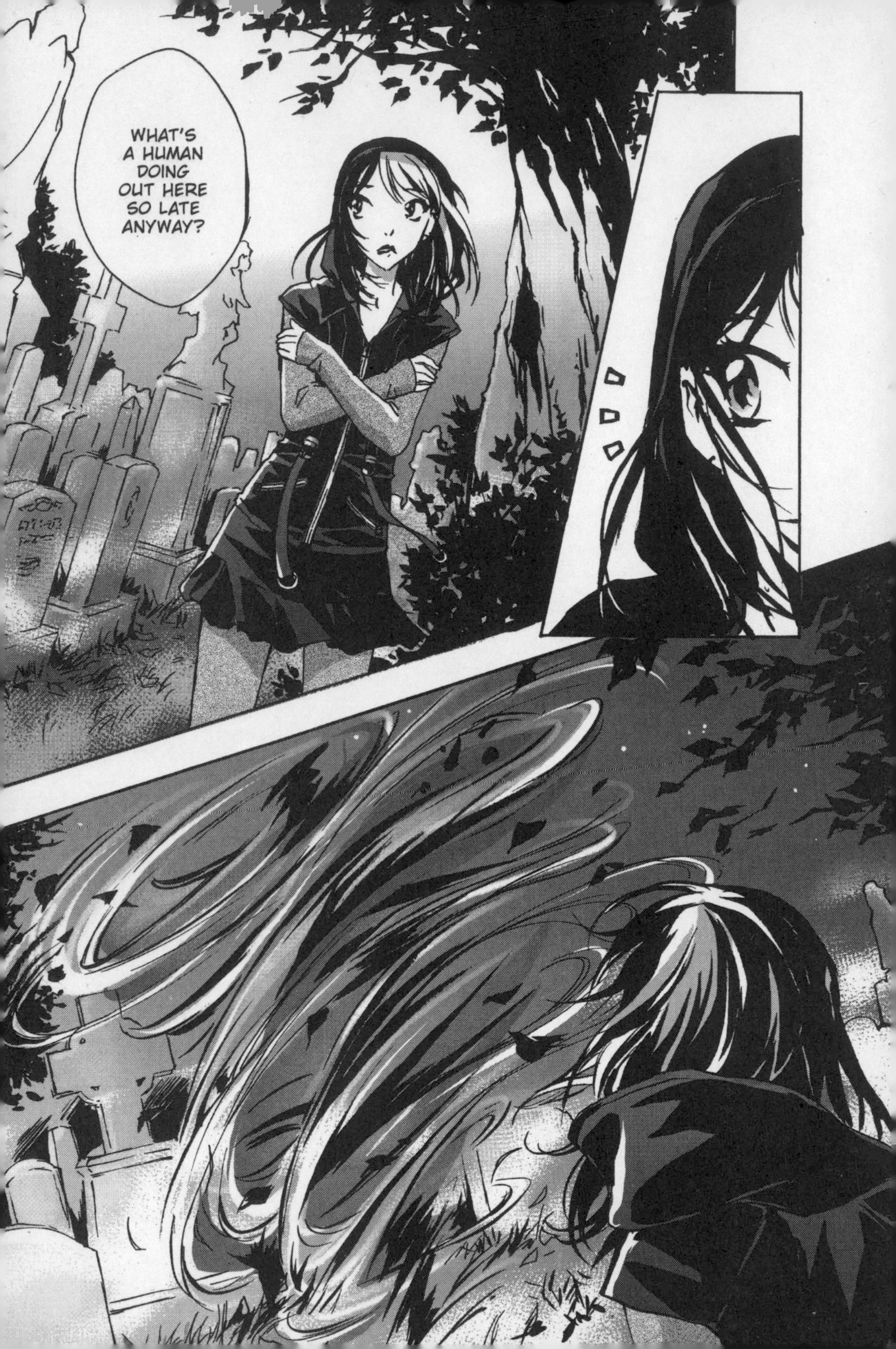
WHAT'S A HUMAN DOING OUT HERE SO LATE ANYWAY?

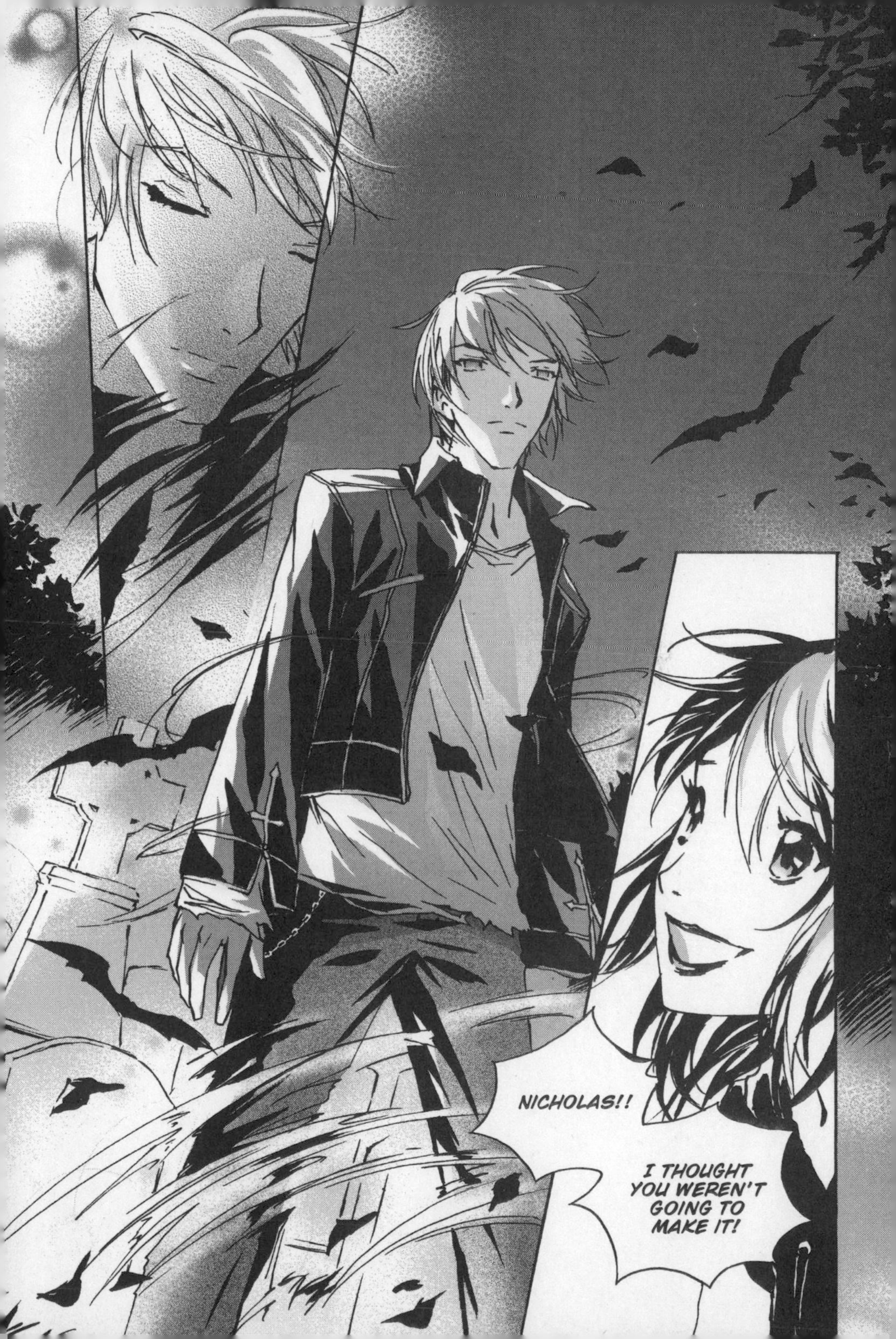
NICHOLAS!!
I THOUGHT YOU WEREN'T GOING TO MAKE IT!

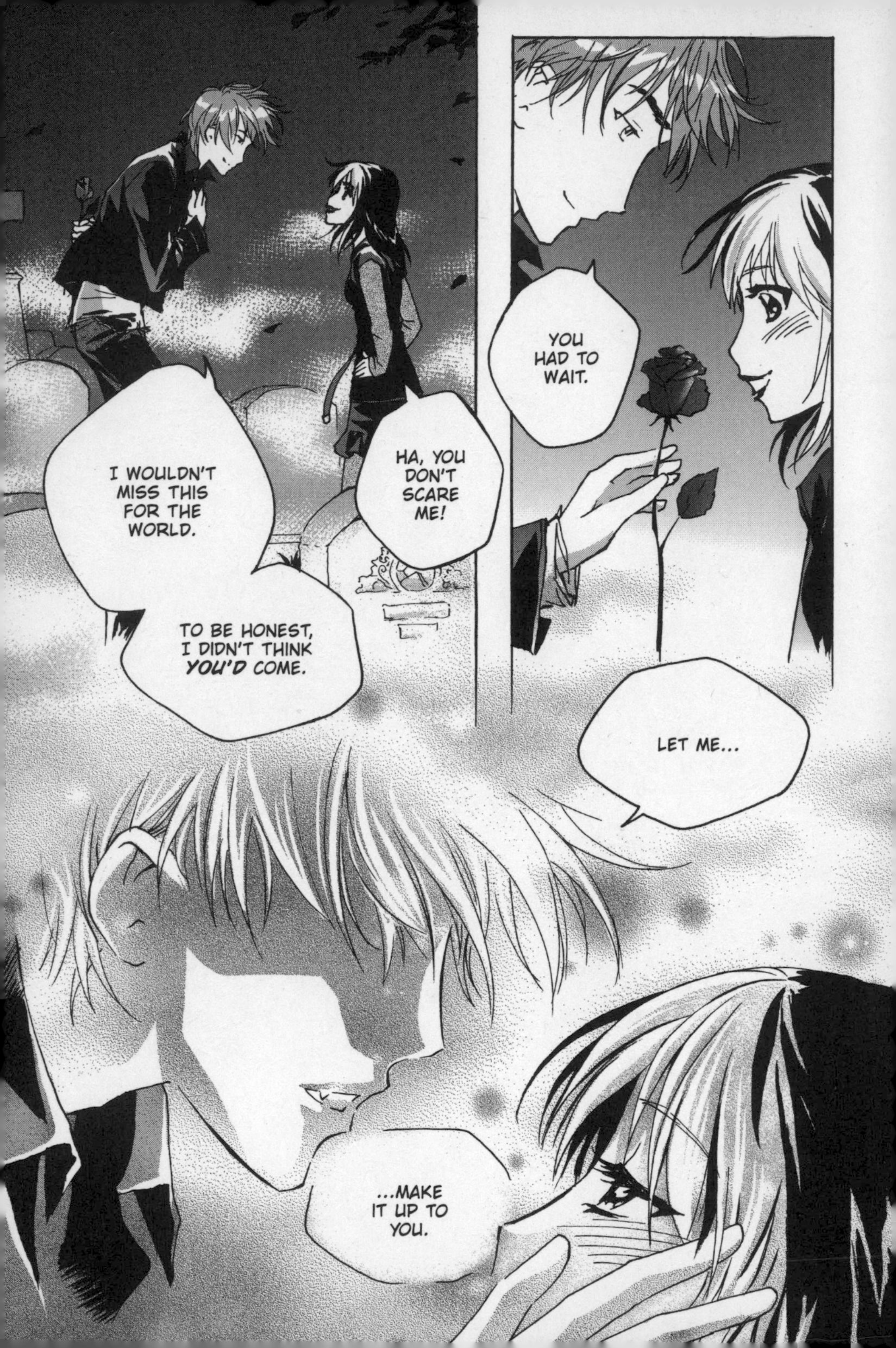
I WOULDN'T MISS THIS FOR THE WORLD.
HA, YOU DON'T SCARE ME!
TO BE HONEST, I DIDN'T THINK *YOU'D* COME.
YOU HAD TO WAIT.
LET ME...
...MAKE IT UP TO YOU.

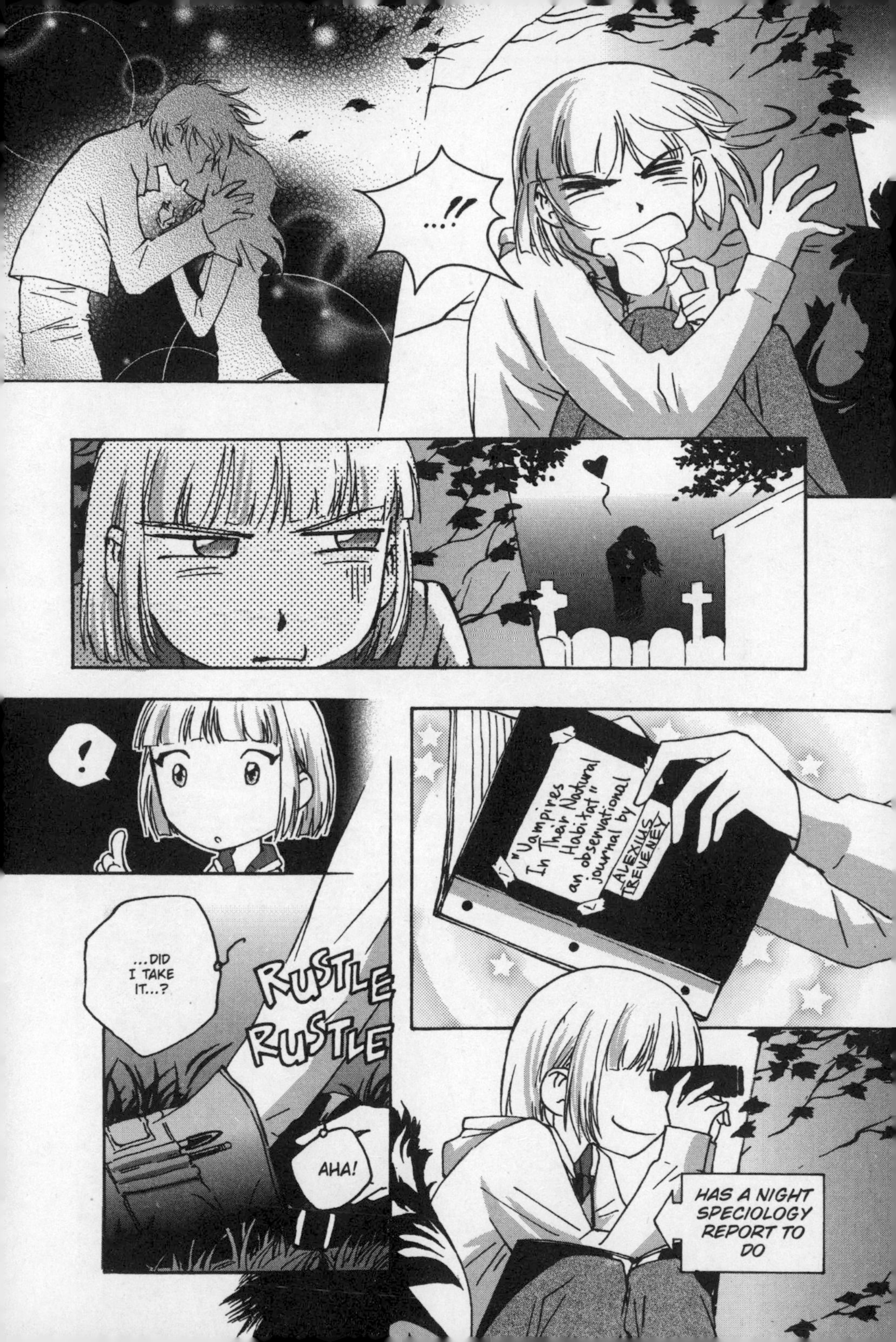

...!!
!
"Vampires In Their Natural Habitat" an observational journal by ALEXIUS TREVENEY
...DID I TAKE IT...?
RUSTLE RUSTLE
AHA!
HAS A NIGHT SPECIOLOGY REPORT TO DO

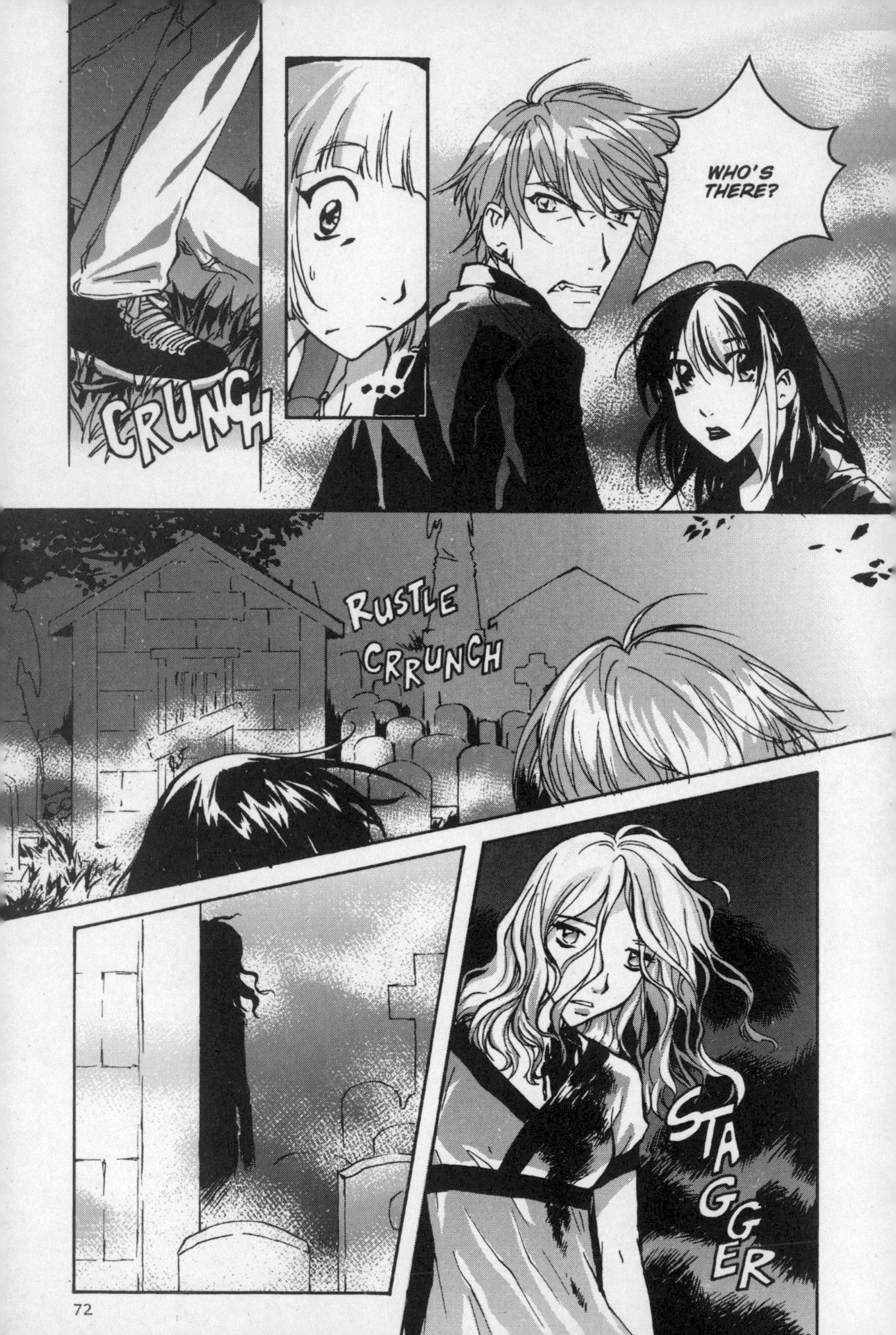
CRUNCH
...!
WHO'S THERE?
RUSTLE
CRRUNCH
STAGGER

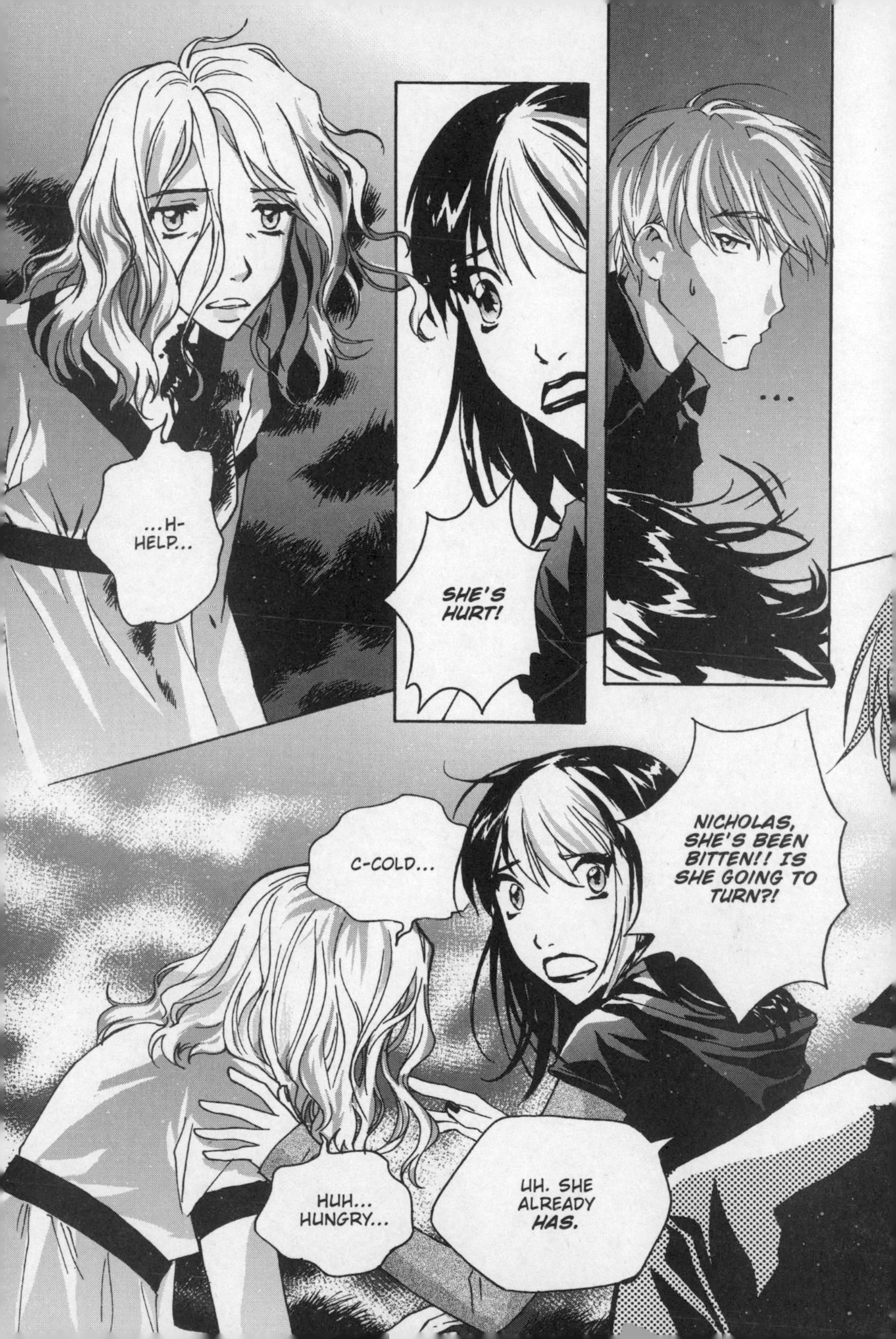
...H-
HELP...
SHE'S
HURT!
...
C-COLD...
NICHOLAS, SHE'S BEEN BITTEN!! IS SHE GOING TO TURN?!
HUH... HUNGRY...
UH. SHE ALREADY HAS.

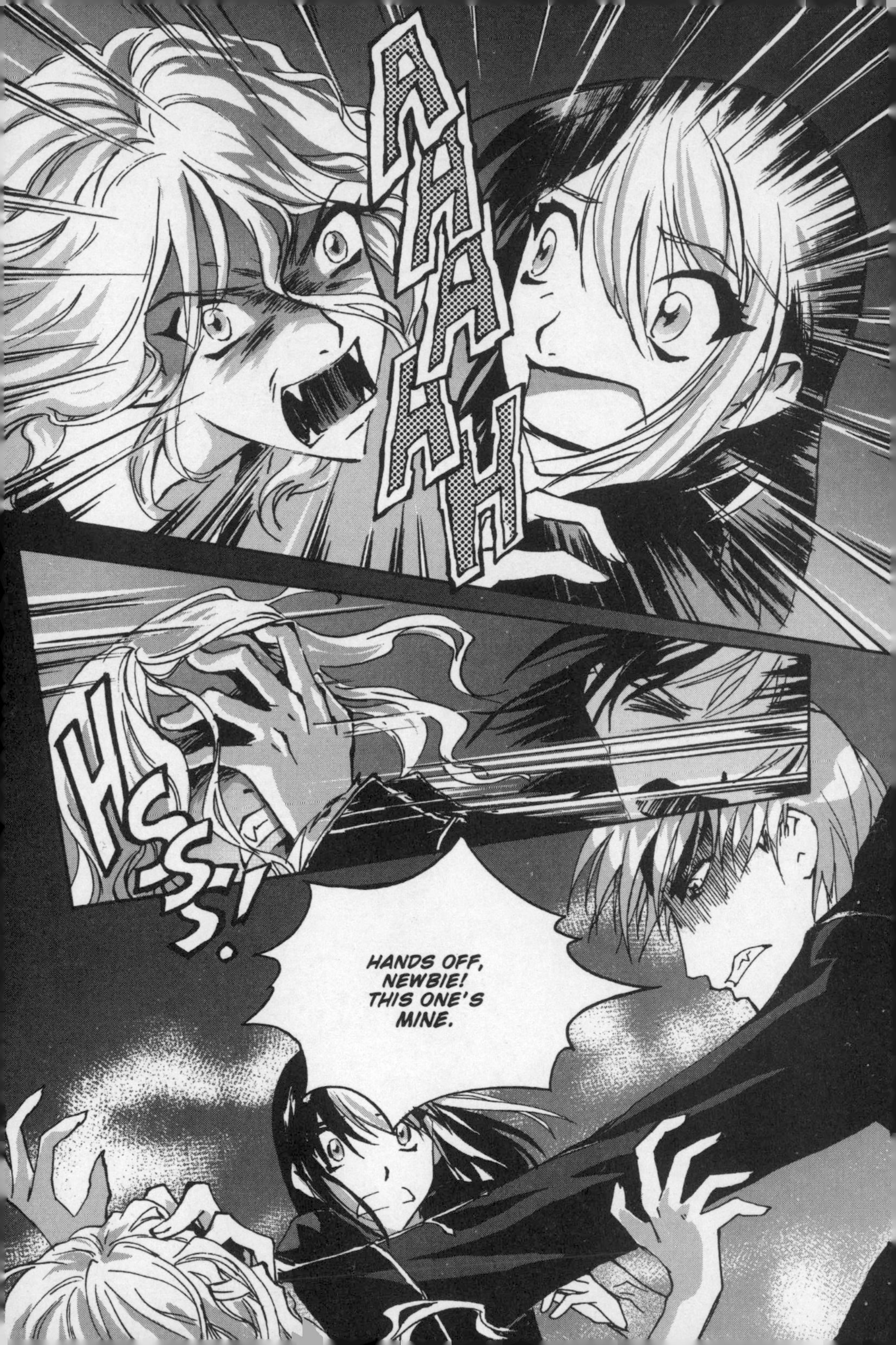
AAAAHH
HSSS!!
HANDS OFF, NEWBIE! THIS ONE'S MINE.

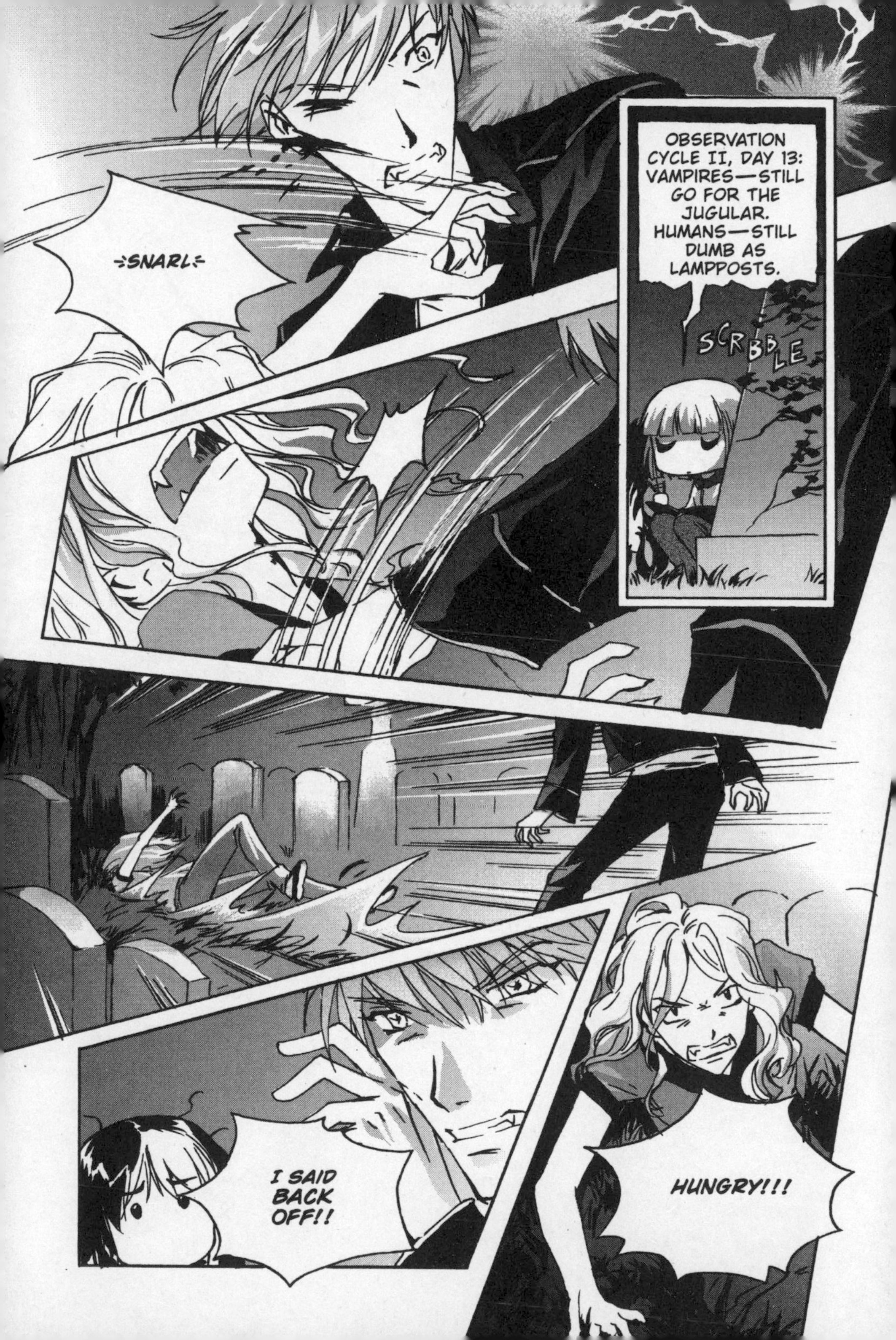

=SNARL=
OBSERVATION CYCLE II, DAY 13: VAMPIRES—STILL GO FOR THE JUGULAR. HUMANS—STILL DUMB AS LAMPPOSTS.
SCRBBLE
I SAID BACK OFF!!
HUNGRY!!!

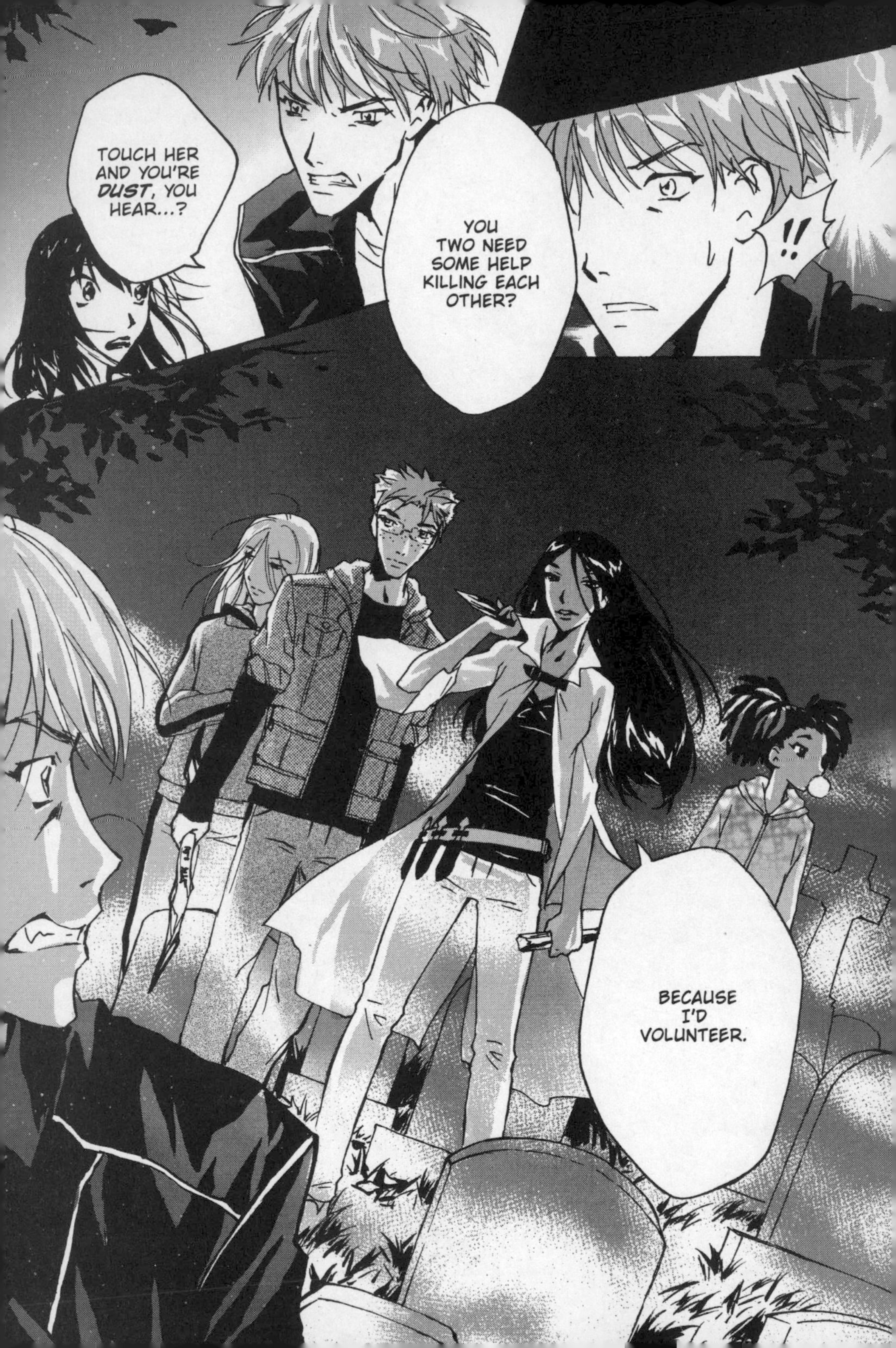
TOUCH HER AND YOU'RE *DUST*, YOU HEAR...?
YOU TWO NEED SOME HELP KILLING EACH OTHER?
!!
BECAUSE I'D VOLUNTEER.

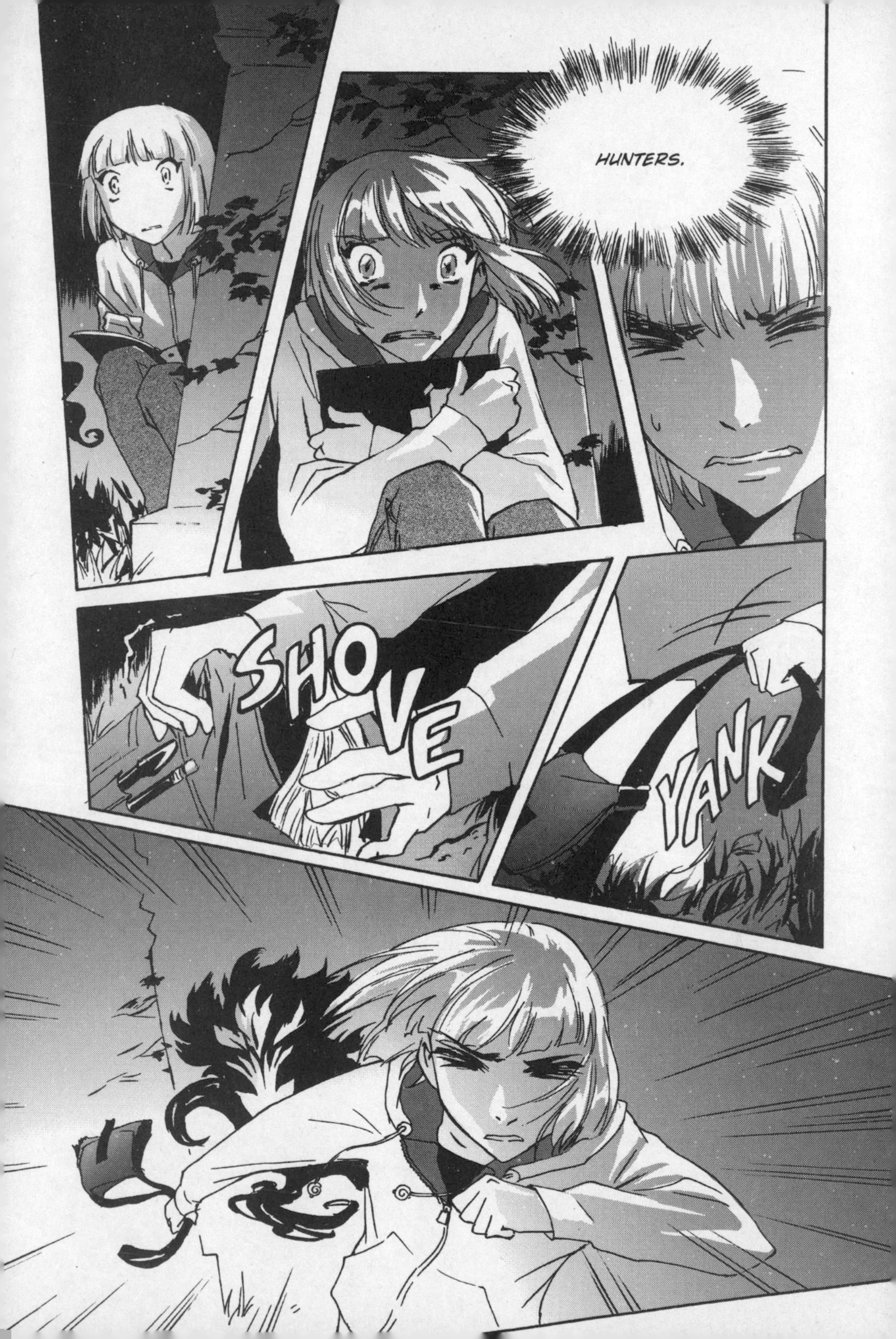

HUNTERS.
SHOVE
YANK

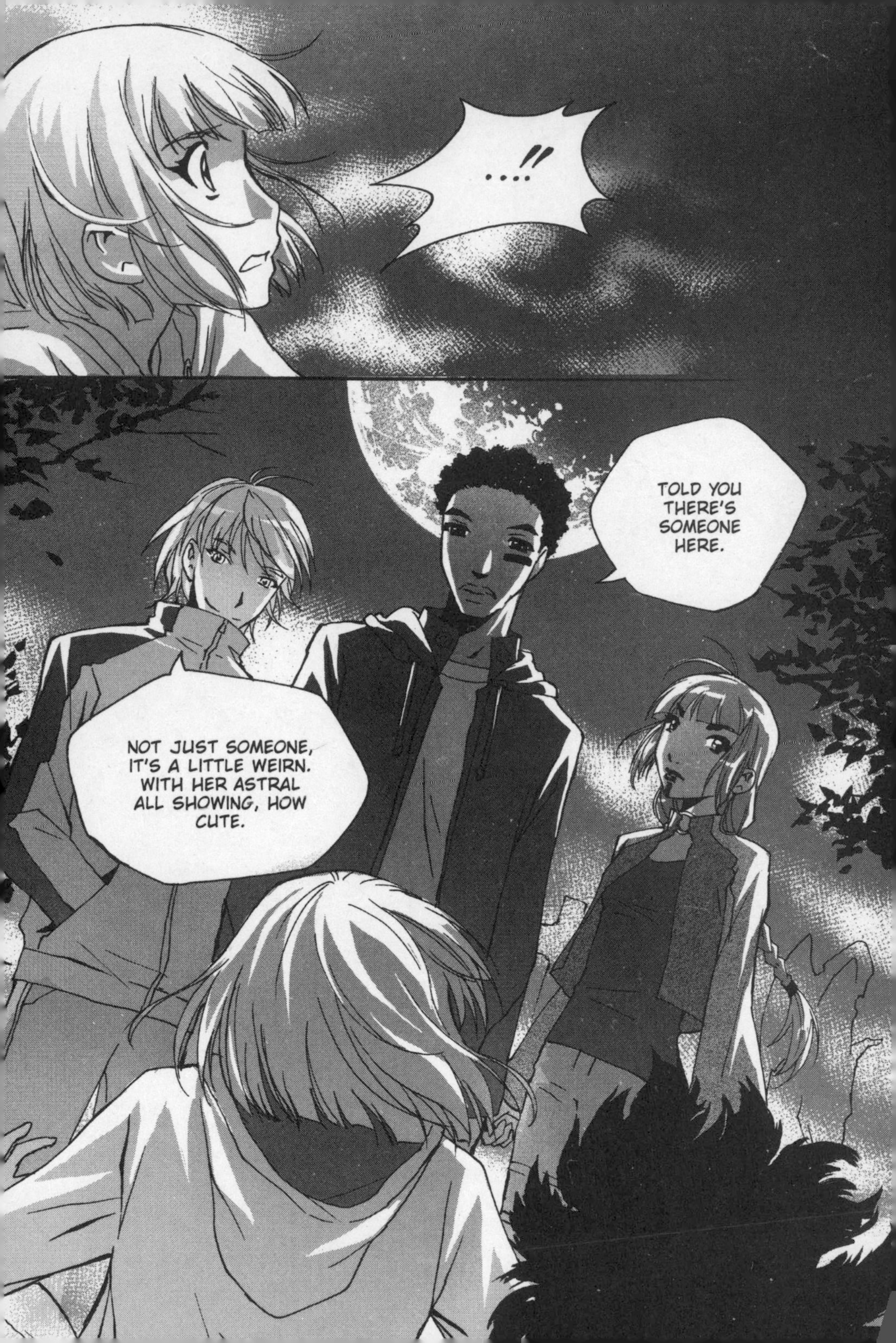
...!!
TOLD YOU THERE'S SOMEONE HERE.
NOT JUST SOMEONE, IT'S A LITTLE WEIRN. WITH HER ASTRAL ALL SHOWING, HOW CUTE.

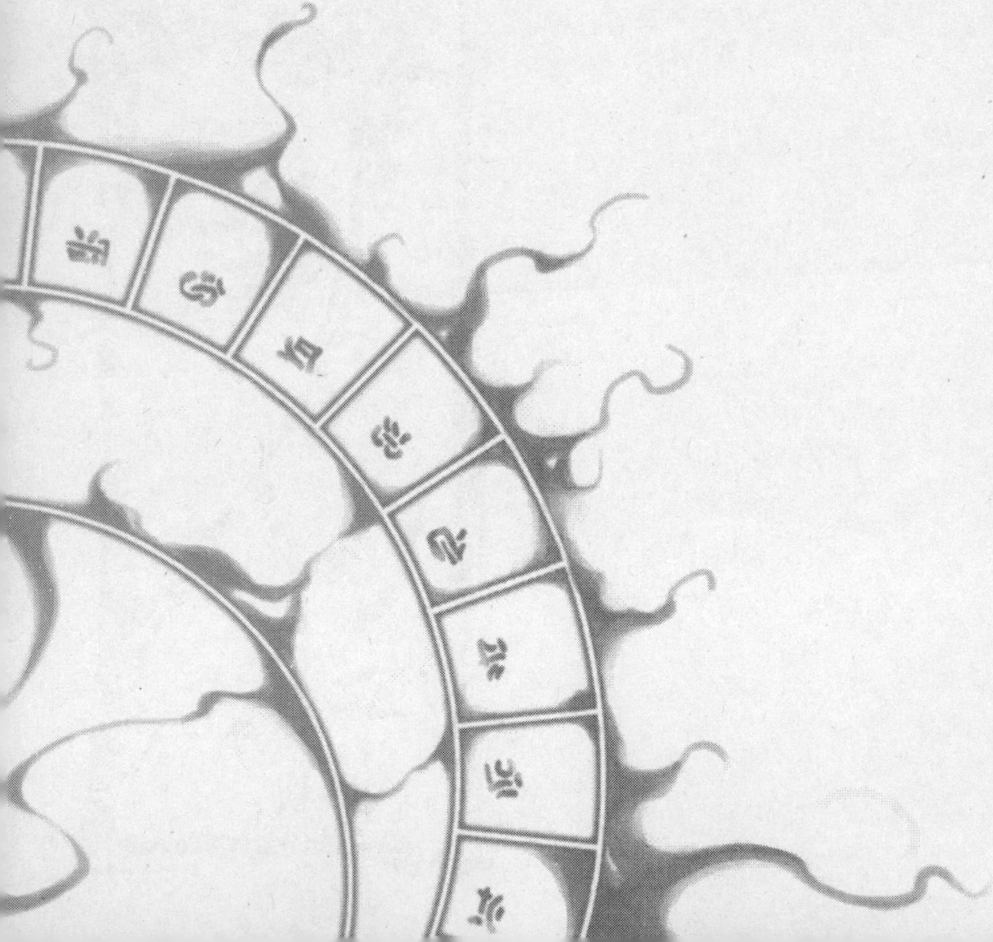

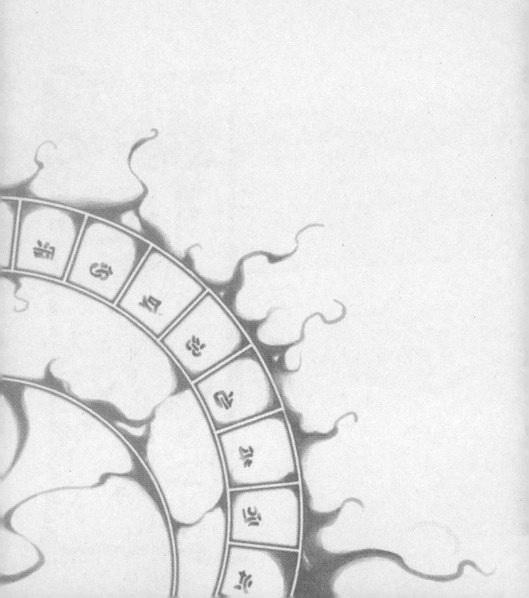

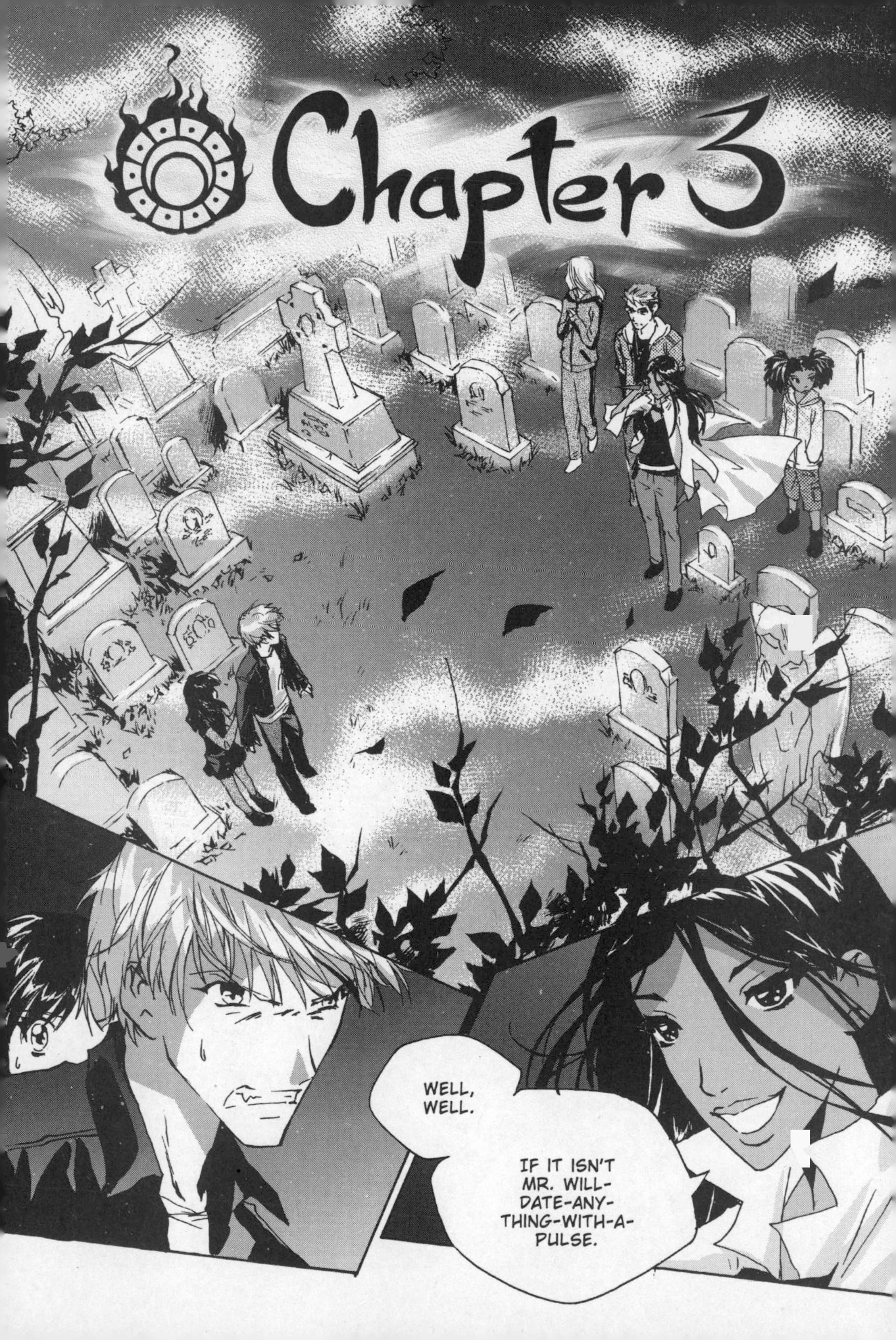
Chapter 3
WELL, WELL.
IF IT ISN'T MR. WILL-DATE-ANY-THING-WITH-A-PULSE.

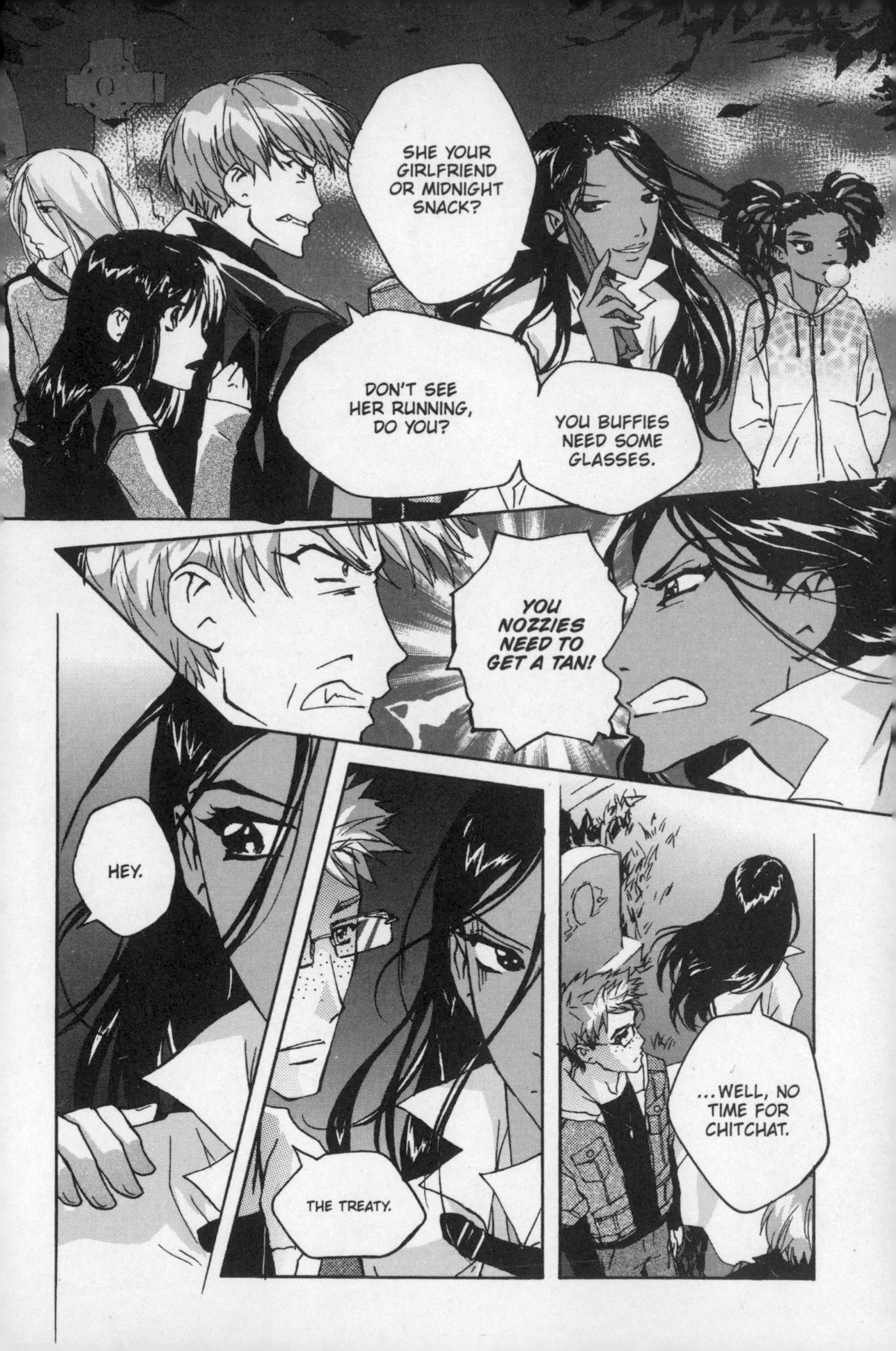
SHE YOUR GIRLFRIEND OR MIDNIGHT SNACK?
DON'T SEE HER RUNNING, DO YOU?
YOU BUFFIES NEED SOME GLASSES.
YOU NOZZIES NEED TO GET A TAN!
HEY.
THE TREATY.
...WELL, NO TIME FOR CHITCHAT.

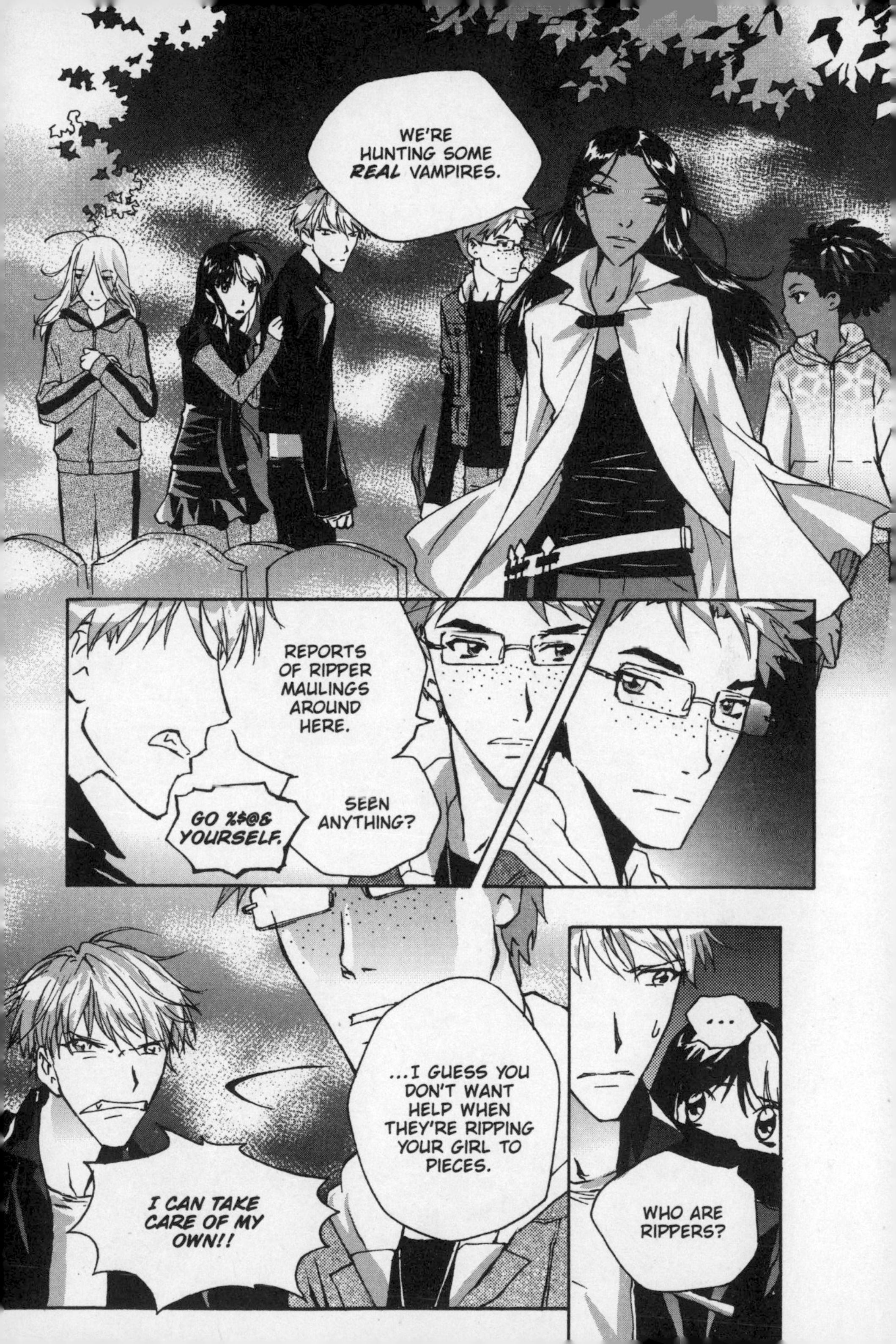
WE'RE HUNTING SOME REAL VAMPIRES.
REPORTS OF RIPPER MAULINGS AROUND HERE.
SEEN ANYTHING?
GO %$@& YOURSELF.
...I GUESS YOU DON'T WANT HELP WHEN THEY'RE RIPPING YOUR GIRL TO PIECES.
I CAN TAKE CARE OF MY OWN!!
...
WHO ARE RIPPERS?

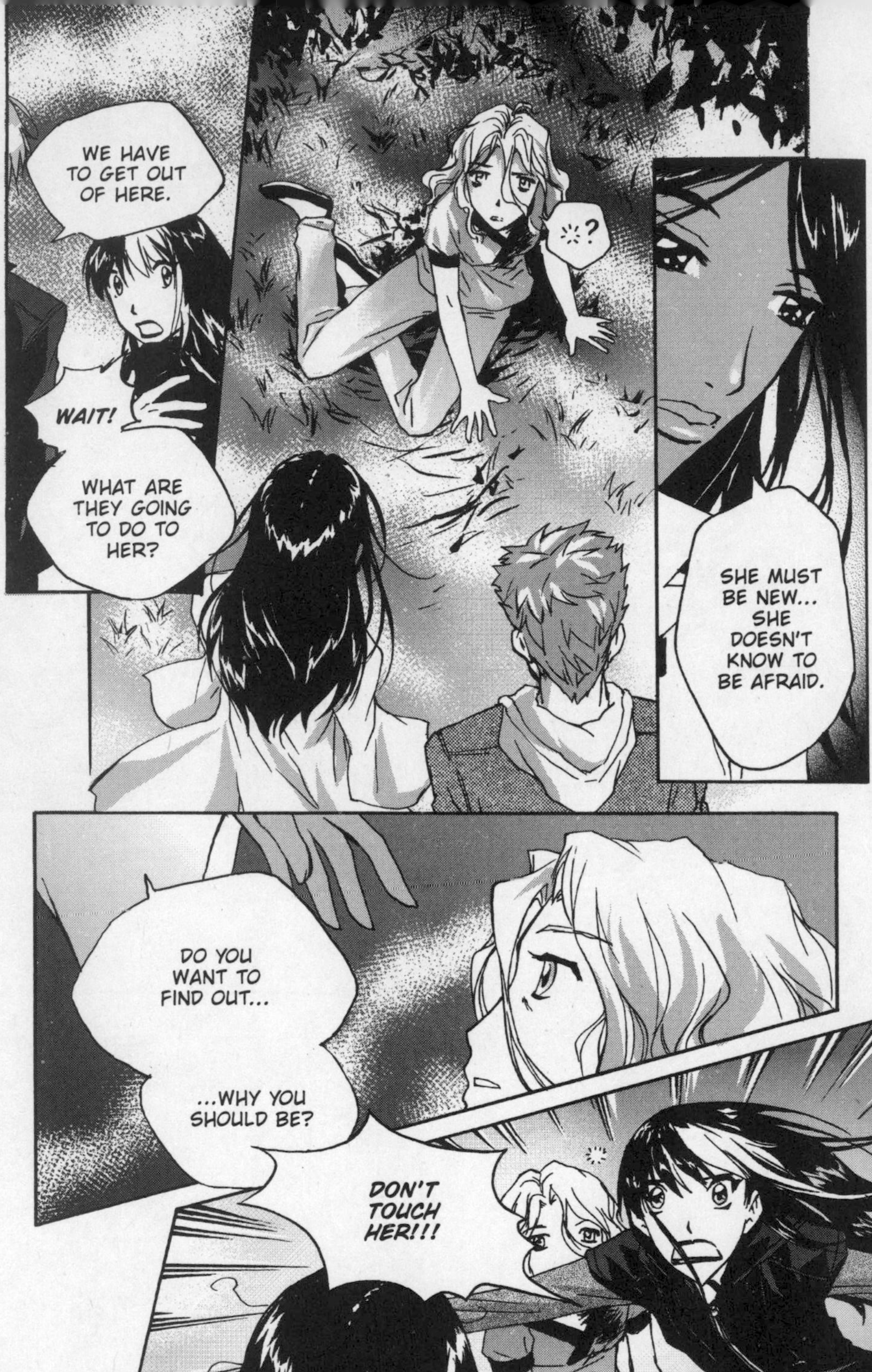
WE HAVE TO GET OUT OF HERE.
WAIT!
WHAT ARE THEY GOING TO DO TO HER?
?
SHE MUST BE NEW... SHE DOESN'T KNOW TO BE AFRAID.
DO YOU WANT TO FIND OUT...
...WHY YOU SHOULD BE?
DON'T TOUCH HER!!!

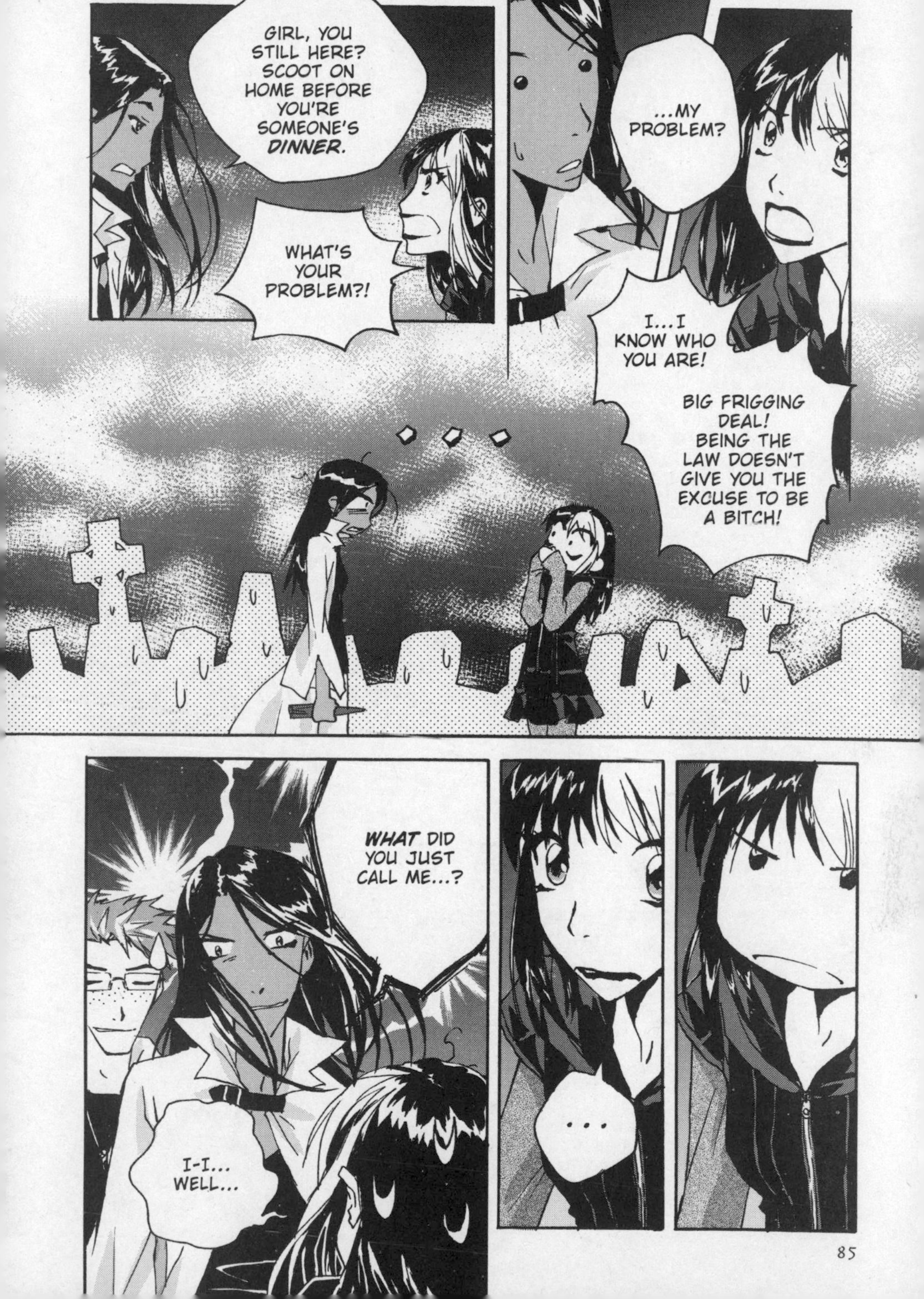
GIRL, YOU STILL HERE? SCOOT ON HOME BEFORE YOU'RE SOMEONE'S *DINNER*.
WHAT'S YOUR PROBLEM?!
...MY PROBLEM?
I...I KNOW WHO YOU ARE!
BIG FRIGGING DEAL! BEING THE LAW DOESN'T GIVE YOU THE EXCUSE TO BE A BITCH!
WHAT DID YOU JUST CALL ME...?
I-I... WELL...
...

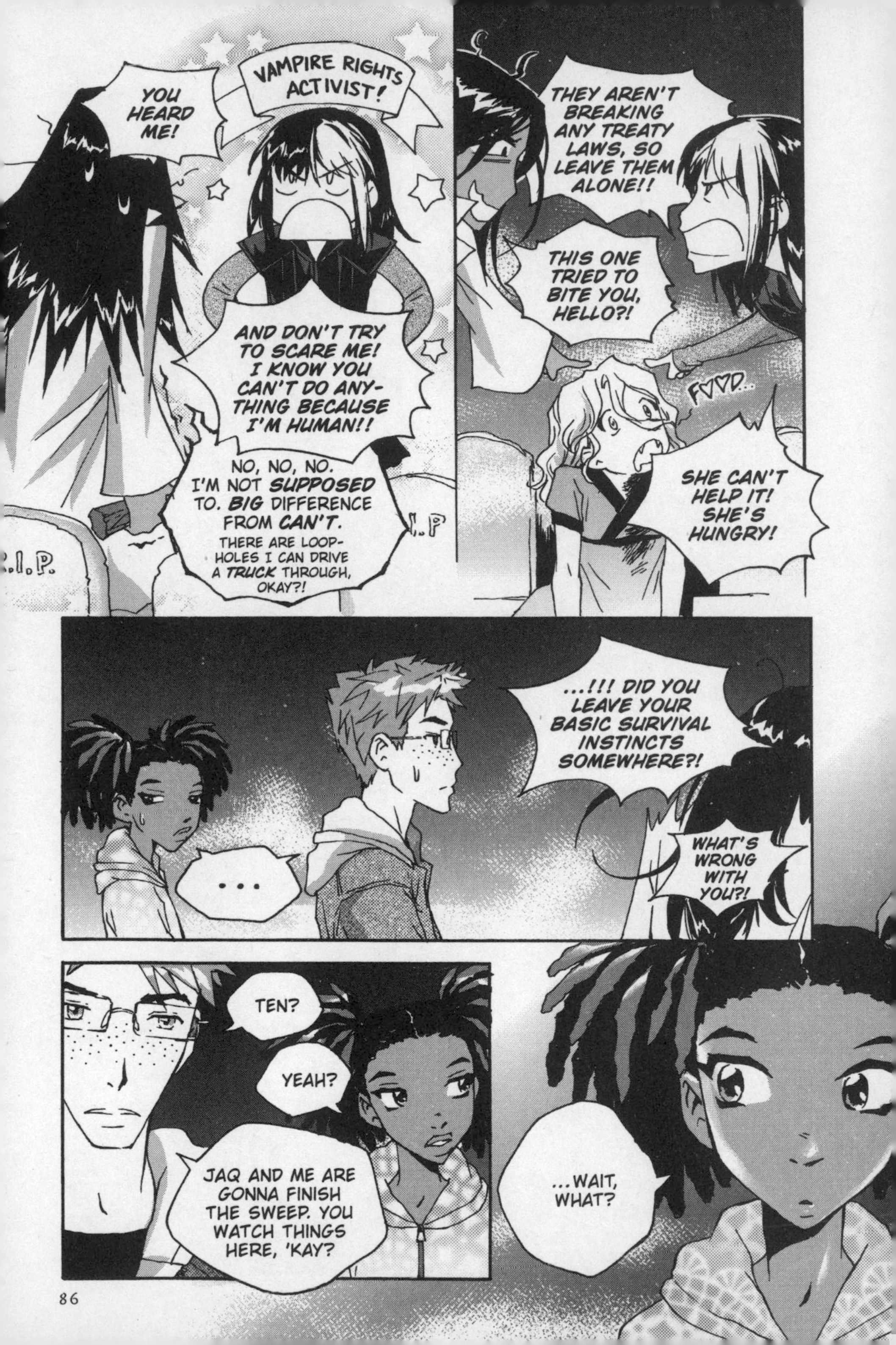
YOU HEARD ME!
VAMPIRE RIGHTS ACTIVIST!
AND DON'T TRY TO SCARE ME! I KNOW YOU CAN'T DO ANY-THING BECAUSE I'M HUMAN!!
NO, NO, NO. I'M NOT SUPPOSED TO. BIG DIFFERENCE FROM CAN'T. THERE ARE LOOP-HOLES I CAN DRIVE A TRUCK THROUGH, OKAY?!
R.I.P.
THEY AREN'T BREAKING ANY TREATY LAWS, SO LEAVE THEM ALONE!!
THIS ONE TRIED TO BITE YOU, HELLO?!
FOOD..
SHE CAN'T HELP IT! SHE'S HUNGRY!
...!!! DID YOU LEAVE YOUR BASIC SURVIVAL INSTINCTS SOMEWHERE?!
...
WHAT'S WRONG WITH YOU?!
TEN?
YEAH?
JAQ AND ME ARE GONNA FINISH THE SWEEP. YOU WATCH THINGS HERE, 'KAY?
...WAIT, WHAT?

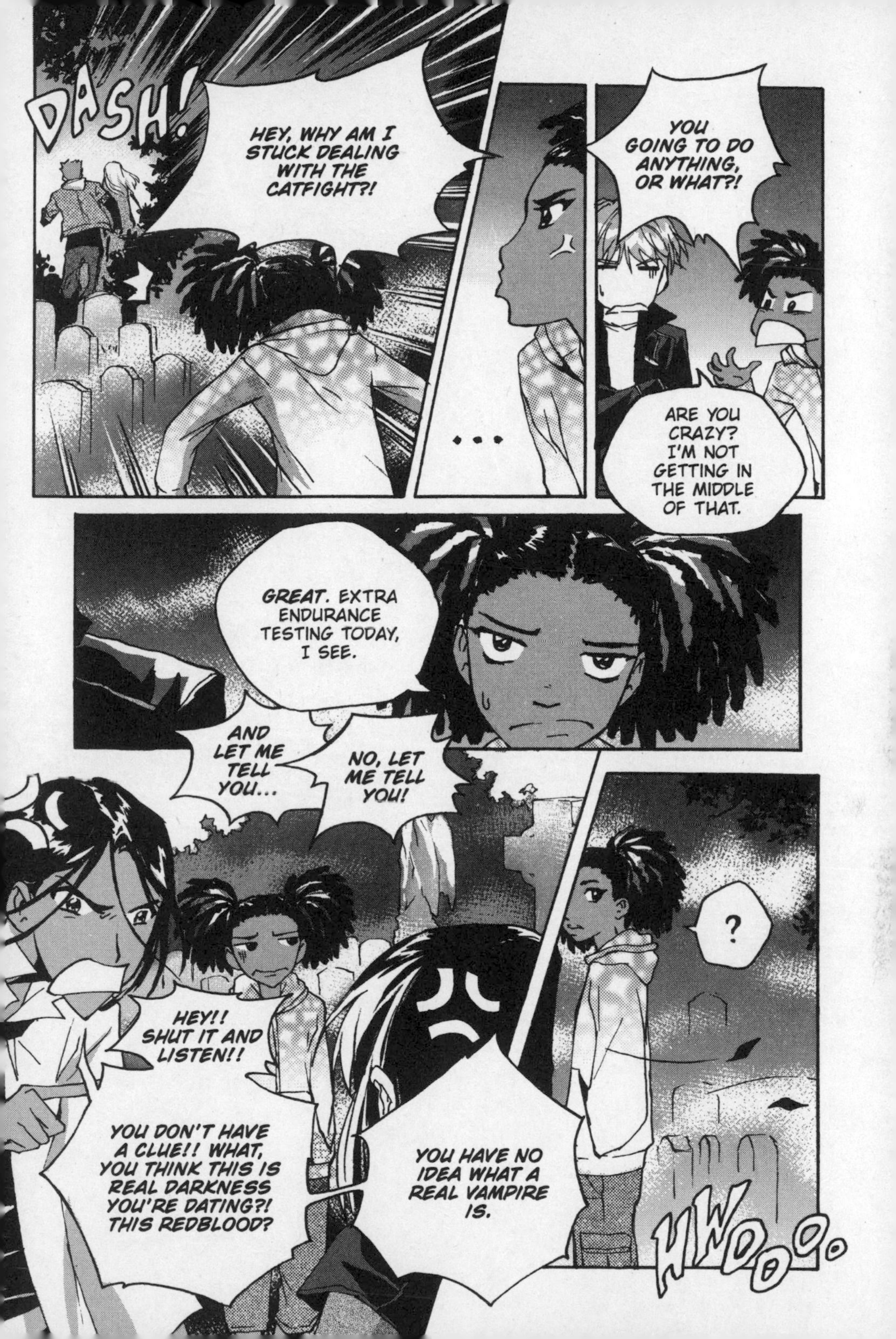
DASH!
HEY, WHY AM I STUCK DEALING WITH THE CATFIGHT?!
...
YOU GOING TO DO ANYTHING, OR WHAT?!
ARE YOU CRAZY? I'M NOT GETTING IN THE MIDDLE OF THAT.
GREAT. EXTRA ENDURANCE TESTING TODAY, I SEE.
AND LET ME TELL YOU...
NO, LET ME TELL YOU!
HEY!! SHUT IT AND LISTEN!!
YOU DON'T HAVE A CLUE!! WHAT, YOU THINK THIS IS REAL DARKNESS YOU'RE DATING?! THIS REDBLOOD?
YOU HAVE NO IDEA WHAT A REAL VAMPIRE IS.
?
HWOOOO

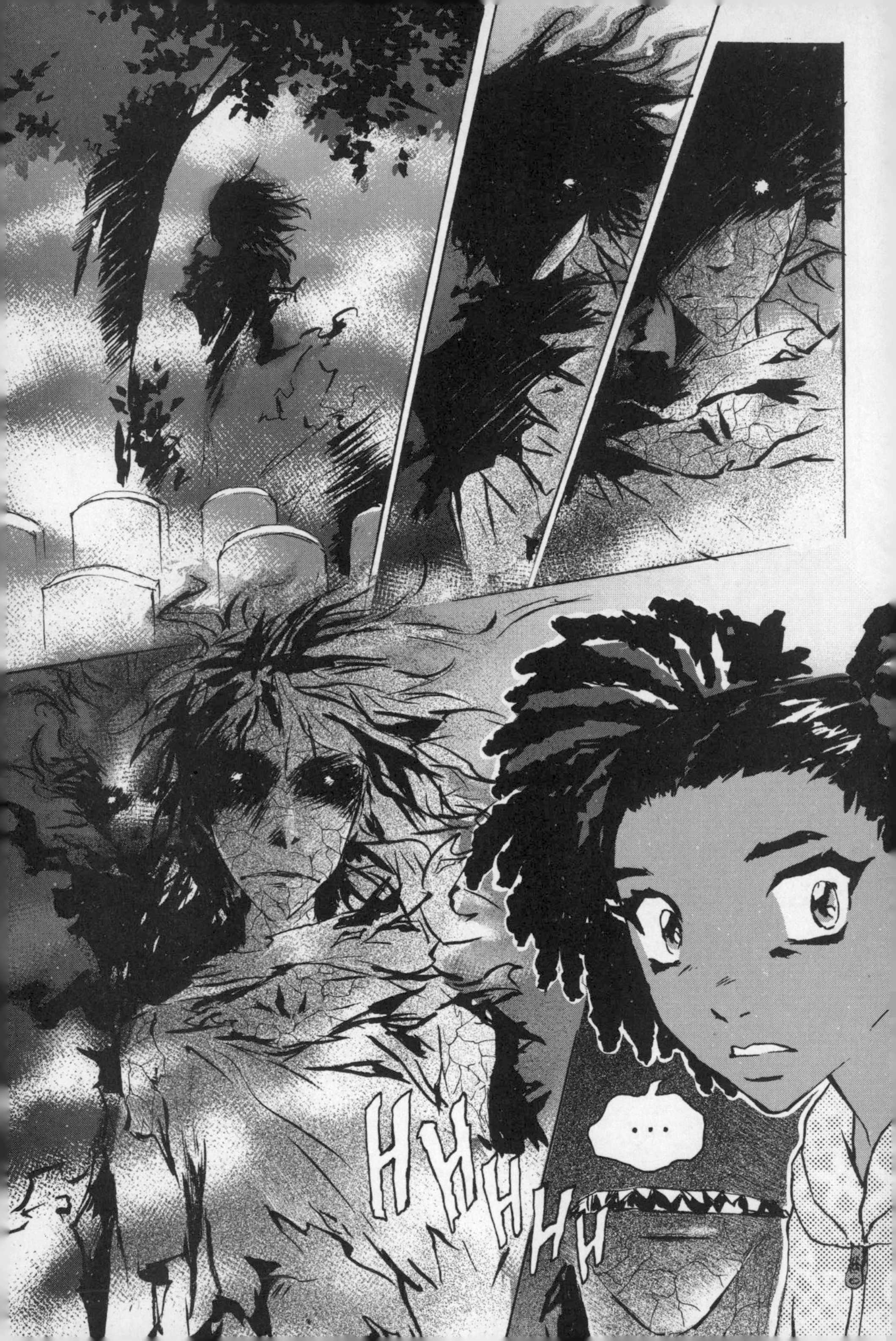
HHHHHH
...

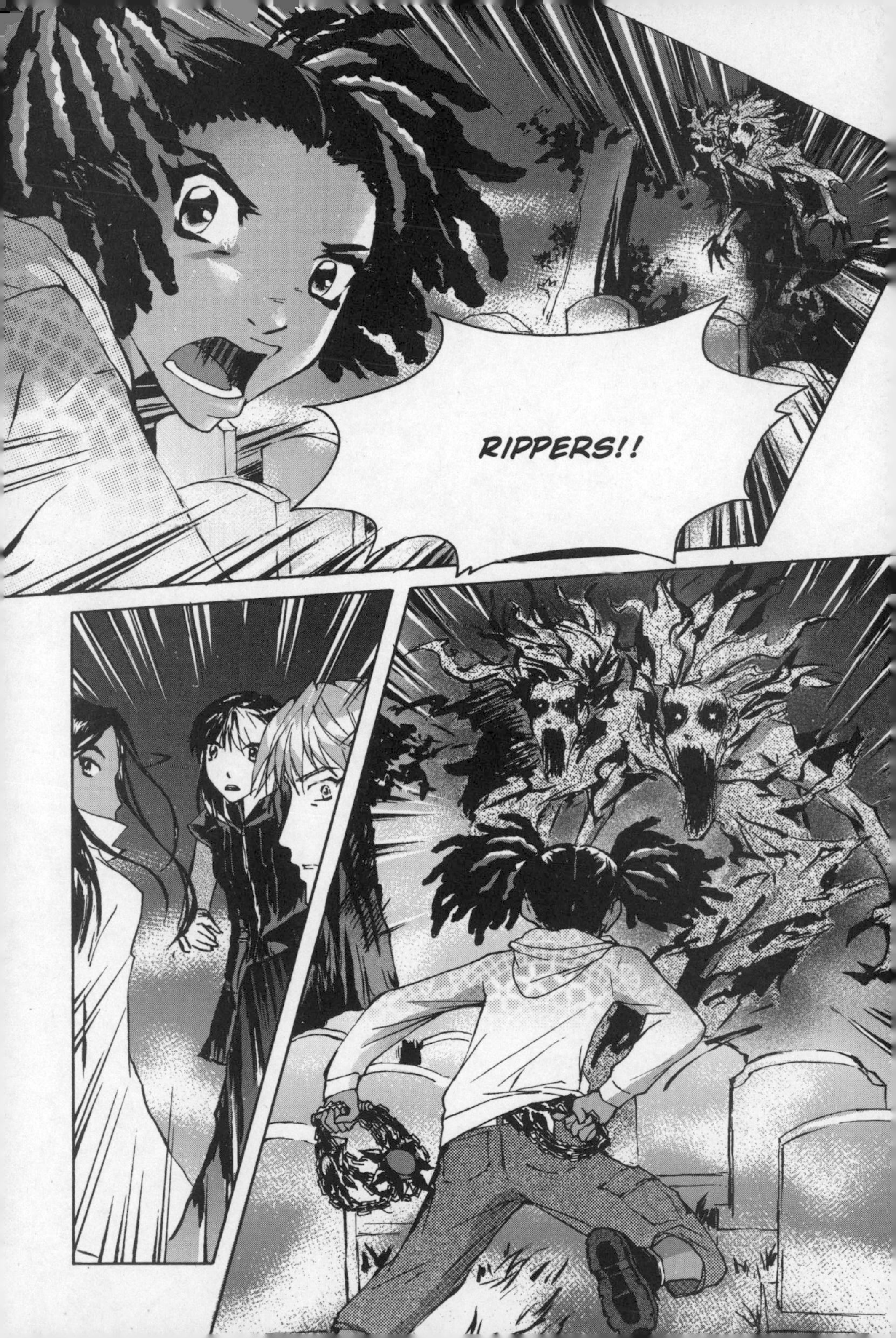
RIPPERS!!

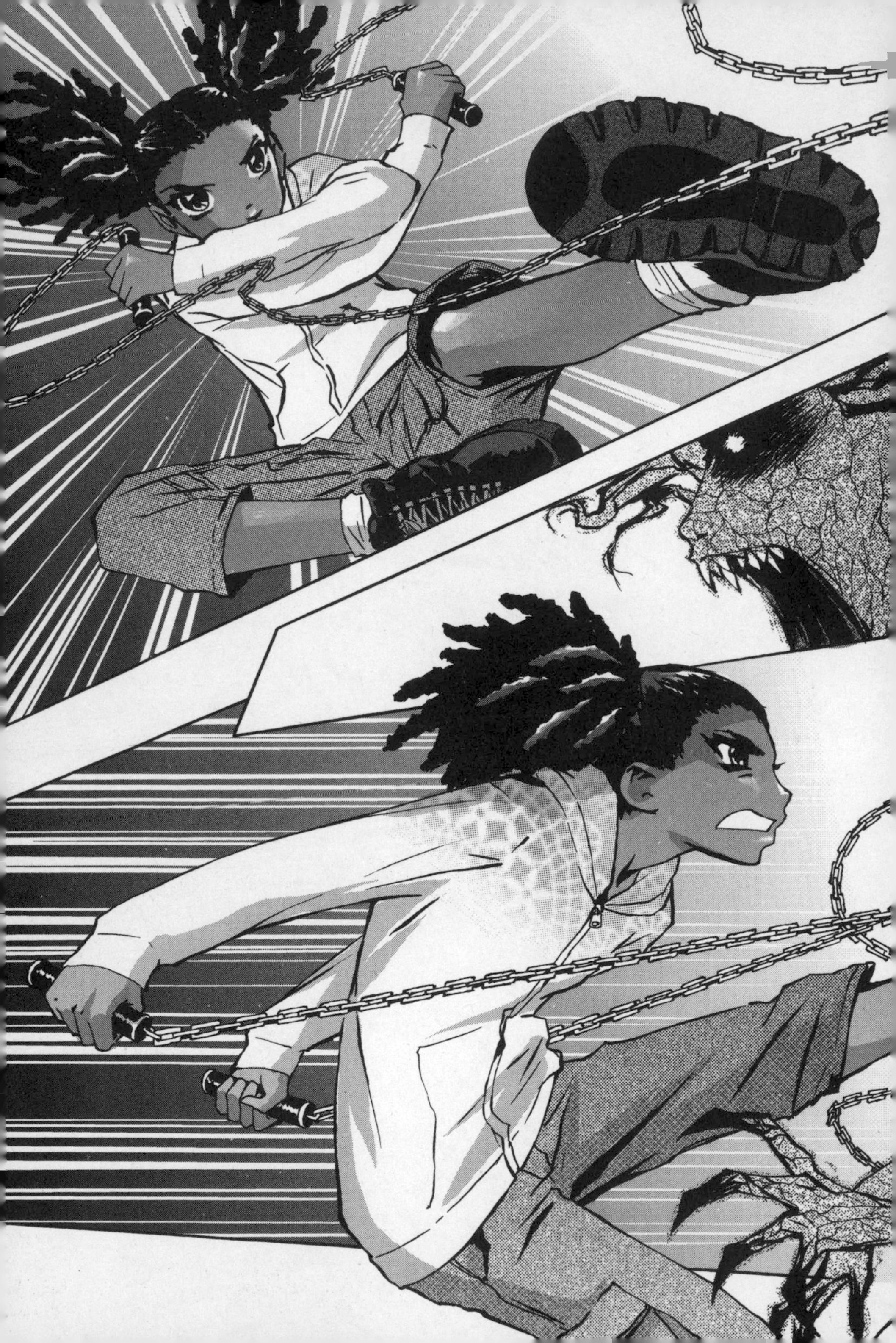

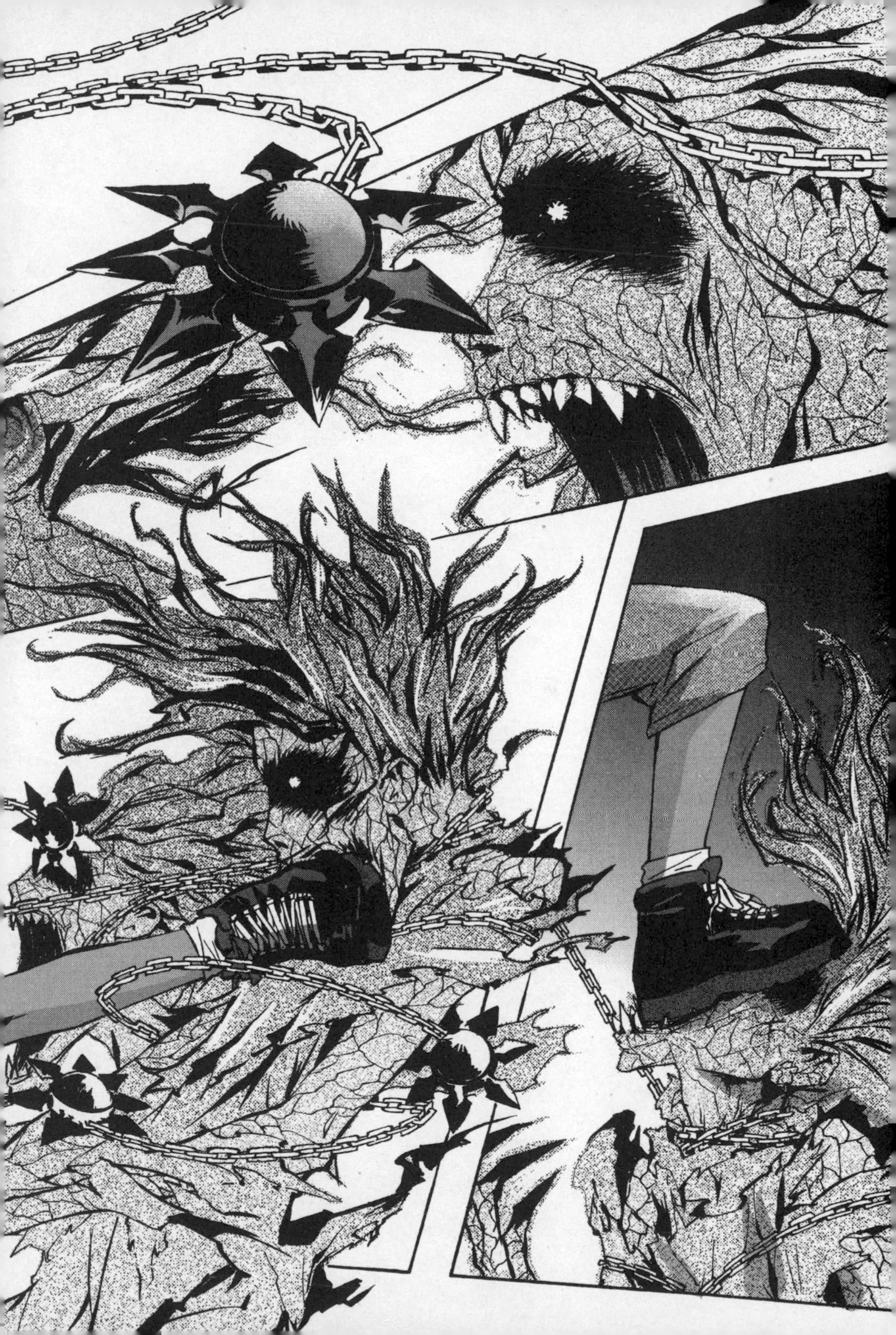

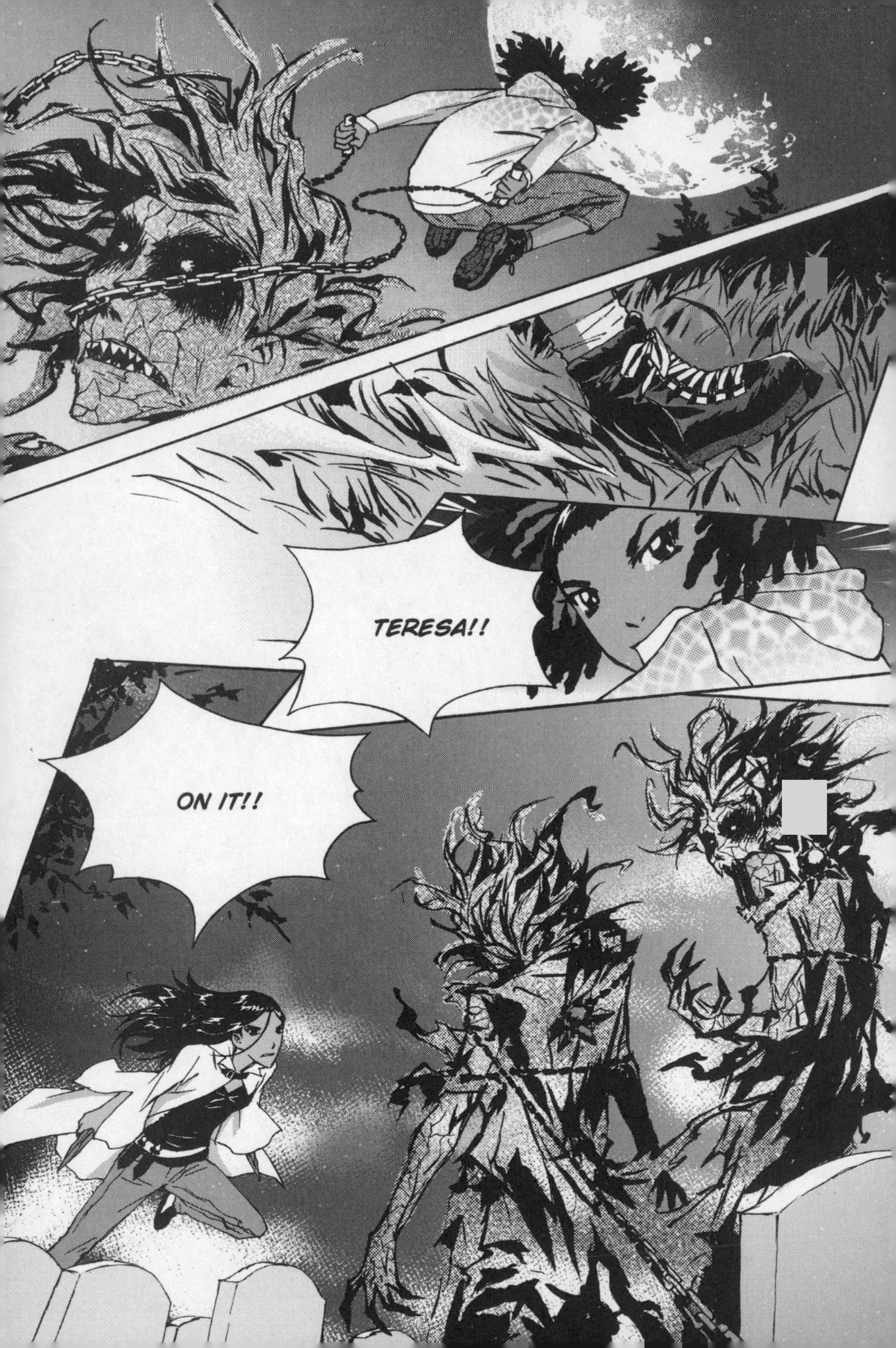
TERESA!!
ON IT!!

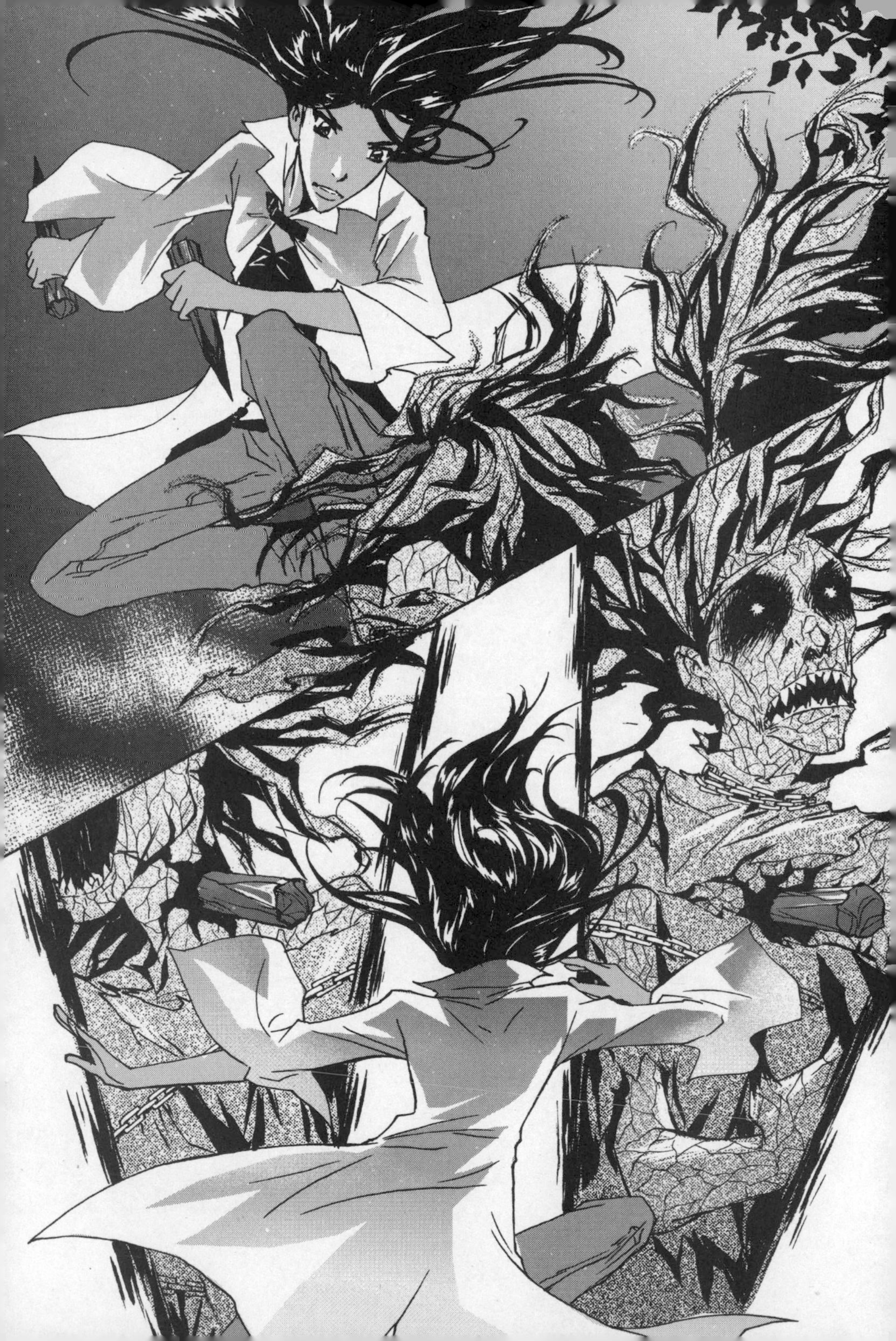

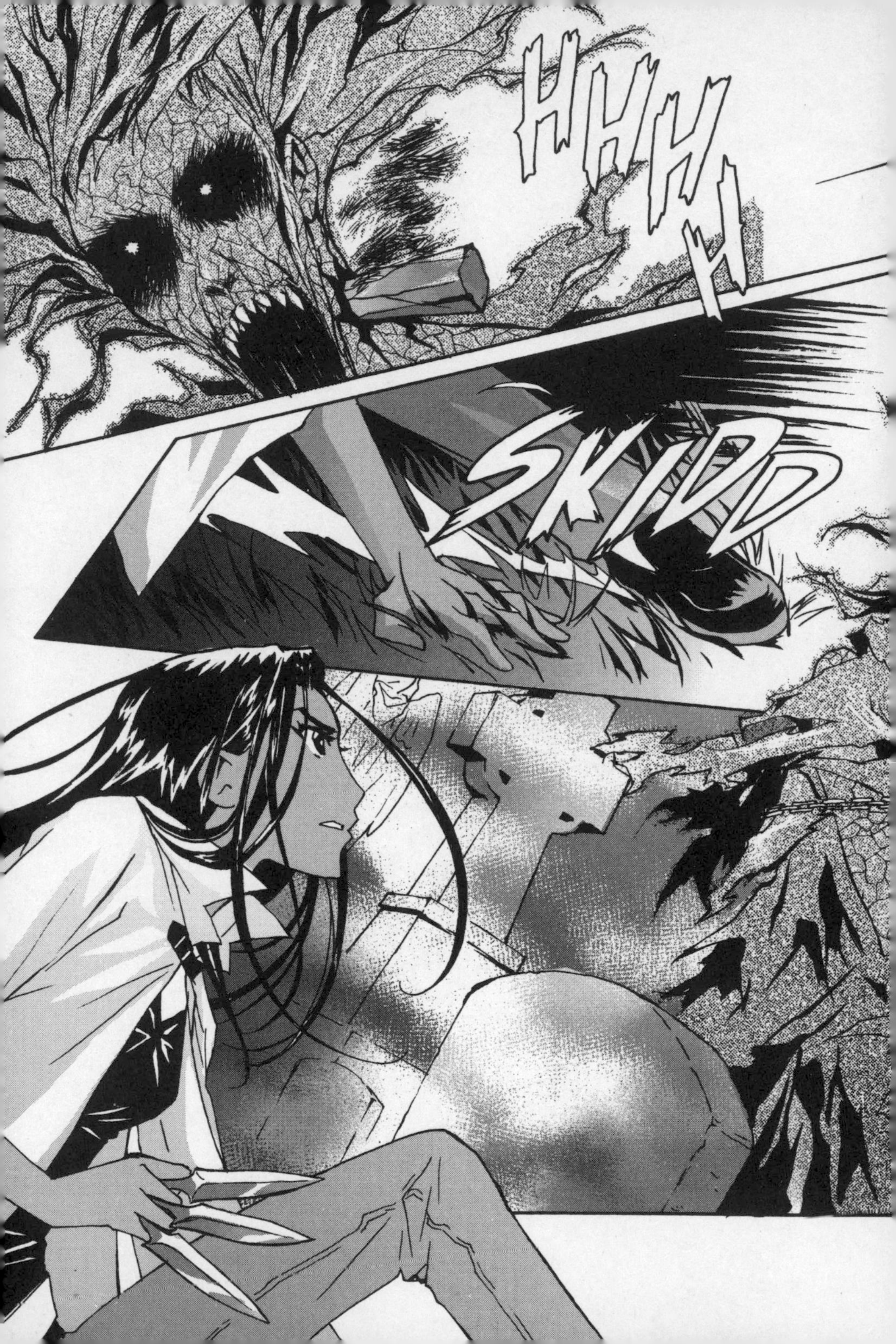
HHHHH
SKIDD

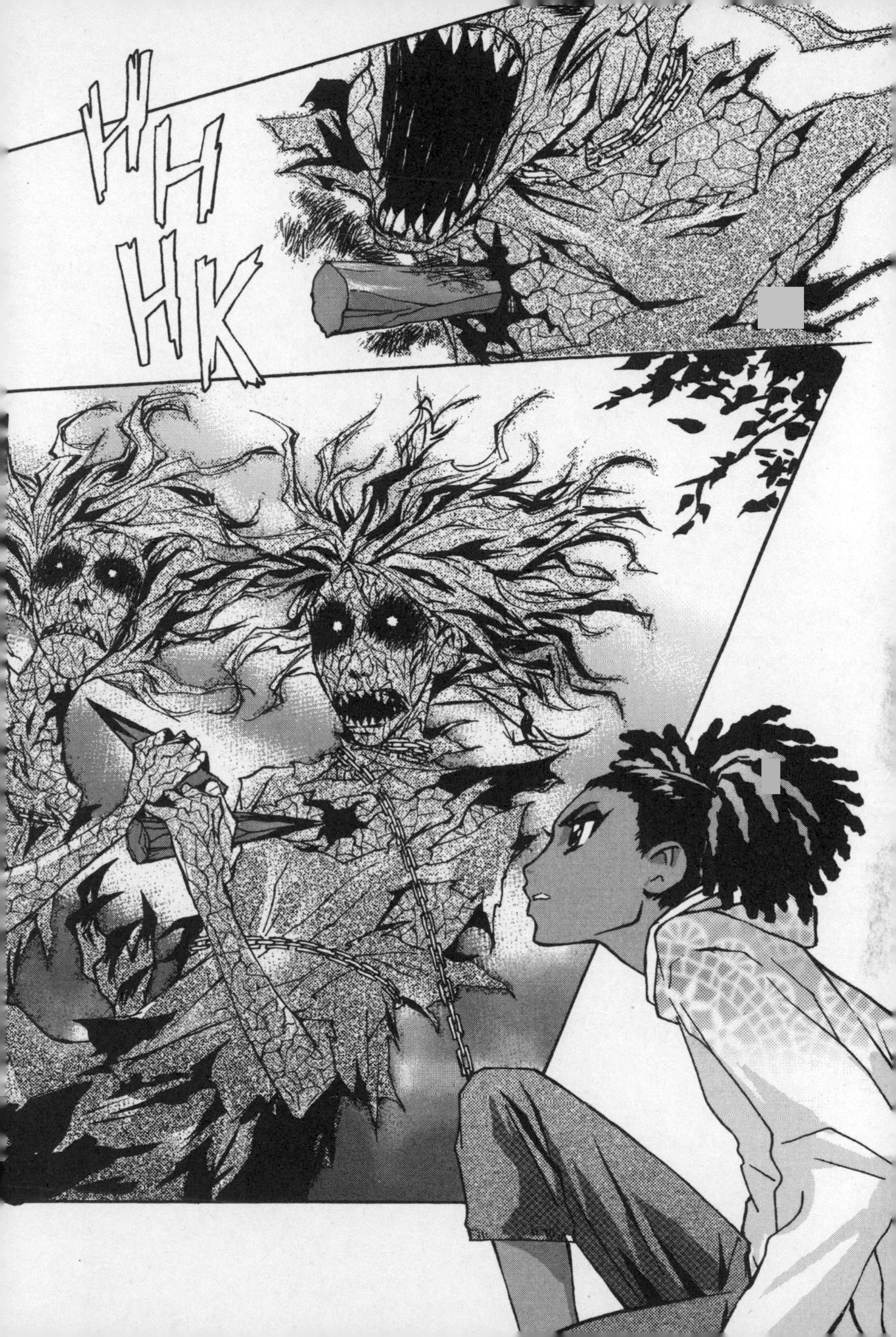
HHHK

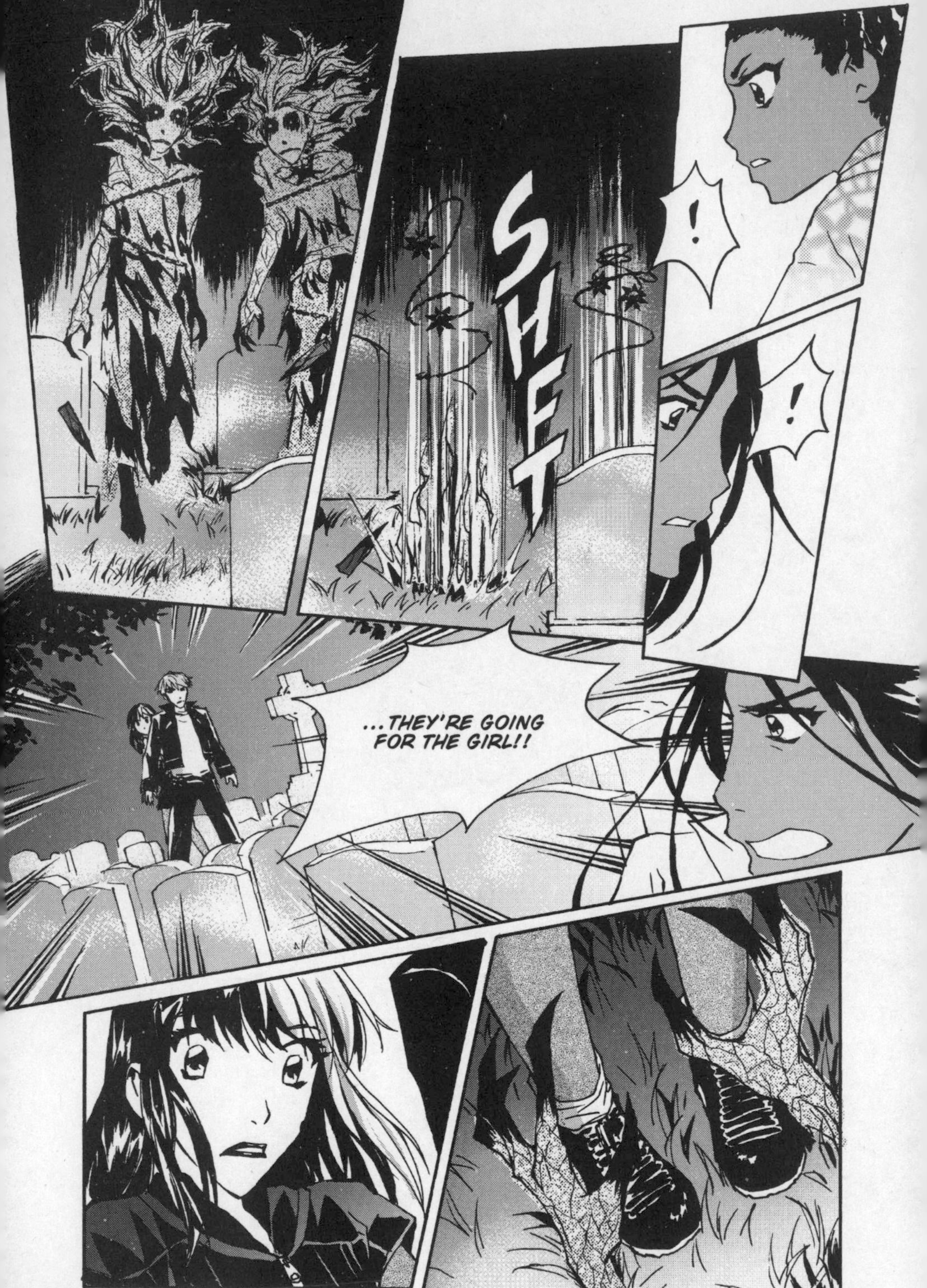

SHFT
!
!
...THEY'RE GOING FOR THE GIRL!!

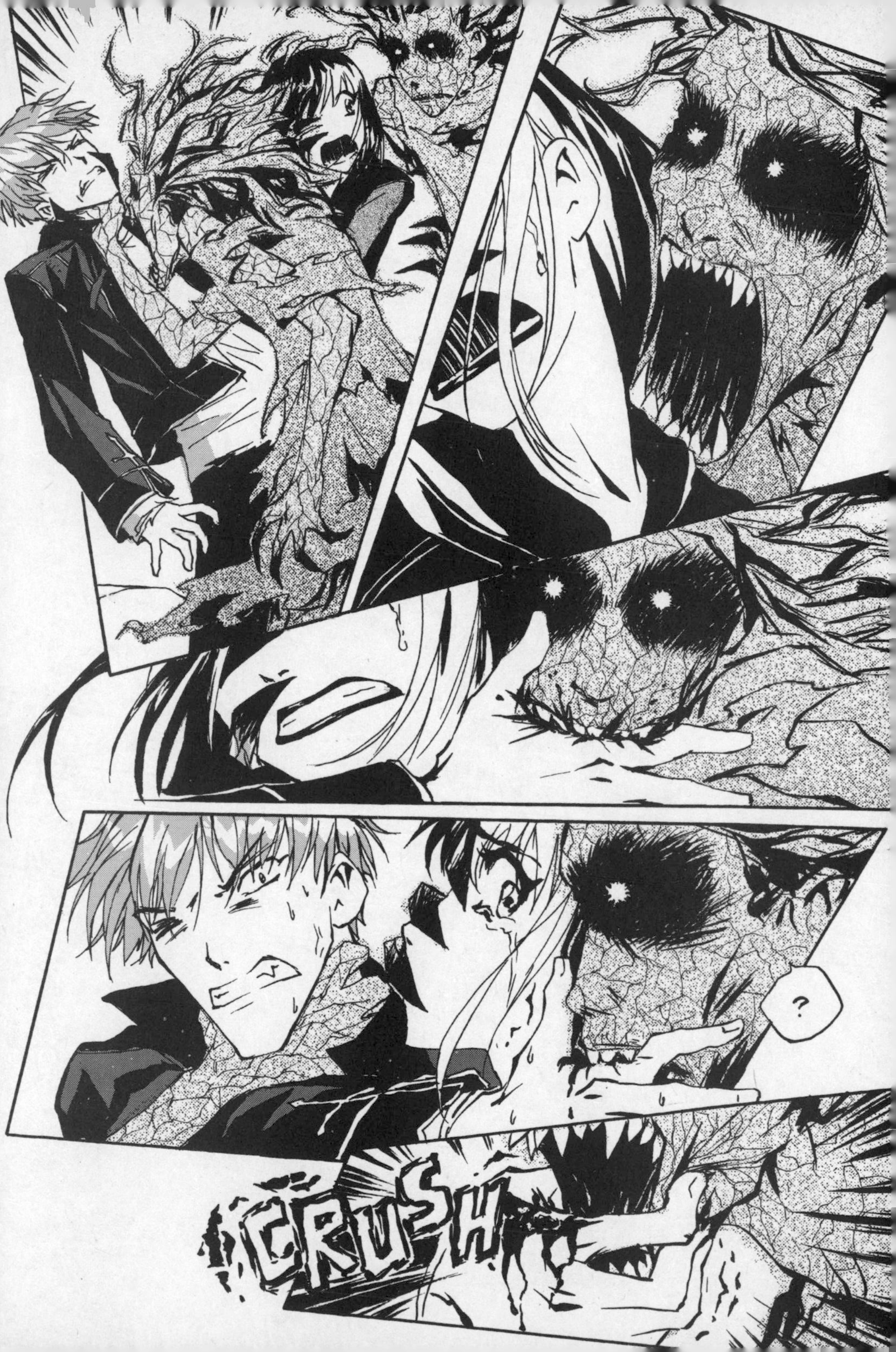
?
CRUSH

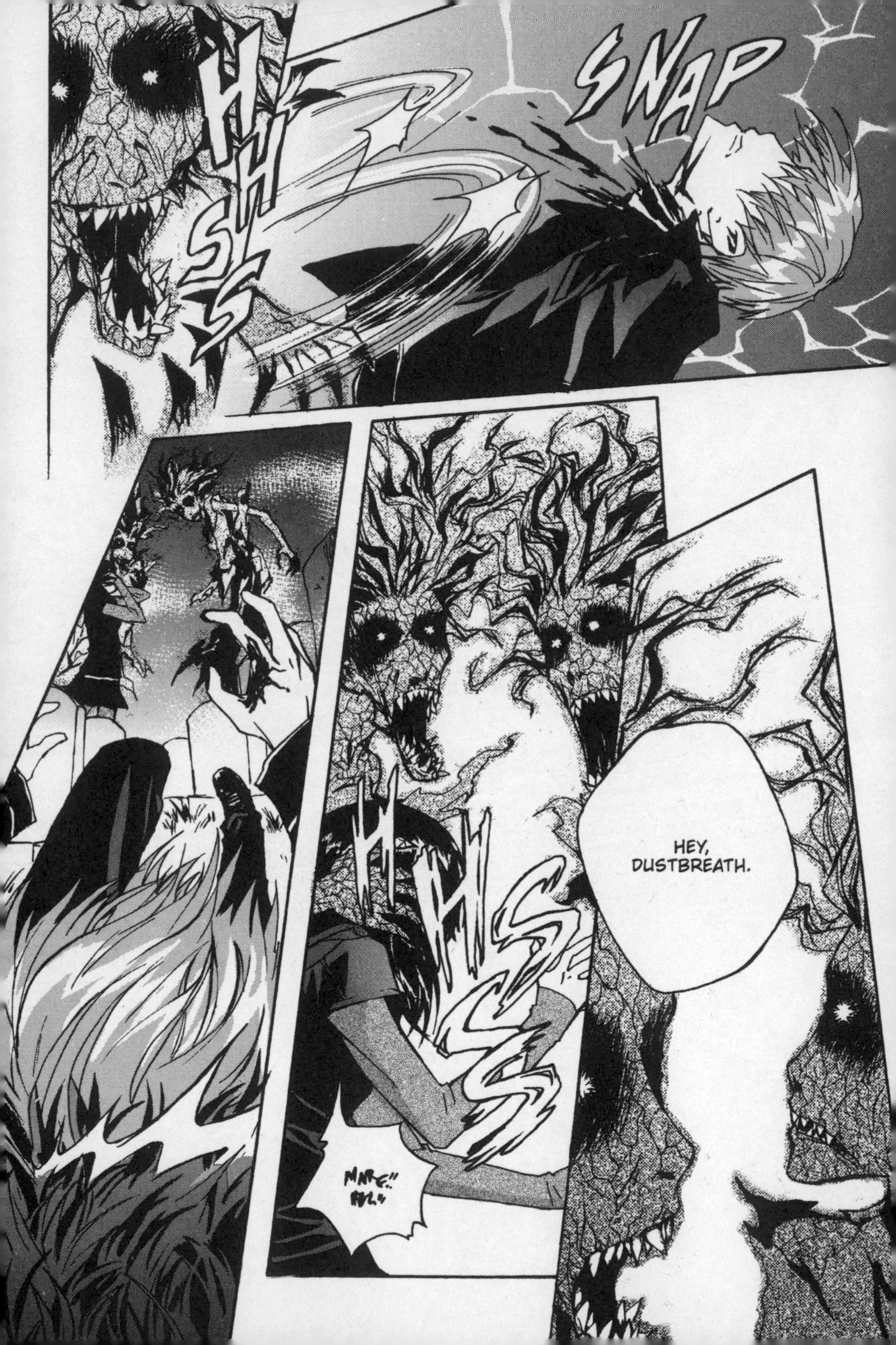
SNAP
HEY, DUSTBREATH.

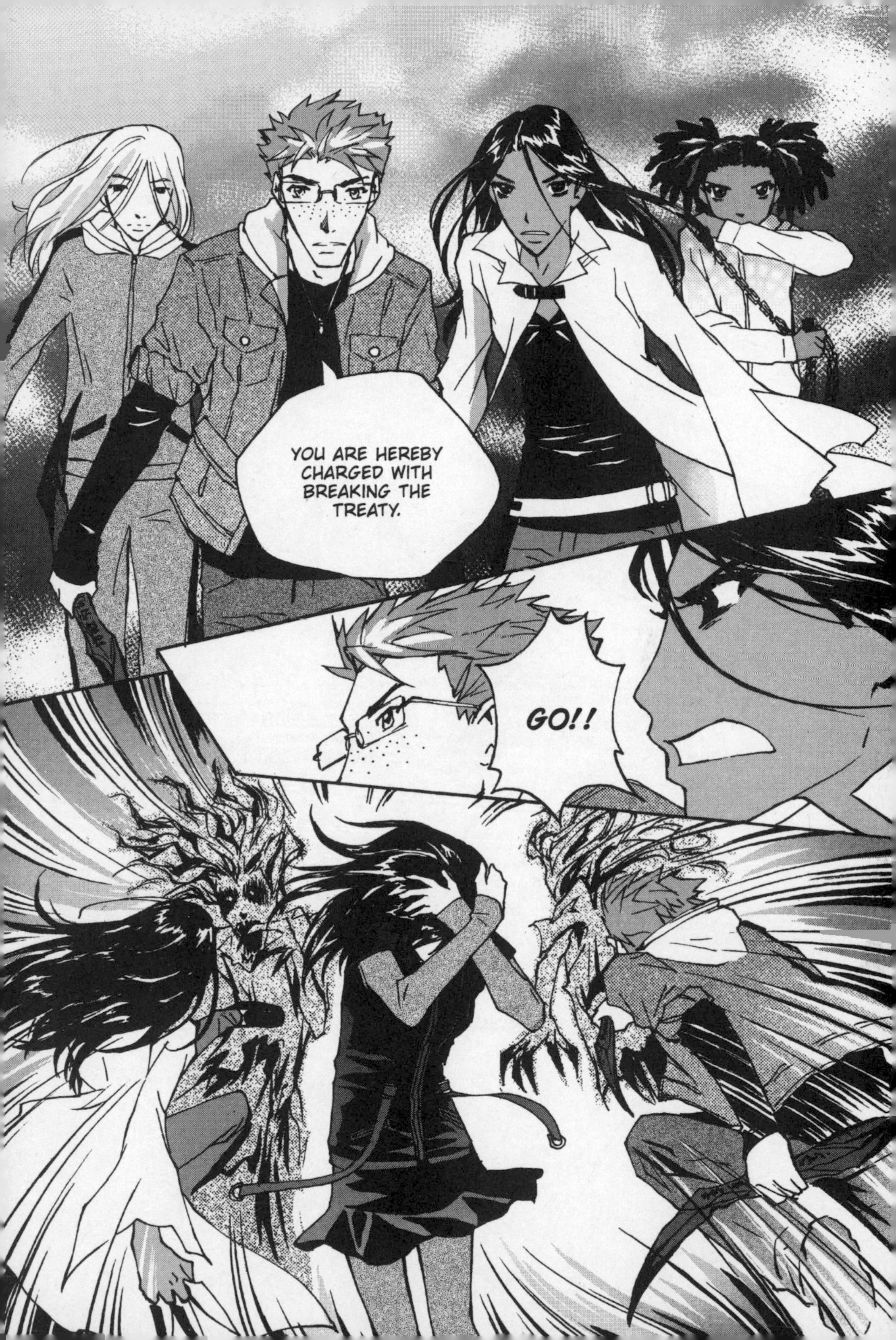
YOU ARE HEREBY CHARGED WITH BREAKING THE TREATY.
GO!!

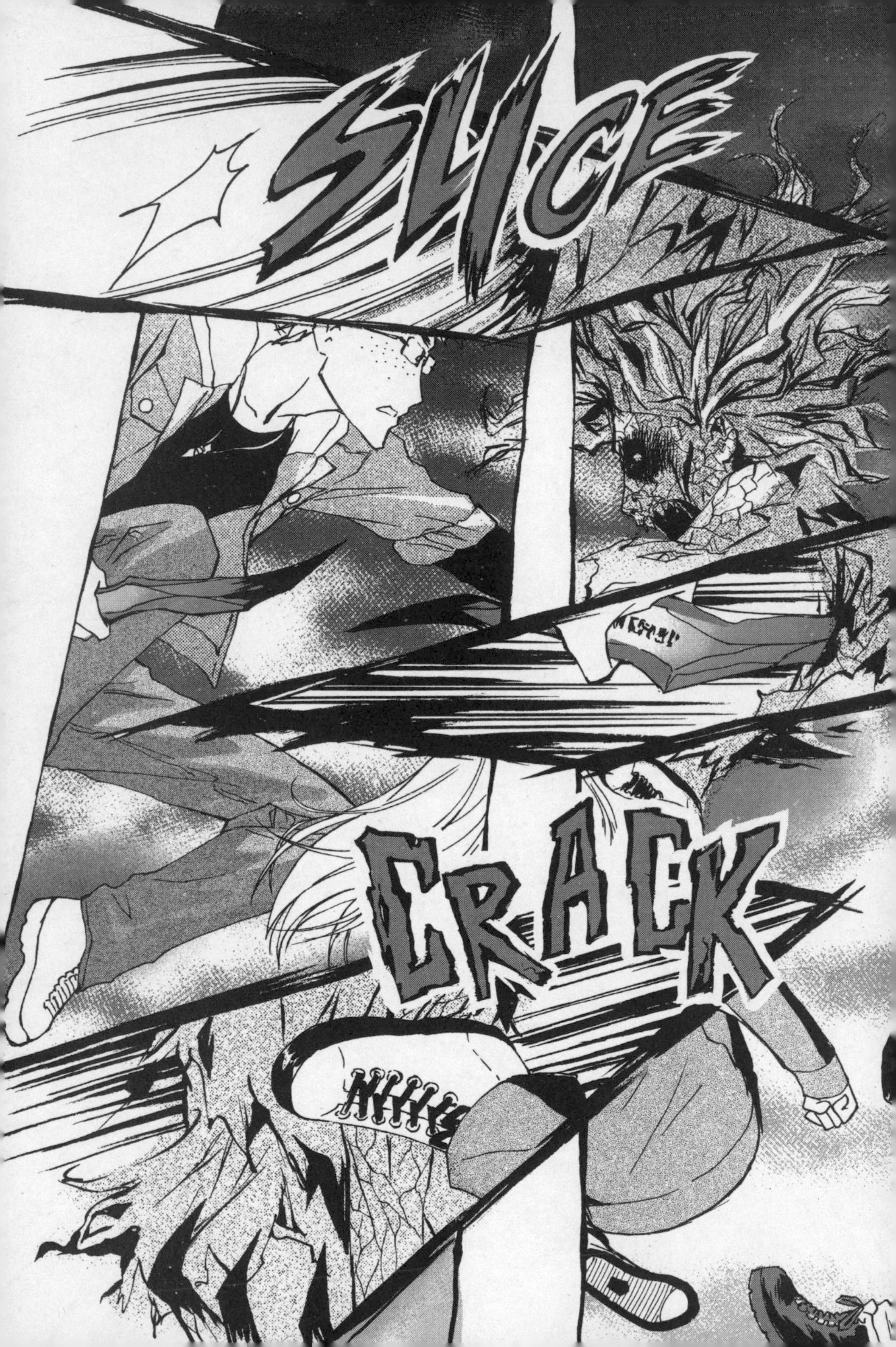
SLICE
CRACK

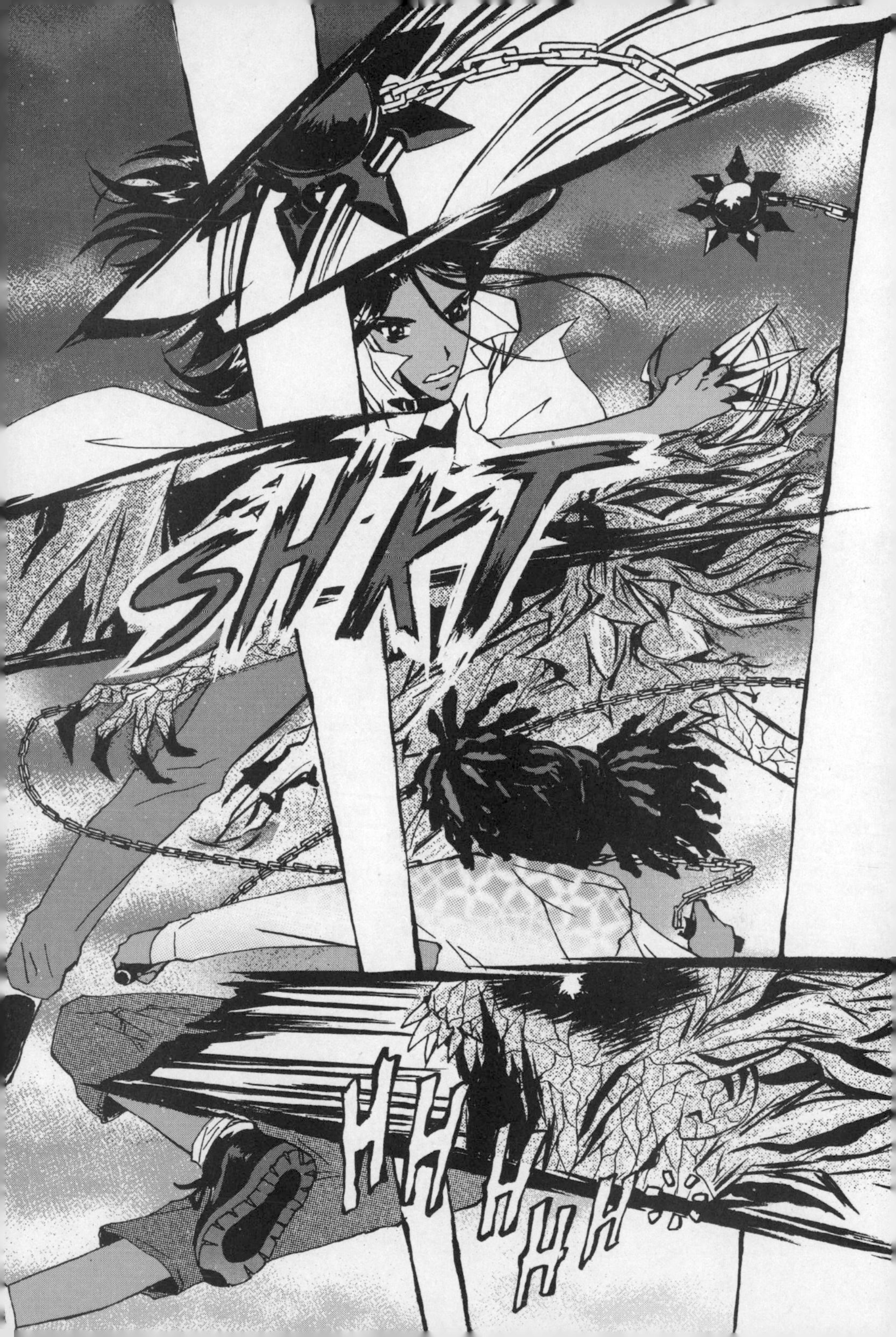
SH-KT
HHHHHH

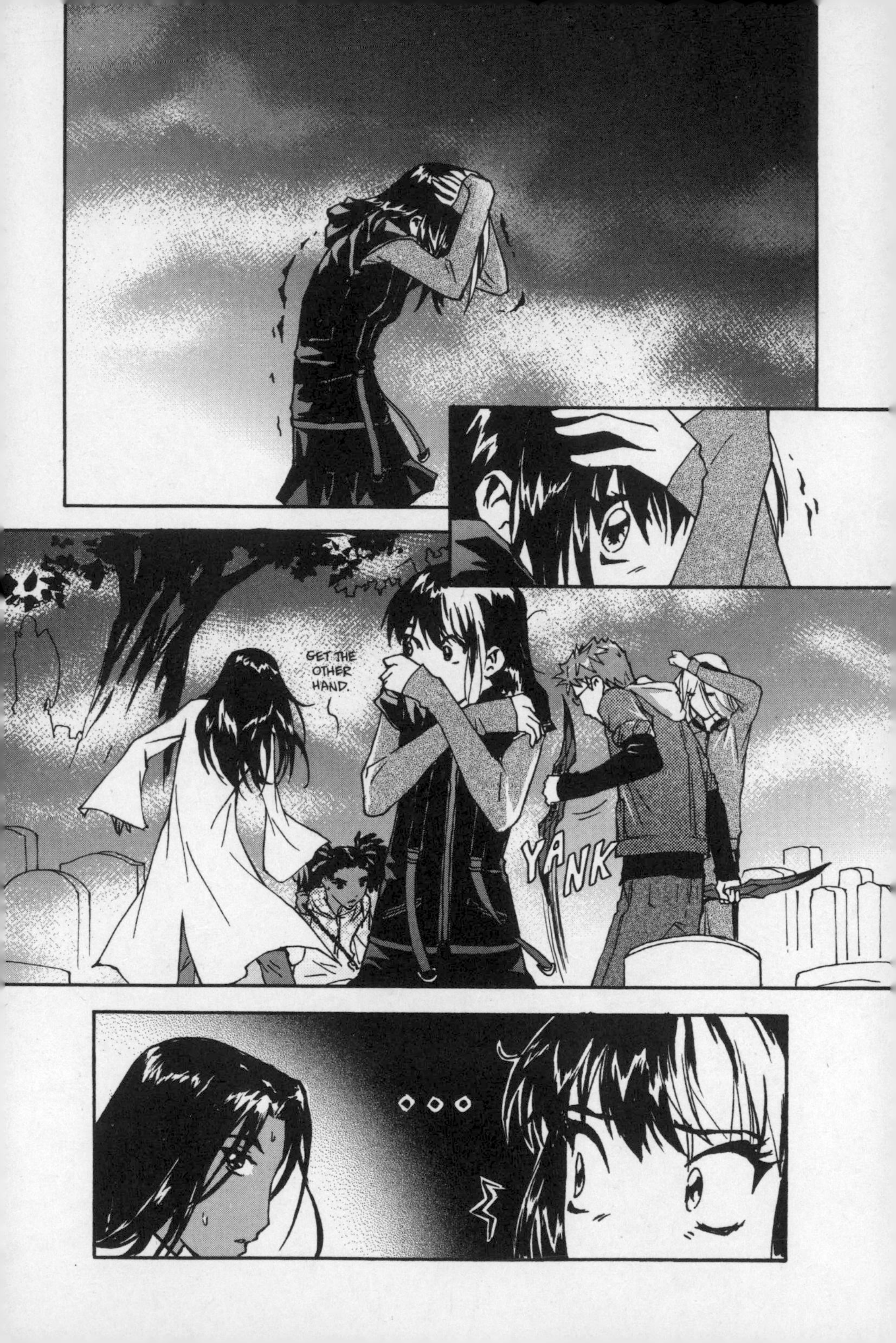

YANK
GET THE OTHER HAND.

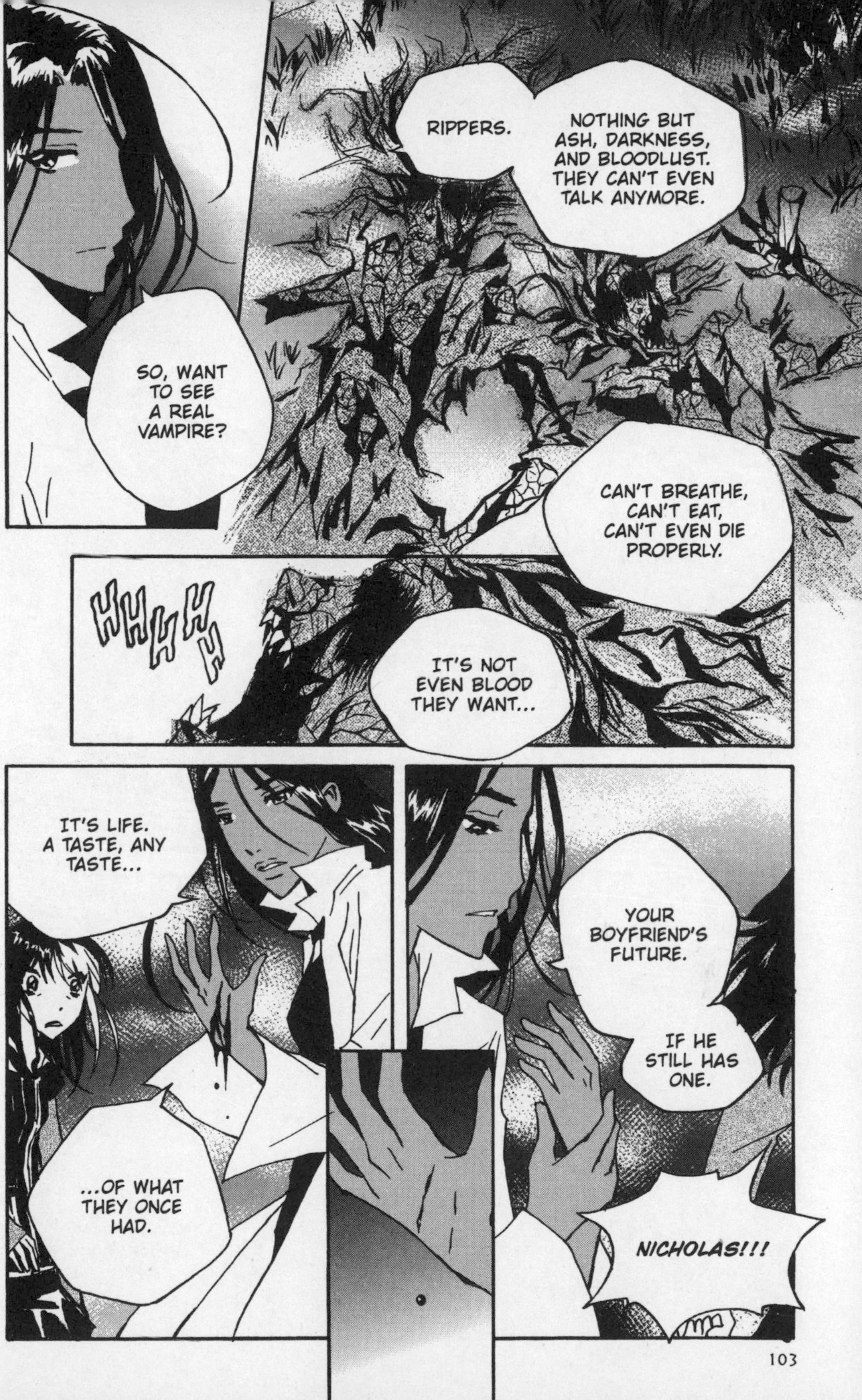

SO, WANT TO SEE A REAL VAMPIRE?
RIPPERS.
NOTHING BUT ASH, DARKNESS, AND BLOODLUST. THEY CAN'T EVEN TALK ANYMORE.
CAN'T BREATHE, CAN'T EAT, CAN'T EVEN DIE PROPERLY.
HHHHH
IT'S NOT EVEN BLOOD THEY WANT...
IT'S LIFE. A TASTE, ANY TASTE...
...OF WHAT THEY ONCE HAD.
YOUR BOYFRIEND'S FUTURE.
IF HE STILL HAS ONE.
NICHOLAS!!!

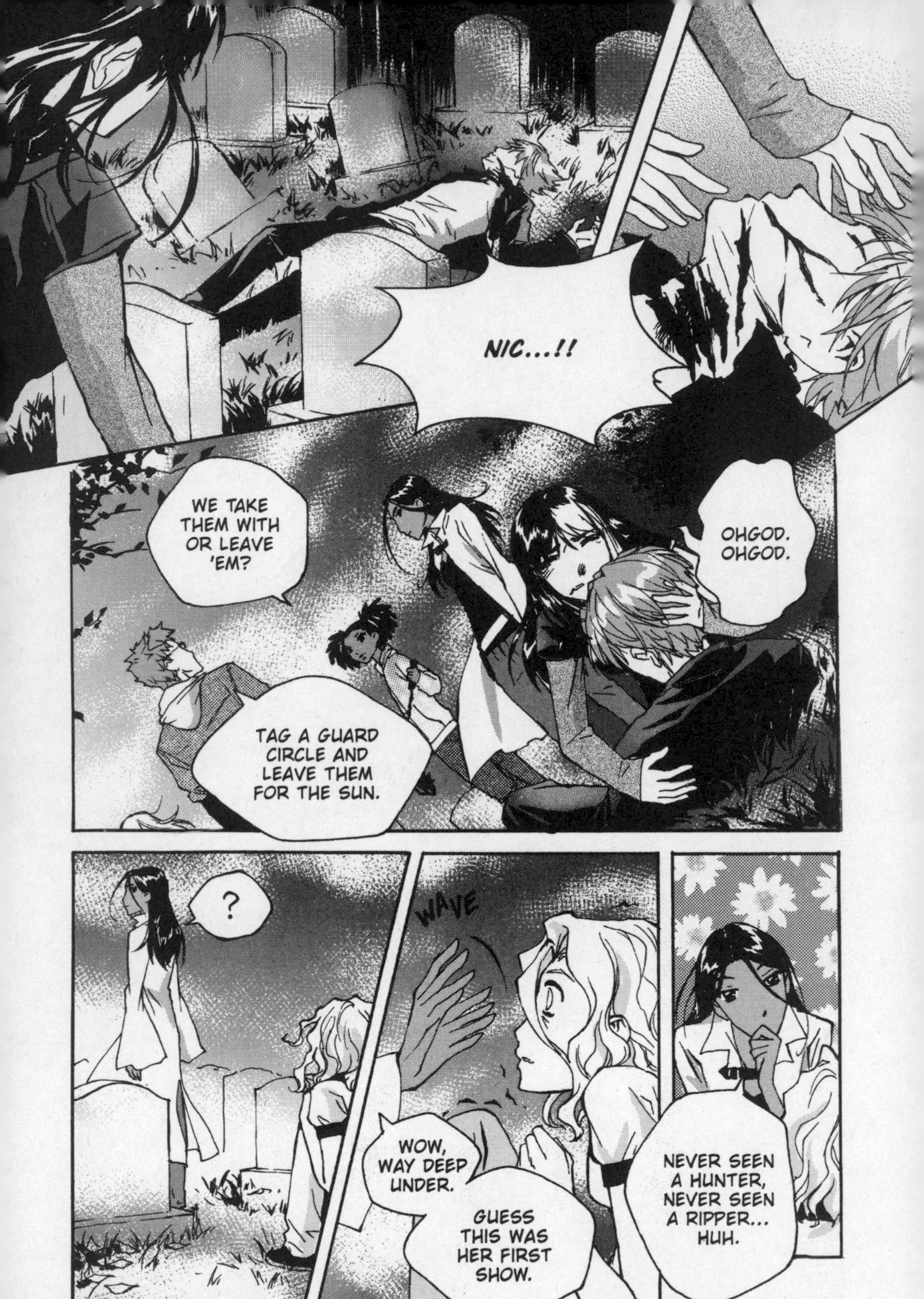
NIC...!!
WE TAKE THEM WITH OR LEAVE 'EM?
OHGOD. OHGOD.
TAG A GUARD CIRCLE AND LEAVE THEM FOR THE SUN.
?
WAVE
WOW, WAY DEEP UNDER.
GUESS THIS WAS HER FIRST SHOW.
NEVER SEEN A HUNTER, NEVER SEEN A RIPPER... HUH.

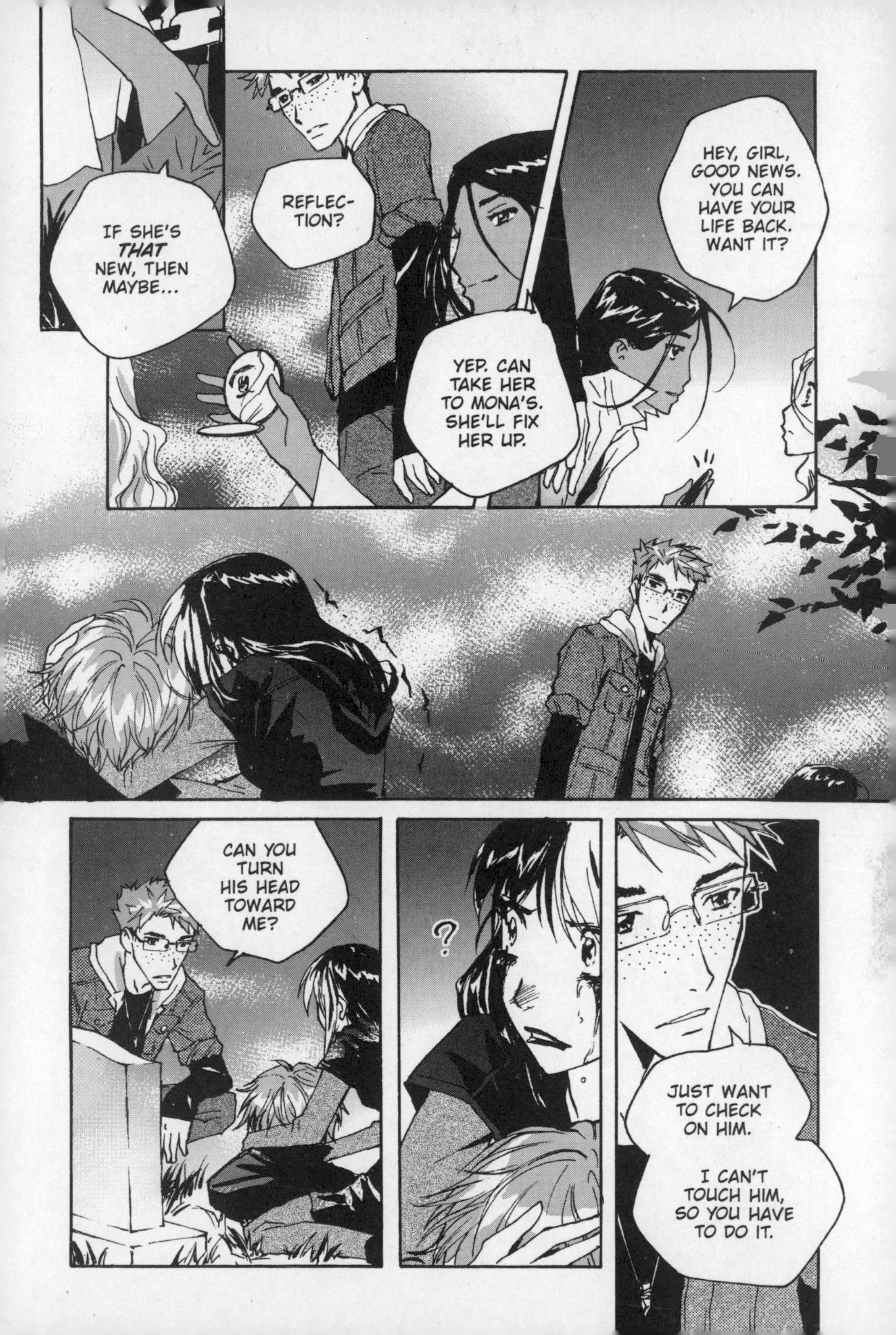
IF SHE'S *THAT* NEW, THEN MAYBE...
REFLECTION?
HEY, GIRL, GOOD NEWS. YOU CAN HAVE YOUR LIFE BACK. WANT IT?
YEP. CAN TAKE HER TO MONA'S. SHE'LL FIX HER UP.
CAN YOU TURN HIS HEAD TOWARD ME?
?
JUST WANT TO CHECK ON HIM.
I CAN'T TOUCH HIM, SO YOU HAVE TO DO IT.

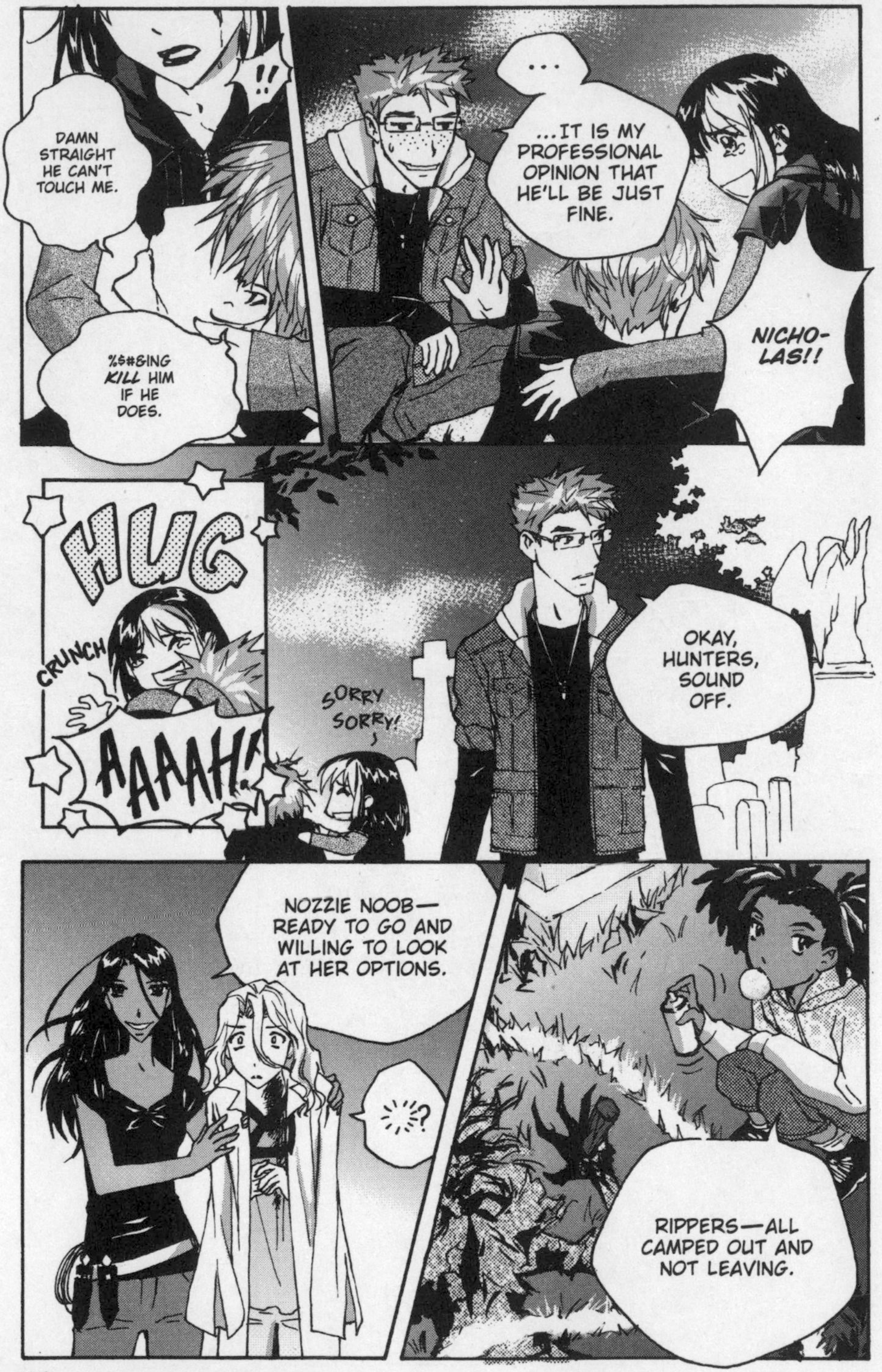
!!
DAMN STRAIGHT HE CAN'T TOUCH ME.
%$#&ING KILL HIM IF HE DOES.
...
...IT IS MY PROFESSIONAL OPINION THAT HE'LL BE JUST FINE.
NICHO-LAS!!
HUG
CRUNCH
AAAAH!
SORRY SORRY!
OKAY, HUNTERS, SOUND OFF.
NOZZIE NOOB—READY TO GO AND WILLING TO LOOK AT HER OPTIONS.
?
RIPPERS—ALL CAMPED OUT AND NOT LEAVING.

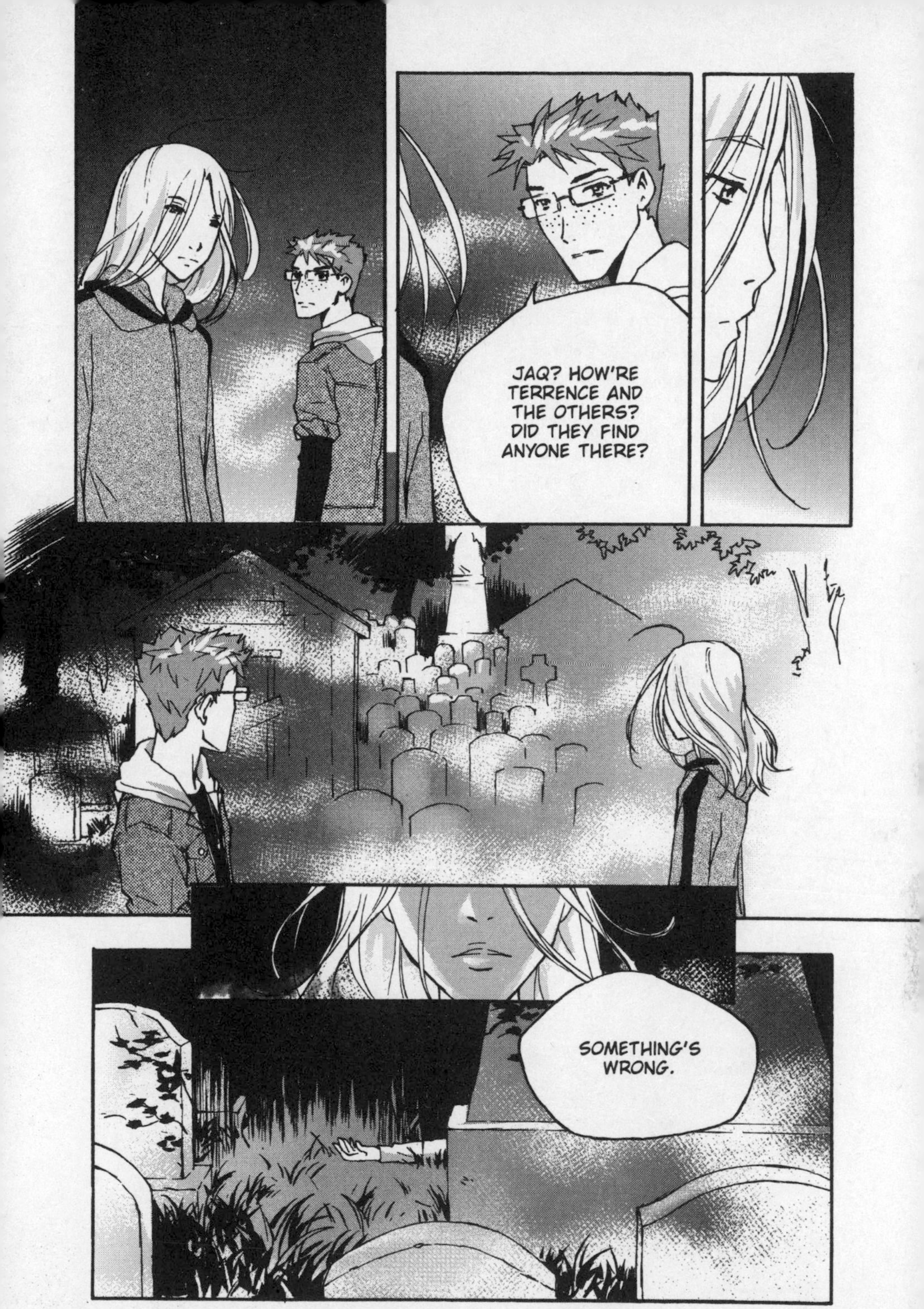
JAQ? HOW'RE TERRENCE AND THE OTHERS? DID THEY FIND ANYONE THERE?
SOMETHING'S WRONG.

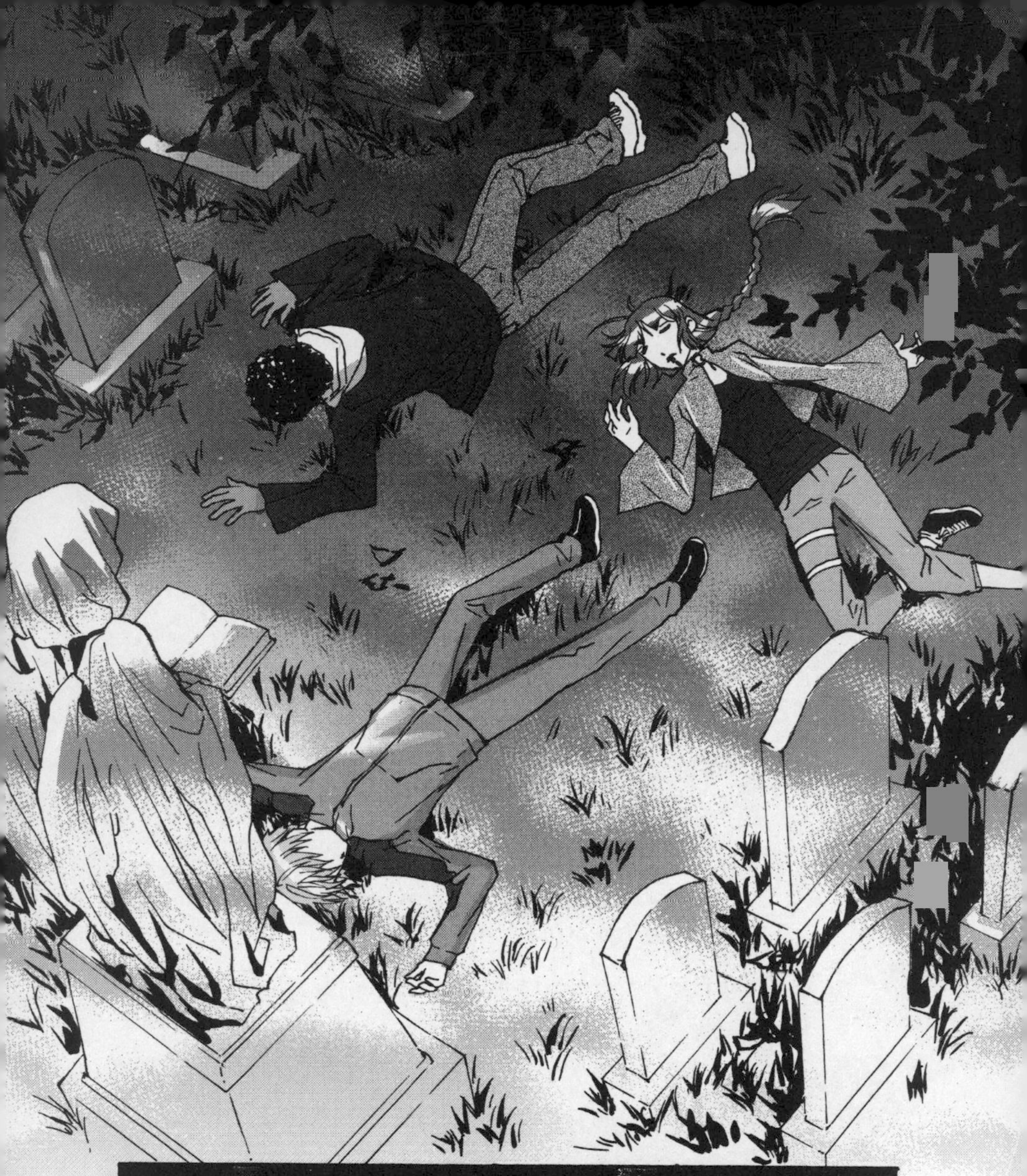
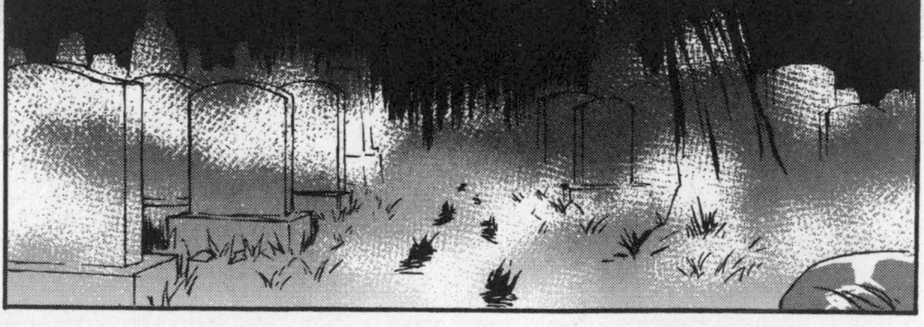

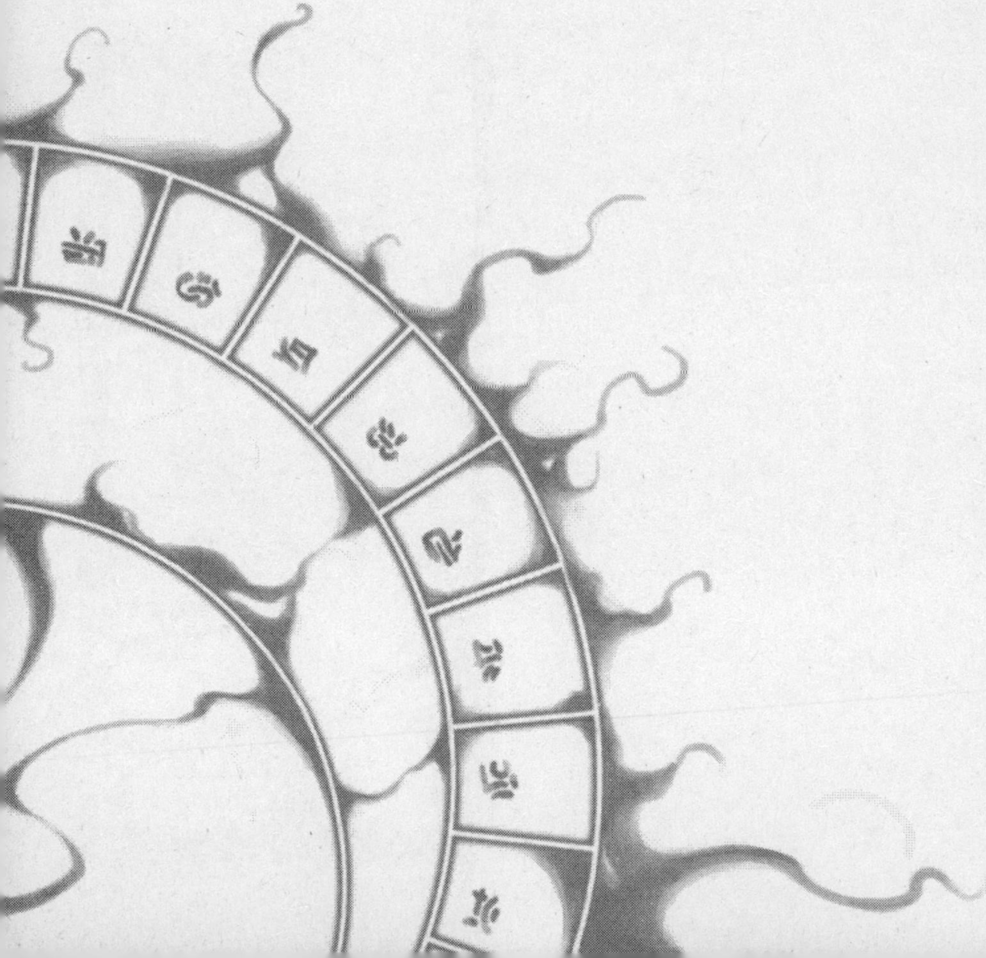

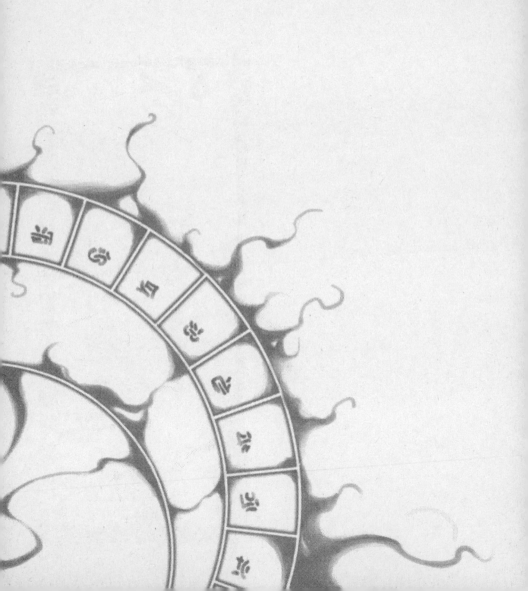

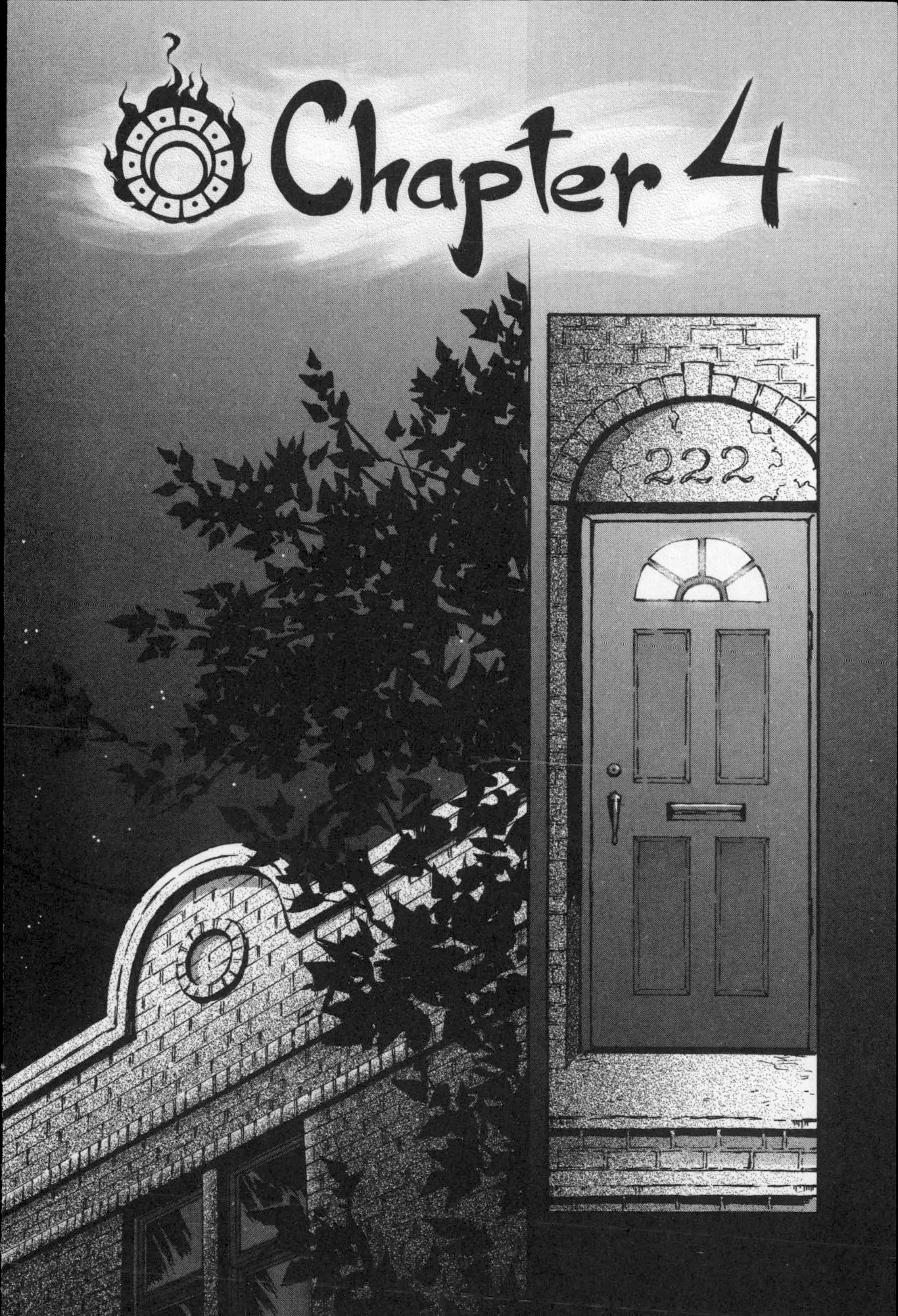
Chapter 4
222

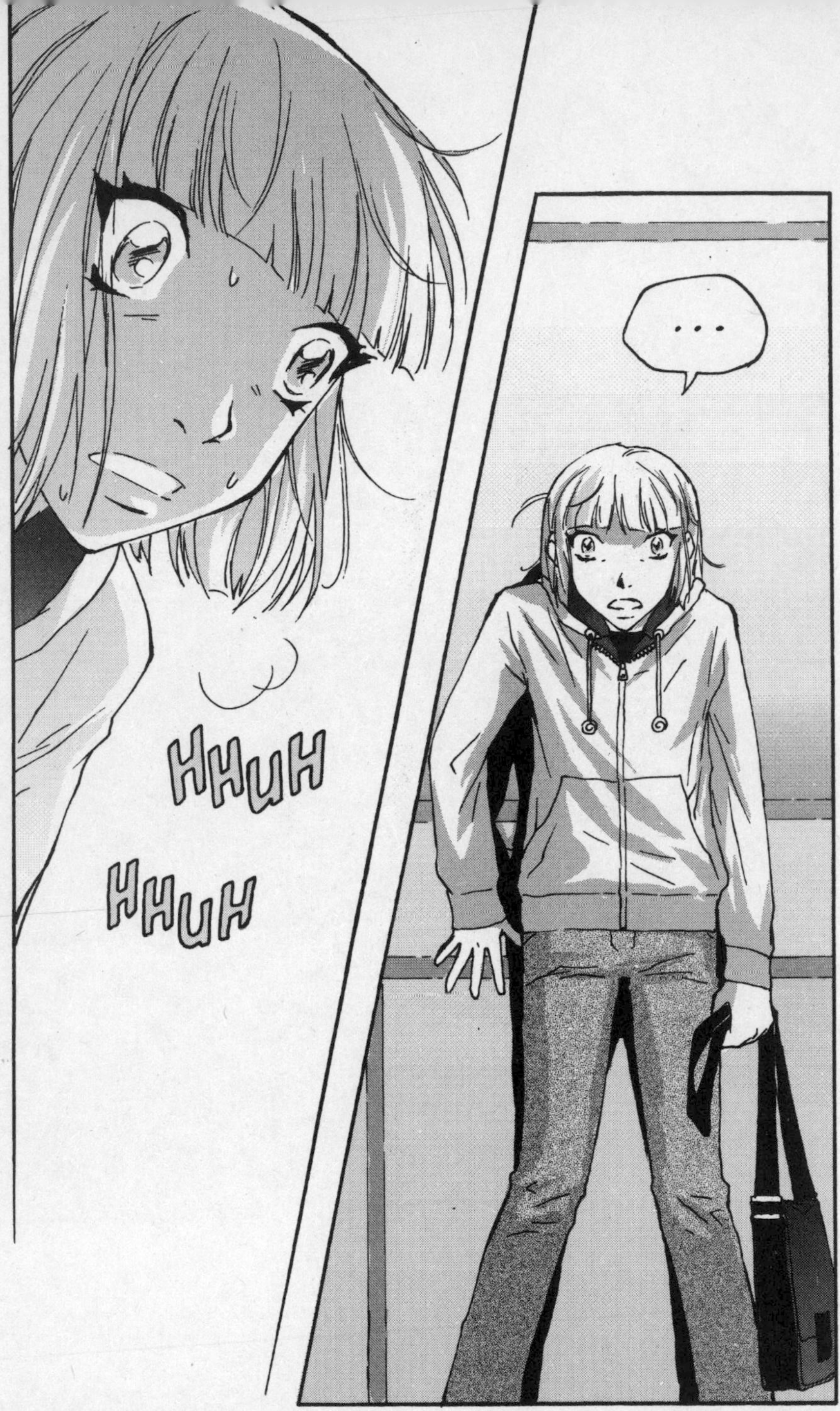
HHUH
HHUH
...

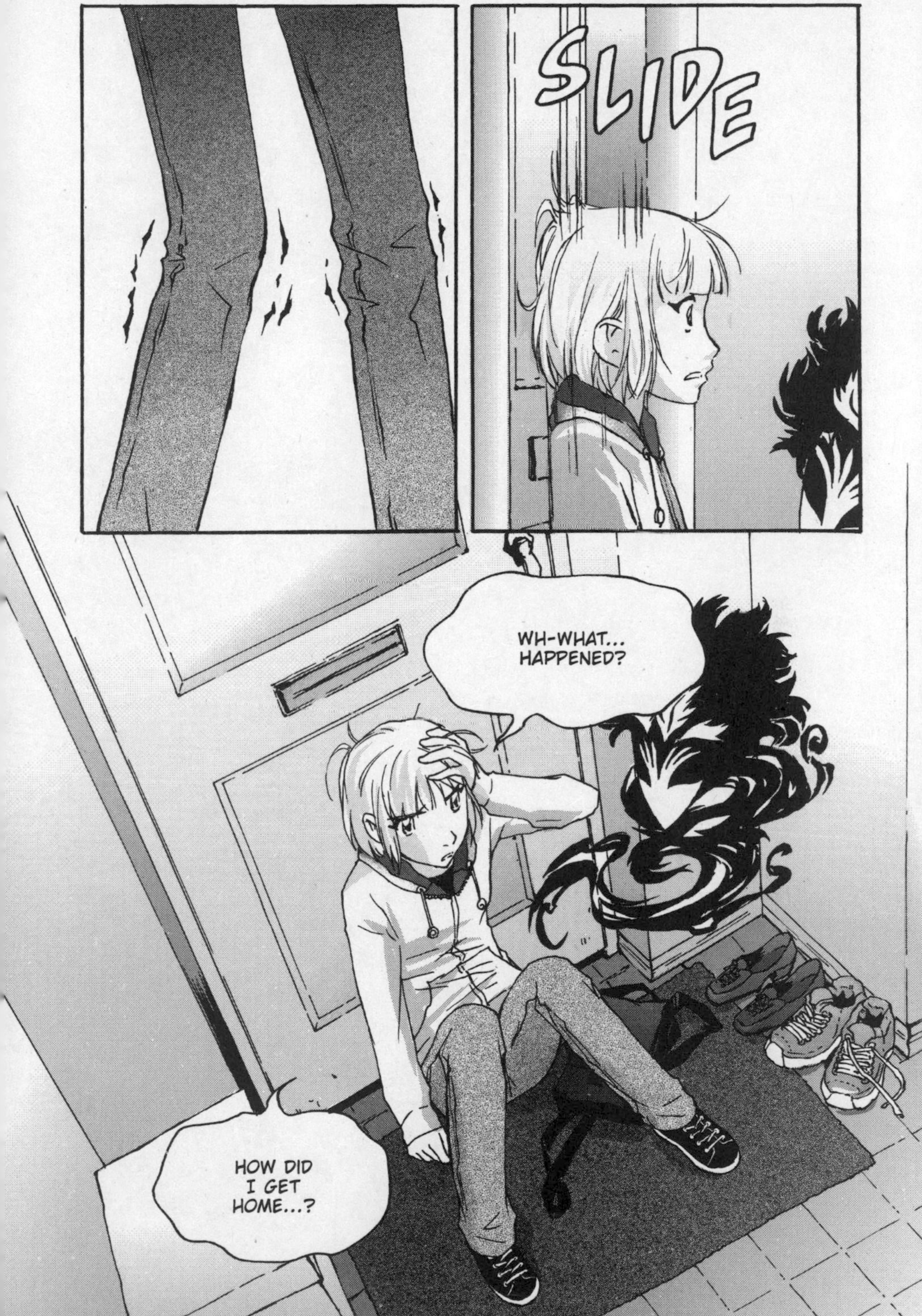
SLIDE
WH-WHAT... HAPPENED?
HOW DID I GET HOME...?

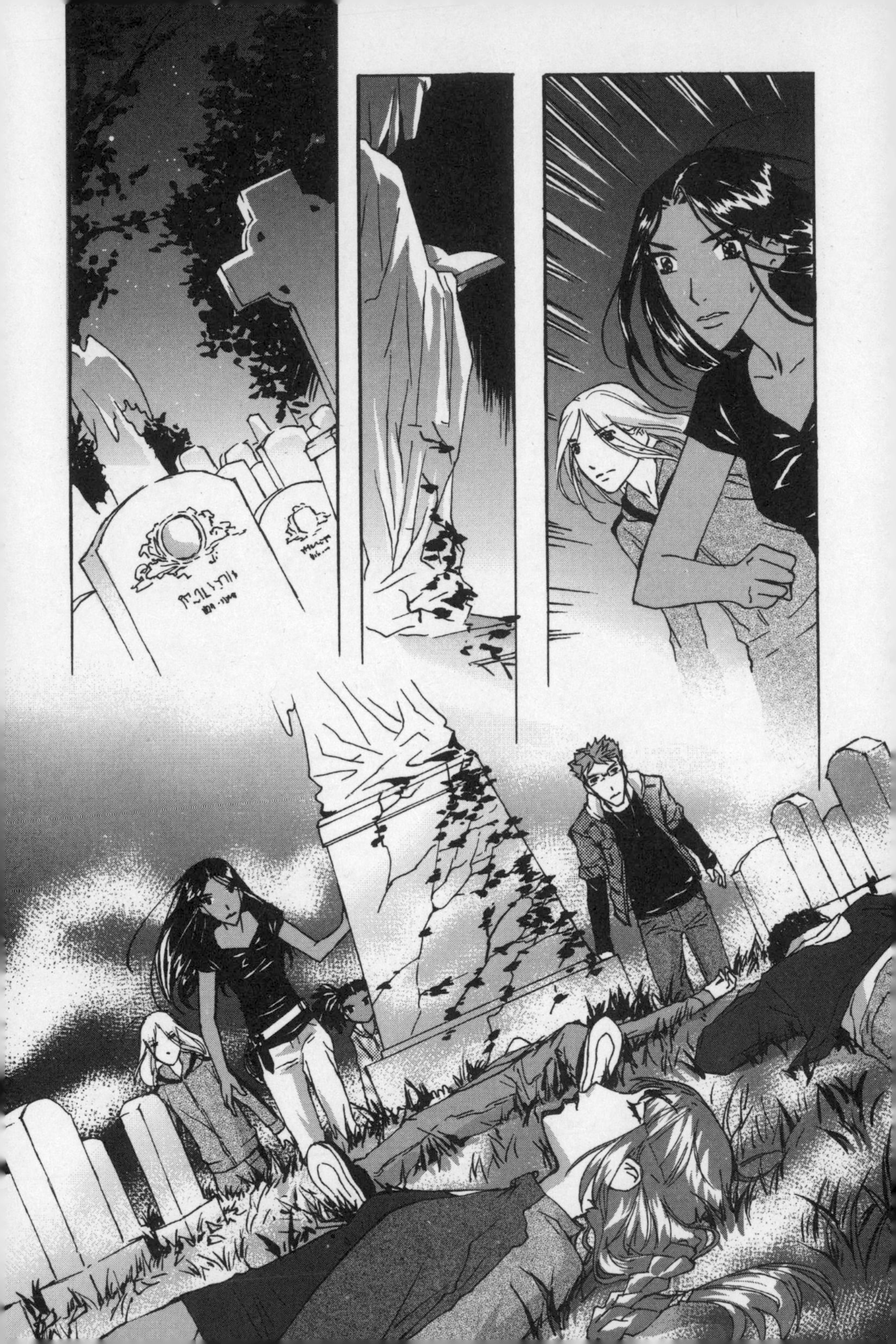

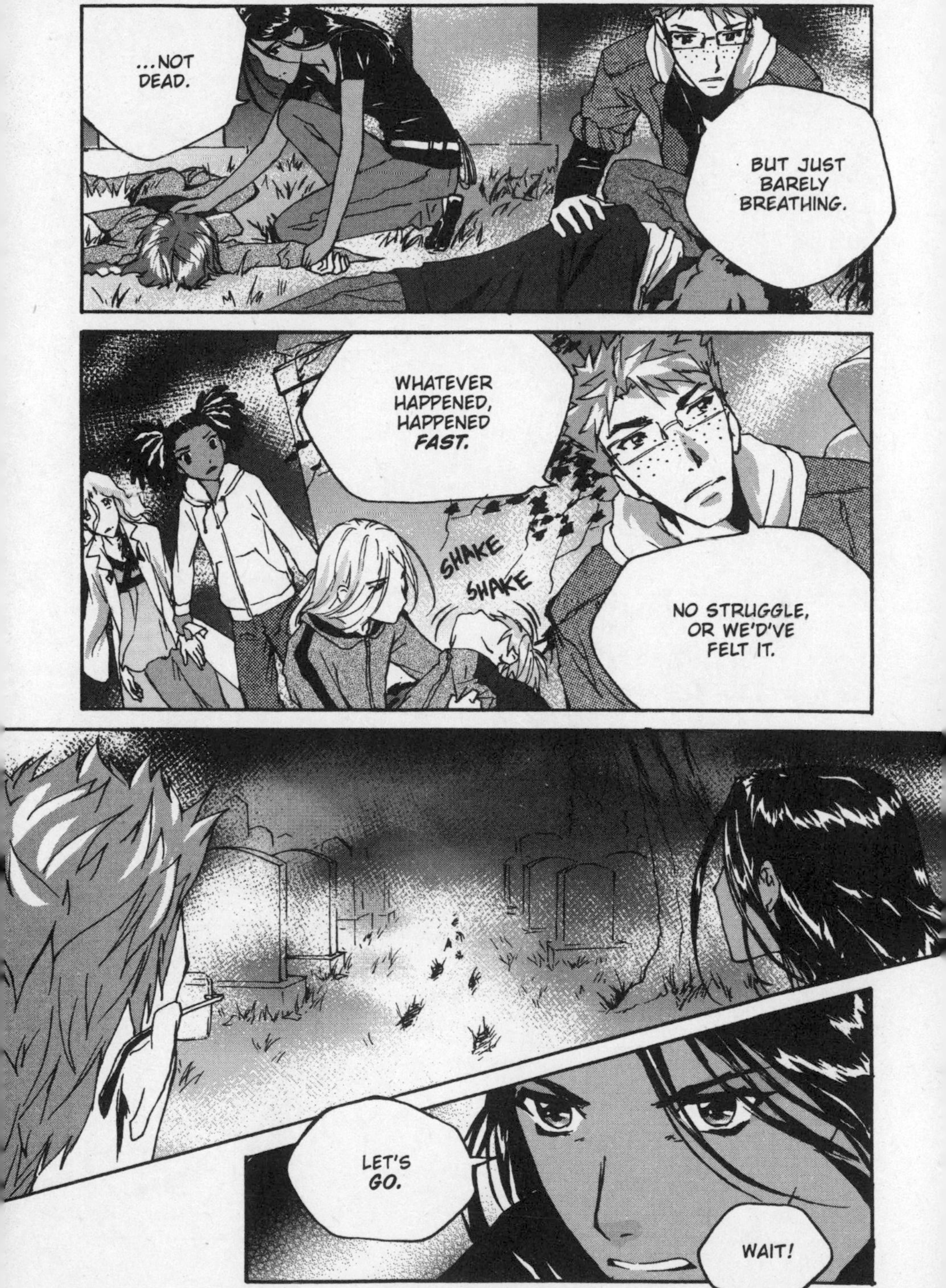
...NOT DEAD.
BUT JUST BARELY BREATHING.
WHATEVER HAPPENED, HAPPENED FAST.
SHAKE SHAKE
NO STRUGGLE, OR WE'D'VE FELT IT.
LET'S GO.
WAIT!

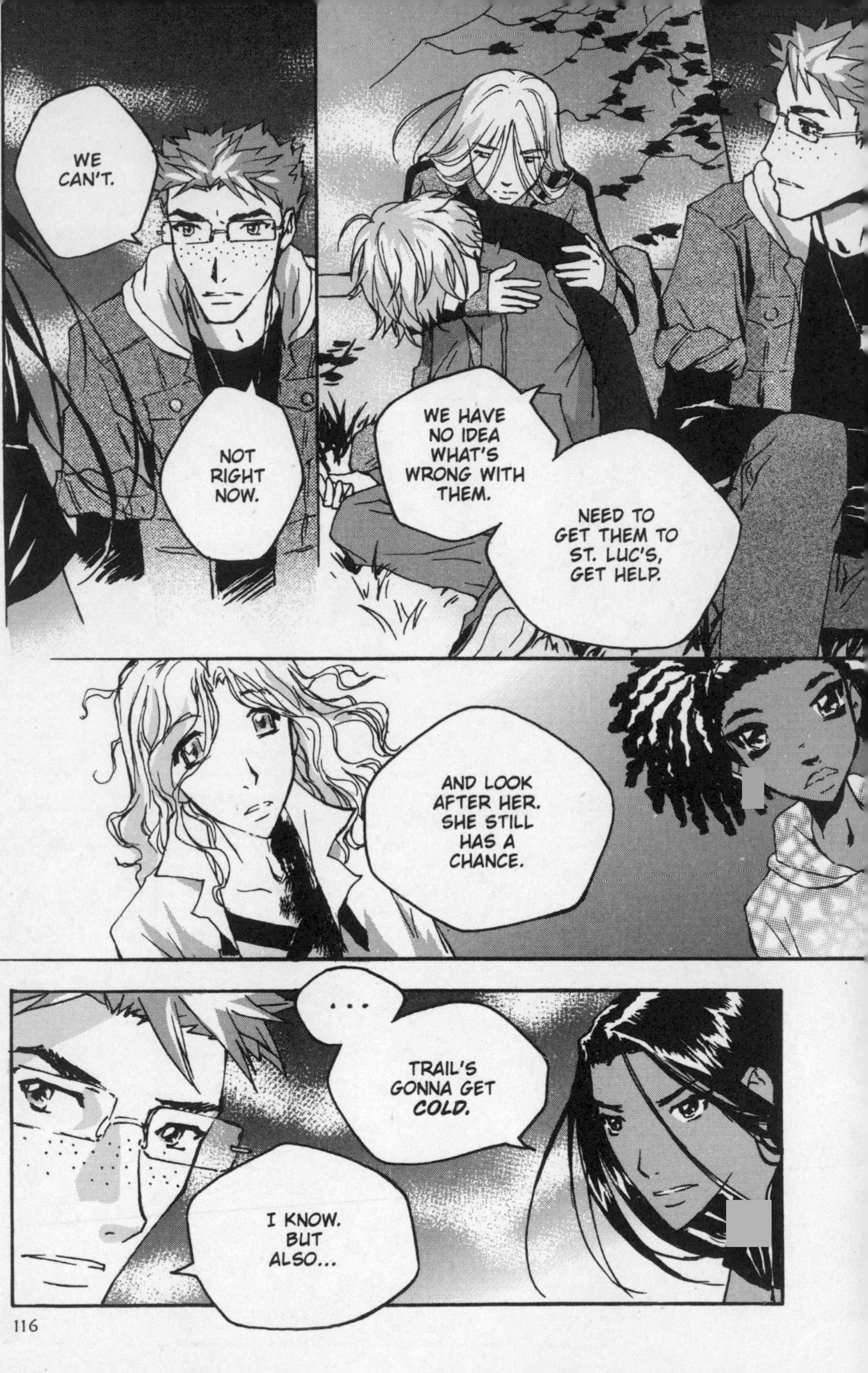
WE CAN'T.
NOT RIGHT NOW.
WE HAVE NO IDEA WHAT'S WRONG WITH THEM.
NEED TO GET THEM TO ST. LUC'S, GET HELP.
AND LOOK AFTER HER. SHE STILL HAS A CHANCE.
...
TRAIL'S GONNA GET *COLD.*
I KNOW. BUT ALSO...

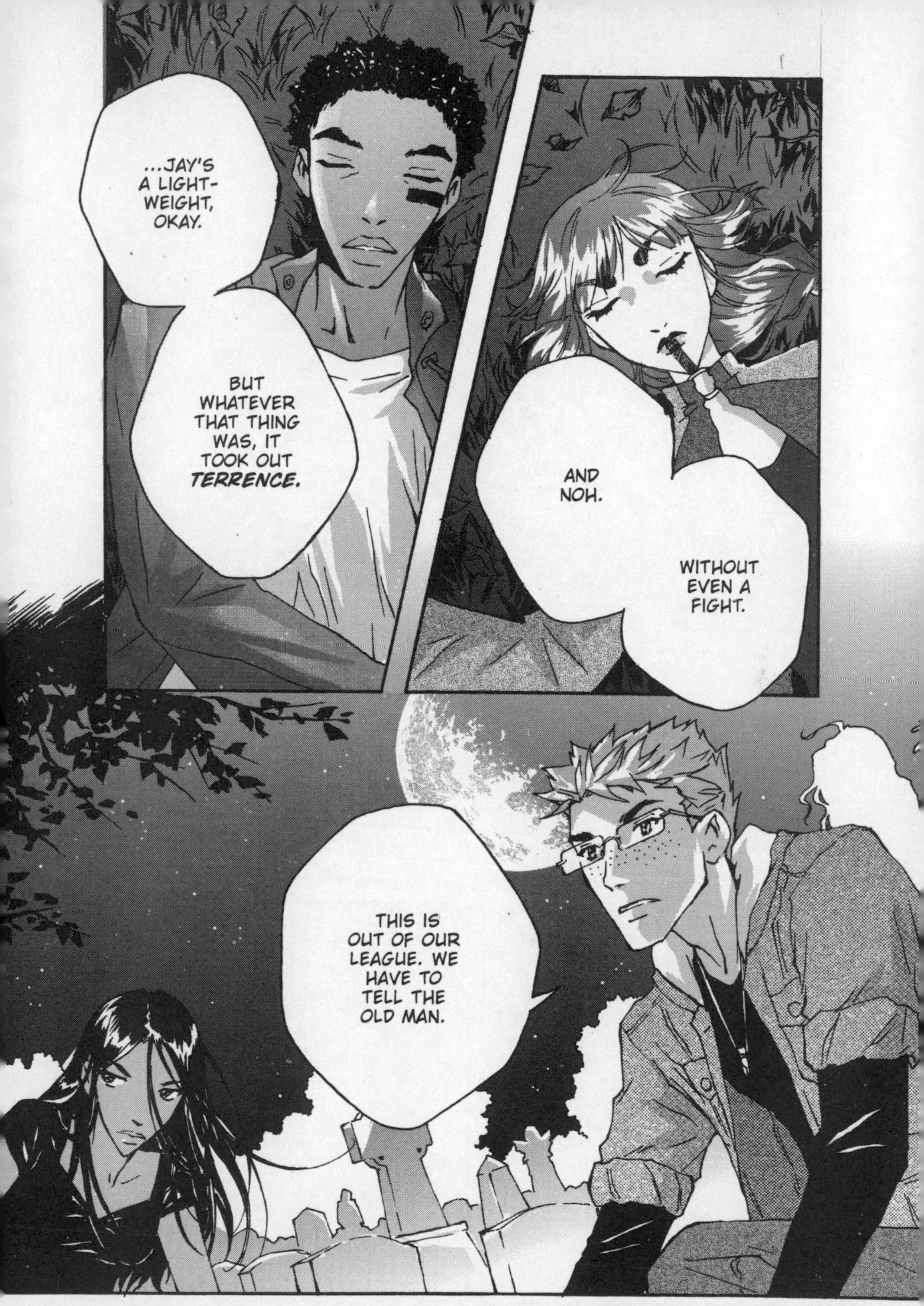
...JAY'S A LIGHT-WEIGHT, OKAY.
BUT WHATEVER THAT THING WAS, IT TOOK OUT *TERRENCE.*
AND NOH.
WITHOUT EVEN A FIGHT.
THIS IS OUT OF OUR LEAGUE. WE HAVE TO TELL THE OLD MAN.

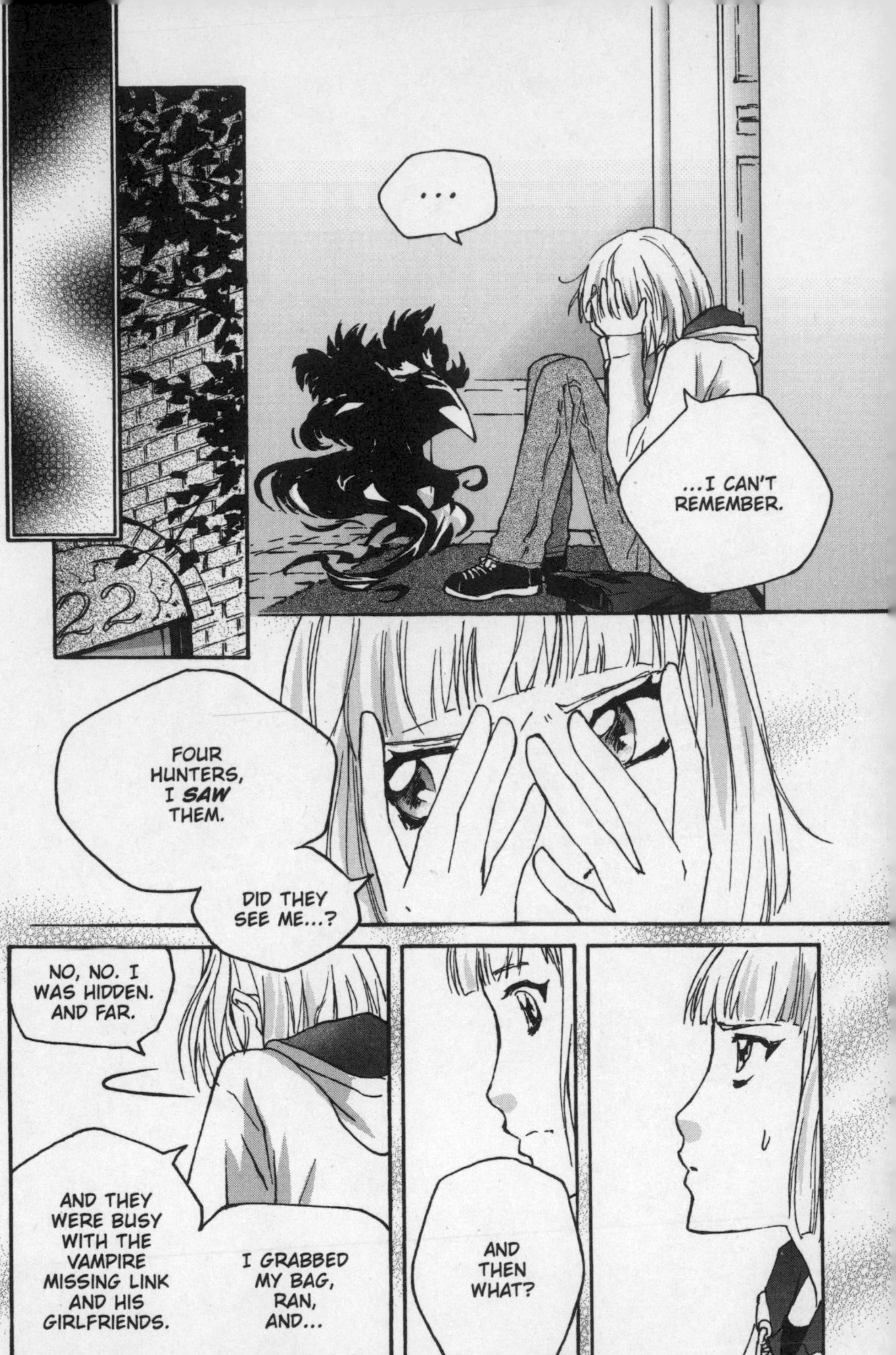
...
...I CAN'T REMEMBER.
FOUR HUNTERS, I SAW THEM.
DID THEY SEE ME...?
NO, NO. I WAS HIDDEN. AND FAR.
AND THEY WERE BUSY WITH THE VAMPIRE MISSING LINK AND HIS GIRLFRIENDS.
I GRABBED MY BAG, RAN, AND...
AND THEN WHAT?

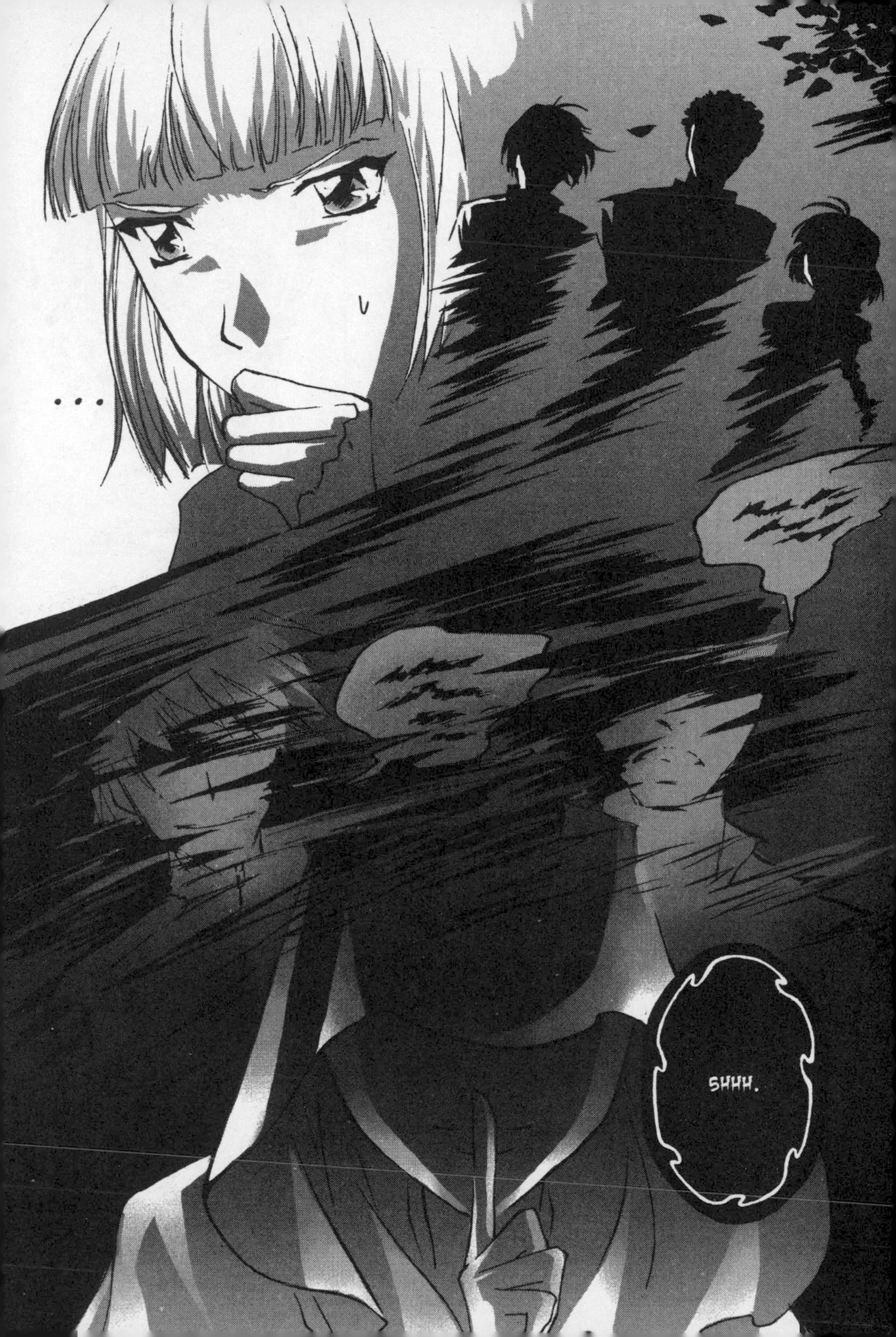
...
SHHH.

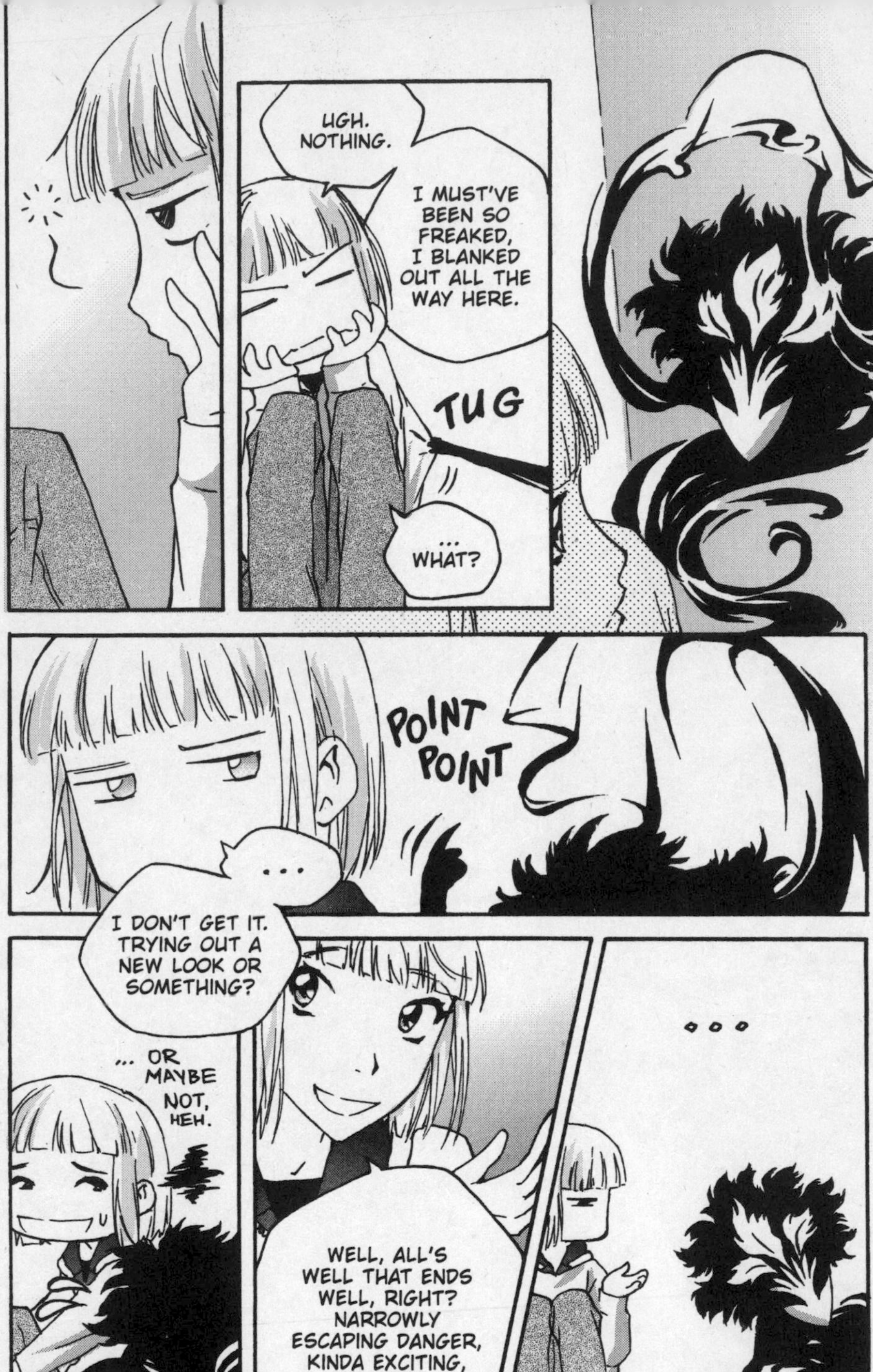
UGH. NOTHING.
I MUST'VE BEEN SO FREAKED, I BLANKED OUT ALL THE WAY HERE.
TUG
... WHAT?
POINT POINT
...
I DON'T GET IT. TRYING OUT A NEW LOOK OR SOMETHING?
... OR MAYBE NOT, HEH.
WELL, ALL'S WELL THAT ENDS WELL, RIGHT? NARROWLY ESCAPING DANGER, KINDA EXCITING, HUH? :D
...

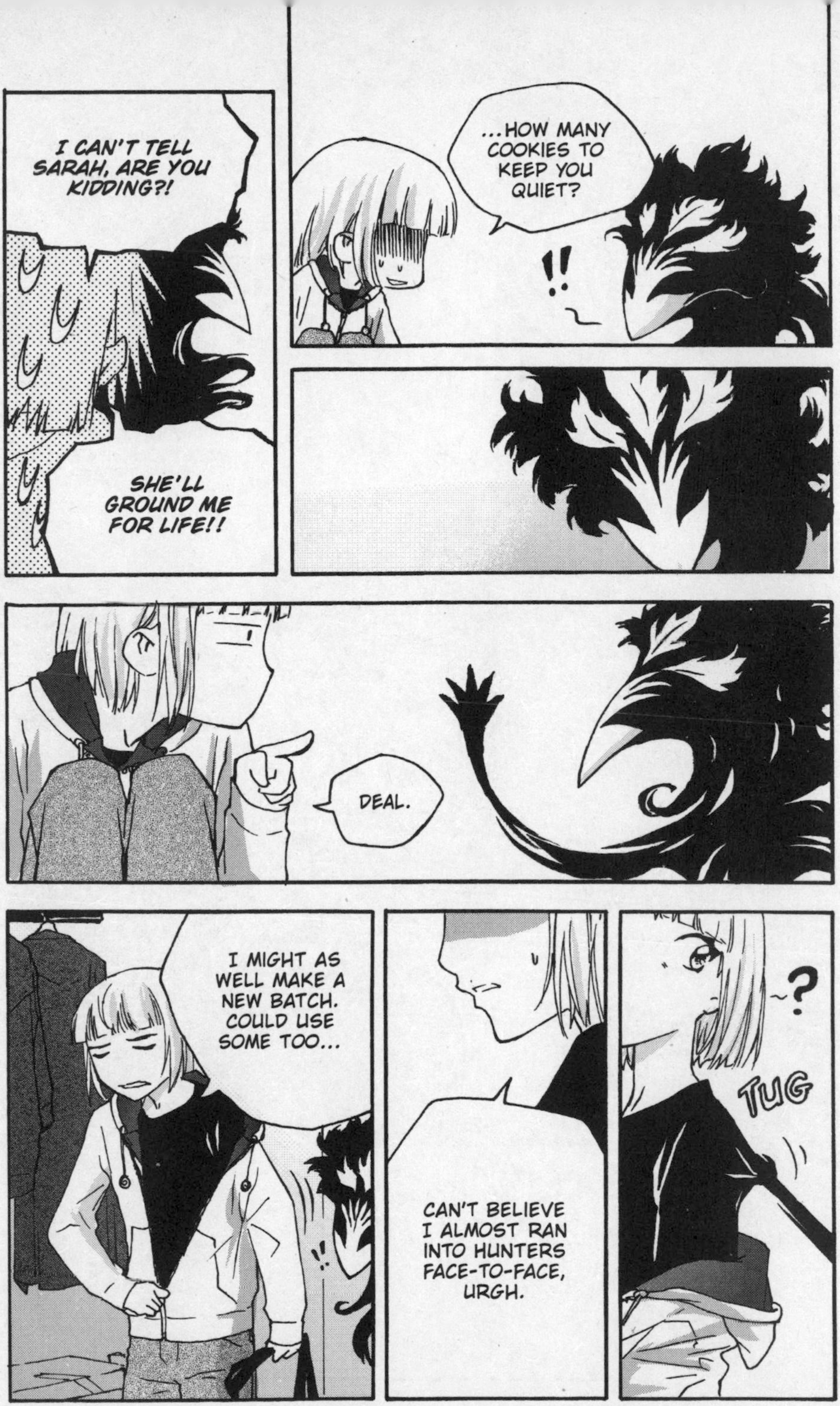
I CAN'T TELL SARAH, ARE YOU KIDDING?!
SHE'LL GROUND ME FOR LIFE!!
...HOW MANY COOKIES TO KEEP YOU QUIET?
!!
DEAL.
I MIGHT AS WELL MAKE A NEW BATCH. COULD USE SOME TOO...
!
CAN'T BELIEVE I ALMOST RAN INTO HUNTERS FACE-TO-FACE, URGH.
?
TUG

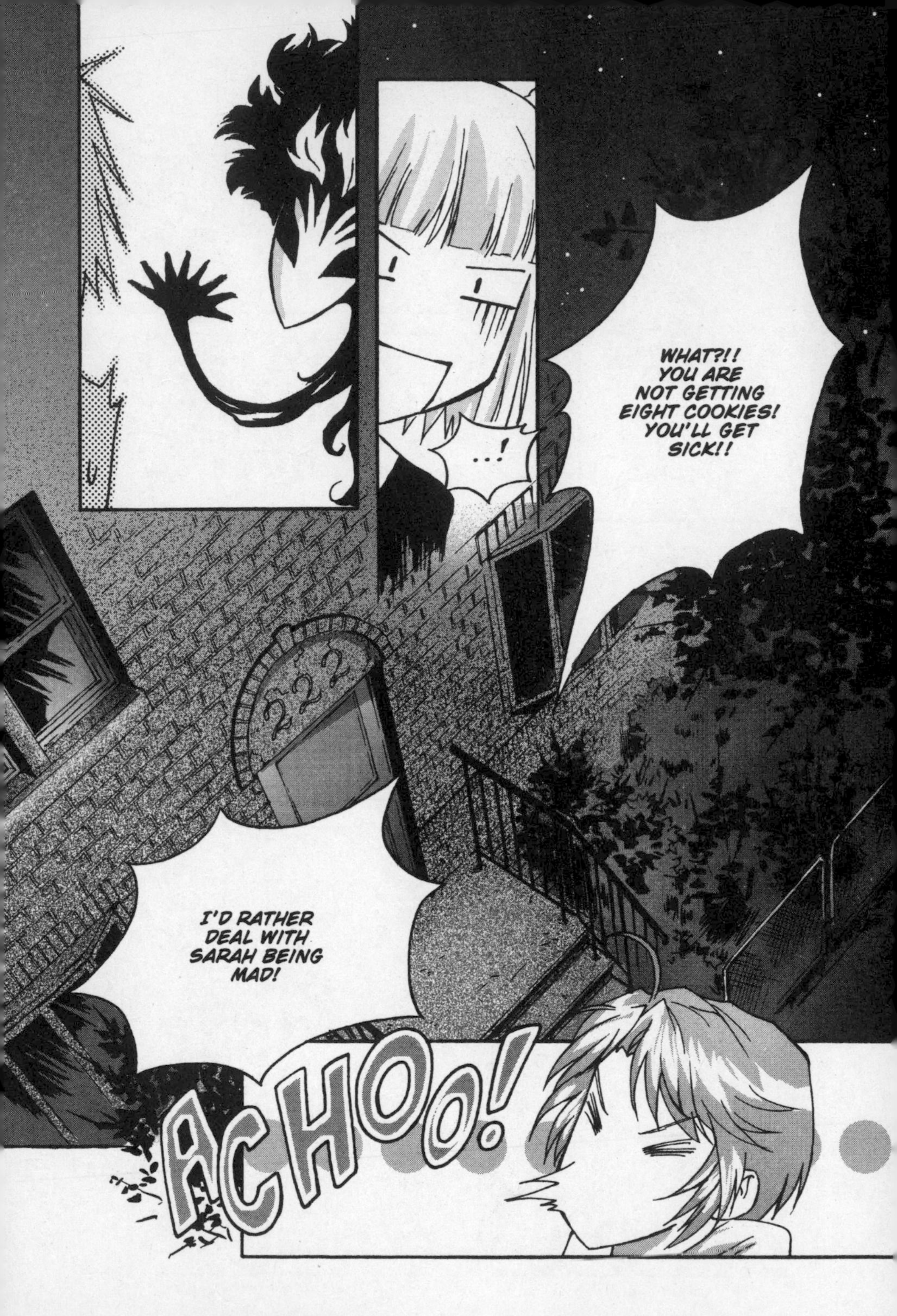
...!
WHAT?!! YOU ARE NOT GETTING EIGHT COOKIES! YOU'LL GET SICK!!
I'D RATHER DEAL WITH SARAH BEING MAD!
ACHOO!

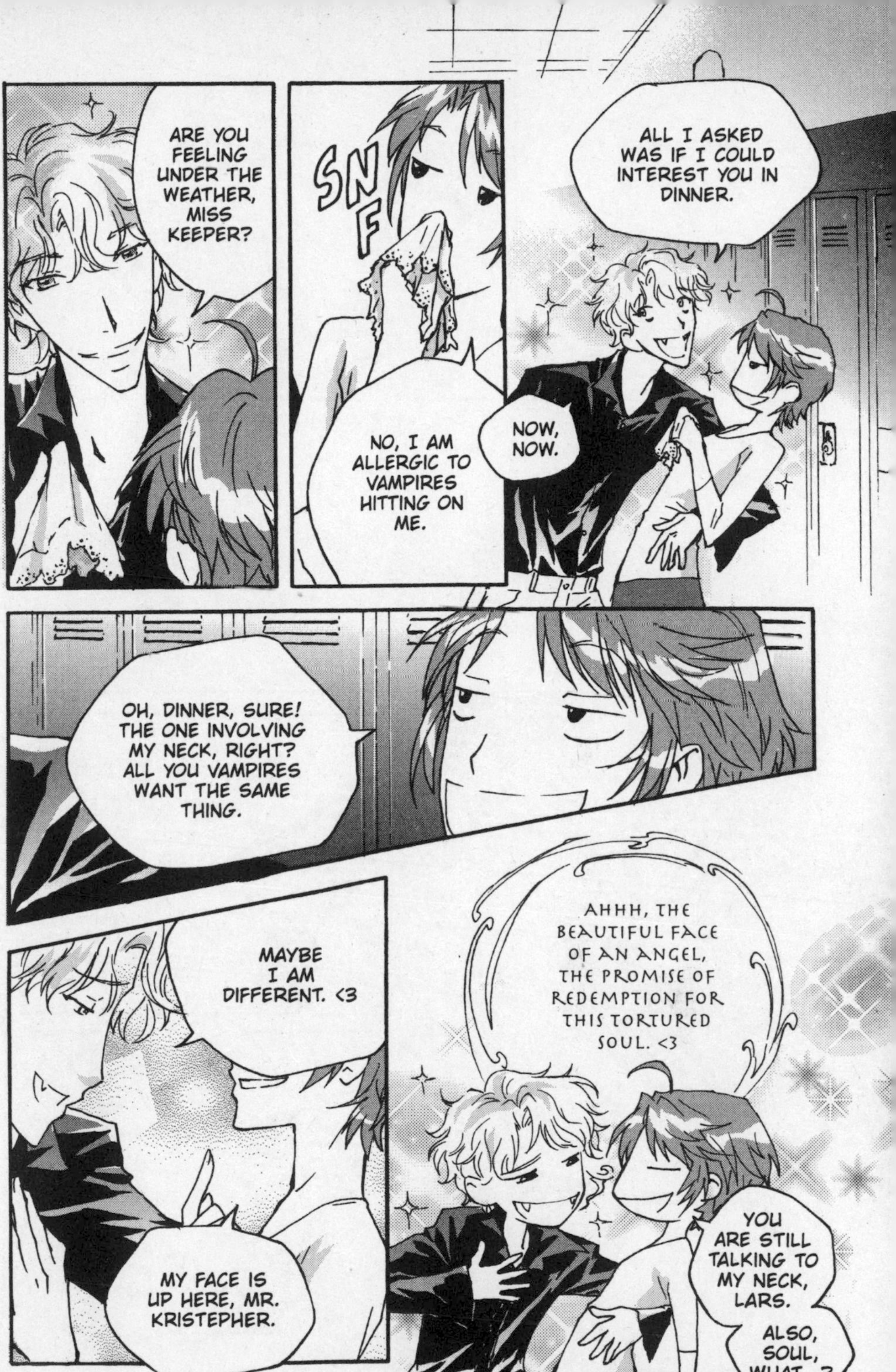
ARE YOU FEELING UNDER THE WEATHER, MISS KEEPER?
SNF
NO, I AM ALLERGIC TO VAMPIRES HITTING ON ME.
ALL I ASKED WAS IF I COULD INTEREST YOU IN DINNER.
NOW, NOW.
OH, DINNER, SURE! THE ONE INVOLVING MY NECK, RIGHT? ALL YOU VAMPIRES WANT THE SAME THING.
MAYBE I AM DIFFERENT. <3
MY FACE IS UP HERE, MR. KRISTEPHER.
AHHH, THE BEAUTIFUL FACE OF AN ANGEL, THE PROMISE OF REDEMPTION FOR THIS TORTURED SOUL. <3
YOU ARE STILL TALKING TO MY NECK, LARS.
ALSO, SOUL, WHAT...?

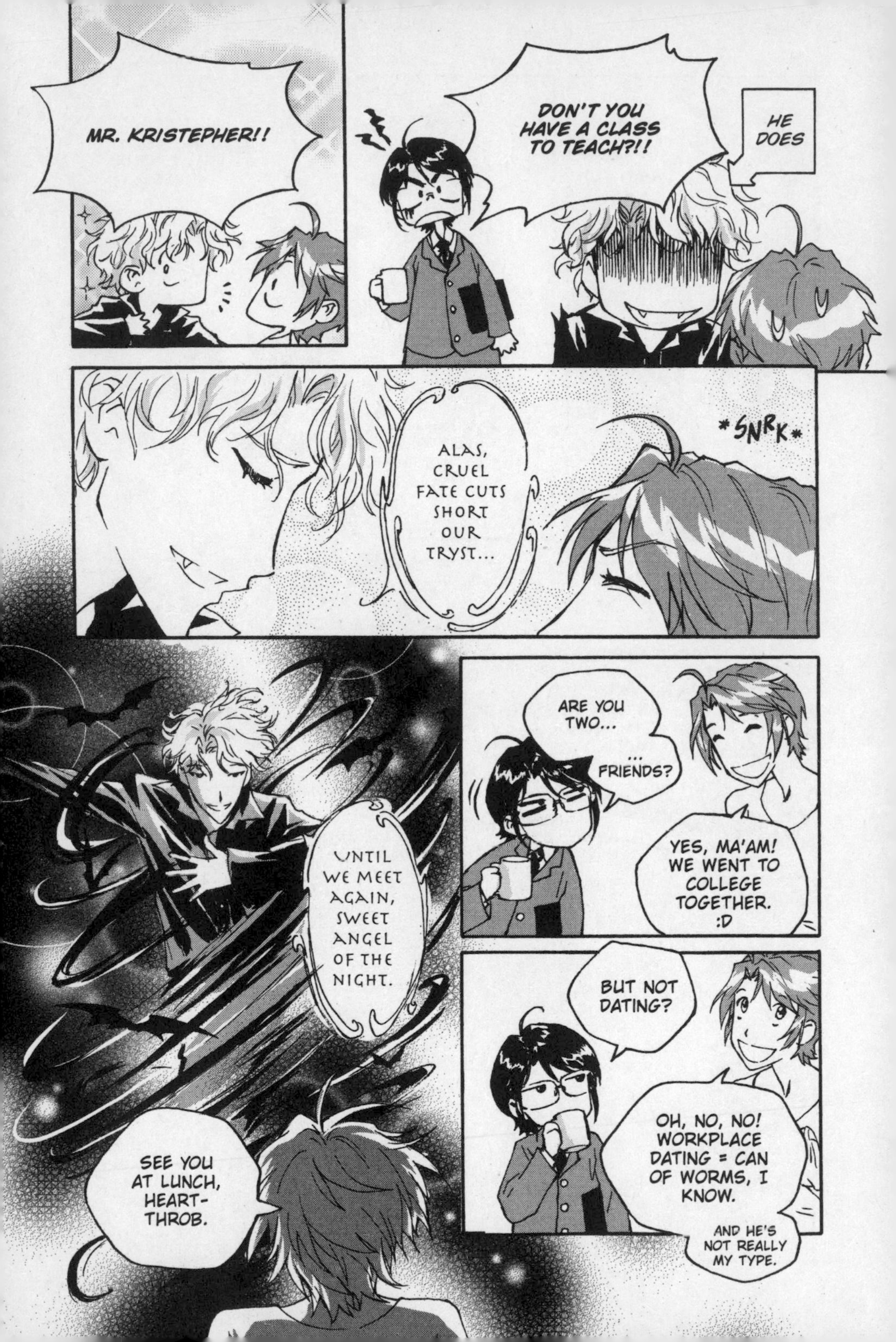
MR. KRISTEPHER!!
DON'T YOU HAVE A CLASS TO TEACH?!!
HE DOES
ALAS, CRUEL FATE CUTS SHORT OUR TRYST...
SNRK
UNTIL WE MEET AGAIN, SWEET ANGEL OF THE NIGHT.
SEE YOU AT LUNCH, HEART-THROB.
ARE YOU TWO...
...FRIENDS?
YES, MA'AM! WE WENT TO COLLEGE TOGETHER. :D
BUT NOT DATING?
OH, NO, NO! WORKPLACE DATING = CAN OF WORMS, I KNOW.
AND HE'S NOT REALLY MY TYPE.

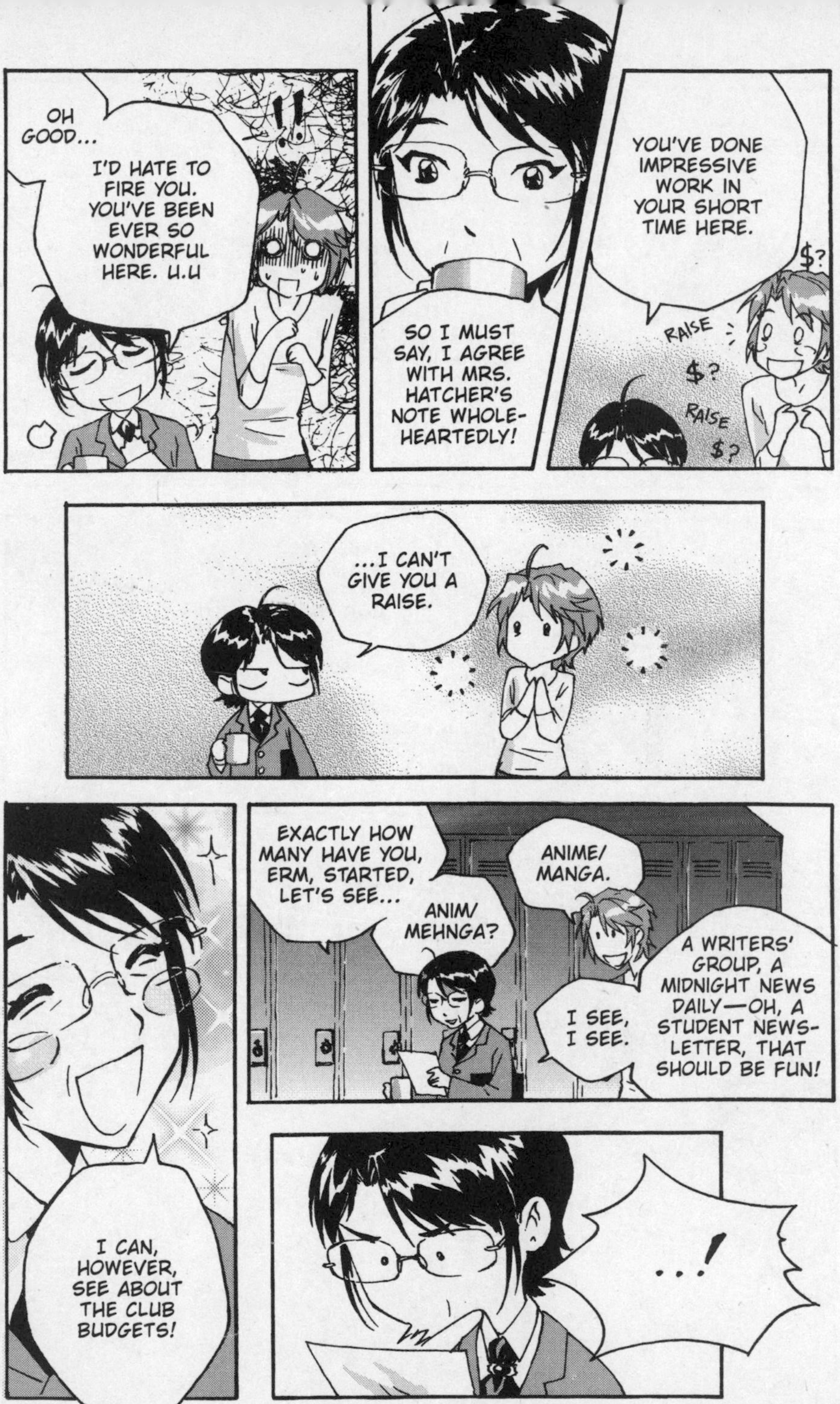
OH GOOD...
I'D HATE TO FIRE YOU. YOU'VE BEEN EVER SO WONDERFUL HERE. u.u
!!
SO I MUST SAY, I AGREE WITH MRS. HATCHER'S NOTE WHOLE-HEARTEDLY!
YOU'VE DONE IMPRESSIVE WORK IN YOUR SHORT TIME HERE.
$?
RAISE
$?
RAISE
$?
...I CAN'T GIVE YOU A RAISE.
I CAN, HOWEVER, SEE ABOUT THE CLUB BUDGETS!
EXACTLY HOW MANY HAVE YOU, ERM, STARTED, LET'S SEE...
ANIME/ MANGA.
ANIM/ MEHNGA?
A WRITERS' GROUP, A MIDNIGHT NEWS DAILY—OH, A STUDENT NEWS-LETTER, THAT SHOULD BE FUN!
I SEE, I SEE.
...!

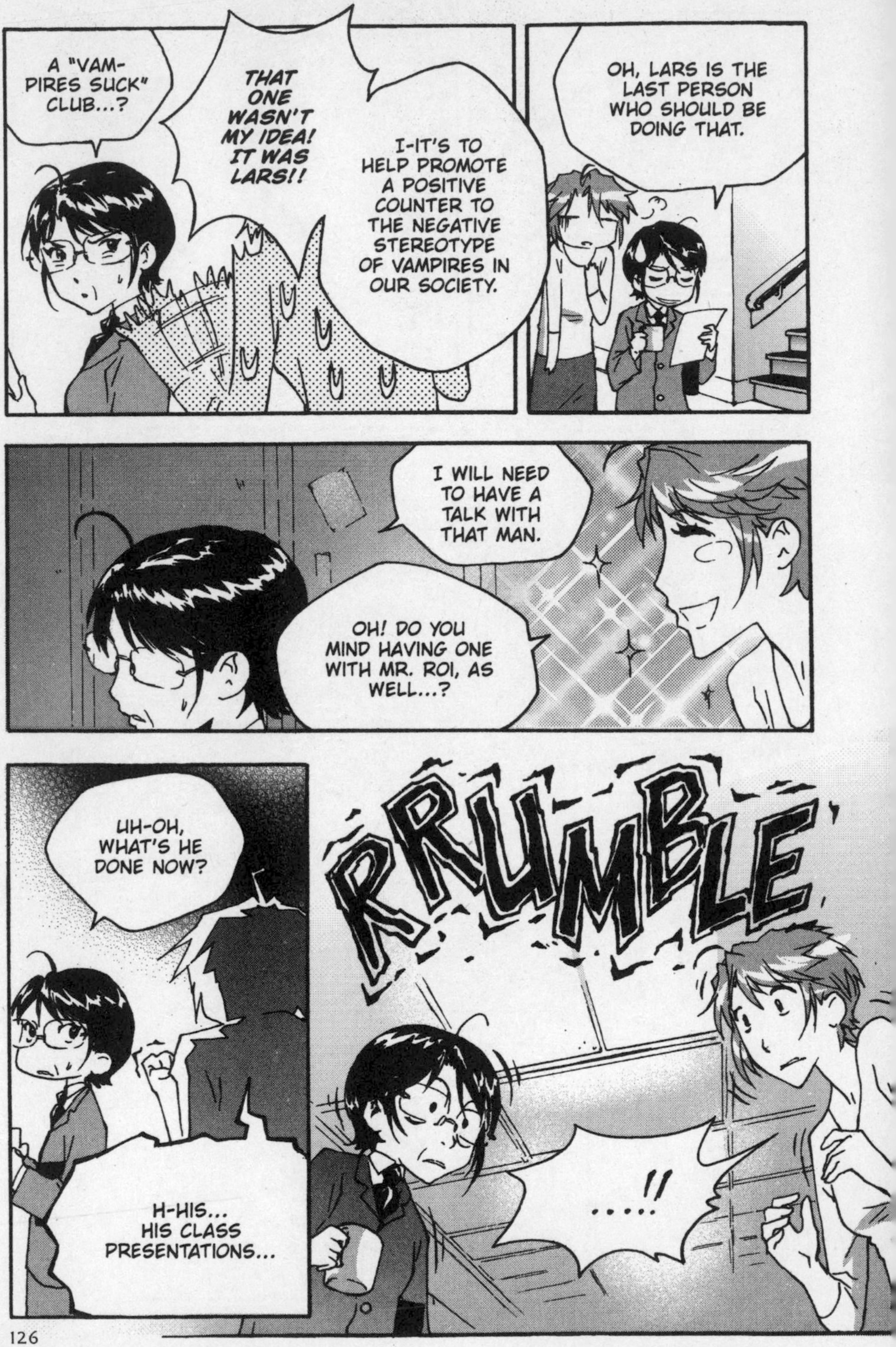

A "VAMPIRES SUCK" CLUB...?
THAT ONE WASN'T MY IDEA! IT WAS LARS!!
I-IT'S TO HELP PROMOTE A POSITIVE COUNTER TO THE NEGATIVE STEREOTYPE OF VAMPIRES IN OUR SOCIETY.
OH, LARS IS THE LAST PERSON WHO SHOULD BE DOING THAT.
I WILL NEED TO HAVE A TALK WITH THAT MAN.
OH! DO YOU MIND HAVING ONE WITH MR. ROI, AS WELL...?
UH-OH, WHAT'S HE DONE NOW?
H-HIS... HIS CLASS PRESENTATIONS...
RRUMBLE
.....!!

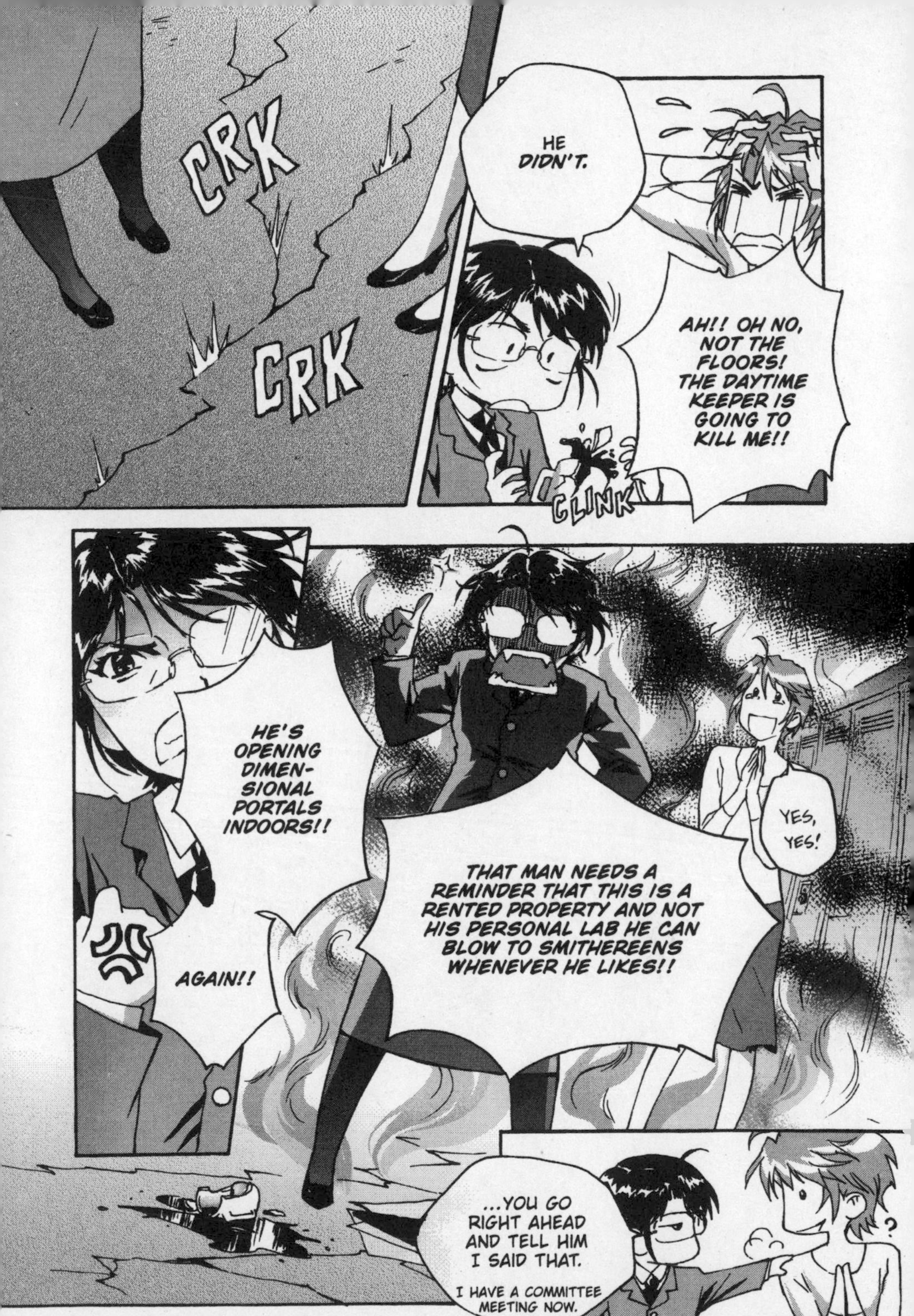
CRK
CRK
HE DIDN'T.
AH!! OH NO, NOT THE FLOORS! THE DAYTIME KEEPER IS GOING TO KILL ME!!
CLINK
HE'S OPENING DIMEN-SIONAL PORTALS INDOORS!!
AGAIN!!
THAT MAN NEEDS A REMINDER THAT THIS IS A RENTED PROPERTY AND NOT HIS PERSONAL LAB HE CAN BLOW TO SMITHEREENS WHENEVER HE LIKES!!
YES, YES!
...YOU GO RIGHT AHEAD AND TELL HIM I SAID THAT.
I HAVE A COMMITTEE MEETING NOW.
?

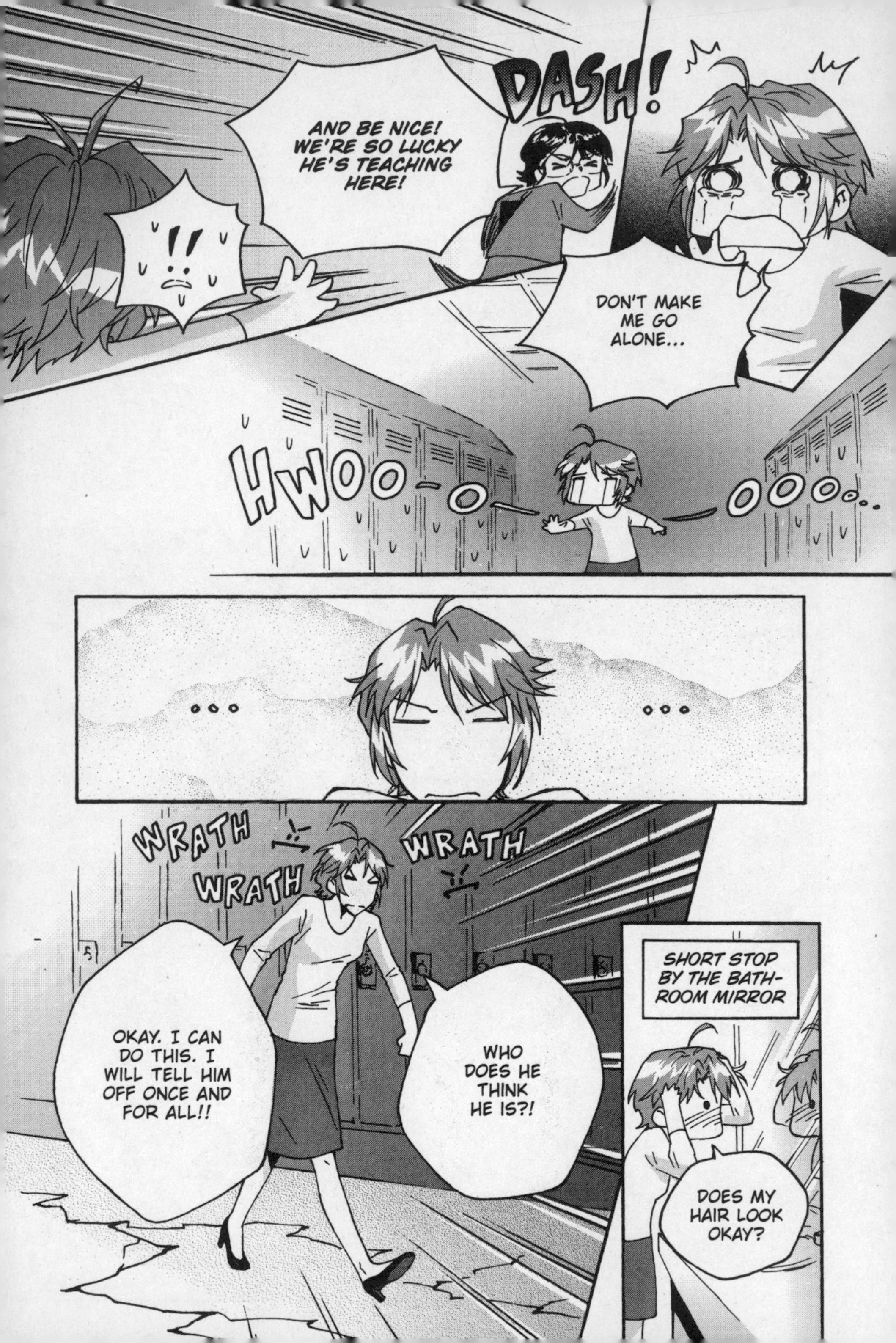
AND BE NICE! WE'RE SO LUCKY HE'S TEACHING HERE!
!!
DASH!
DON'T MAKE ME GO ALONE...
HWOO-O-OOOO...
...
...
WRATH
WRATH
WRATH
OKAY. I CAN DO THIS. I WILL TELL HIM OFF ONCE AND FOR ALL!!
WHO DOES HE THINK HE IS?!
SHORT STOP BY THE BATH-ROOM MIRROR
DOES MY HAIR LOOK OKAY?

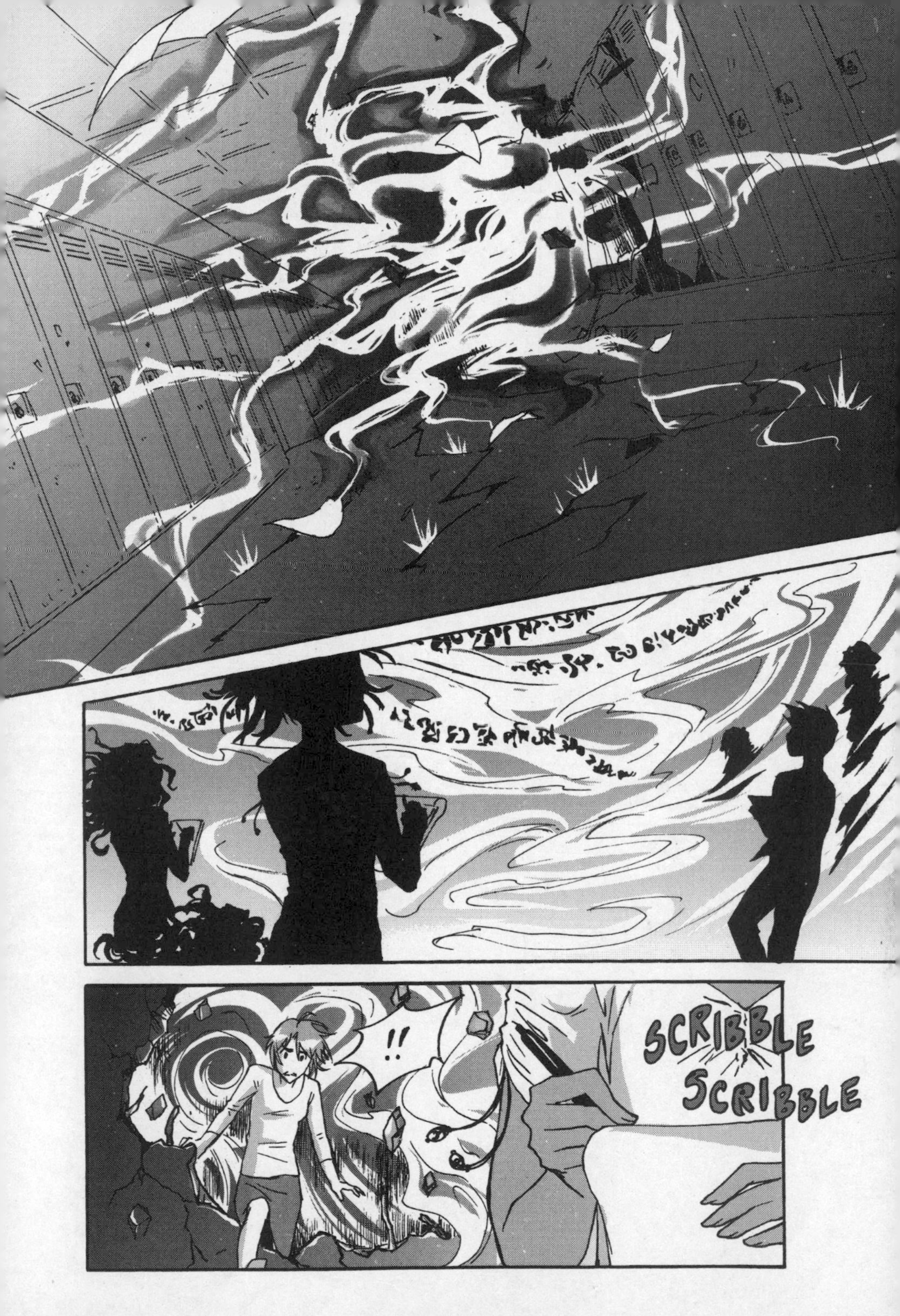
!!
SCRIBBLE
SCRIBBLE

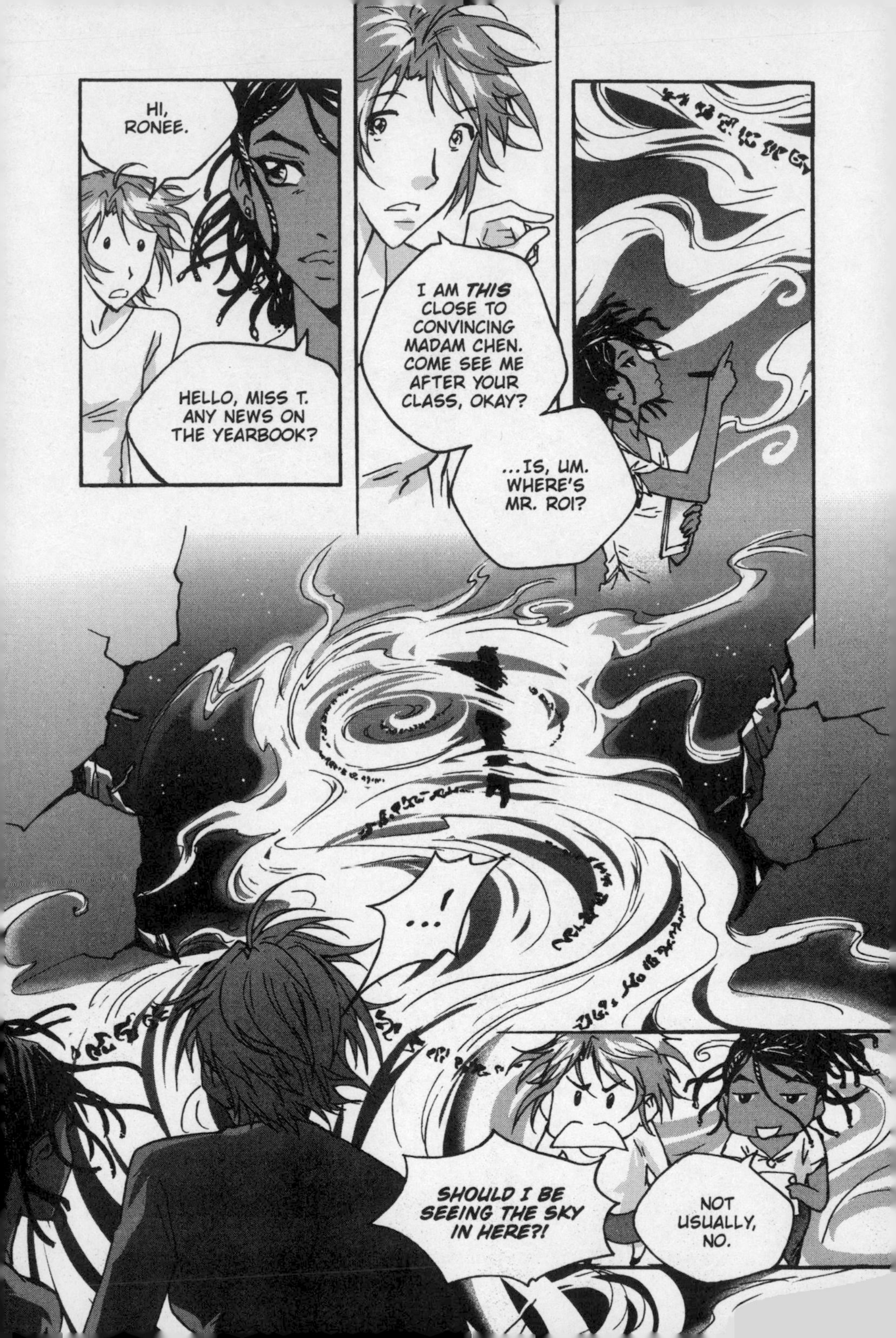
HI, RONEE.
HELLO, MISS T. ANY NEWS ON THE YEARBOOK?
I AM *THIS* CLOSE TO CONVINCING MADAM CHEN. COME SEE ME AFTER YOUR CLASS, OKAY?
...IS, UM. WHERE'S MR. ROI?
...!
SHOULD I BE SEEING THE SKY IN HERE?!
NOT USUALLY, NO.

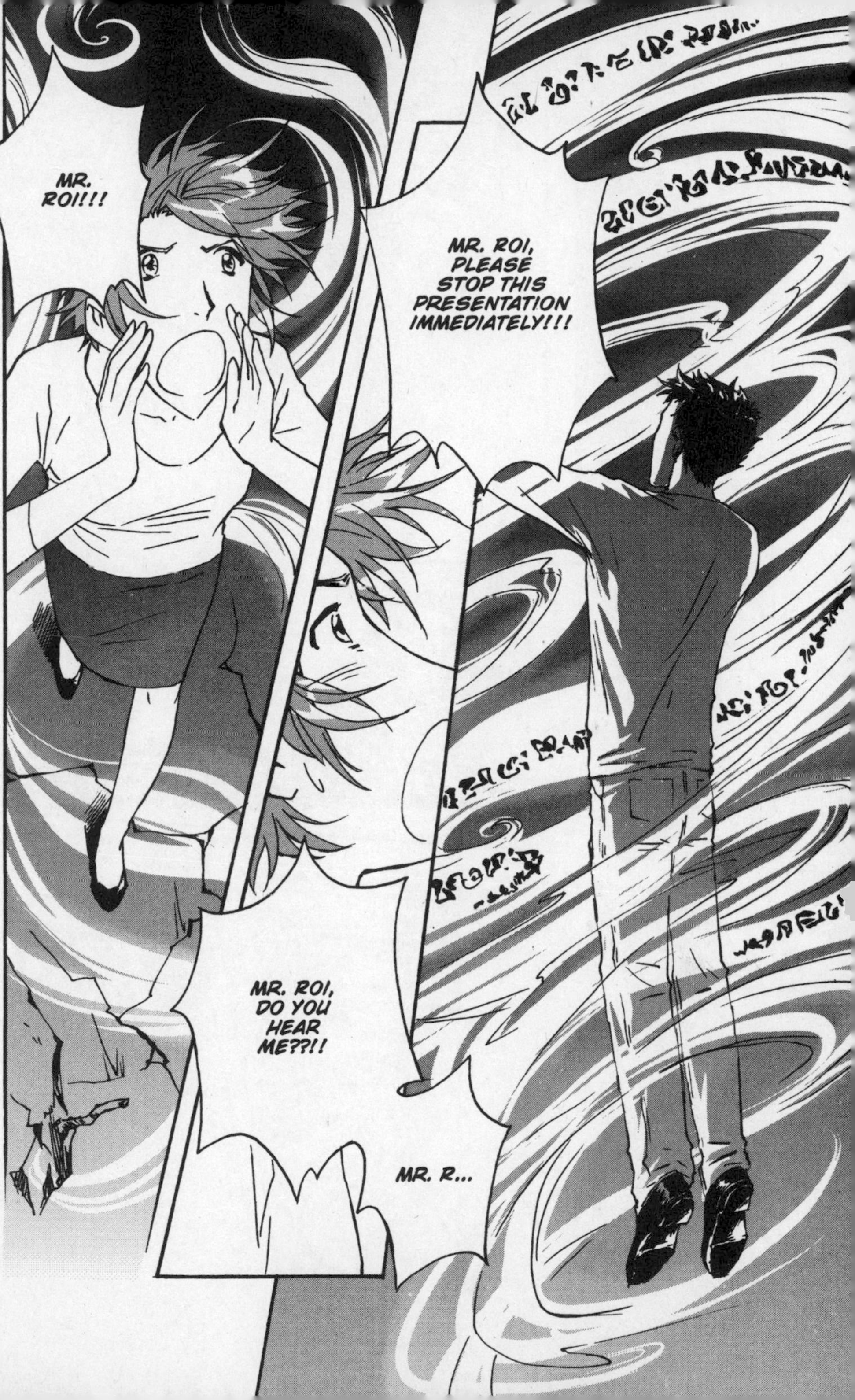
MR. ROI!!!
MR. ROI, PLEASE STOP THIS PRESENTATION IMMEDIATELY!!!
MR. ROI, DO YOU HEAR ME??!!
MR. R...

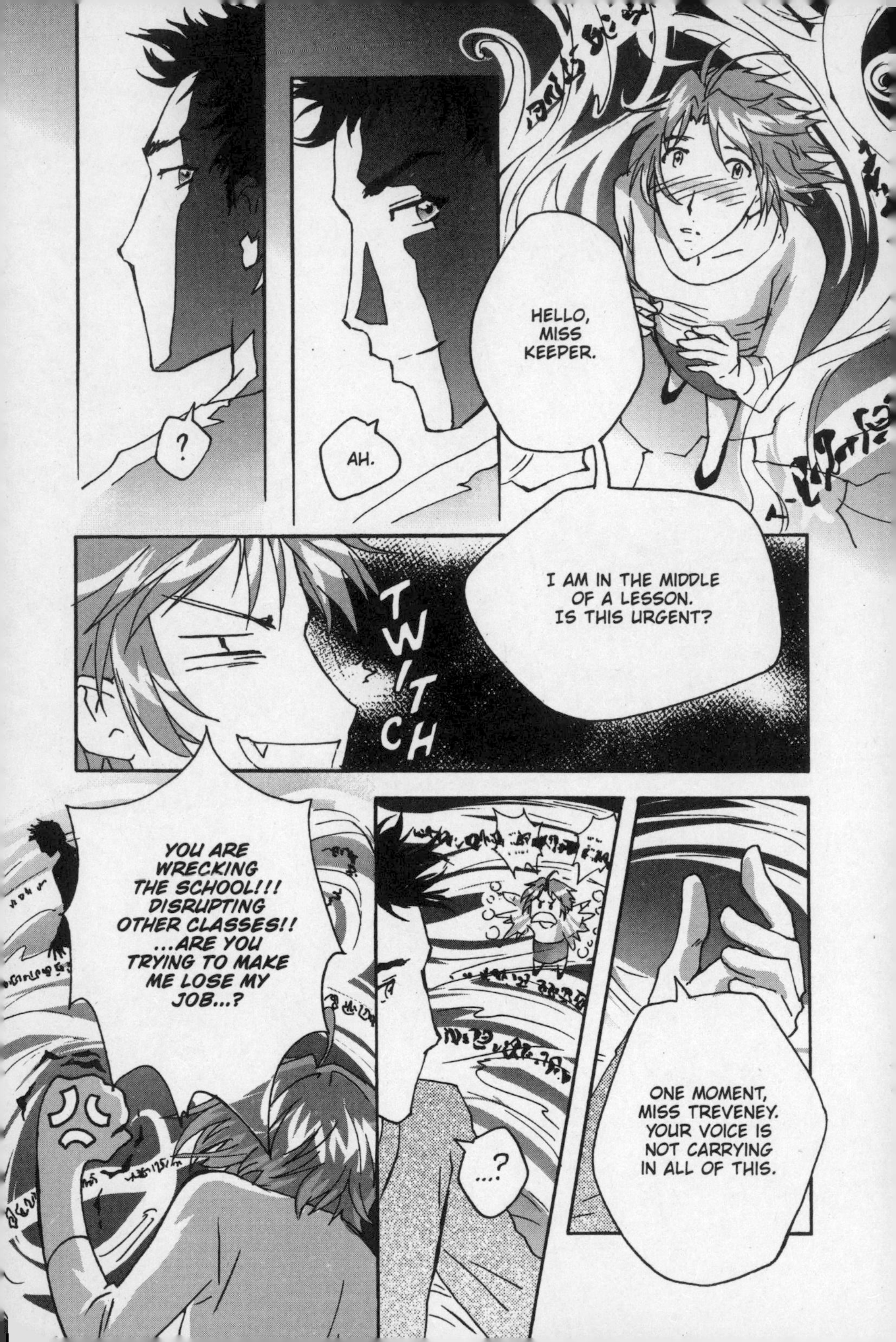
?
AH.
HELLO, MISS KEEPER.
I AM IN THE MIDDLE OF A LESSON. IS THIS URGENT?
TWITCH
YOU ARE WRECKING THE SCHOOL!!! DISRUPTING OTHER CLASSES!! ...ARE YOU TRYING TO MAKE ME LOSE MY JOB...?
....?
ONE MOMENT, MISS TREVENEY. YOUR VOICE IS NOT CARRYING IN ALL OF THIS.

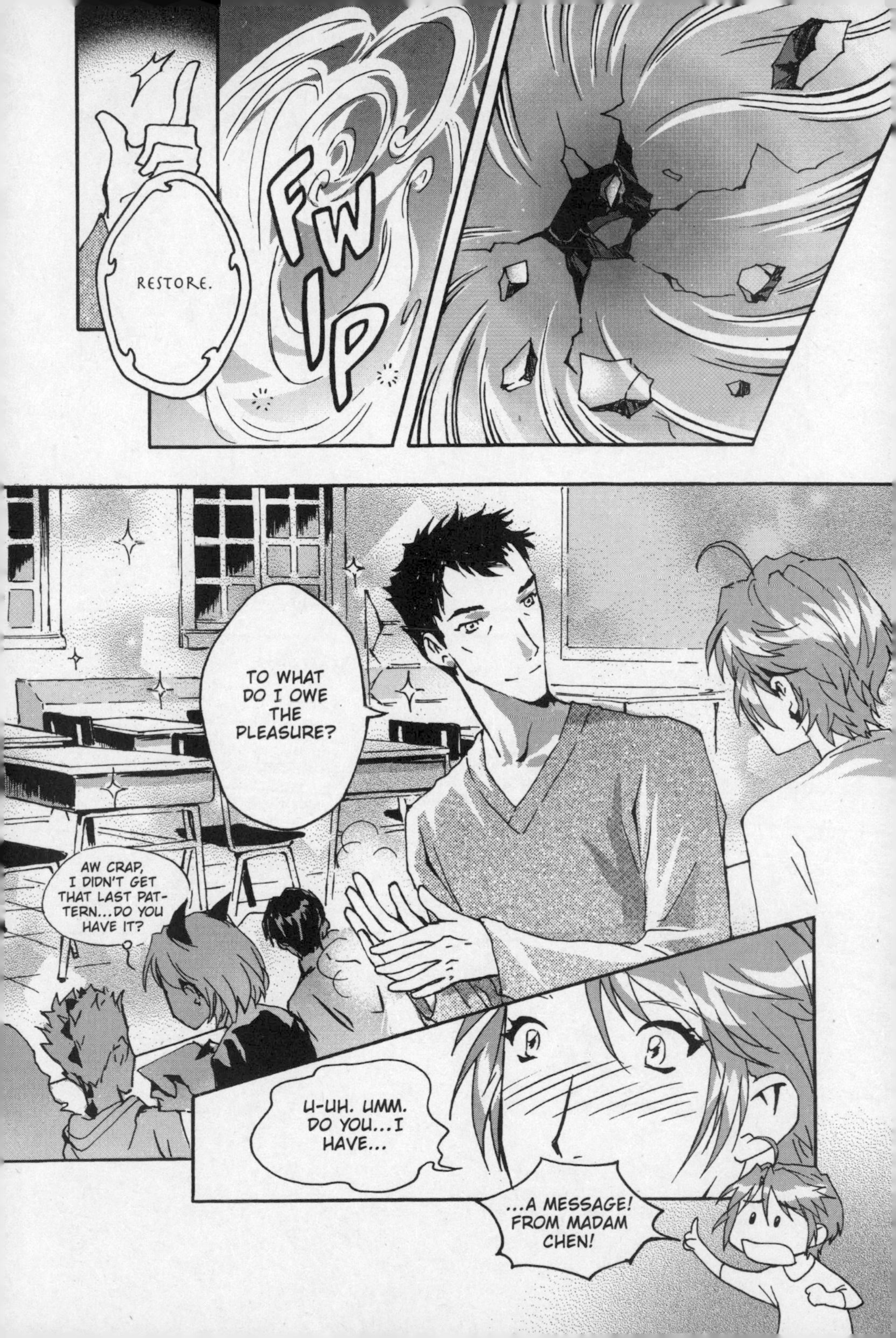
RESTORE.
FWIP
TO WHAT DO I OWE THE PLEASURE?
AW CRAP, I DIDN'T GET THAT LAST PATTERN...DO YOU HAVE IT?
U-UH. UMM. DO YOU...I HAVE...
...A MESSAGE! FROM MADAM CHEN!

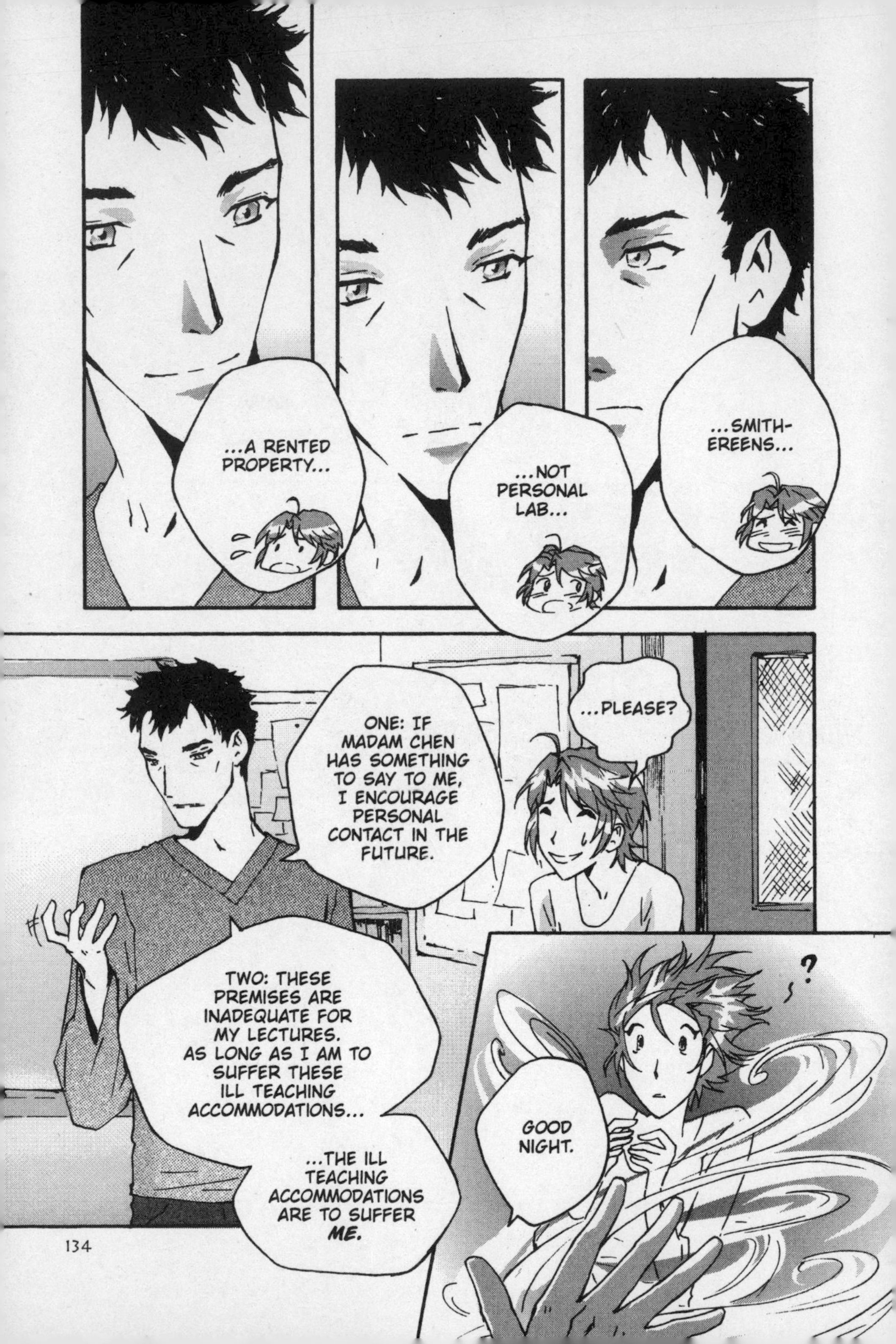
...A RENTED PROPERTY...
...NOT PERSONAL LAB...
...SMITH-EREENS...
ONE: IF MADAM CHEN HAS SOMETHING TO SAY TO ME, I ENCOURAGE PERSONAL CONTACT IN THE FUTURE.
...PLEASE?
TWO: THESE PREMISES ARE INADEQUATE FOR MY LECTURES. AS LONG AS I AM TO SUFFER THESE ILL TEACHING ACCOMMODATIONS...
...THE ILL TEACHING ACCOMMODATIONS ARE TO SUFFER *ME.*
?
GOOD NIGHT.

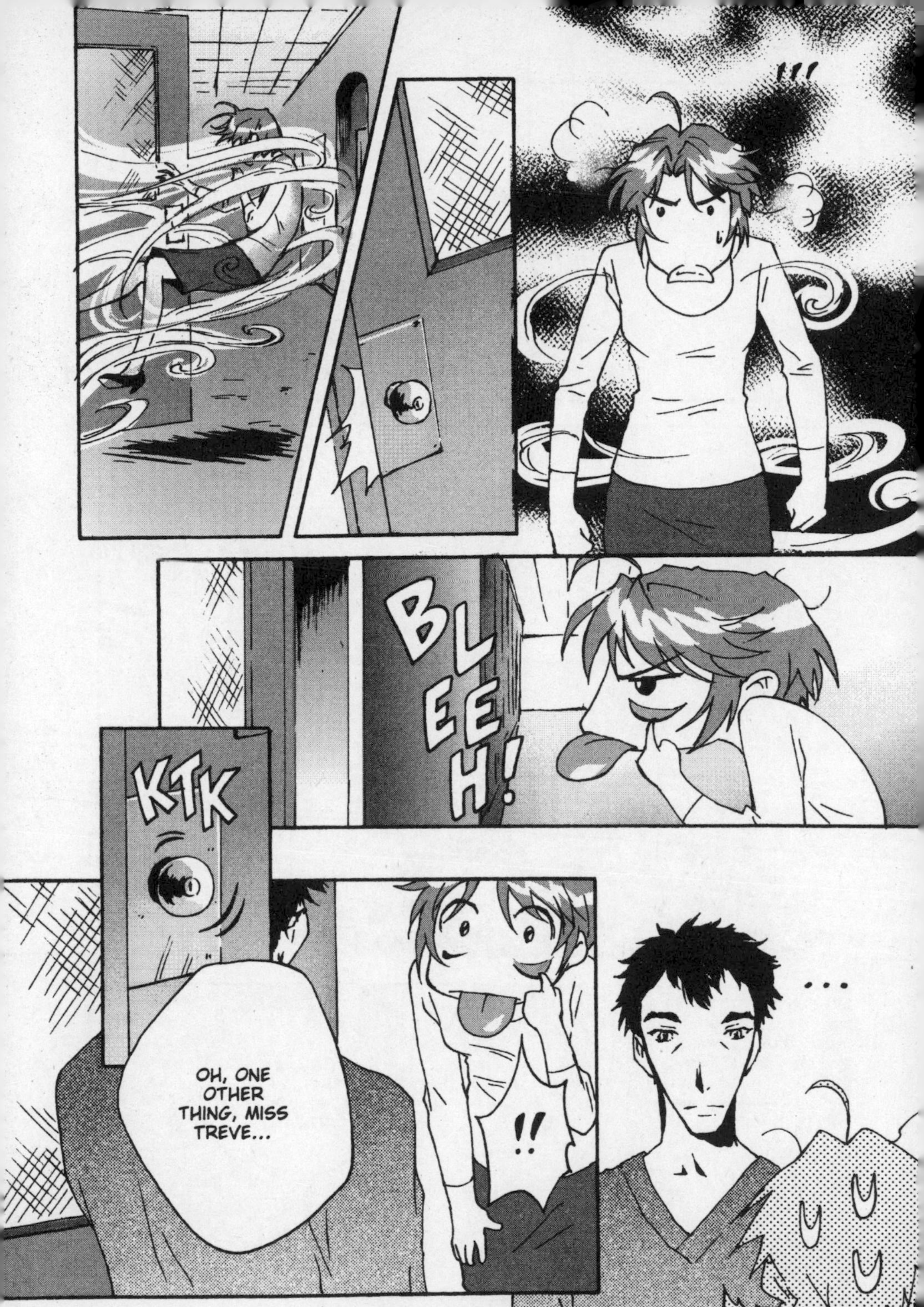
!!!
BLEEH!
KTK
OH, ONE OTHER THING, MISS TREVE...
!!
...

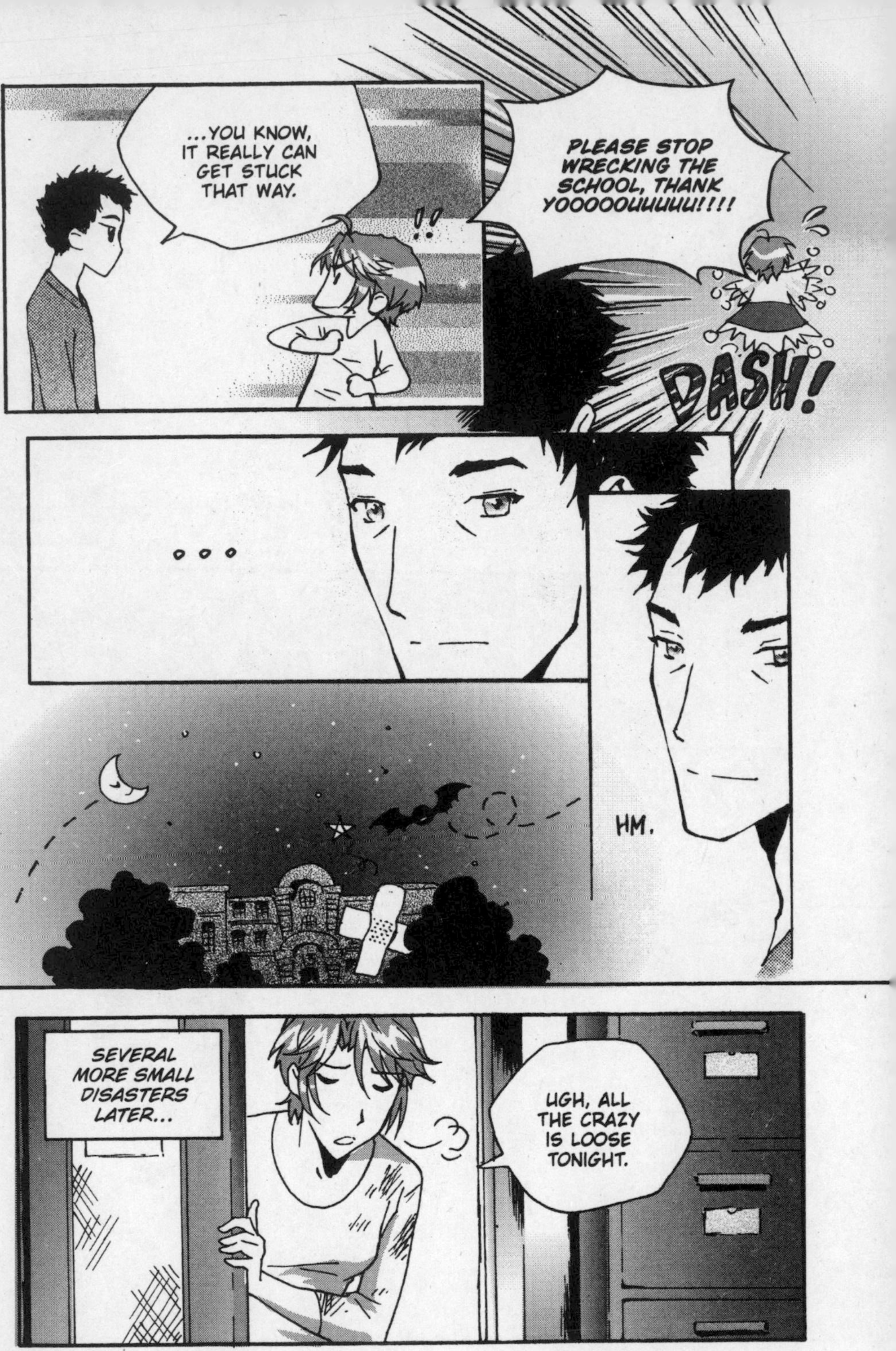
...YOU KNOW, IT REALLY CAN GET STUCK THAT WAY.
!!
PLEASE STOP WRECKING THE SCHOOL, THANK YOOOOOUUUUU!!!!
DASH!
...
HM.
SEVERAL MORE SMALL DISASTERS LATER...
UGH, ALL THE CRAZY IS LOOSE TONIGHT.

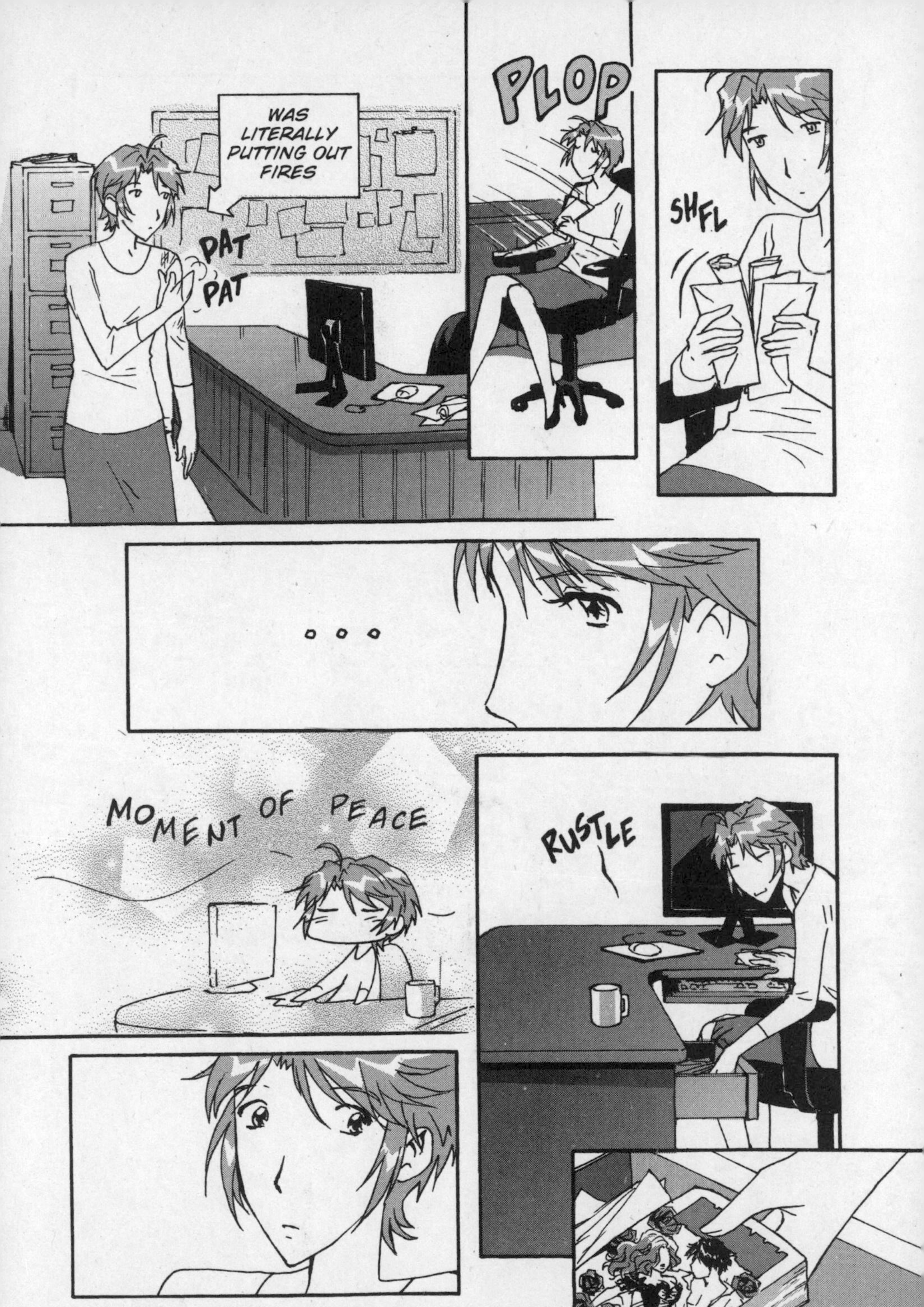

WAS LITERALLY PUTTING OUT FIRES
PAT PAT
PLOP
SHFL
...
MOMENT OF PEACE
RUSTLE

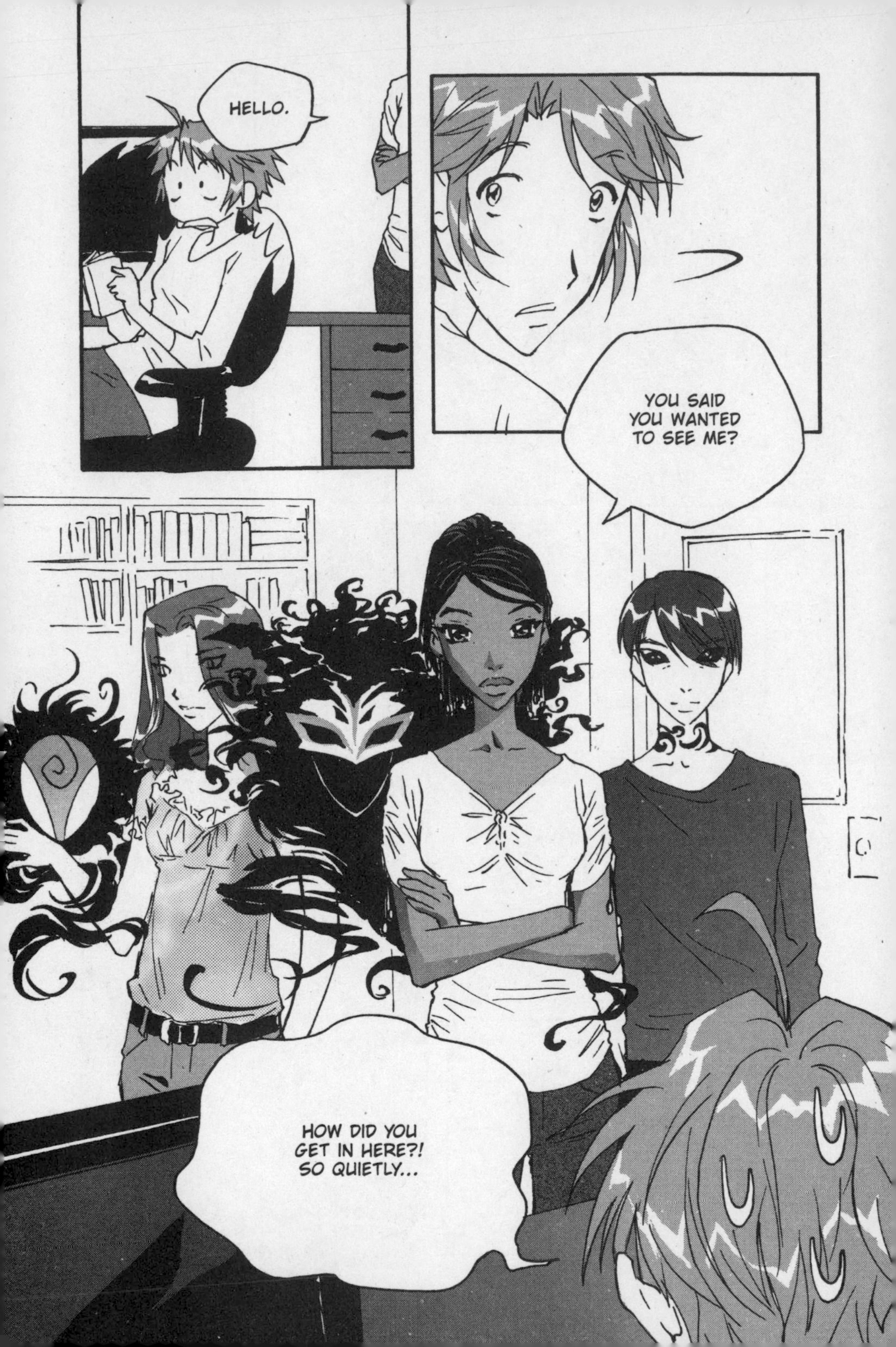
HELLO.
YOU SAID YOU WANTED TO SEE ME?
HOW DID YOU GET IN HERE?! SO QUIETLY...

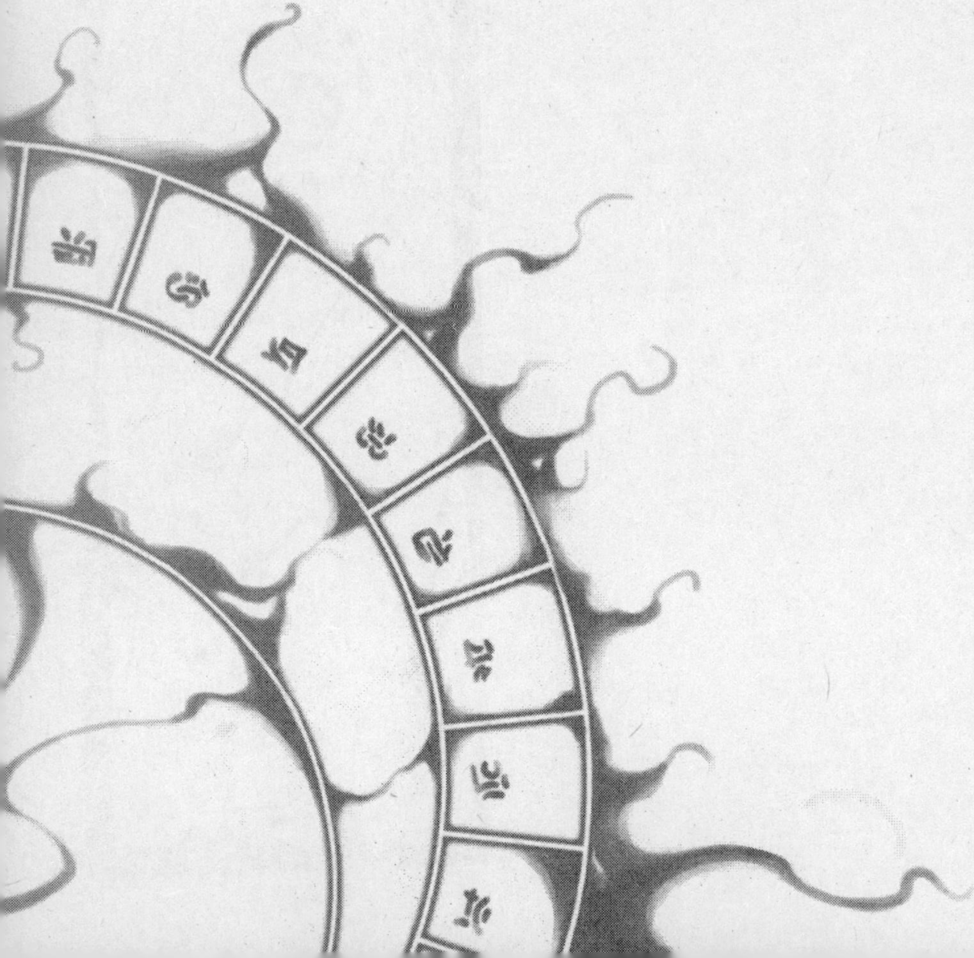

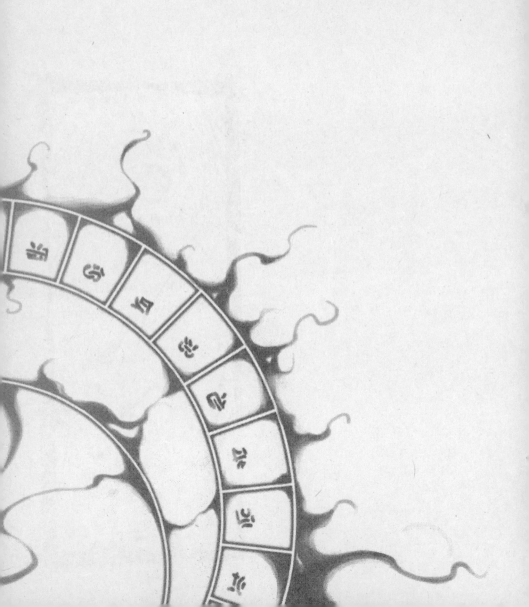

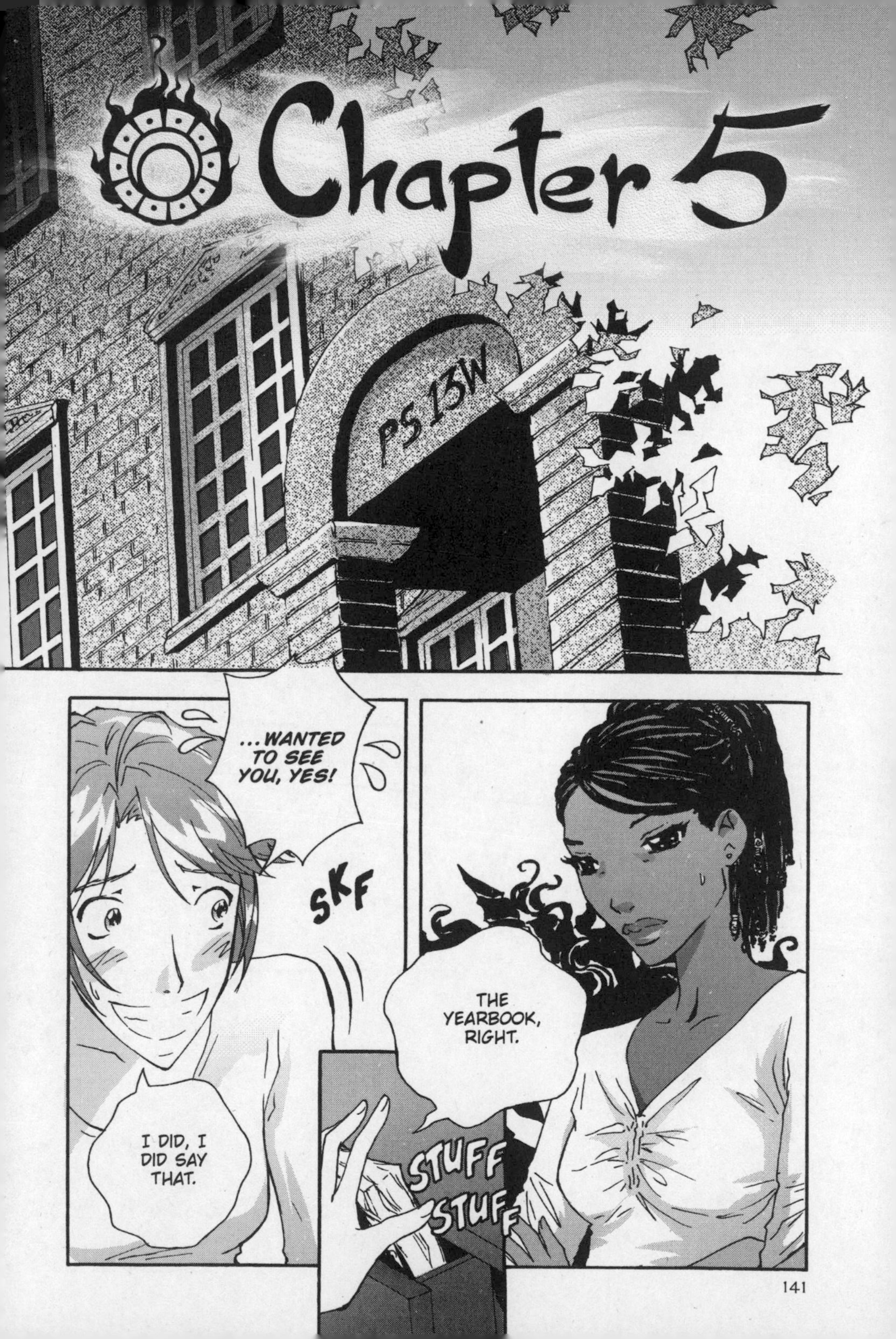
Chapter 5
PS 13W
...WANTED TO SEE YOU, YES!
SKF
I DID, I DID SAY THAT.
THE YEARBOOK, RIGHT.
STUFF STUFF

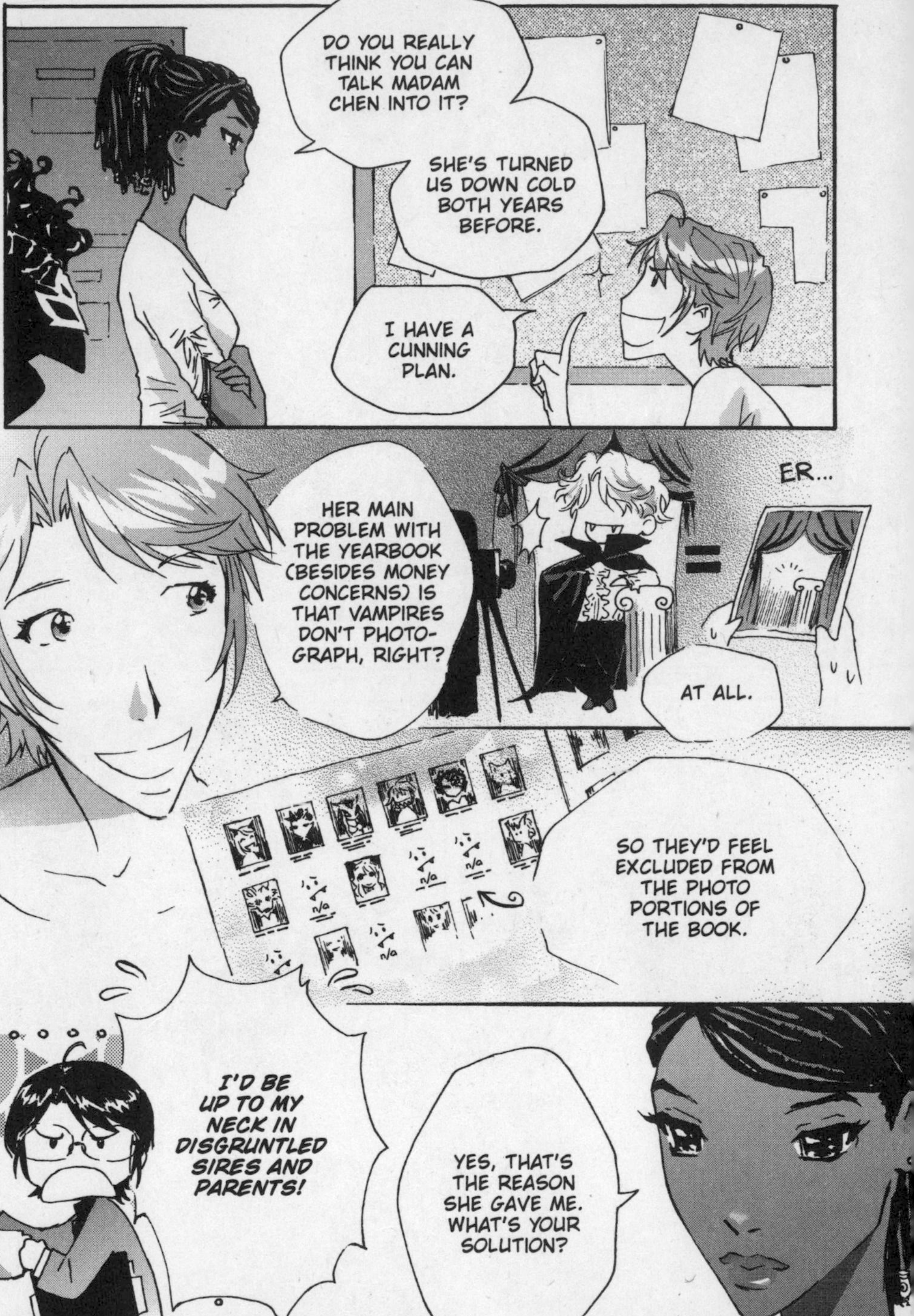
DO YOU REALLY THINK YOU CAN TALK MADAM CHEN INTO IT?
SHE'S TURNED US DOWN COLD BOTH YEARS BEFORE.
I HAVE A CUNNING PLAN.
HER MAIN PROBLEM WITH THE YEARBOOK (BESIDES MONEY CONCERNS) IS THAT VAMPIRES DON'T PHOTOGRAPH, RIGHT?
ER...
AT ALL.
SO THEY'D FEEL EXCLUDED FROM THE PHOTO PORTIONS OF THE BOOK.
I'D BE UP TO MY NECK IN DISGRUNTLED SIRES AND PARENTS!
YES, THAT'S THE REASON SHE GAVE ME. WHAT'S YOUR SOLUTION?

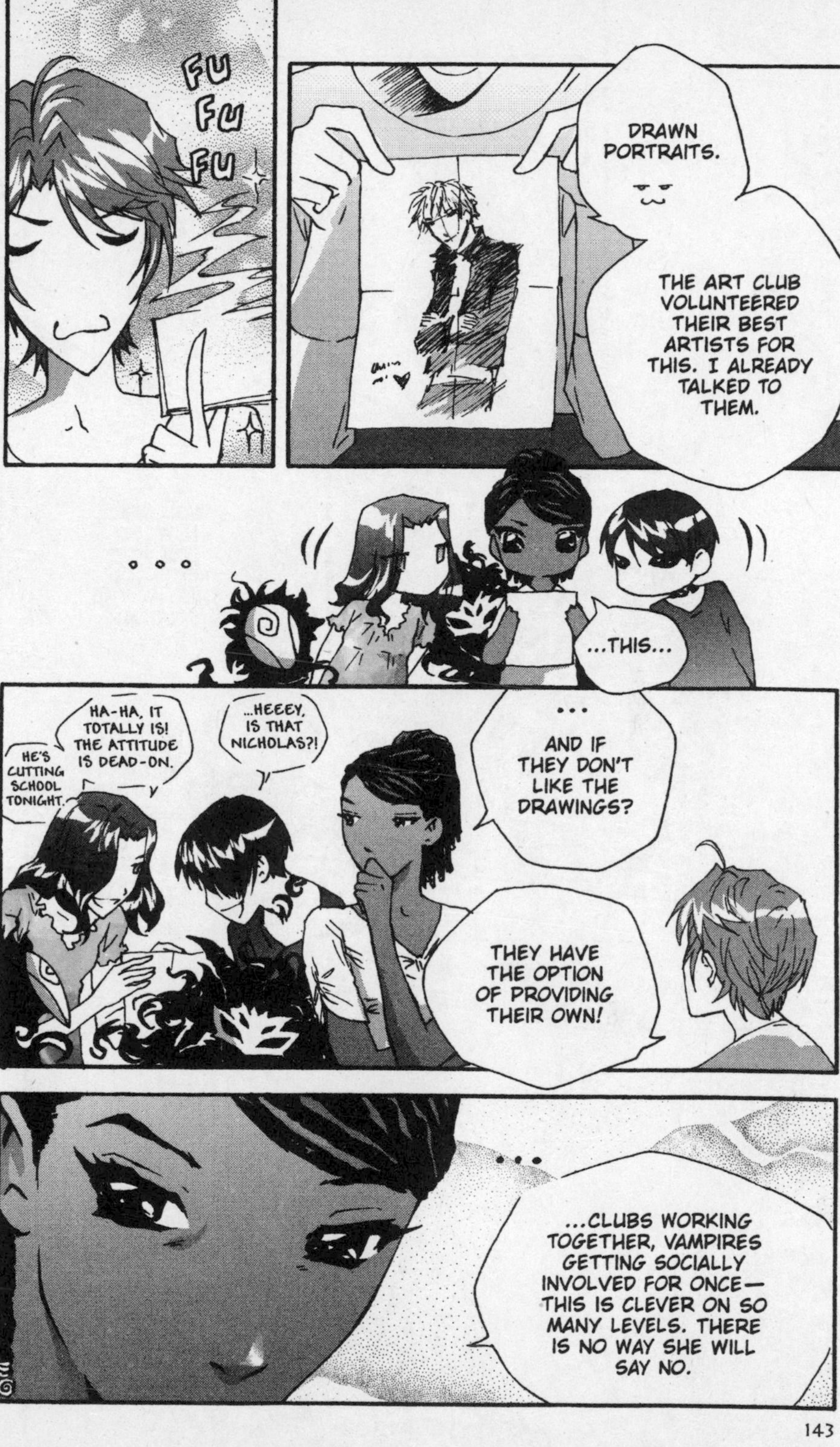
FU FU FU
DRAWN PORTRAITS.
THE ART CLUB VOLUNTEERED THEIR BEST ARTISTS FOR THIS. I ALREADY TALKED TO THEM.
...
...THIS...
HE'S CUTTING SCHOOL TONIGHT.
HA-HA, IT TOTALLY IS! THE ATTITUDE IS DEAD-ON.
...HEEEY, IS THAT NICHOLAS?!
... AND IF THEY DON'T LIKE THE DRAWINGS?
THEY HAVE THE OPTION OF PROVIDING THEIR OWN!
...
...CLUBS WORKING TOGETHER, VAMPIRES GETTING SOCIALLY INVOLVED FOR ONCE—THIS IS CLEVER ON SO MANY LEVELS. THERE IS NO WAY SHE WILL SAY NO.

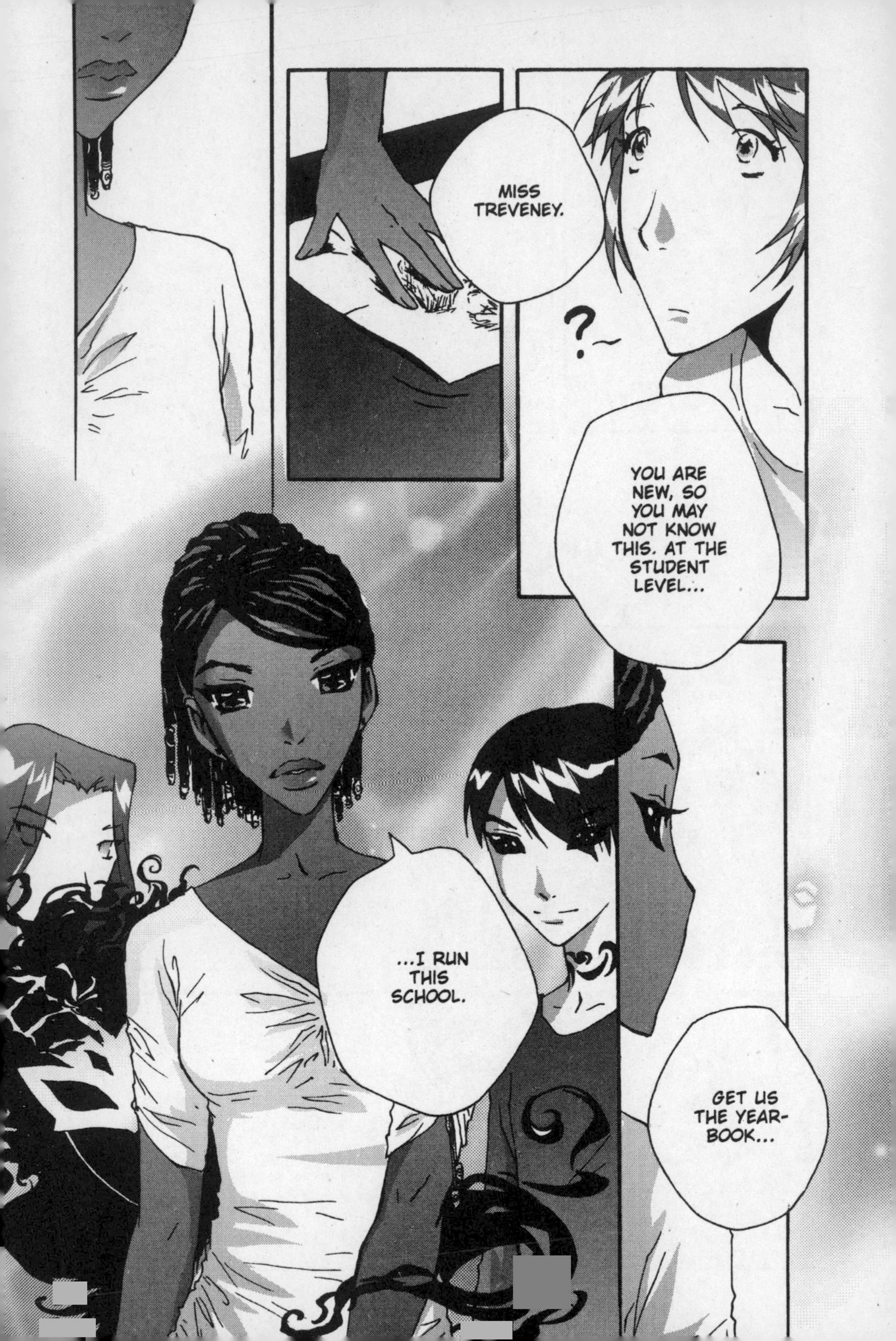
MISS TREVENEY.
?~
YOU ARE NEW, SO YOU MAY NOT KNOW THIS. AT THE STUDENT LEVEL...
...I RUN THIS SCHOOL.
GET US THE YEAR-BOOK...

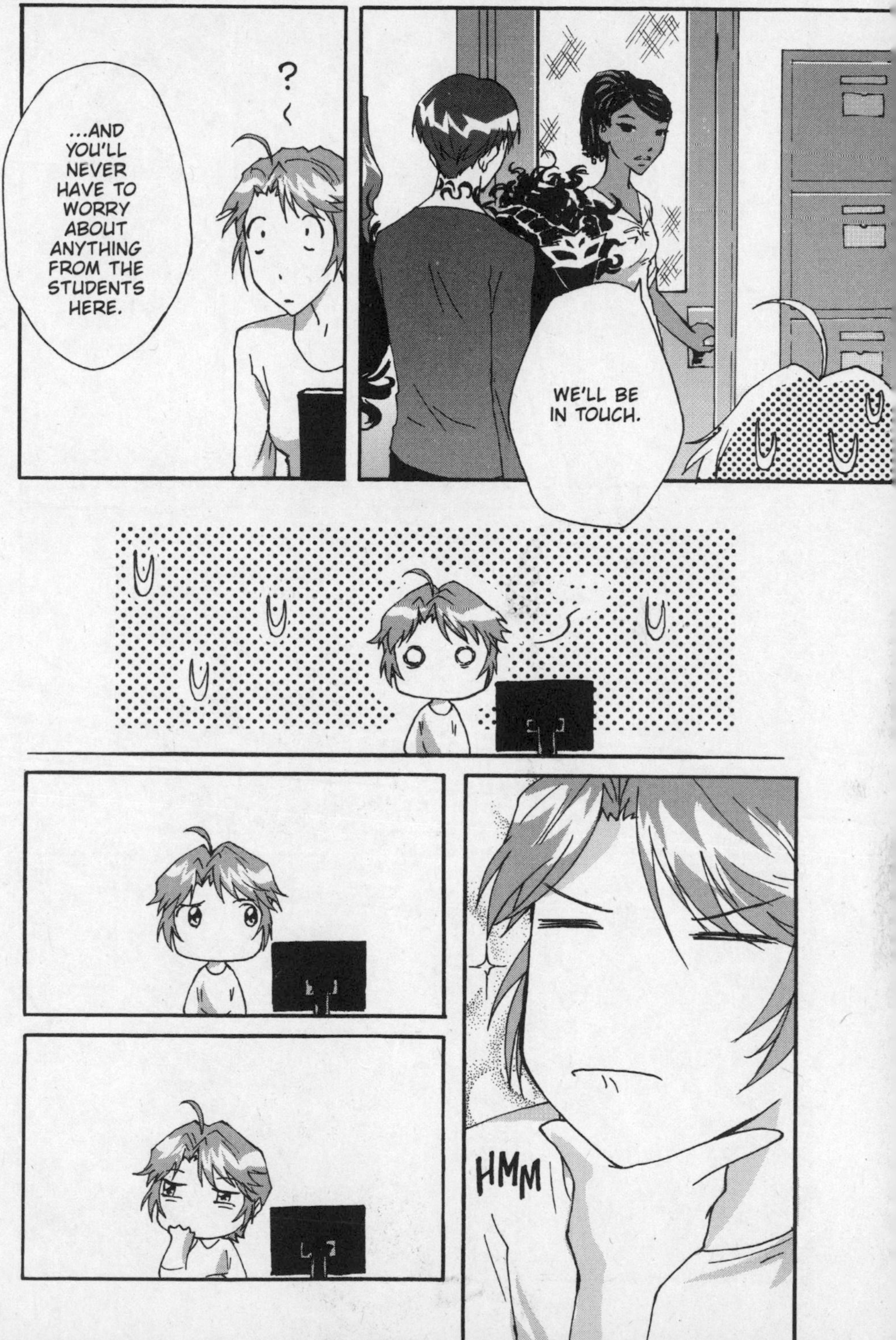

...AND YOU'LL NEVER HAVE TO WORRY ABOUT ANYTHING FROM THE STUDENTS HERE.
?
WE'LL BE IN TOUCH.
HMM

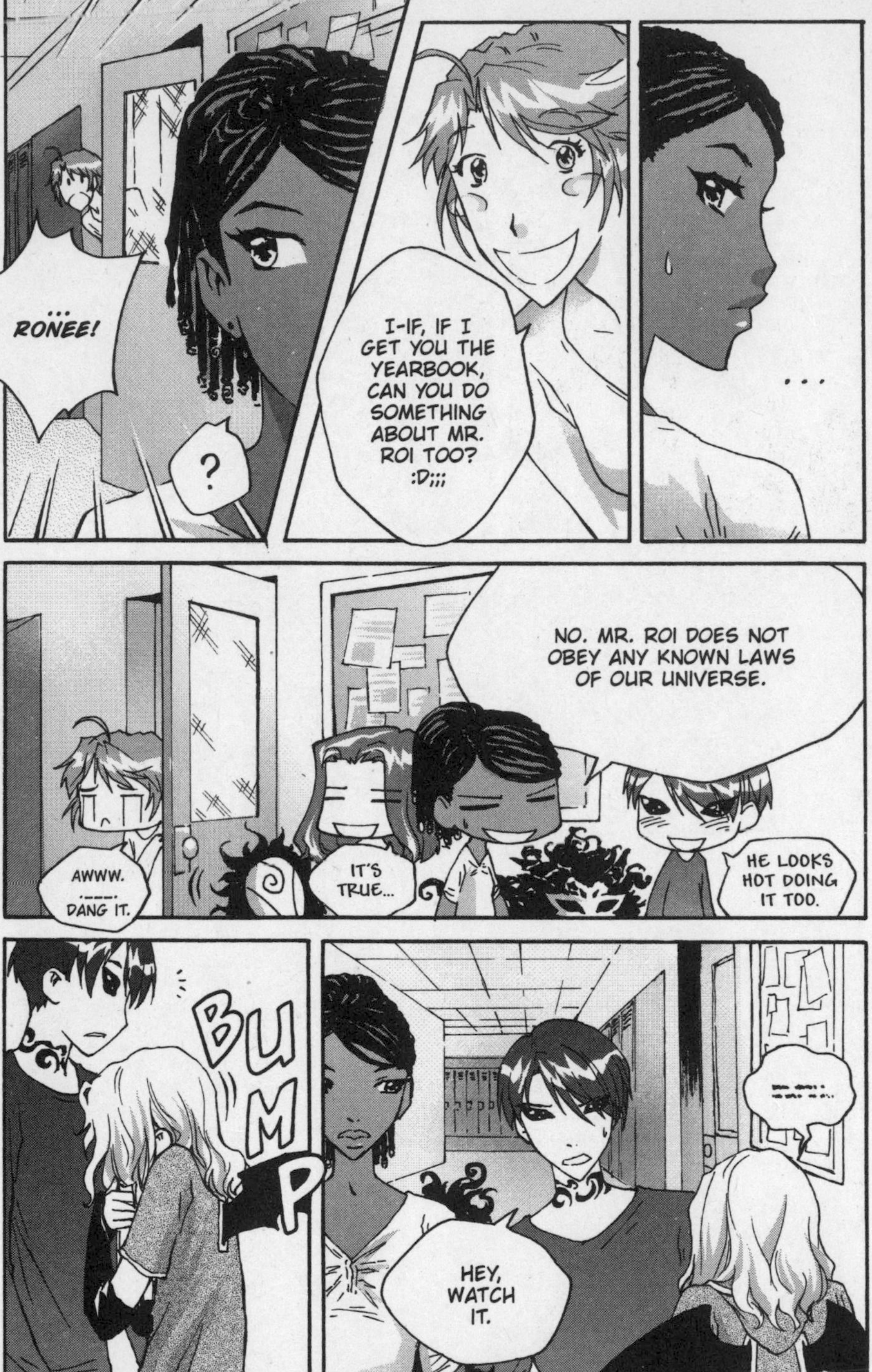

...
RONEE!
?
I-IF, IF I GET YOU THE YEARBOOK, CAN YOU DO SOMETHING ABOUT MR. ROI TOO? :D;;;
. . .
NO. MR. ROI DOES NOT OBEY ANY KNOWN LAWS OF OUR UNIVERSE.
AWWW. ._____. DANG IT.
IT'S TRUE...
HE LOOKS HOT DOING IT TOO.
BUMP
HEY, WATCH IT.

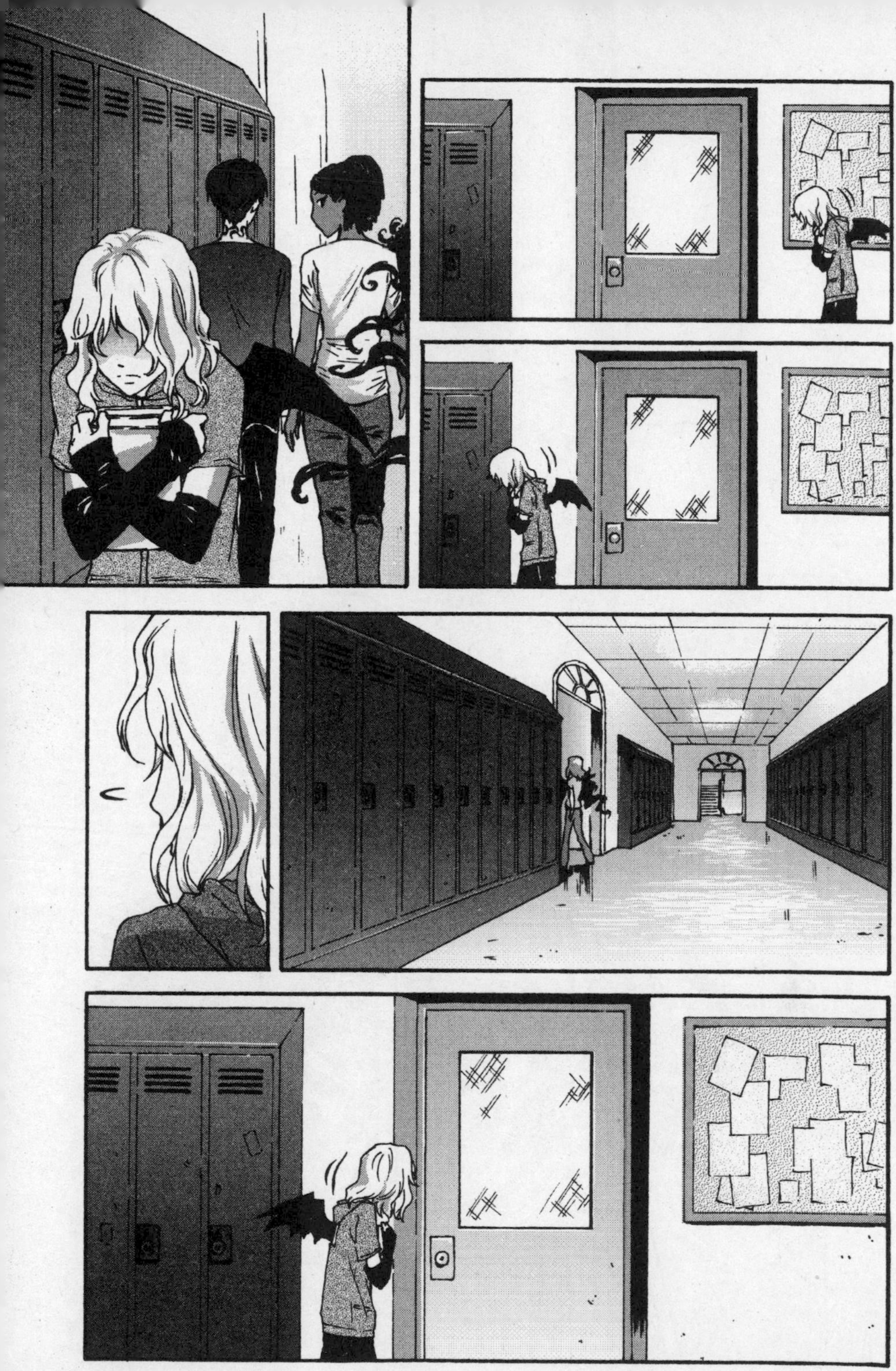

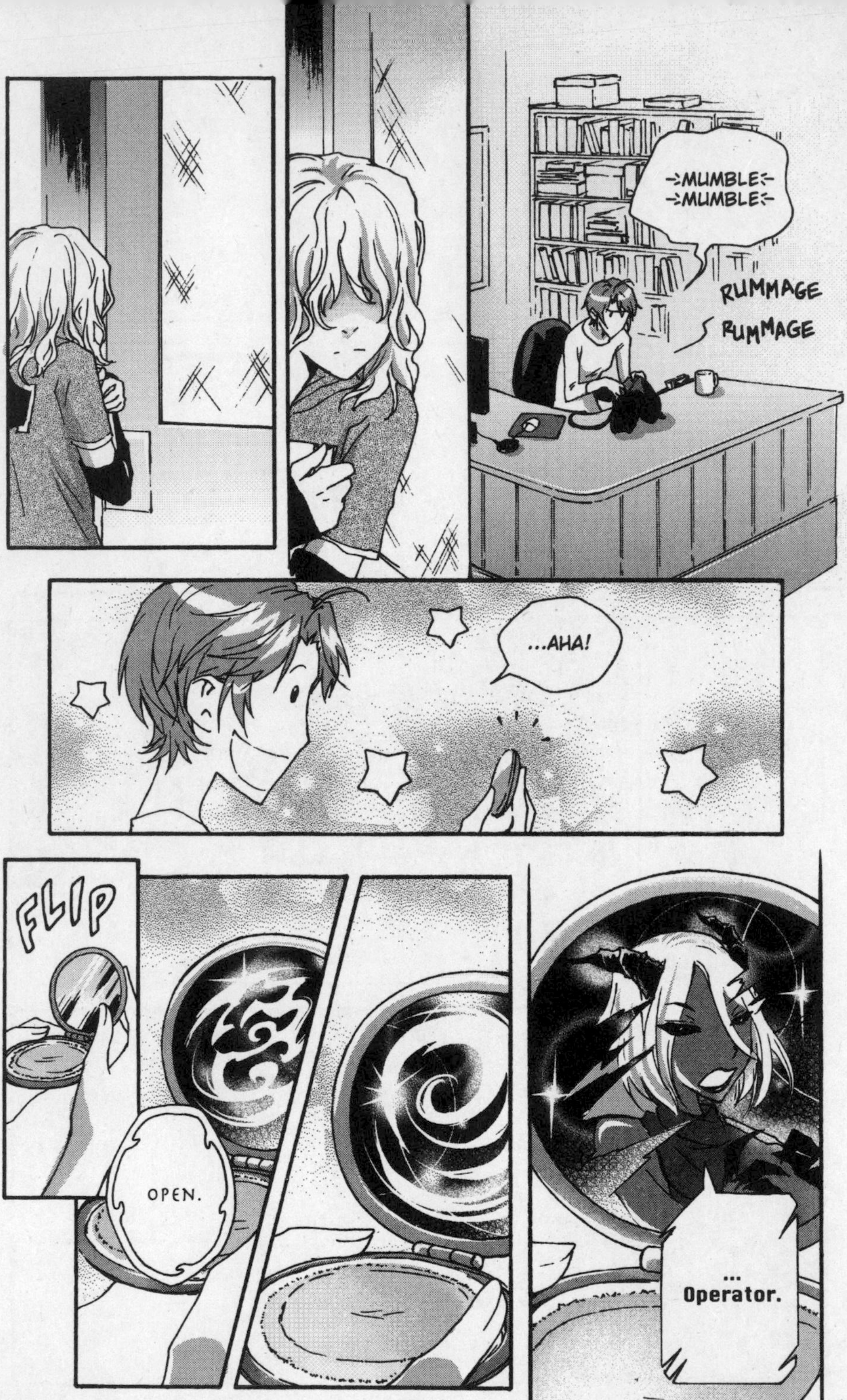
MUMBLE
MUMBLE
RUMMAGE
RUMMAGE
...AHA!
FLIP
OPEN.
...
Operator.

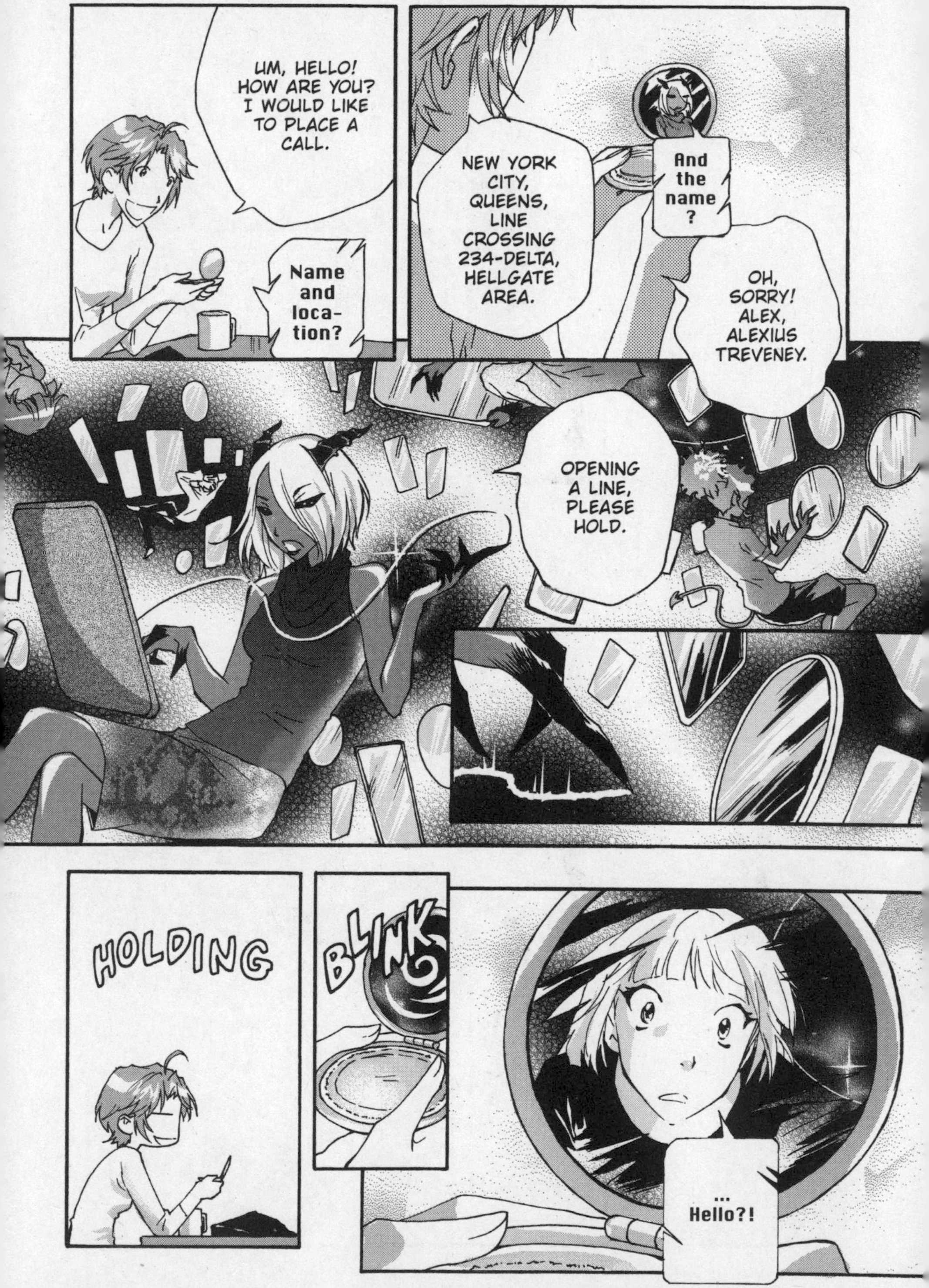
UM, HELLO! HOW ARE YOU? I WOULD LIKE TO PLACE A CALL.
Name and loca-tion?
NEW YORK CITY, QUEENS, LINE CROSSING 234-DELTA, HELLGATE AREA.
And the name?
OH, SORRY! ALEX, ALEXIUS TREVENEY.
OPENING A LINE, PLEASE HOLD.
HOLDING
BLINK
... Hello?!

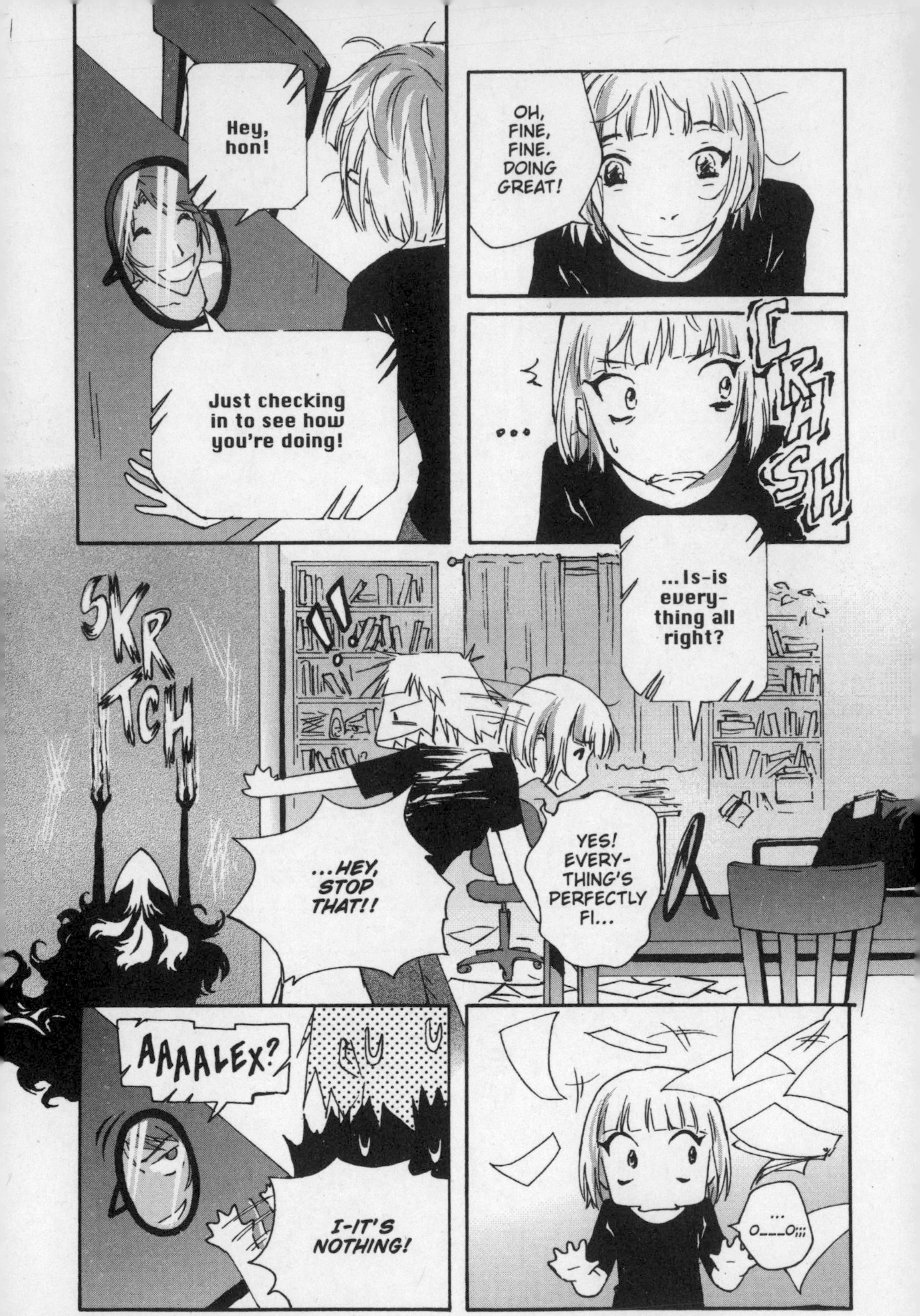
Hey, hon!
Just checking in to see how you're doing!
OH, FINE, FINE. DOING GREAT!
...
CRASH
...Is-is every-thing all right?
SKRTCH
...HEY, STOP THAT!!
YES! EVERY-THING'S PERFECTLY FI...
AAAALEX?
I-IT'S NOTHING!
... O___O;;;

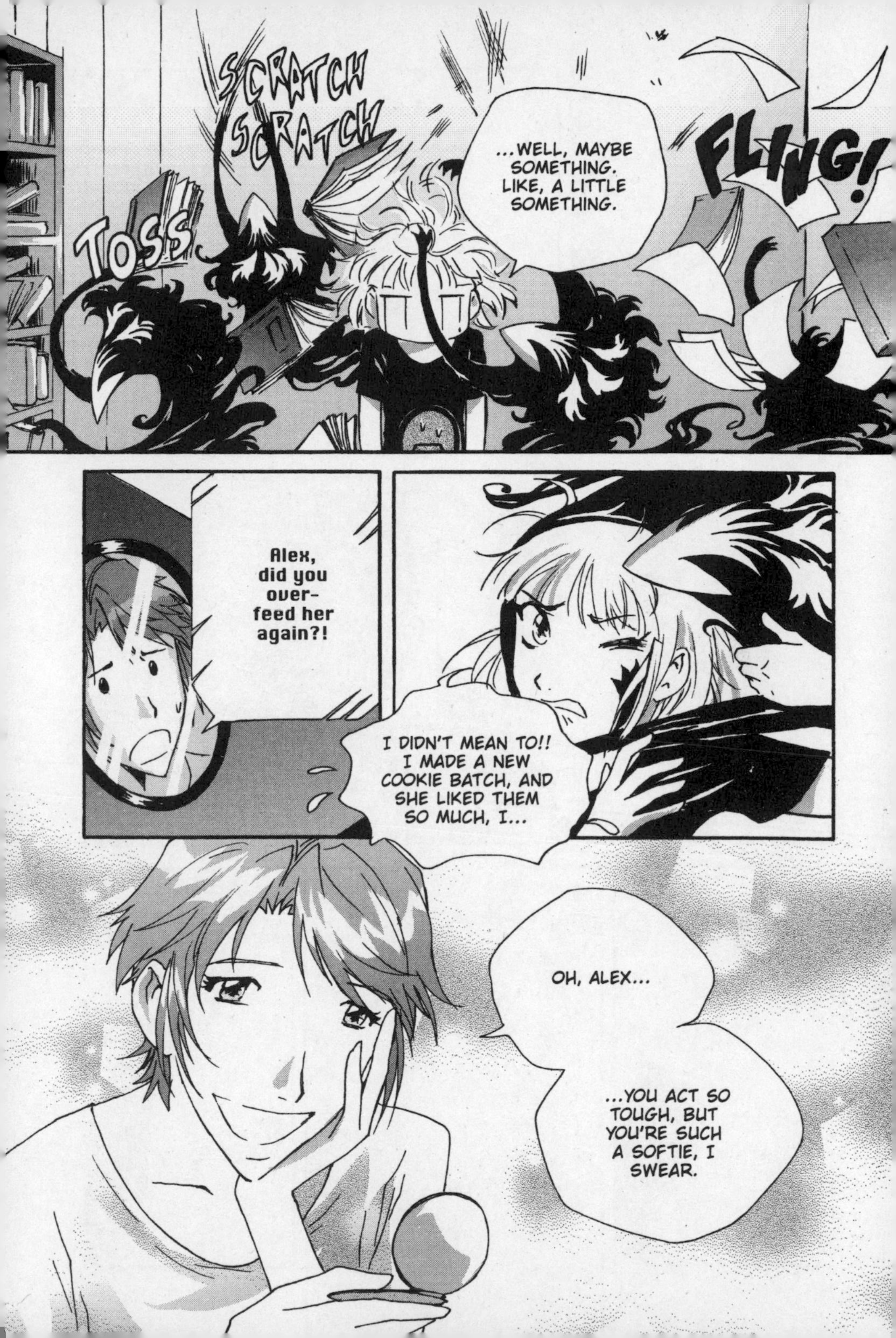
SCRATCH SCRATCH
TOSS
...WELL, MAYBE SOMETHING. LIKE, A LITTLE SOMETHING.
FLING!
Alex, did you over-feed her again?!
I DIDN'T MEAN TO!! I MADE A NEW COOKIE BATCH, AND SHE LIKED THEM SO MUCH, I...
OH, ALEX...
...YOU ACT SO TOUGH, BUT YOU'RE SUCH A SOFTIE, I SWEAR.

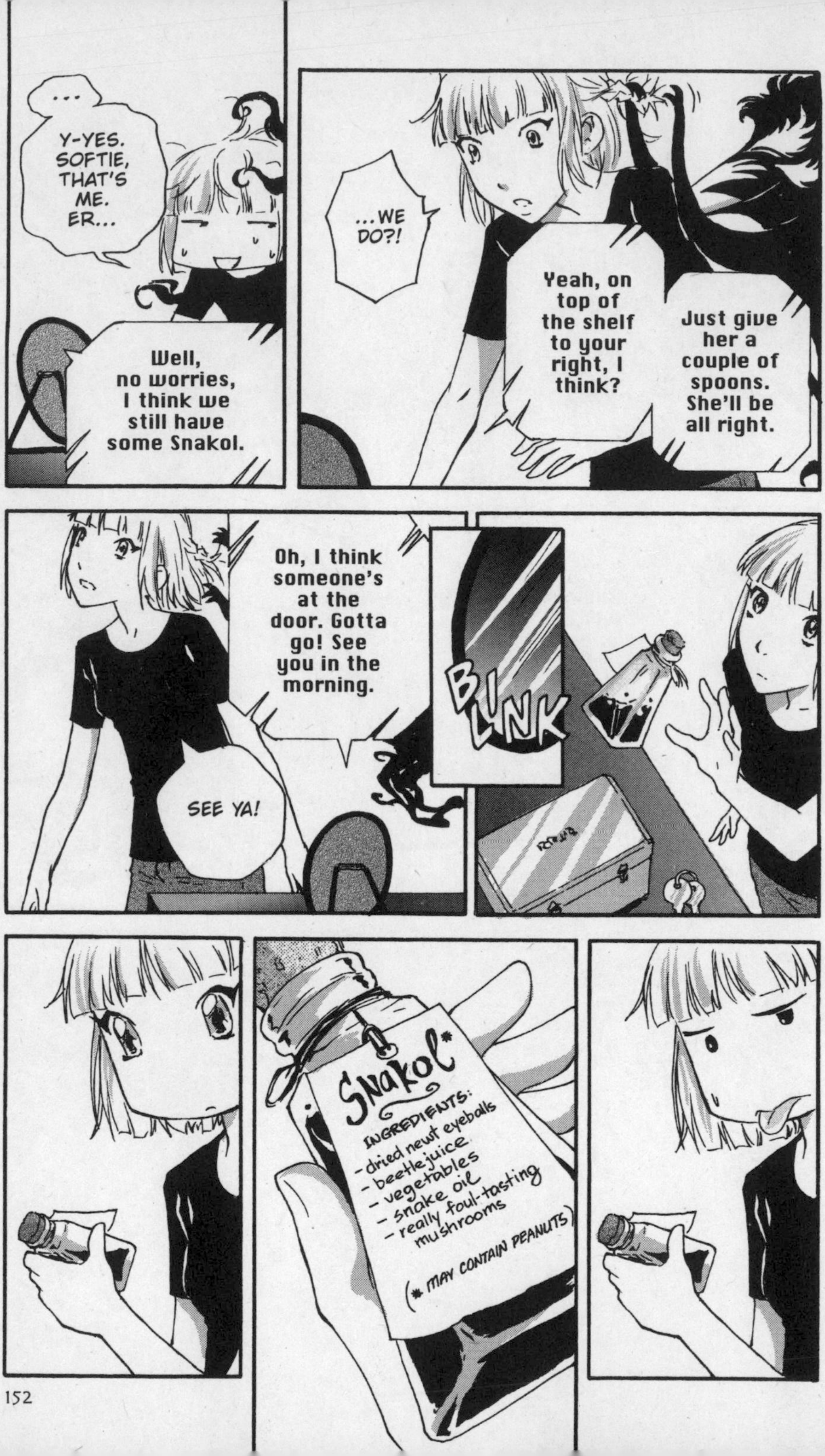
...
Y-YES. SOFTIE, THAT'S ME. ER...
Well, no worries, I think we still have some Snakol.
...WE DO?!
Yeah, on top of the shelf to your right, I think?
Just give her a couple of spoons. She'll be all right.
Oh, I think someone's at the door. Gotta go! See you in the morning.
SEE YA!
BLINK
Snakol*
INGREDIENTS:
- dried newt eyeballs
- beetlejuice
- vegetables
- snake oil
- really foul-tasting mushrooms
(* MAY CONTAIN PEANUTS)

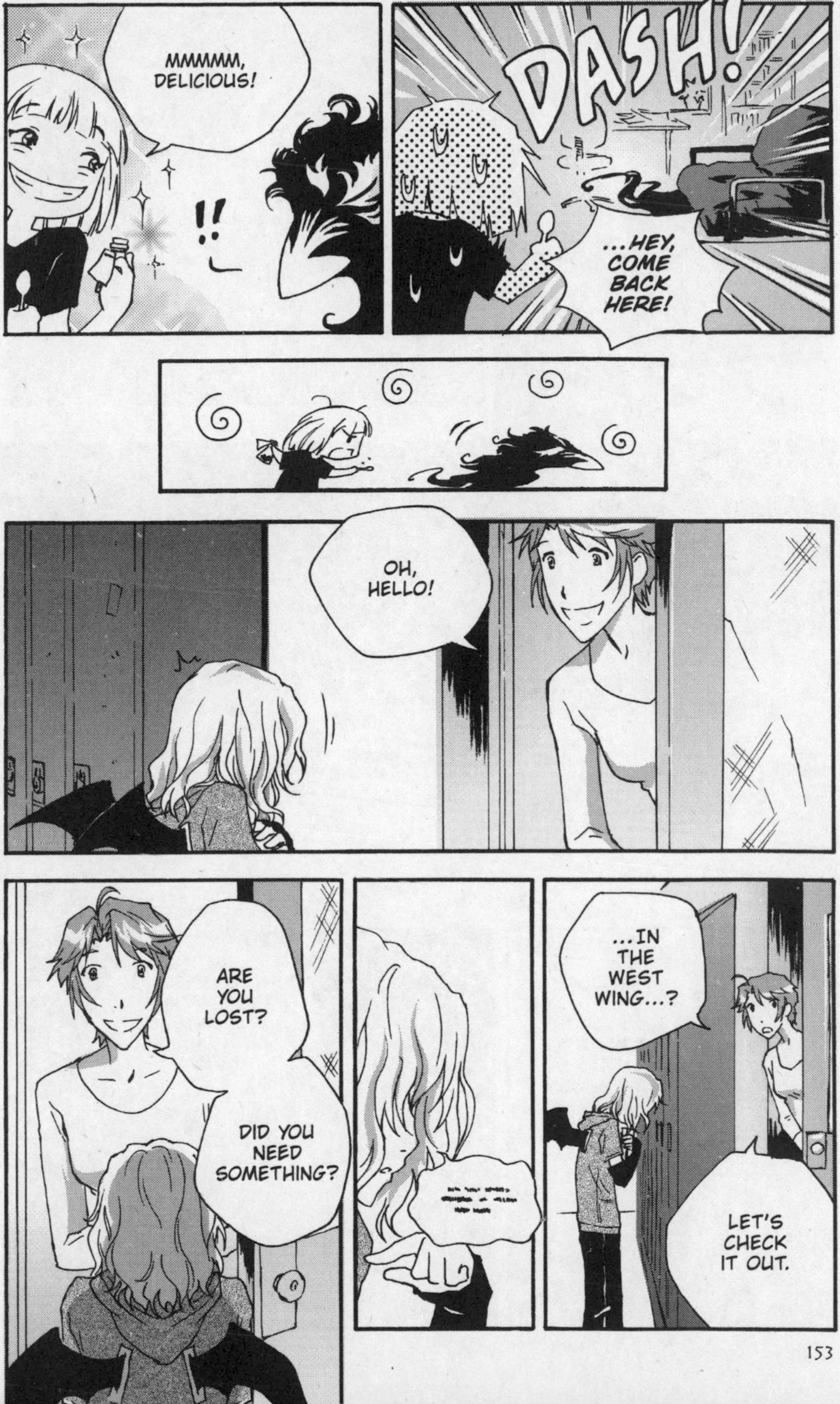
MMMMM, DELICIOUS!
!!
DASH!
...HEY, COME BACK HERE!
OH, HELLO!
ARE YOU LOST?
DID YOU NEED SOMETHING?
...IN THE WEST WING...?
LET'S CHECK IT OUT.

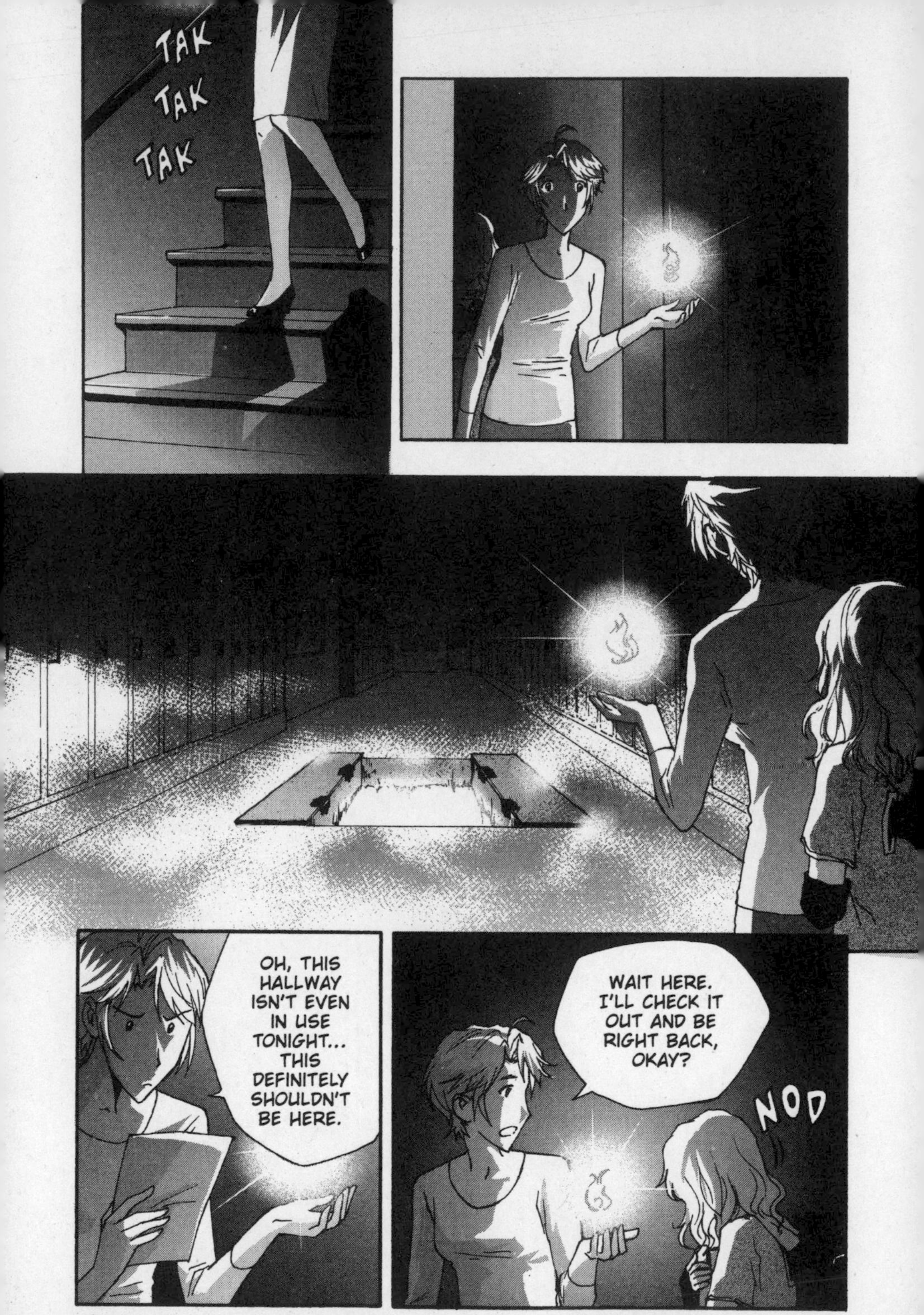

TAK
TAK
TAK
OH, THIS HALLWAY ISN'T EVEN IN USE TONIGHT... THIS DEFINITELY SHOULDN'T BE HERE.
WAIT HERE. I'LL CHECK IT OUT AND BE RIGHT BACK, OKAY?
NOD

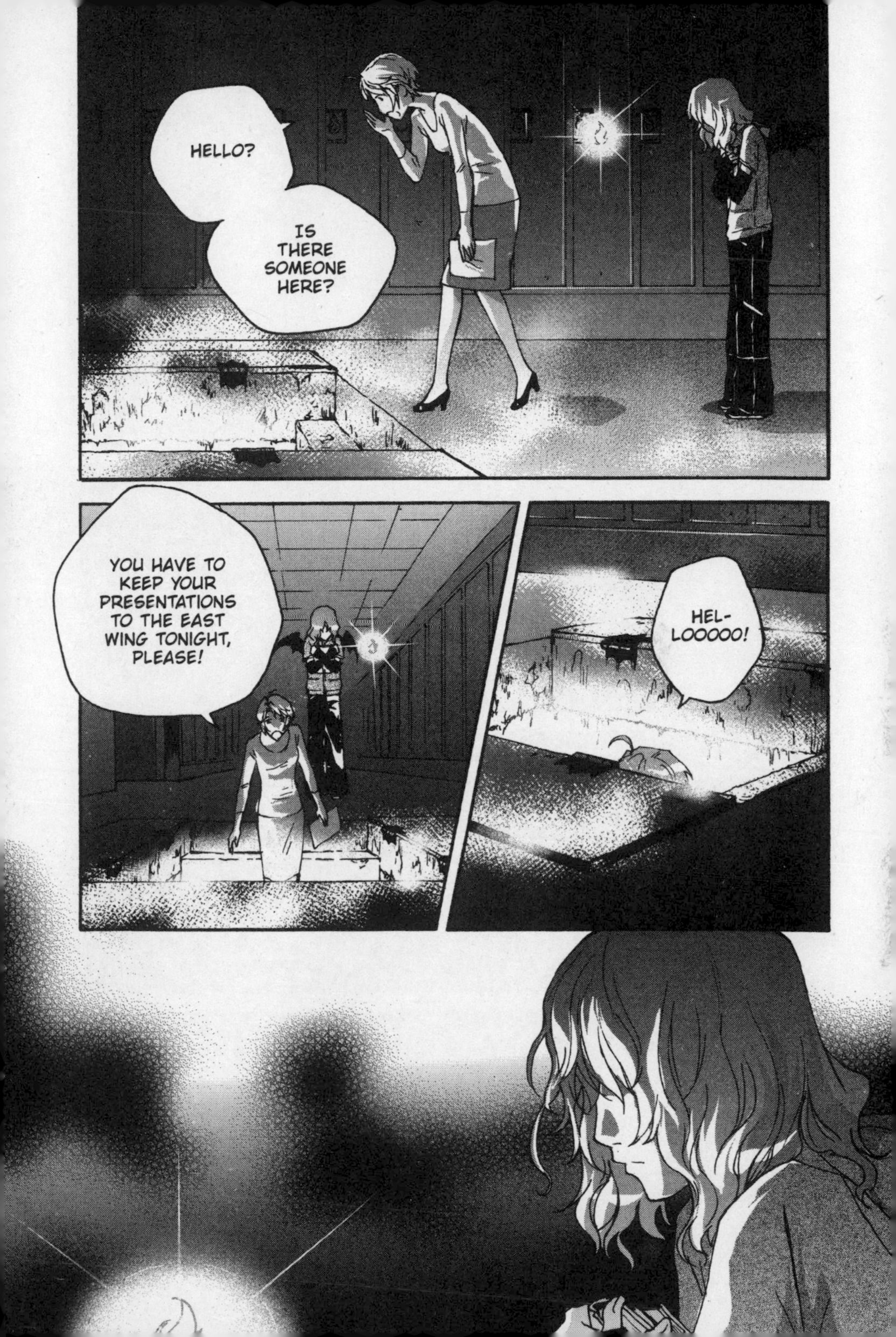
HELLO?
IS THERE SOMEONE HERE?
YOU HAVE TO KEEP YOUR PRESENTATIONS TO THE EAST WING TONIGHT, PLEASE!
HEL-LOOOOO!

CREAK
KTK

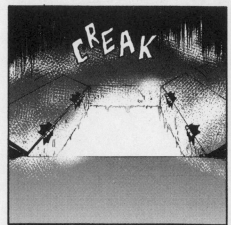

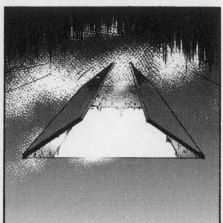

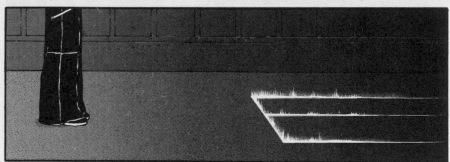

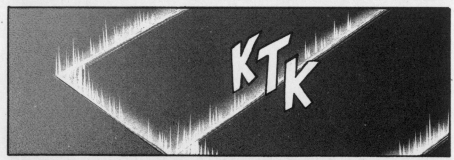

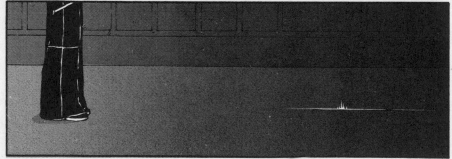

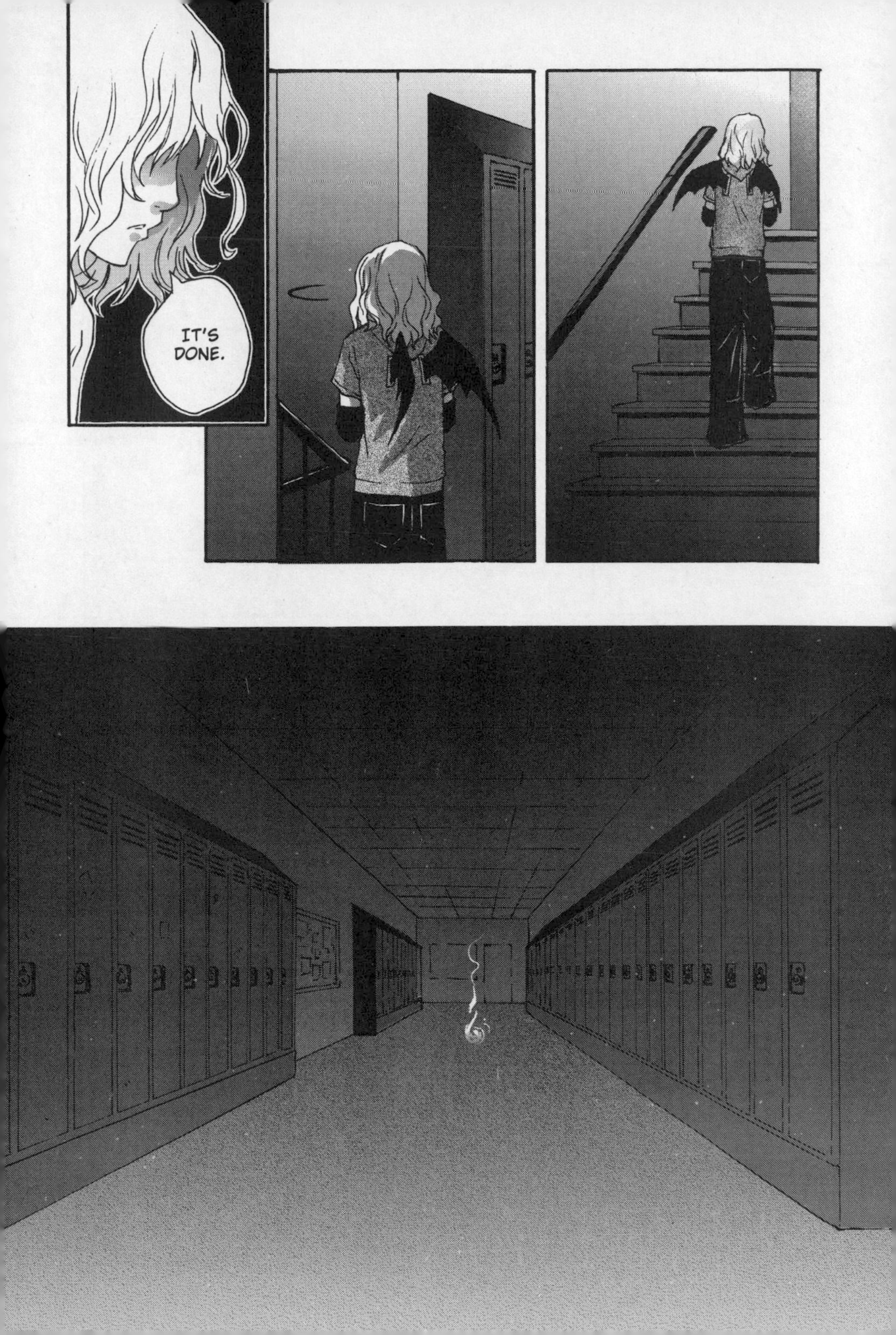
IT'S DONE.

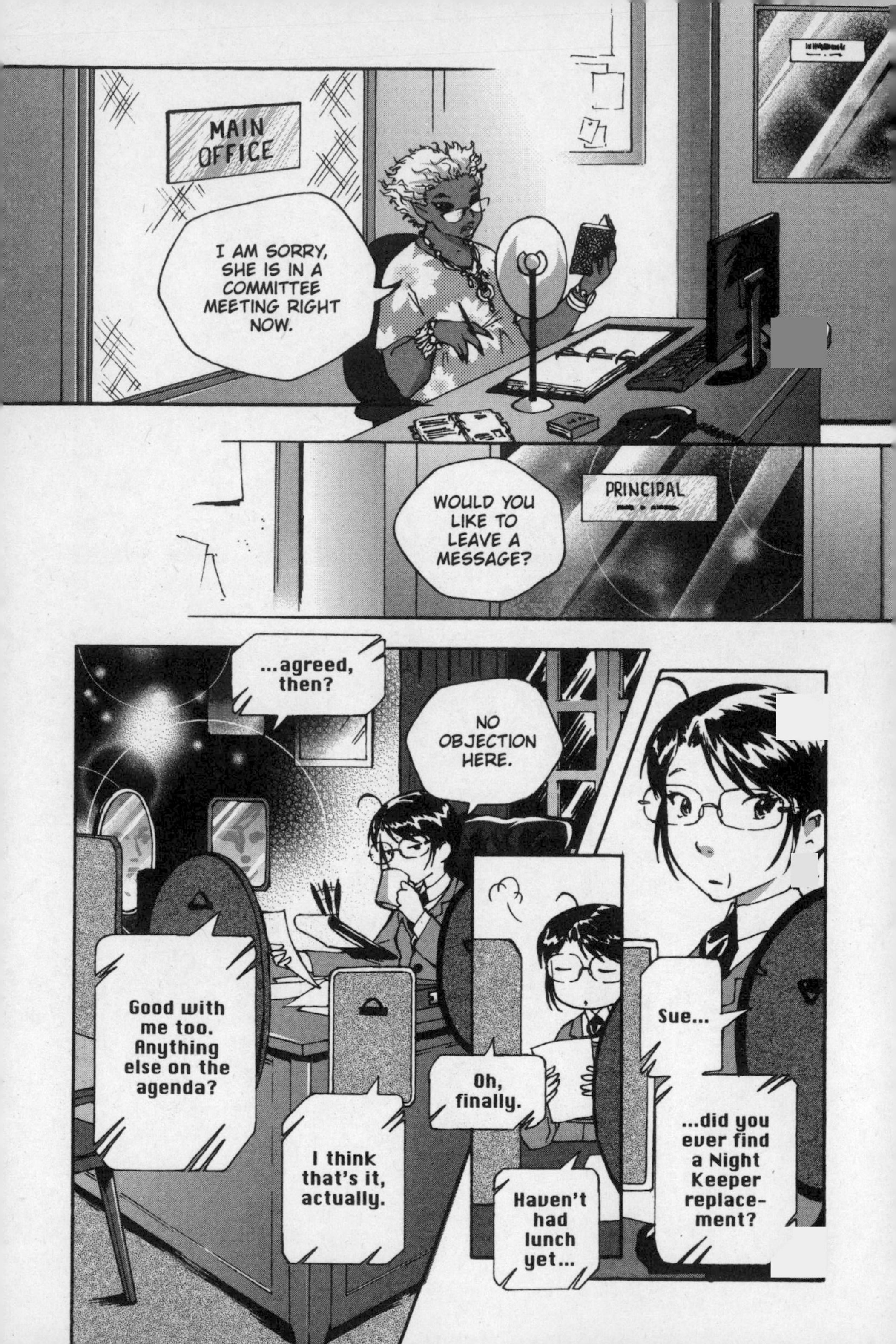
MAIN OFFICE
I AM SORRY, SHE IS IN A COMMITTEE MEETING RIGHT NOW.
PRINCIPAL
WOULD YOU LIKE TO LEAVE A MESSAGE?
...agreed, then?
NO OBJECTION HERE.
Good with me too. Anything else on the agenda?
I think that's it, actually.
Oh, finally.
Haven't had lunch yet...
Sue...
...did you ever find a Night Keeper replacement?

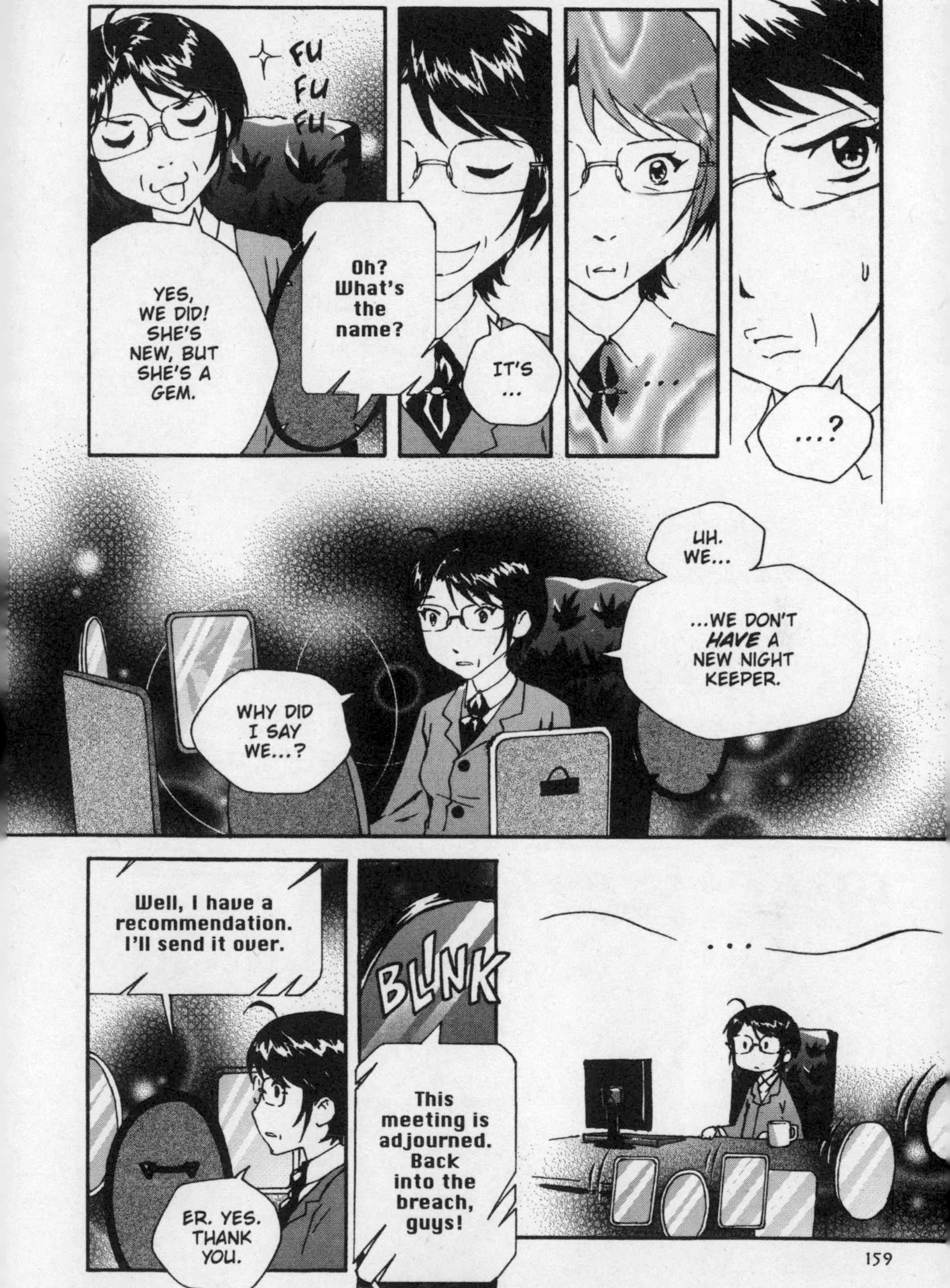
FU FU FU
YES, WE DID! SHE'S NEW, BUT SHE'S A GEM.
Oh? What's the name?
IT'S ...
...
...?
UH. WE...
...WE DON'T *HAVE* A NEW NIGHT KEEPER.
WHY DID I SAY WE...?
Well, I have a recommendation. I'll send it over.
ER. YES. THANK YOU.
BLINK
This meeting is adjourned. Back into the breach, guys!
...

SHELLY, DO WE HAVE A NIGHT KEEPER?

NOT SINCE YOU FIRED THE LAST ONE A MONTH AGO. REALLY NEED ONE, THOUGH.

HUH.

I WAS SO *SURE*. HM.

WELL, THERE IS DEFINITELY A CONTRACT... IT MUST HAVE A NAME.

FLIP FLIP

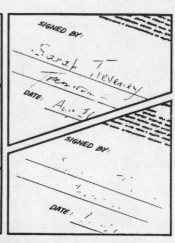

SIGNED BY:

Sarah T. Trevenry
Trevenon

DATE: Aug 31

SIGNED BY:

DATE:

IT'S BLANK ...?

...

... WAS I LOOKING AT THIS AGAIN?

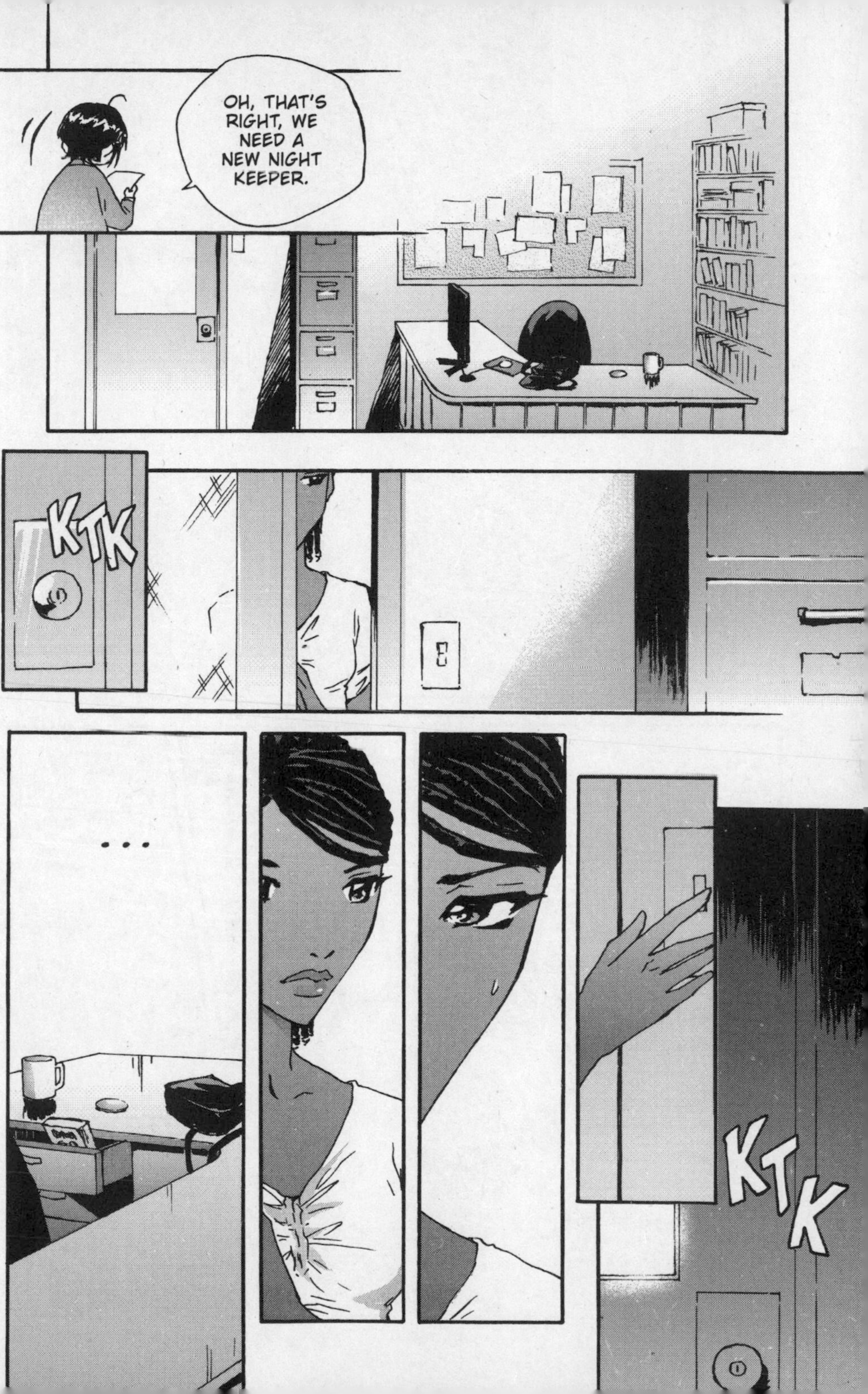
OH, THAT'S RIGHT, WE NEED A NEW NIGHT KEEPER.
KTK
...
KTK

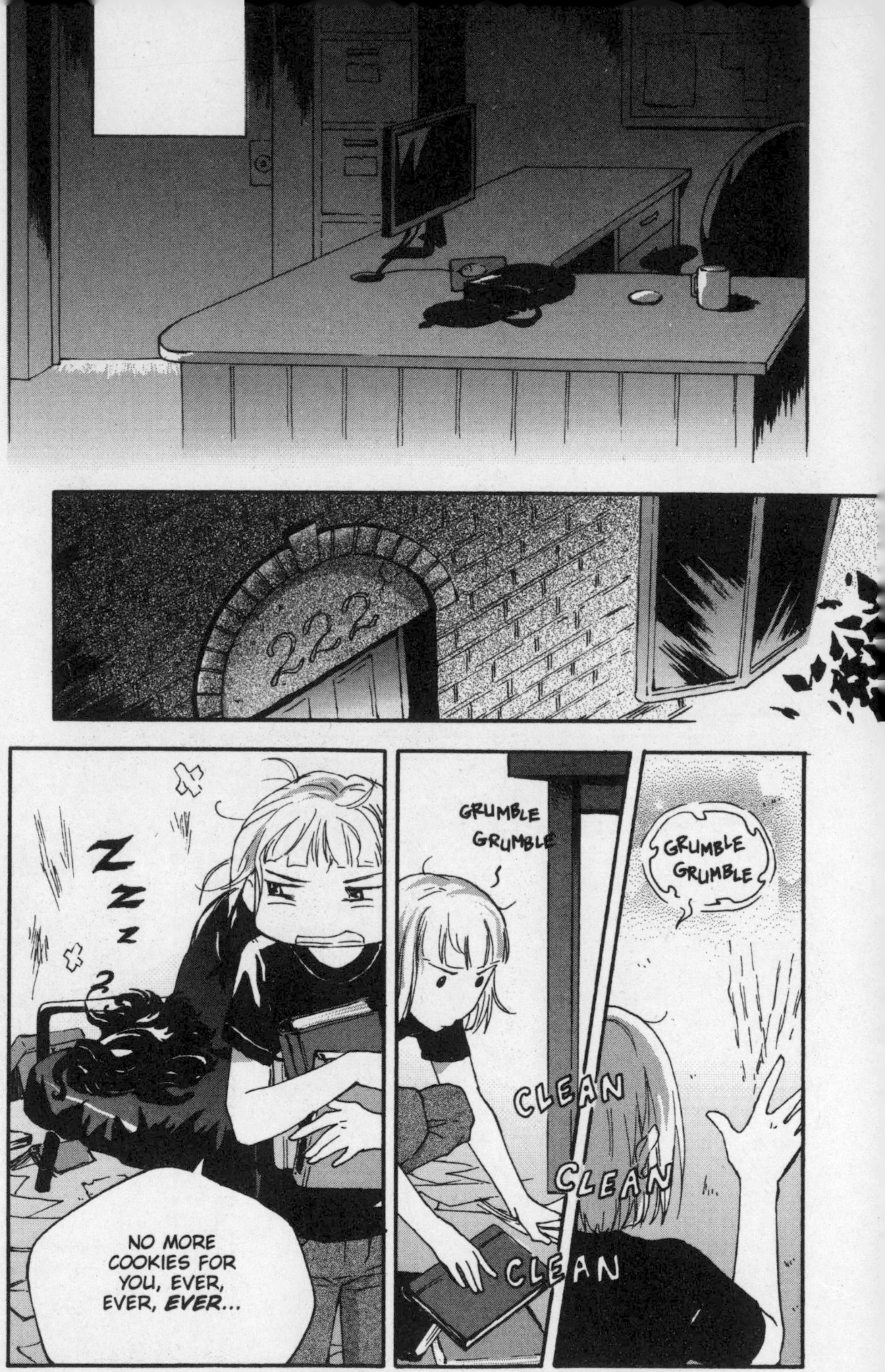
222
ZZZ
NO MORE COOKIES FOR YOU, EVER, EVER, **EVER**...
GRUMBLE GRUMBLE
CLEAN
CLEAN
CLEAN
GRUMBLE GRUMBLE

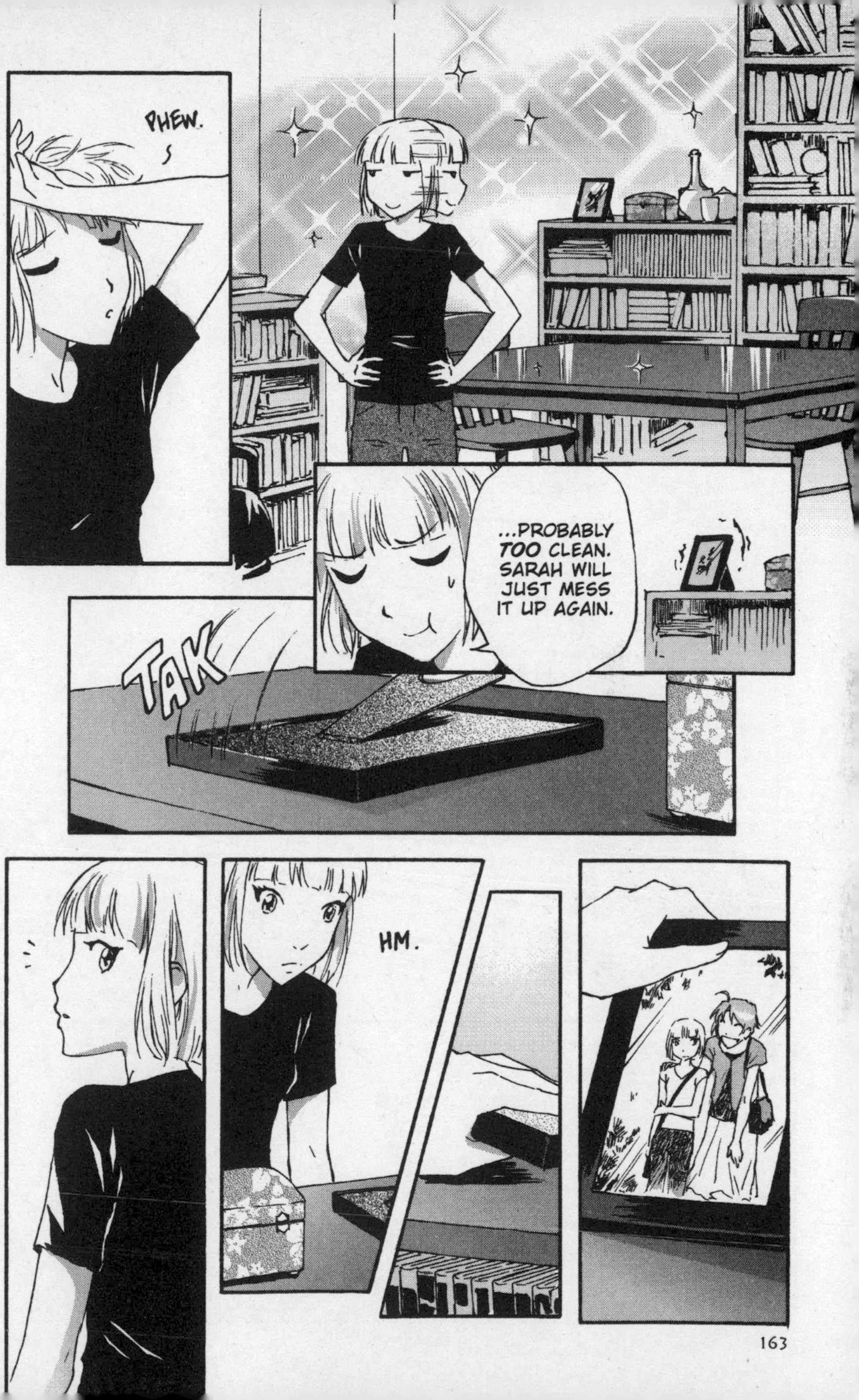
PHEW.
...PROBABLY TOO CLEAN. SARAH WILL JUST MESS IT UP AGAIN.
TAK
HM.

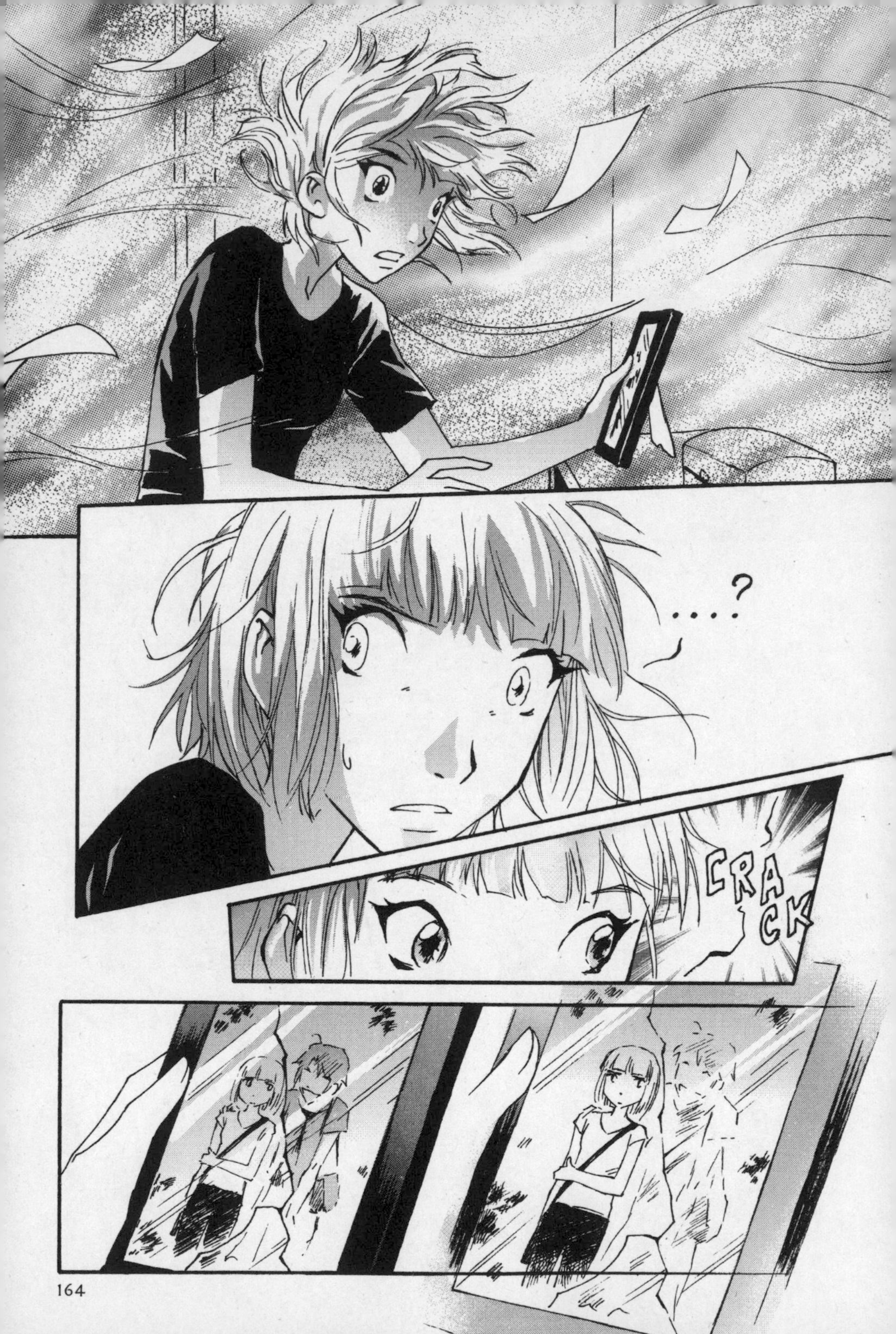
...?
CRACK

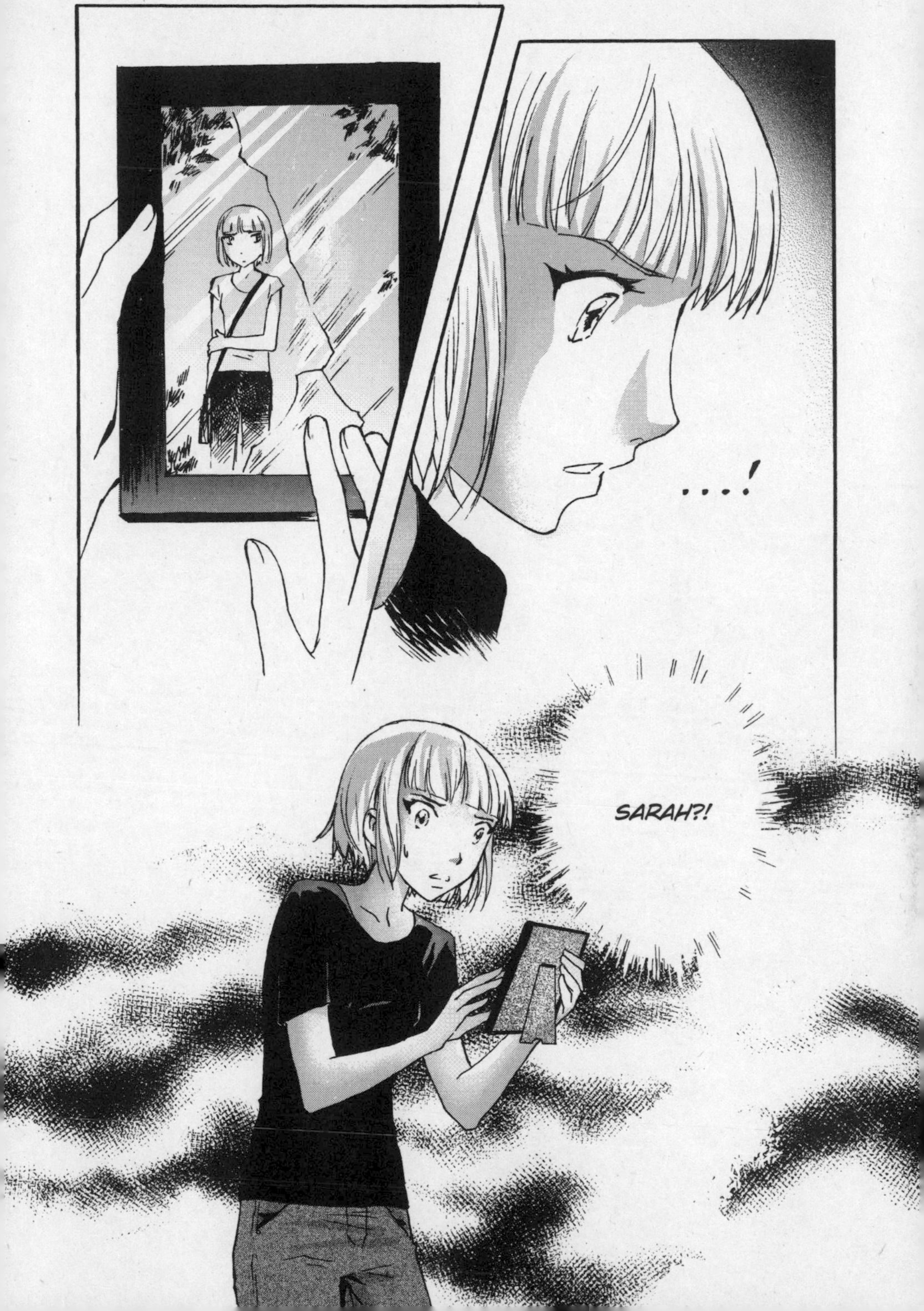
...!
SARAH?!

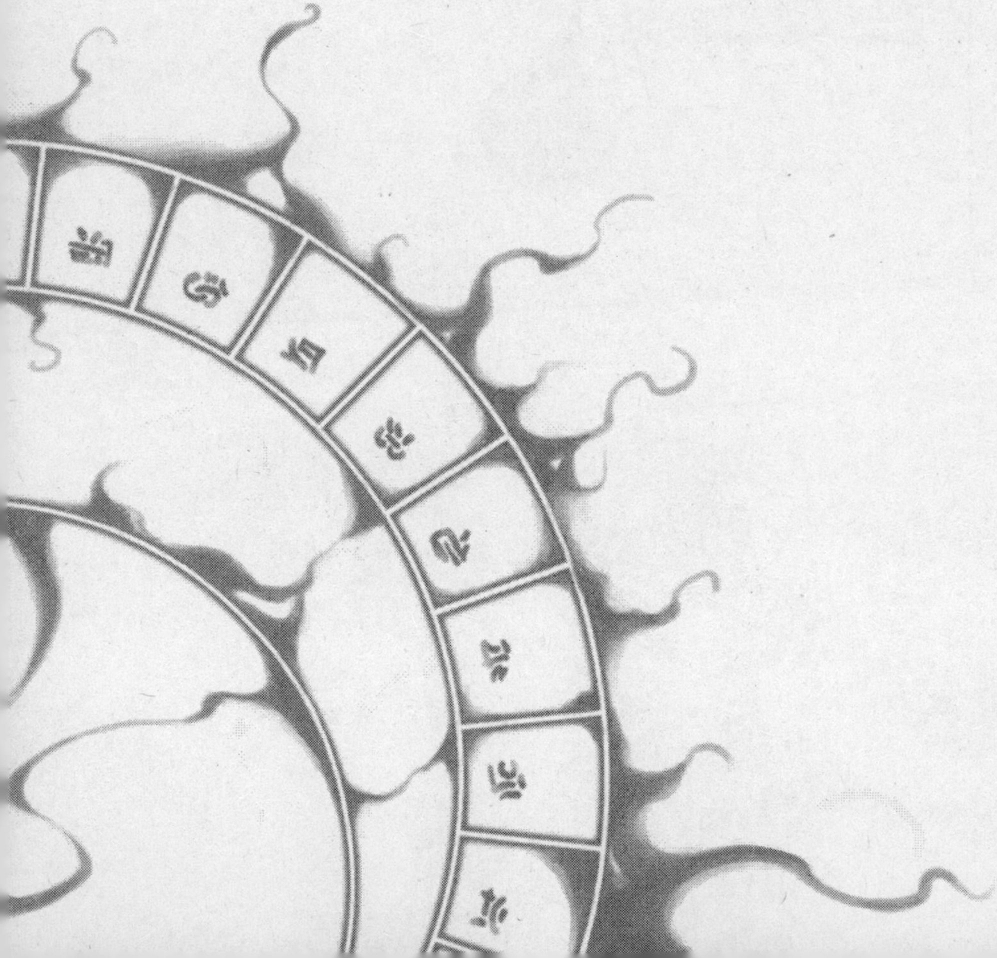

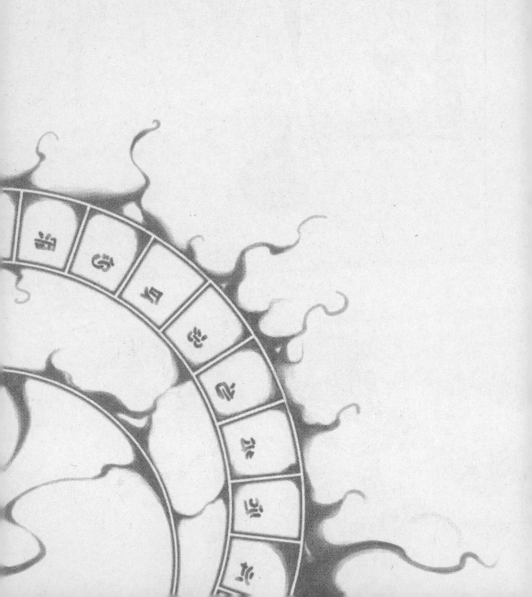

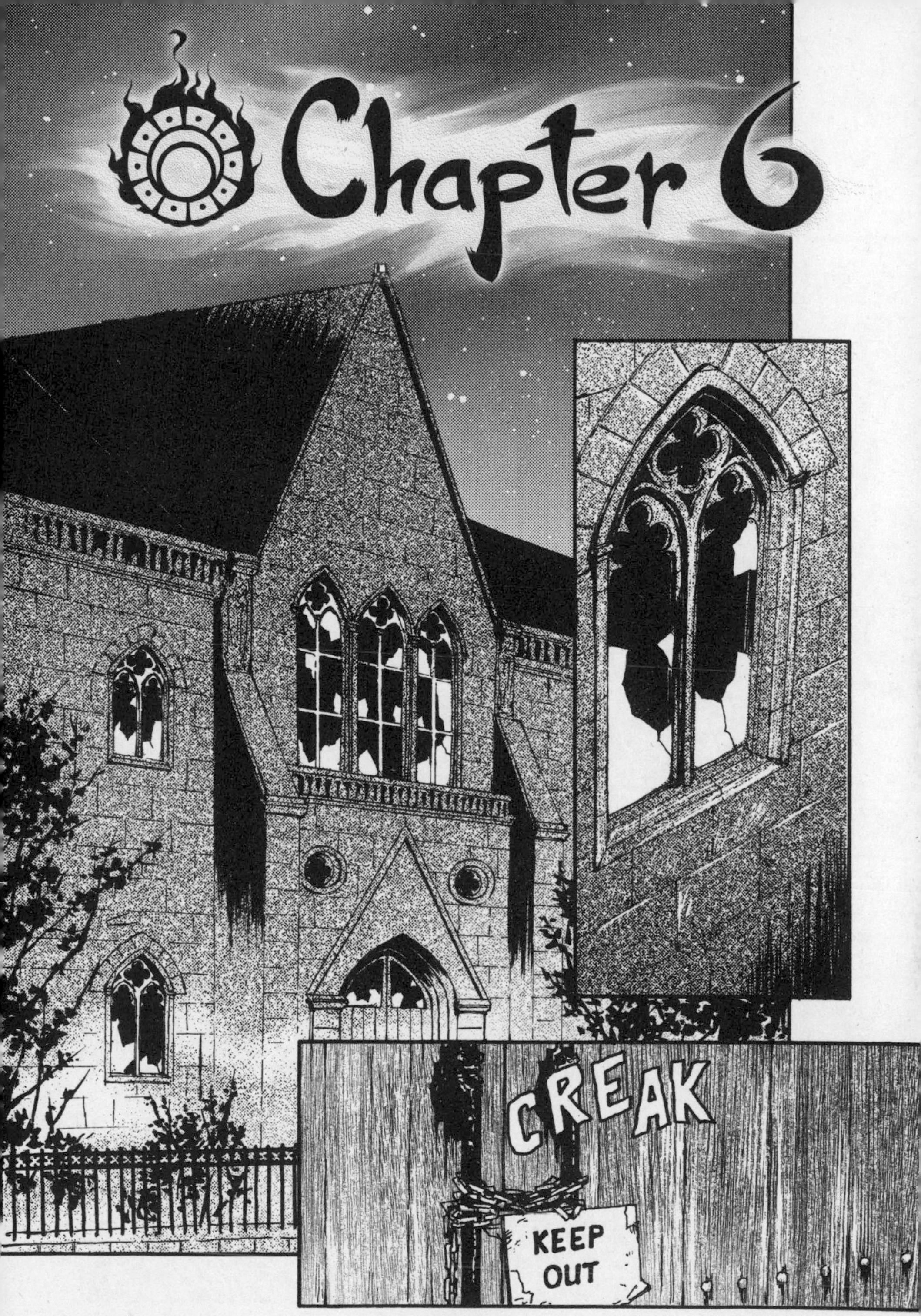
Chapter 6
CREAK
KEEP
OUT

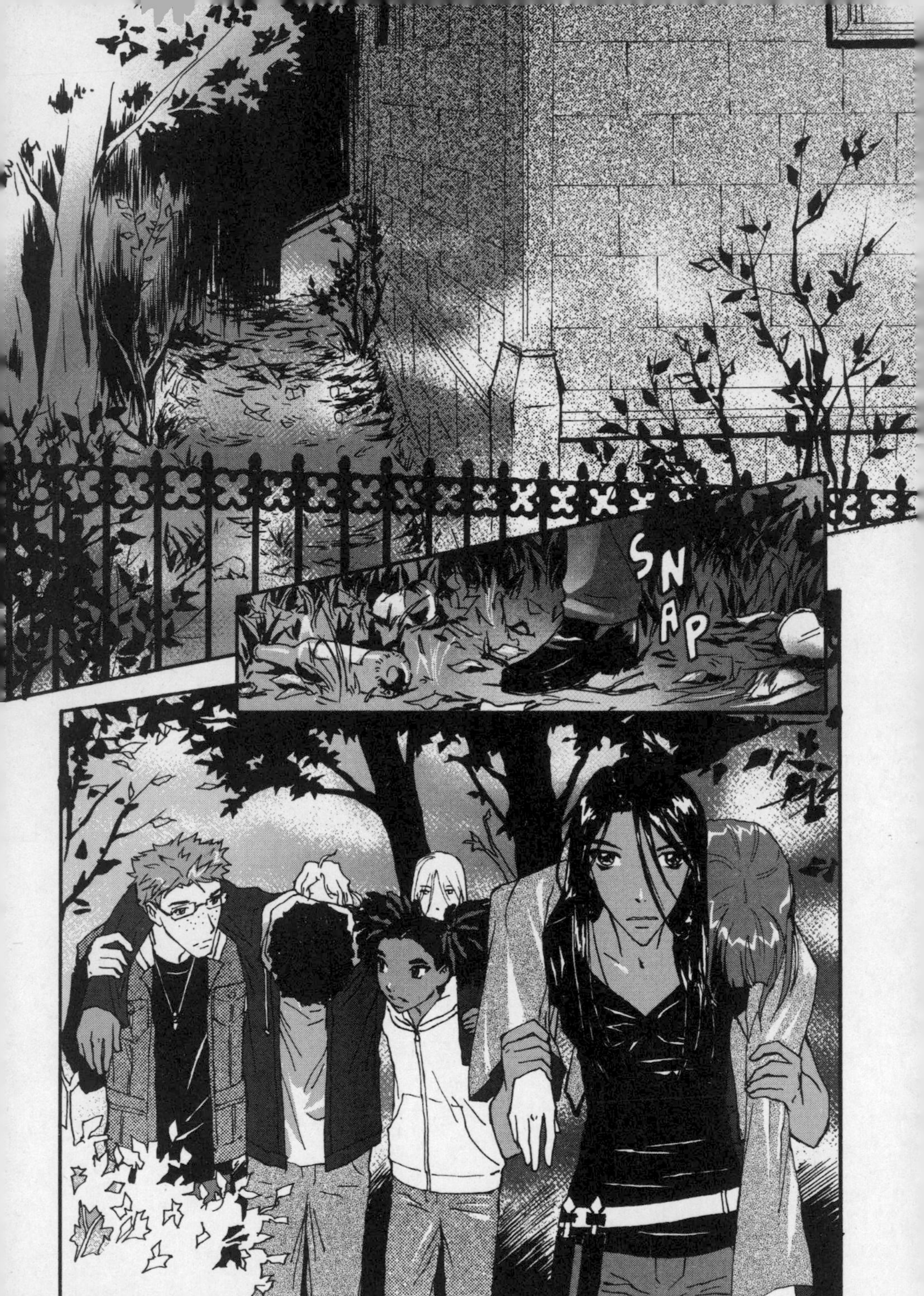
SNAP

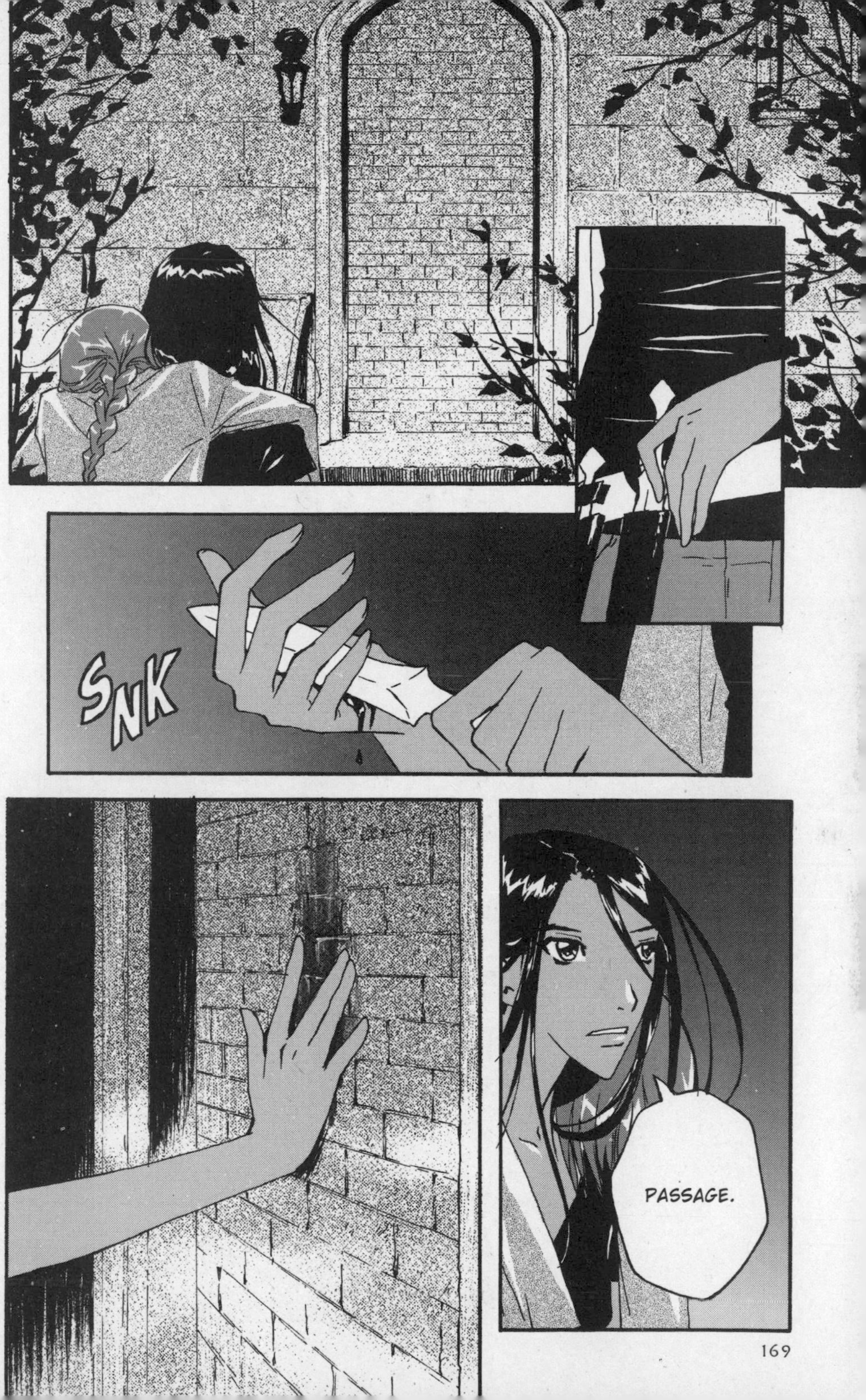
SNK
PASSAGE.

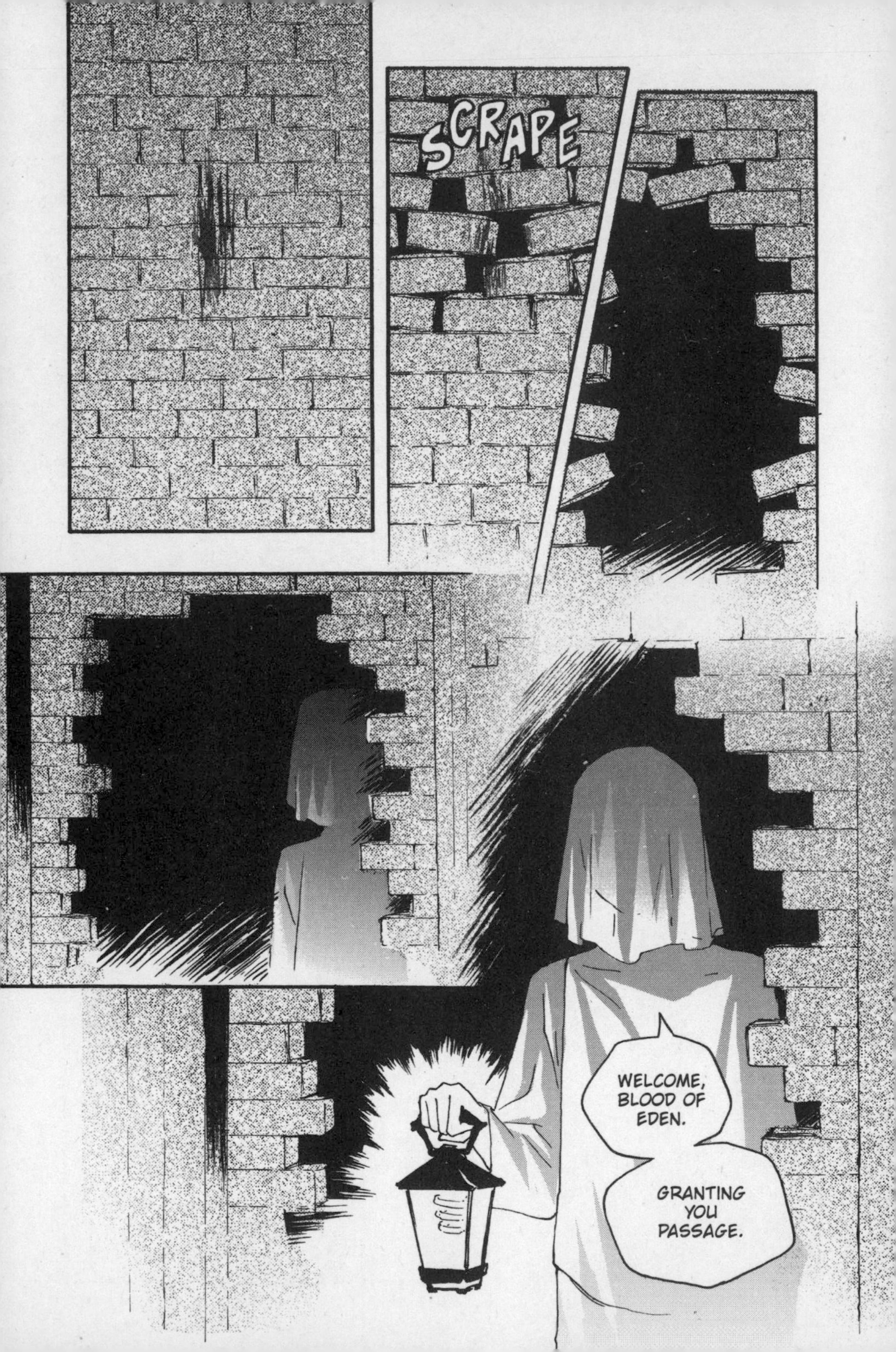
SCRAPE
WELCOME, BLOOD OF EDEN.
GRANTING YOU PASSAGE.

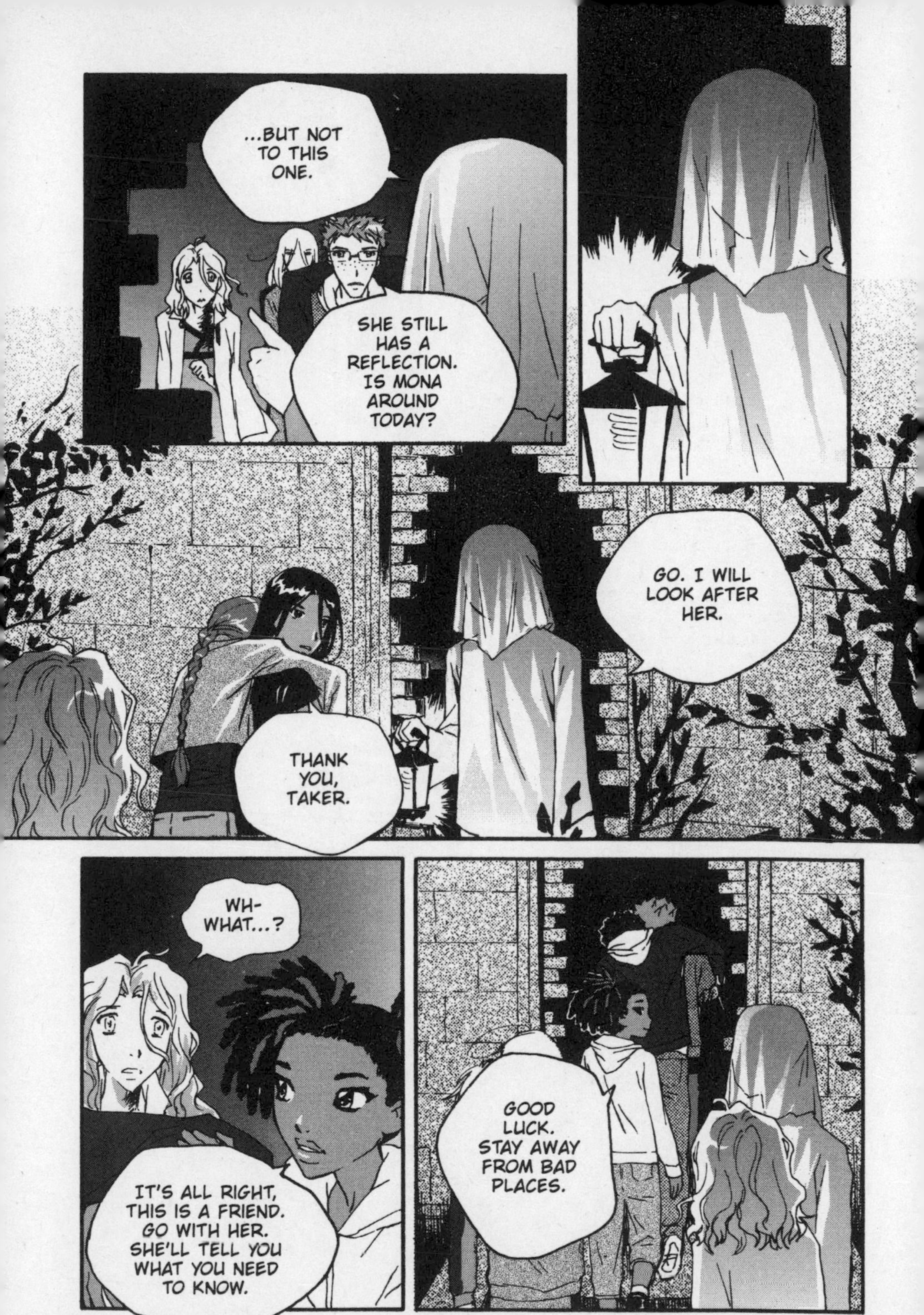
...BUT NOT TO THIS ONE.
SHE STILL HAS A REFLECTION. IS MONA AROUND TODAY?
GO. I WILL LOOK AFTER HER.
THANK YOU, TAKER.
WH-WHAT...?
IT'S ALL RIGHT, THIS IS A FRIEND. GO WITH HER. SHE'LL TELL YOU WHAT YOU NEED TO KNOW.
GOOD LUCK. STAY AWAY FROM BAD PLACES.

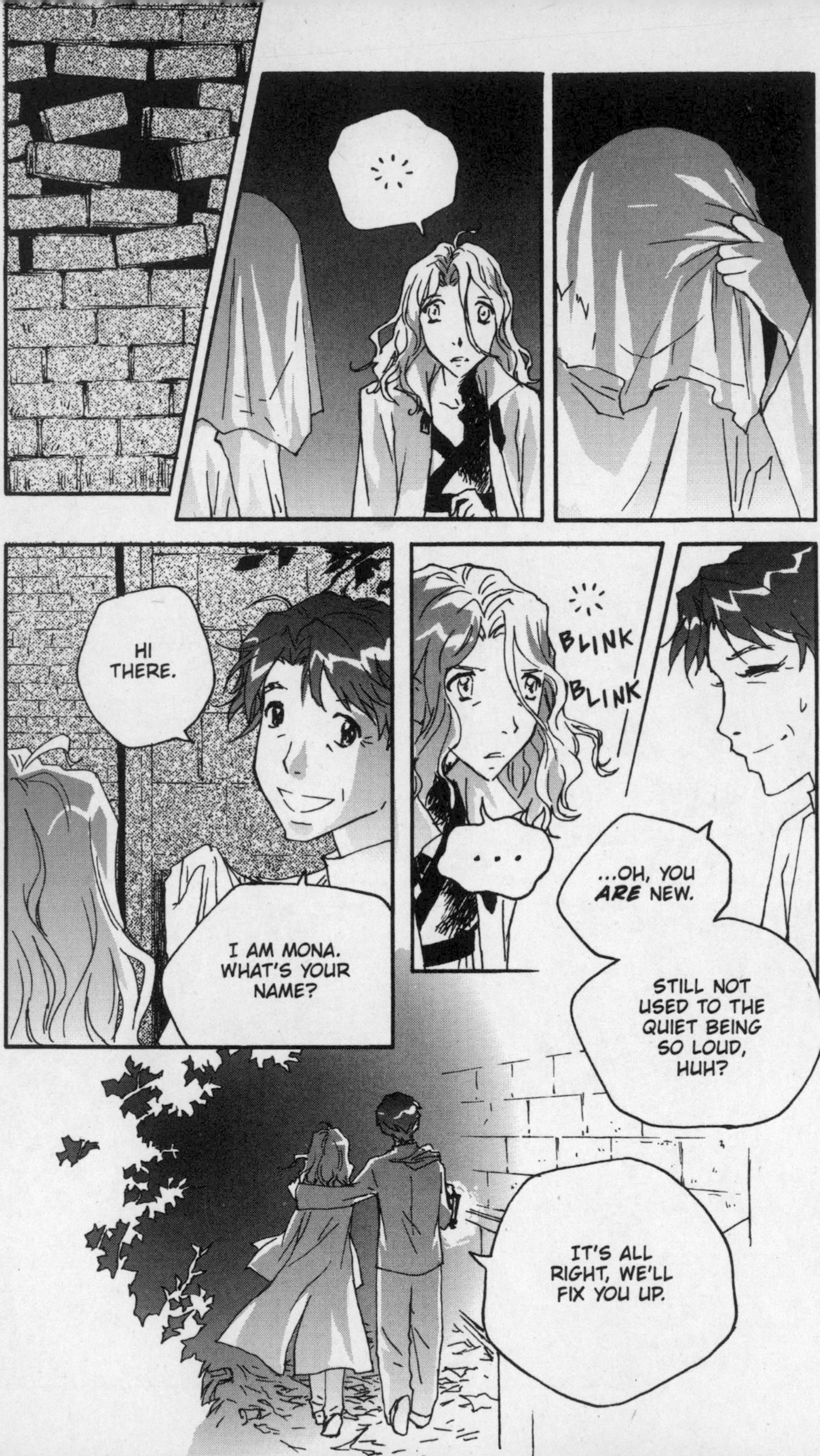
BLINK
BLINK
HI THERE.
I AM MONA. WHAT'S YOUR NAME?
...
...OH, YOU *ARE* NEW.
STILL NOT USED TO THE QUIET BEING SO LOUD, HUH?
IT'S ALL RIGHT, WE'LL FIX YOU UP.

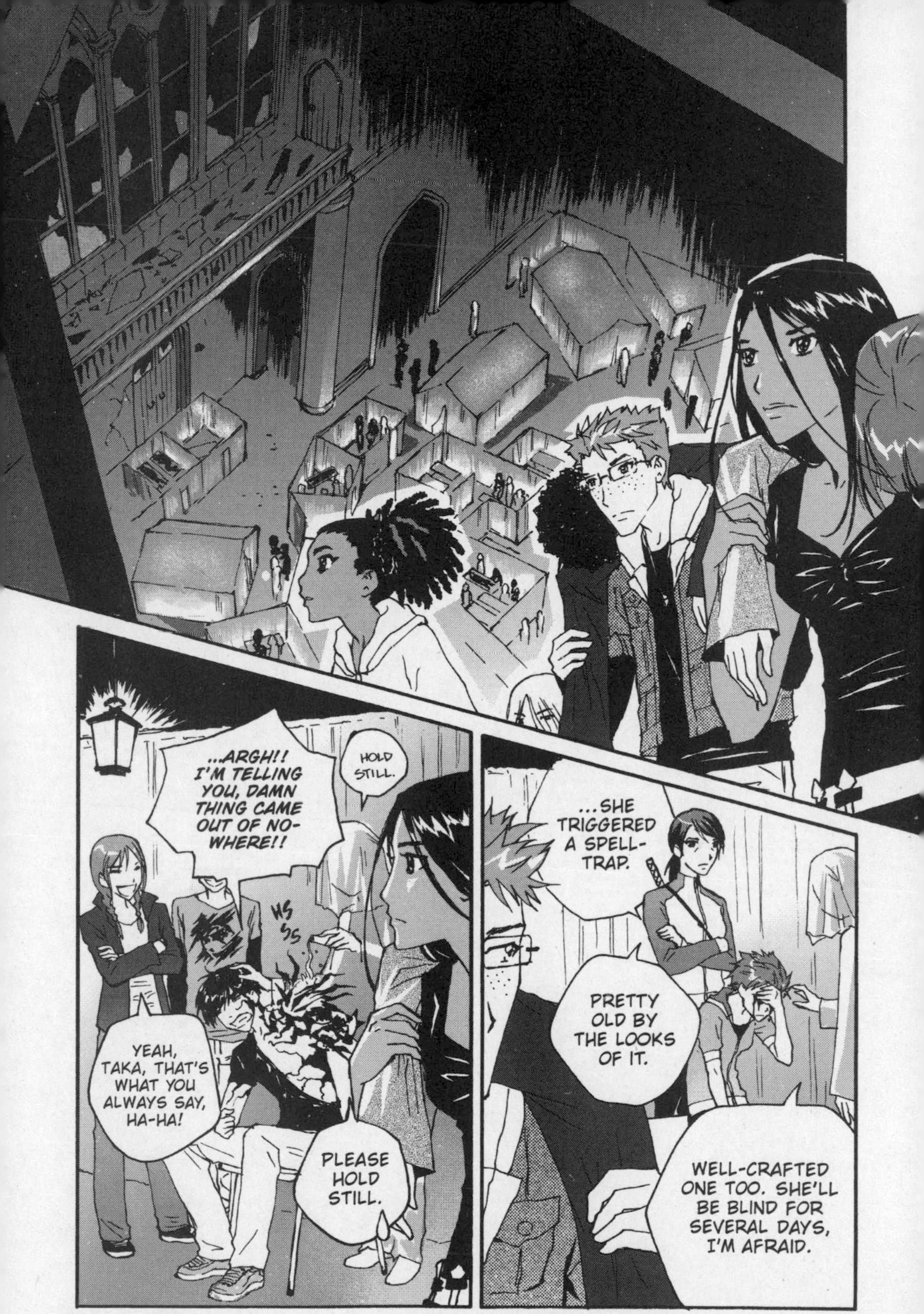
...ARGH!! I'M TELLING YOU, DAMN THING CAME OUT OF NO-WHERE!!
HOLD STILL.
YEAH, TAKA, THAT'S WHAT YOU ALWAYS SAY, HA-HA!
PLEASE HOLD STILL.
...SHE TRIGGERED A SPELL-TRAP.
PRETTY OLD BY THE LOOKS OF IT.
WELL-CRAFTED ONE TOO. SHE'LL BE BLIND FOR SEVERAL DAYS, I'M AFRAID.

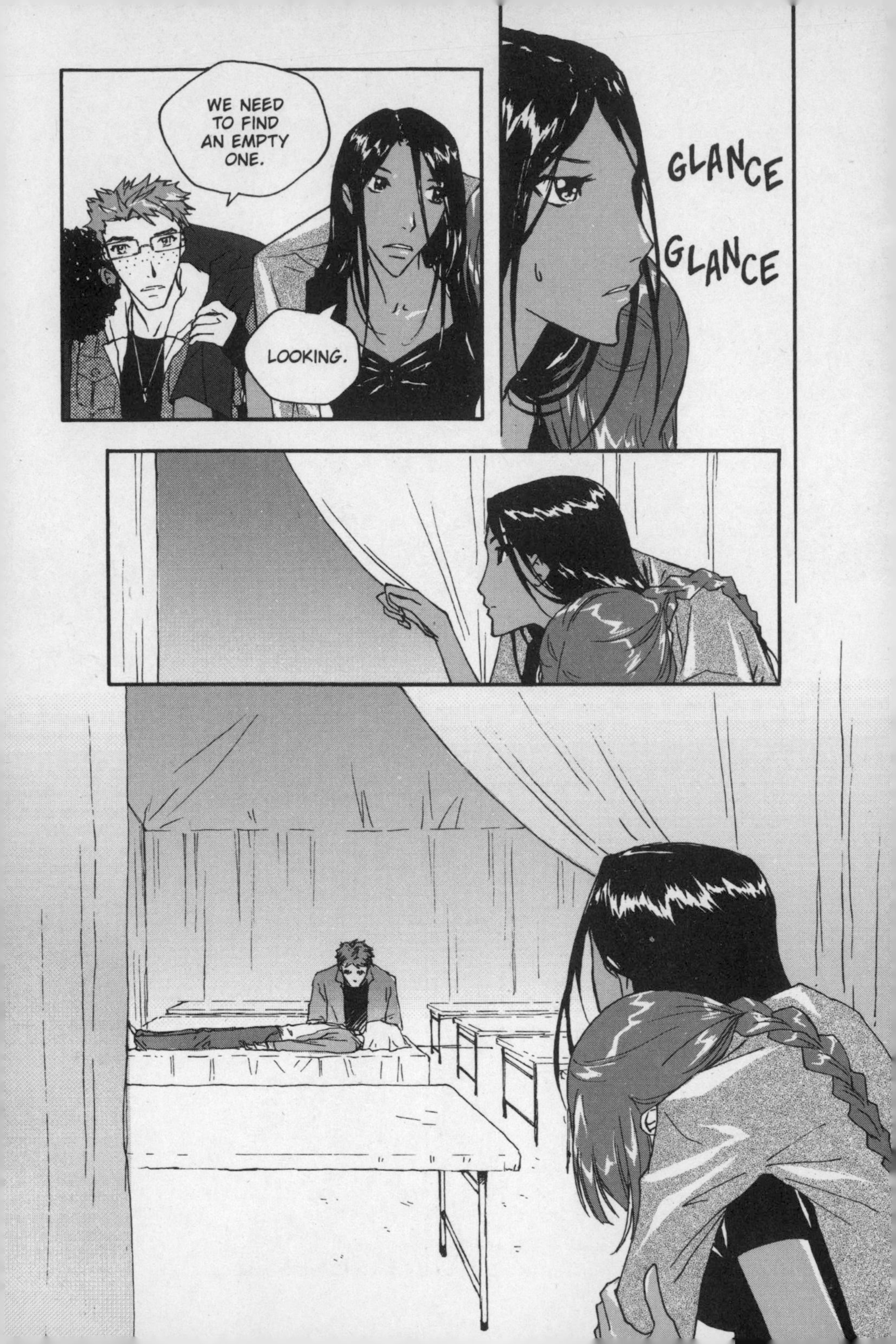
WE NEED TO FIND AN EMPTY ONE.
LOOKING.
GLANCE
GLANCE

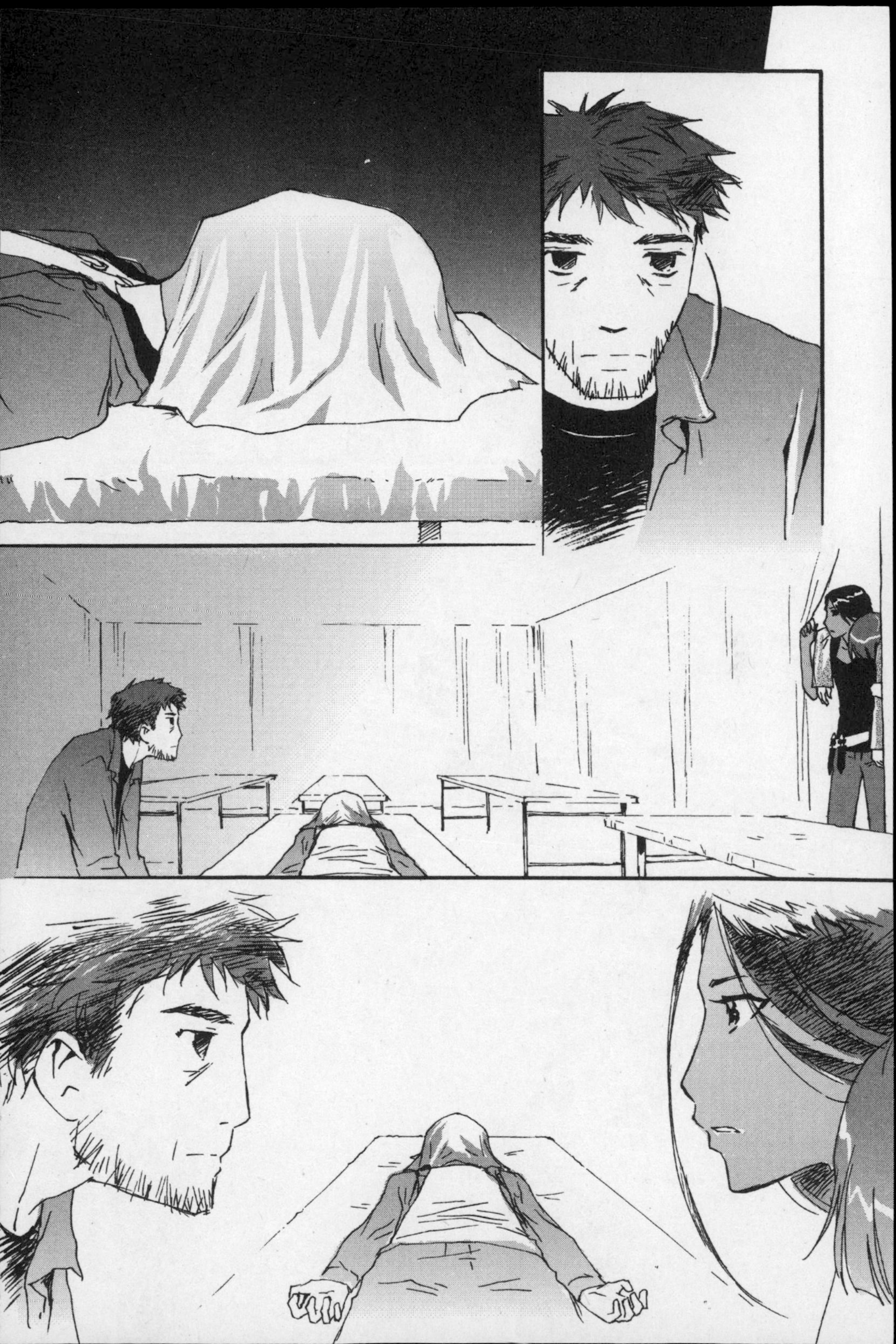

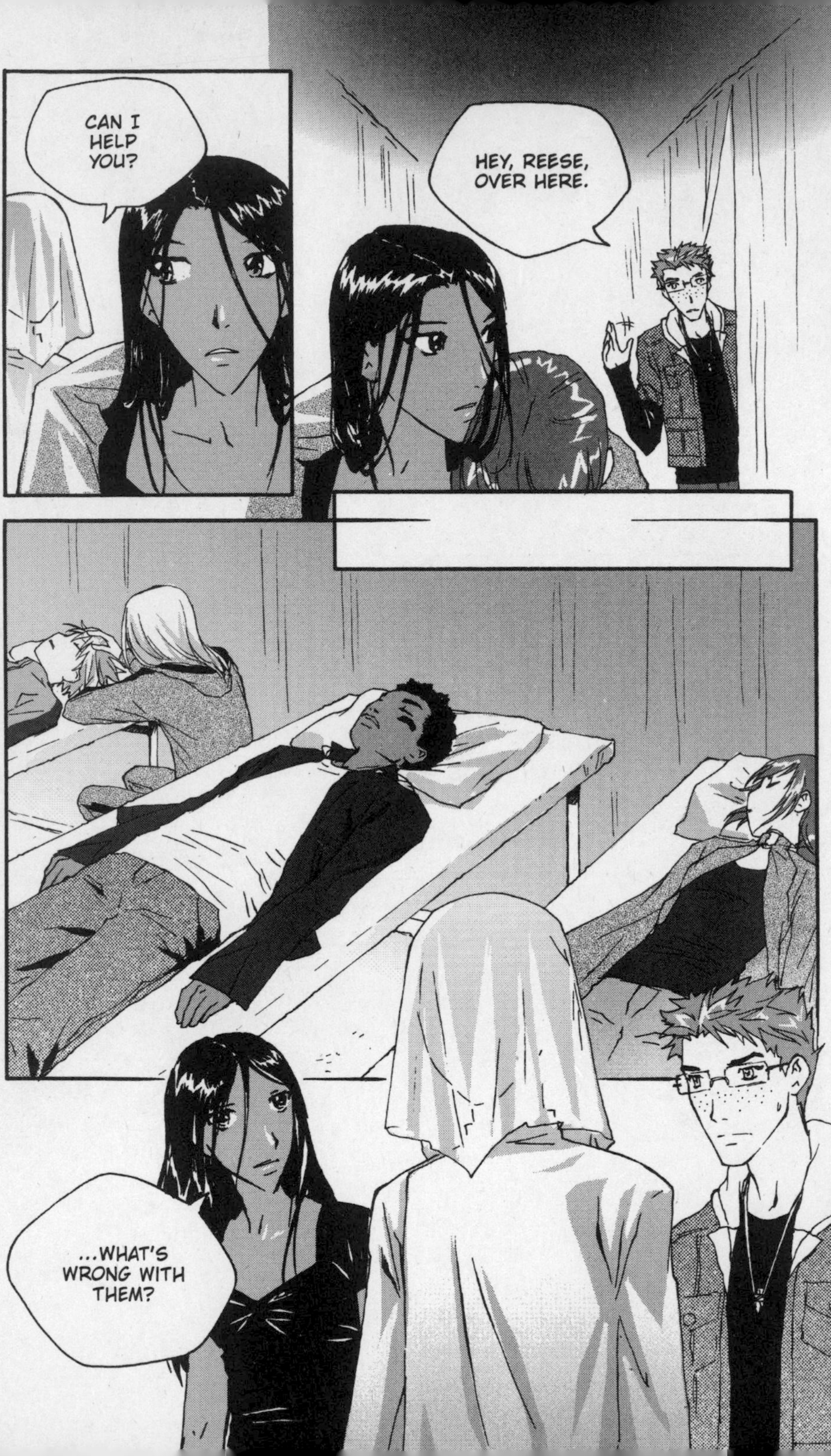
CAN I HELP YOU?
HEY, REESE, OVER HERE.
...WHAT'S WRONG WITH THEM?

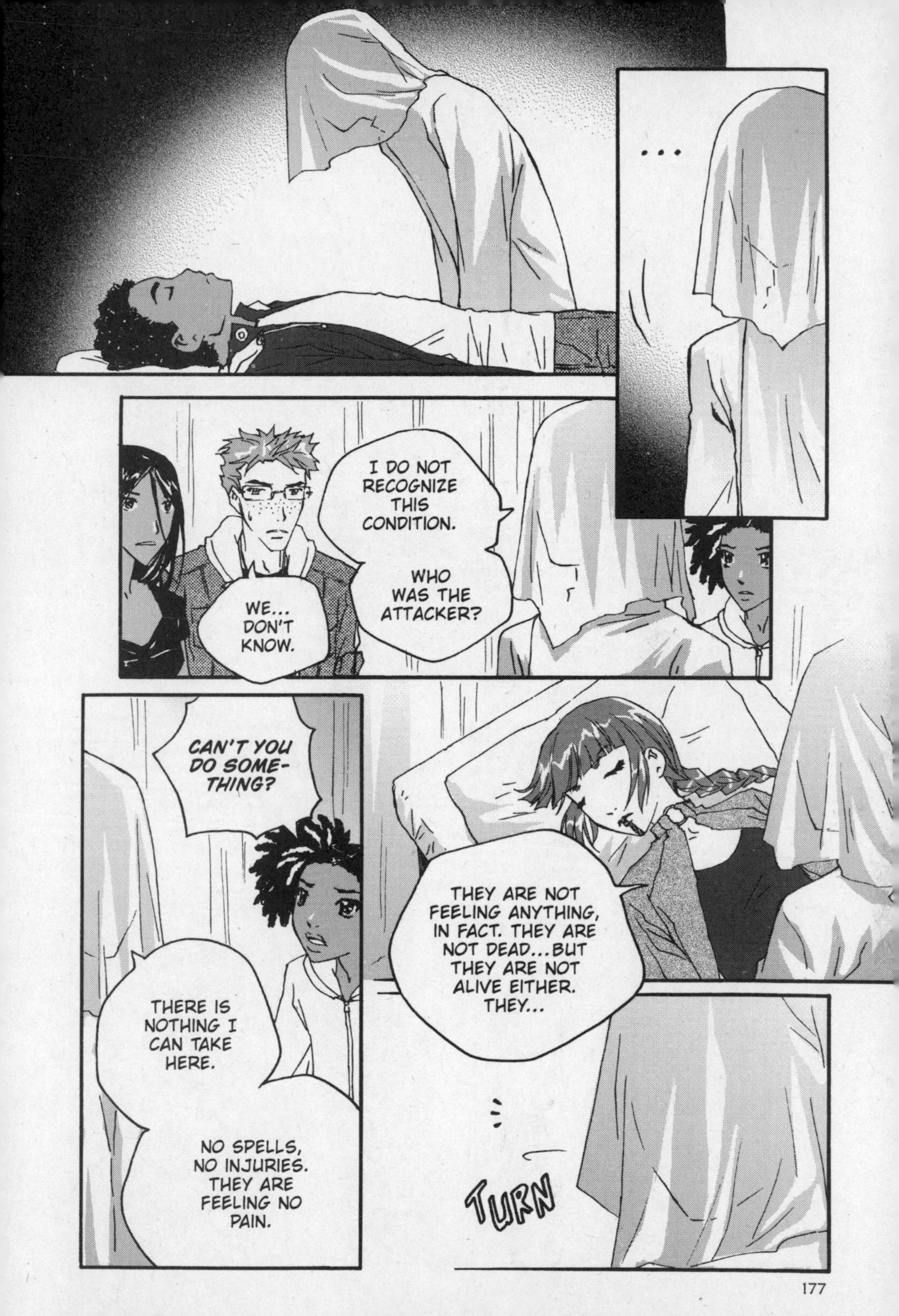
...
I DO NOT RECOGNIZE THIS CONDITION.
WHO WAS THE ATTACKER?
WE... DON'T KNOW.
CAN'T YOU DO SOME-THING?
THERE IS NOTHING I CAN TAKE HERE.
NO SPELLS, NO INJURIES. THEY ARE FEELING NO PAIN.
THEY ARE NOT FEELING ANYTHING, IN FACT. THEY ARE NOT DEAD...BUT THEY ARE NOT ALIVE EITHER. THEY...
TURN

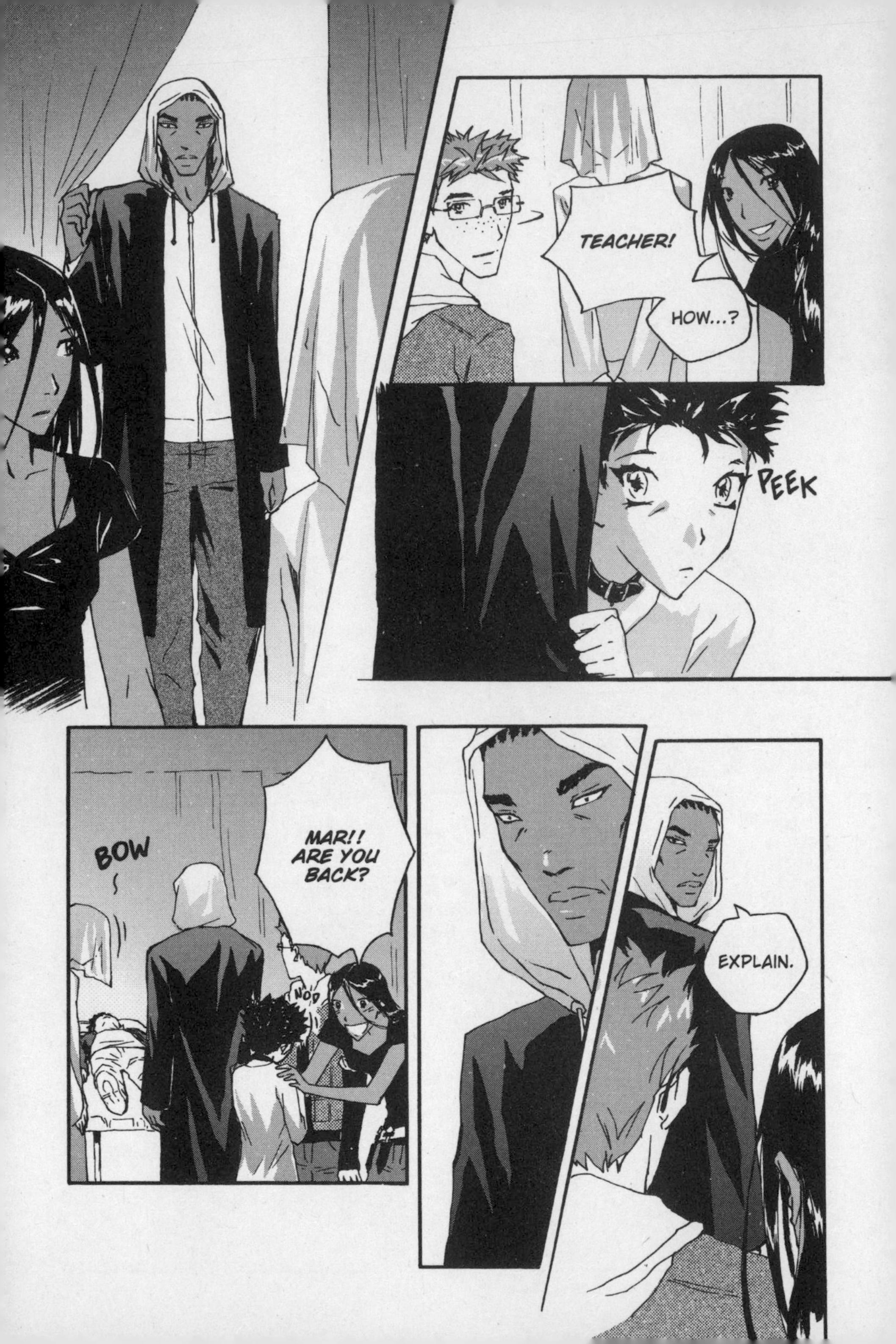
TEACHER!
HOW...?
PEEK
BOW
MAR!! ARE YOU BACK?
NOD
EXPLAIN.

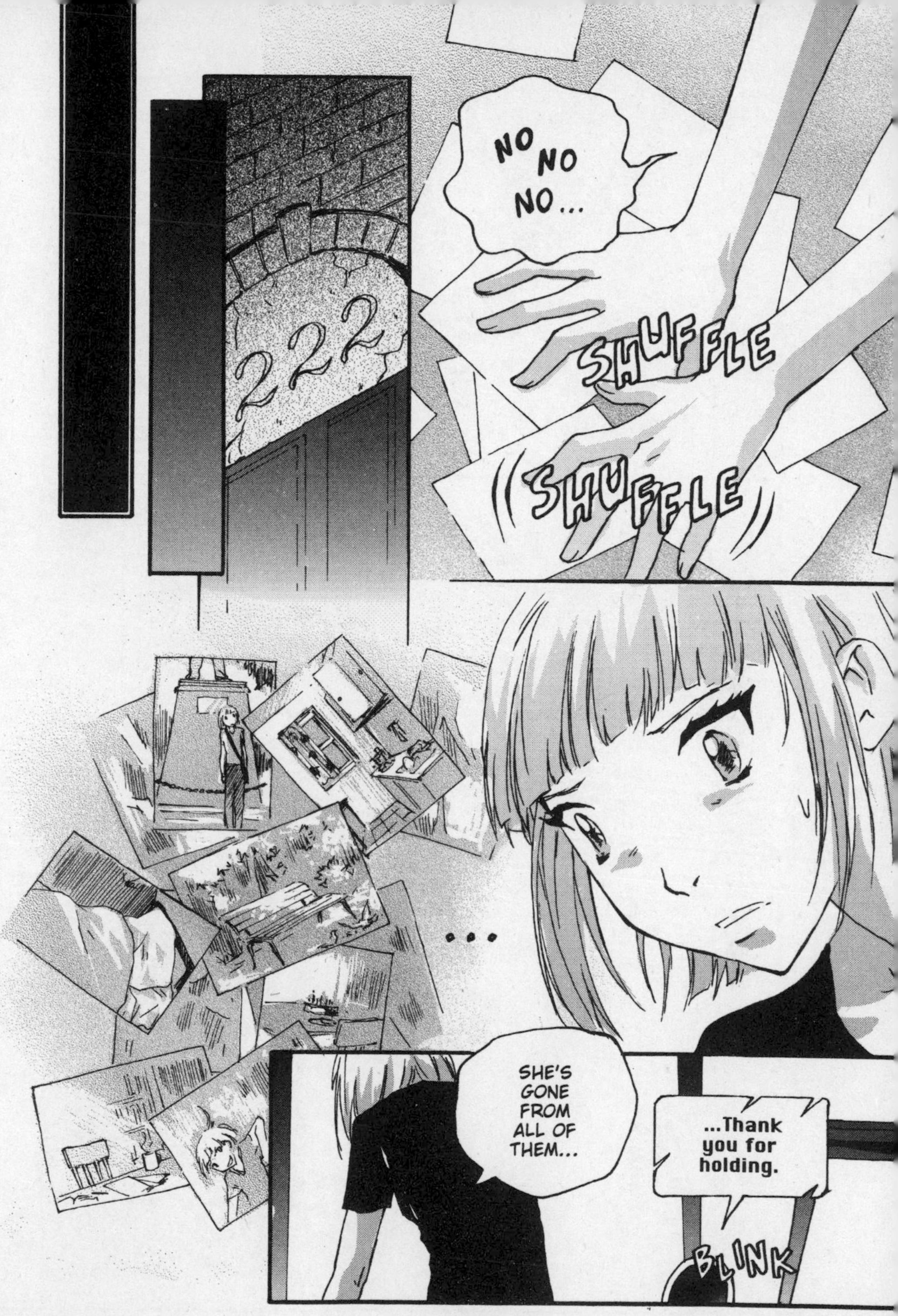
NO NO NO...
SHUFFLE
SHUFFLE
...
SHE'S GONE FROM ALL OF THEM...
...Thank you for holding.
BLINK

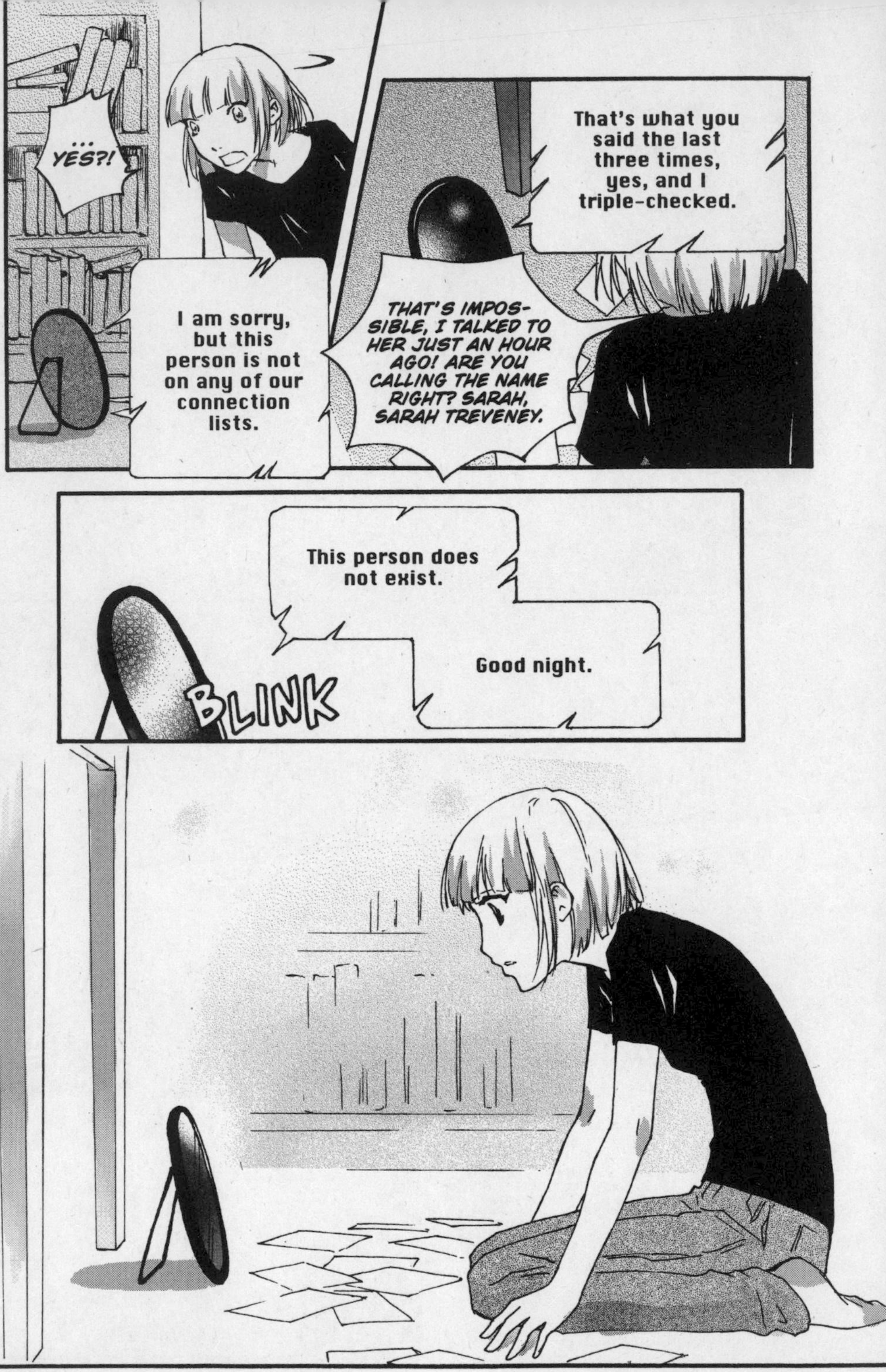
...YES?!
I am sorry, but this person is not on any of our connection lists.
That's what you said the last three times, yes, and I triple-checked.
THAT'S IMPOSSIBLE, I TALKED TO HER JUST AN HOUR AGO! ARE YOU CALLING THE NAME RIGHT? SARAH, SARAH TREVENEY.
This person does not exist.
Good night.
BLINK

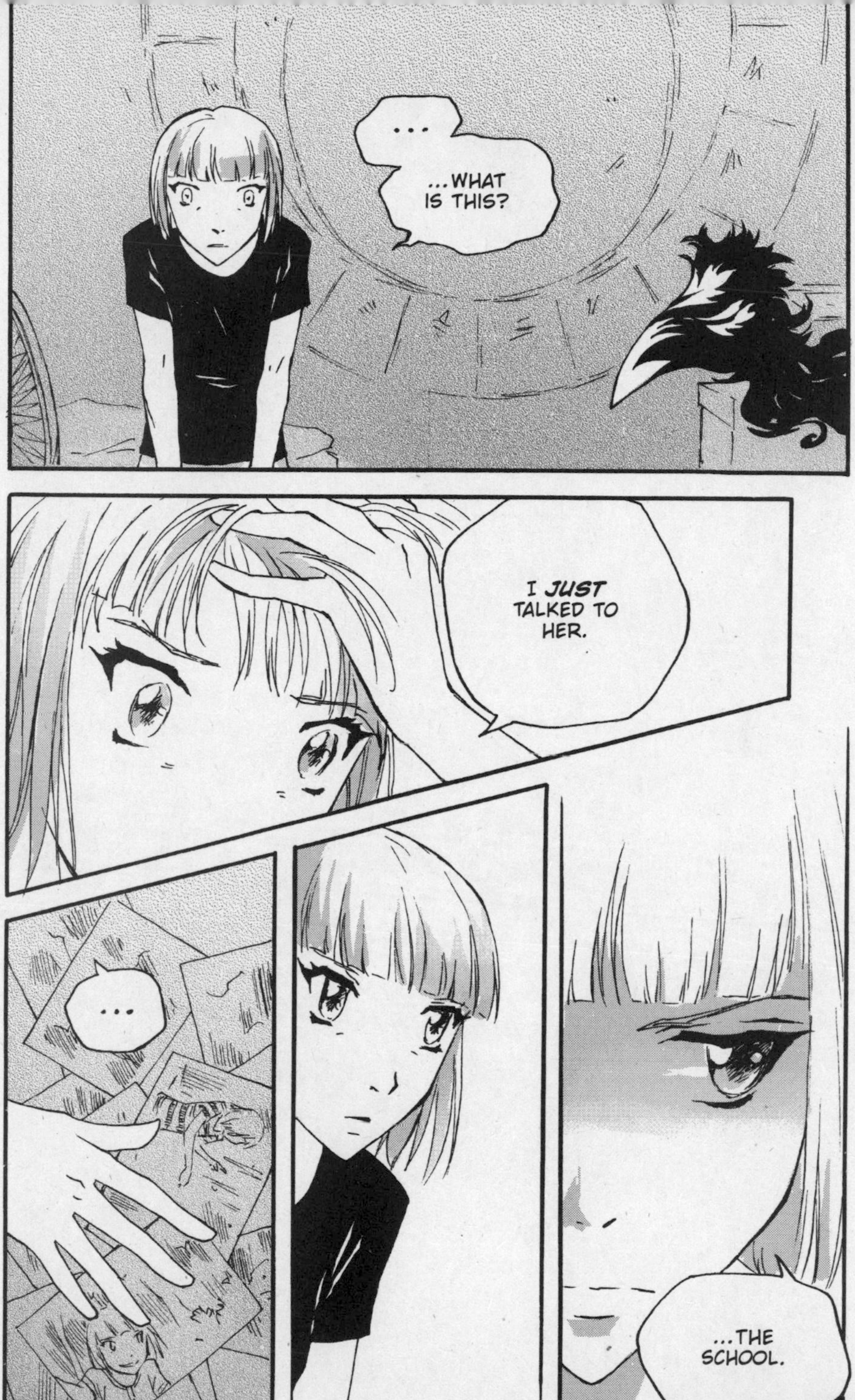
...
...WHAT IS THIS?
I *JUST* TALKED TO HER.
...
...THE SCHOOL.

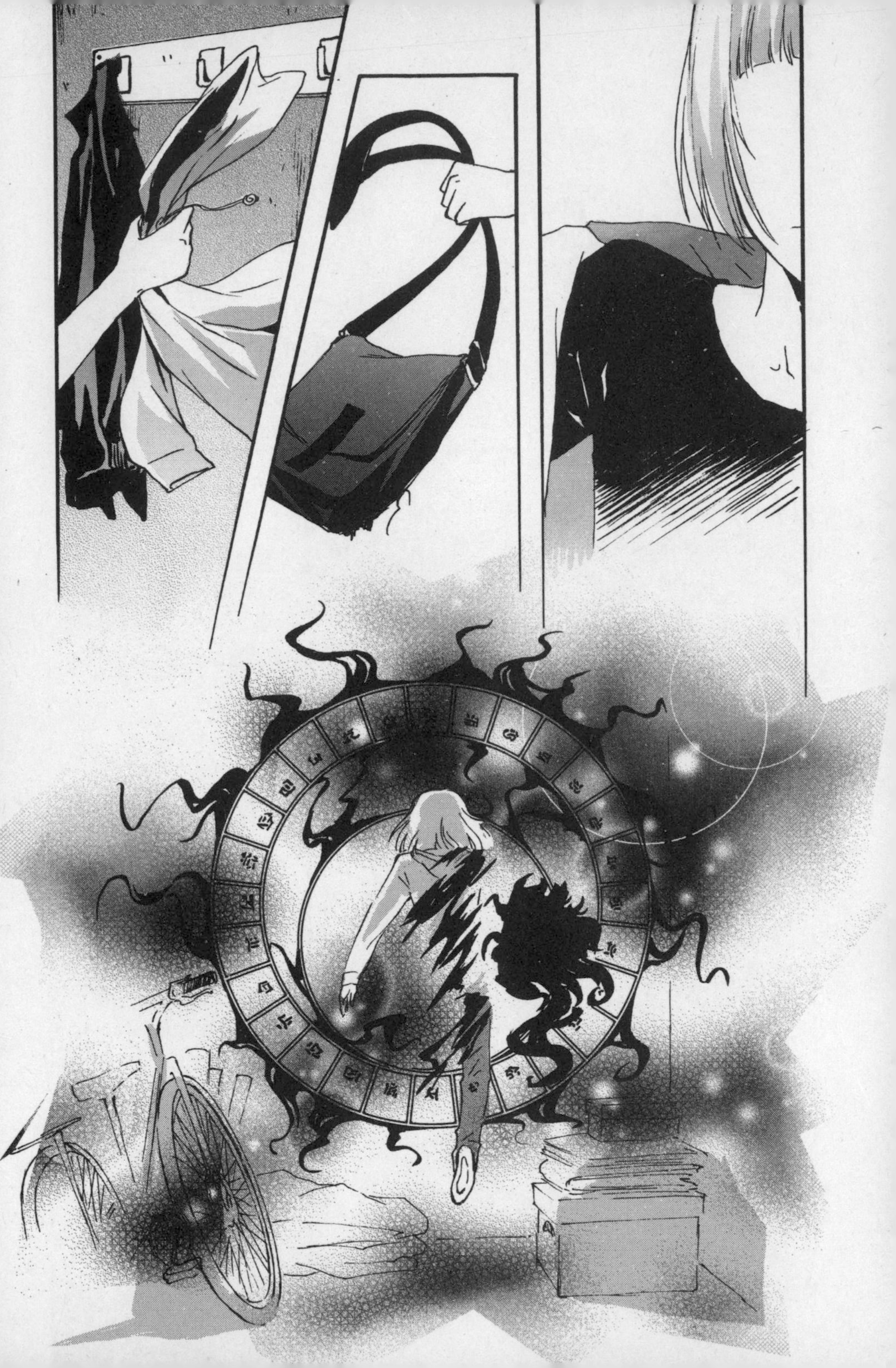

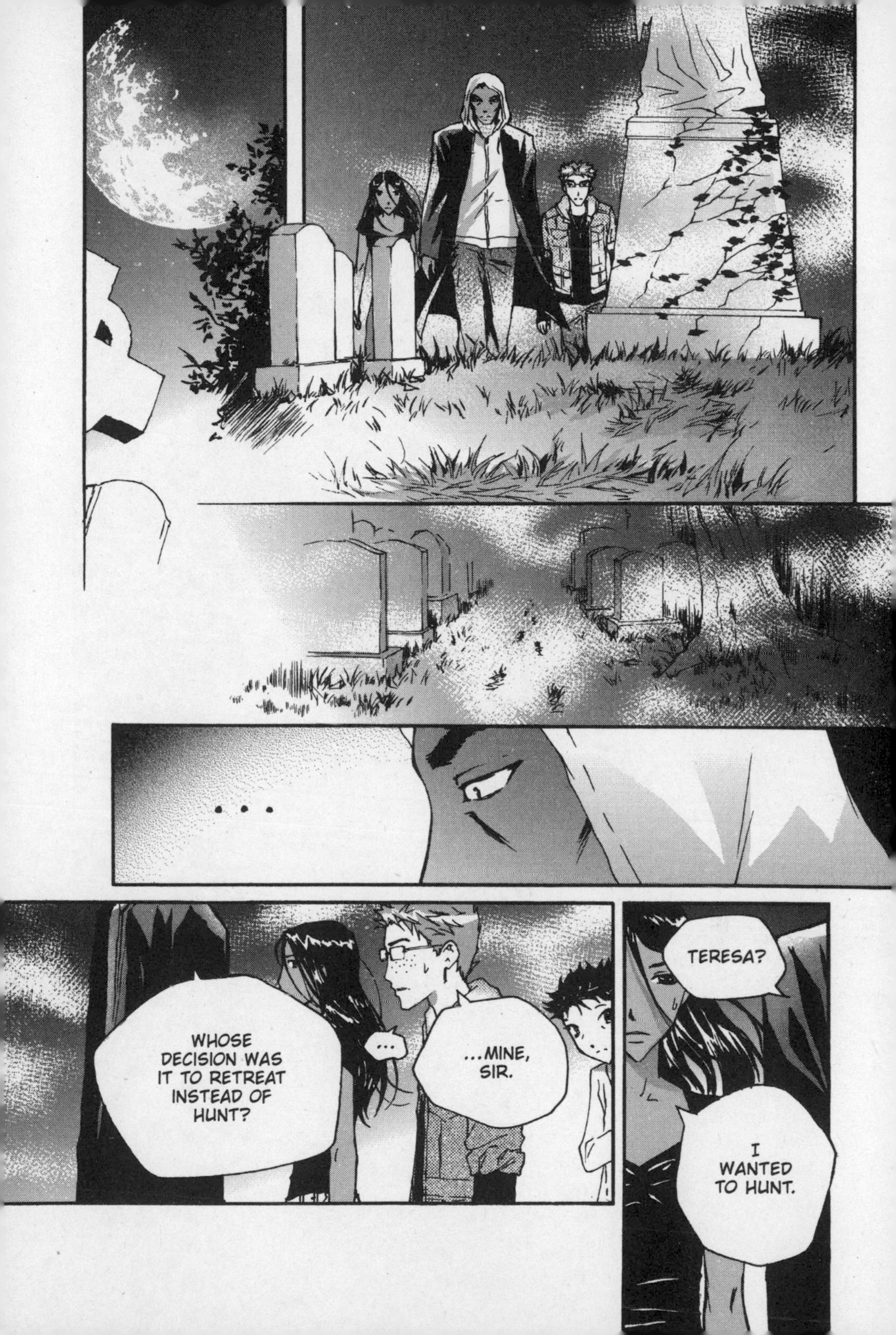
...
WHOSE DECISION WAS IT TO RETREAT INSTEAD OF HUNT?
...
...MINE, SIR.
TERESA?
I WANTED TO HUNT.

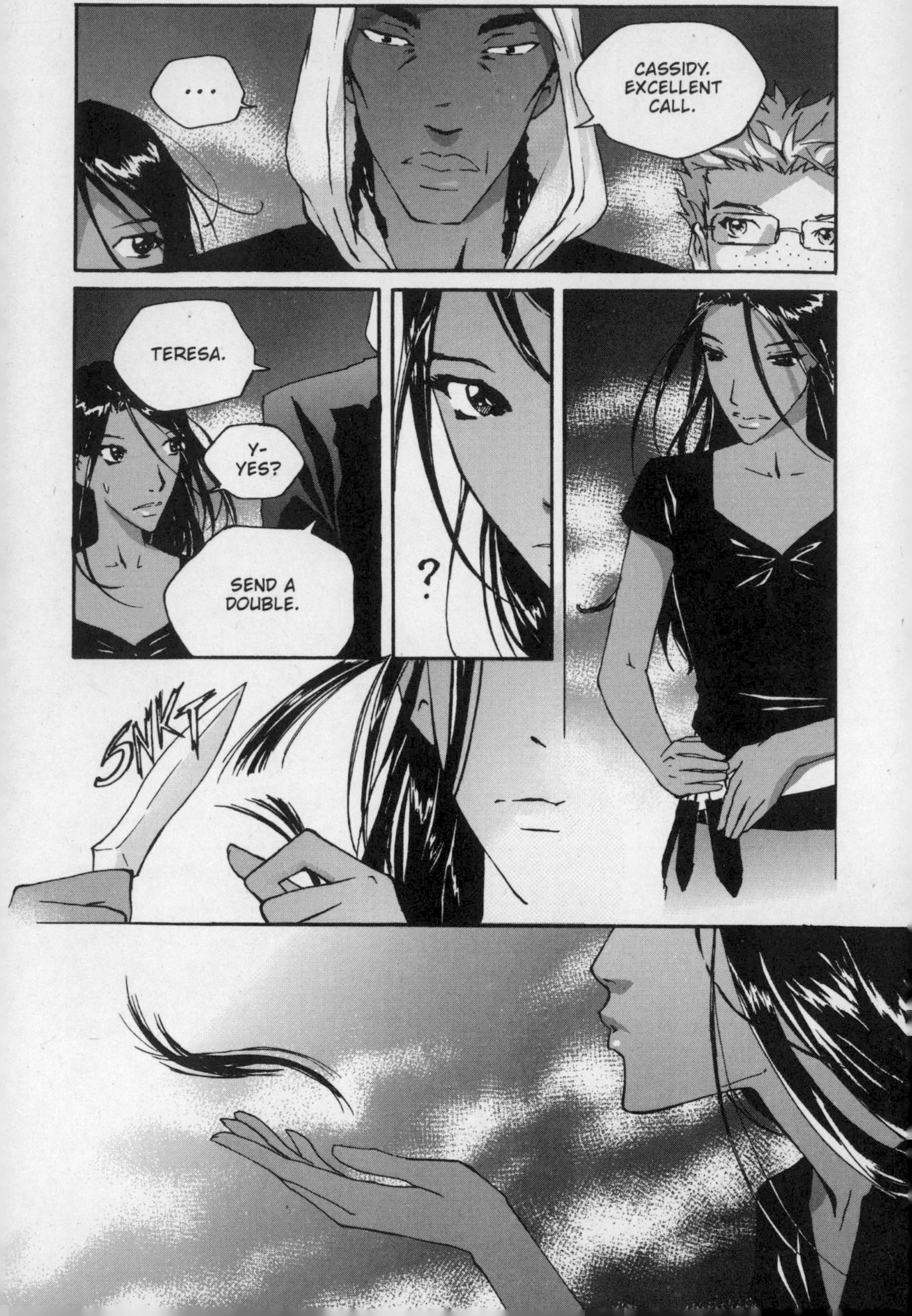
...
CASSIDY. EXCELLENT CALL.
TERESA.
Y-YES?
SEND A DOUBLE.
?
SNKT

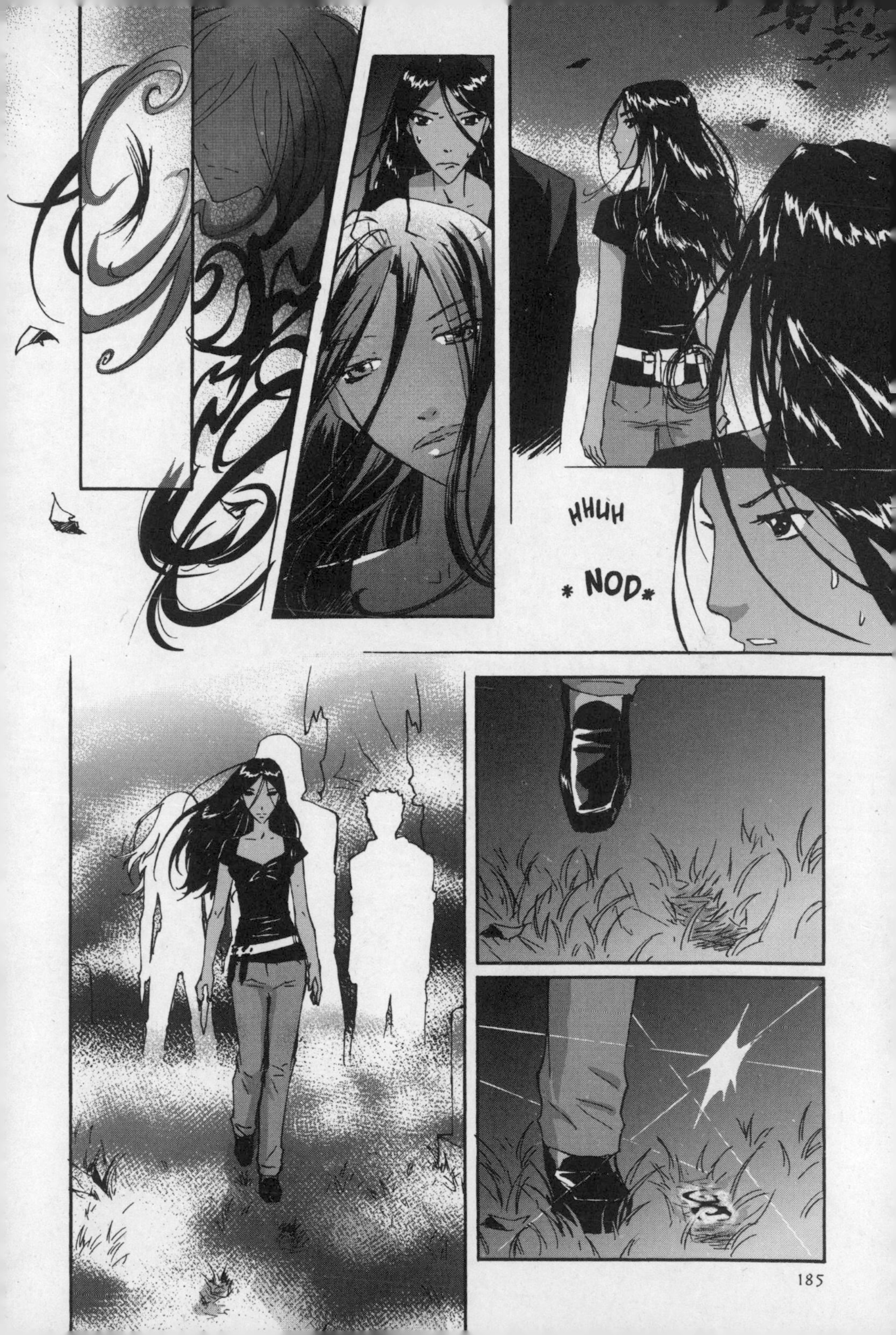
HHUH
NOD

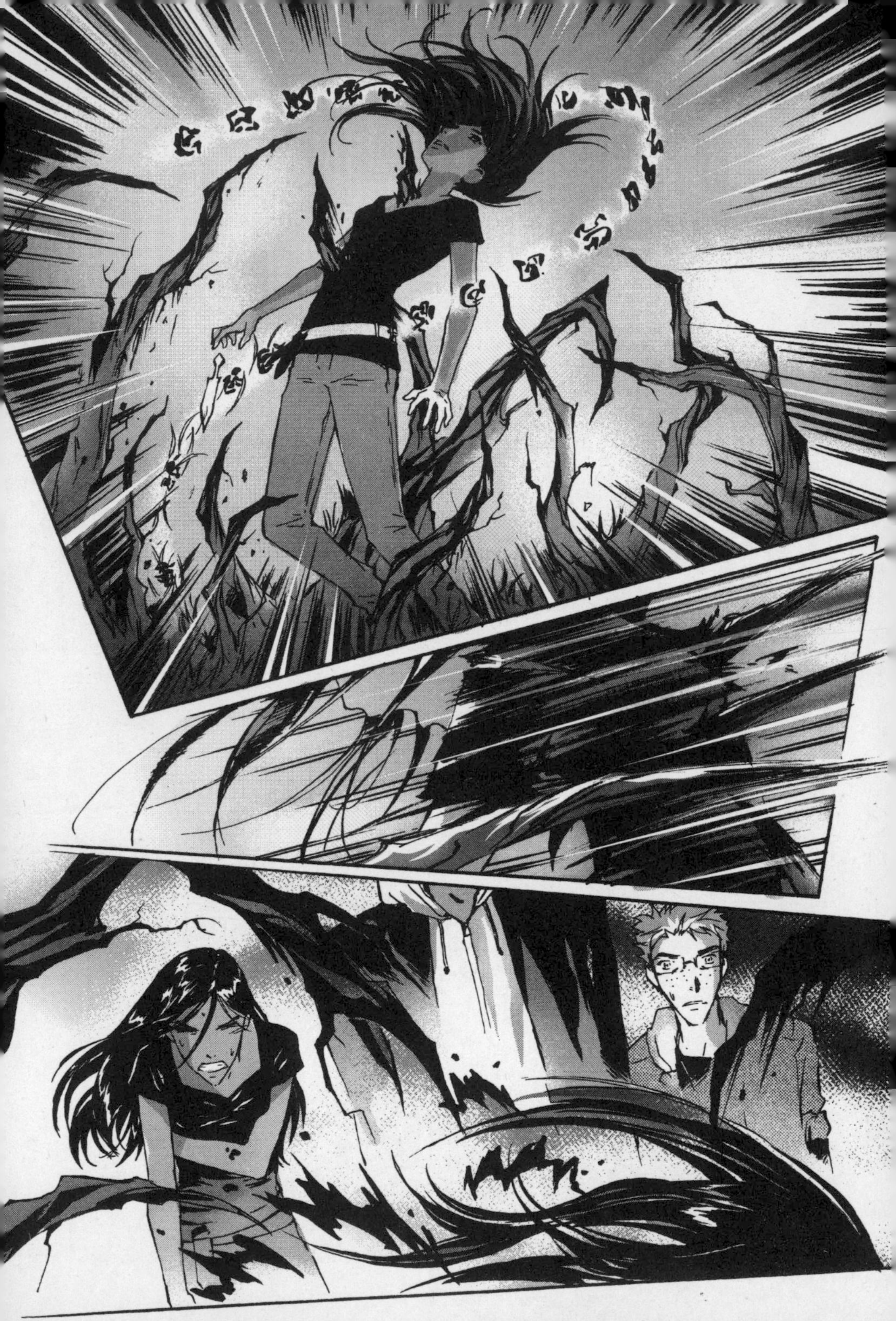

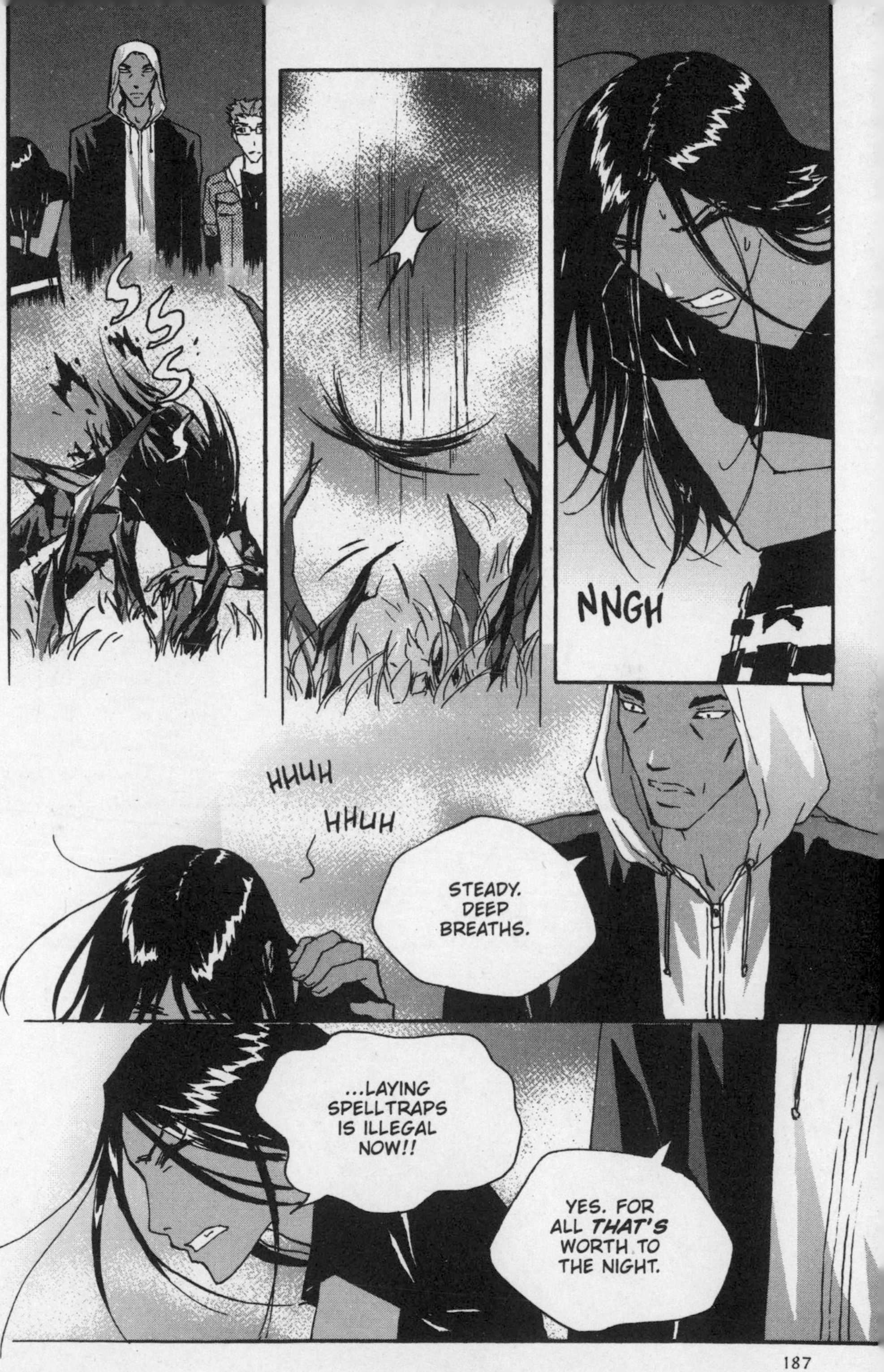
NNGH
HHUH
HHUH
STEADY. DEEP BREATHS.
...LAYING SPELLTRAPS IS ILLEGAL NOW!!
YES. FOR ALL THAT'S WORTH TO THE NIGHT.

DAMMIT...

ARE YOU OKAY?

I'M FINE!!

...

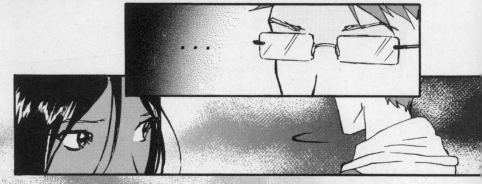

SEE ANYTHING?

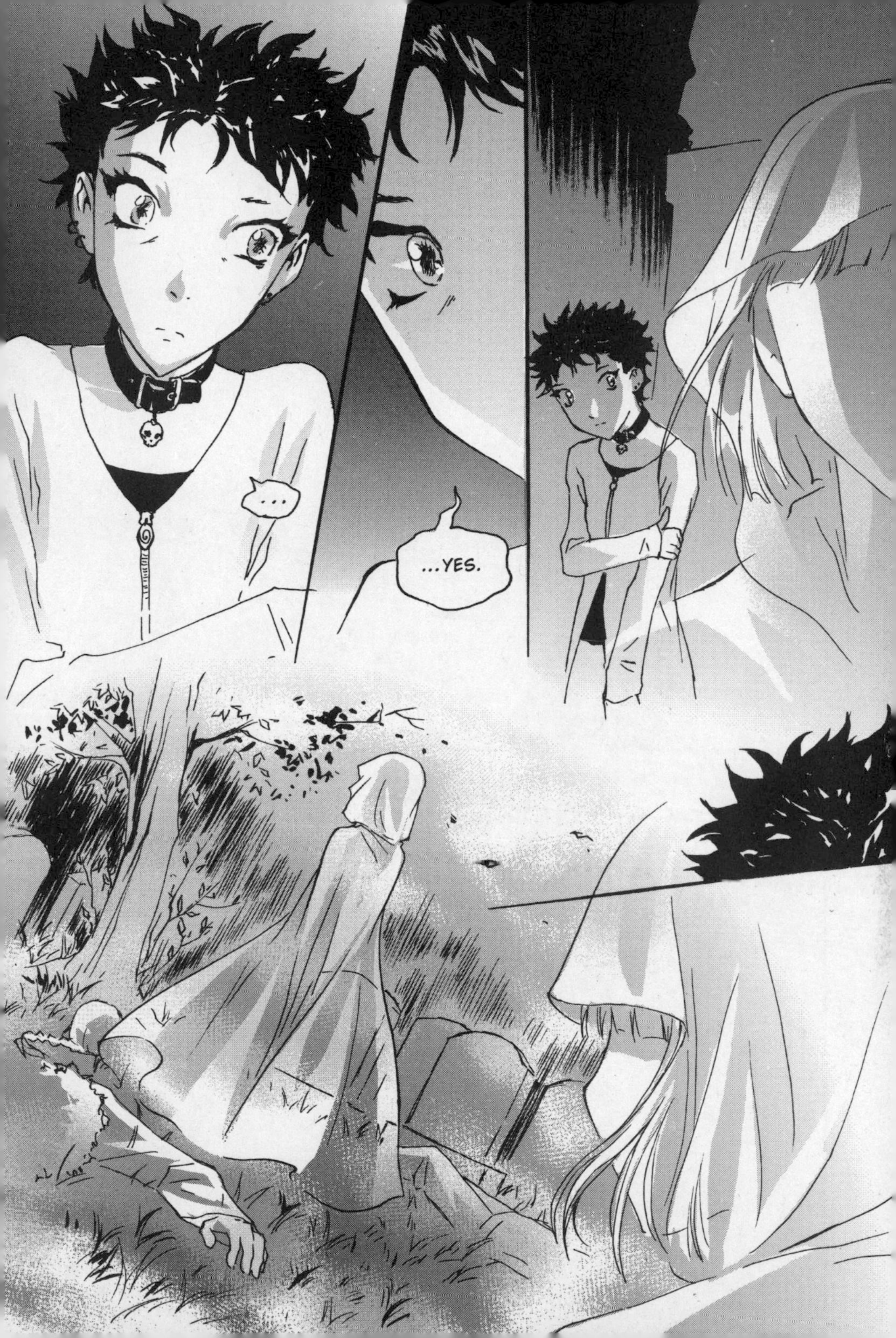
...
...YES.

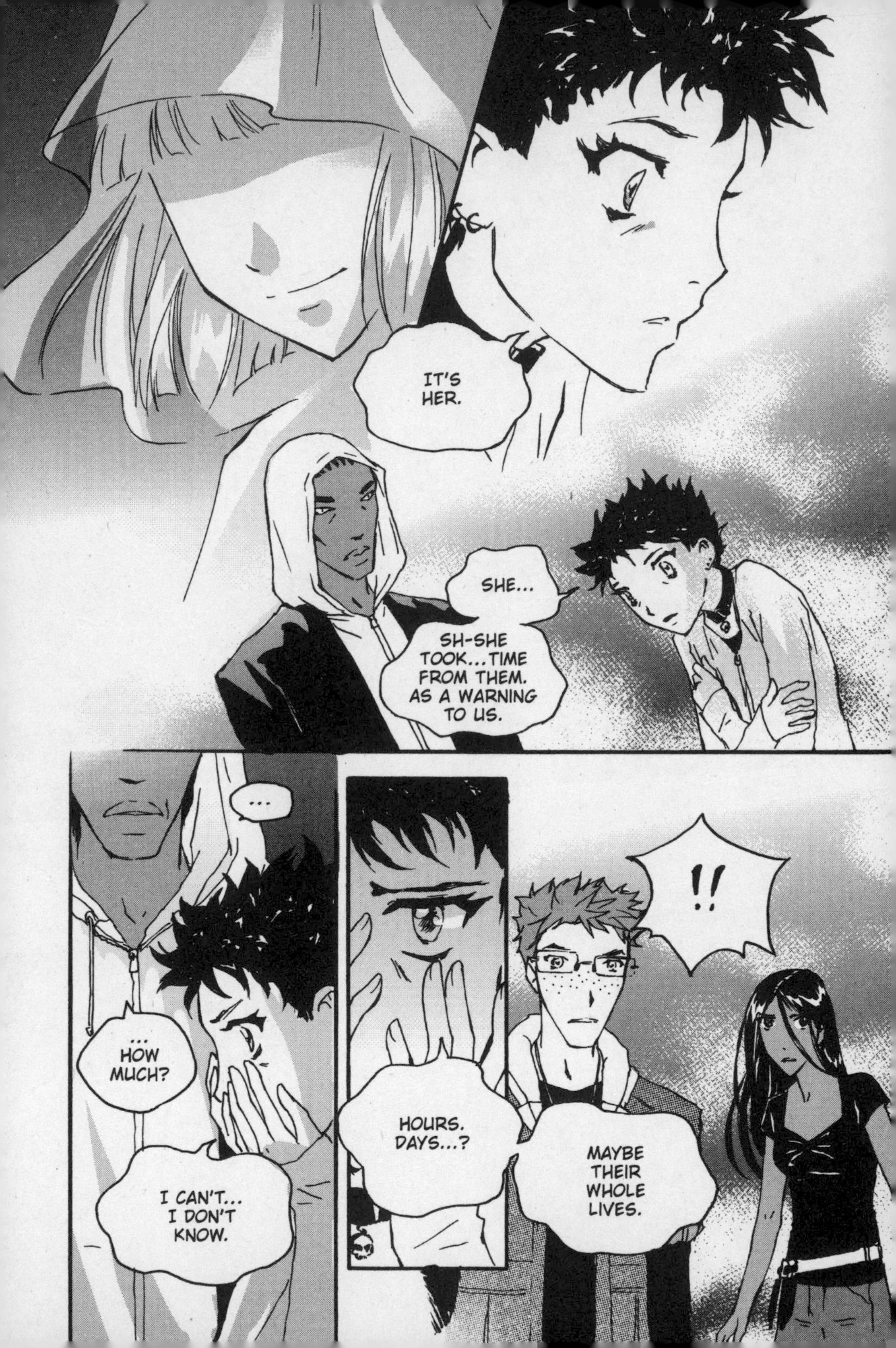
IT'S HER.
SHE...
SH-SHE TOOK...TIME FROM THEM. AS A WARNING TO US.
...
...HOW MUCH?
I CAN'T... I DON'T KNOW.
HOURS. DAYS...?
!!
MAYBE THEIR WHOLE LIVES.

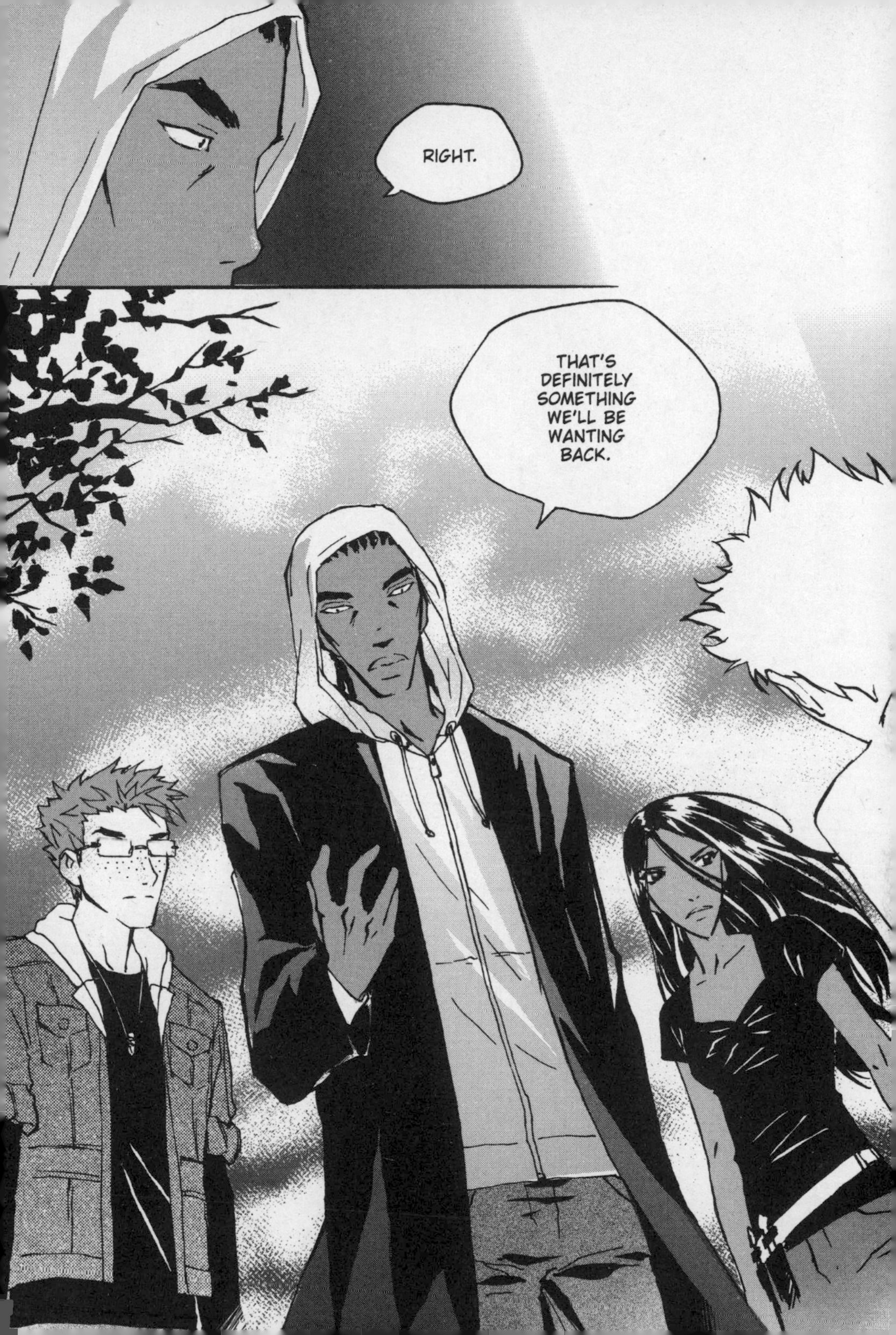
RIGHT.
THAT'S DEFINITELY SOMETHING WE'LL BE WANTING BACK.

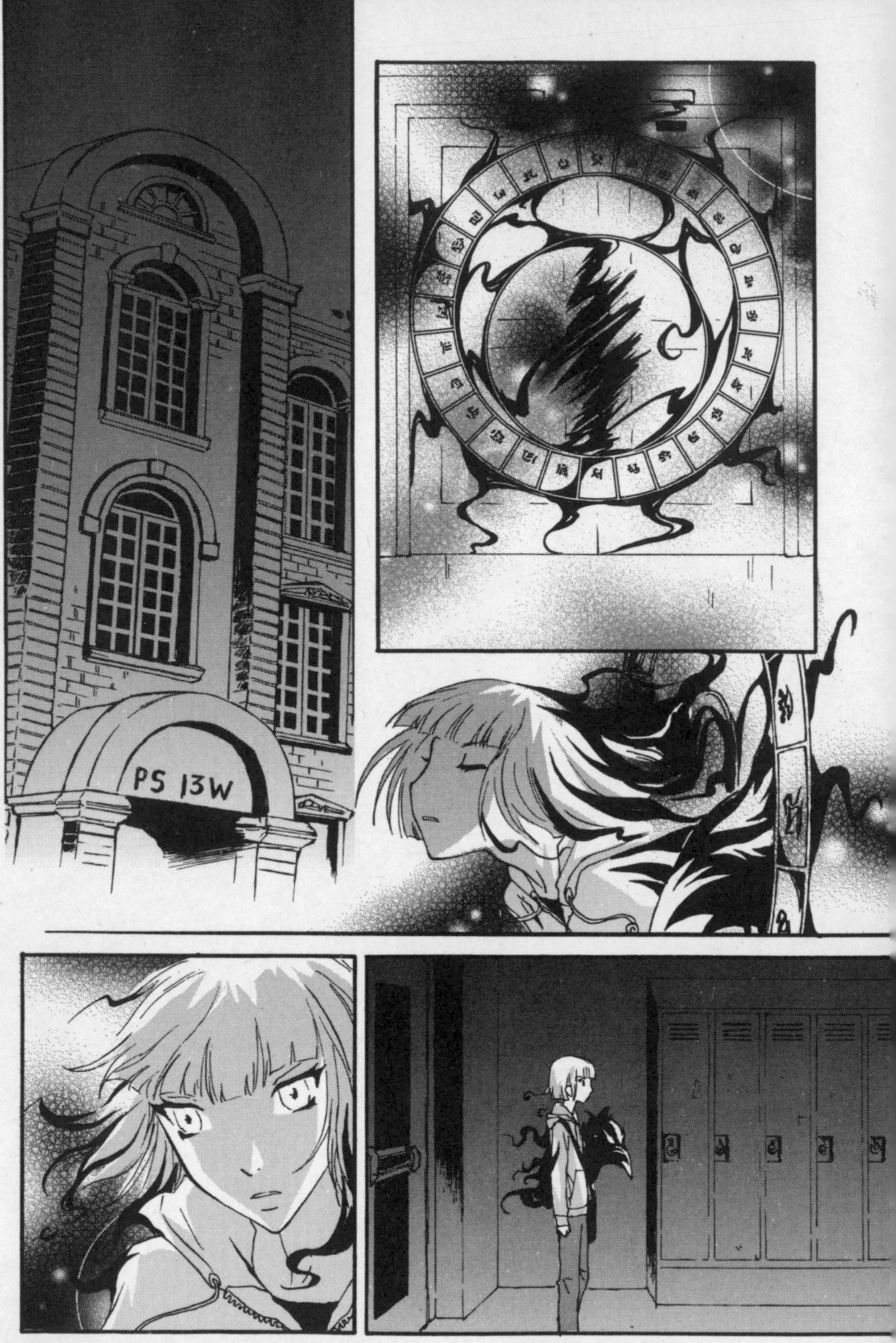
PS 13W

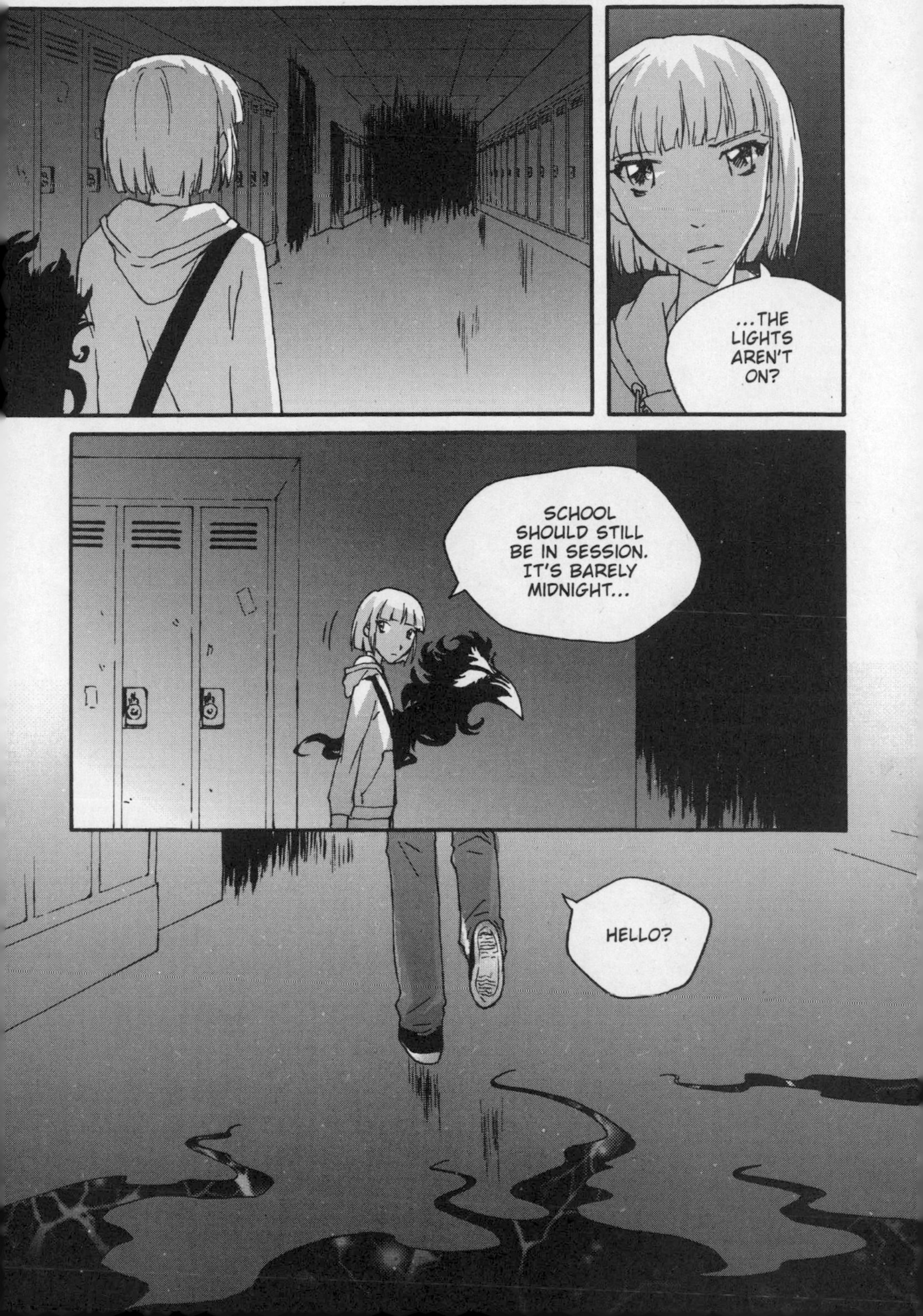
...THE LIGHTS AREN'T ON?
SCHOOL SHOULD STILL BE IN SESSION. IT'S BARELY MIDNIGHT...
HELLO?

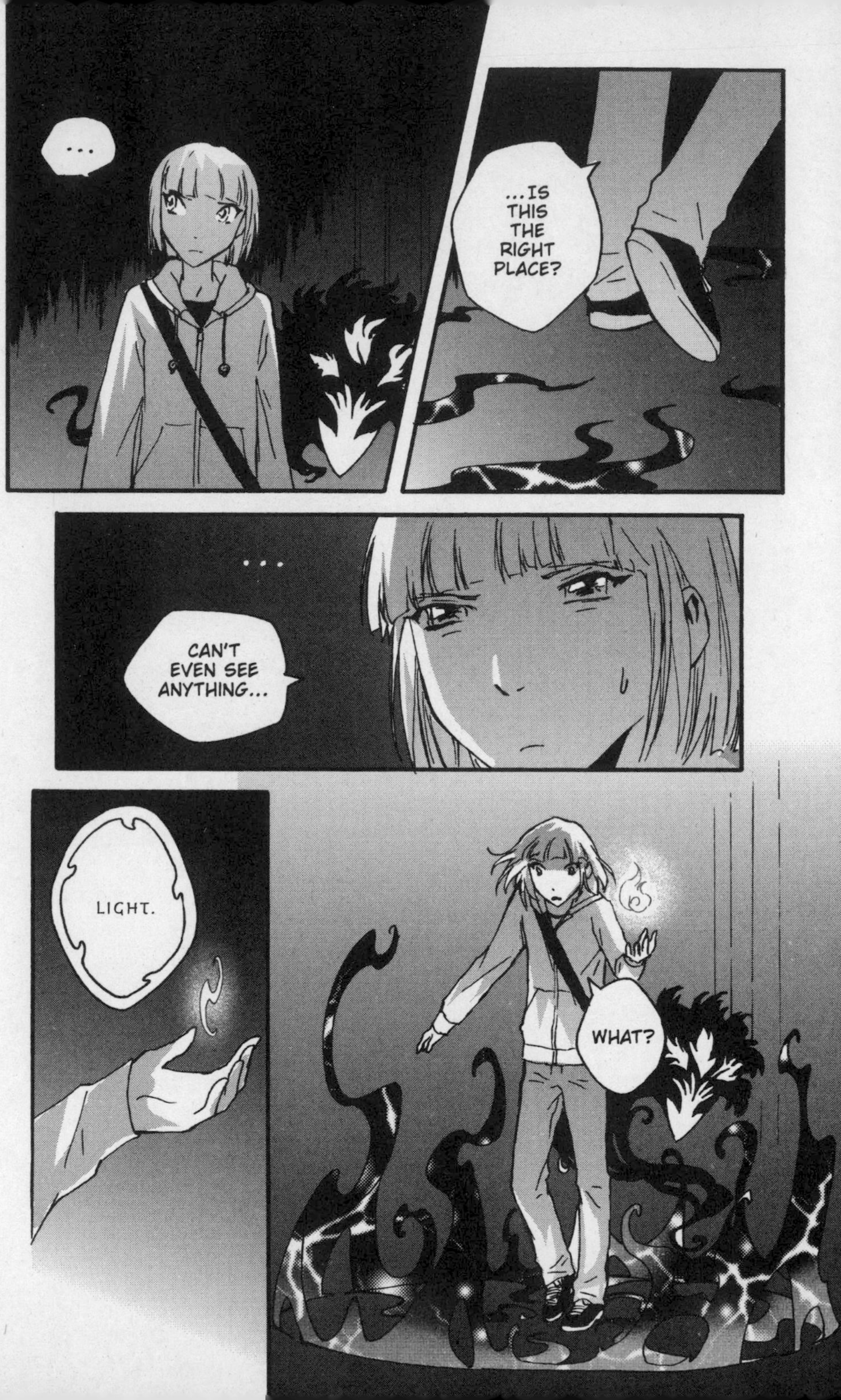
...
...IS THIS THE RIGHT PLACE?
...
CAN'T EVEN SEE ANYTHING...
LIGHT.
WHAT?

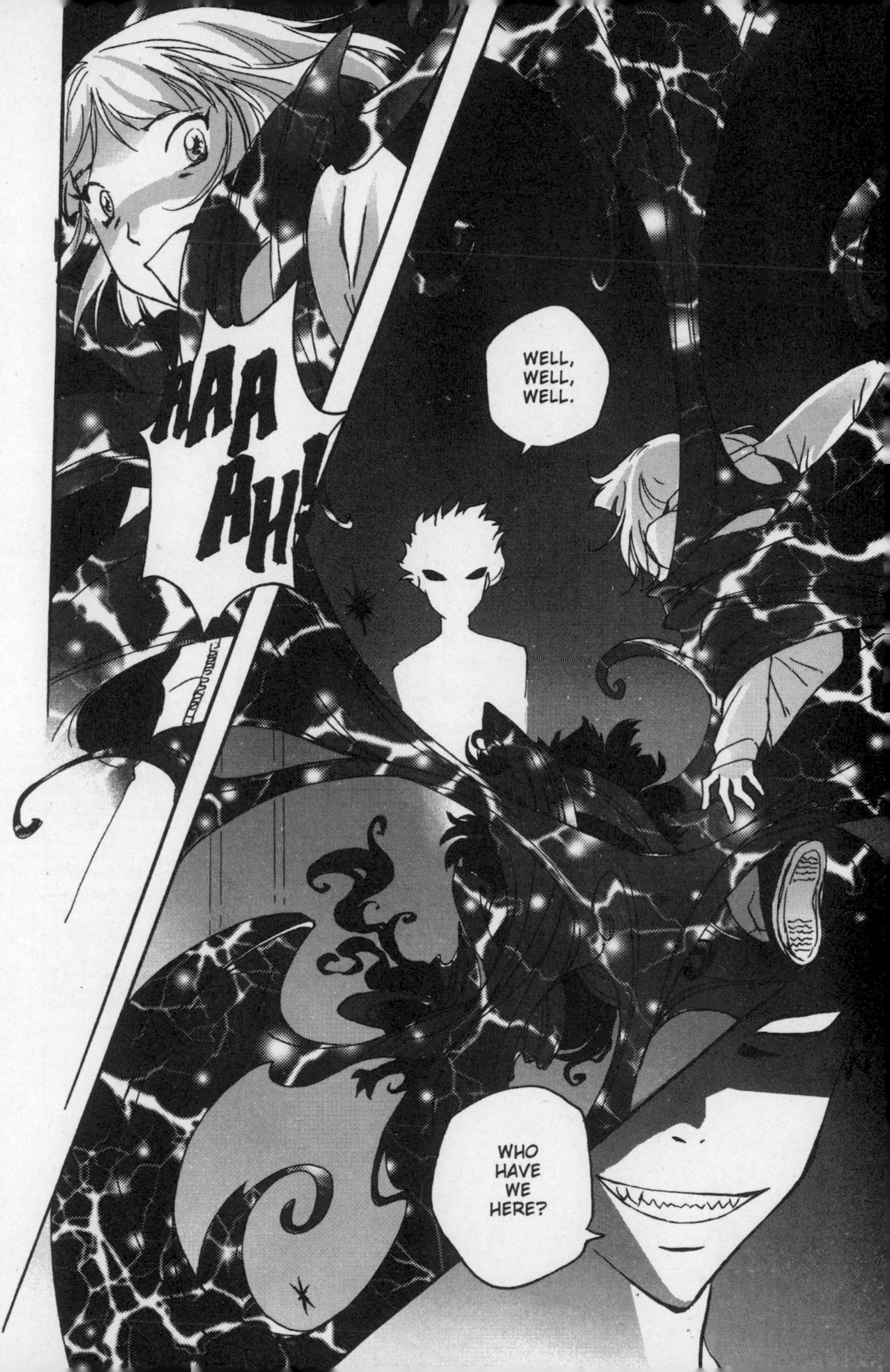
AAAAH!
WELL, WELL, WELL.
WHO HAVE WE HERE?

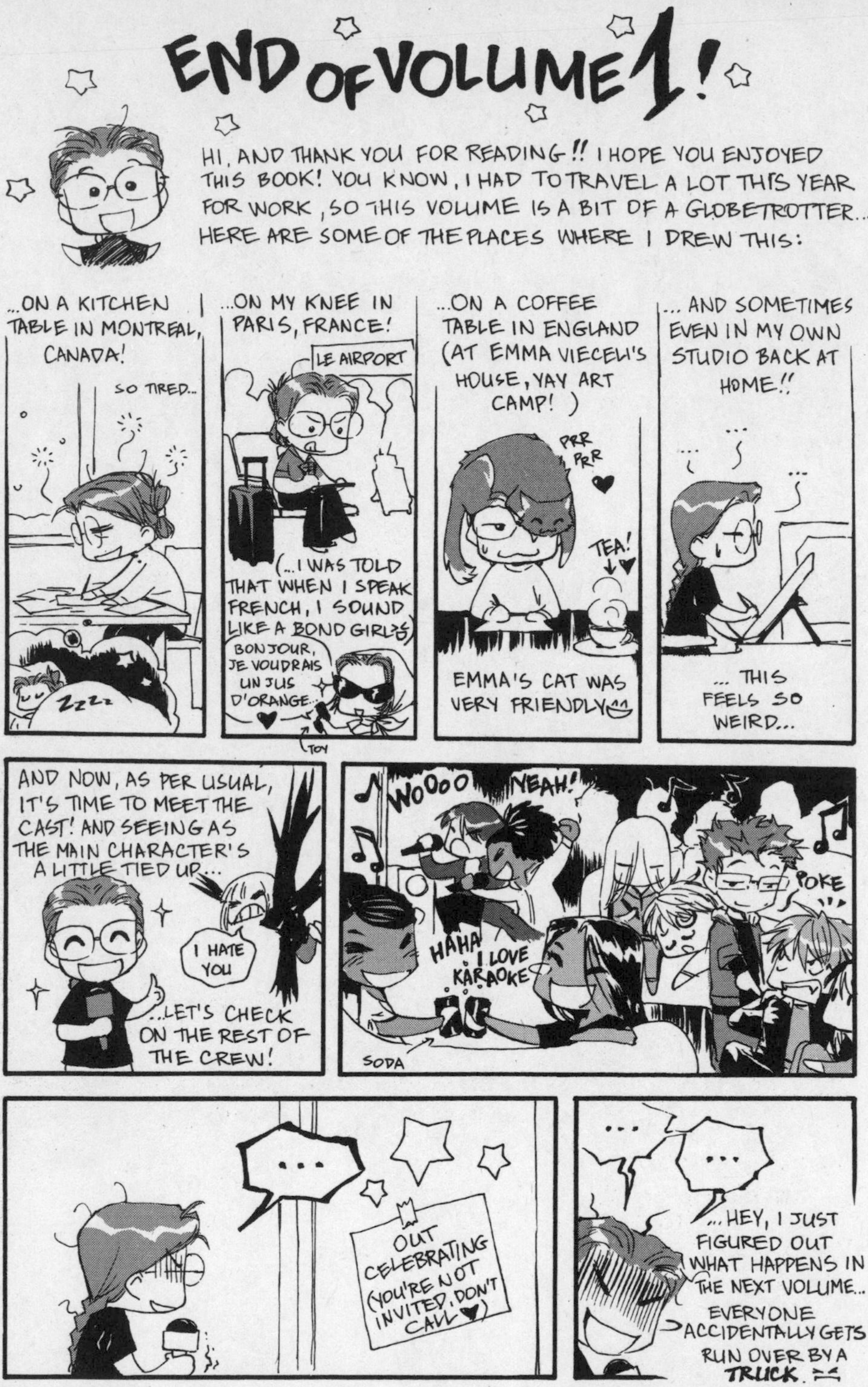
END OF VOLUME 1!
HI, AND THANK YOU FOR READING!! I HOPE YOU ENJOYED THIS BOOK! YOU KNOW, I HAD TO TRAVEL A LOT THIS YEAR FOR WORK, SO THIS VOLUME IS A BIT OF A GLOBETROTTER... HERE ARE SOME OF THE PLACES WHERE I DREW THIS:
...ON A KITCHEN TABLE IN MONTREAL, CANADA!
SO TIRED...
ZZZZ
...ON MY KNEE IN PARIS, FRANCE!
LE AIRPORT
(...I WAS TOLD THAT WHEN I SPEAK FRENCH, I SOUND LIKE A BOND GIRL
BONJOUR, JE VOUDRAIS UN JUS D'ORANGE...
TOY
...ON A COFFEE TABLE IN ENGLAND (AT EMMA VIECELI'S HOUSE, YAY ART CAMP!)
PRR PRR
TEA!
EMMA'S CAT WAS VERY FRIENDLY
... AND SOMETIMES EVEN IN MY OWN STUDIO BACK AT HOME!!
...
...
...
... THIS FEELS SO WEIRD...
AND NOW, AS PER USUAL, IT'S TIME TO MEET THE CAST! AND SEEING AS THE MAIN CHARACTER'S A LITTLE TIED UP...
I HATE YOU
...LET'S CHECK ON THE REST OF THE CREW!
WOOOO
YEAH!
POKE
HAHA
I LOVE KARAOKE
SODA
...
OUT CELEBRATING (YOU'RE NOT INVITED, DON'T CALL)
...
...
...HEY, I JUST FIGURED OUT WHAT HAPPENS IN THE NEXT VOLUME...
EVERYONE ACCIDENTALLY GETS RUN OVER BY A TRUCK.

~THANQ's~

Barry McCarthy -- my high school art teacher. Thank you, Mr. McCarthy, for showing me that I could be an artist and for letting me draw cartoons. (And for making me draw stuff other than cartoons... You were right, it was important :D;;;)

My family and friends -- for being the rocking foundation of the whirlwind that is my life, I couldn't do this half as well without you.

(...Especially without Dee, my long-suffering tone artist with a hunted look in her eyes, and Sasha, my invaluable little sister and life-saver <3)

Yen Press crew ♥ -- this book would not be the same elsewhere. Thank you for helping me run amok on the pages of Yen Plus!!

(...Especially to my editor JuYoun, for guiding me through this very different writing process and for putting up with my loose grasp on the concept of "deadline"... Yes, Lillian, I see you smiling there!! Also, huge thanks to Kurt, for supporting my work all these years and for the encouragement at a time when I really needed it. Thank you, sir!)

Judy! -- my wonderful agent. Thank you for always looking out for me! *HUGS*

Dave and Raina -- those reference pictures helped So Much, I can't even say. Yay!!

Everyone who read this book! ^^ --you, dear readers, are a huge reason for why I am able to do this. Thank you so much for reading, for writing wonderful letters and for sending such amazing art.

I LOVE YOU!!

Jan. 12, 2009
(hope I didn't forget anyone...!)
Svetlana
ALEX WUZ HERE
SEE YOU NEXT TIME!
VAMPIRES R PEEPLE 2
TEN WUZ HERE
WHERE ARE MY PAGES!..
EDITOR'S OFFICE
BUSY POSING FOR AUTHOR PICTURE

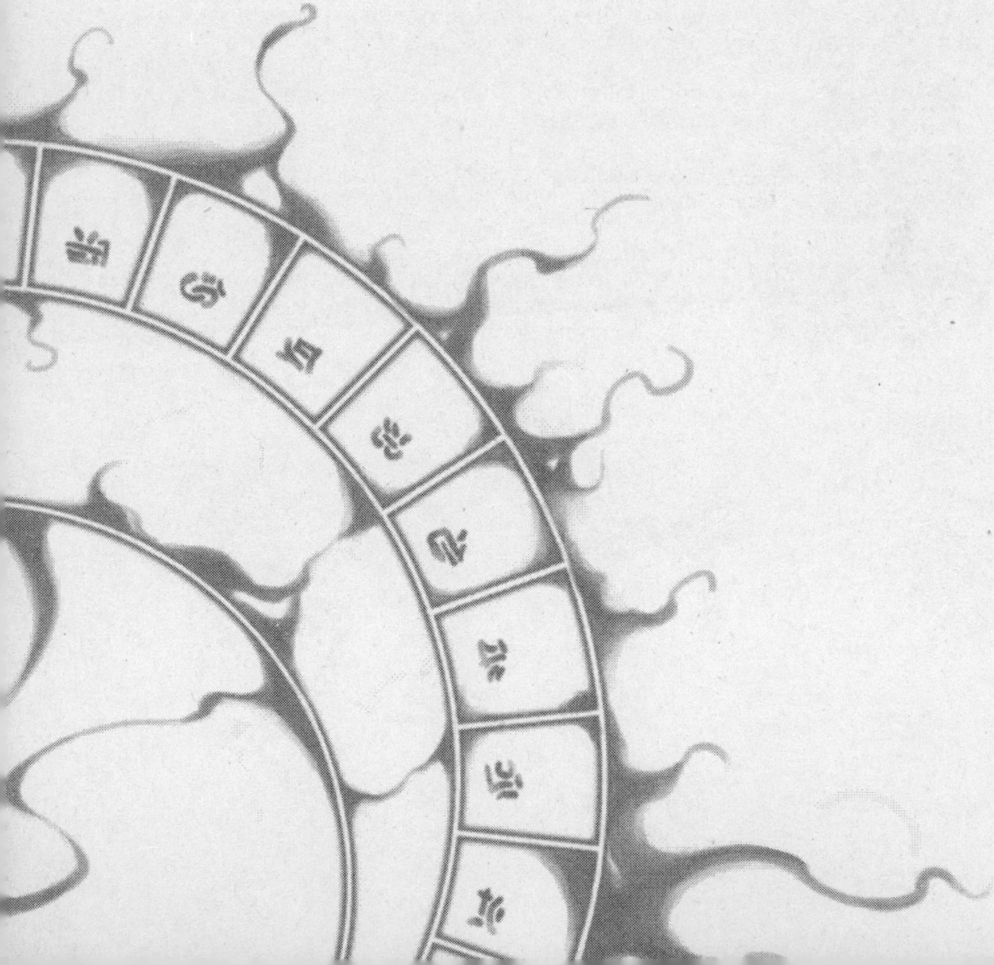

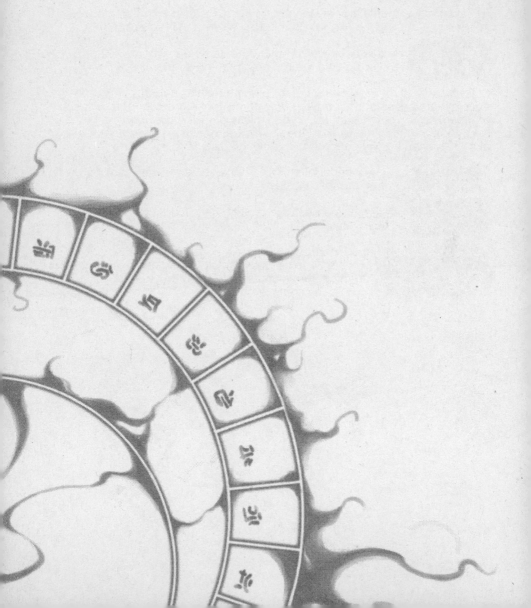

Chapter 7

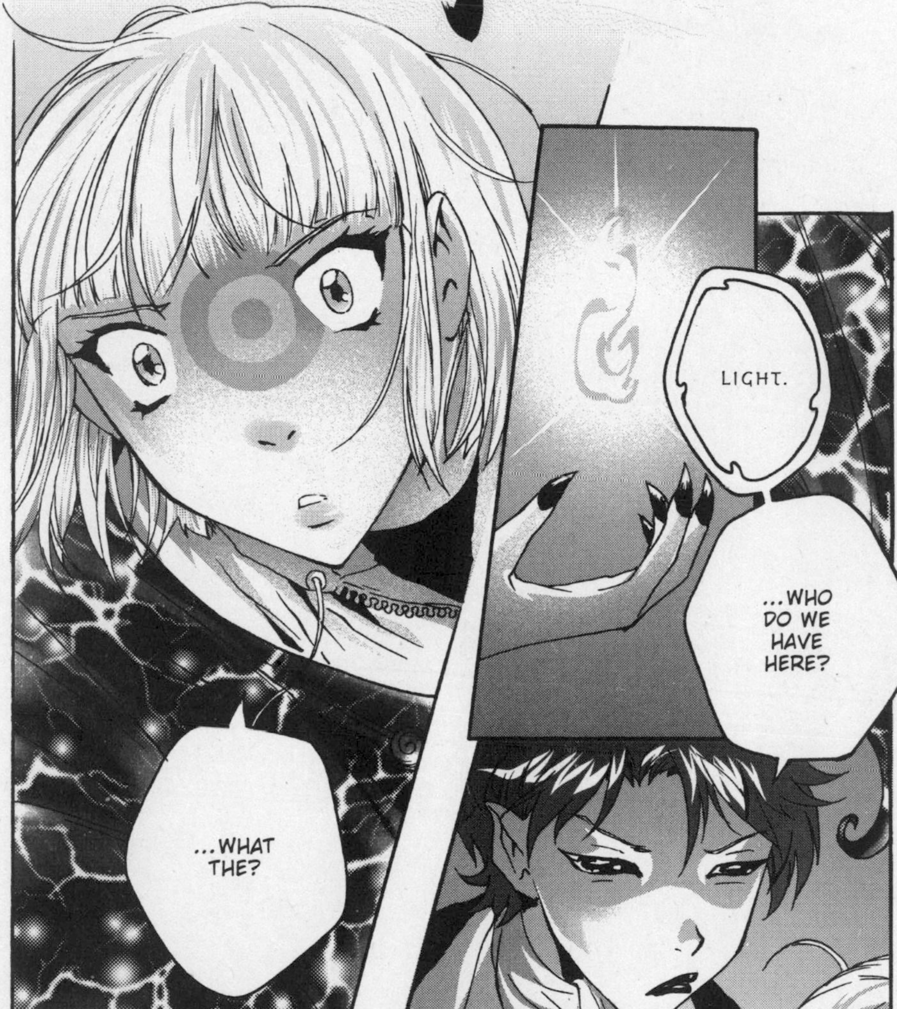
...WHAT THE?
LIGHT.
...WHO DO WE HAVE HERE?

ARE YOU A STUDENT HERE?

UM, NO. I-I'M LOOKING FOR MY SISTER? SARAH TREVENEY? SHE IS THE NIGHT KEEPER HERE?

WHERE IS YOUR NIGHT-PASS?

SARAH TWEENY, SARAH TWEENY...

TREVENEY!

NO, I DON'T KNOW ANYONE BY THAT NAME. AND WE HAVEN'T HAD A NIGHT KEEPER FOR A MONTH.

WHICH IS WHY I AM FORCED TO MAKE THE ROUNDS *MYSELF*, OF ALL THE...

CLAP CLAP

CLARICE, RELEASE THEM.

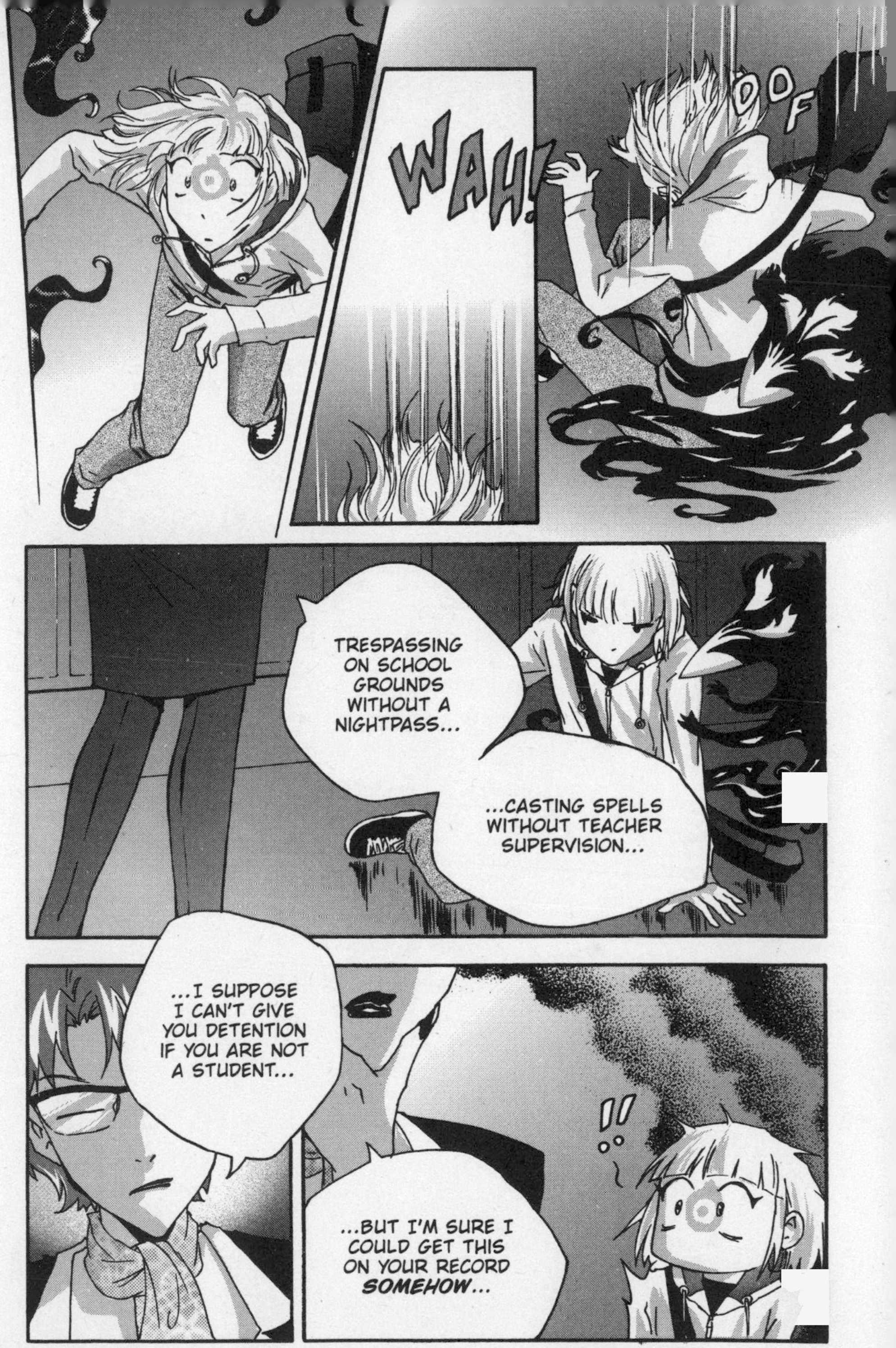
WAH!
OOF
TRESPASSING ON SCHOOL GROUNDS WITHOUT A NIGHTPASS...
...CASTING SPELLS WITHOUT TEACHER SUPERVISION...
...I SUPPOSE I CAN'T GIVE YOU DETENTION IF YOU ARE NOT A STUDENT...
!!
...BUT I'M SURE I COULD GET THIS ON YOUR RECORD ***SOMEHOW***...

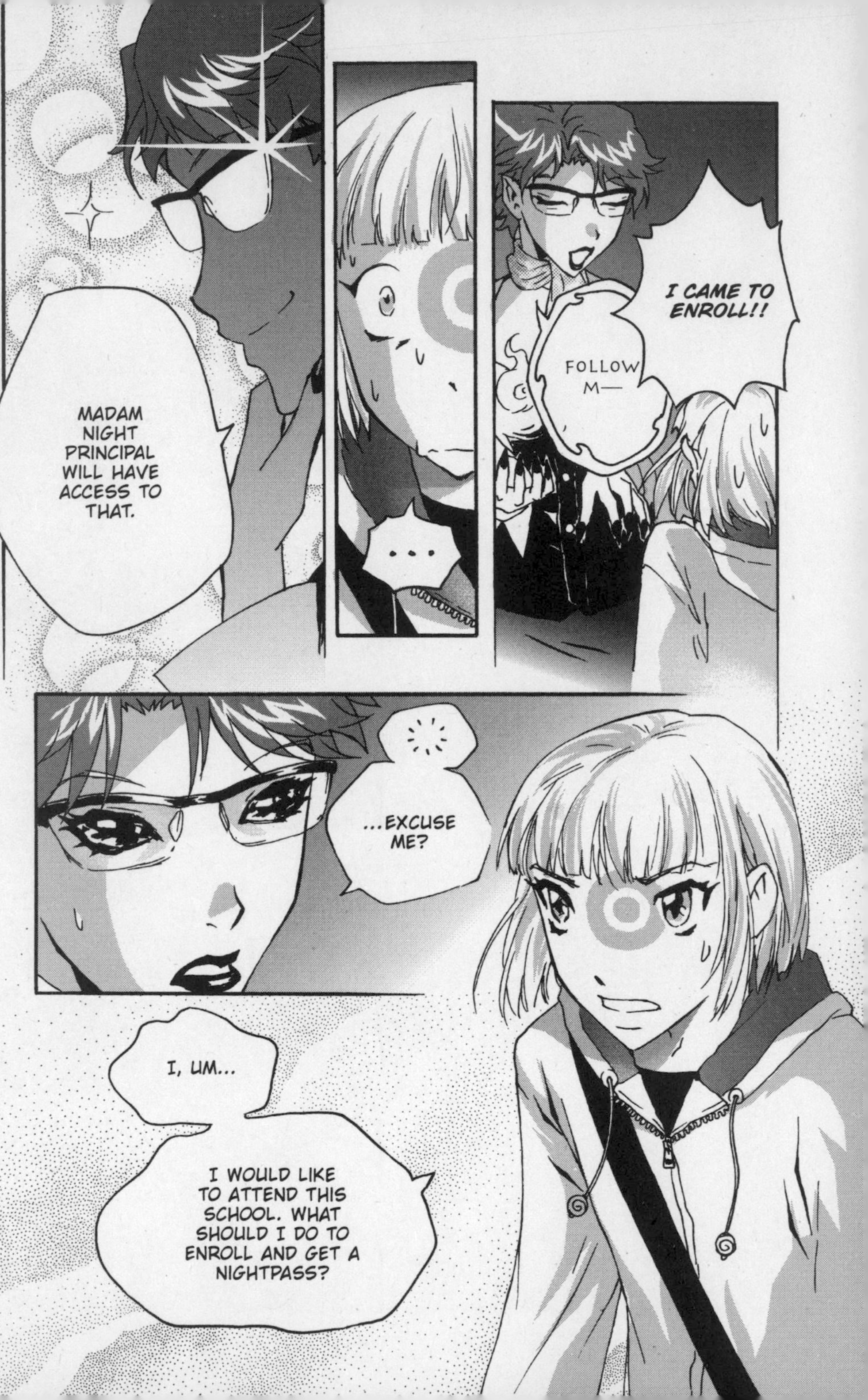
MADAM NIGHT PRINCIPAL WILL HAVE ACCESS TO THAT.
...
FOLLOW M—
I CAME TO ENROLL!!
...EXCUSE ME?
I, UM...
I WOULD LIKE TO ATTEND THIS SCHOOL. WHAT SHOULD I DO TO ENROLL AND GET A NIGHTPASS?

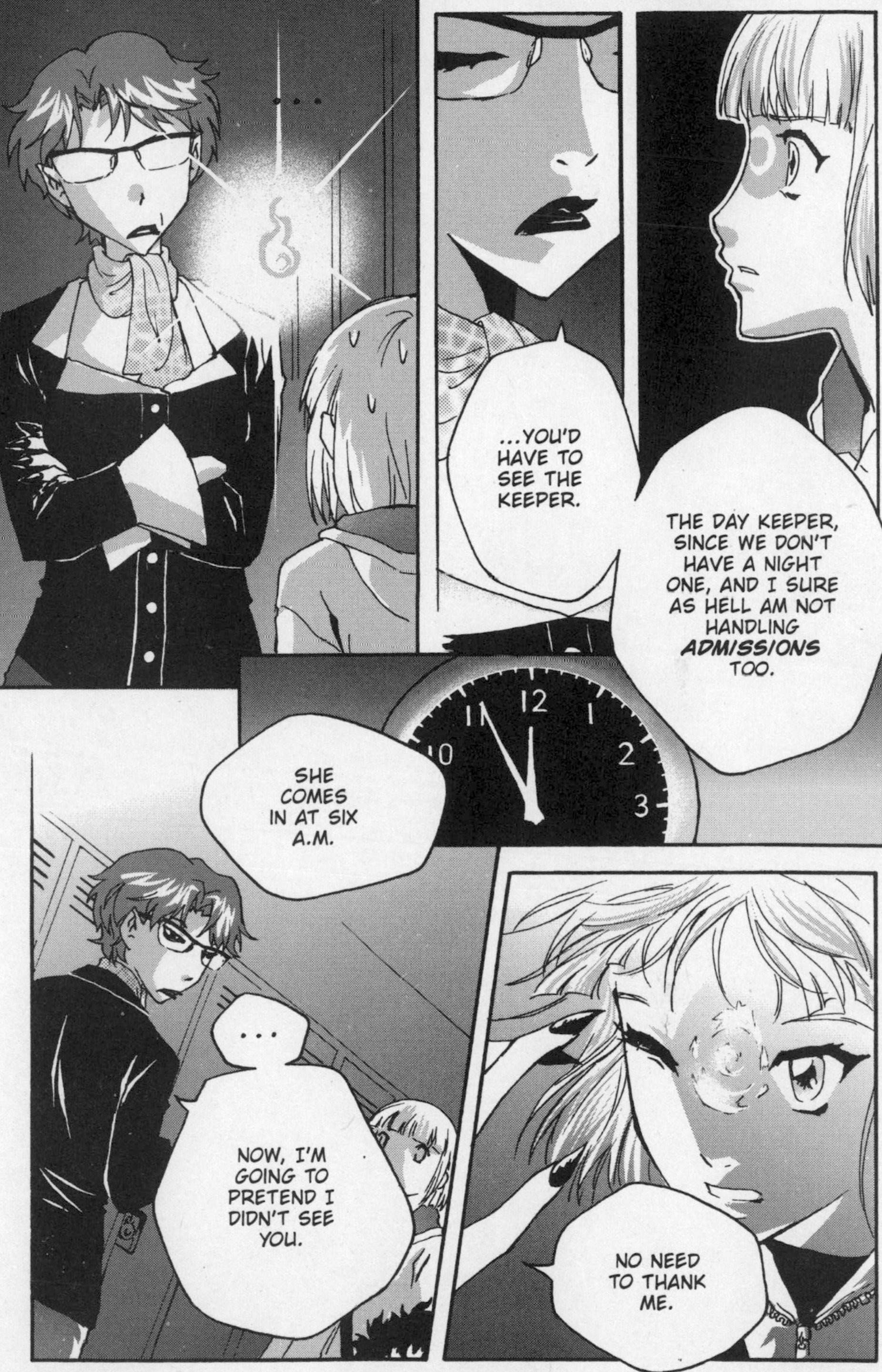
...YOU'D HAVE TO SEE THE KEEPER.
THE DAY KEEPER, SINCE WE DON'T HAVE A NIGHT ONE, AND I SURE AS HELL AM NOT HANDLING ***ADMISSIONS*** TOO.
12 1 2 3 10 11
SHE COMES IN AT SIX A.M.
...
NOW, I'M GOING TO PRETEND I DIDN'T SEE YOU.
NO NEED TO THANK ME.

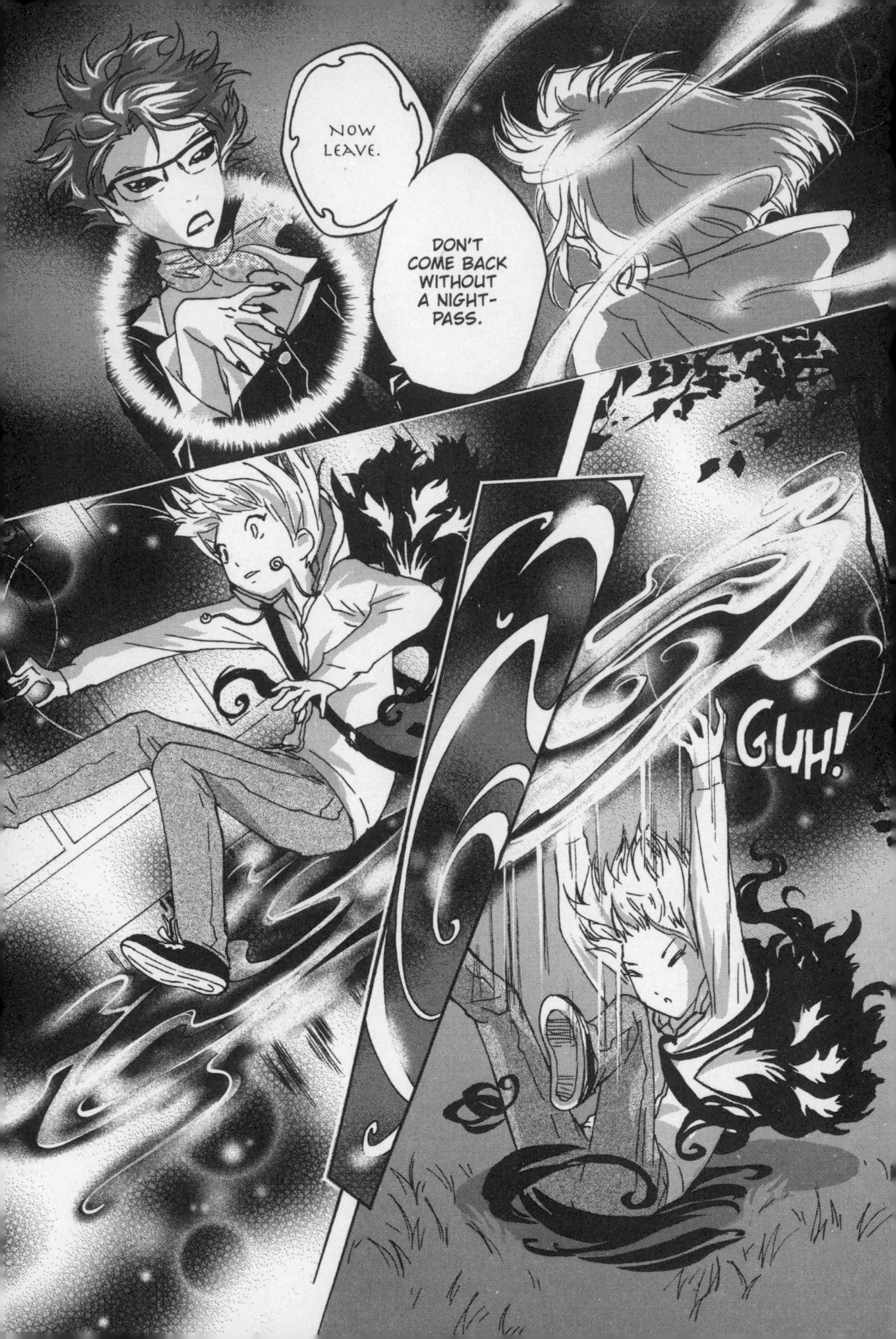
NOW LEAVE.
DON'T COME BACK WITHOUT A NIGHT-PASS.
GUH!

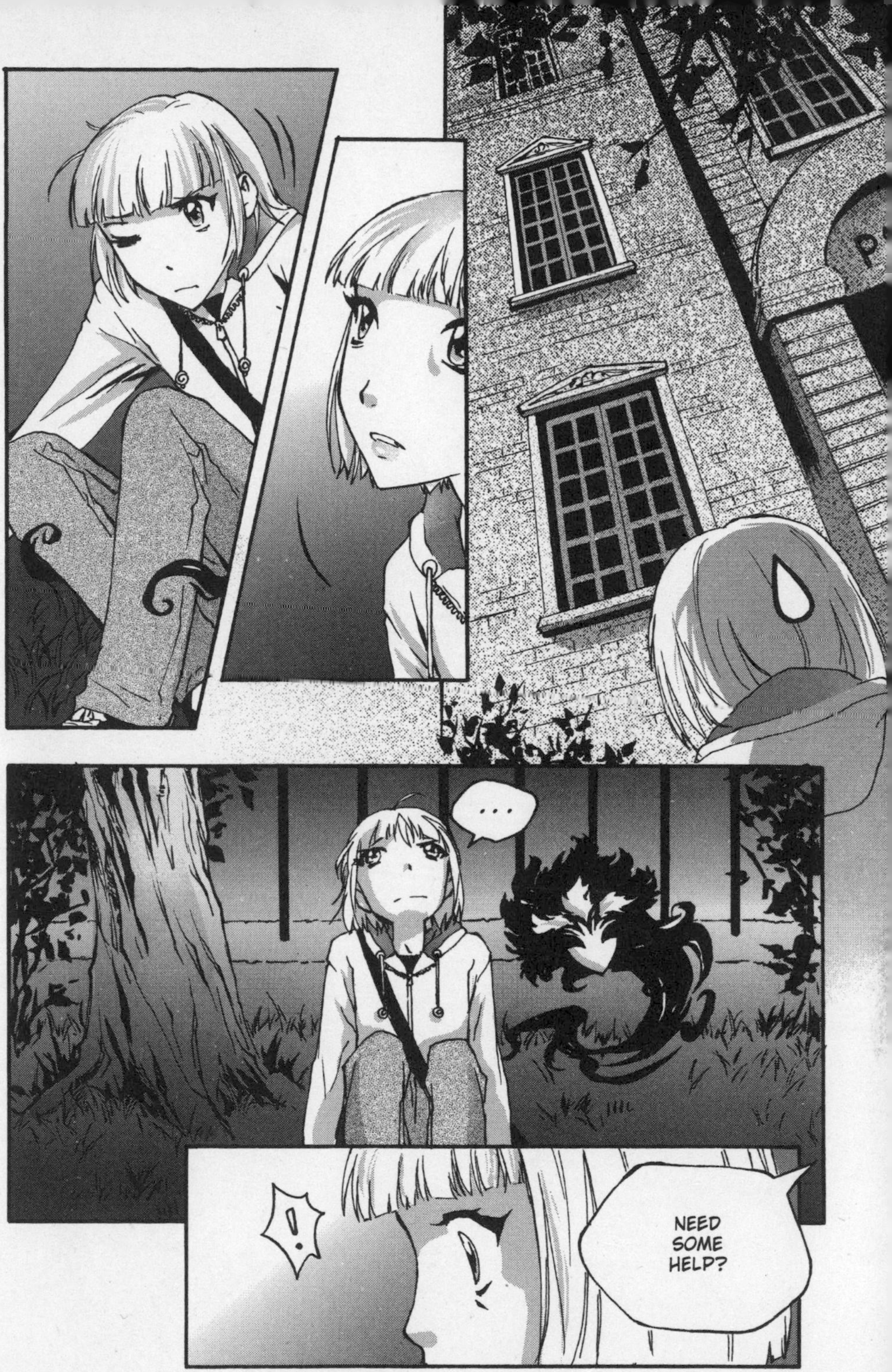
...
!
NEED SOME HELP?

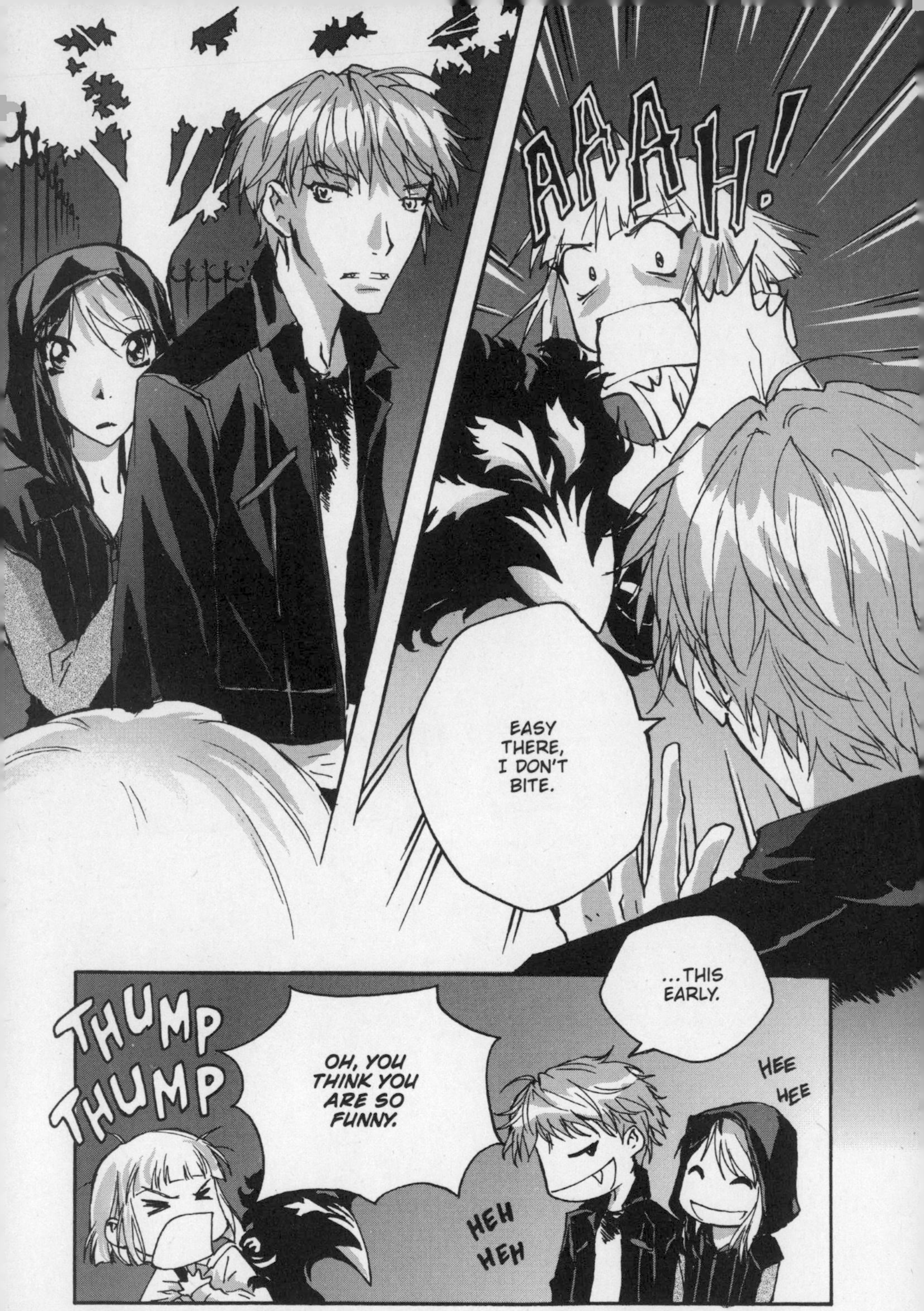
AAAH!
EASY THERE, I DON'T BITE.
THUMP THUMP
...THIS EARLY.
OH, YOU THINK YOU ARE SO FUNNY.
HEE HEE
HEH HEH

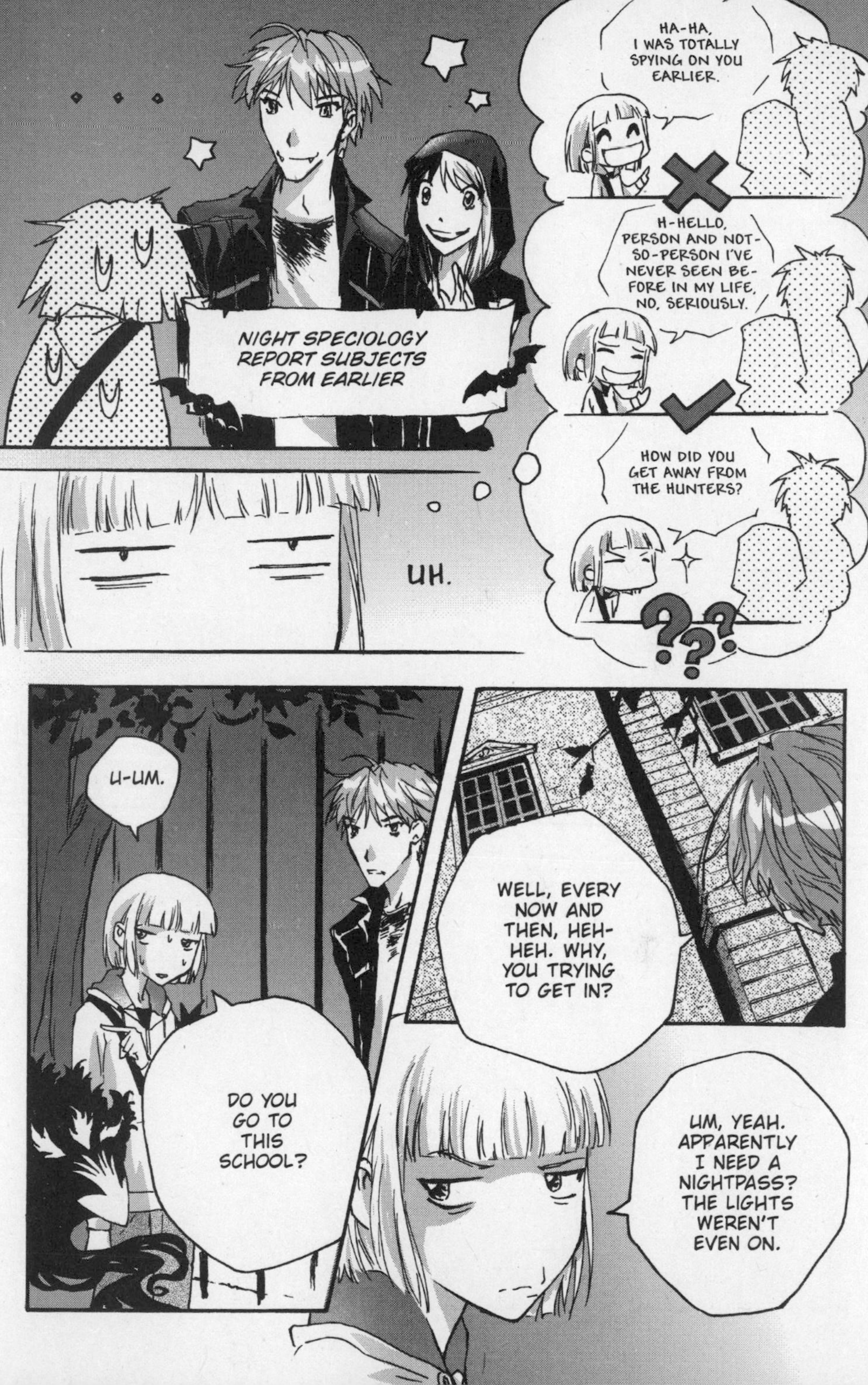
NIGHT SPECIOLOGY REPORT SUBJECTS FROM EARLIER
HA-HA, I WAS TOTALLY SPYING ON YOU EARLIER.
H-HELLO, PERSON AND NOT-SO-PERSON I'VE NEVER SEEN BEFORE IN MY LIFE, NO, SERIOUSLY.
HOW DID YOU GET AWAY FROM THE HUNTERS?
UH.
U-UM.
DO YOU GO TO THIS SCHOOL?
WELL, EVERY NOW AND THEN, HEH-HEH. WHY, YOU TRYING TO GET IN?
UM, YEAH. APPARENTLY I NEED A NIGHTPASS? THE LIGHTS WEREN'T EVEN ON.

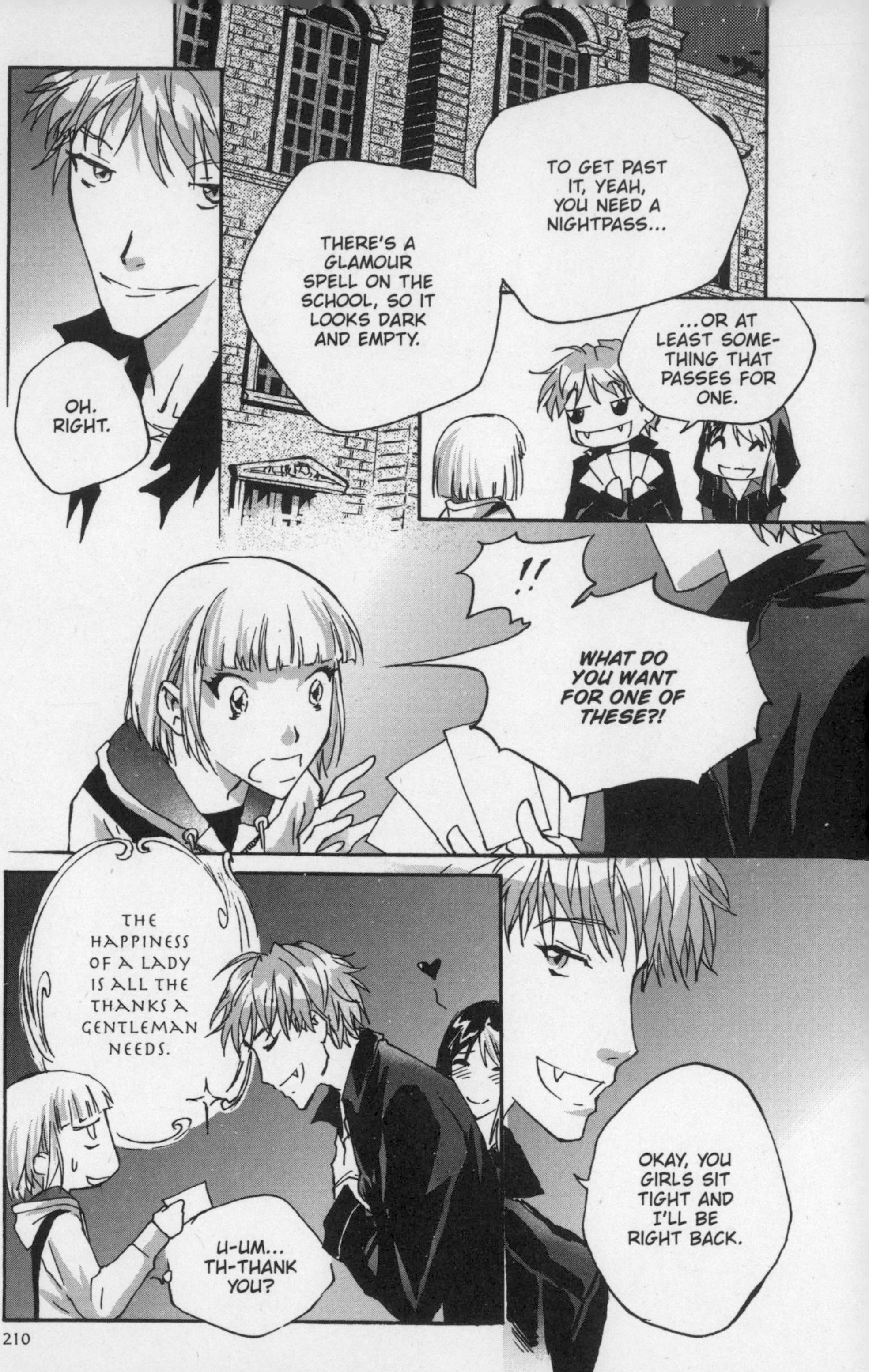
OH. RIGHT.
THERE'S A GLAMOUR SPELL ON THE SCHOOL, SO IT LOOKS DARK AND EMPTY.
TO GET PAST IT, YEAH, YOU NEED A NIGHTPASS...
...OR AT LEAST SOME-THING THAT PASSES FOR ONE.
!!
WHAT DO YOU WANT FOR ONE OF THESE?!
THE HAPPINESS OF A LADY IS ALL THE THANKS A GENTLEMAN NEEDS.
U-UM... TH-THANK YOU?
OKAY, YOU GIRLS SIT TIGHT AND I'LL BE RIGHT BACK.

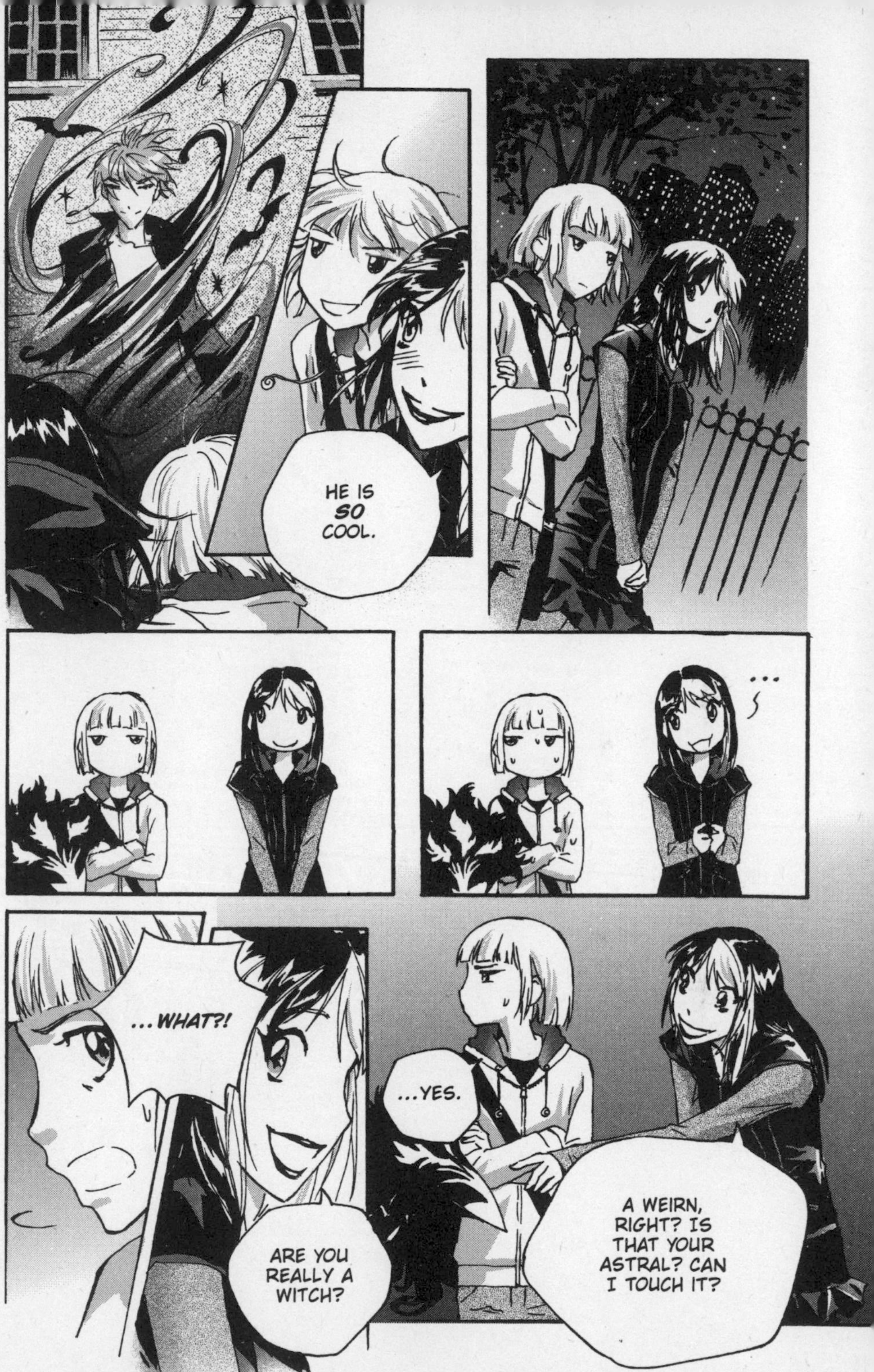
HE IS SO COOL.
...
...WHAT?!
ARE YOU REALLY A WITCH?
...YES.
A WEIRN, RIGHT? IS THAT YOUR ASTRAL? CAN I TOUCH IT?

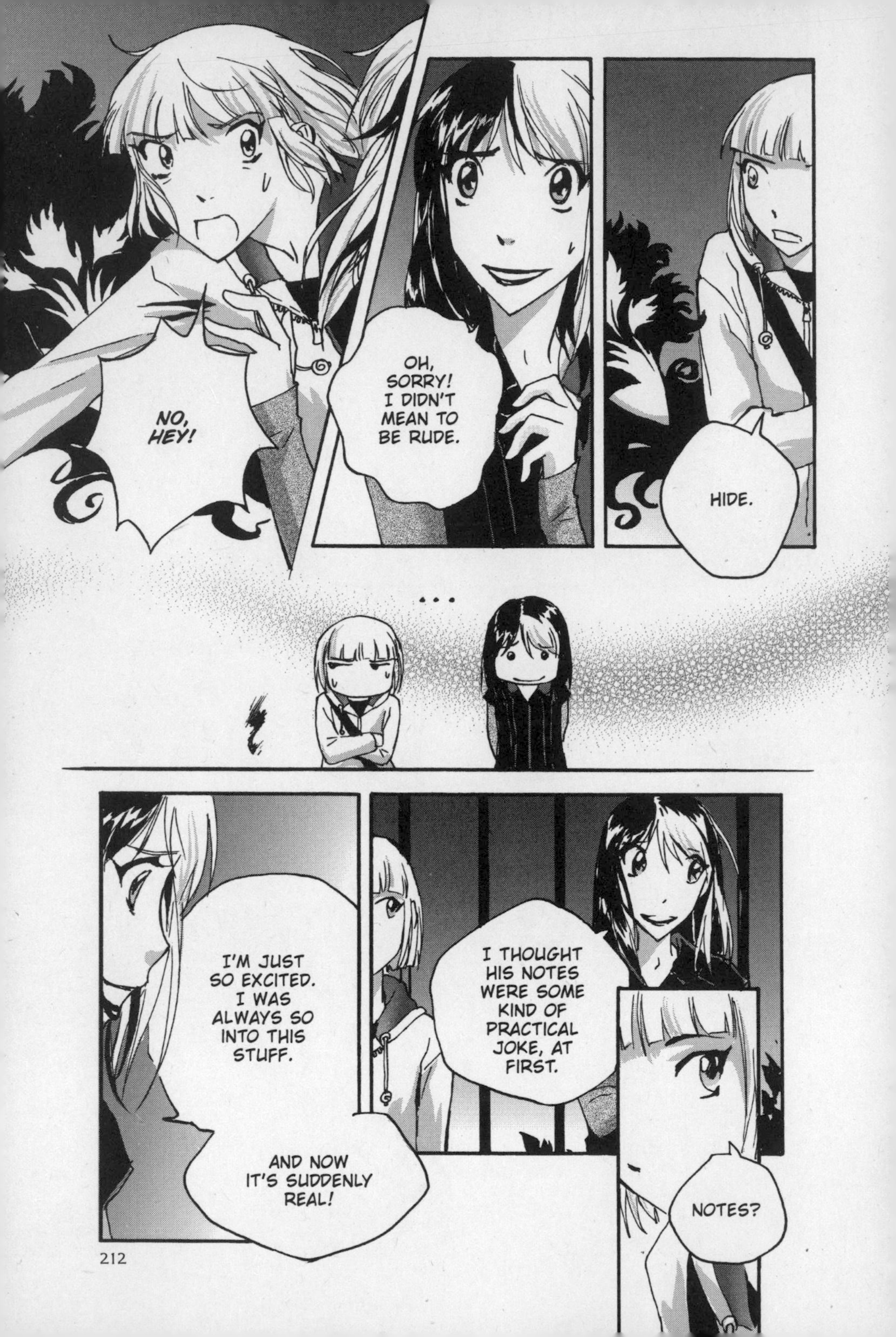
NO, HEY!
OH, SORRY! I DIDN'T MEAN TO BE RUDE.
HIDE.
...
I'M JUST SO EXCITED. I WAS ALWAYS SO INTO THIS STUFF.
AND NOW IT'S SUDDENLY REAL!
I THOUGHT HIS NOTES WERE SOME KIND OF PRACTICAL JOKE, AT FIRST.
NOTES?

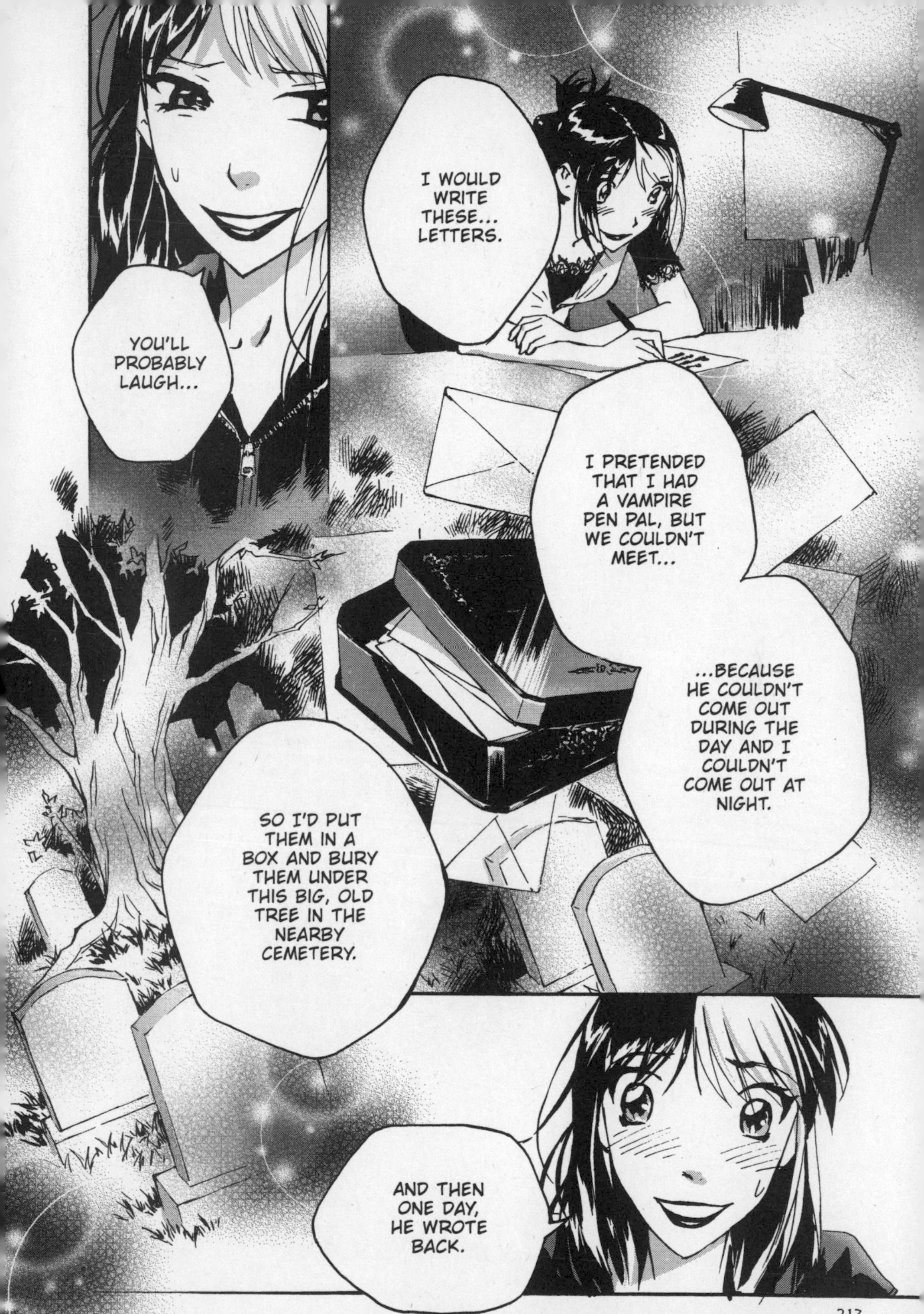
YOU'LL PROBABLY LAUGH...
I WOULD WRITE THESE... LETTERS.
I PRETENDED THAT I HAD A VAMPIRE PEN PAL, BUT WE COULDN'T MEET...
...BECAUSE HE COULDN'T COME OUT DURING THE DAY AND I COULDN'T COME OUT AT NIGHT.
SO I'D PUT THEM IN A BOX AND BURY THEM UNDER THIS BIG, OLD TREE IN THE NEARBY CEMETERY.
AND THEN ONE DAY, HE WROTE BACK.

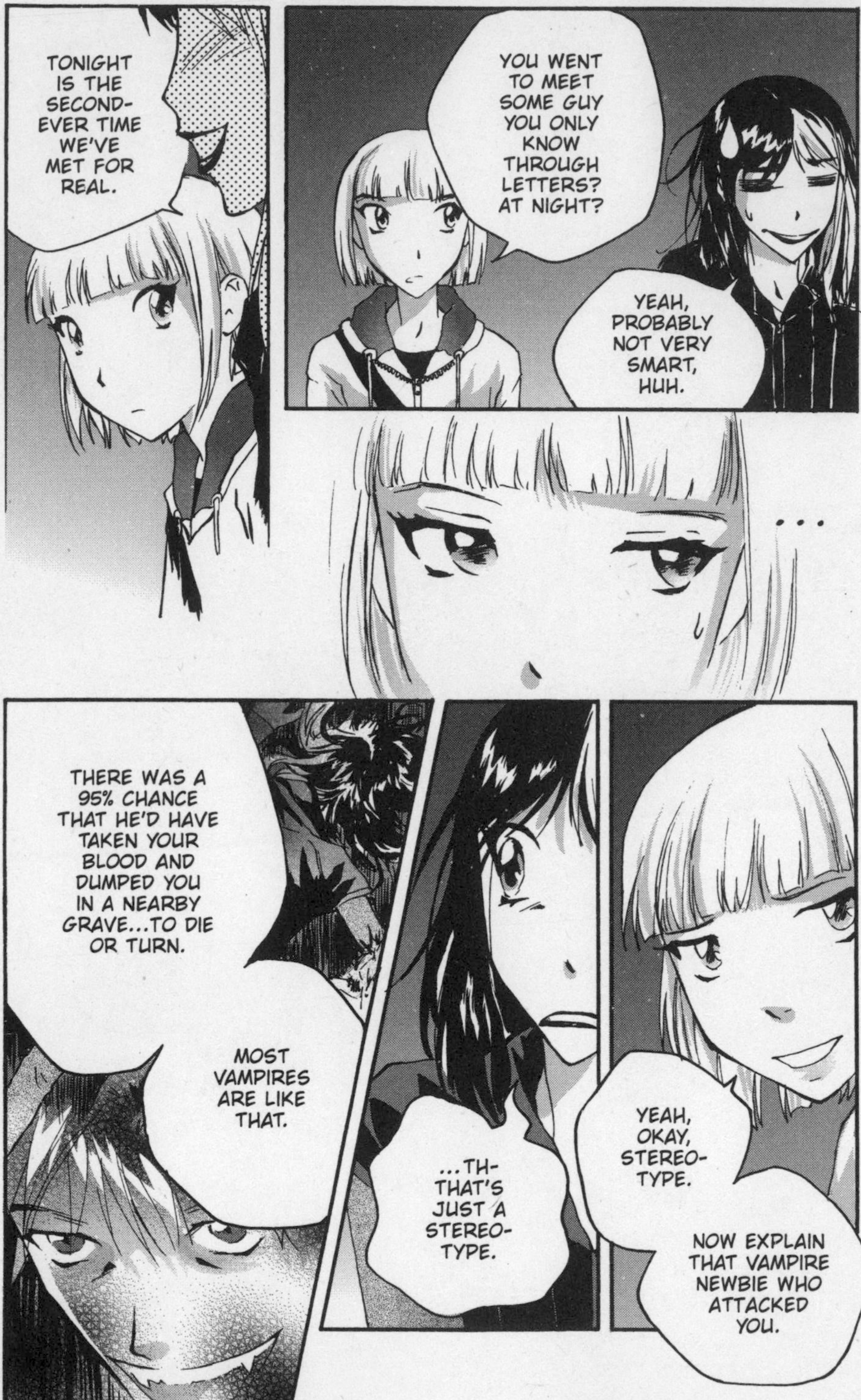
TONIGHT IS THE SECOND-EVER TIME WE'VE MET FOR REAL.
YOU WENT TO MEET SOME GUY YOU ONLY KNOW THROUGH LETTERS? AT NIGHT?
YEAH, PROBABLY NOT VERY SMART, HUH.
...
THERE WAS A 95% CHANCE THAT HE'D HAVE TAKEN YOUR BLOOD AND DUMPED YOU IN A NEARBY GRAVE...TO DIE OR TURN.
MOST VAMPIRES ARE LIKE THAT.
...TH-THAT'S JUST A STEREO-TYPE.
YEAH, OKAY, STEREO-TYPE.
NOW EXPLAIN THAT VAMPIRE NEWBIE WHO ATTACKED YOU.

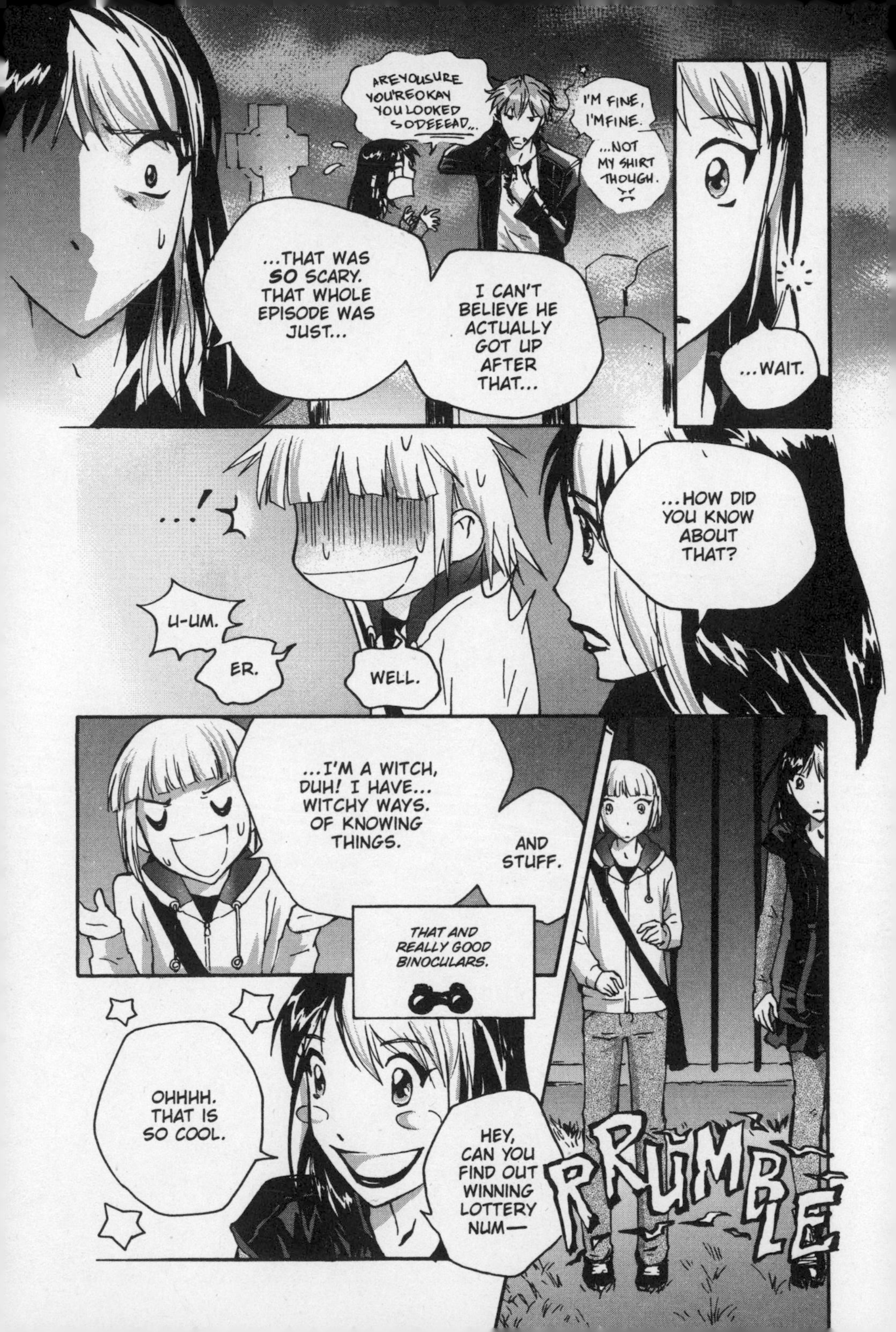

ARE YOU SURE YOU'RE OKAY YOU LOOKED SO DEEEEAD...
I'M FINE, I'M FINE.
...NOT MY SHIRT THOUGH.
...THAT WAS SO SCARY. THAT WHOLE EPISODE WAS JUST...
I CAN'T BELIEVE HE ACTUALLY GOT UP AFTER THAT...
...WAIT.
...!
...HOW DID YOU KNOW ABOUT THAT?
U-UM.
ER.
WELL.
...I'M A WITCH, DUH! I HAVE... WITCHY WAYS. OF KNOWING THINGS.
AND STUFF.
THAT AND REALLY GOOD BINOCULARS.
OHHHH. THAT IS SO COOL.
HEY, CAN YOU FIND OUT WINNING LOTTERY NUM—
RRUMBLE

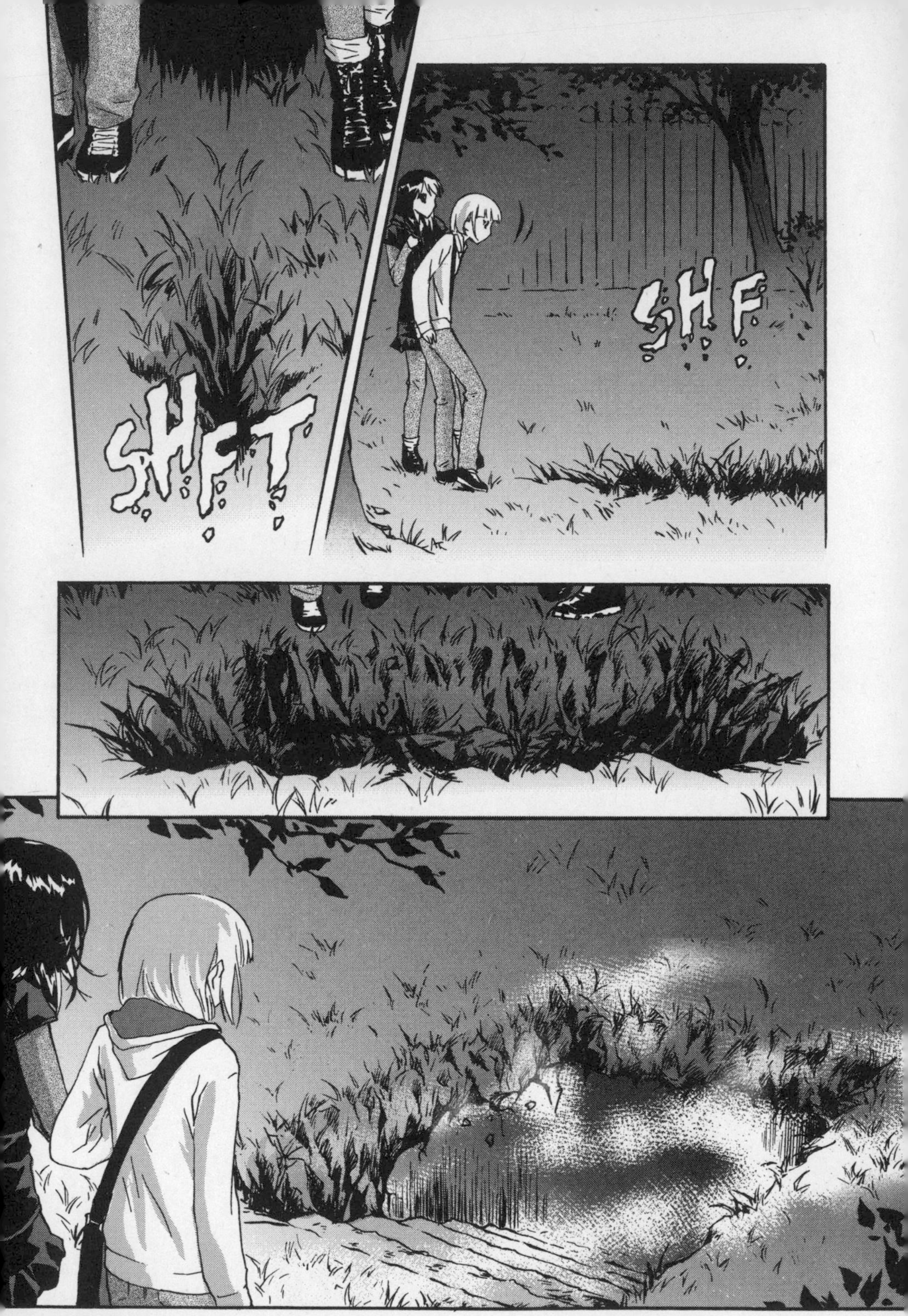
SHFT
SHF

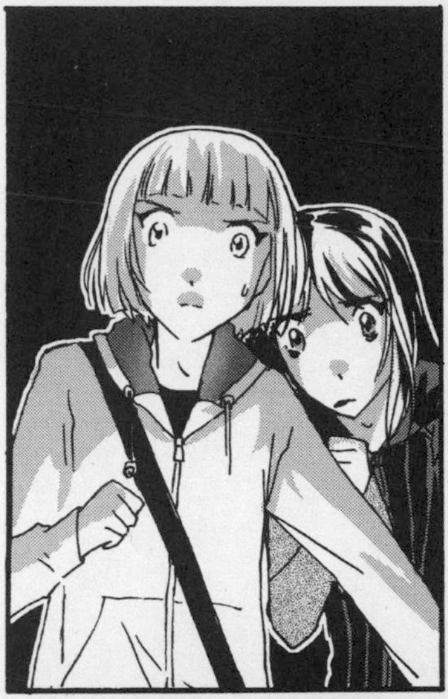
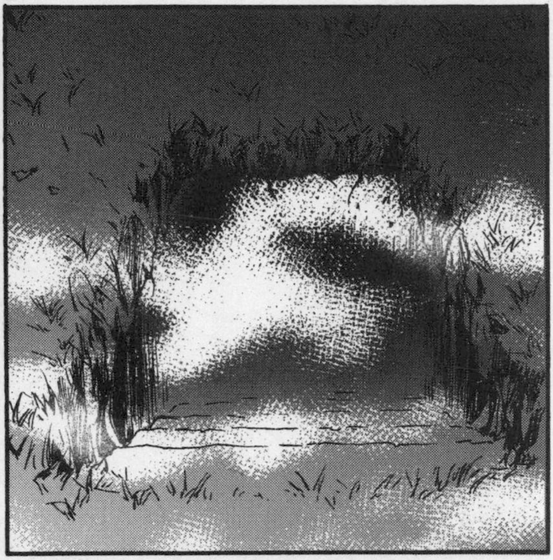
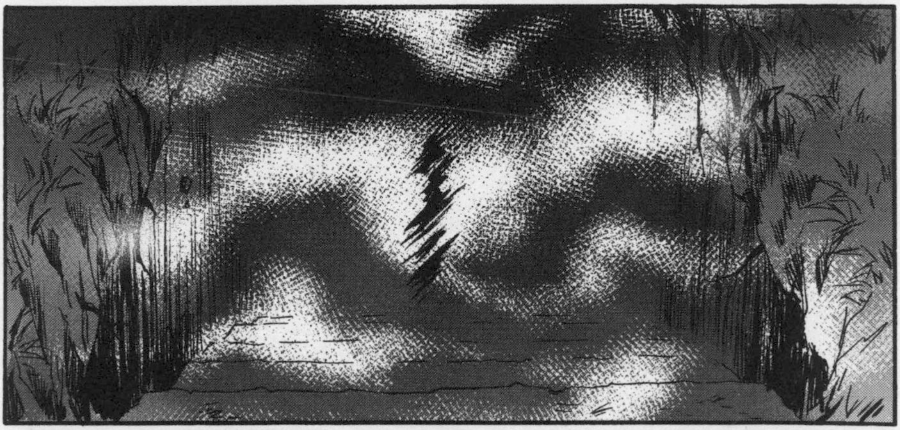
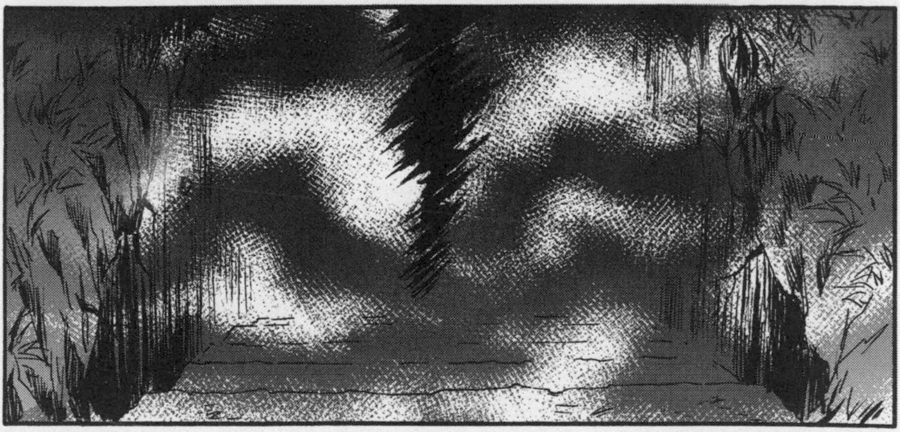

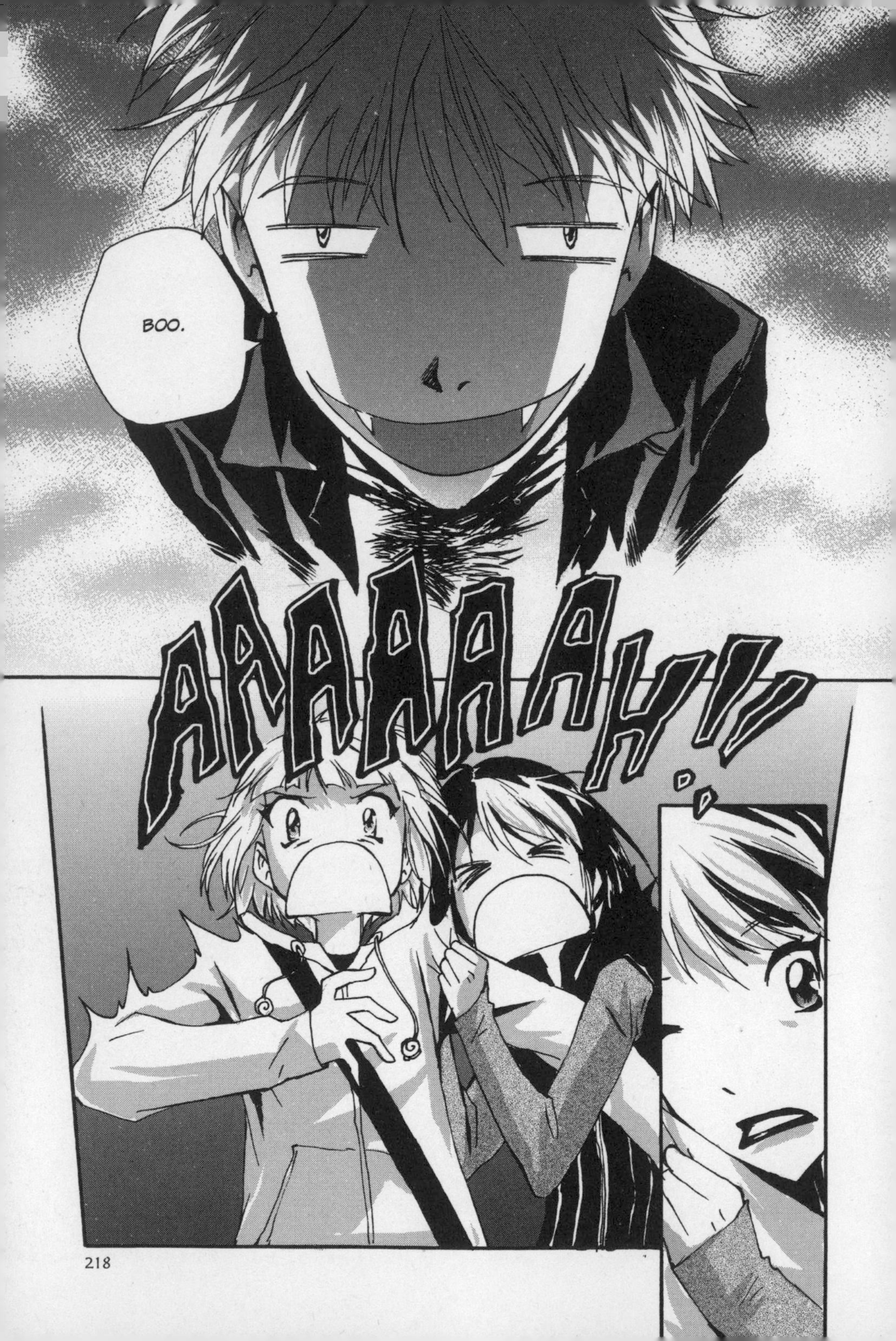
BOO.
AAAAAAH!!

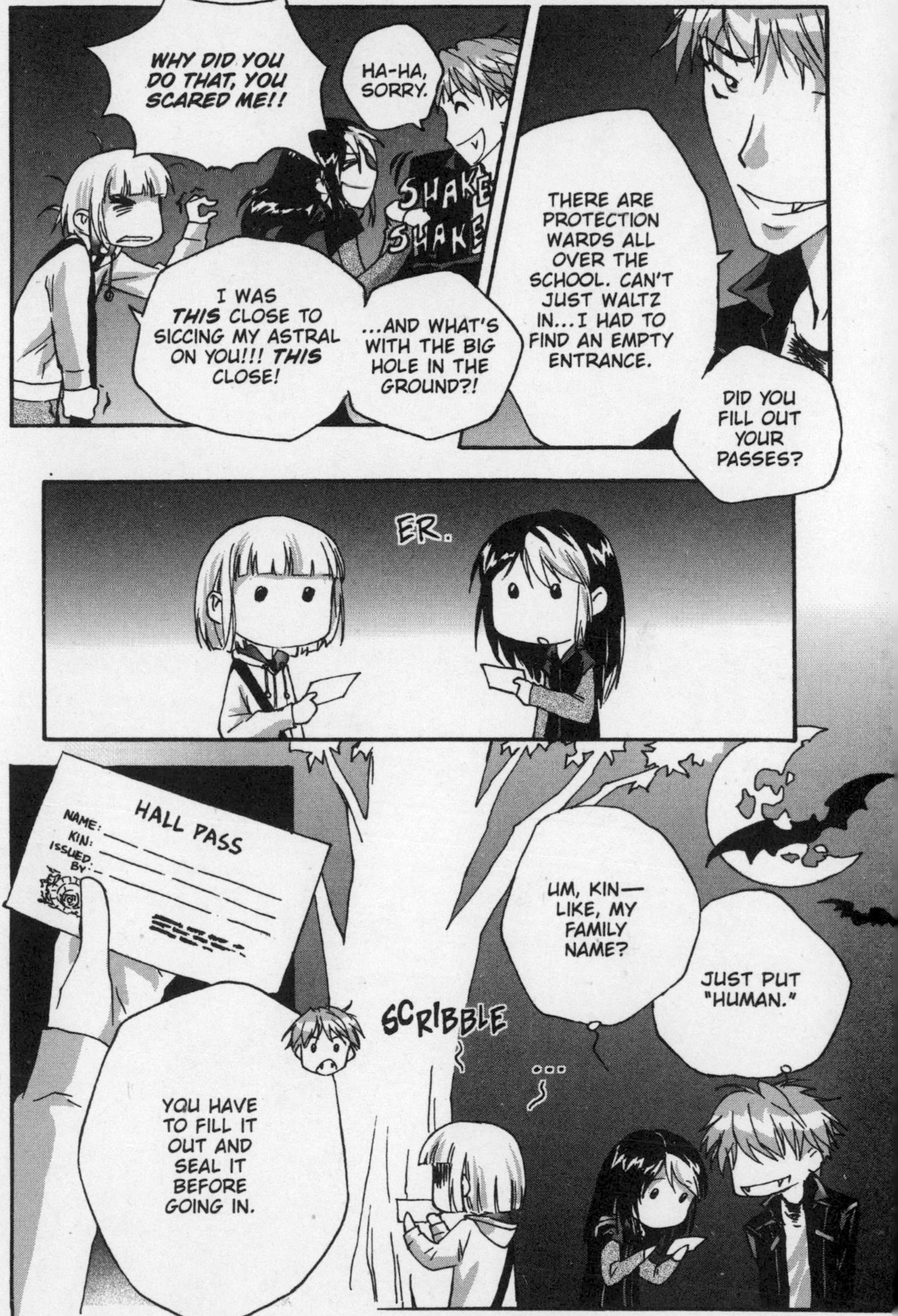
WHY DID YOU DO THAT, YOU SCARED ME!!
HA-HA, SORRY.
SHAKE SHAKE
I WAS THIS CLOSE TO SICCING MY ASTRAL ON YOU!!! THIS CLOSE!
...AND WHAT'S WITH THE BIG HOLE IN THE GROUND?!
THERE ARE PROTECTION WARDS ALL OVER THE SCHOOL. CAN'T JUST WALTZ IN...I HAD TO FIND AN EMPTY ENTRANCE.
DID YOU FILL OUT YOUR PASSES?
ER.
HALL PASS
NAME:
KIN:
ISSUED BY:
YOU HAVE TO FILL IT OUT AND SEAL IT BEFORE GOING IN.
SCRIBBLE
...
UM, KIN— LIKE, MY FAMILY NAME?
JUST PUT "HUMAN."

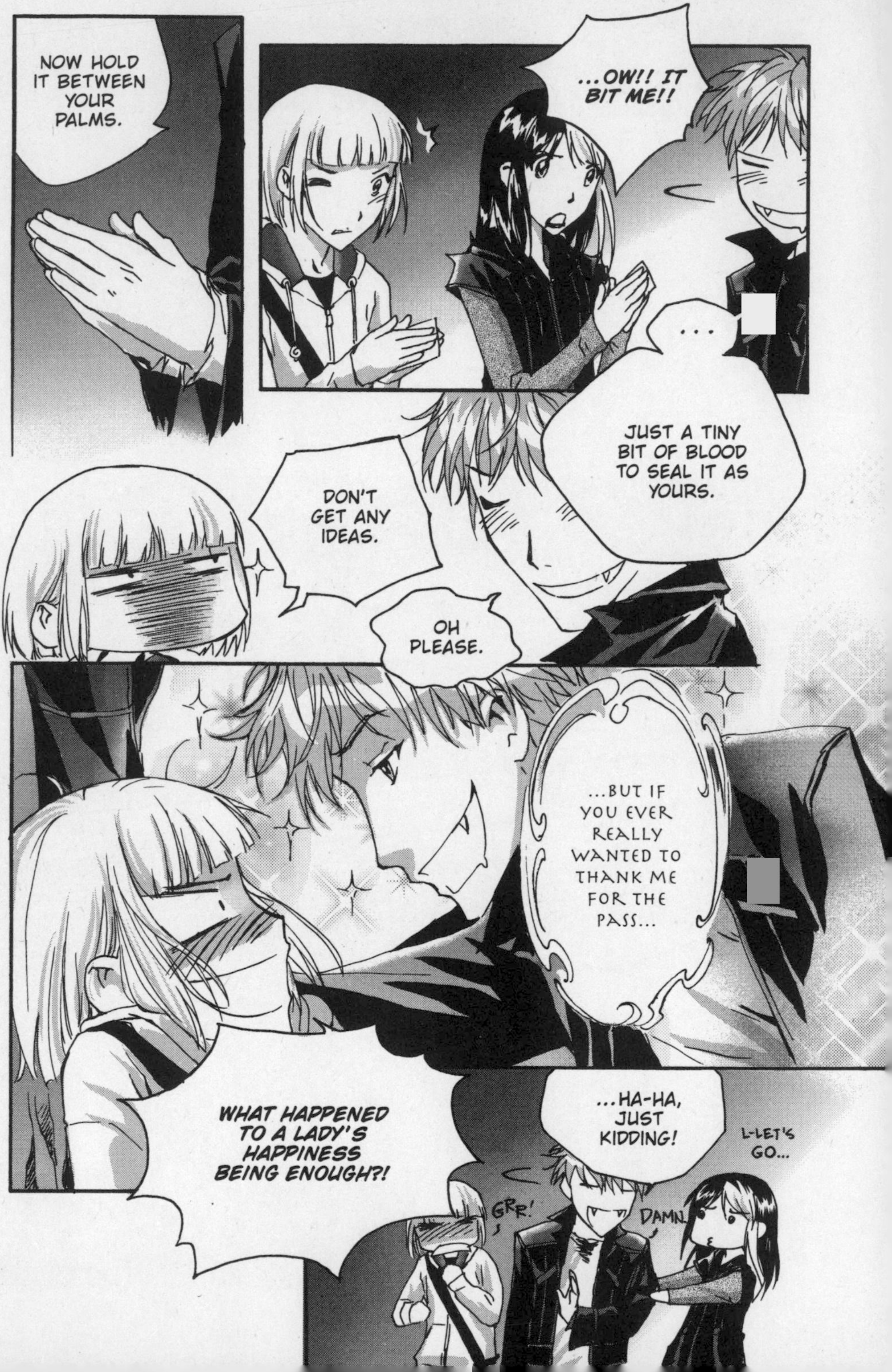
NOW HOLD IT BETWEEN YOUR PALMS.
...OW!! IT BIT ME!!
...
JUST A TINY BIT OF BLOOD TO SEAL IT AS YOURS.
DON'T GET ANY IDEAS.
OH PLEASE.
...BUT IF YOU EVER REALLY WANTED TO THANK ME FOR THE PASS...
WHAT HAPPENED TO A LADY'S HAPPINESS BEING ENOUGH?!
...HA-HA, JUST KIDDING!
GRR!
DAMN.
L-LET'S GO...

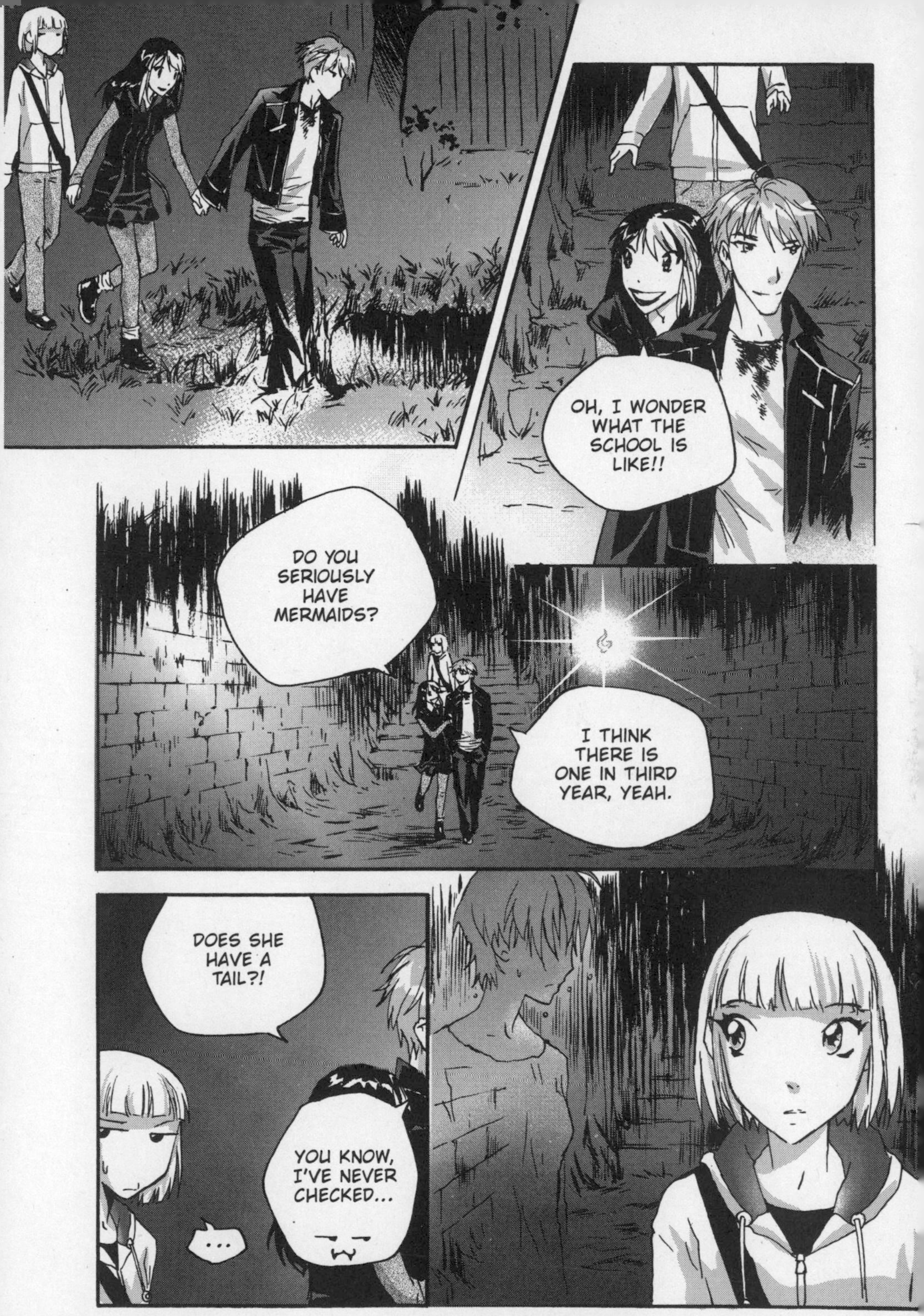
OH, I WONDER WHAT THE SCHOOL IS LIKE!!
DO YOU SERIOUSLY HAVE MERMAIDS?
I THINK THERE IS ONE IN THIRD YEAR, YEAH.
DOES SHE HAVE A TAIL?!
...
YOU KNOW, I'VE NEVER CHECKED...

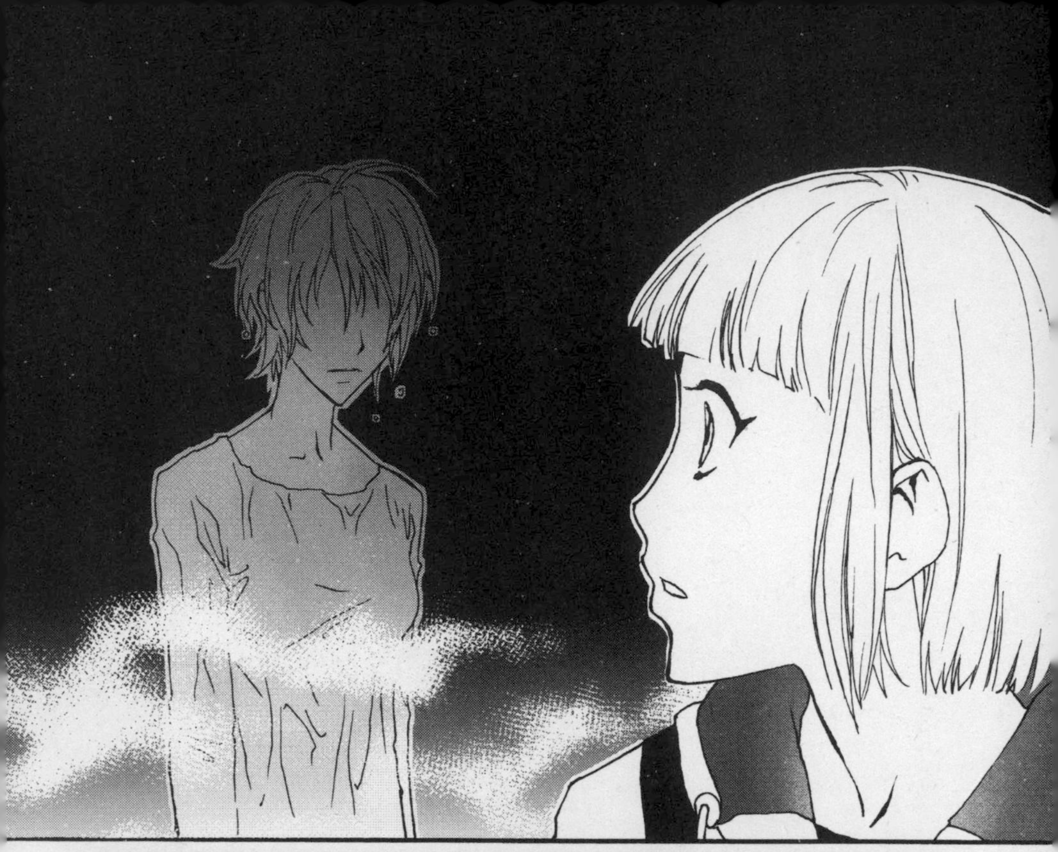

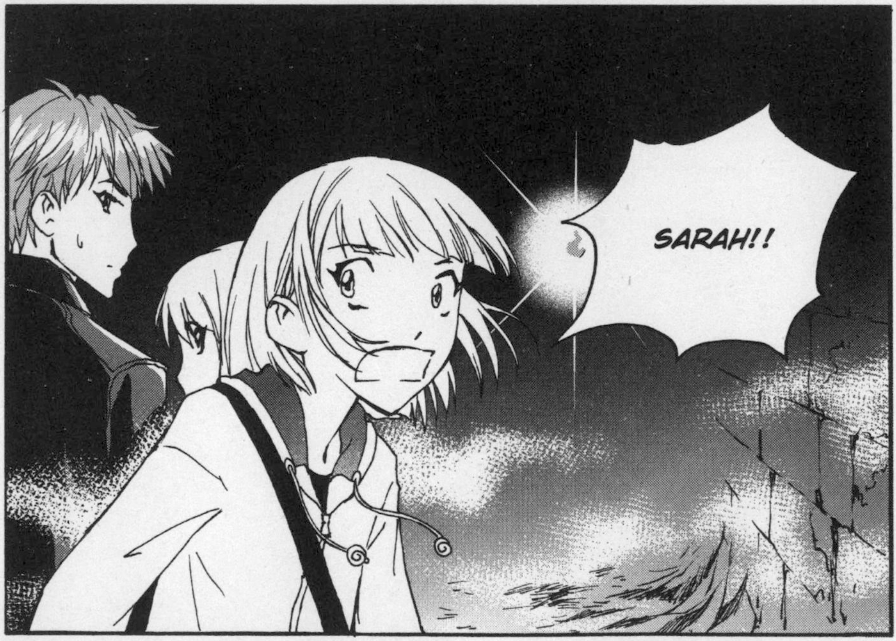
SARAH!!

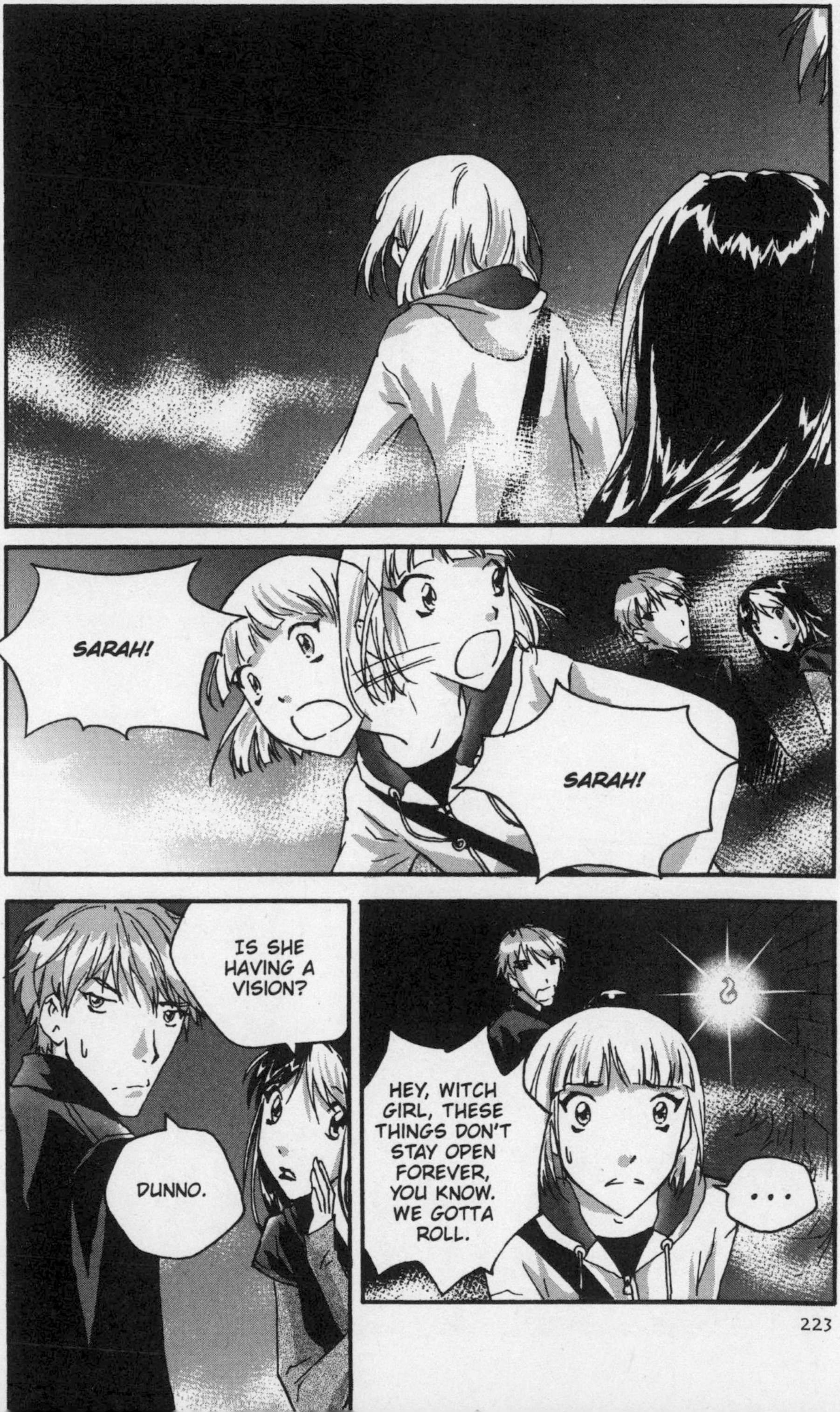
SARAH!
SARAH!
IS SHE HAVING A VISION?
DUNNO.
HEY, WITCH GIRL, THESE THINGS DON'T STAY OPEN FOREVER, YOU KNOW. WE GOTTA ROLL.
...

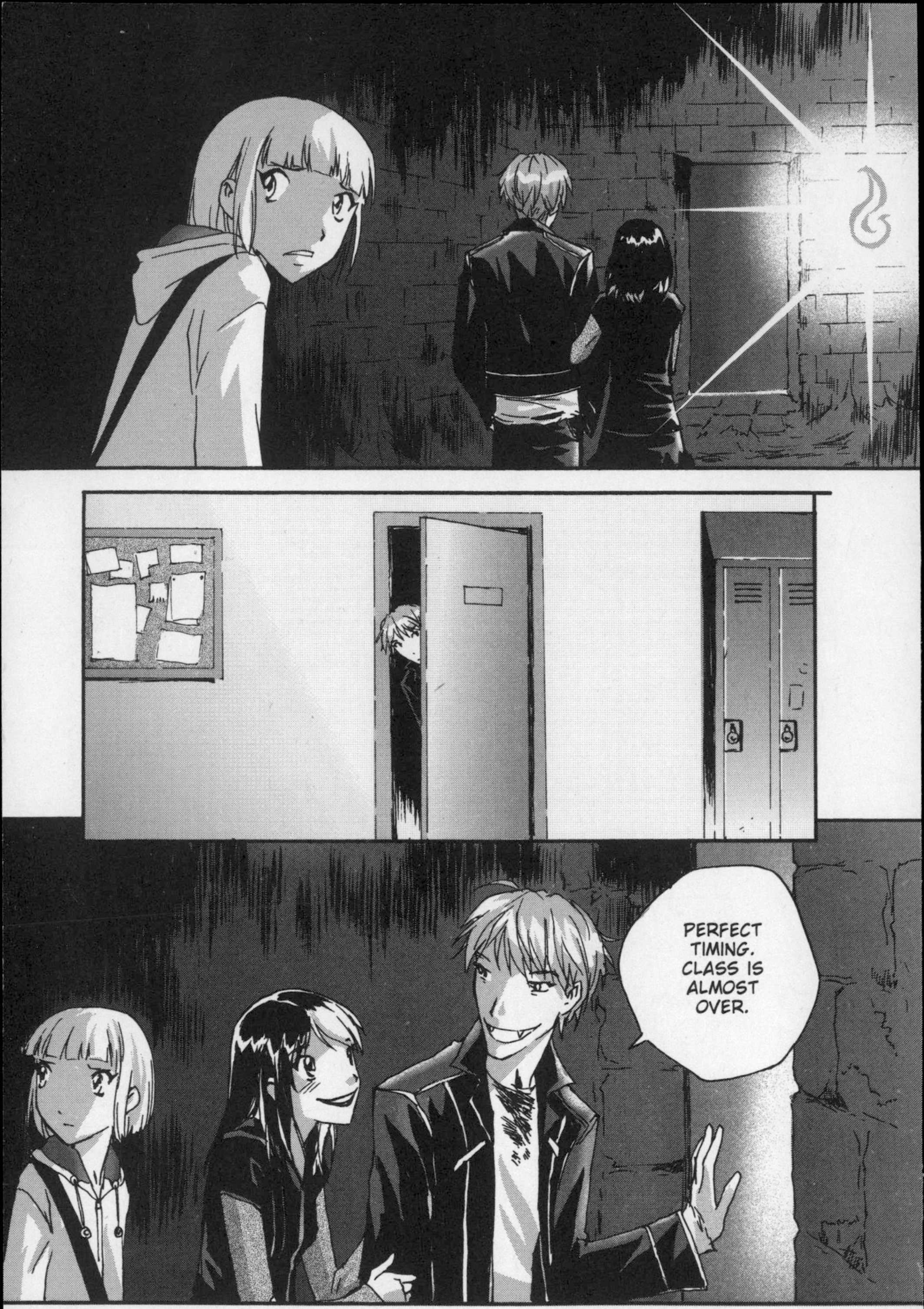
PERFECT TIMING. CLASS IS ALMOST OVER.

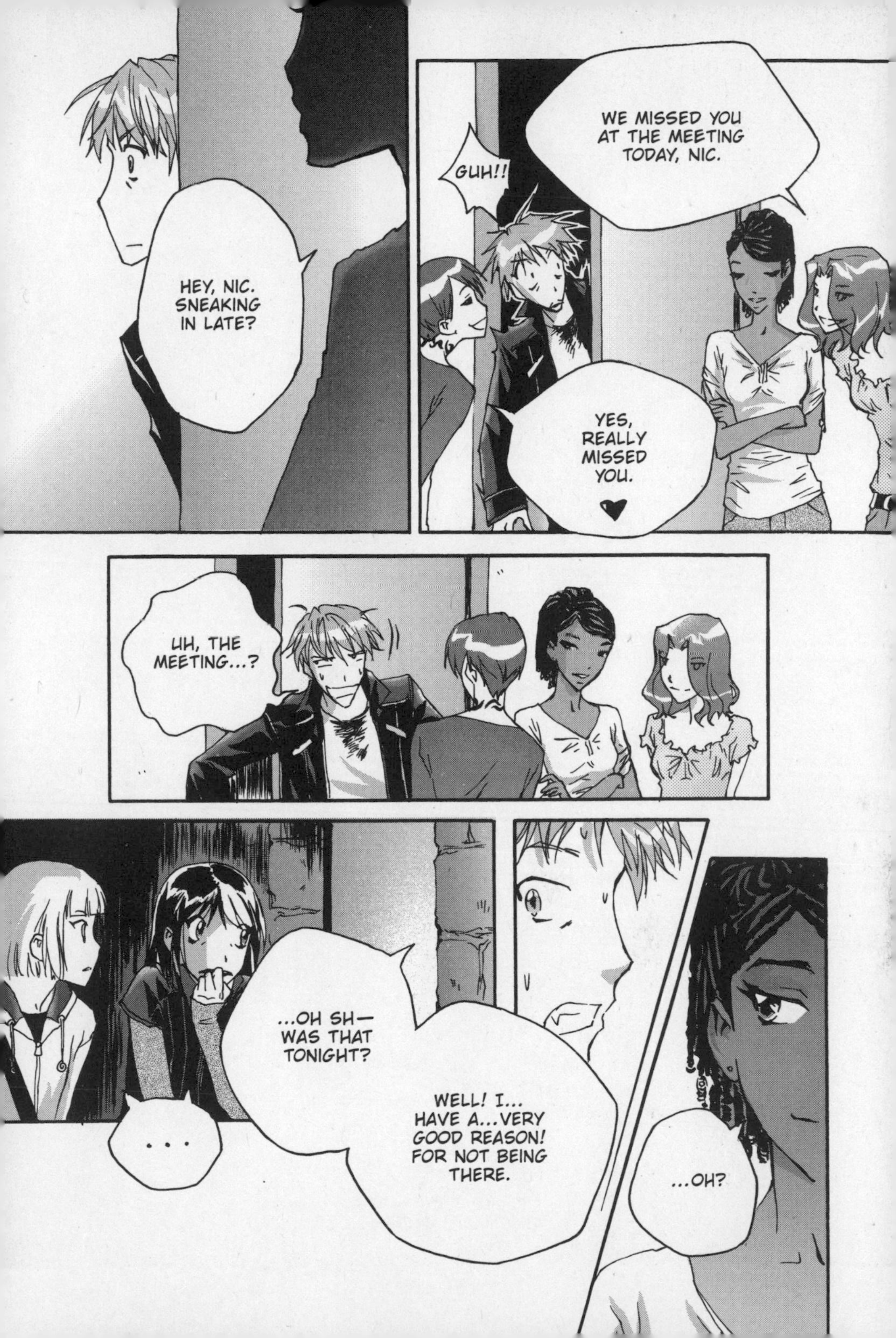
HEY, NIC. SNEAKING IN LATE?
GUH!!
WE MISSED YOU AT THE MEETING TODAY, NIC.
YES, REALLY MISSED YOU.
UH, THE MEETING...?
...OH SH— WAS THAT TONIGHT?
...
WELL! I... HAVE A...VERY GOOD REASON! FOR NOT BEING THERE.
...OH?

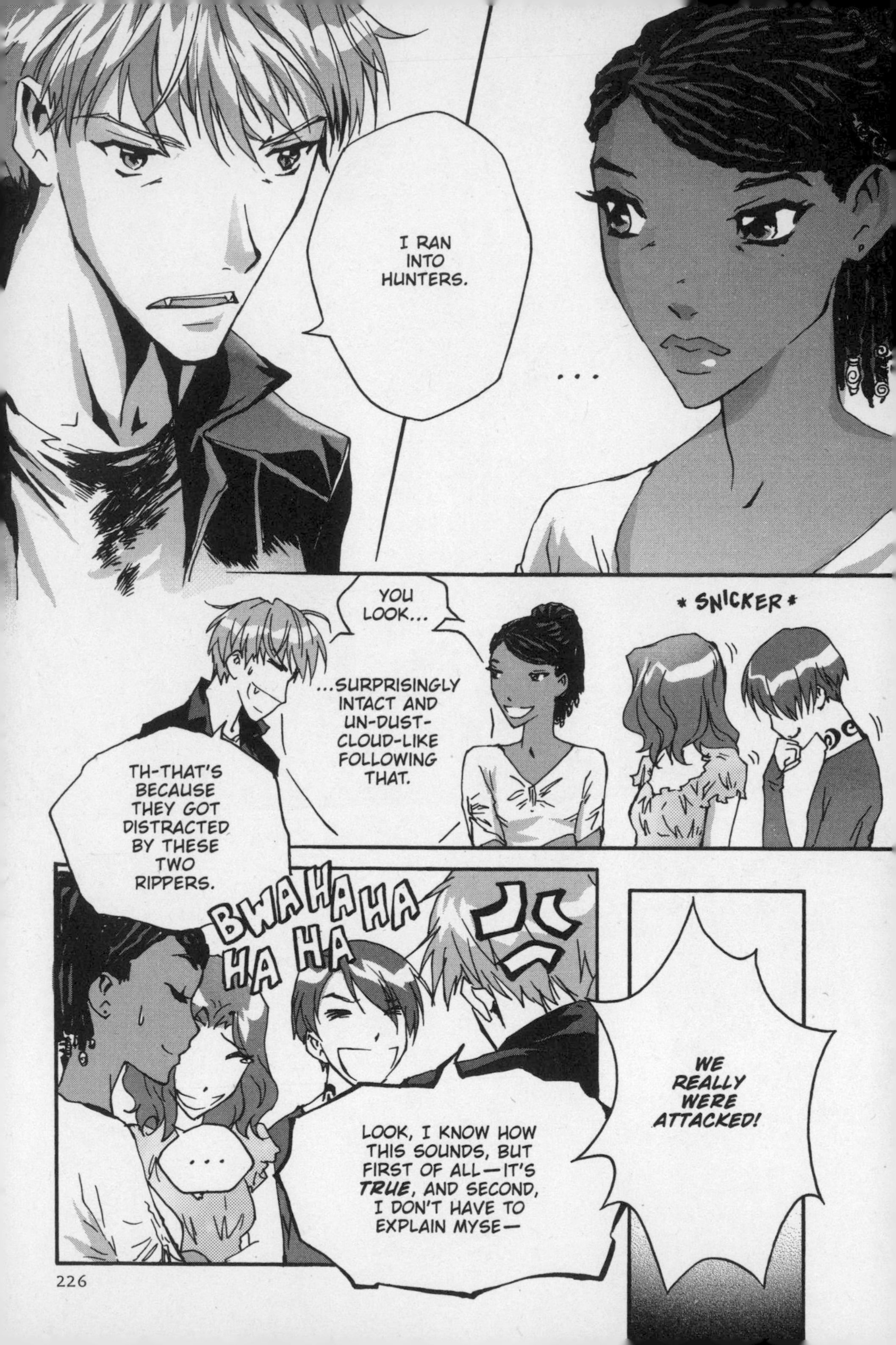
I RAN INTO HUNTERS.
...
YOU LOOK...
...SURPRISINGLY INTACT AND UN-DUST-CLOUD-LIKE FOLLOWING THAT.
* SNICKER *
TH-THAT'S BECAUSE THEY GOT DISTRACTED BY THESE TWO RIPPERS.
BWAHAHAHA HA HA
...
LOOK, I KNOW HOW THIS SOUNDS, BUT FIRST OF ALL—IT'S *TRUE*, AND SECOND, I DON'T HAVE TO EXPLAIN MYSE—
WE REALLY WERE ATTACKED!

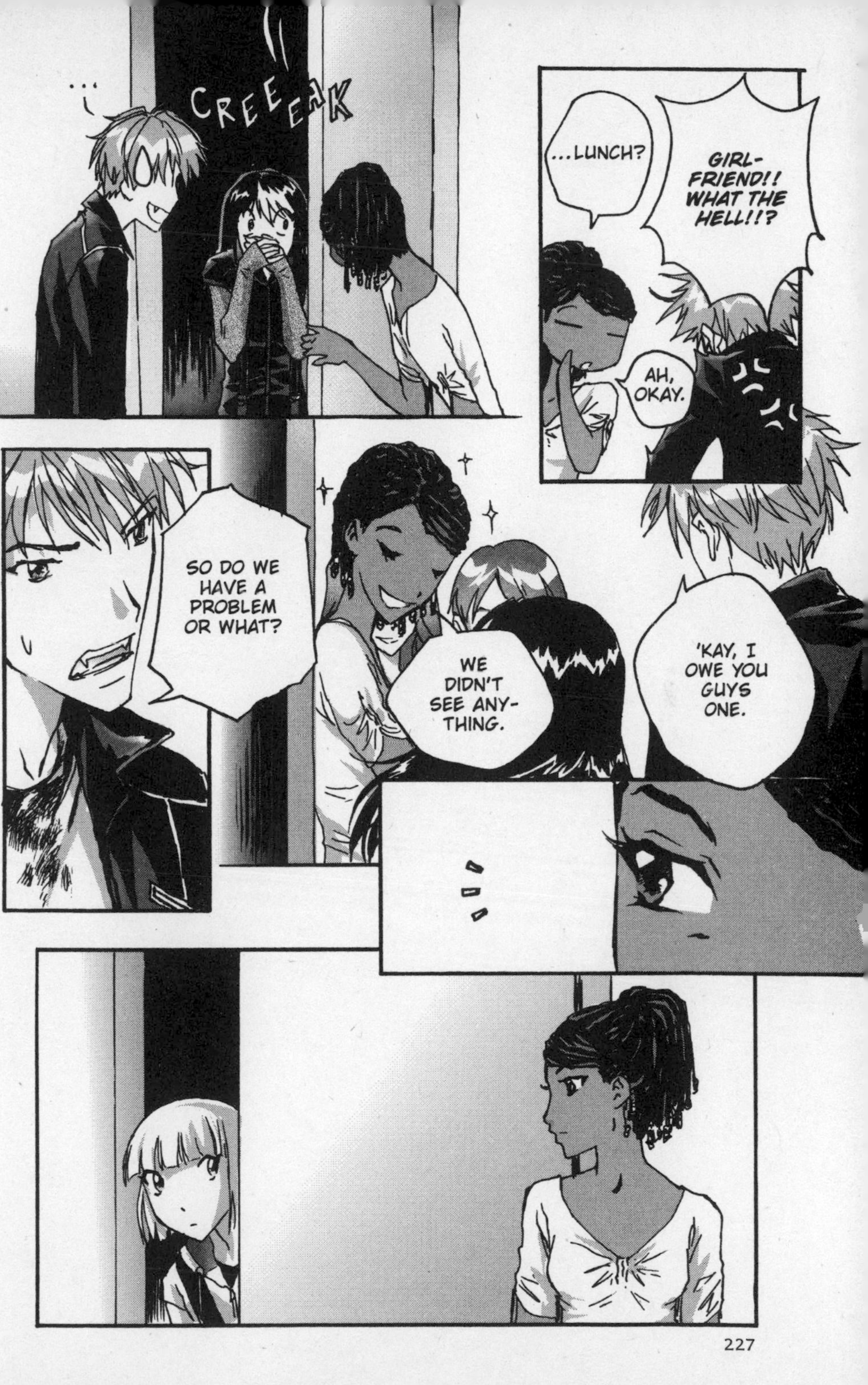
...
CREEEAK
...LUNCH?
GIRL-FRIEND!! WHAT THE HELL!!?
AH, OKAY.
SO DO WE HAVE A PROBLEM OR WHAT?
WE DIDN'T SEE ANY-THING.
'KAY, I OWE YOU GUYS ONE.

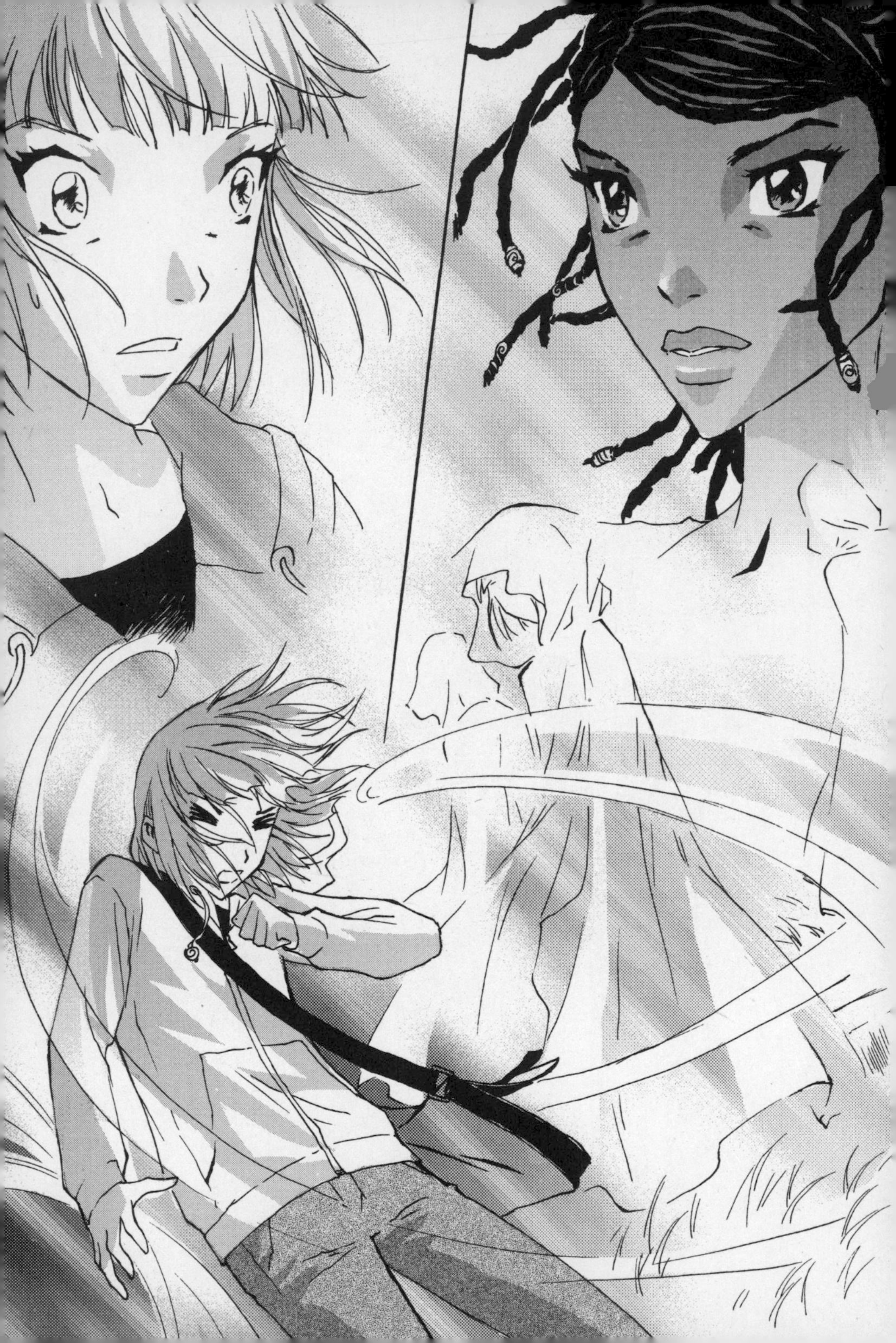

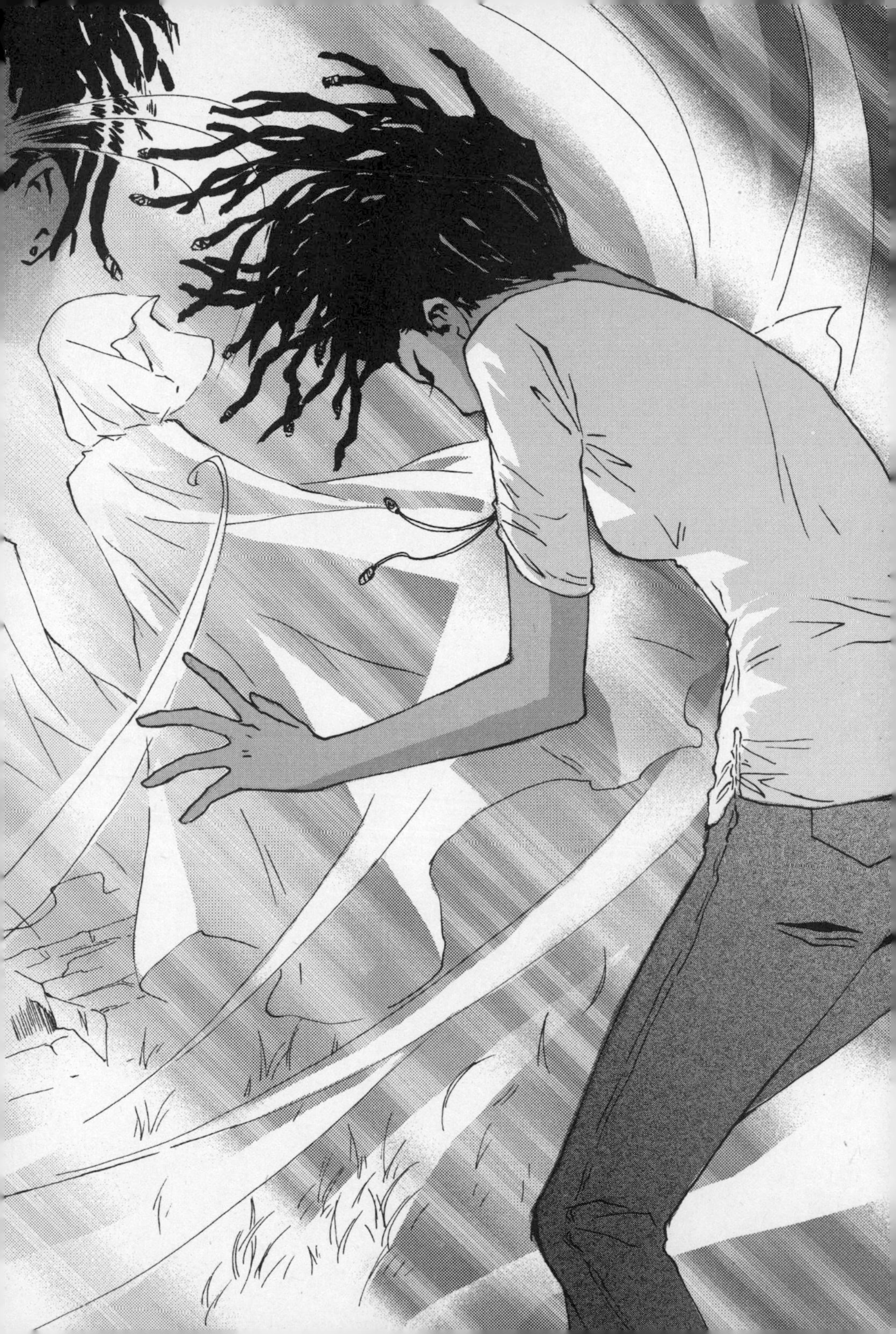

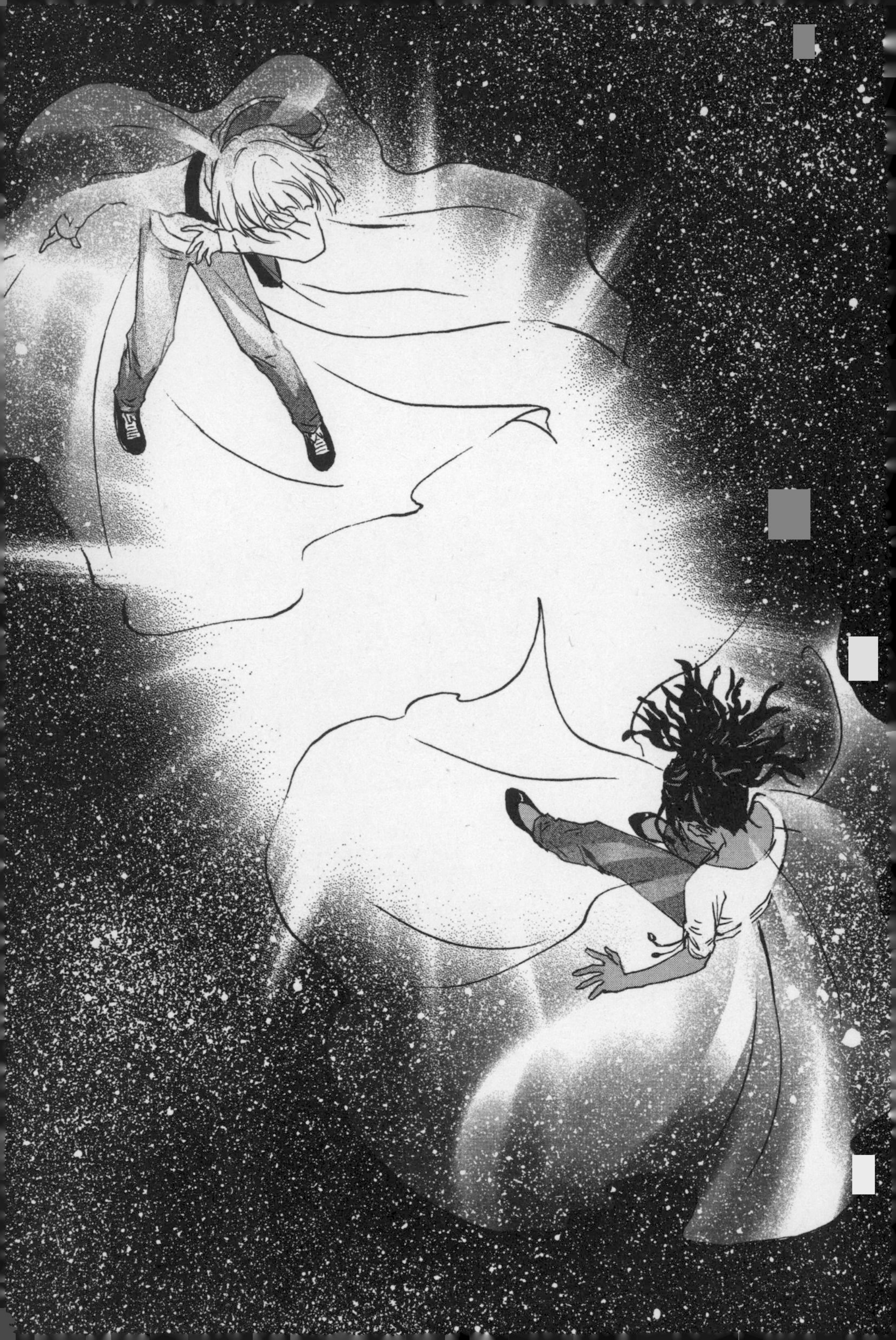

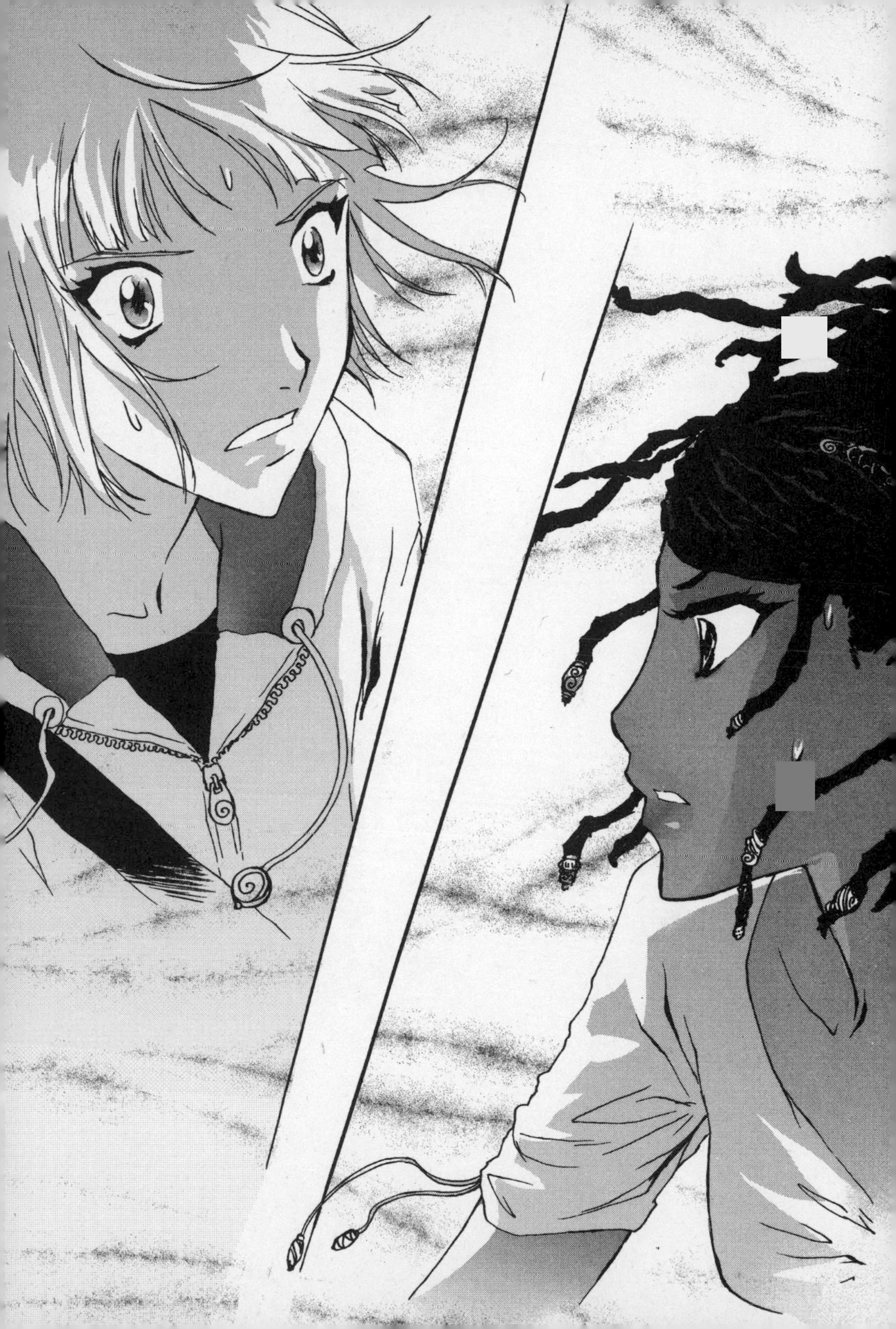

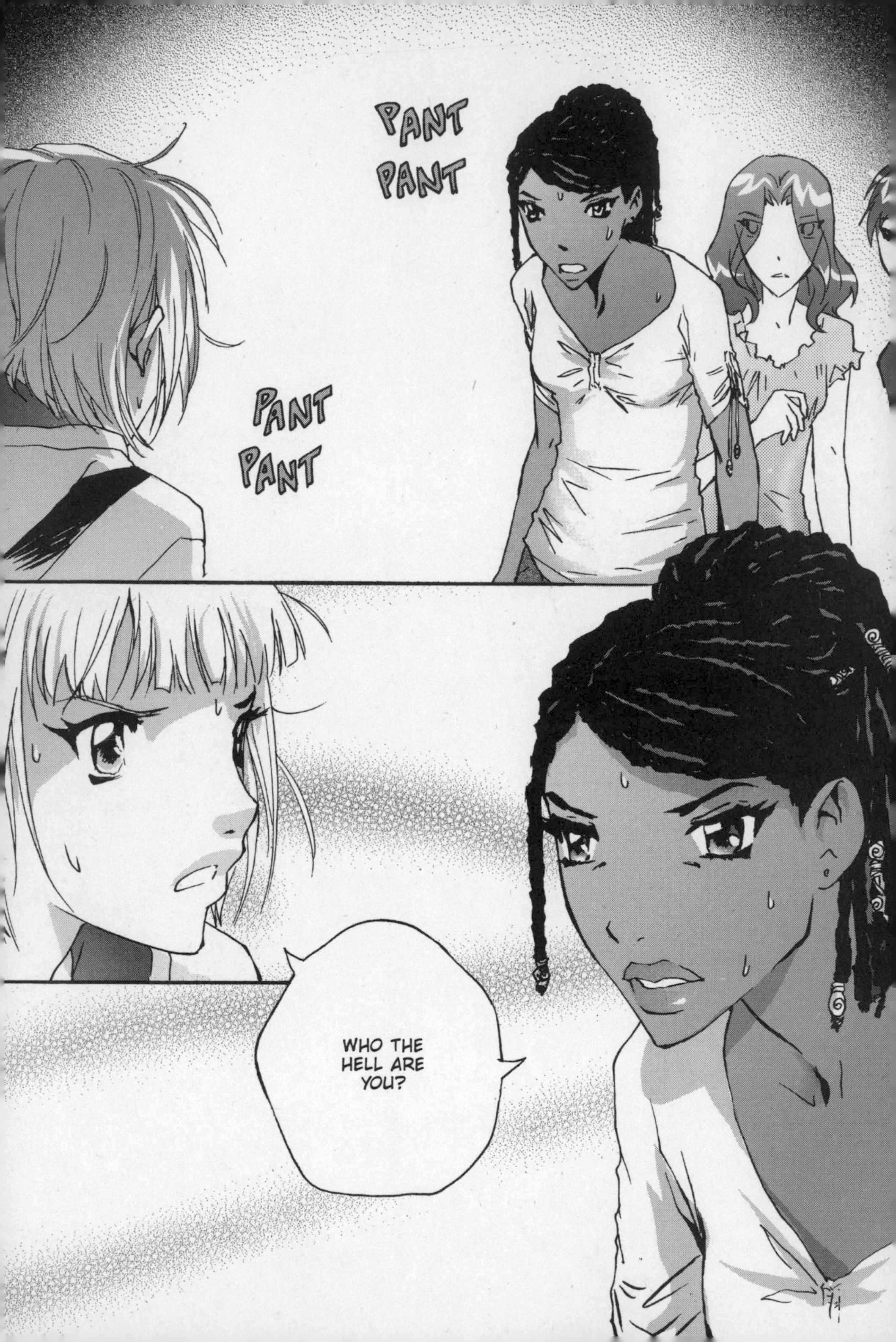
PANT PANT
PANT PANT
WHO THE HELL ARE YOU?

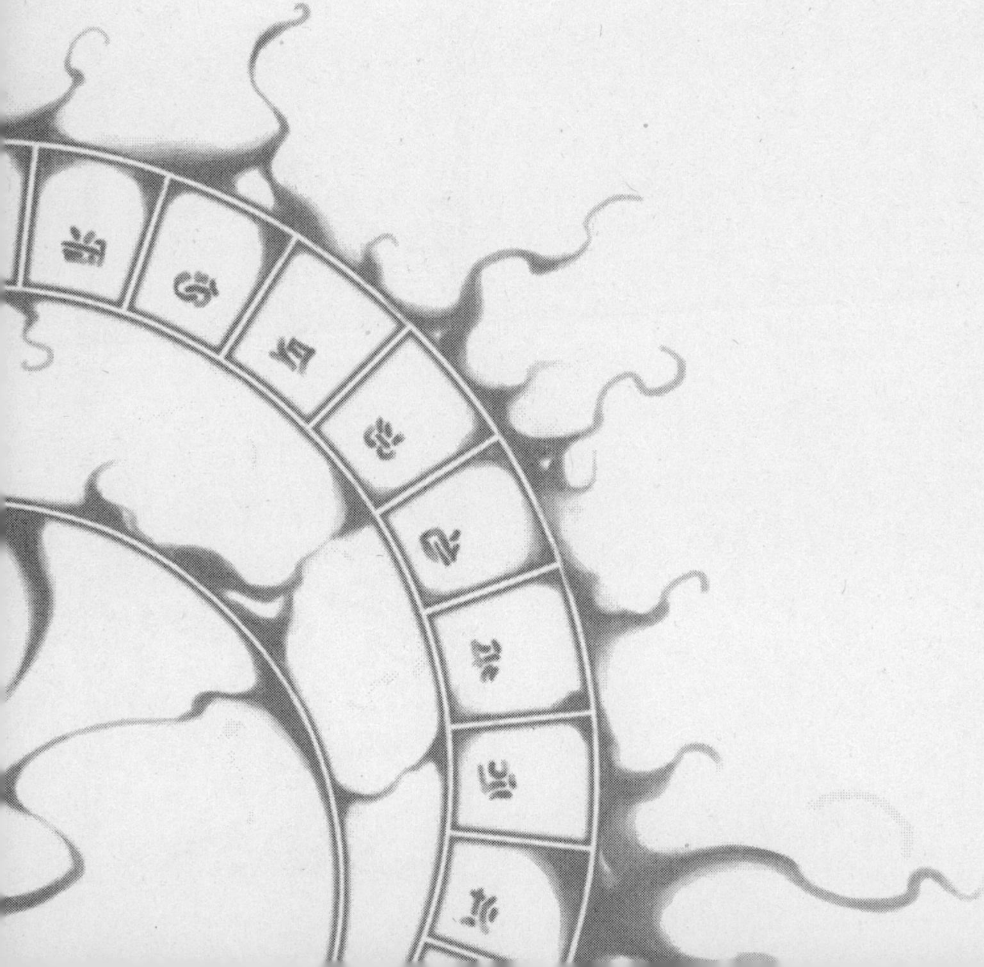

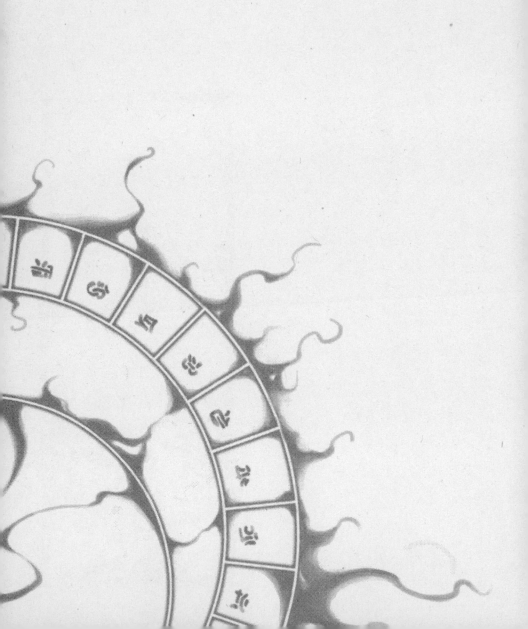

Chapter 8

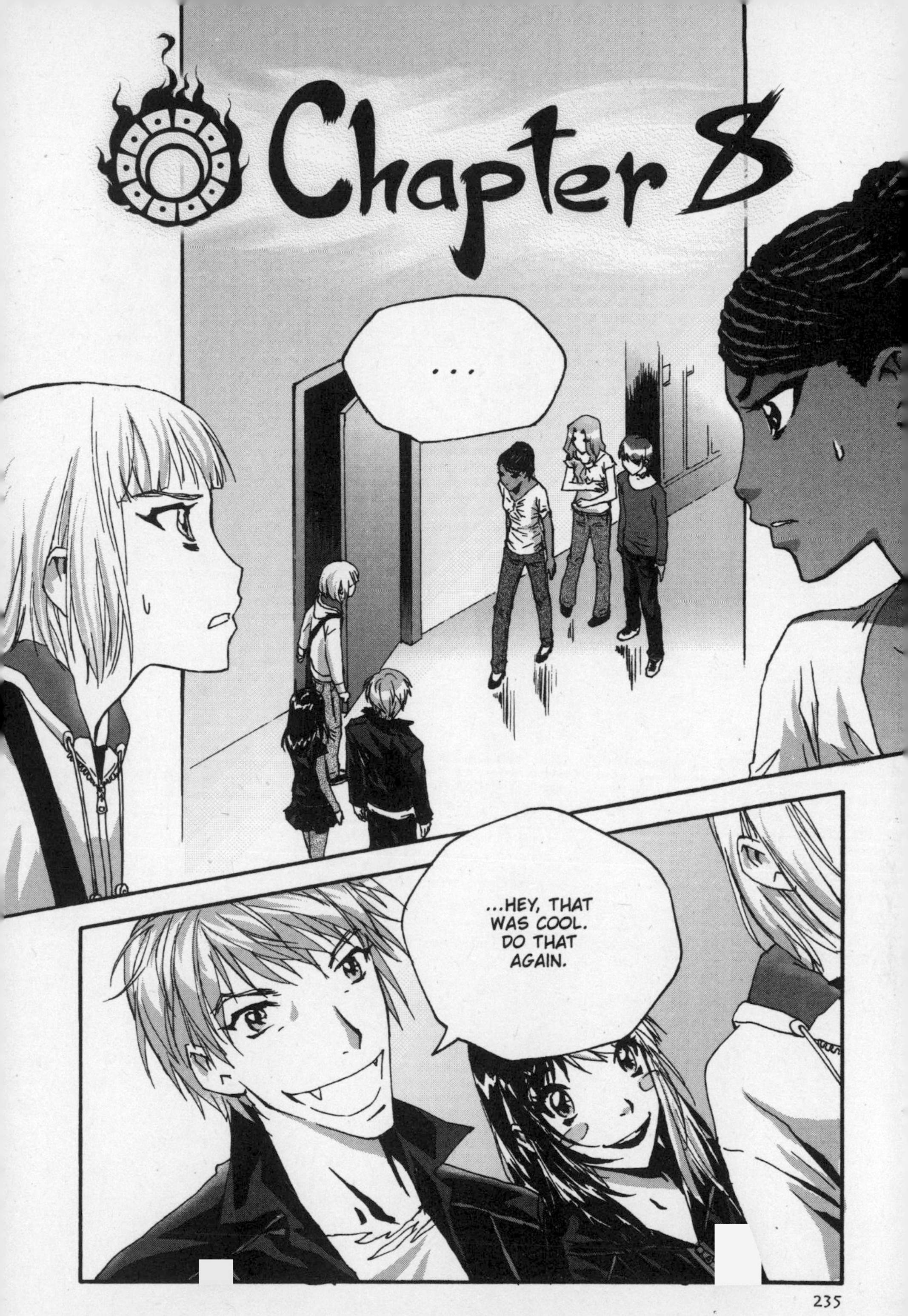
...
...HEY, THAT WAS COOL. DO THAT AGAIN.

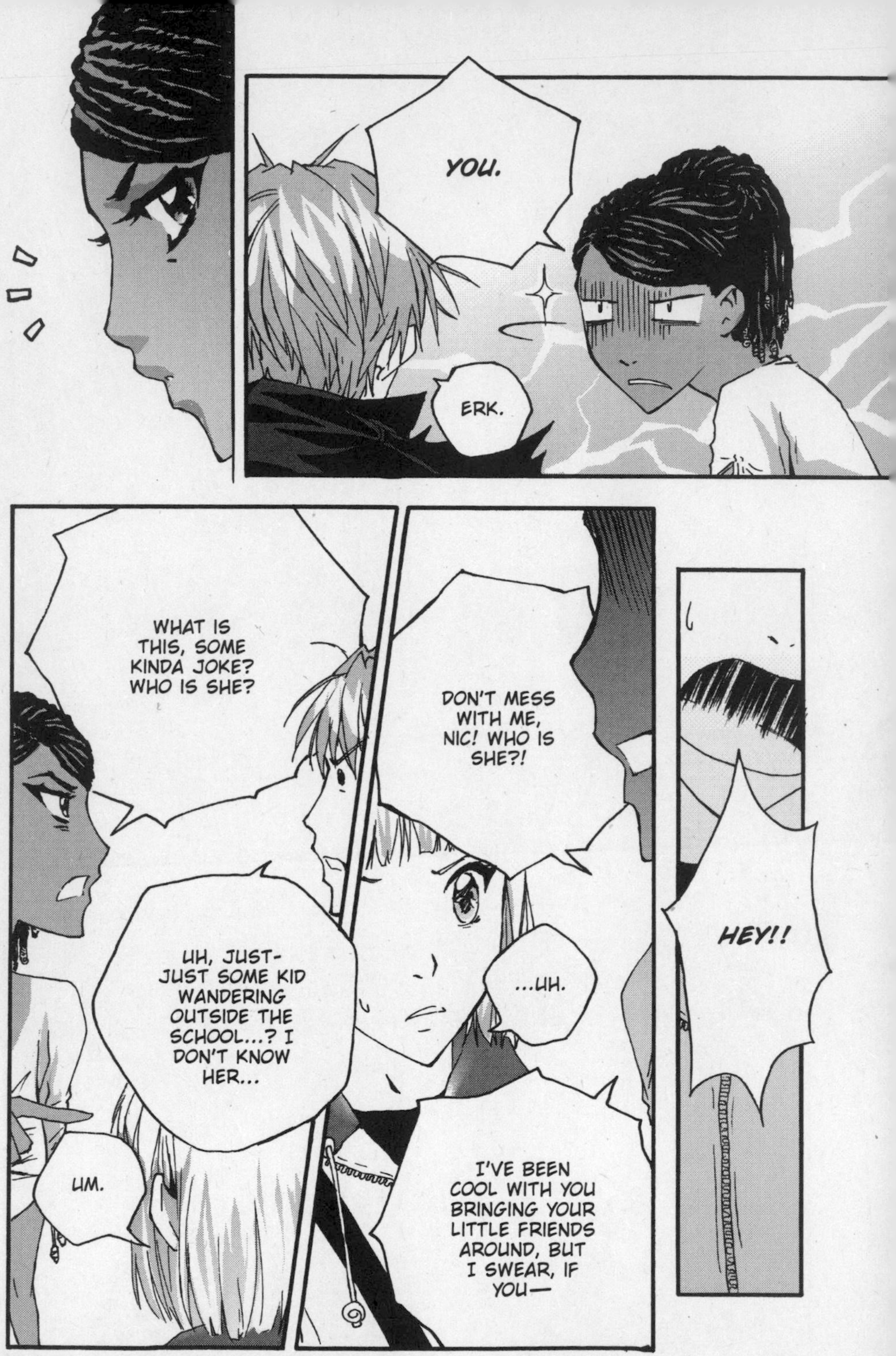
YOU.
ERK.
WHAT IS THIS, SOME KINDA JOKE? WHO IS SHE?
UH, JUST- JUST SOME KID WANDERING OUTSIDE THE SCHOOL...? I DON'T KNOW HER...
UM.
DON'T MESS WITH ME, NIC! WHO IS SHE?!
...UH.
I'VE BEEN COOL WITH YOU BRINGING YOUR LITTLE FRIENDS AROUND, BUT I SWEAR, IF YOU—
HEY!!

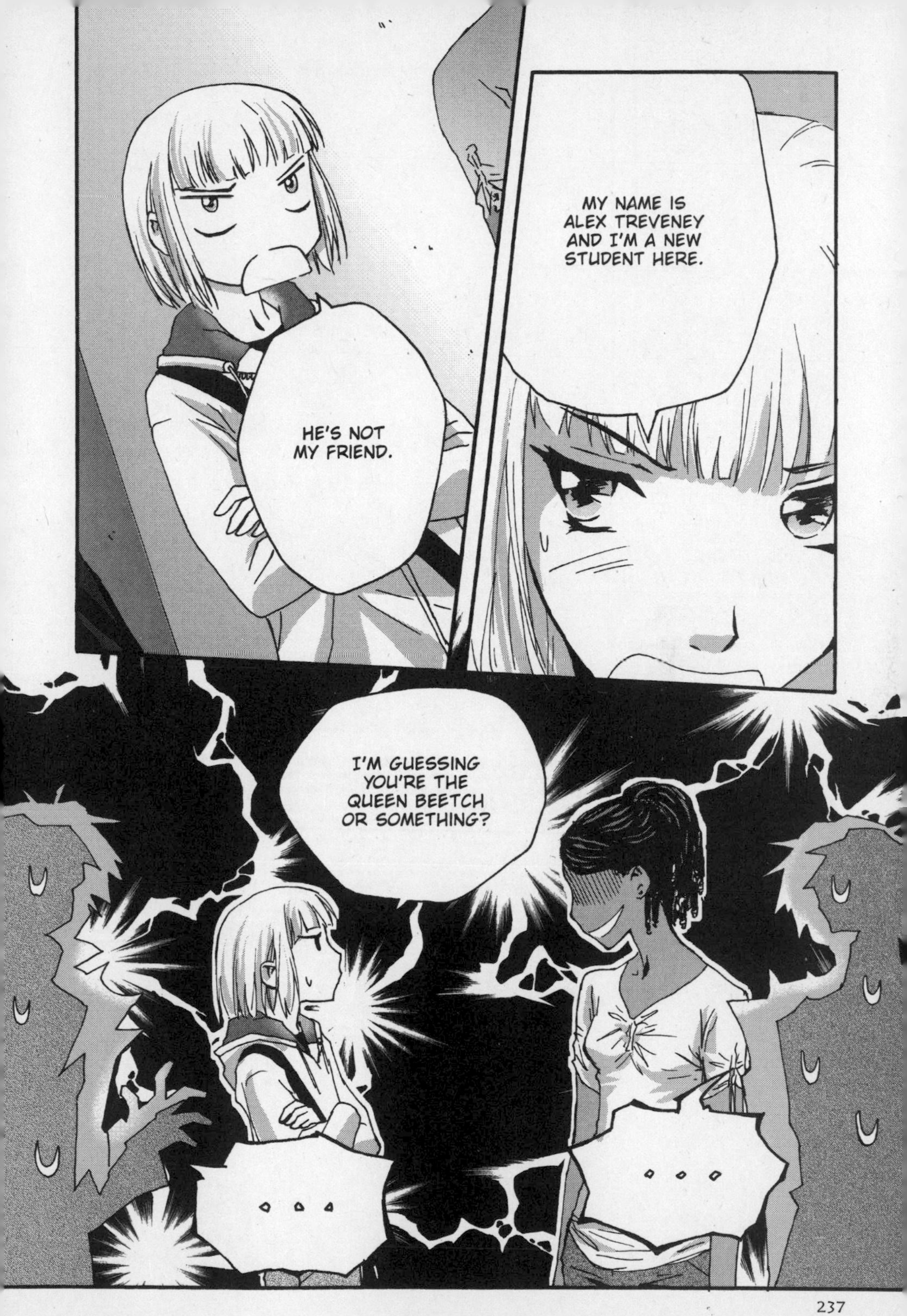
HE'S NOT MY FRIEND.
MY NAME IS ALEX TREVENEY AND I'M A NEW STUDENT HERE.
I'M GUESSING YOU'RE THE QUEEN BEETCH OR SOMETHING?
...
...

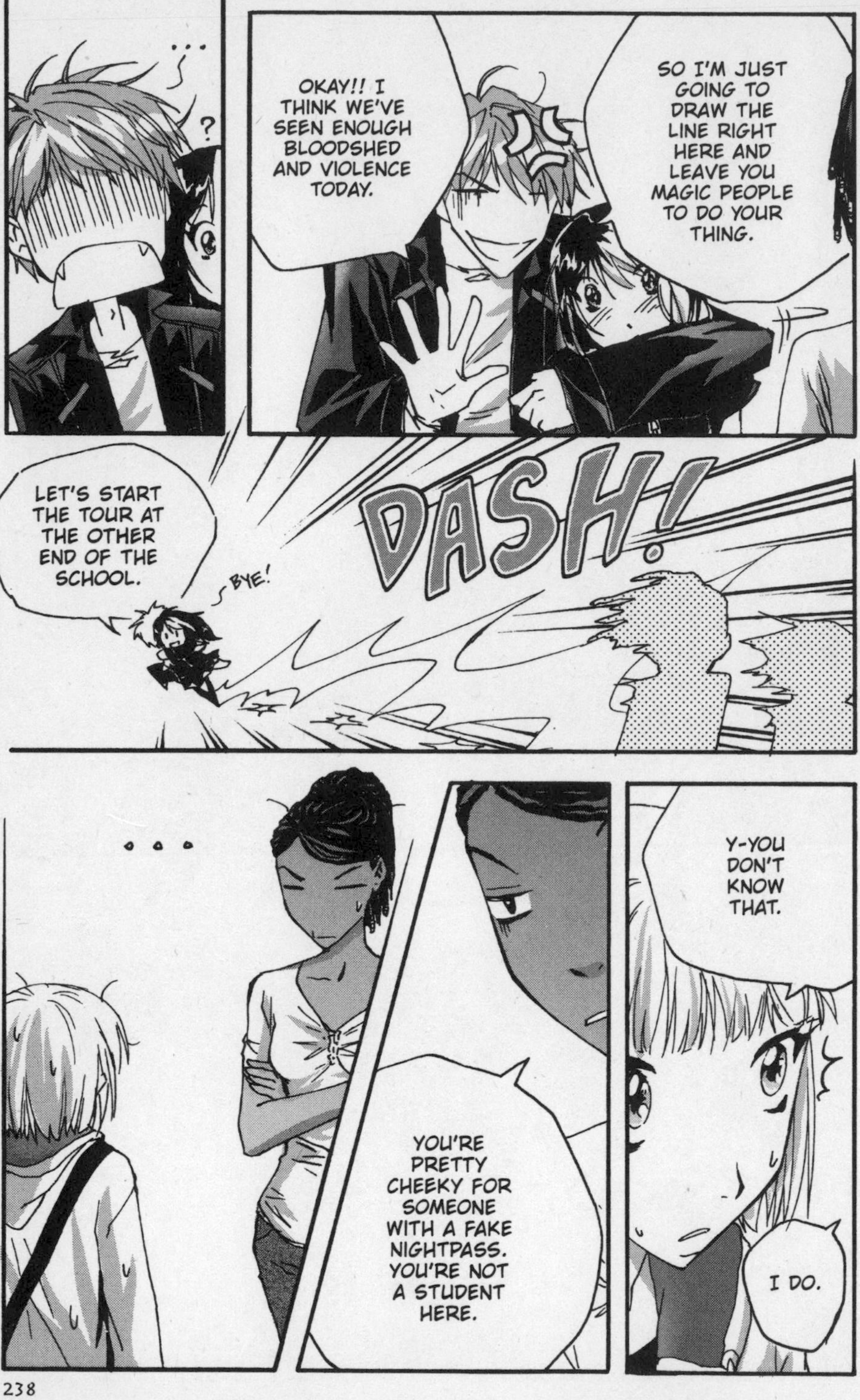
...
?
OKAY!! I THINK WE'VE SEEN ENOUGH BLOODSHED AND VIOLENCE TODAY.
SO I'M JUST GOING TO DRAW THE LINE RIGHT HERE AND LEAVE YOU MAGIC PEOPLE TO DO YOUR THING.
LET'S START THE TOUR AT THE OTHER END OF THE SCHOOL.
BYE!
DASH!
...
YOU'RE PRETTY CHEEKY FOR SOMEONE WITH A FAKE NIGHTPASS. YOU'RE NOT A STUDENT HERE.
Y-YOU DON'T KNOW THAT.
I DO.

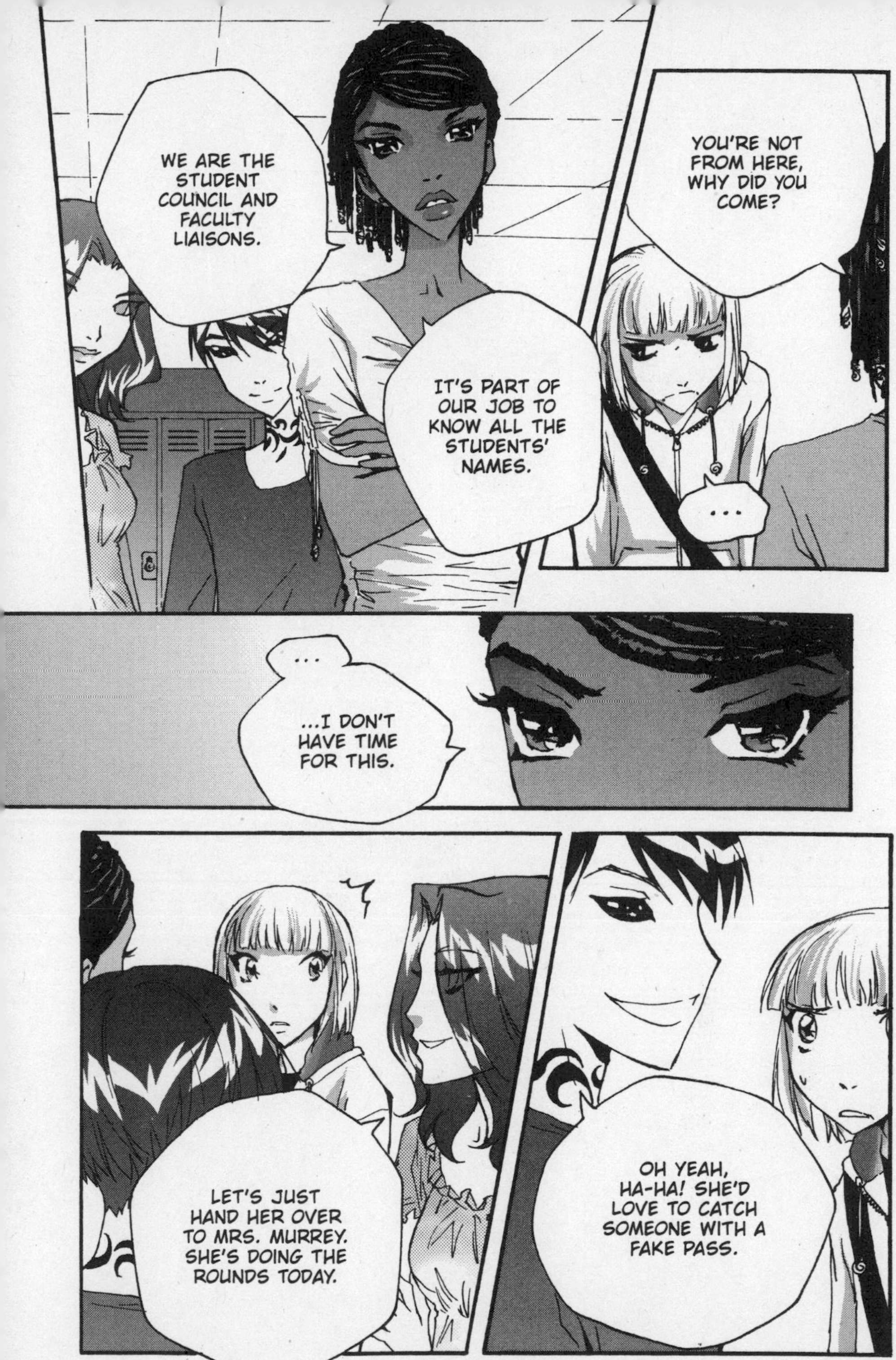
WE ARE THE STUDENT COUNCIL AND FACULTY LIAISONS.
IT'S PART OF OUR JOB TO KNOW ALL THE STUDENTS' NAMES.
YOU'RE NOT FROM HERE, WHY DID YOU COME?
...
...
...I DON'T HAVE TIME FOR THIS.
LET'S JUST HAND HER OVER TO MRS. MURREY. SHE'S DOING THE ROUNDS TODAY.
OH YEAH, HA-HA! SHE'D LOVE TO CATCH SOMEONE WITH A FAKE PASS.

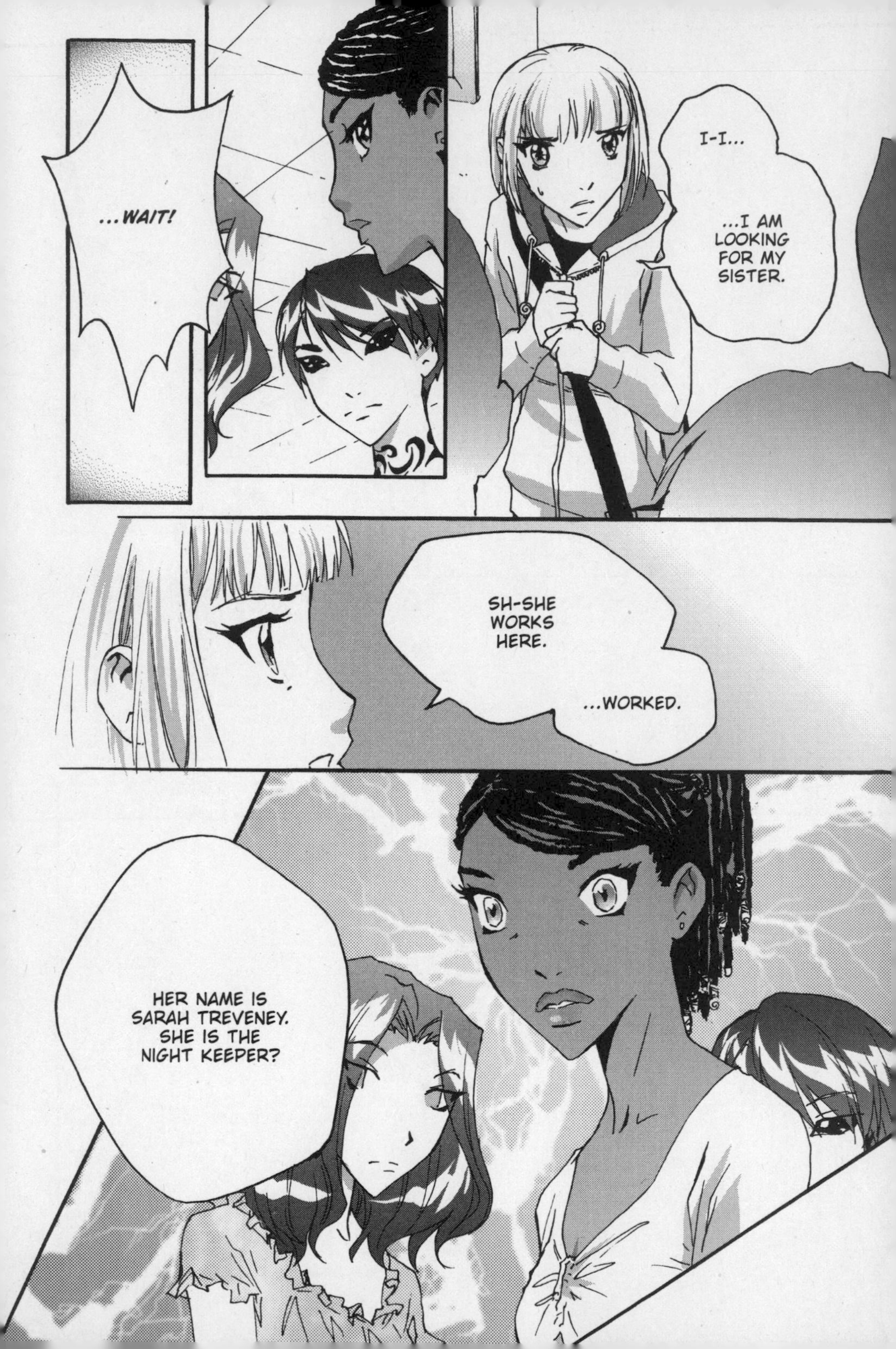
...WAIT!
I-I...
...I AM LOOKING FOR MY SISTER.
SH-SHE WORKS HERE.
...WORKED.
HER NAME IS SARAH TREVENEY. SHE IS THE NIGHT KEEPER?

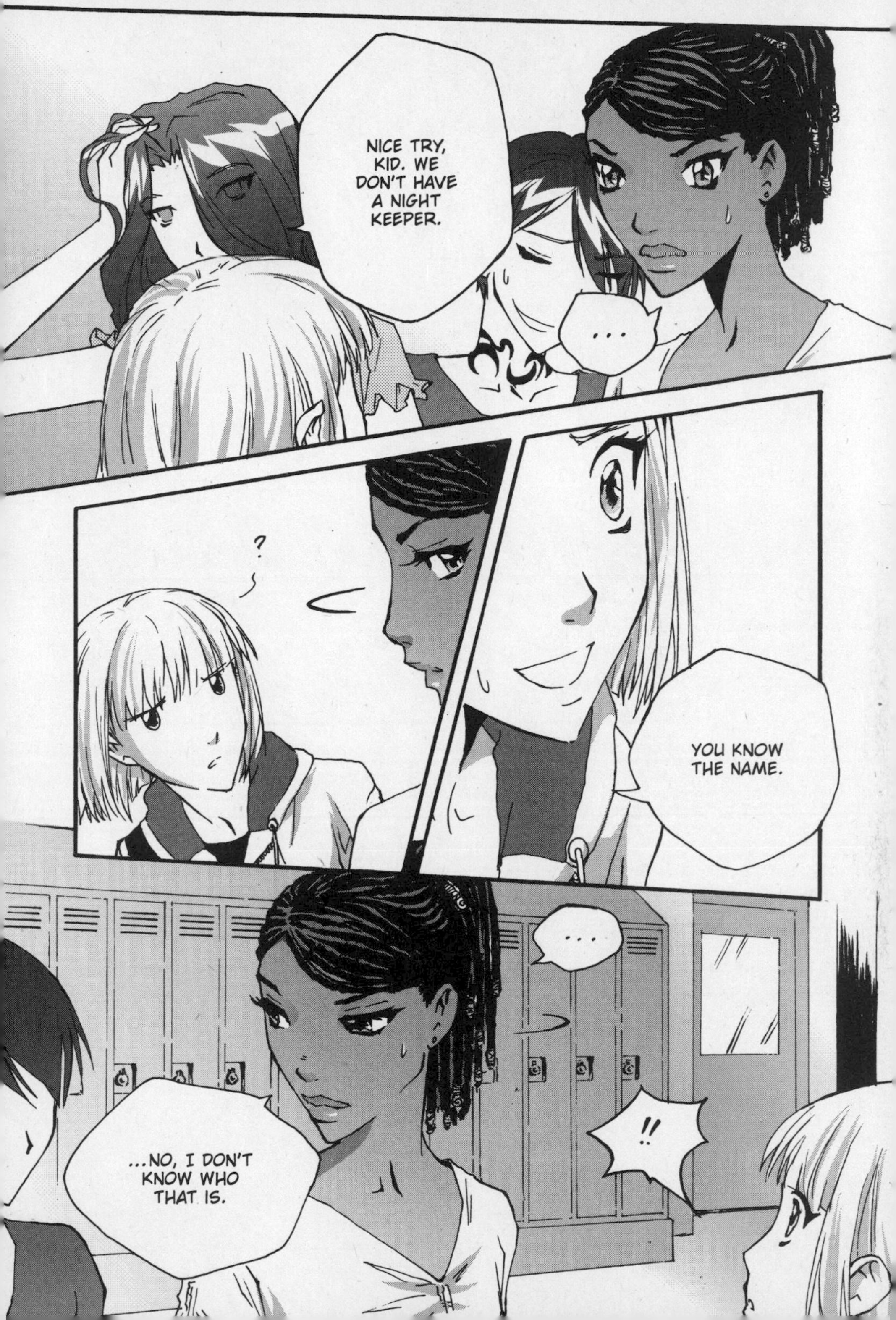
NICE TRY, KID. WE DON'T HAVE A NIGHT KEEPER.
...
?
YOU KNOW THE NAME.
...
...NO, I DON'T KNOW WHO THAT IS.
!!

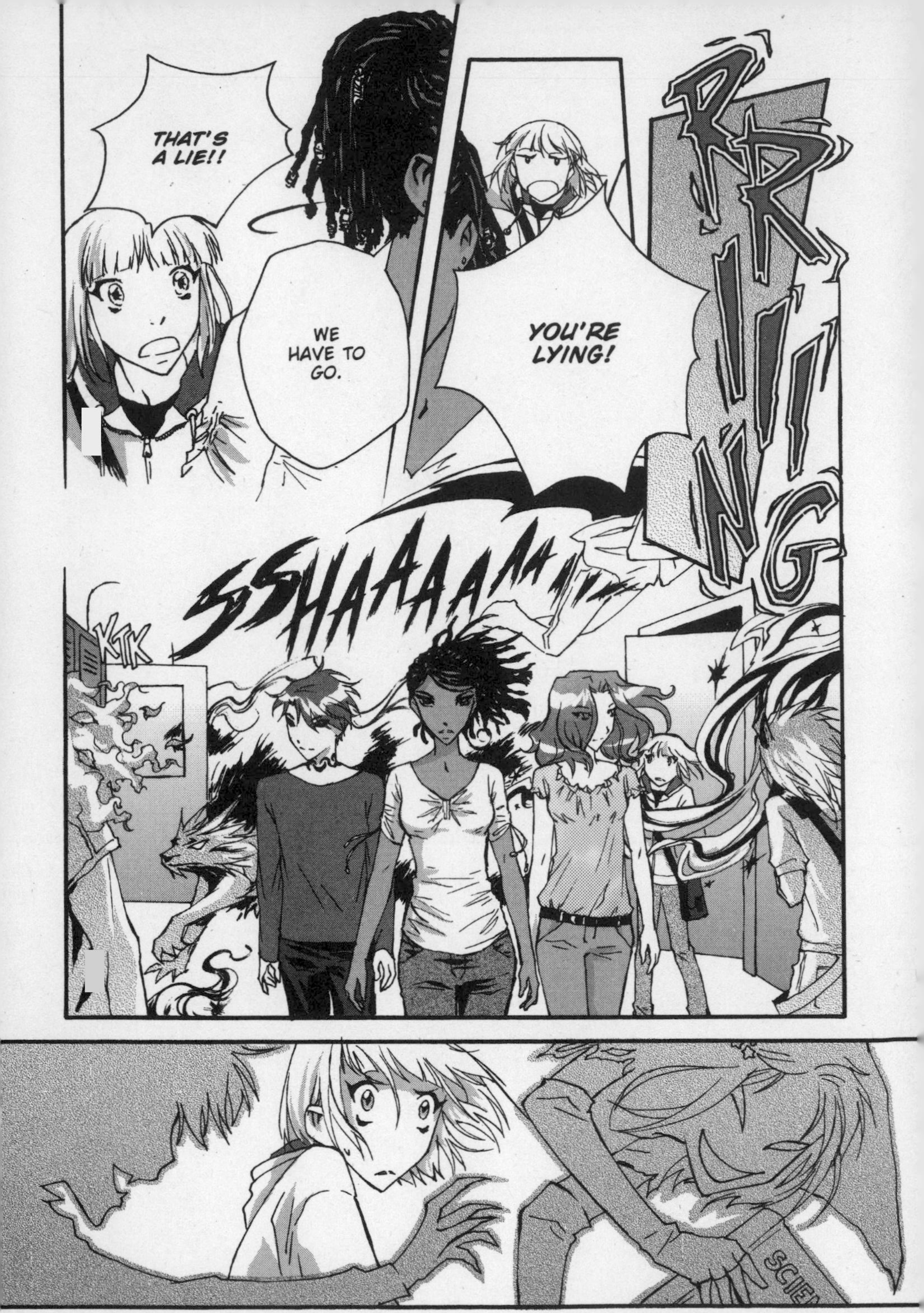
THAT'S A LIE!!
WE HAVE TO GO.
YOU'RE LYING!
RRIIING
SSHAAAAA
KTK

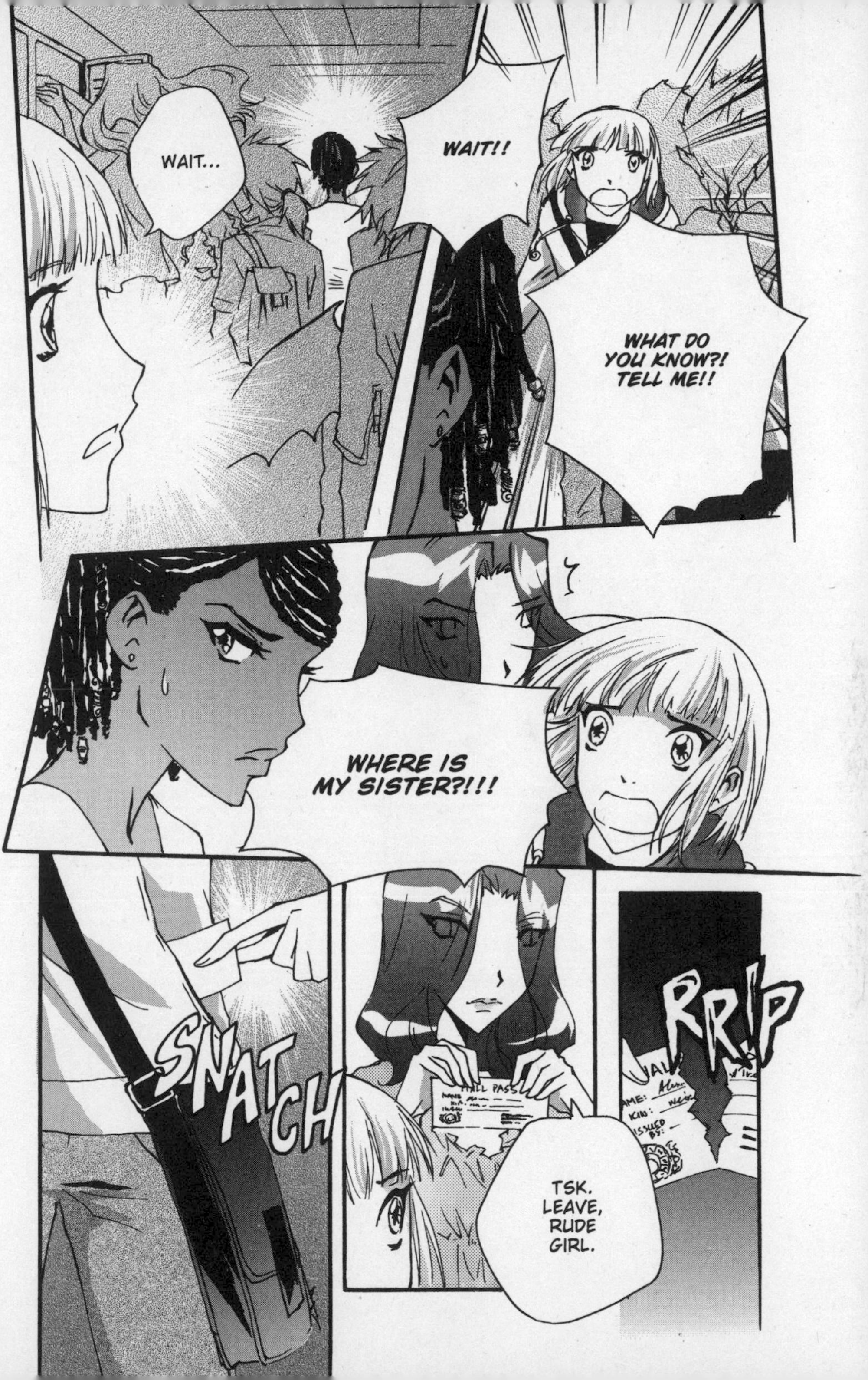
WAIT...
WAIT!!
WHAT DO YOU KNOW?! TELL ME!!
WHERE IS MY SISTER?!!!
SNATCH
HALL PASS
TSK. LEAVE, RUDE GIRL.
RRIP

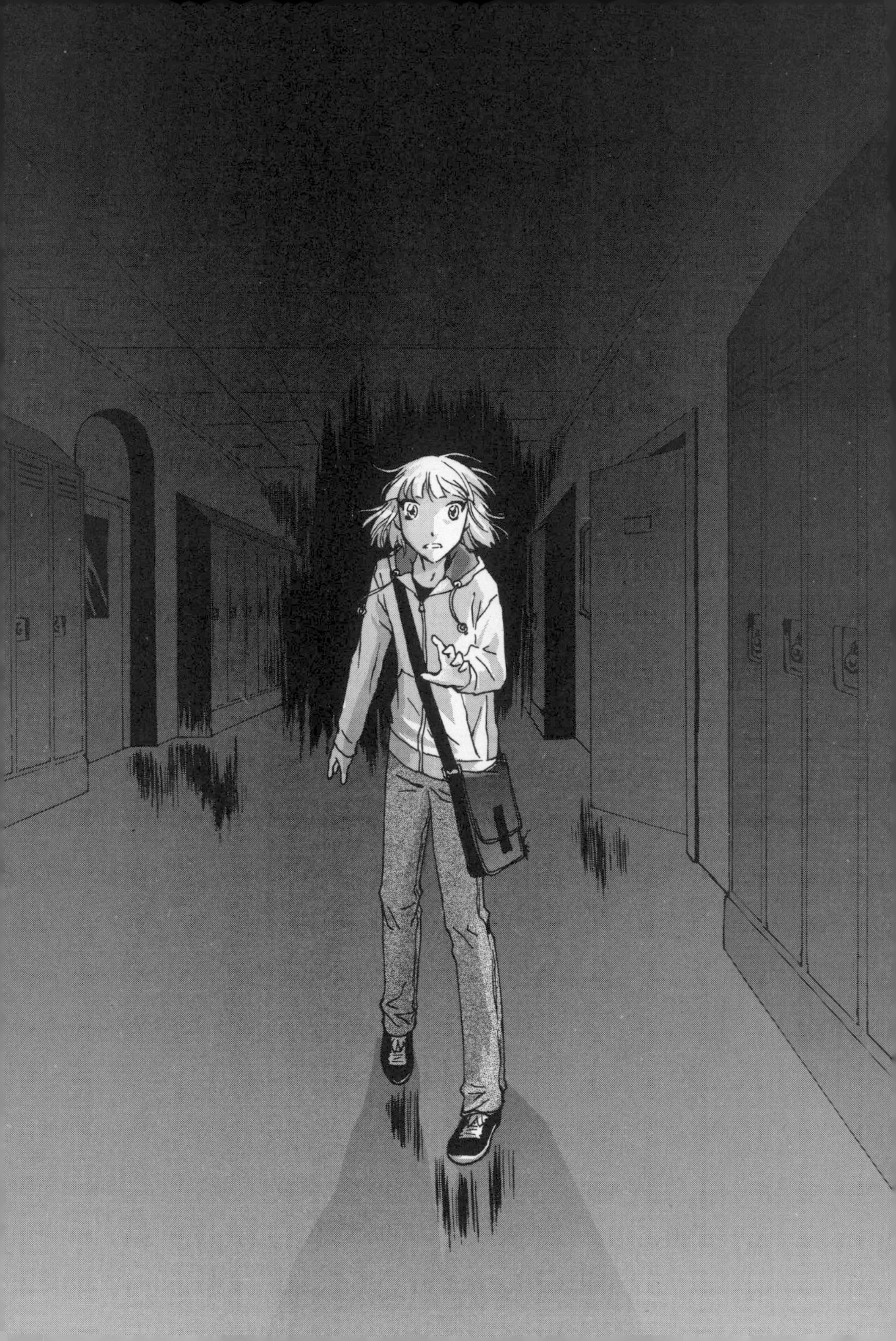

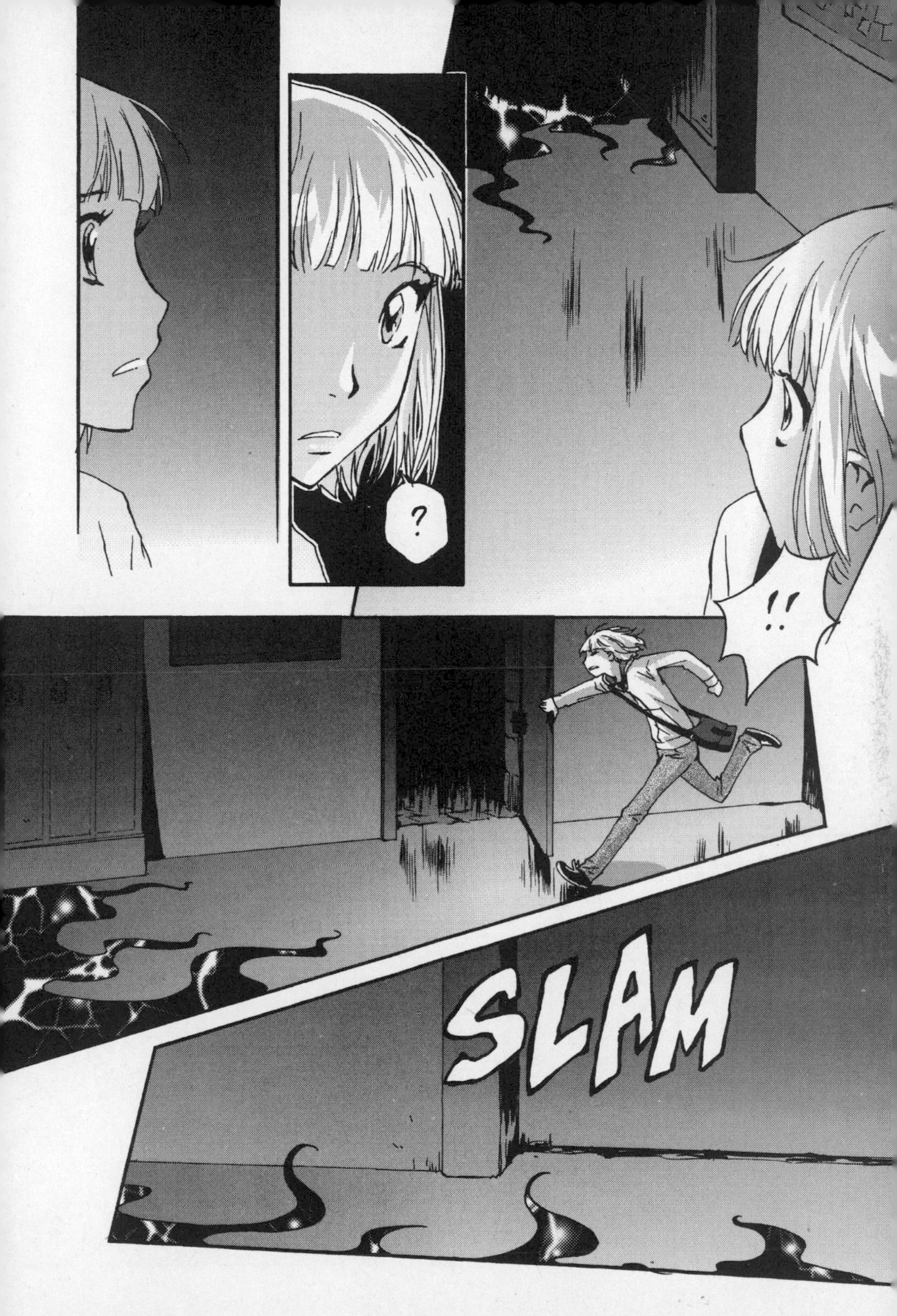
?
!!
SLAM

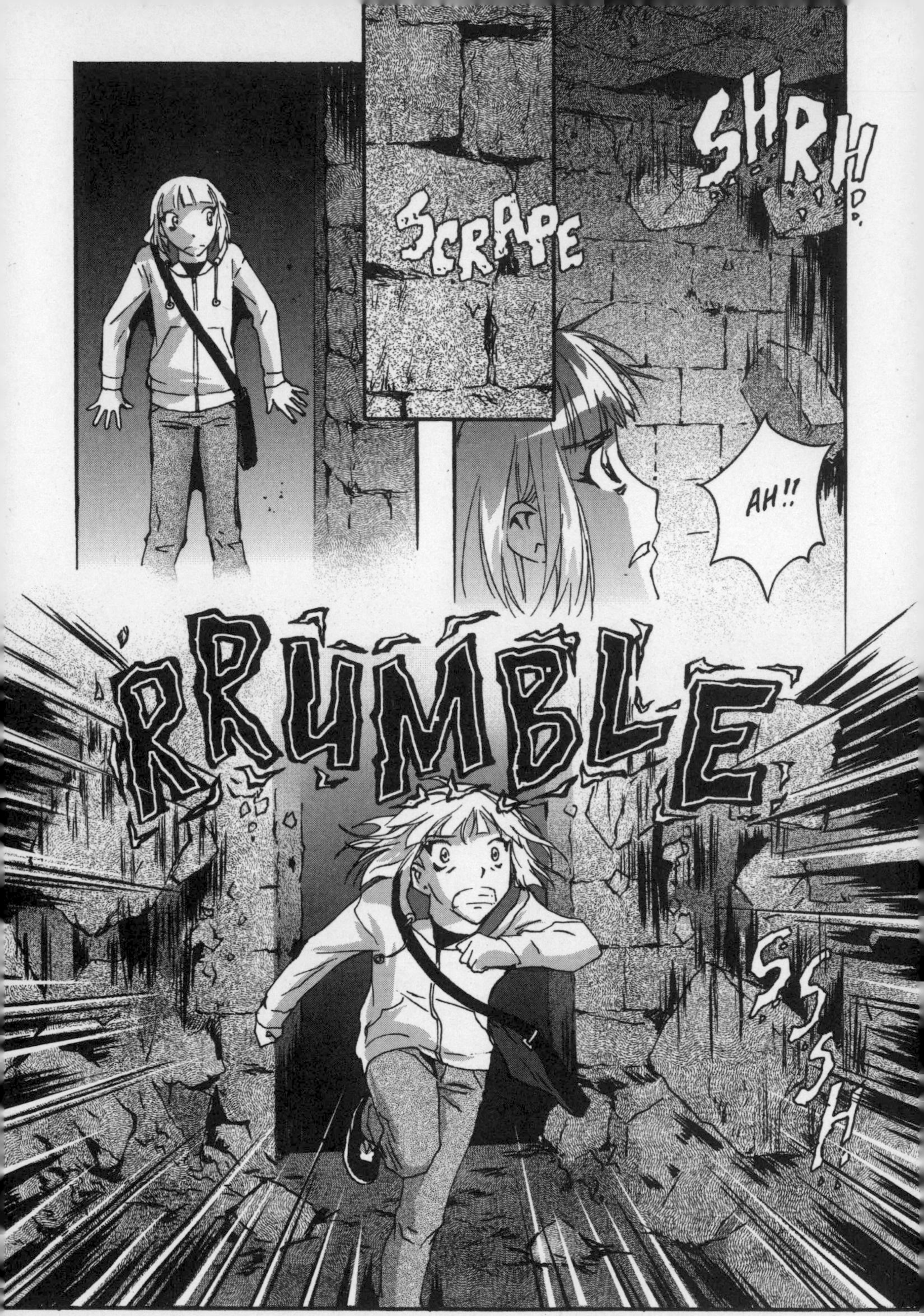
SCRAPE
SHRH
AH!!
RRUMBLE
SSSH

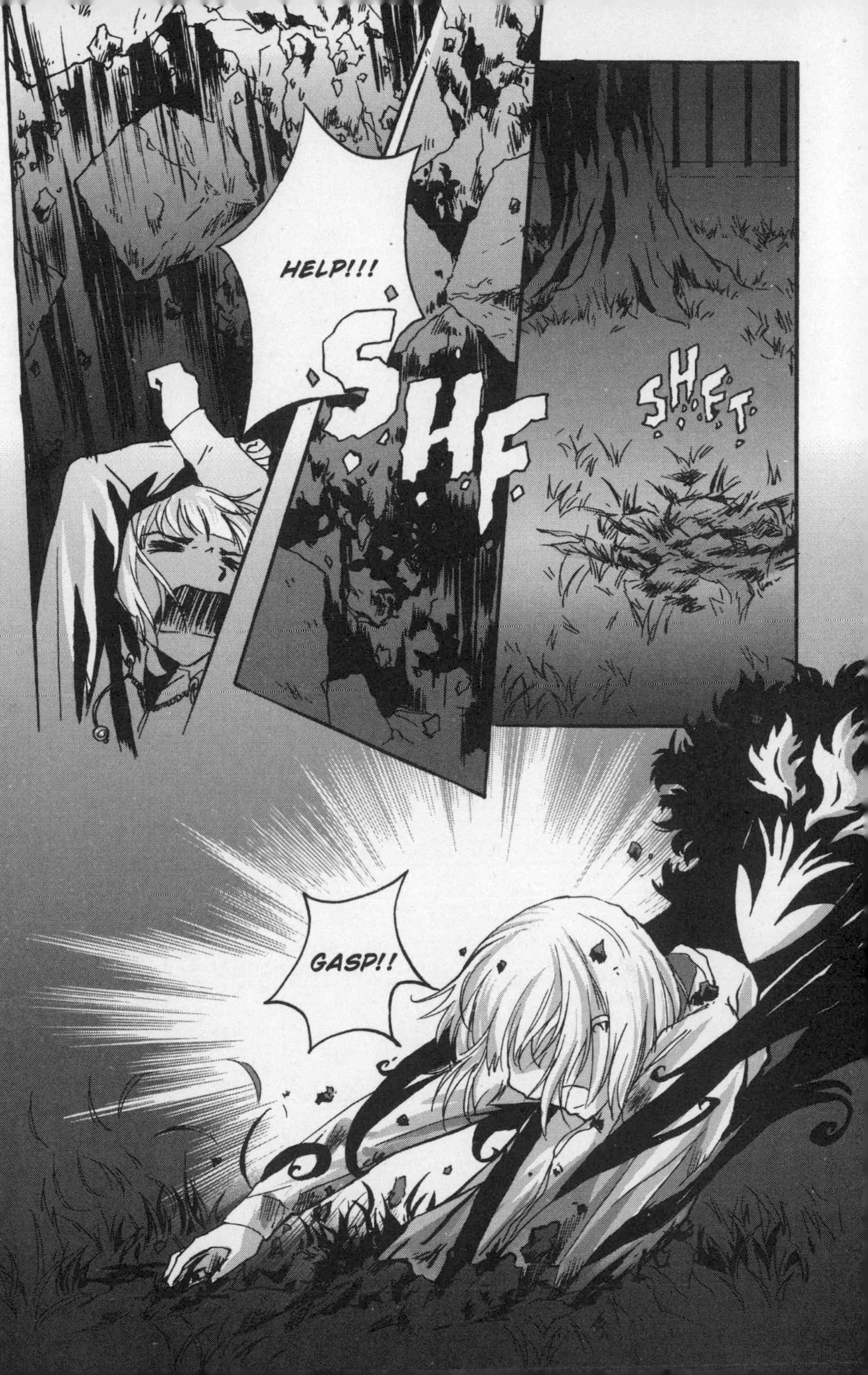
HELP!!!
SHF
SHFT
GASP!!

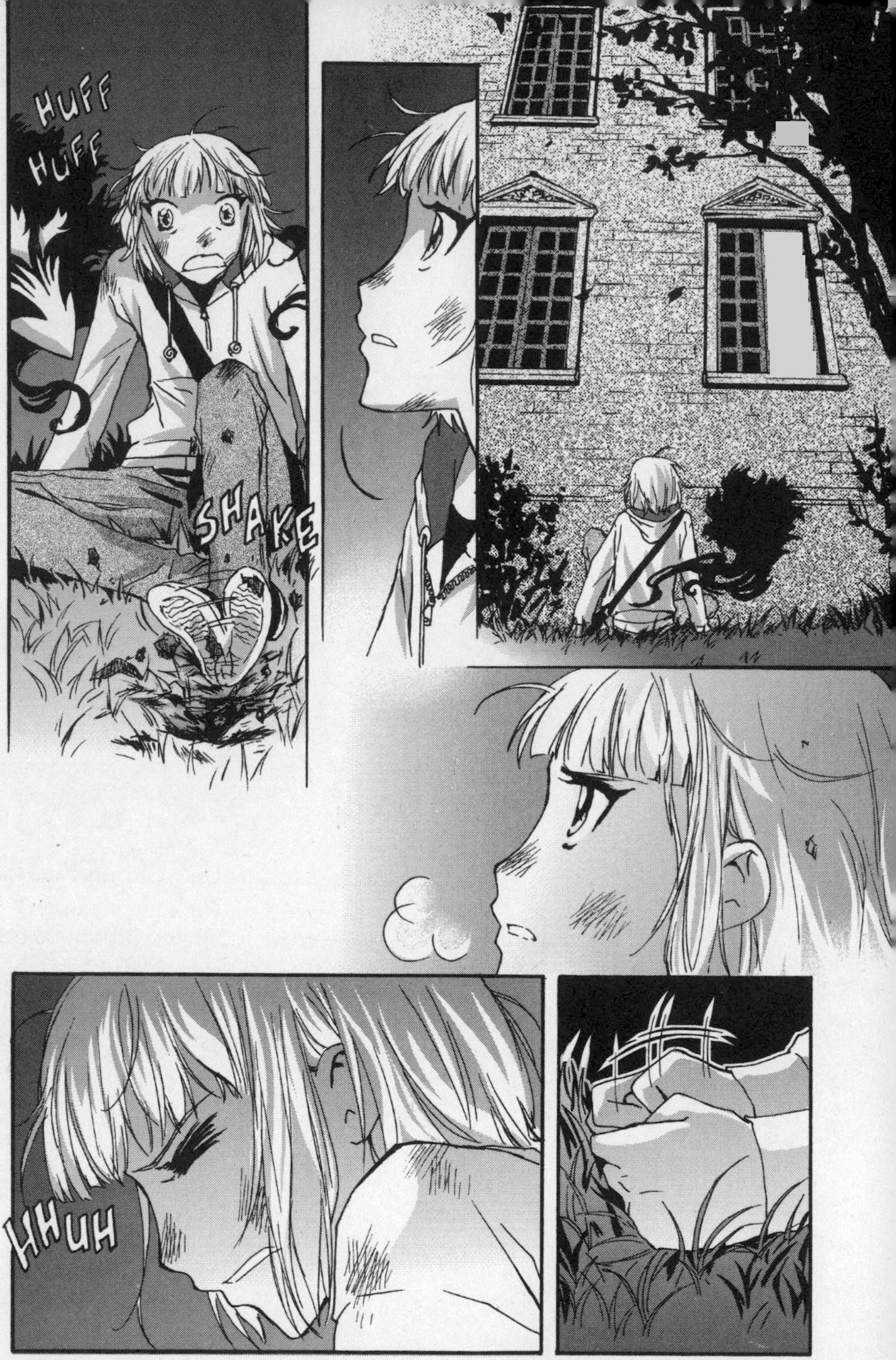
HUFF HUFF
SHAKE
HHUH

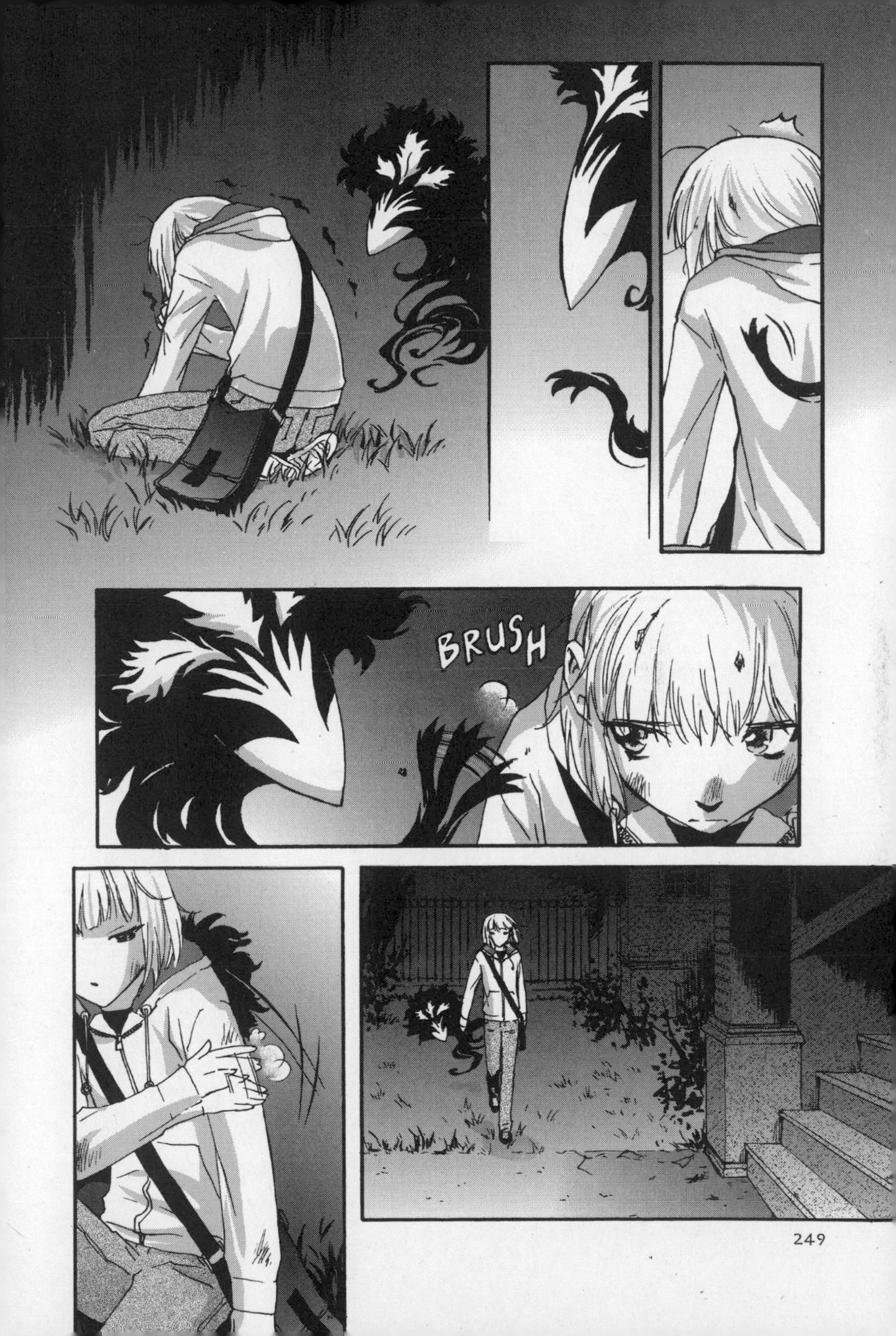
BRUSH

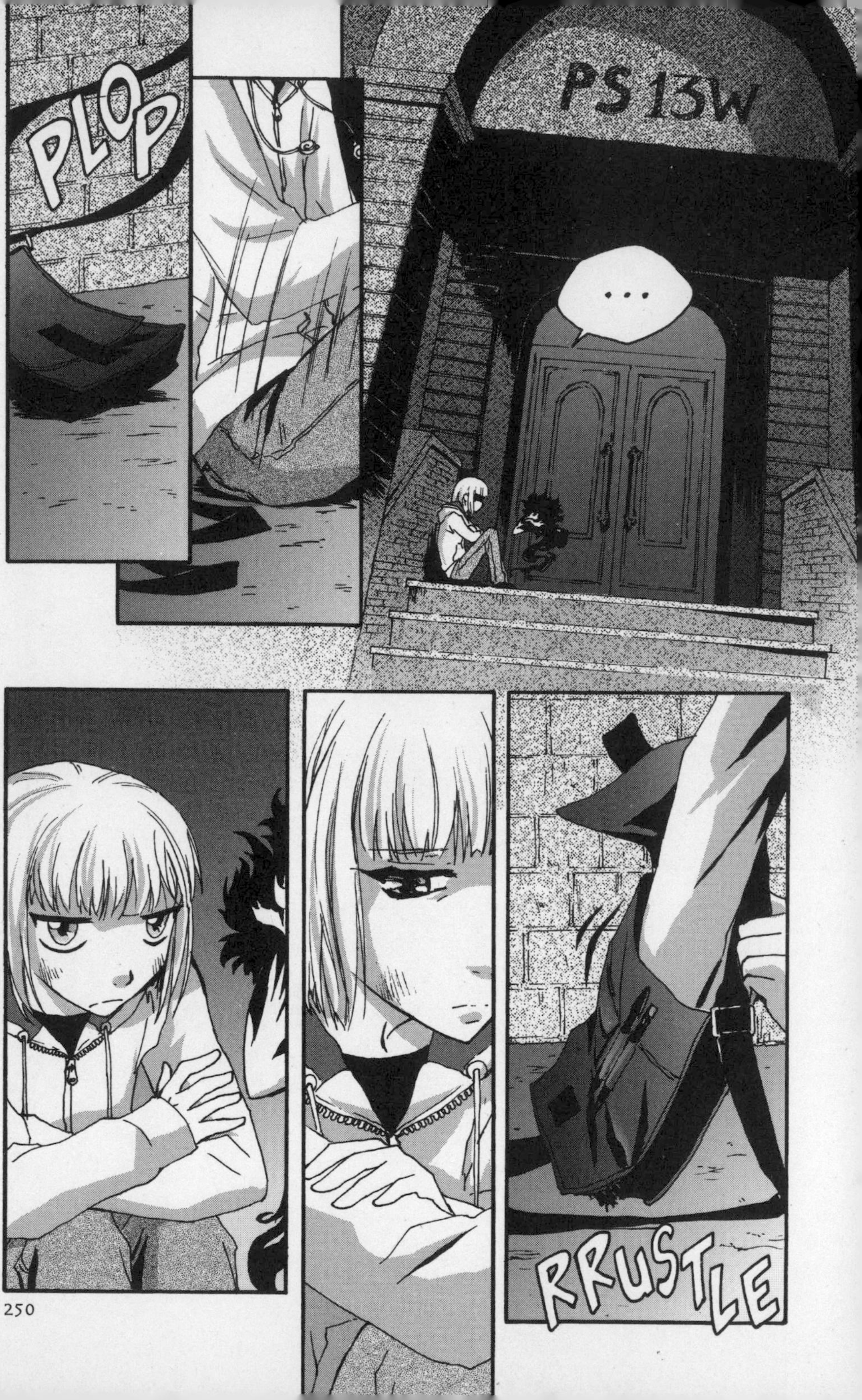
PLOP
PS 13W
...
RRUSTLE

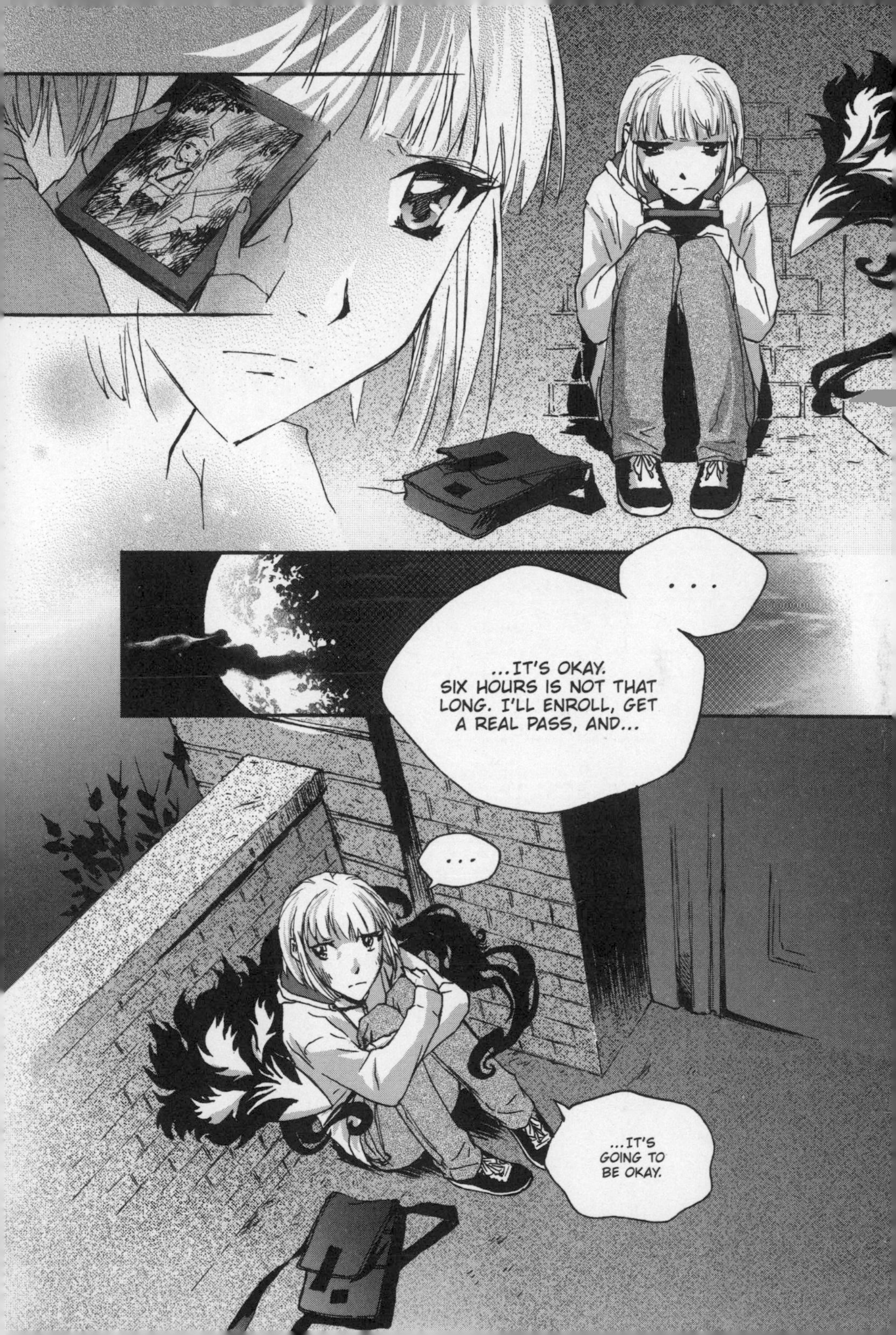
. . .
...IT'S OKAY. SIX HOURS IS NOT THAT LONG. I'LL ENROLL, GET A REAL PASS, AND...
. . .
...IT'S GOING TO BE OKAY.

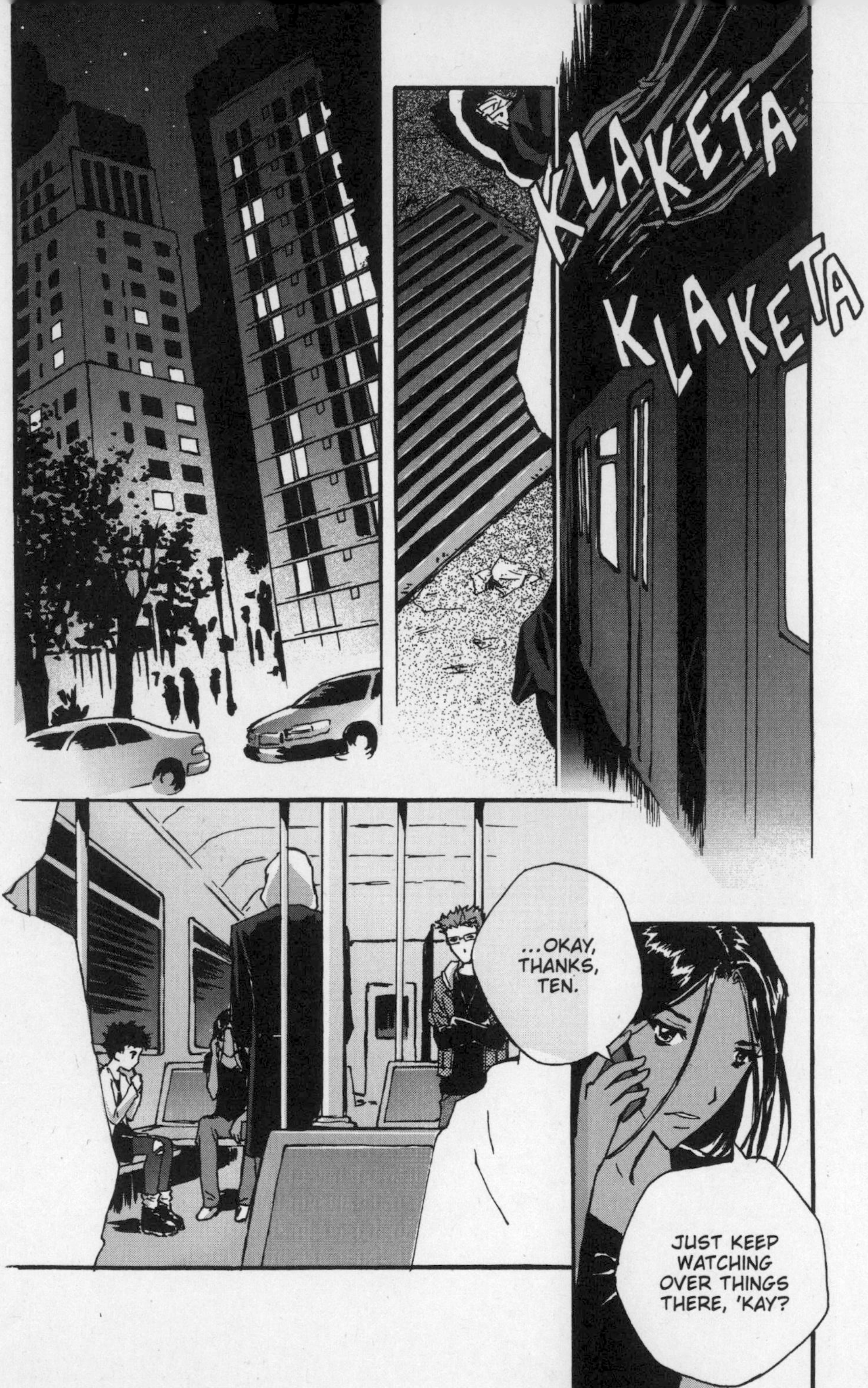
KLAKETA
KLAKETA
...OKAY, THANKS, TEN.
JUST KEEP WATCHING OVER THINGS THERE, 'KAY?

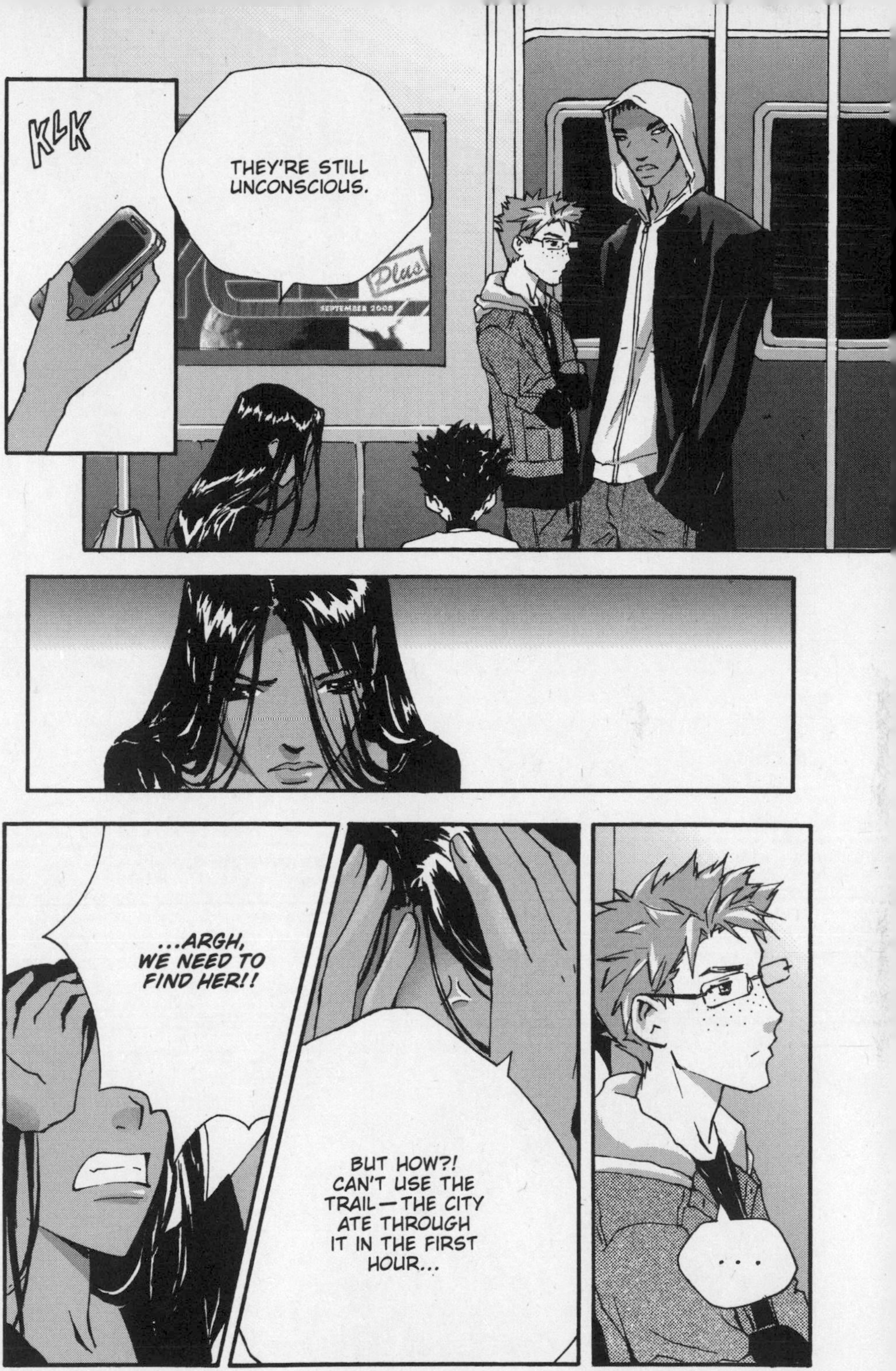
KLK
THEY'RE STILL UNCONSCIOUS.
...ARGH, WE NEED TO FIND HER!!
BUT HOW?! CAN'T USE THE TRAIL—THE CITY ATE THROUGH IT IN THE FIRST HOUR...
...

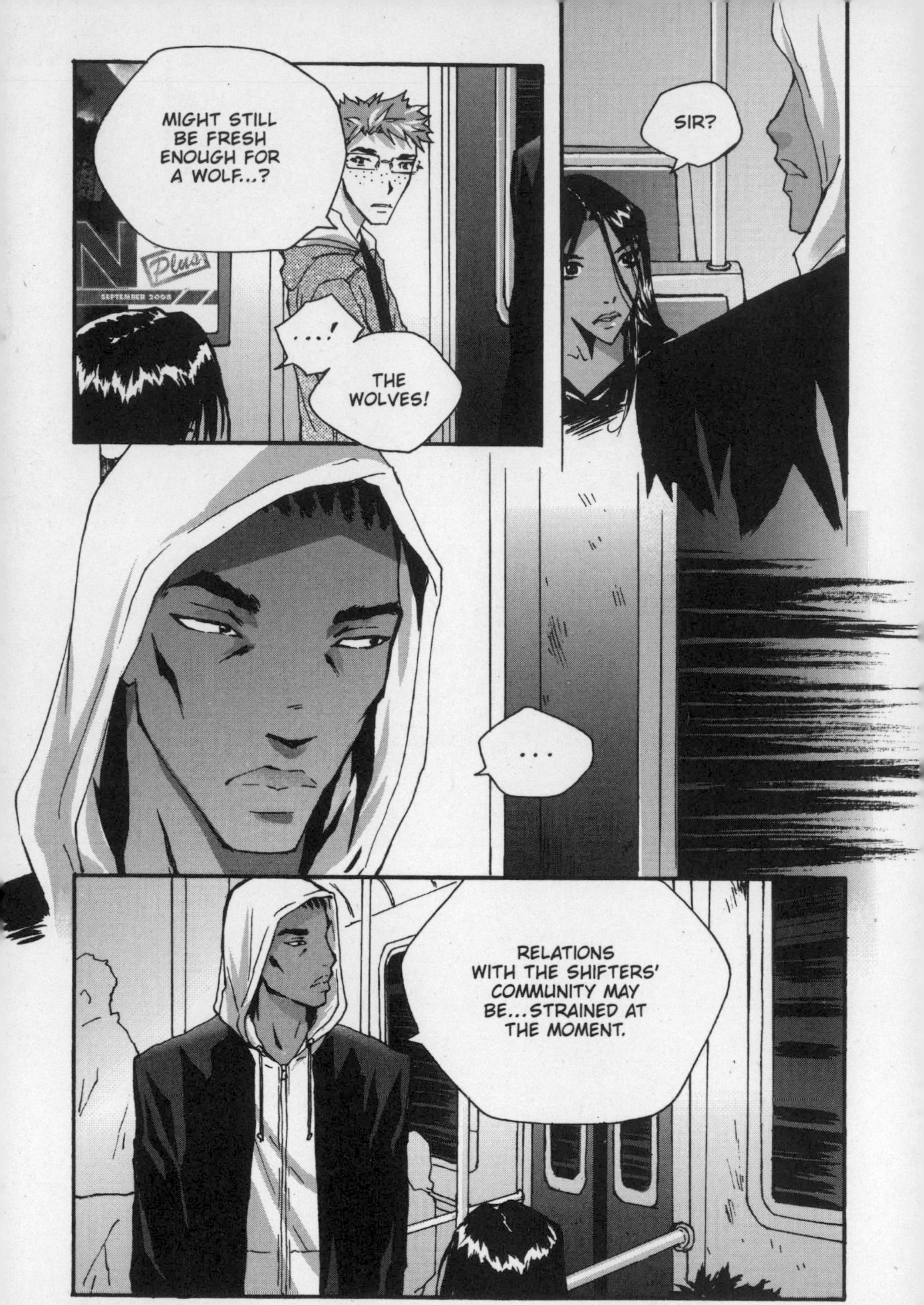
MIGHT STILL BE FRESH ENOUGH FOR A WOLF...?
...!
THE WOLVES!
SIR?
...
RELATIONS WITH THE SHIFTERS' COMMUNITY MAY BE...STRAINED AT THE MOMENT.

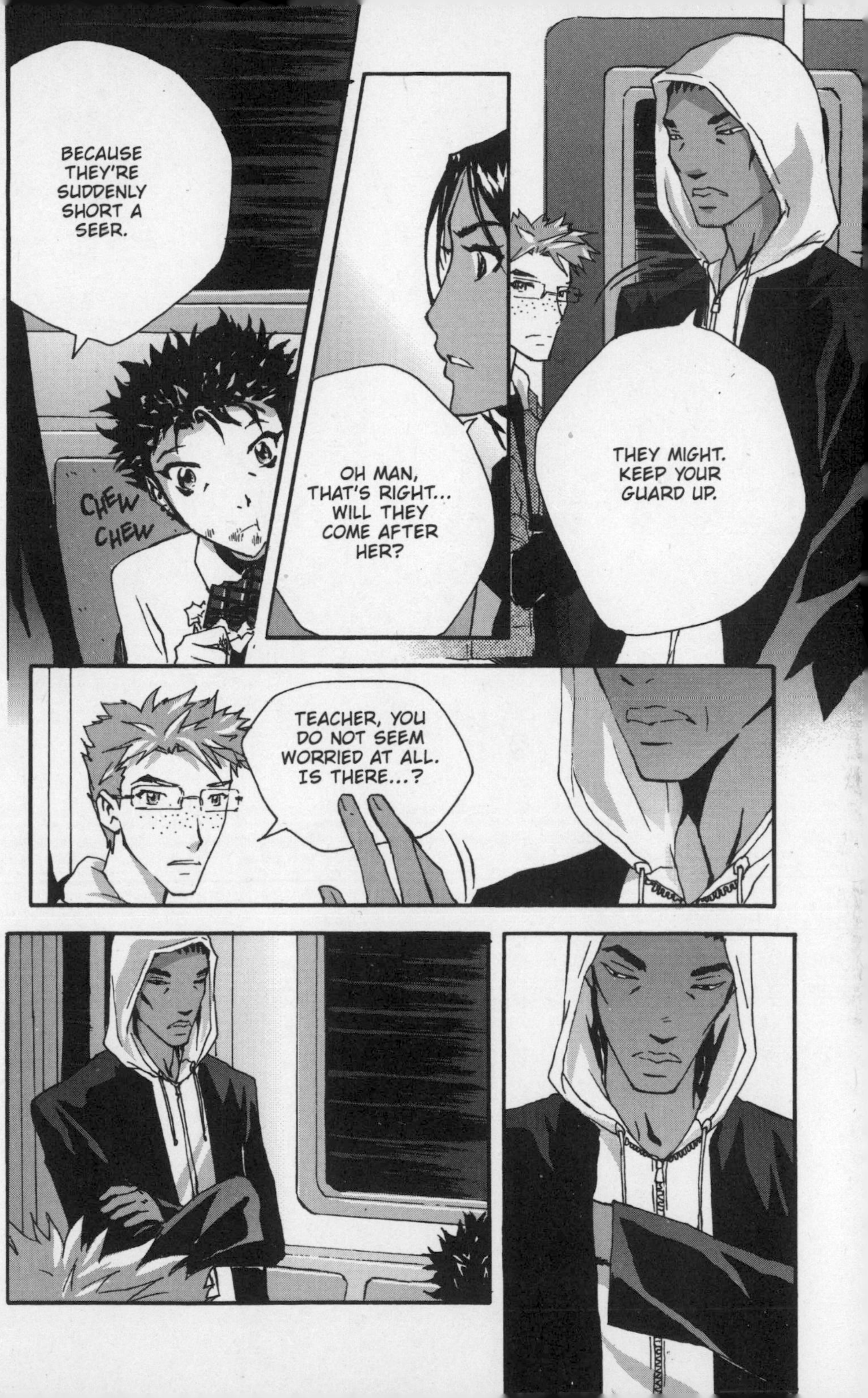

BECAUSE THEY'RE SUDDENLY SHORT A SEER.
CHEW CHEW
OH MAN, THAT'S RIGHT... WILL THEY COME AFTER HER?
THEY MIGHT. KEEP YOUR GUARD UP.
TEACHER, YOU DO NOT SEEM WORRIED AT ALL. IS THERE...?

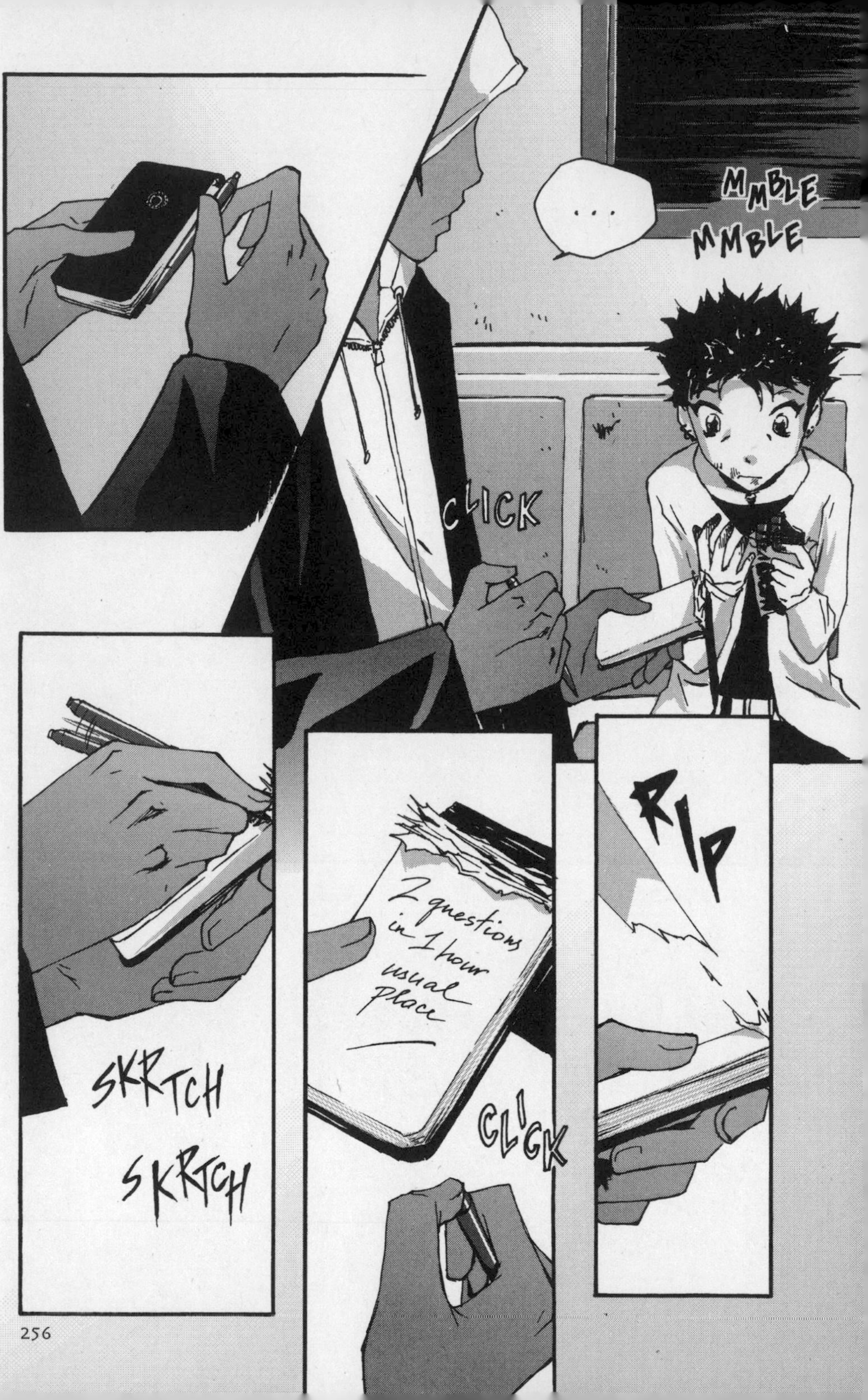
...
MMBLE
MMBLE
CLICK
SKRTCH
SKRTCH
2 questions in 1 hour usual place
CLICK
RIP

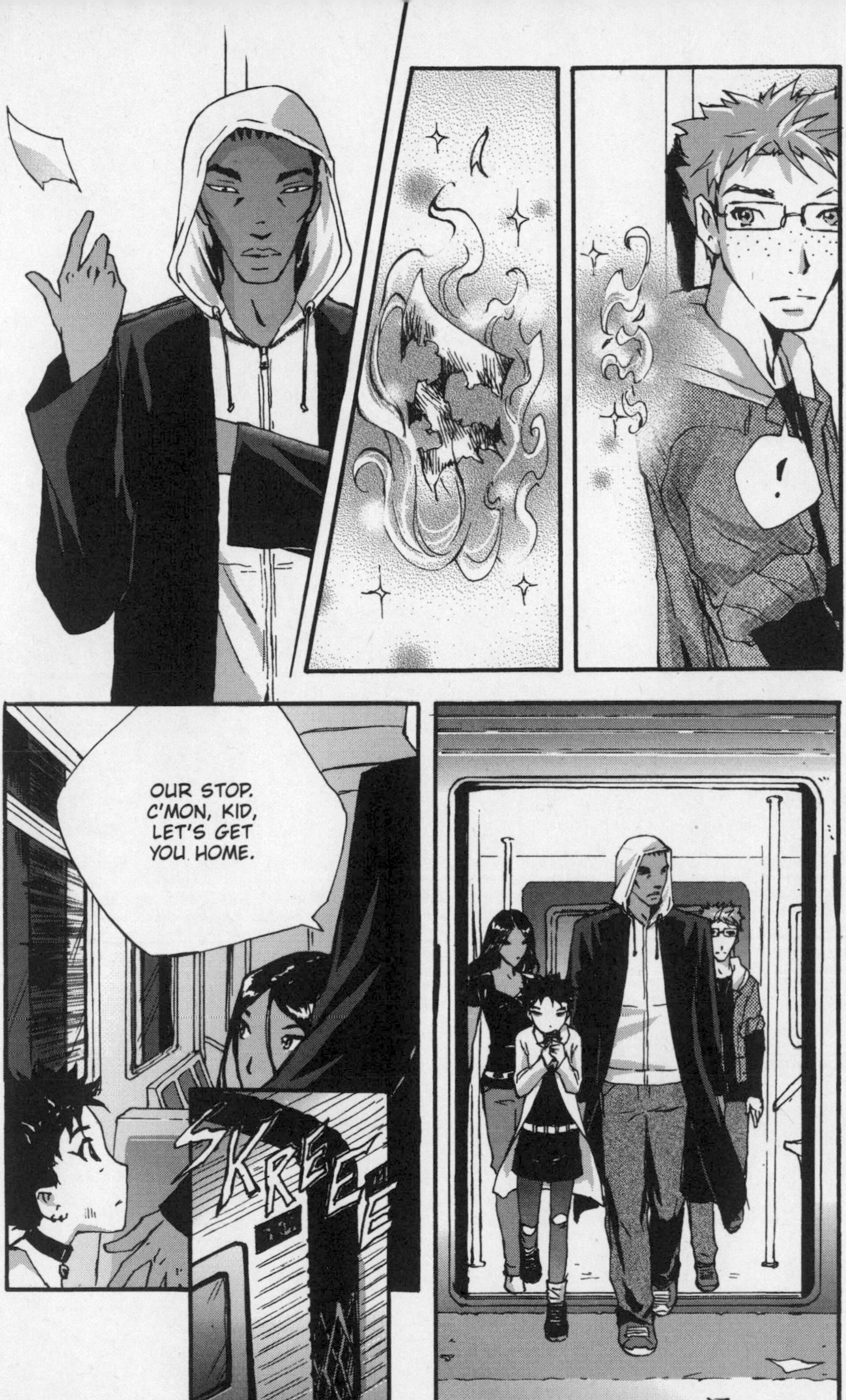
!
OUR STOP. C'MON, KID, LET'S GET YOU HOME.
SKREEEE

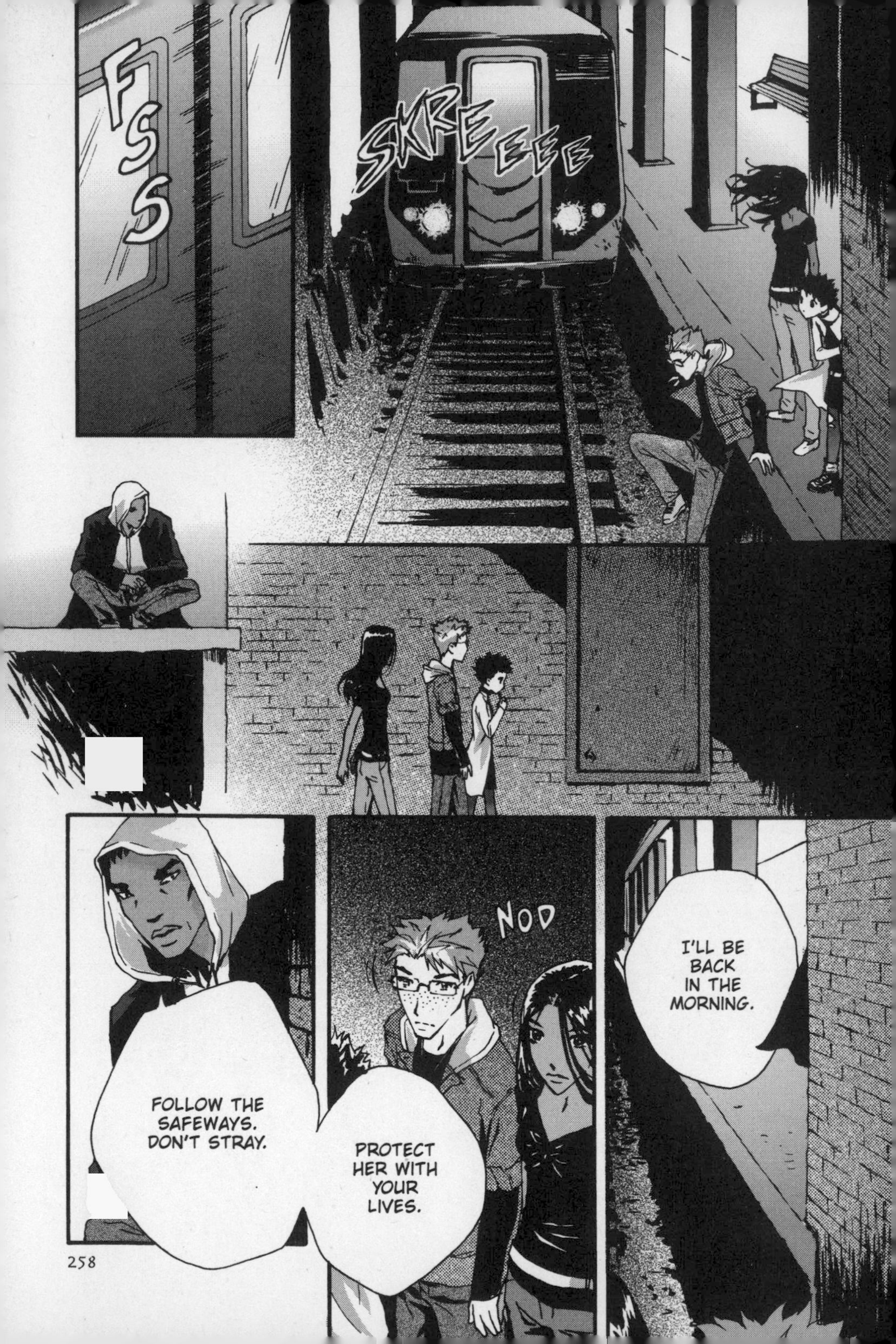
FSS
SKREEEEE
NOD
FOLLOW THE SAFEWAYS. DON'T STRAY.
PROTECT HER WITH YOUR LIVES.
I'LL BE BACK IN THE MORNING.

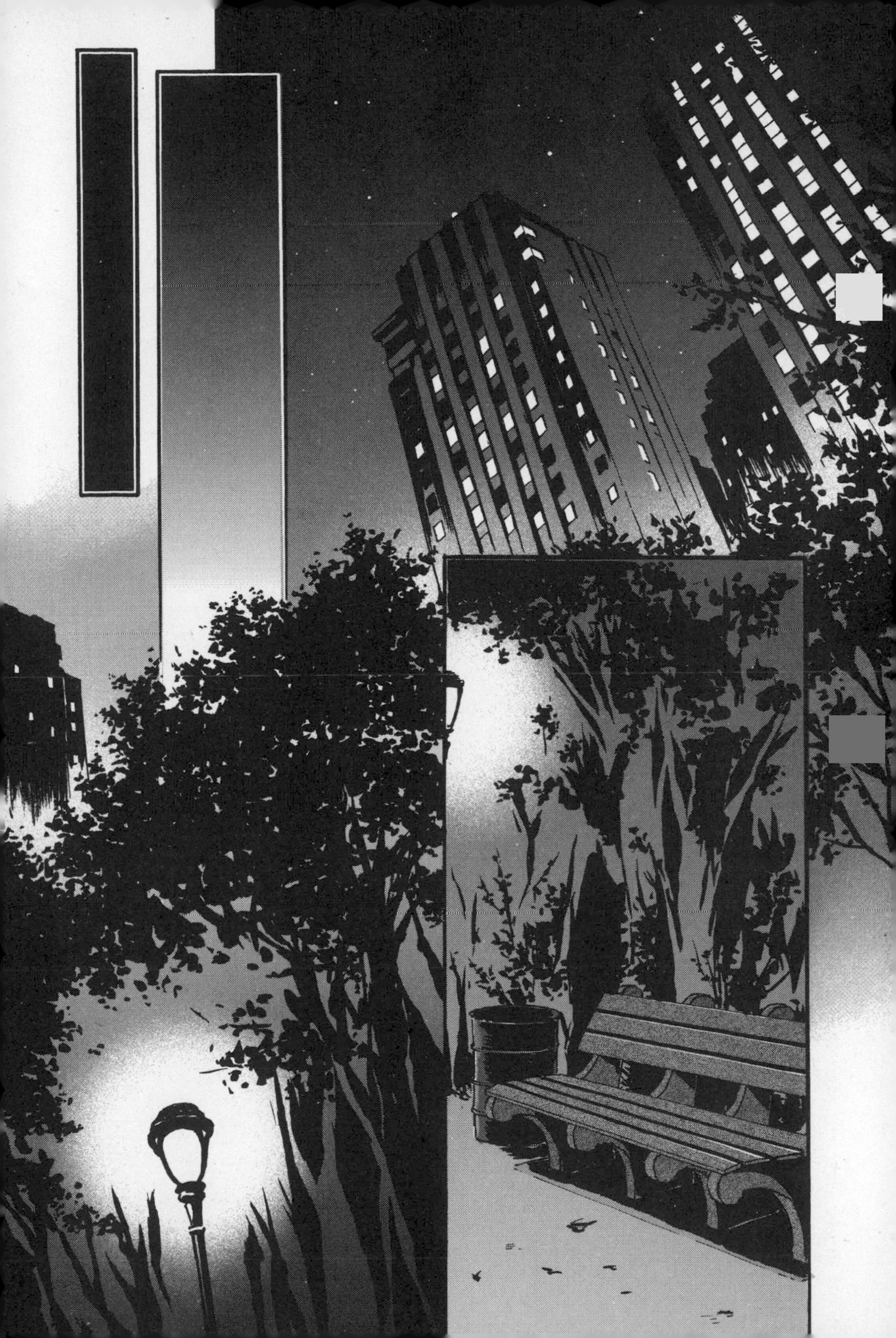

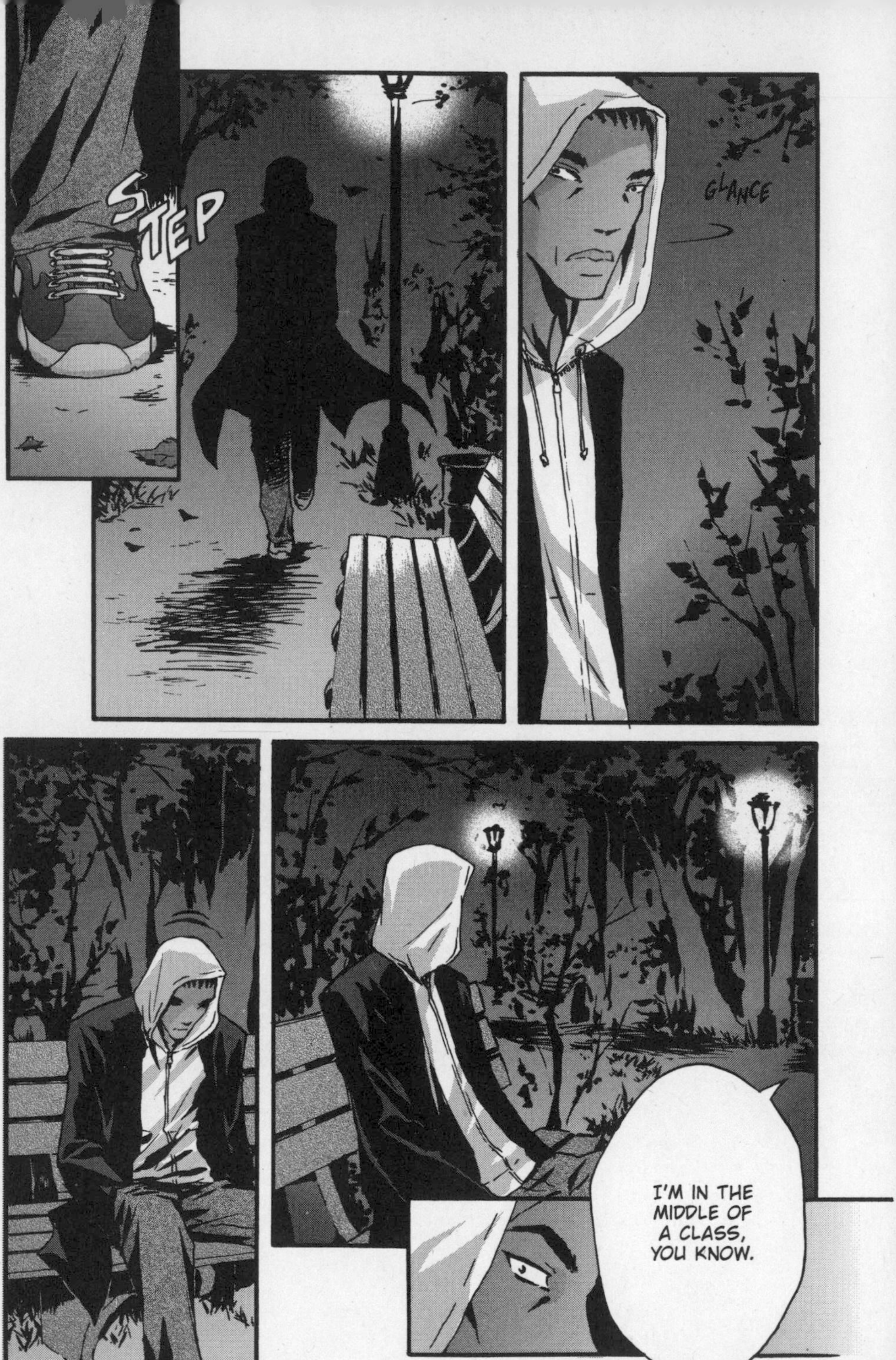
STEP
GLANCE
I'M IN THE MIDDLE OF A CLASS, YOU KNOW.

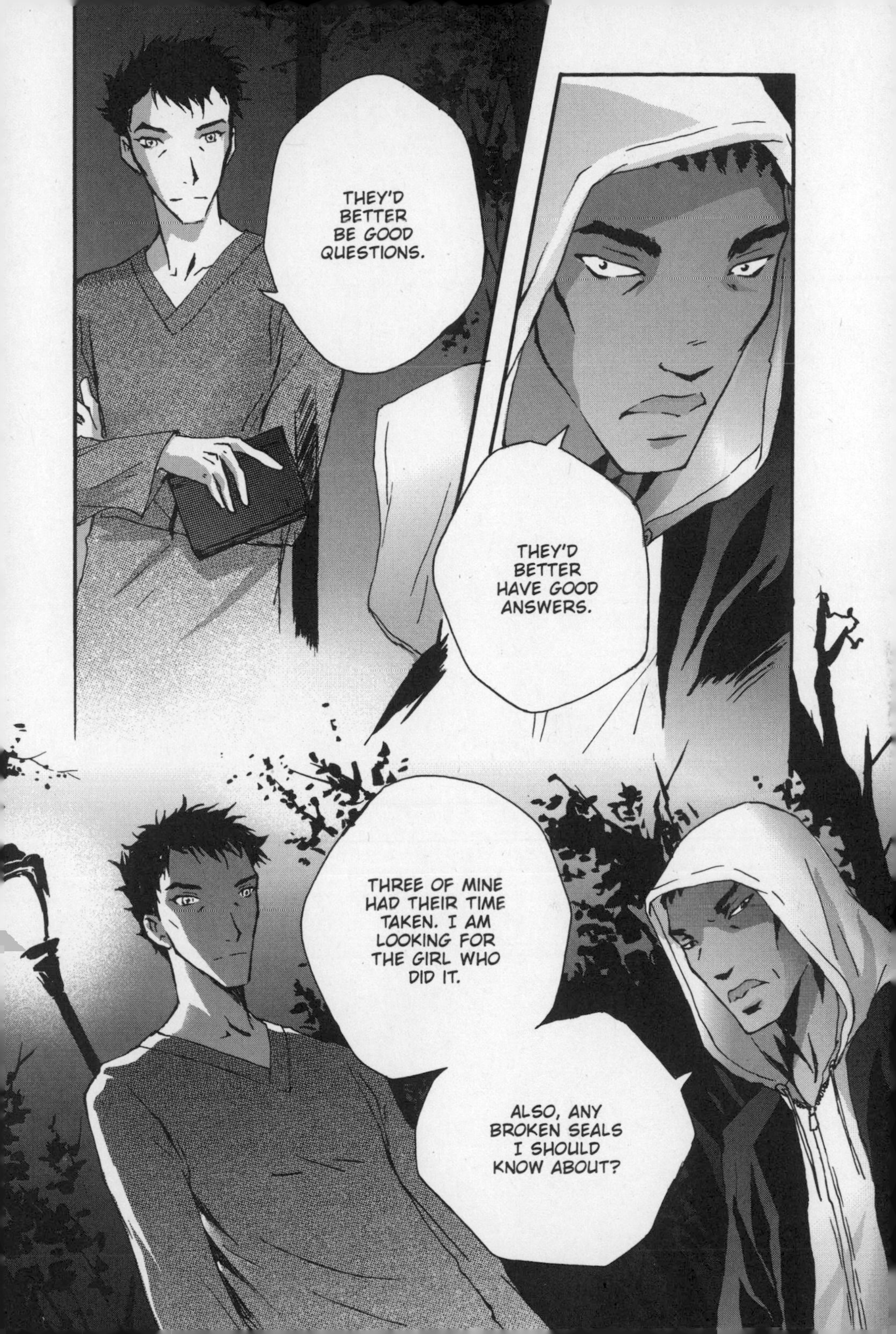
THEY'D BETTER BE GOOD QUESTIONS.
THEY'D BETTER HAVE GOOD ANSWERS.
THREE OF MINE HAD THEIR TIME TAKEN. I AM LOOKING FOR THE GIRL WHO DID IT.
ALSO, ANY BROKEN SEALS I SHOULD KNOW ABOUT?

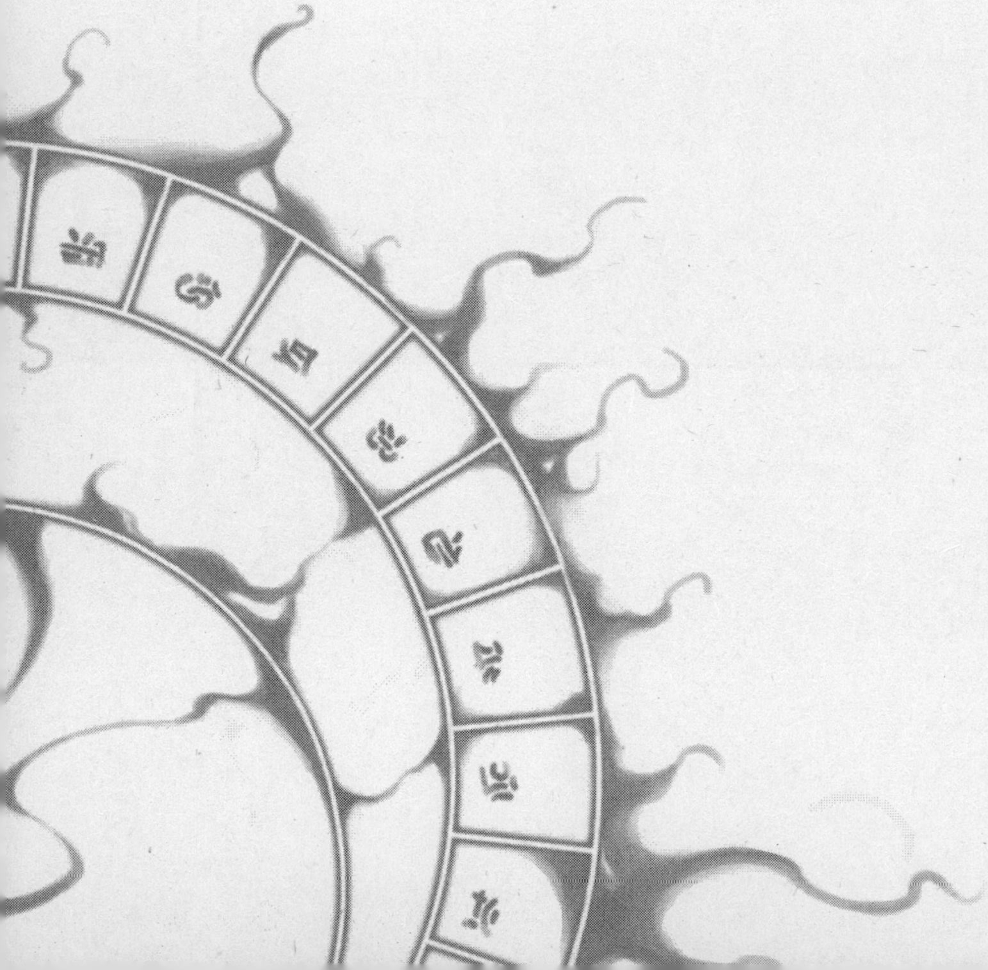

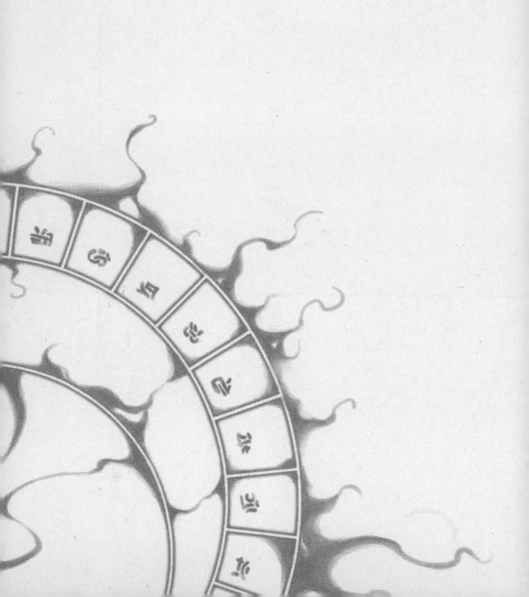

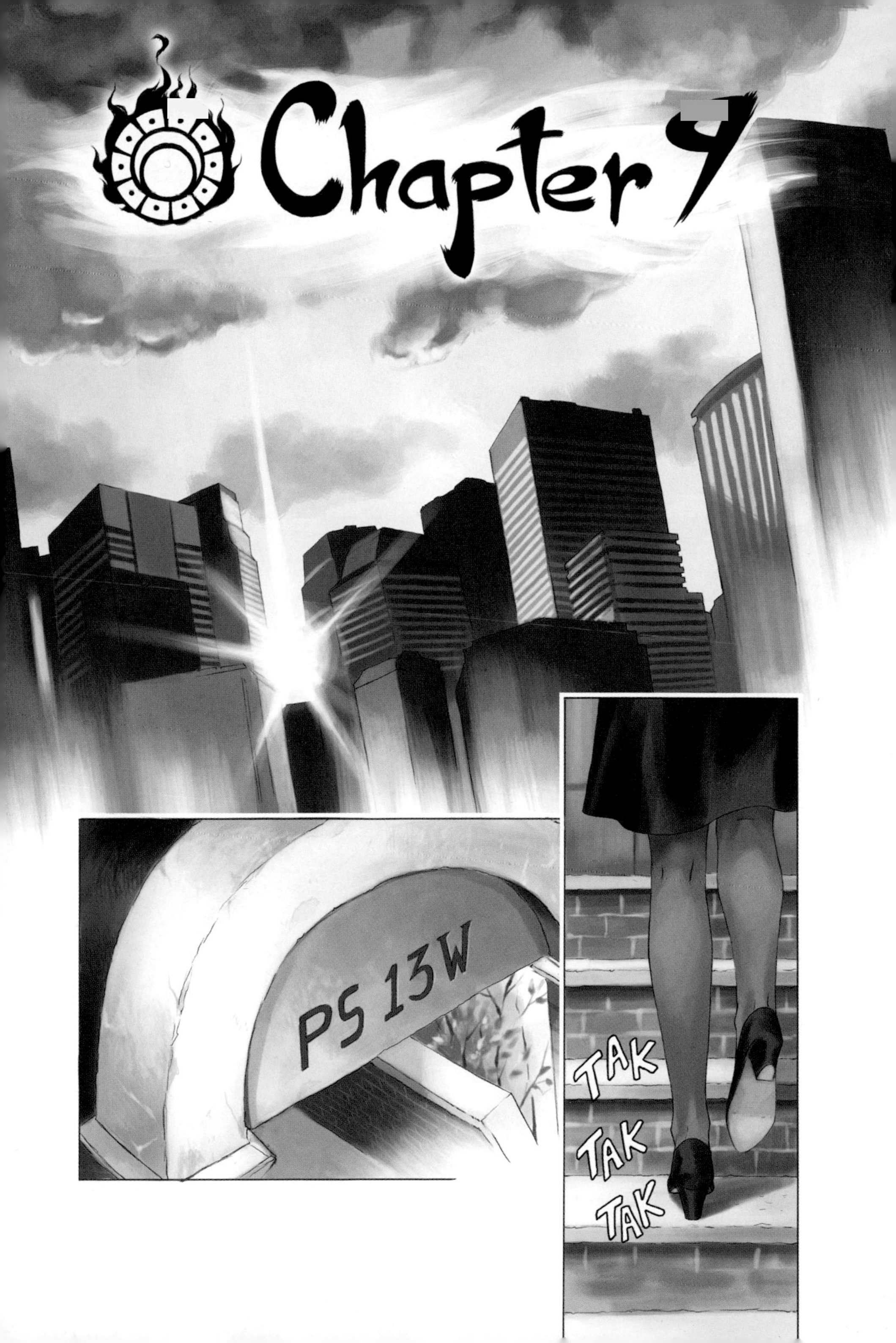
Chapter 9
PS 13W
TAK
TAK
TAK

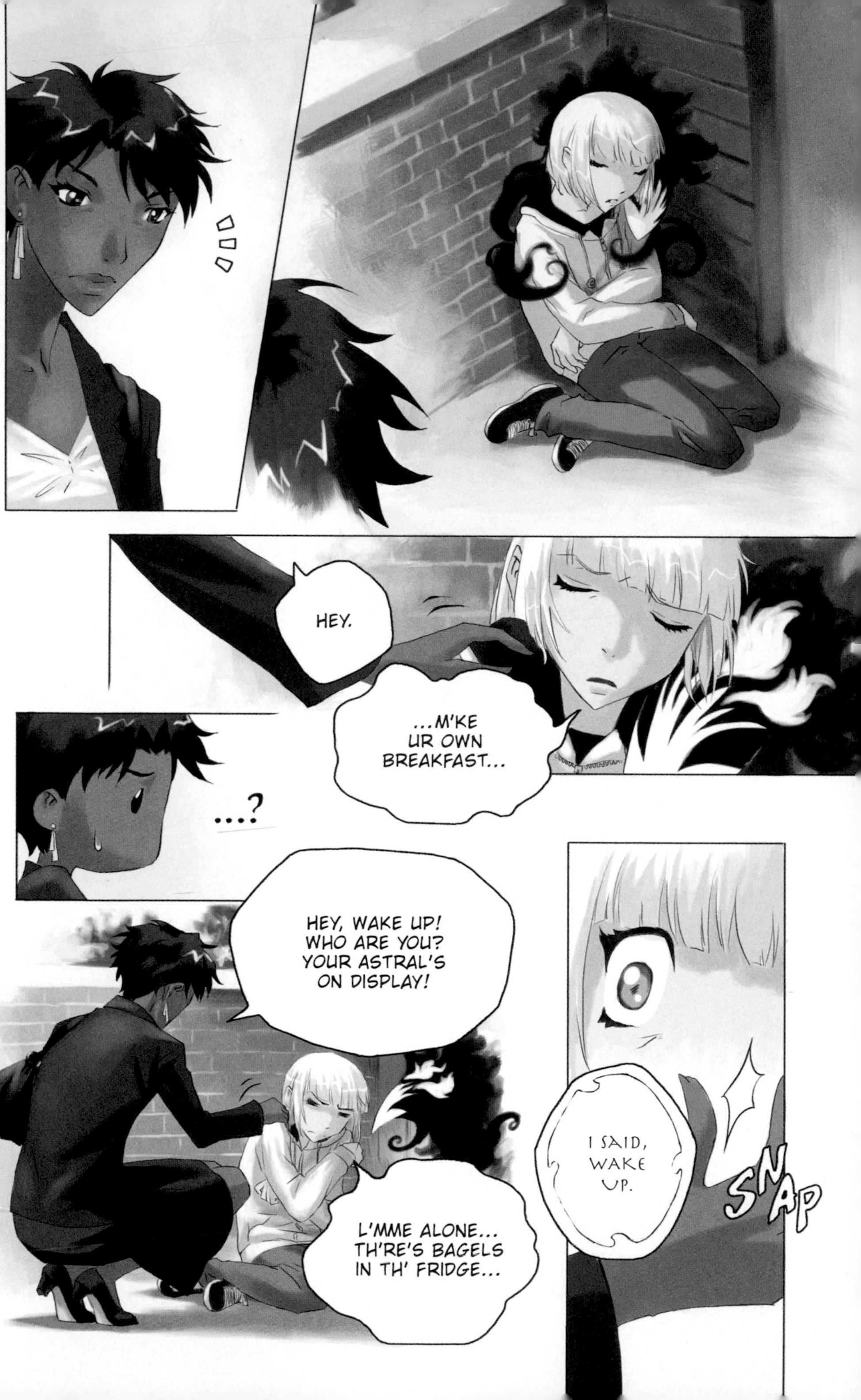
HEY.
...M'KE UR OWN BREAKFAST...
...?
HEY, WAKE UP! WHO ARE YOU? YOUR ASTRAL'S ON DISPLAY!
L'MME ALONE... TH'RE'S BAGELS IN TH' FRIDGE...
I SAID, WAKE UP.
SNAP

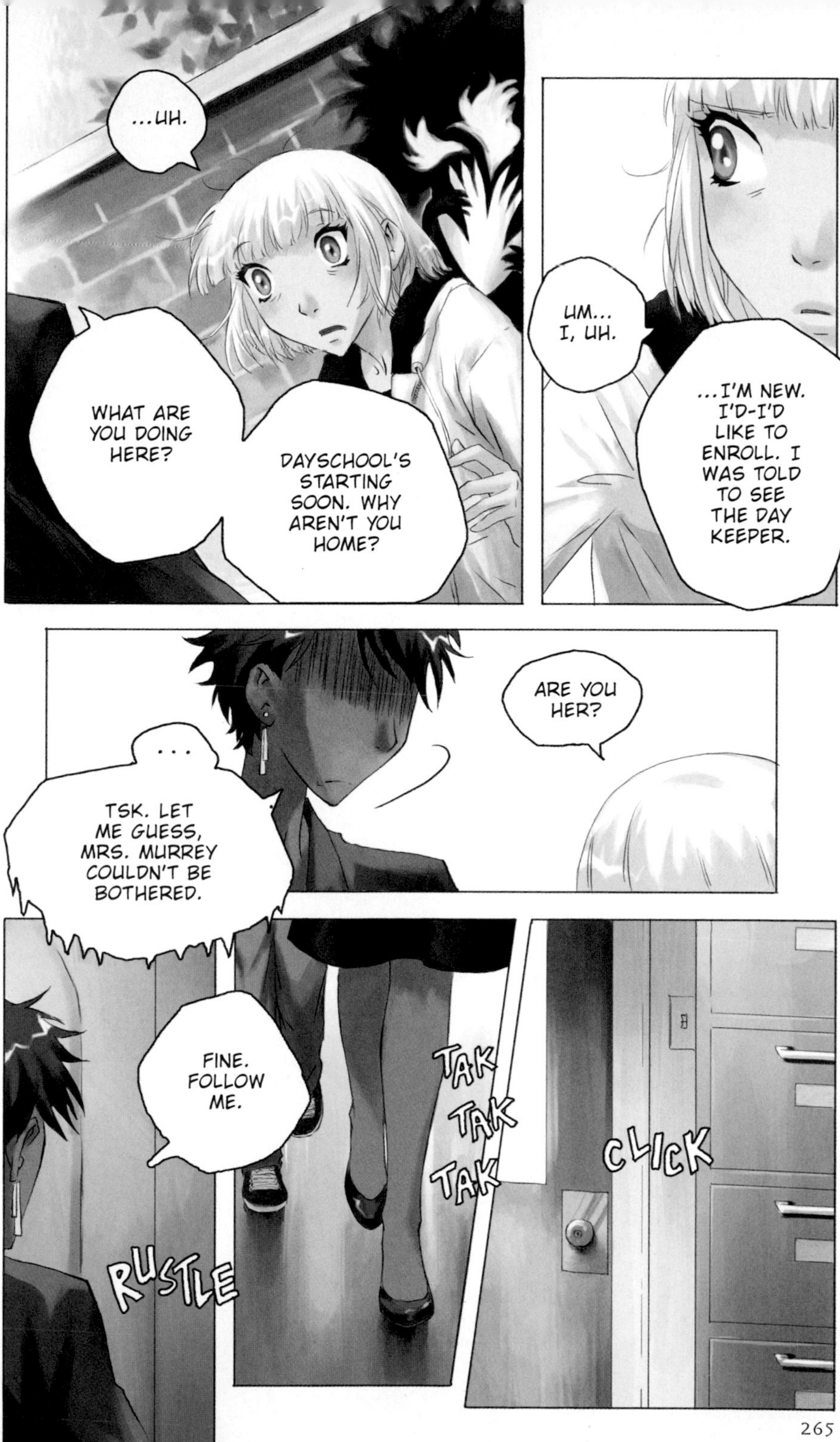
...UH.
WHAT ARE YOU DOING HERE?
DAYSCHOOL'S STARTING SOON. WHY AREN'T YOU HOME?
UM... I, UH.
...I'M NEW. I'D-I'D LIKE TO ENROLL. I WAS TOLD TO SEE THE DAY KEEPER.
...
TSK. LET ME GUESS, MRS. MURREY COULDN'T BE BOTHERED.
ARE YOU HER?
FINE. FOLLOW ME.
RUSTLE
TAK TAK TAK
CLICK

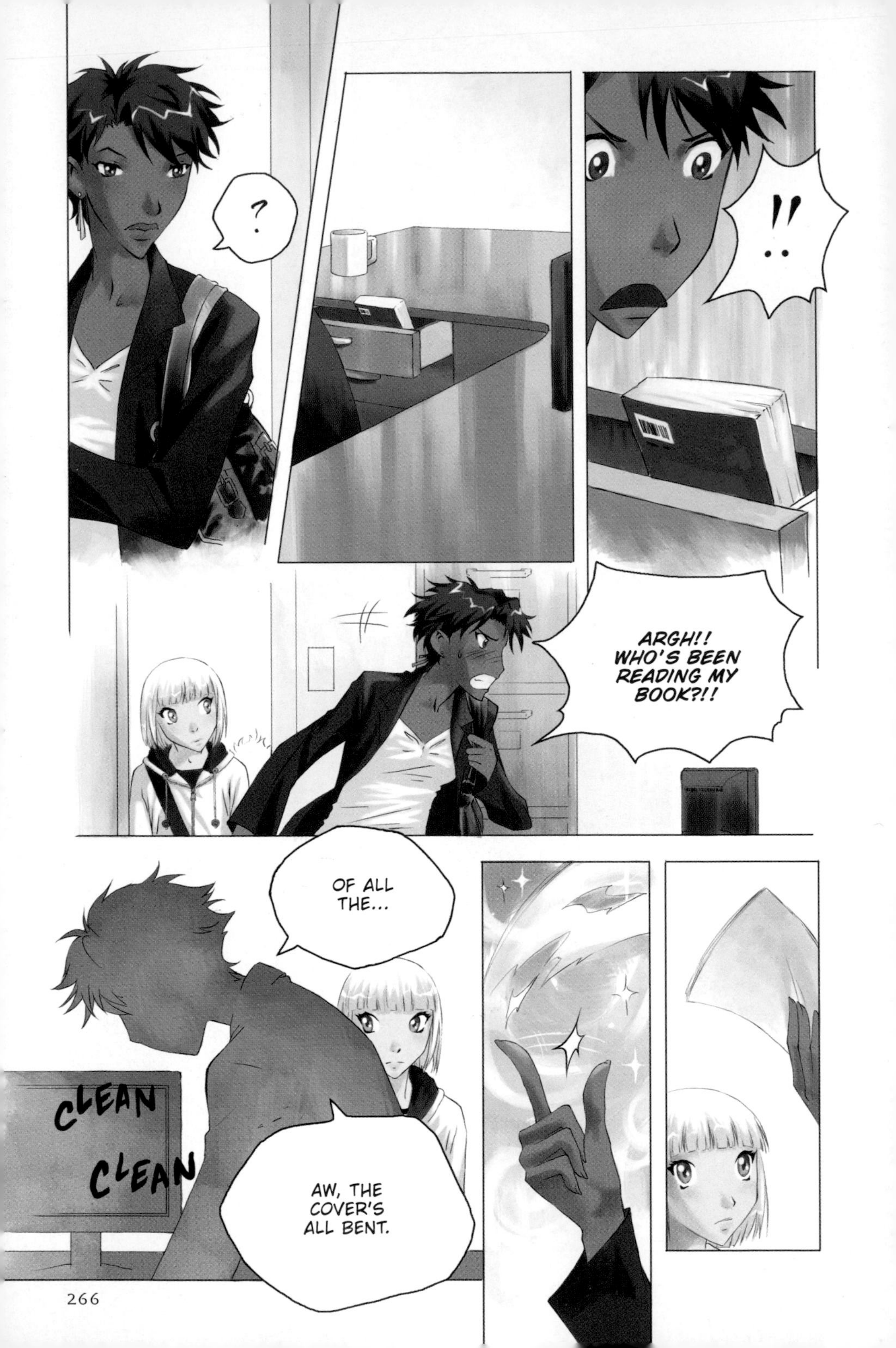
?
!!
ARGH!! WHO'S BEEN READING MY BOOK?!!
OF ALL THE...
CLEAN
CLEAN
AW, THE COVER'S ALL BENT.

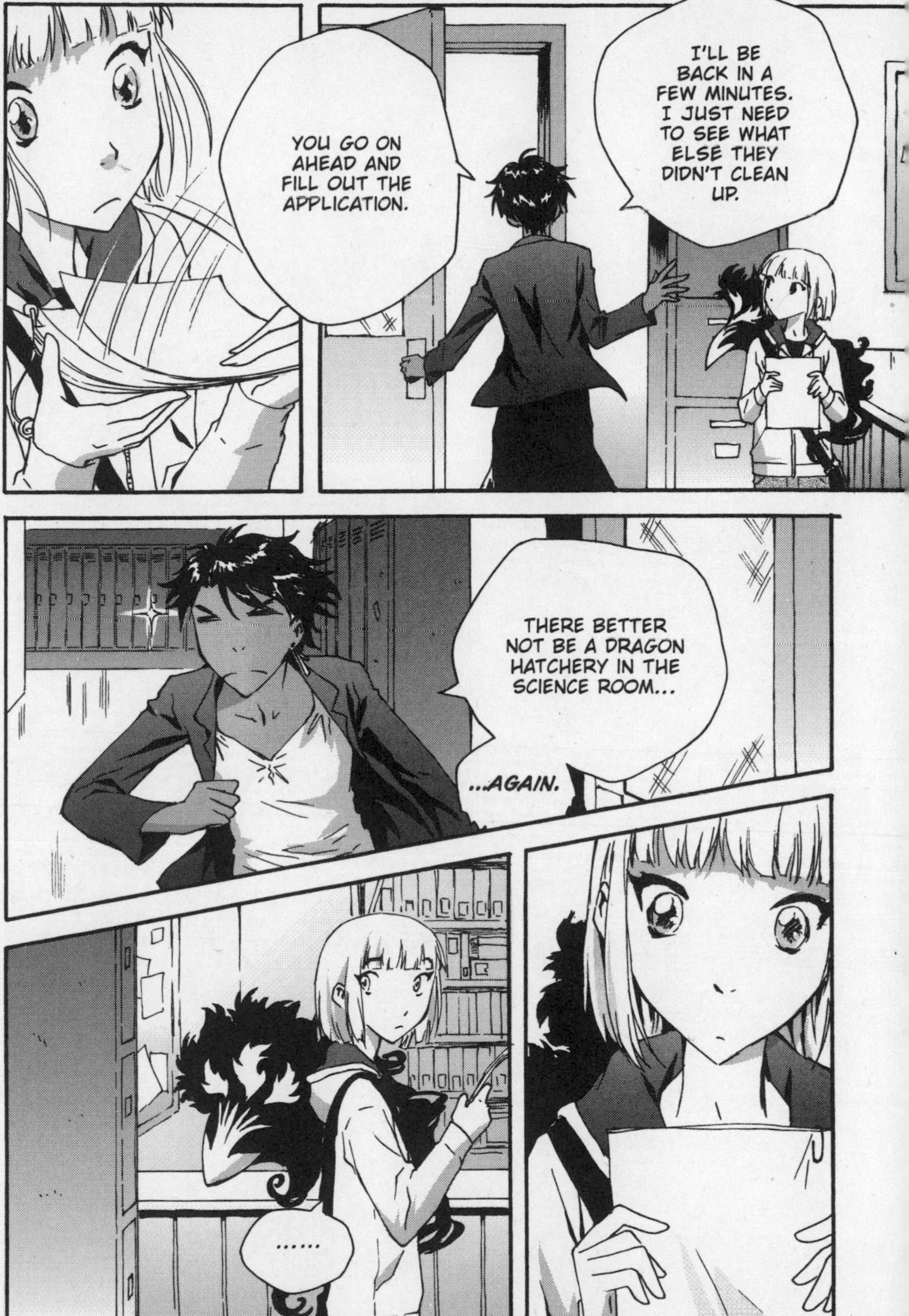
YOU GO ON AHEAD AND FILL OUT THE APPLICATION.
I'LL BE BACK IN A FEW MINUTES. I JUST NEED TO SEE WHAT ELSE THEY DIDN'T CLEAN UP.
THERE BETTER NOT BE A DRAGON HATCHERY IN THE SCIENCE ROOM...
...AGAIN.
......

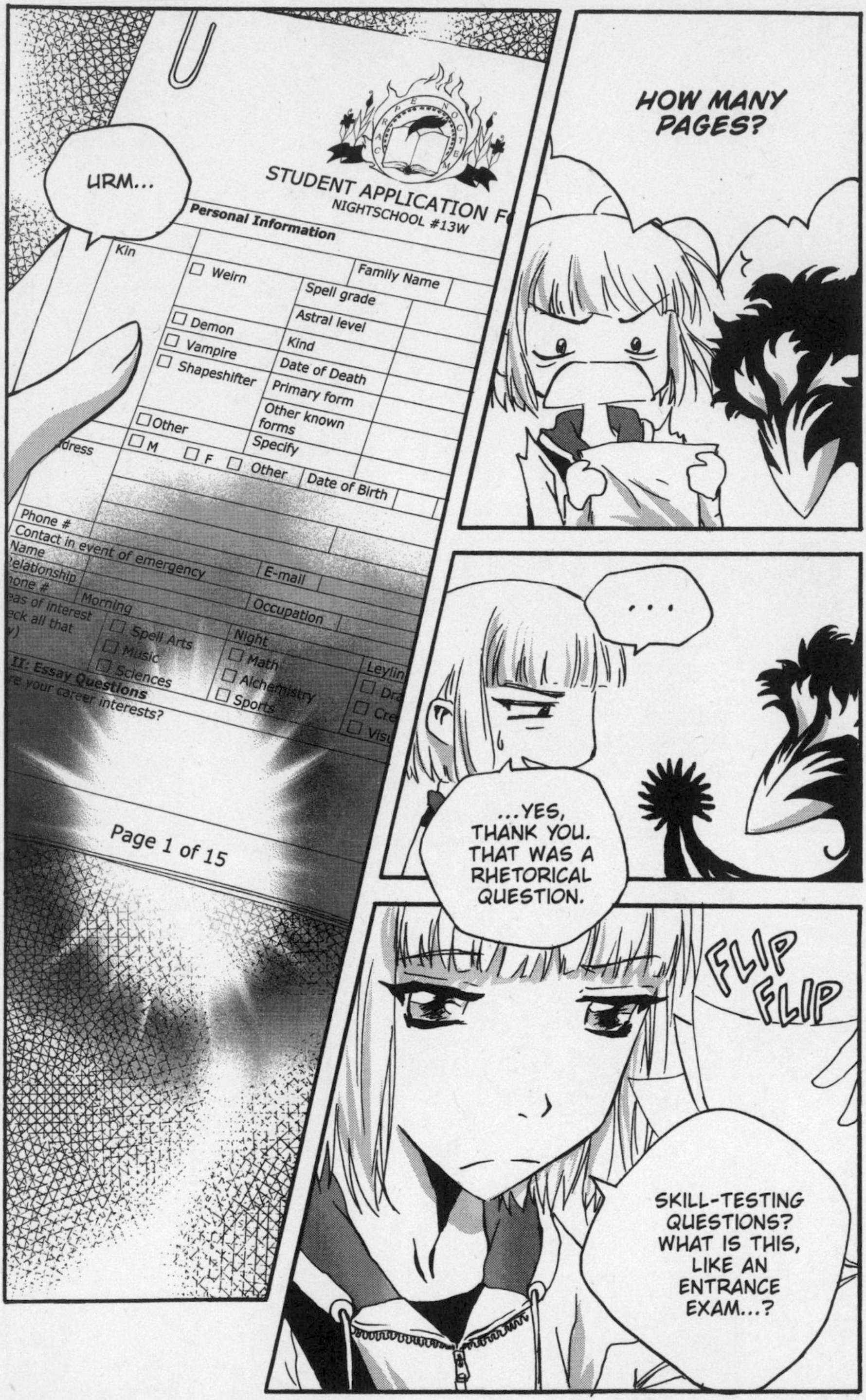
URM...
STUDENT APPLICATION
NIGHTSCHOOL #13W
Personal Information
Kin
Weirn
Demon
Vampire
Shapeshifter
Other
Family Name
Spell grade
Astral level
Kind
Date of Death
Primary form
Other known forms
Specify
M
F
Other
Date of Birth
Phone #
Contact in event of emergency
E-mail
Morning
Occupation
Spell Arts
Music
Sciences
Night
Math
Alchemistry
Sports
Page 1 of 15
HOW MANY PAGES?
...
...YES, THANK YOU. THAT WAS A RHETORICAL QUESTION.
FLIP FLIP
SKILL-TESTING QUESTIONS? WHAT IS THIS, LIKE AN ENTRANCE EXAM...?

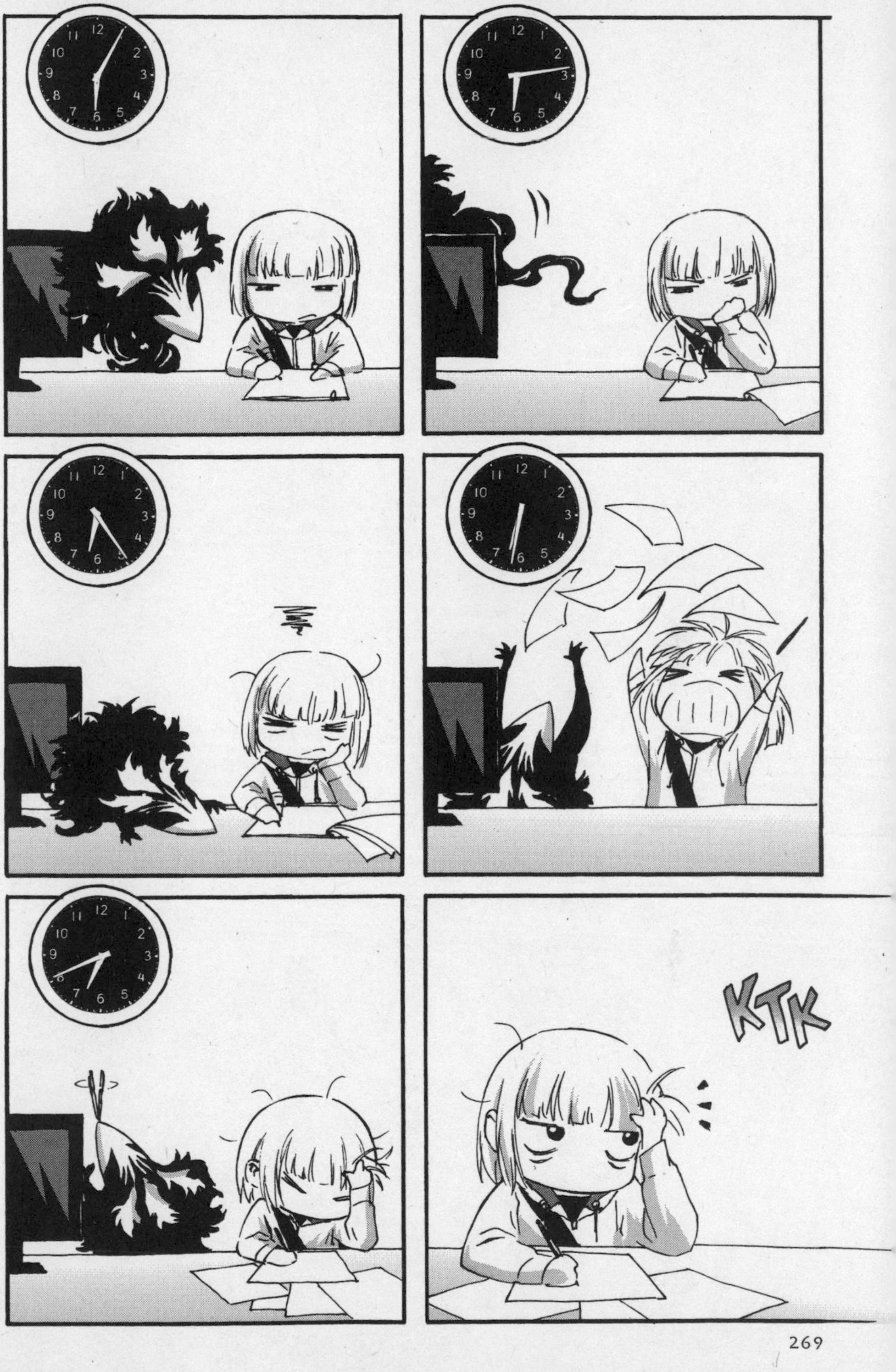
KTK

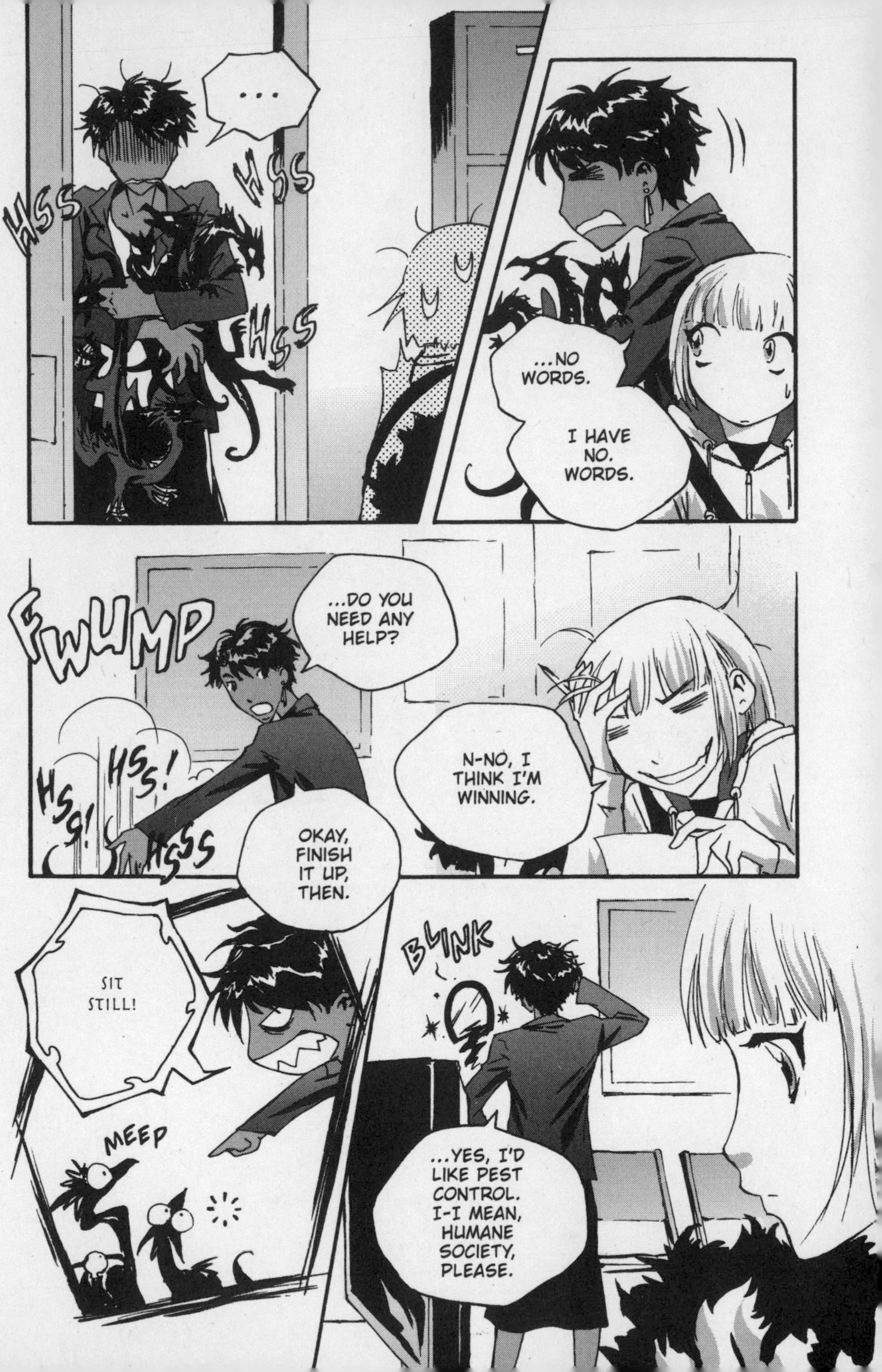
...
HSS
HSS
HSS
...NO WORDS.
I HAVE NO. WORDS.
FWUMP
...DO YOU NEED ANY HELP?
HSS!
HSS!
HSSS
N-NO, I THINK I'M WINNING.
OKAY, FINISH IT UP, THEN.
SIT STILL!
MEEP
BLINK
...YES, I'D LIKE PEST CONTROL. I-I MEAN, HUMANE SOCIETY, PLEASE.

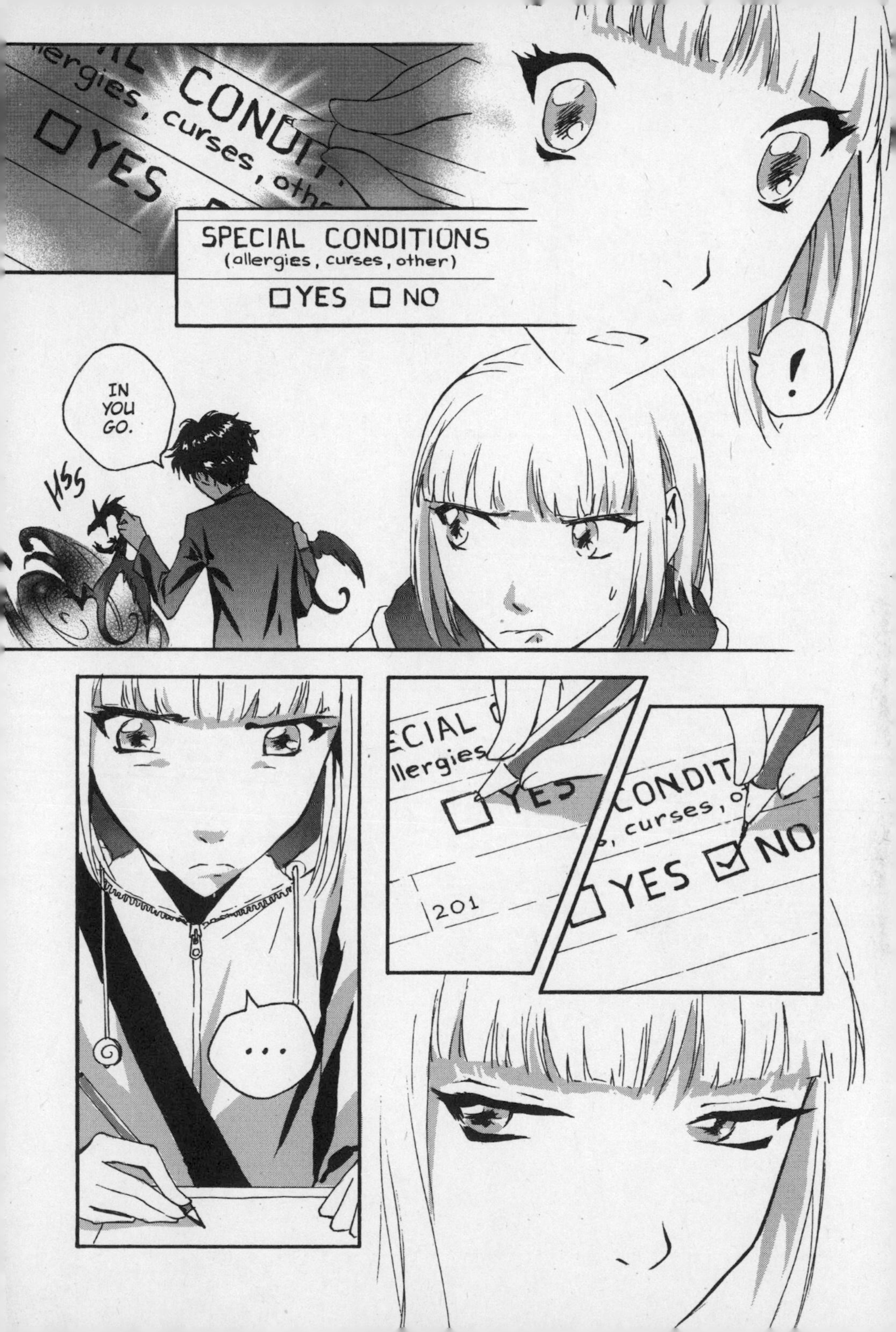

CONDIT
allergies, curses, othe
YES
SPECIAL CONDITIONS
(allergies, curses, other)
YES NO
!
IN YOU GO.
HSS
ECIAL
llergies
YES
CONDIT
, curses, o
YES NO
201
...

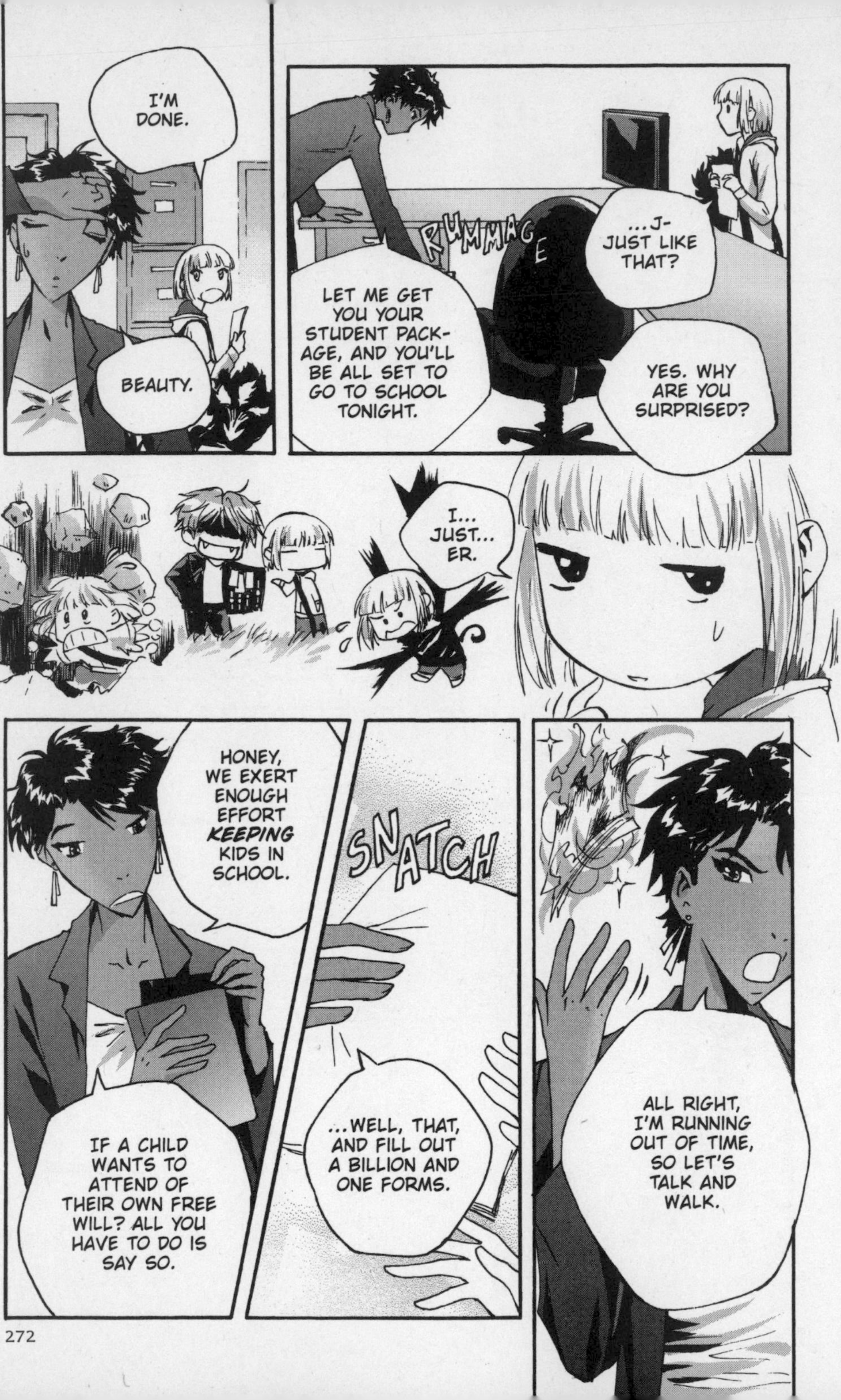
I'M DONE.
BEAUTY.
RUMMAGE
LET ME GET YOU YOUR STUDENT PACKAGE, AND YOU'LL BE ALL SET TO GO TO SCHOOL TONIGHT.
...J-JUST LIKE THAT?
YES. WHY ARE YOU SURPRISED?
I... JUST... ER.
HONEY, WE EXERT ENOUGH EFFORT *KEEPING* KIDS IN SCHOOL.
IF A CHILD WANTS TO ATTEND OF THEIR OWN FREE WILL? ALL YOU HAVE TO DO IS SAY SO.
SNATCH
...WELL, THAT, AND FILL OUT A BILLION AND ONE FORMS.
ALL RIGHT, I'M RUNNING OUT OF TIME, SO LET'S TALK AND WALK.

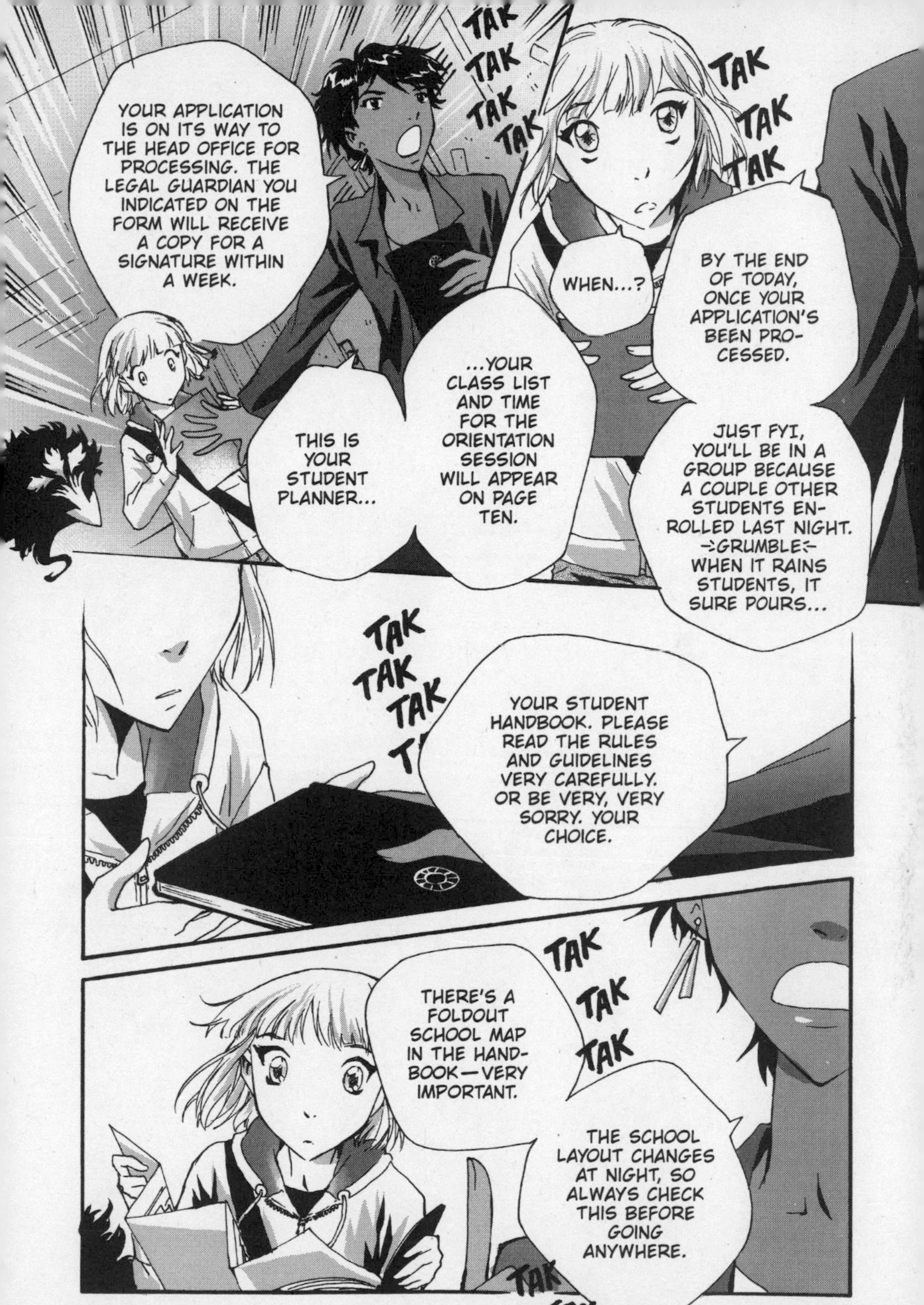
YOUR APPLICATION IS ON ITS WAY TO THE HEAD OFFICE FOR PROCESSING. THE LEGAL GUARDIAN YOU INDICATED ON THE FORM WILL RECEIVE A COPY FOR A SIGNATURE WITHIN A WEEK.
TAK TAK TAK TAK
TAK TAK TAK
WHEN...?
BY THE END OF TODAY, ONCE YOUR APPLICATION'S BEEN PRO-CESSED.
THIS IS YOUR STUDENT PLANNER...
...YOUR CLASS LIST AND TIME FOR THE ORIENTATION SESSION WILL APPEAR ON PAGE TEN.
JUST FYI, YOU'LL BE IN A GROUP BECAUSE A COUPLE OTHER STUDENTS EN-ROLLED LAST NIGHT.
GRUMBLE
WHEN IT RAINS STUDENTS, IT SURE POURS...
TAK TAK TAK
YOUR STUDENT HANDBOOK. PLEASE READ THE RULES AND GUIDELINES VERY CAREFULLY. OR BE VERY, VERY SORRY. YOUR CHOICE.
THERE'S A FOLDOUT SCHOOL MAP IN THE HAND-BOOK—VERY IMPORTANT.
TAK TAK TAK
THE SCHOOL LAYOUT CHANGES AT NIGHT, SO ALWAYS CHECK THIS BEFORE GOING ANYWHERE.
TAK TAK

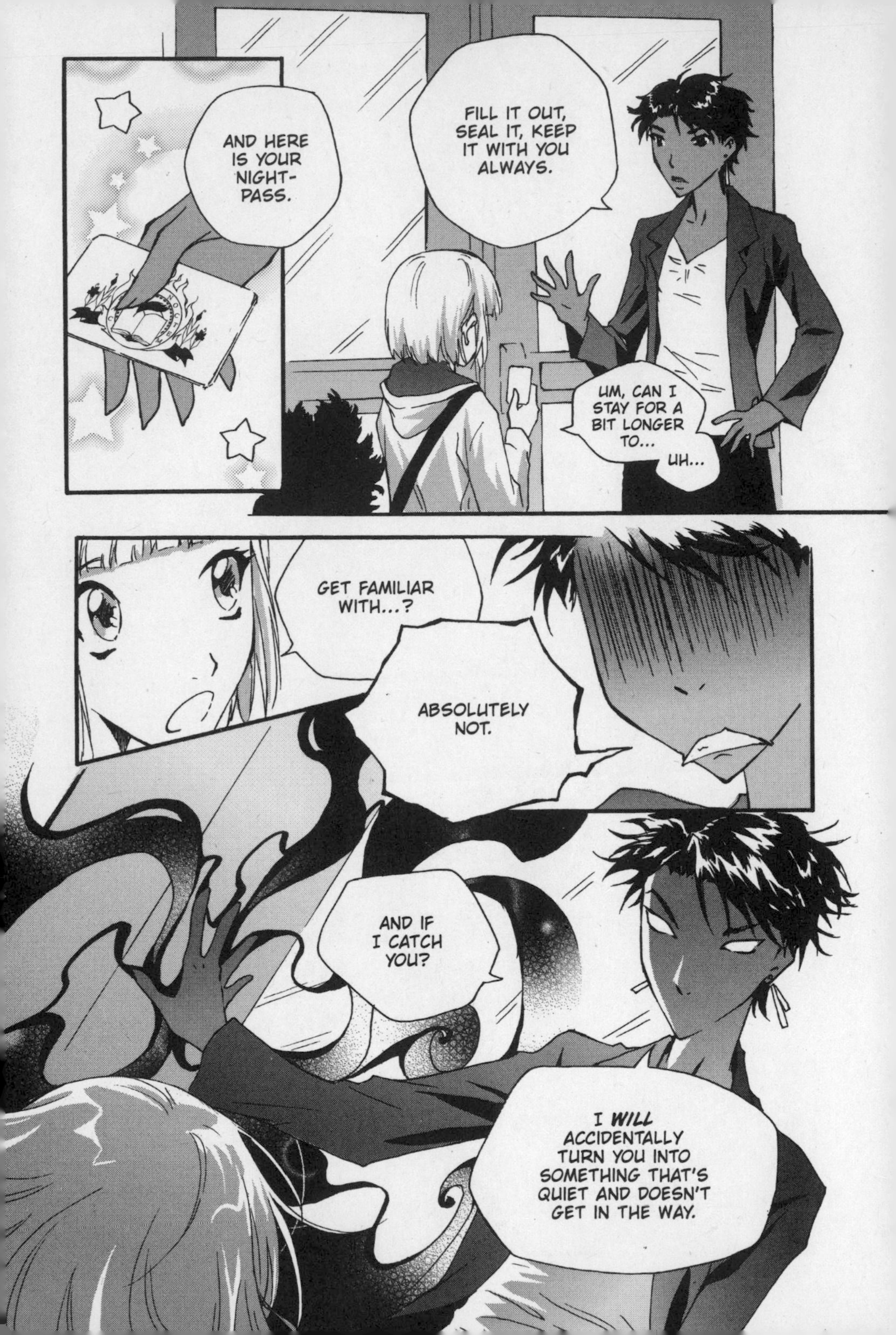
AND HERE IS YOUR NIGHT-PASS.
FILL IT OUT, SEAL IT, KEEP IT WITH YOU ALWAYS.
UM, CAN I STAY FOR A BIT LONGER TO...
UH...
GET FAMILIAR WITH...?
ABSOLUTELY NOT.
AND IF I CATCH YOU?
I WILL ACCIDENTALLY TURN YOU INTO SOMETHING THAT'S QUIET AND DOESN'T GET IN THE WAY.

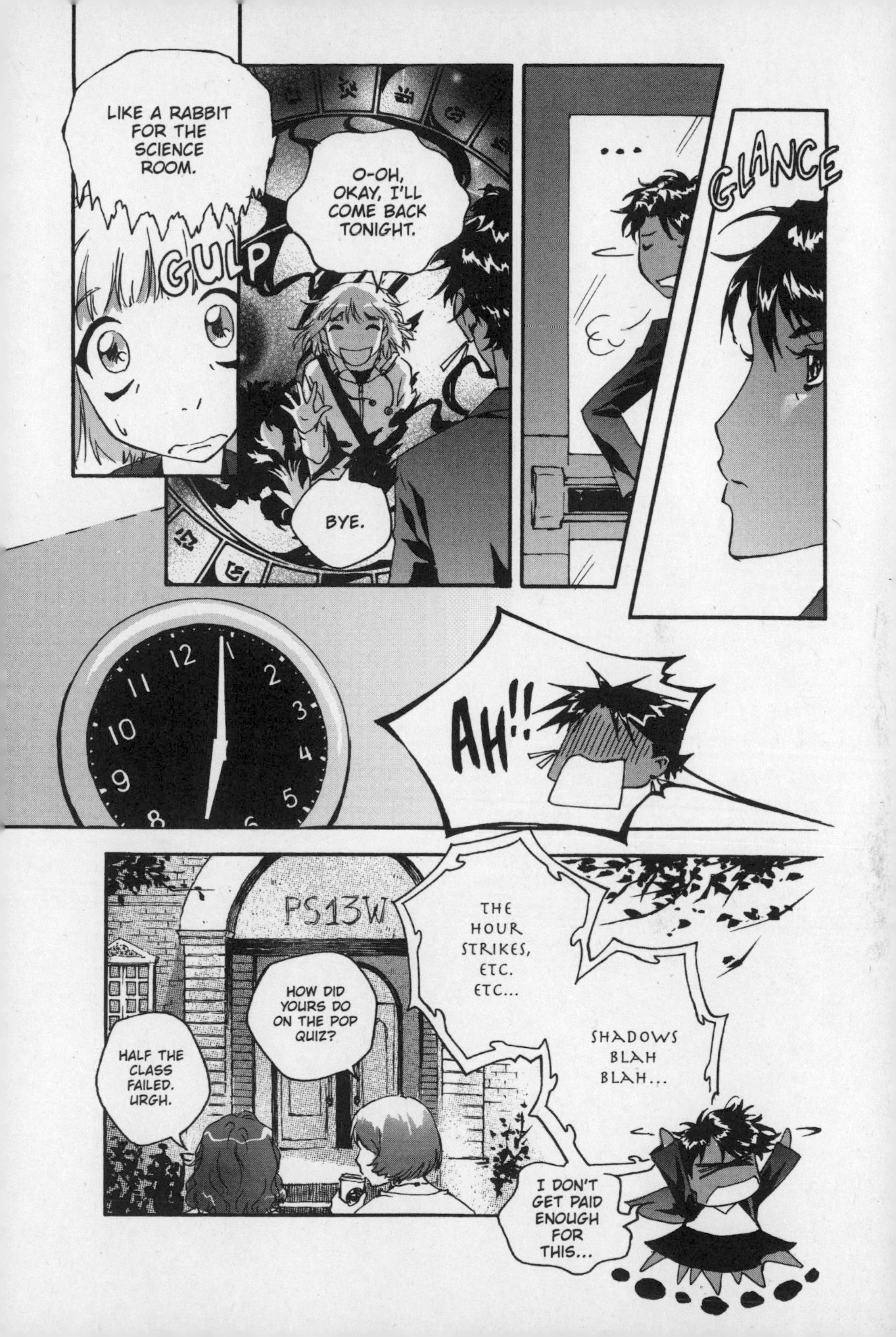
LIKE A RABBIT FOR THE SCIENCE ROOM.
GULP
O-OH, OKAY, I'LL COME BACK TONIGHT.
BYE.
...
GLANCE
AH!!
PS13W
HOW DID YOURS DO ON THE POP QUIZ?
HALF THE CLASS FAILED. URGH.
THE HOUR STRIKES, ETC. ETC...
SHADOWS BLAH BLAH...
I DON'T GET PAID ENOUGH FOR THIS...

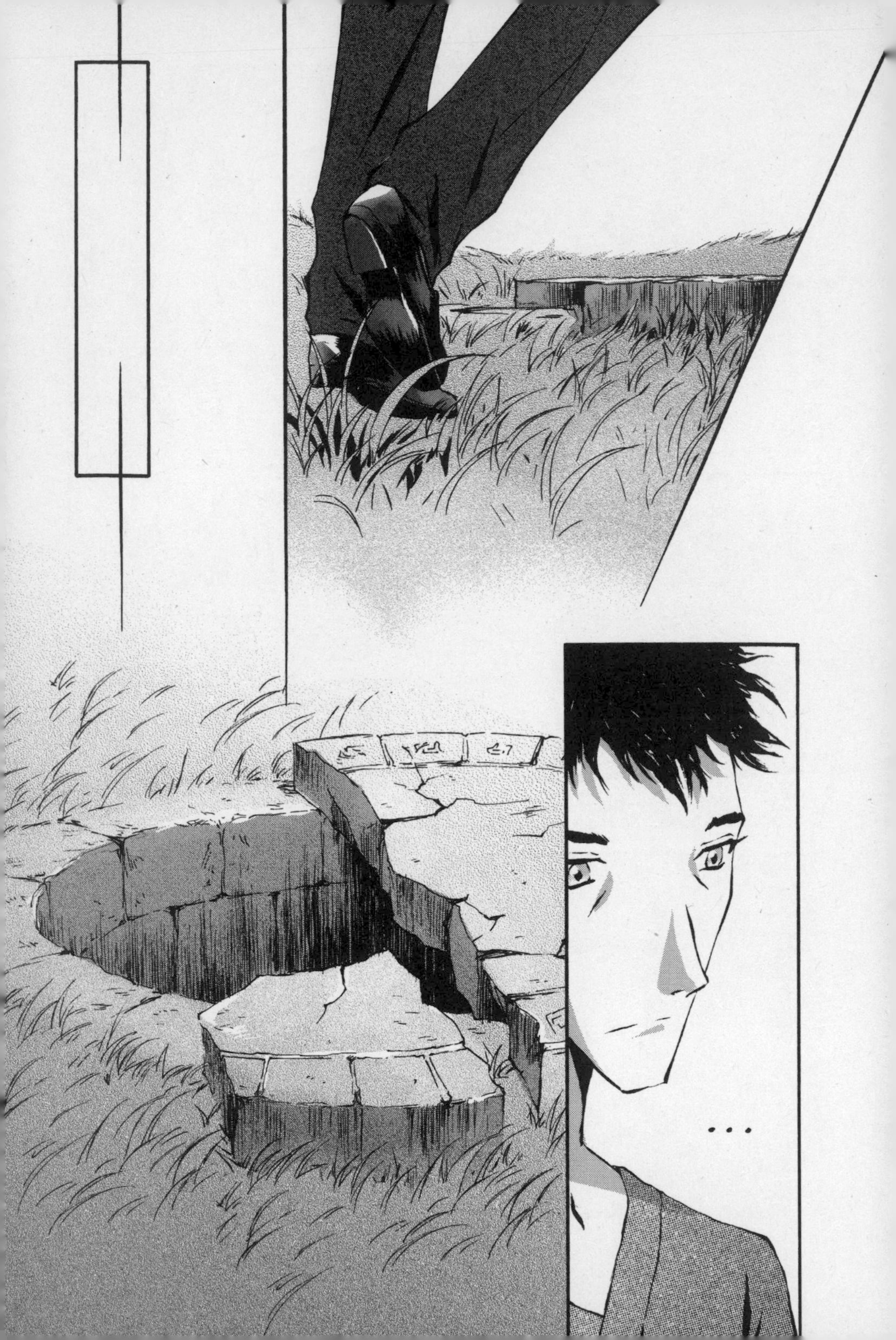
• • •

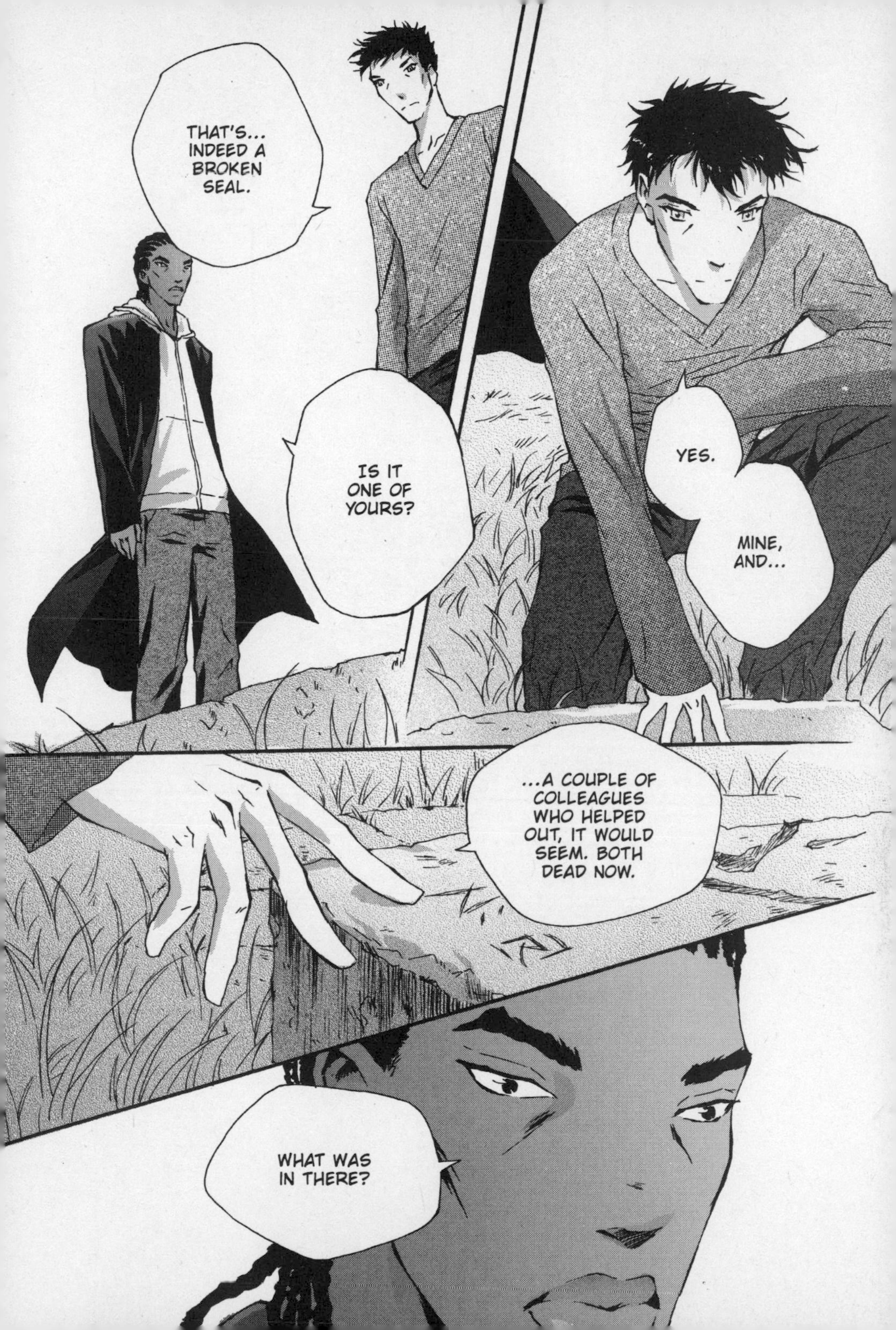
THAT'S... INDEED A BROKEN SEAL.
IS IT ONE OF YOURS?
YES.
MINE, AND...
...A COUPLE OF COLLEAGUES WHO HELPED OUT, IT WOULD SEEM. BOTH DEAD NOW.
WHAT WAS IN THERE?

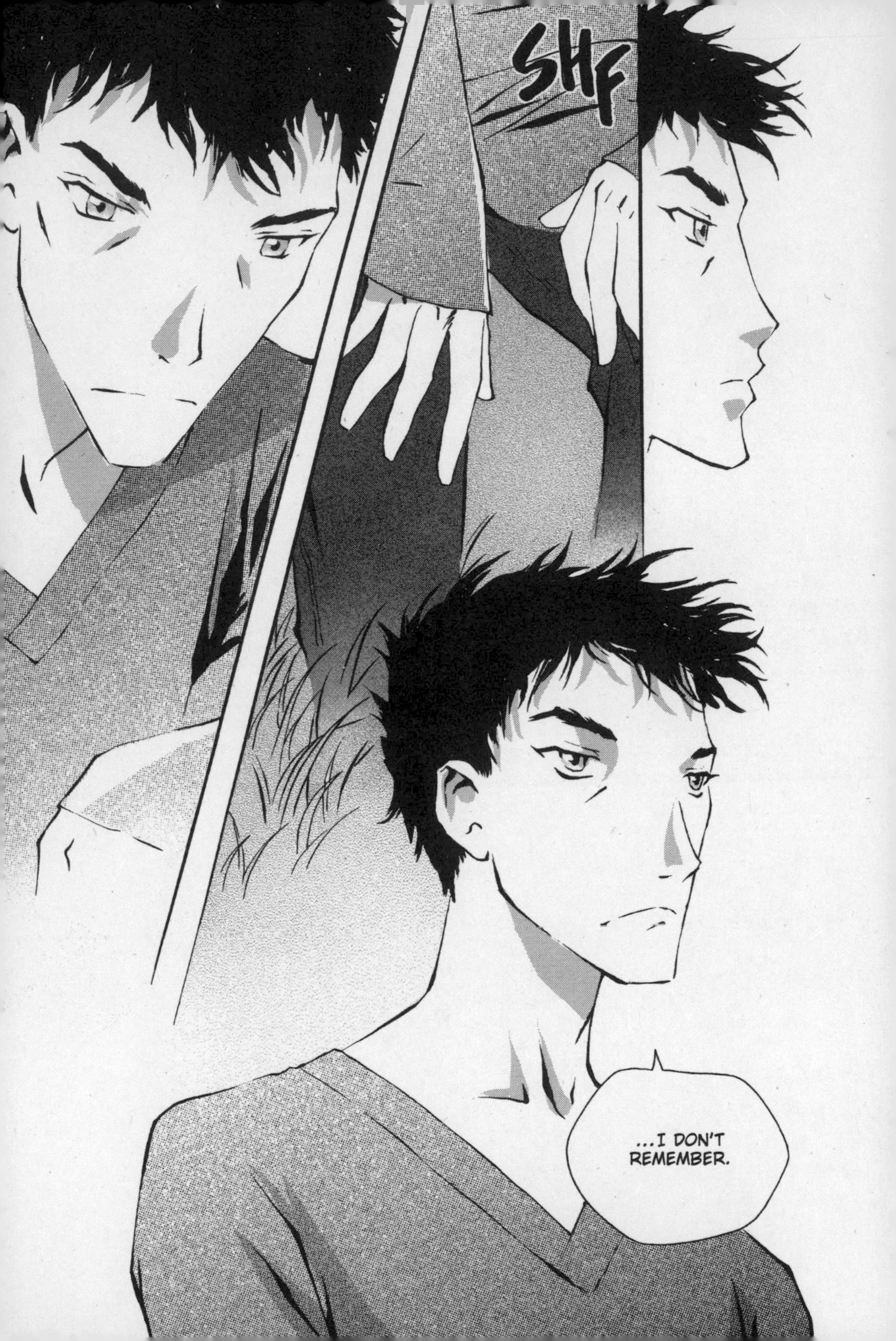
SHF
...I DON'T REMEMBER.

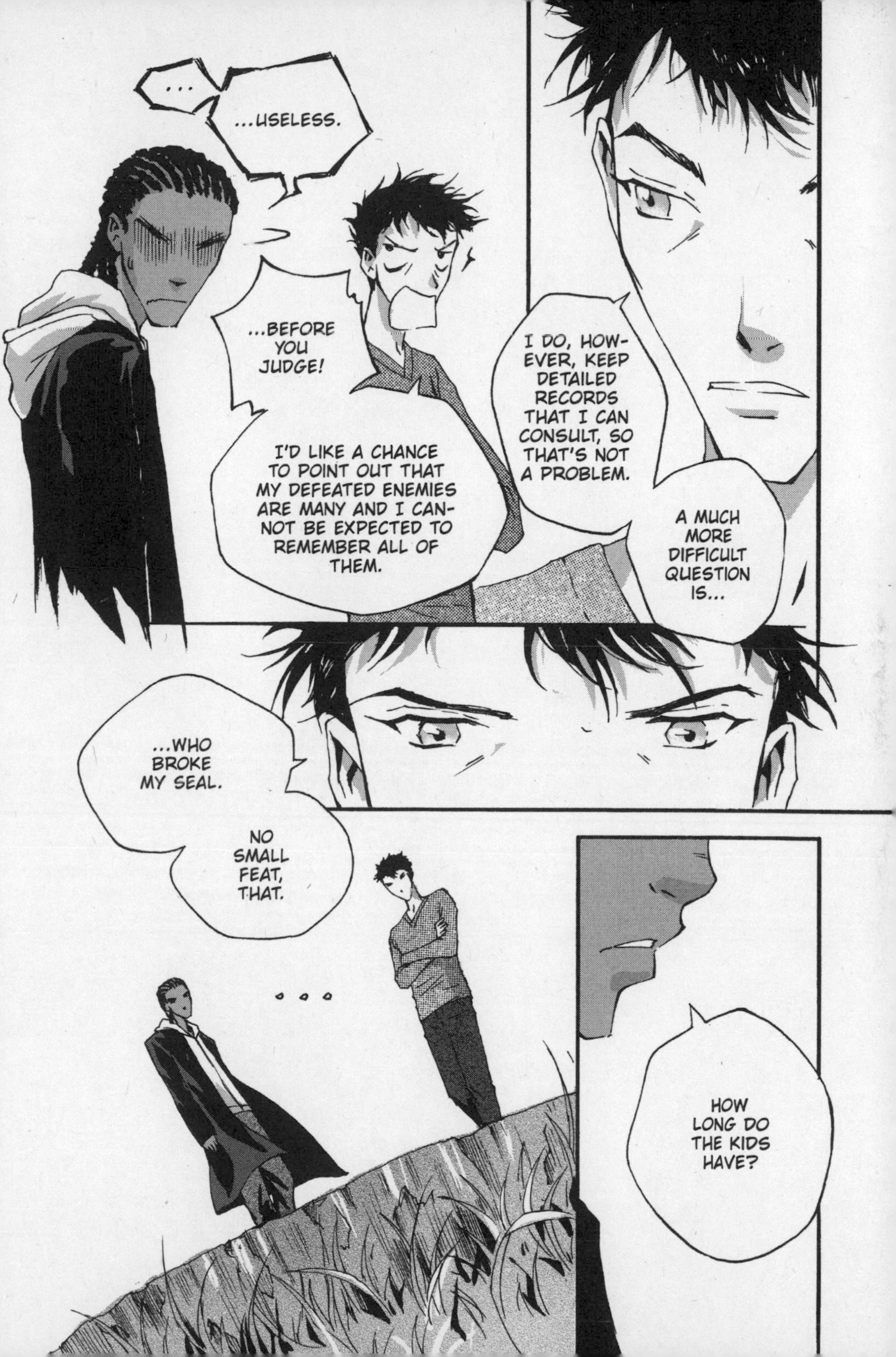
...
...USELESS.
...BEFORE YOU JUDGE!
I'D LIKE A CHANCE TO POINT OUT THAT MY DEFEATED ENEMIES ARE MANY AND I CAN-NOT BE EXPECTED TO REMEMBER ALL OF THEM.
I DO, HOW-EVER, KEEP DETAILED RECORDS THAT I CAN CONSULT, SO THAT'S NOT A PROBLEM.
A MUCH MORE DIFFICULT QUESTION IS...
...WHO BROKE MY SEAL.
NO SMALL FEAT, THAT.
...
HOW LONG DO THE KIDS HAVE?

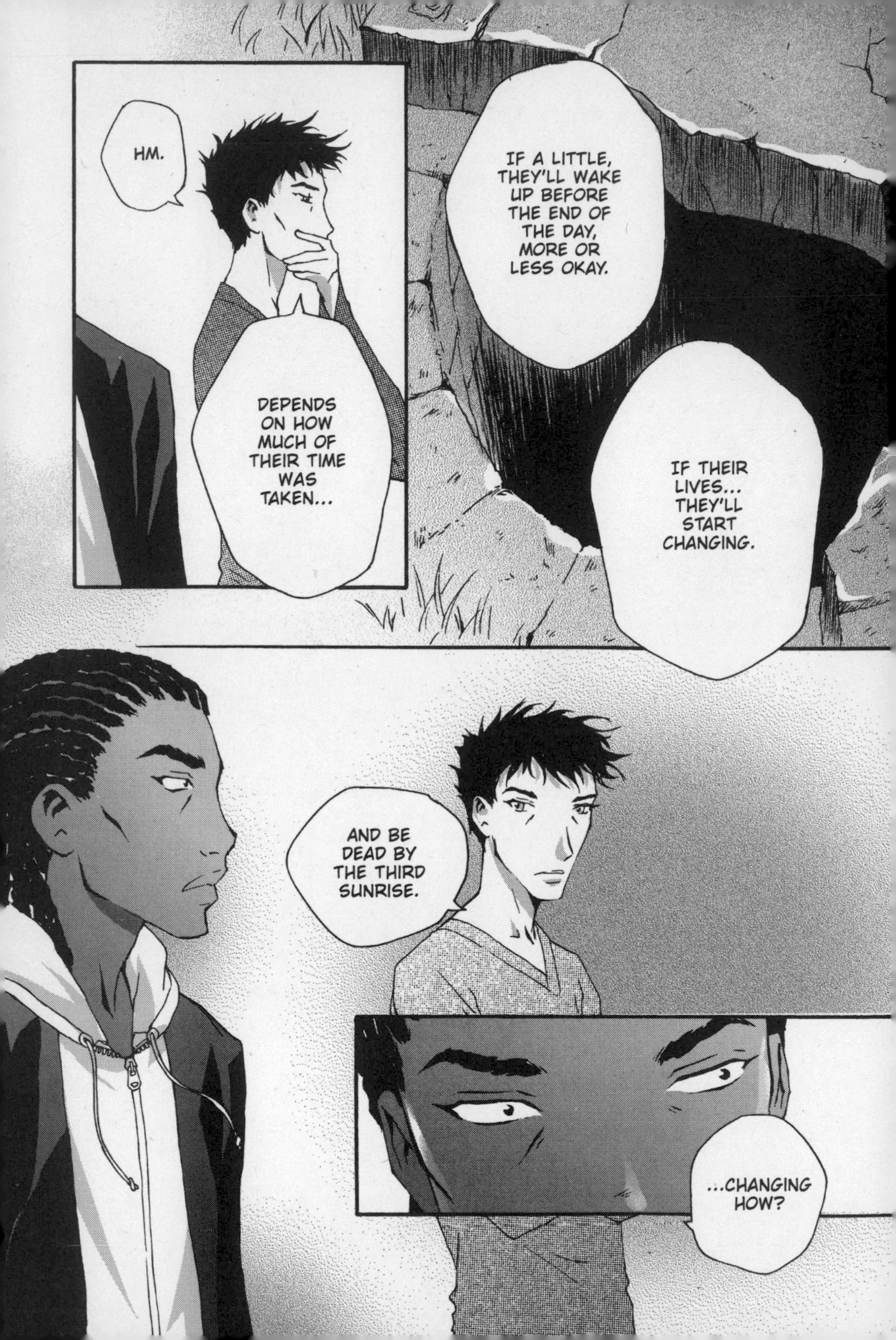
HM.
DEPENDS ON HOW MUCH OF THEIR TIME WAS TAKEN...
IF A LITTLE, THEY'LL WAKE UP BEFORE THE END OF THE DAY, MORE OR LESS OKAY.
IF THEIR LIVES... THEY'LL START CHANGING.
AND BE DEAD BY THE THIRD SUNRISE.
...CHANGING HOW?

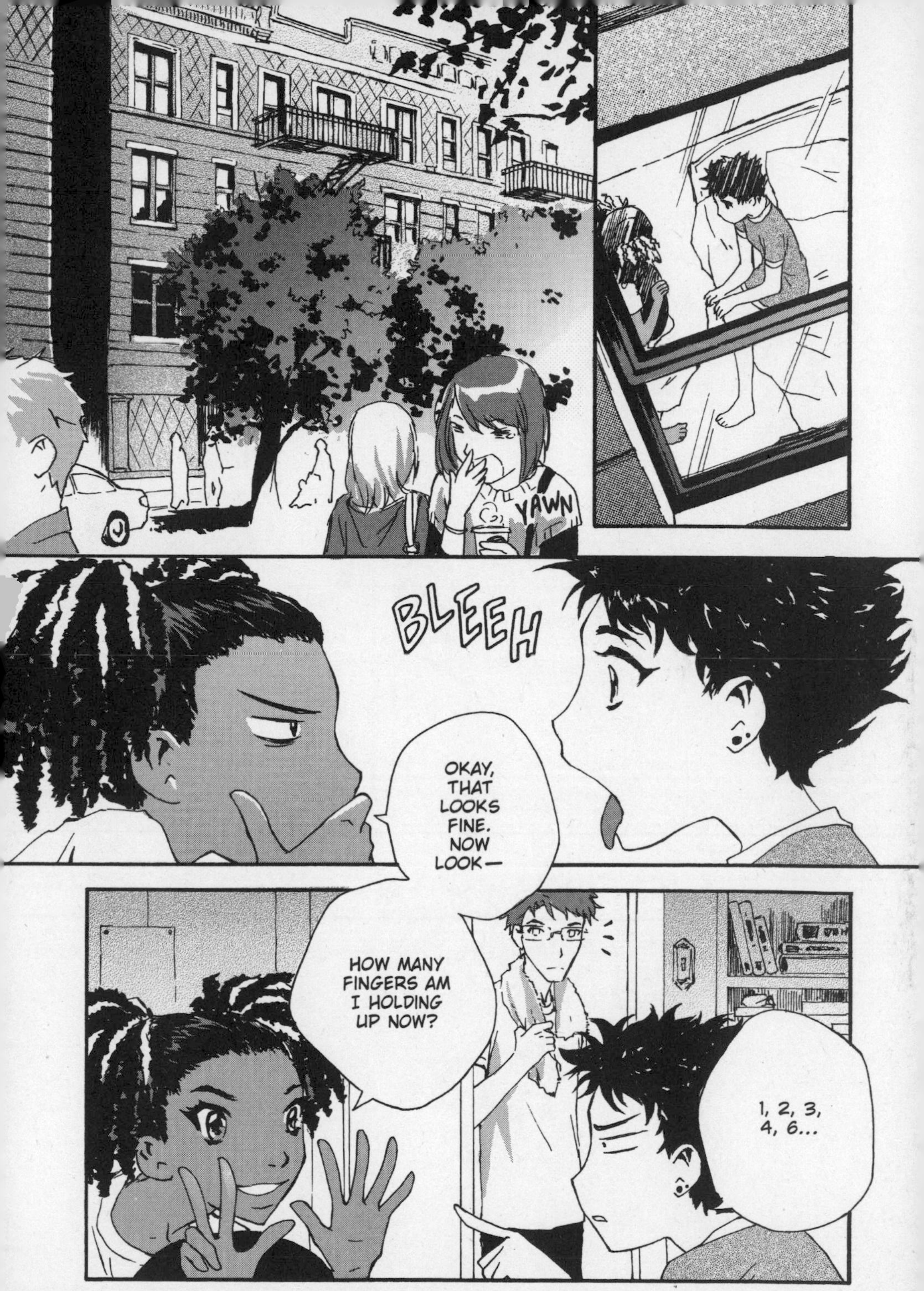
YAWN
BLEEH
OKAY, THAT LOOKS FINE. NOW LOOK—
HOW MANY FINGERS AM I HOLDING UP NOW?
1, 2, 3, 4, 6...

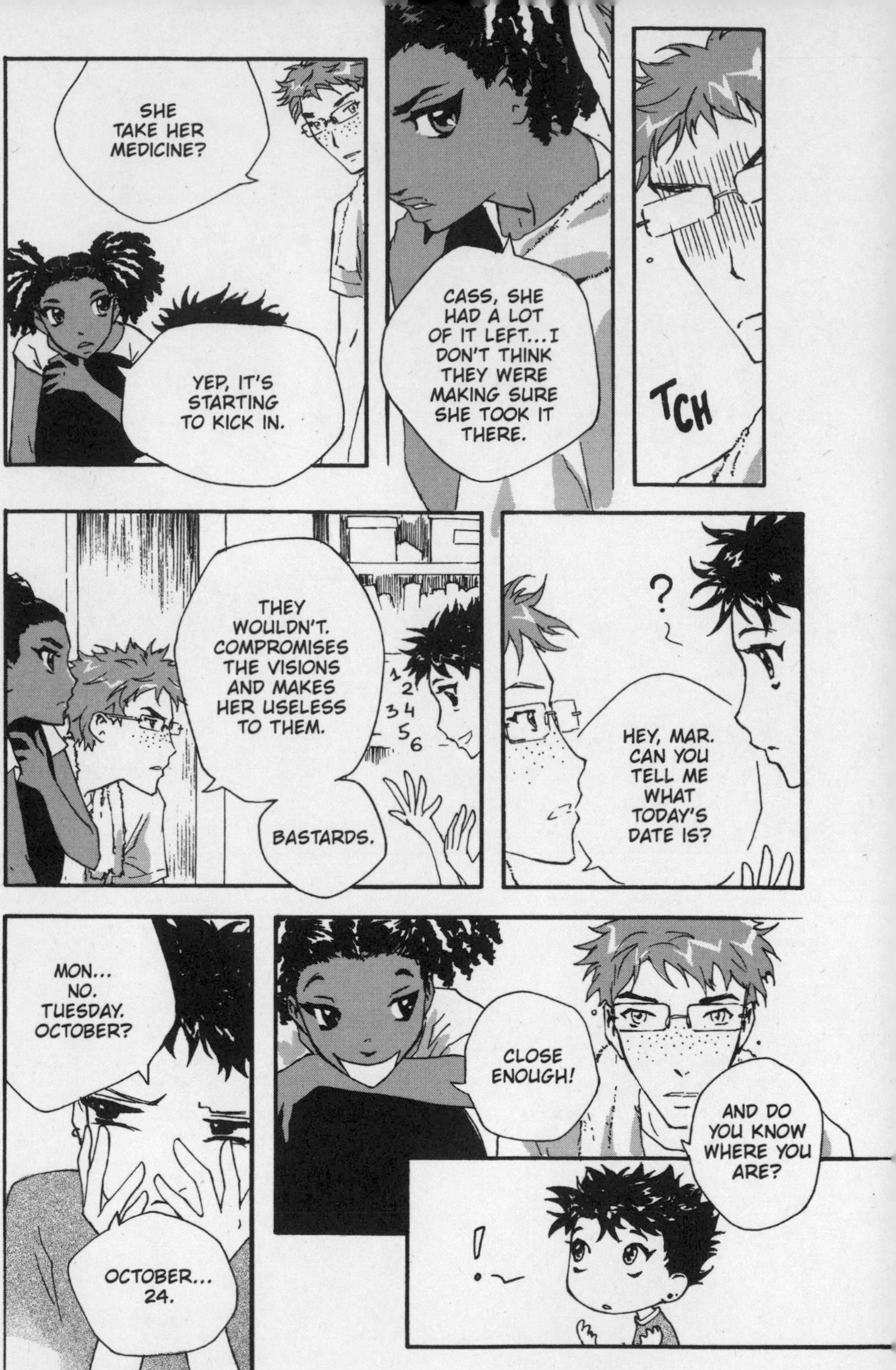
SHE TAKE HER MEDICINE?
YEP, IT'S STARTING TO KICK IN.
CASS, SHE HAD A LOT OF IT LEFT...I DON'T THINK THEY WERE MAKING SURE SHE TOOK IT THERE.
TCH
THEY WOULDN'T. COMPROMISES THE VISIONS AND MAKES HER USELESS TO THEM.
BASTARDS.
1 2 3 4 5 6
?
HEY, MAR. CAN YOU TELL ME WHAT TODAY'S DATE IS?
MON... NO. TUESDAY. OCTOBER?
OCTOBER... 24.
CLOSE ENOUGH!
AND DO YOU KNOW WHERE YOU ARE?
!

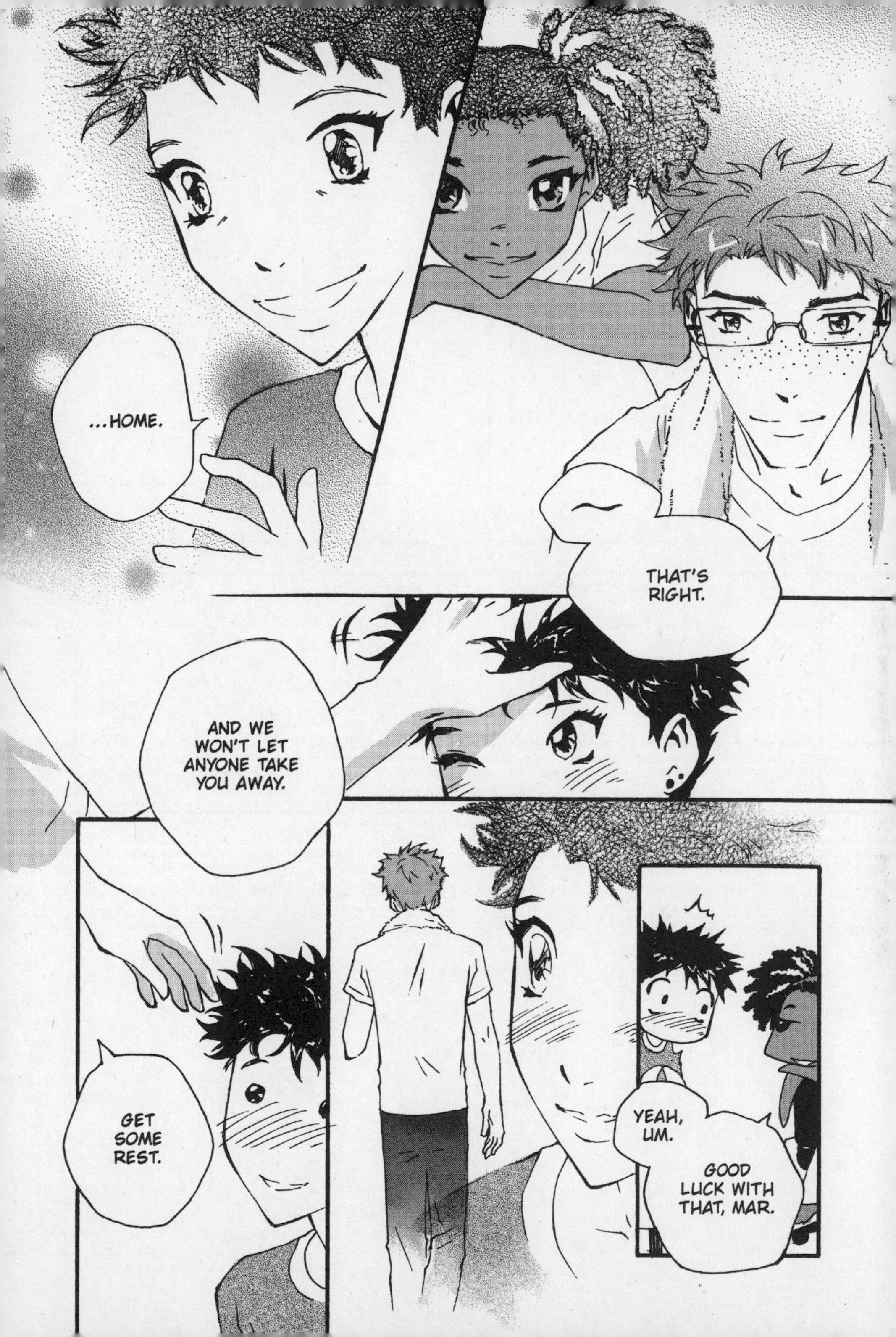
...HOME.
THAT'S RIGHT.
AND WE WON'T LET ANYONE TAKE YOU AWAY.
GET SOME REST.
YEAH, UM.
GOOD LUCK WITH THAT, MAR.

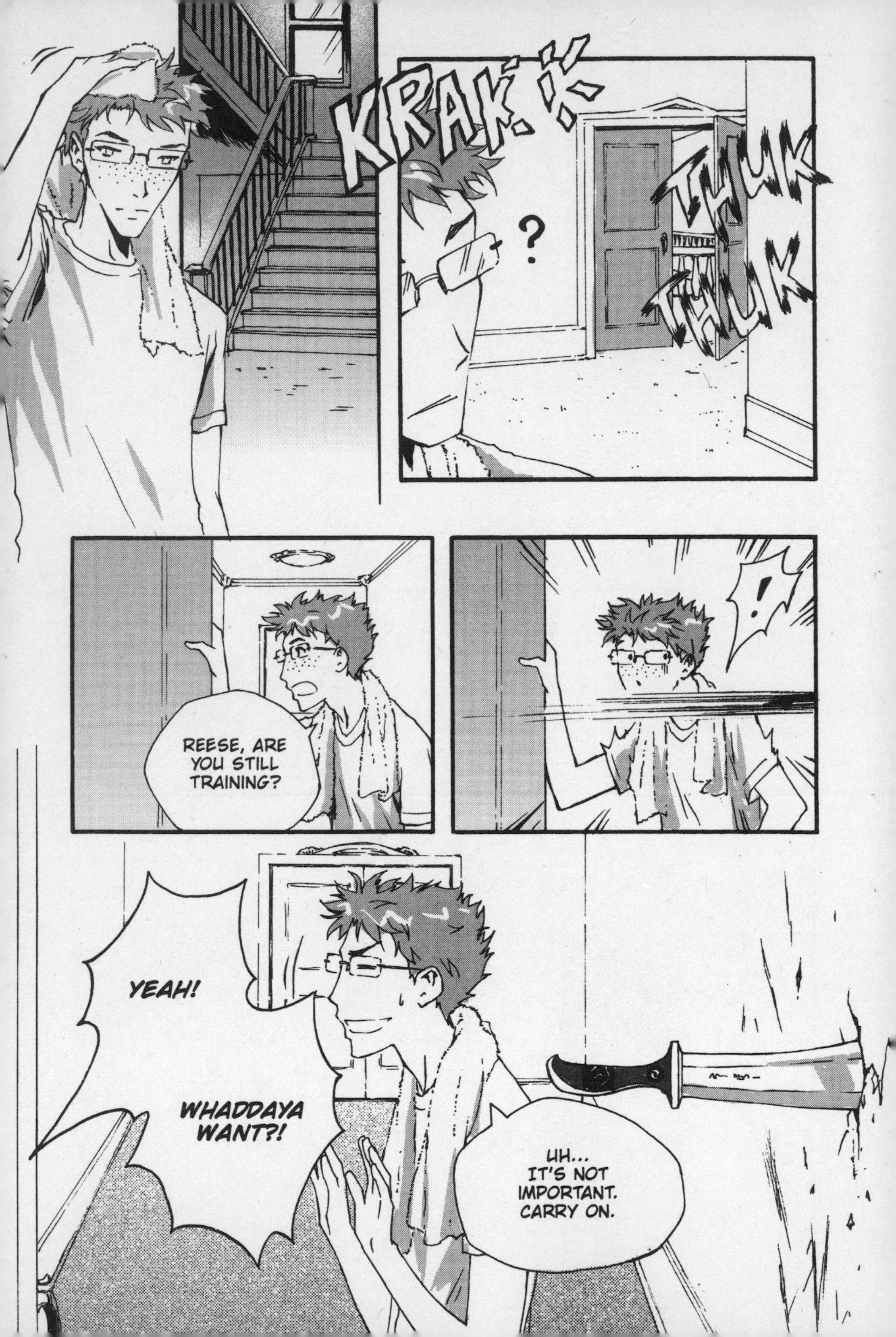
KRAK!!
?
THUK THUK
REESE, ARE YOU STILL TRAINING?
!
YEAH!
WHADDAYA WANT?!
UH... IT'S NOT IMPORTANT. CARRY ON.

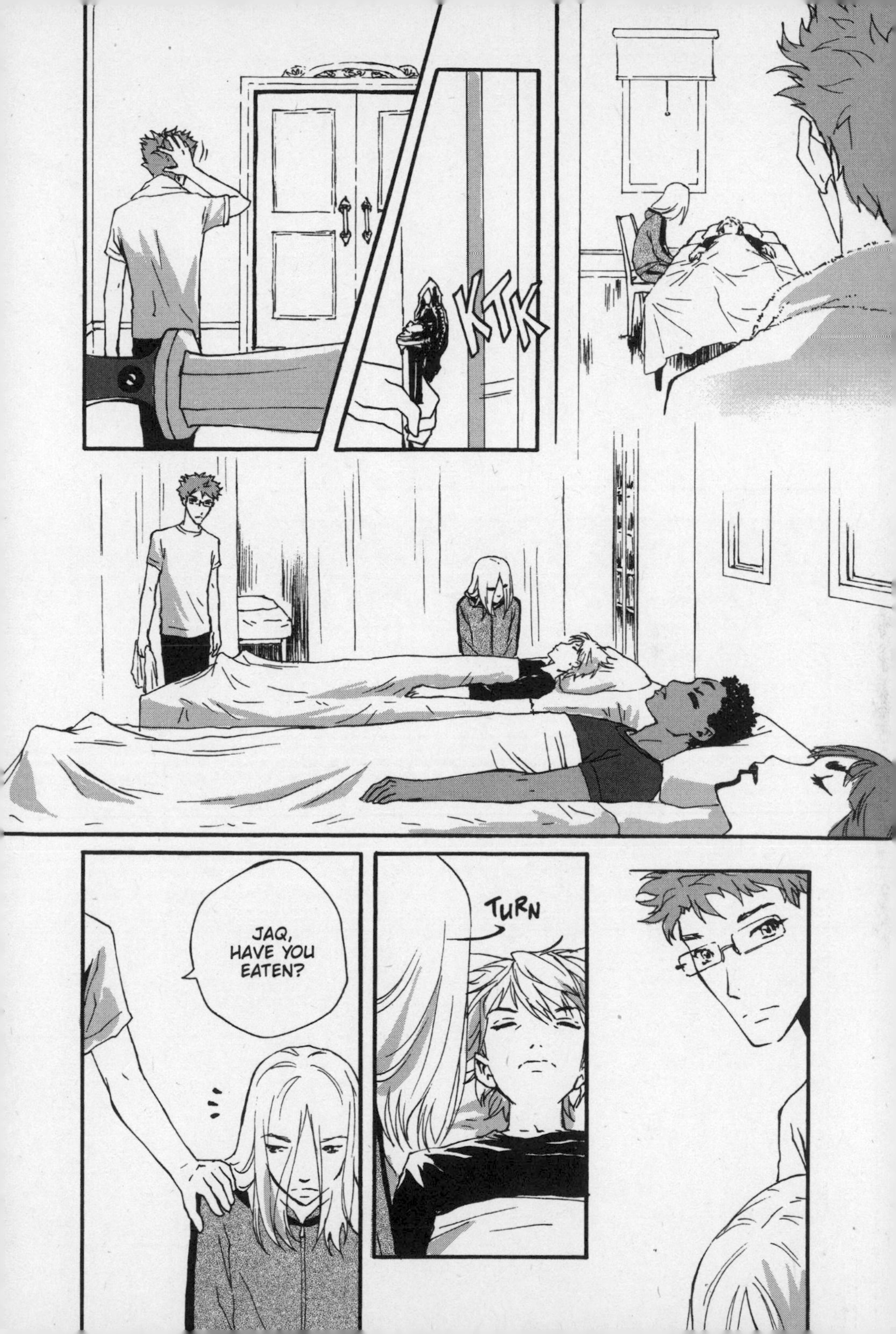
KTK
JAQ, HAVE YOU EATEN?
TURN

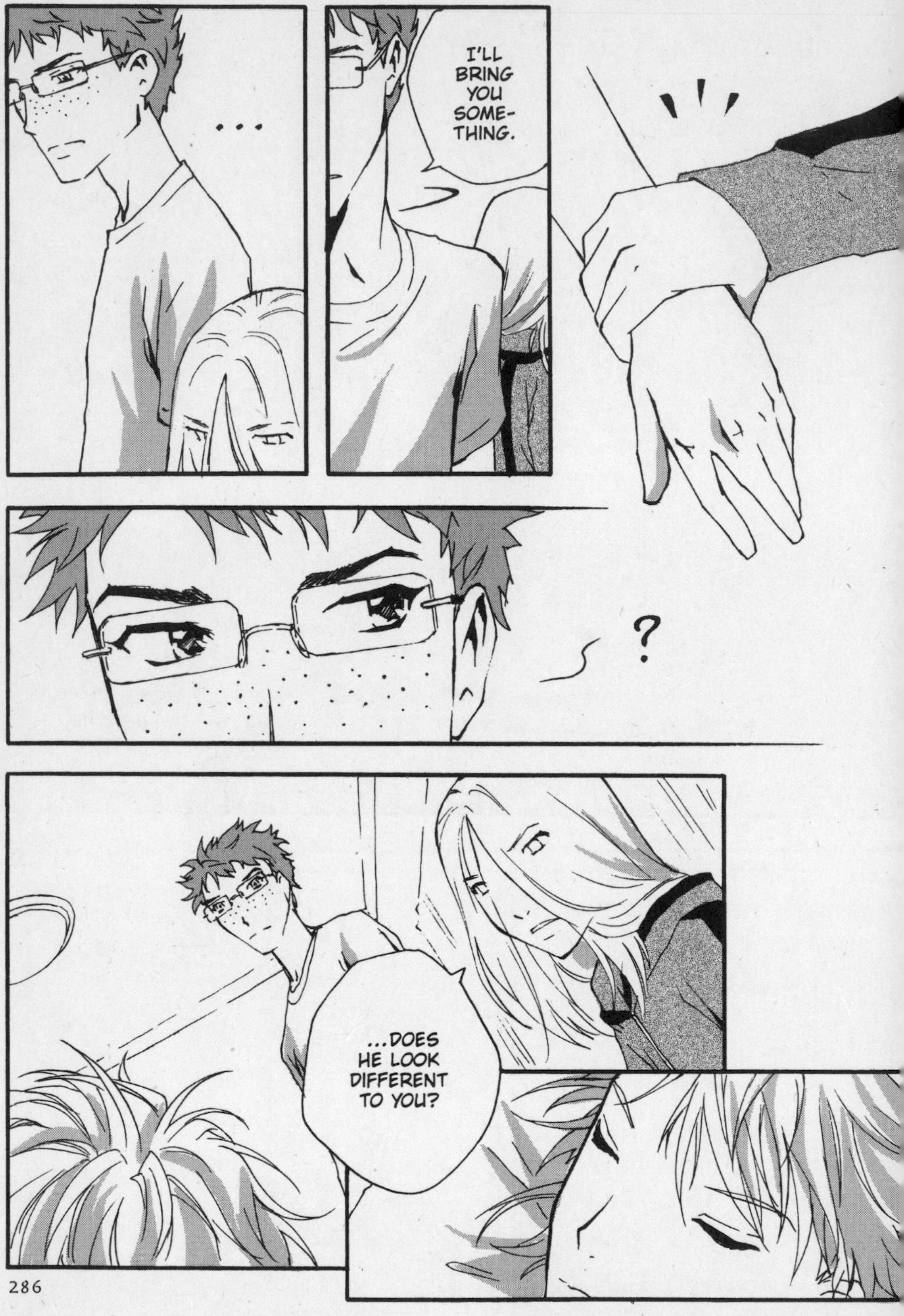
...
I'LL BRING YOU SOMETHING.
?
...DOES HE LOOK DIFFERENT TO YOU?

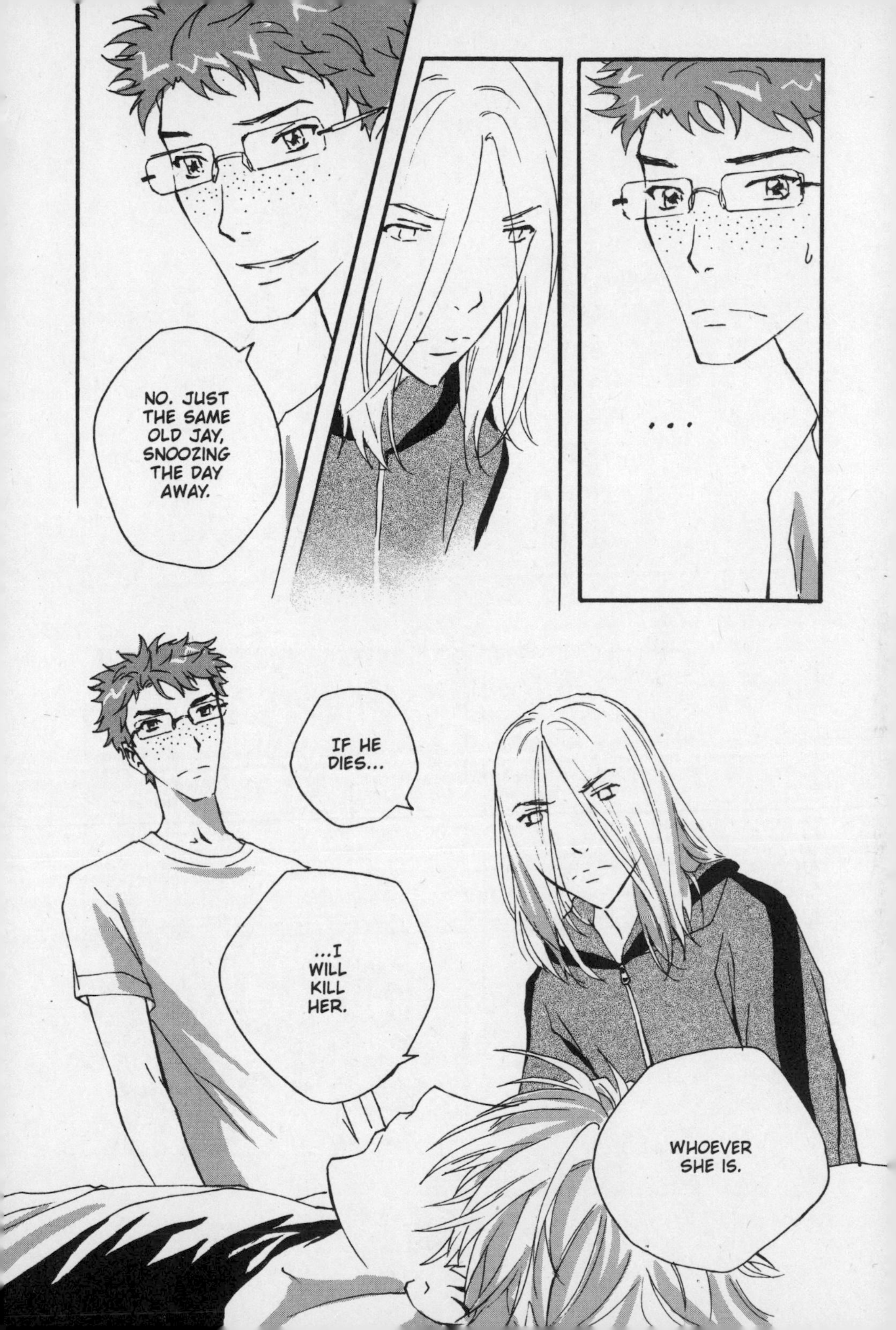
NO. JUST THE SAME OLD JAY, SNOOZING THE DAY AWAY.
...
IF HE DIES...
...I WILL KILL HER.
WHOEVER SHE IS.

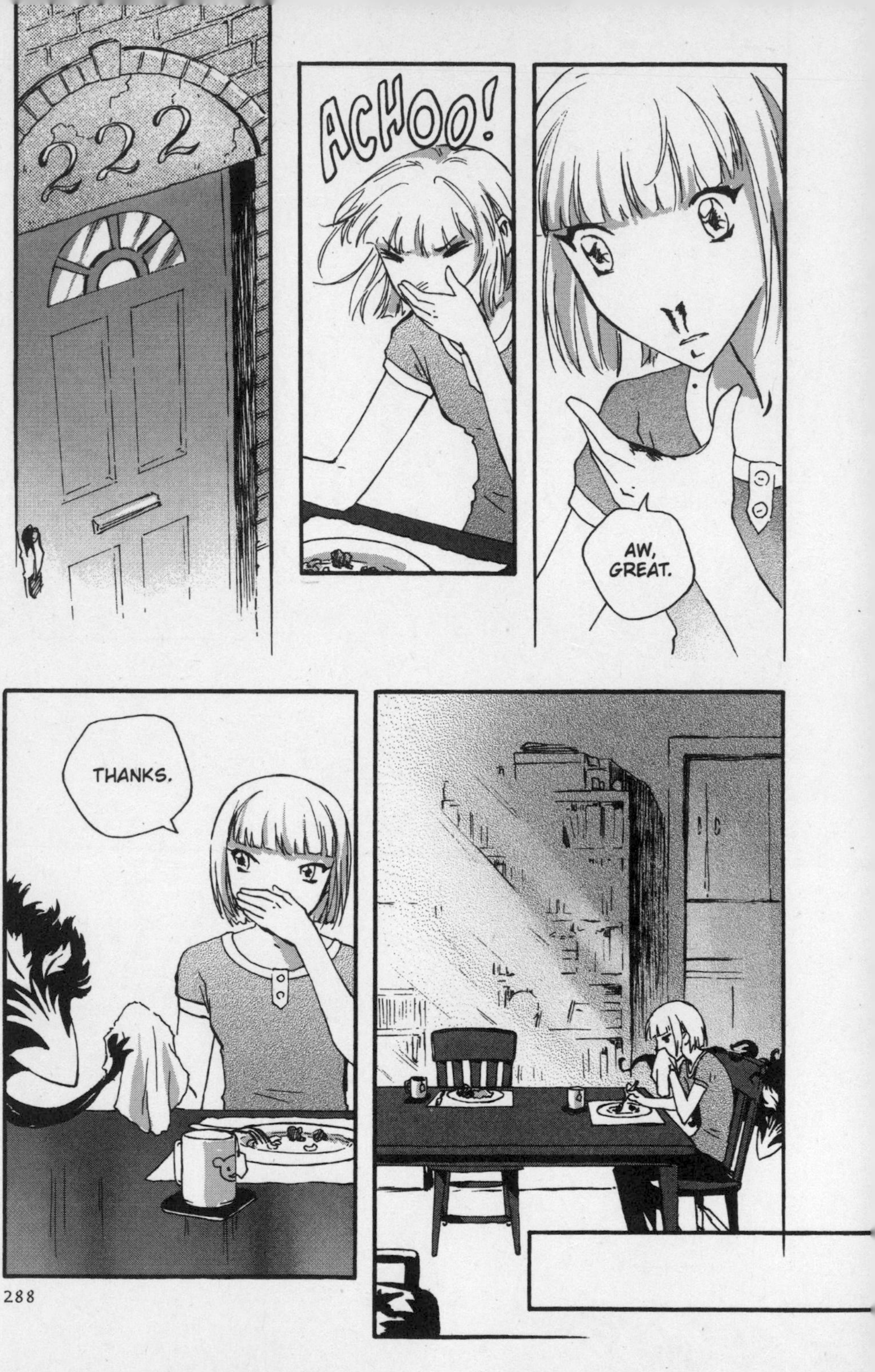

222
ACHOO!
AW, GREAT.
THANKS.

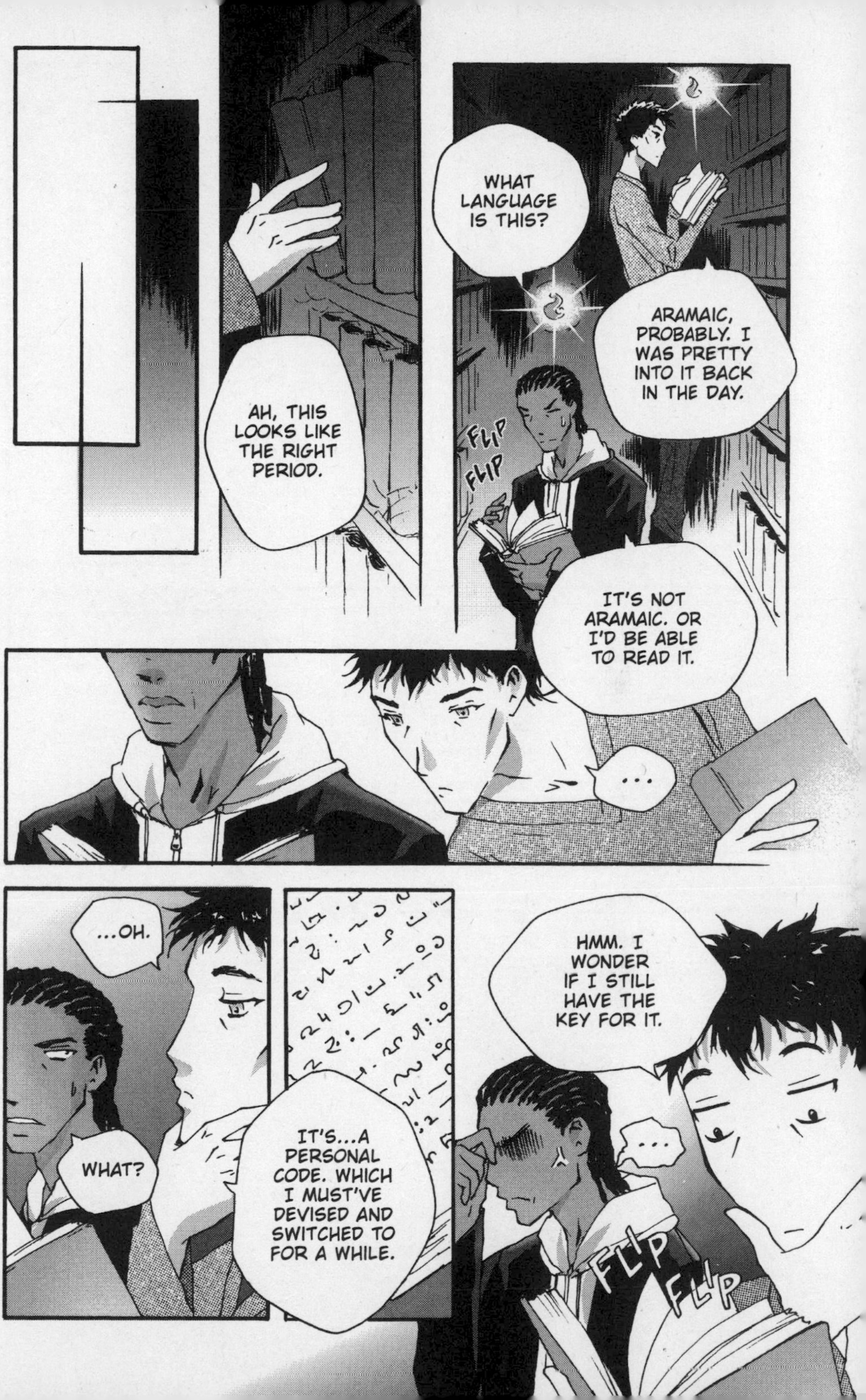

AH, THIS LOOKS LIKE THE RIGHT PERIOD.
WHAT LANGUAGE IS THIS?
ARAMAIC, PROBABLY. I WAS PRETTY INTO IT BACK IN THE DAY.
FLIP FLIP
IT'S NOT ARAMAIC. OR I'D BE ABLE TO READ IT.
...
...OH.
WHAT?
IT'S...A PERSONAL CODE. WHICH I MUST'VE DEVISED AND SWITCHED TO FOR A WHILE.
HMM. I WONDER IF I STILL HAVE THE KEY FOR IT.
...
FLIP FLIP

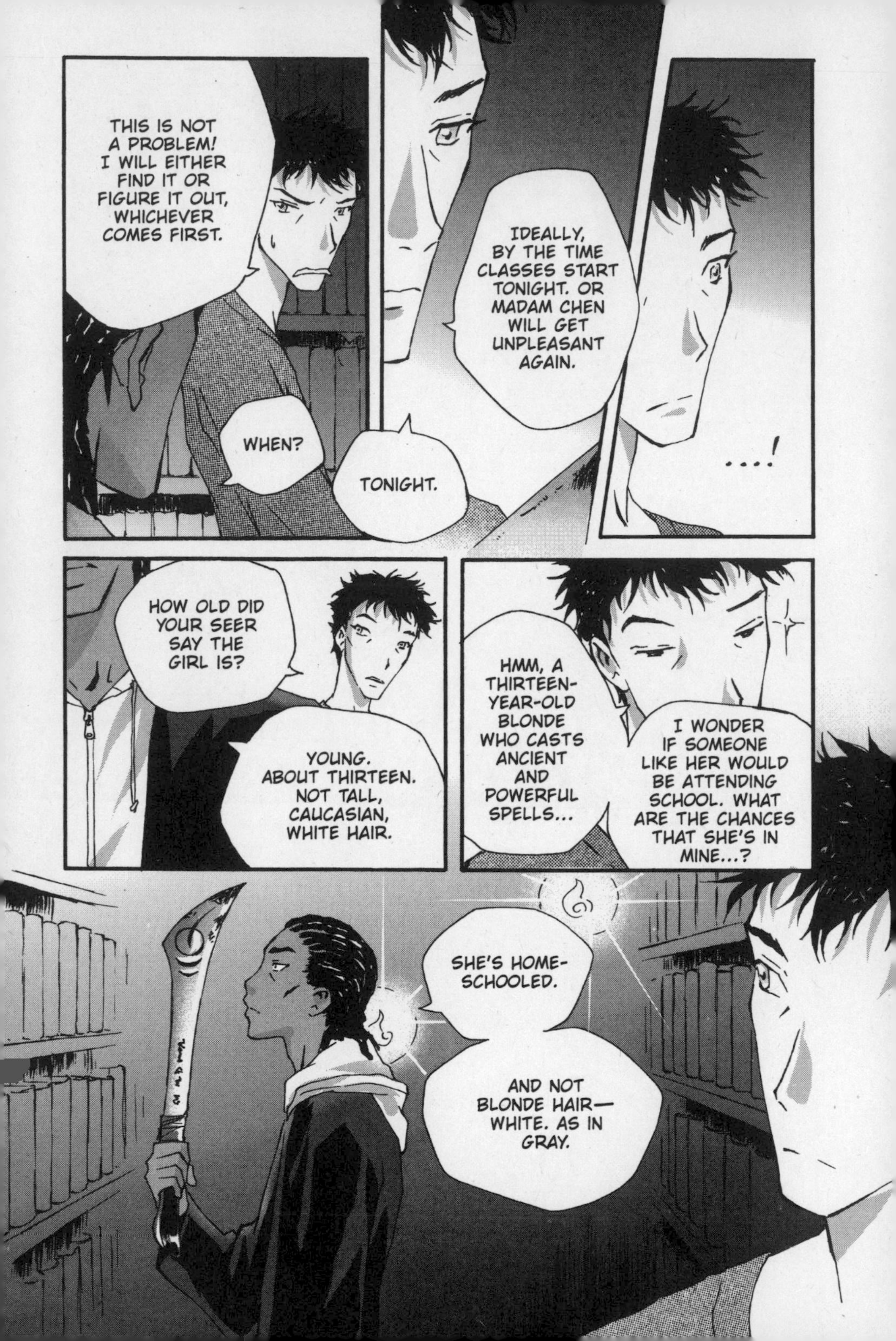
THIS IS NOT A PROBLEM! I WILL EITHER FIND IT OR FIGURE IT OUT, WHICHEVER COMES FIRST.
WHEN?
TONIGHT.
IDEALLY, BY THE TIME CLASSES START TONIGHT. OR MADAM CHEN WILL GET UNPLEASANT AGAIN.
...!
HOW OLD DID YOUR SEER SAY THE GIRL IS?
YOUNG. ABOUT THIRTEEN. NOT TALL, CAUCASIAN, WHITE HAIR.
HMM, A THIRTEEN-YEAR-OLD BLONDE WHO CASTS ANCIENT AND POWERFUL SPELLS...
I WONDER IF SOMEONE LIKE HER WOULD BE ATTENDING SCHOOL. WHAT ARE THE CHANCES THAT SHE'S IN MINE...?
SHE'S HOME-SCHOOLED.
AND NOT BLONDE HAIR—WHITE. AS IN GRAY.

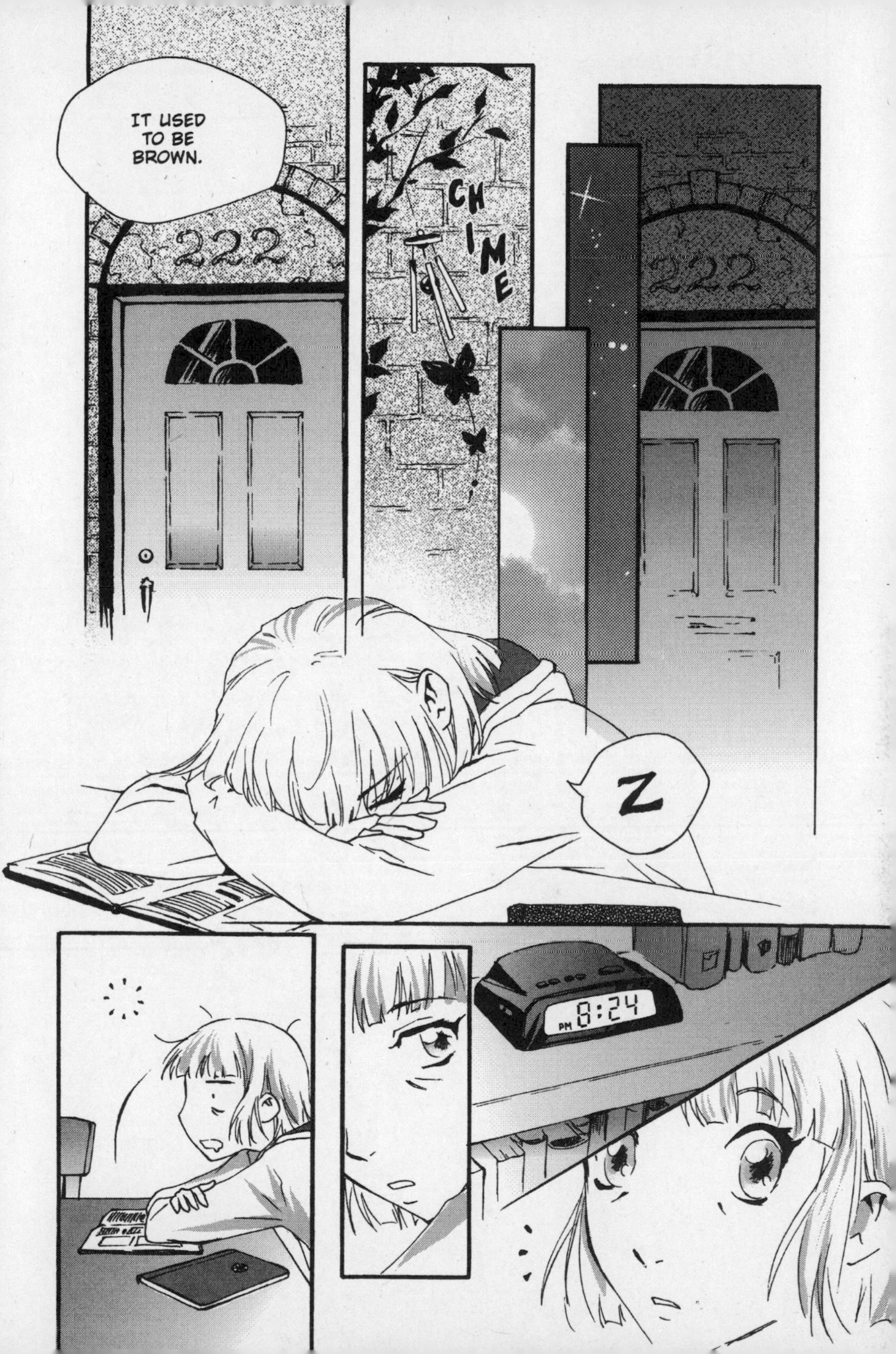
IT USED TO BE BROWN.
222
CHIME
222
Z
PM 8:24

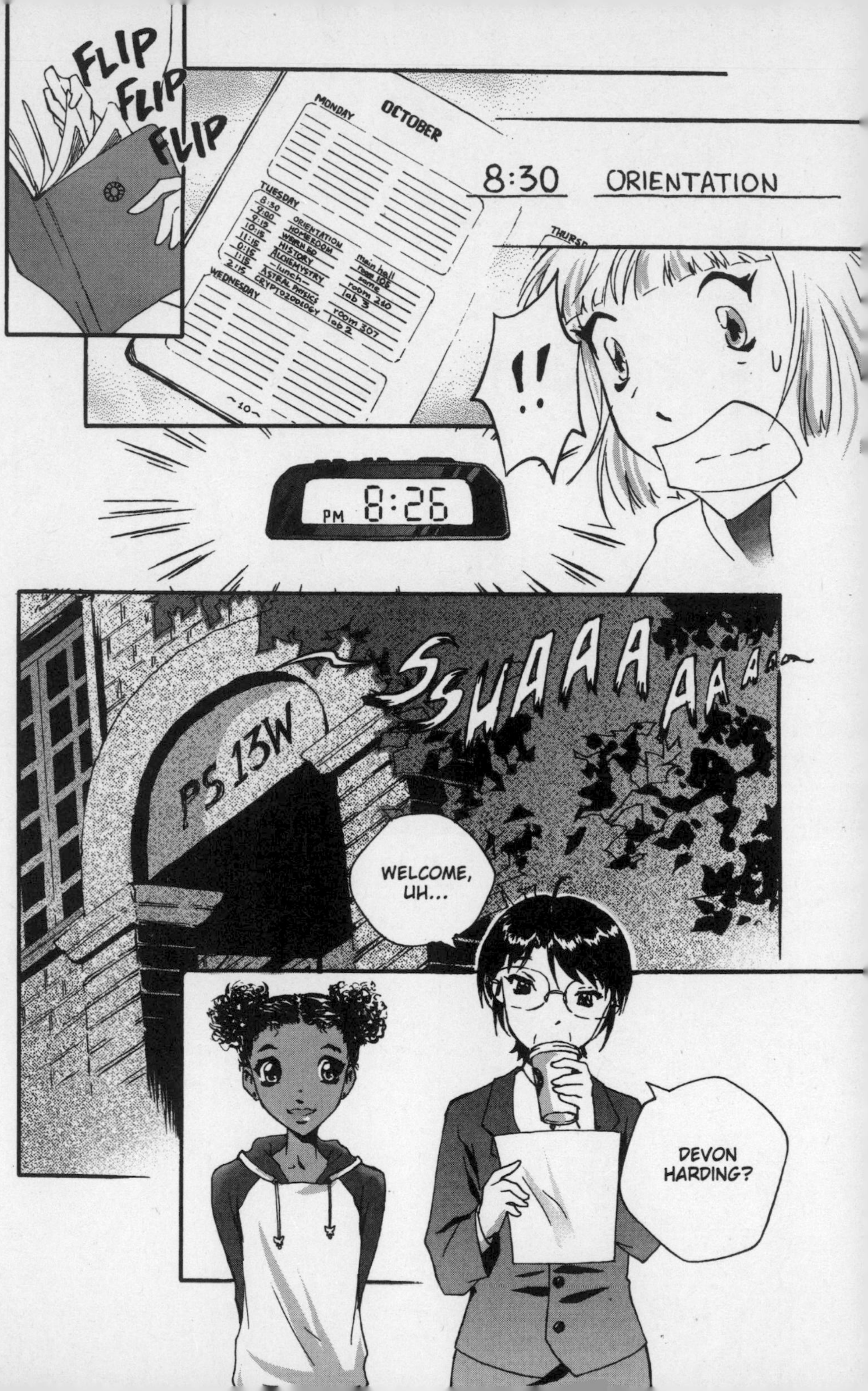
FLIP FLIP FLIP
MONDAY
OCTOBER
TUESDAY
8:30 ORIENTATION main hall
9:00 HOMEROOM room 105
10:15 HISTORY
11:15 ALCHEMYSTRY
–lunch–
1:15 ASTRAL PHYSICS
2:15 CRYPTOZOOLOGY
WEDNESDAY
~10~
8:30 ORIENTATION
THURSD
!!
PM 8:26
PS 13W
SSHAAAAAAA
WELCOME, UH...
DEVON HARDING?

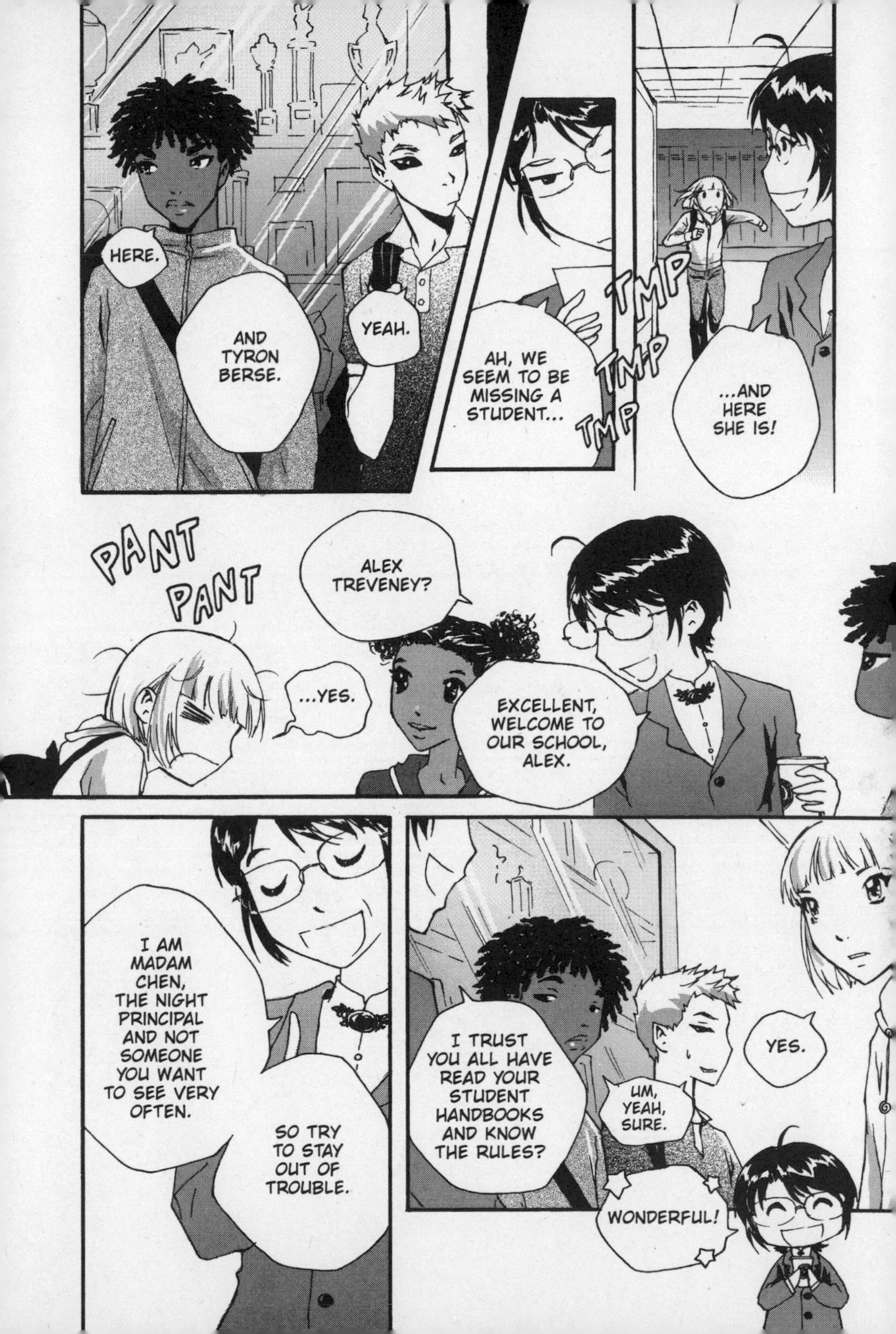
HERE.
AND TYRON BERSE.
YEAH.
AH, WE SEEM TO BE MISSING A STUDENT...
TMP TMP TMP
...AND HERE SHE IS!
PANT PANT
ALEX TREVENEY?
...YES.
EXCELLENT, WELCOME TO OUR SCHOOL, ALEX.
I AM MADAM CHEN, THE NIGHT PRINCIPAL AND NOT SOMEONE YOU WANT TO SEE VERY OFTEN.
SO TRY TO STAY OUT OF TROUBLE.
I TRUST YOU ALL HAVE READ YOUR STUDENT HANDBOOKS AND KNOW THE RULES?
UM, YEAH, SURE.
YES.
WONDERFUL!

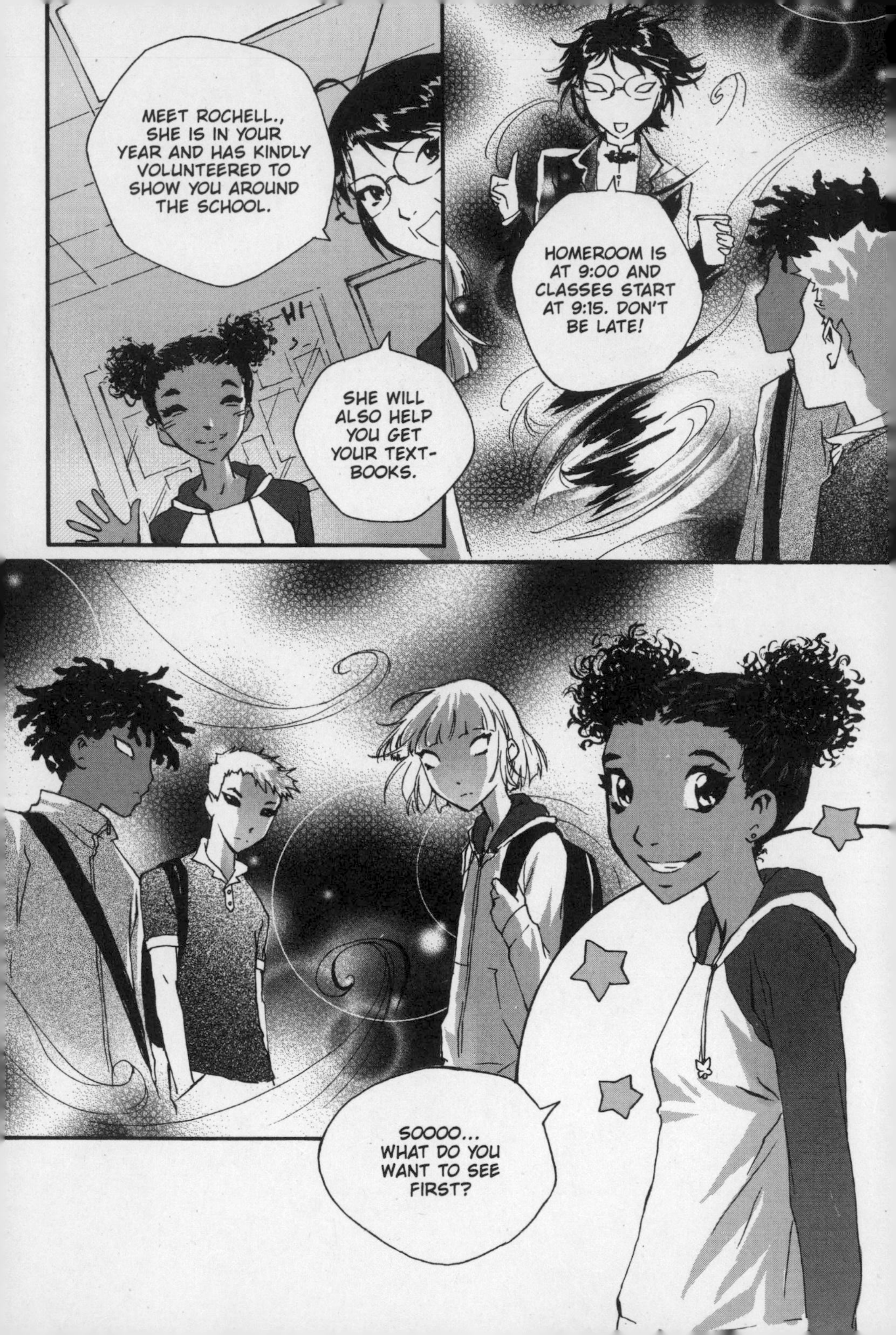
MEET ROCHELL., SHE IS IN YOUR YEAR AND HAS KINDLY VOLUNTEERED TO SHOW YOU AROUND THE SCHOOL.
HI
SHE WILL ALSO HELP YOU GET YOUR TEXT-BOOKS.
HOMEROOM IS AT 9:00 AND CLASSES START AT 9:15. DON'T BE LATE!
SOOOO... WHAT DO YOU WANT TO SEE FIRST?

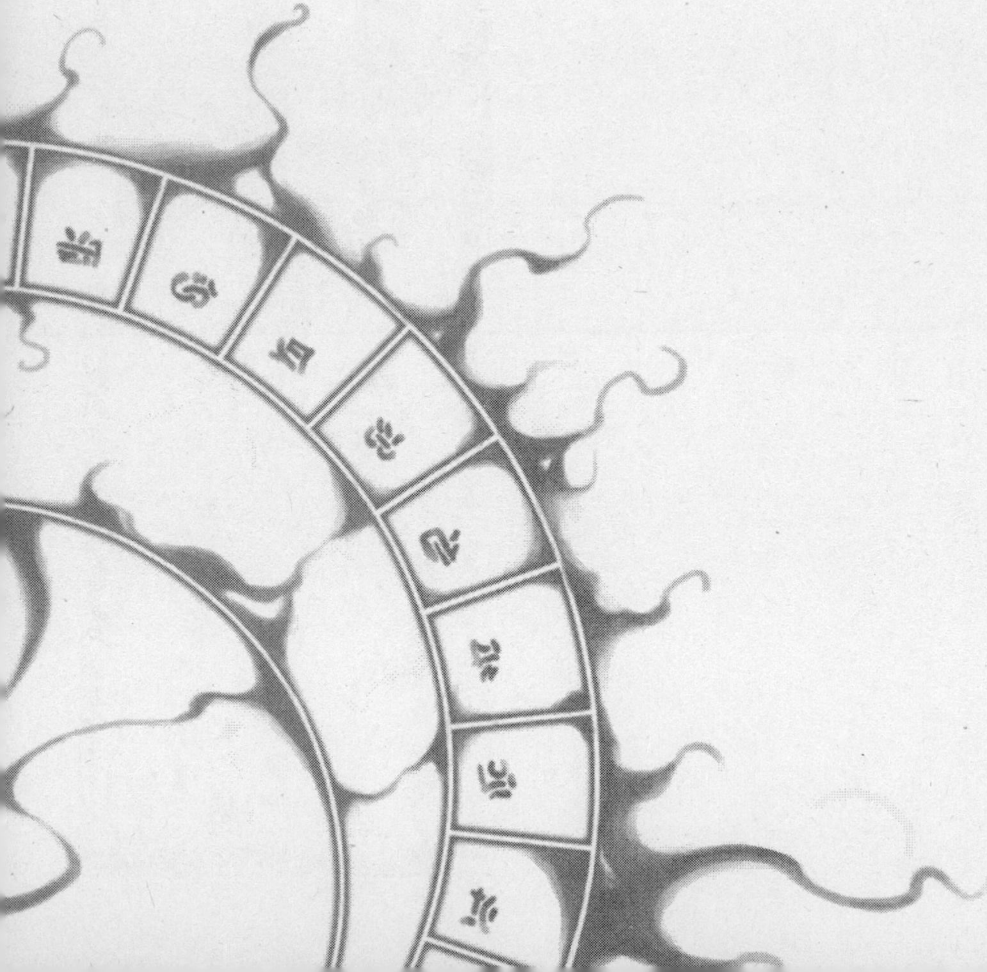

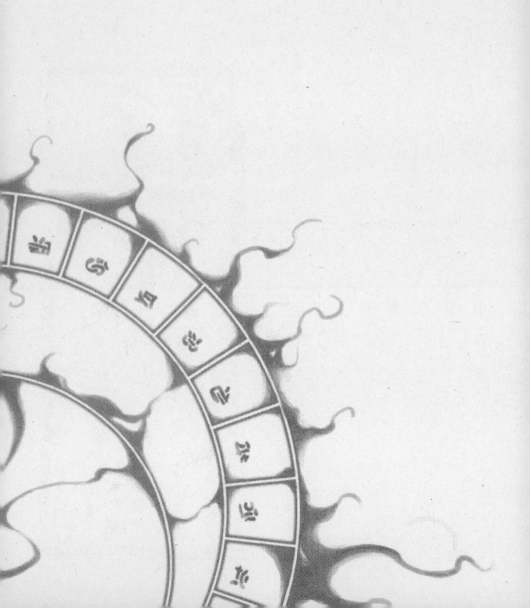

Chapter 10

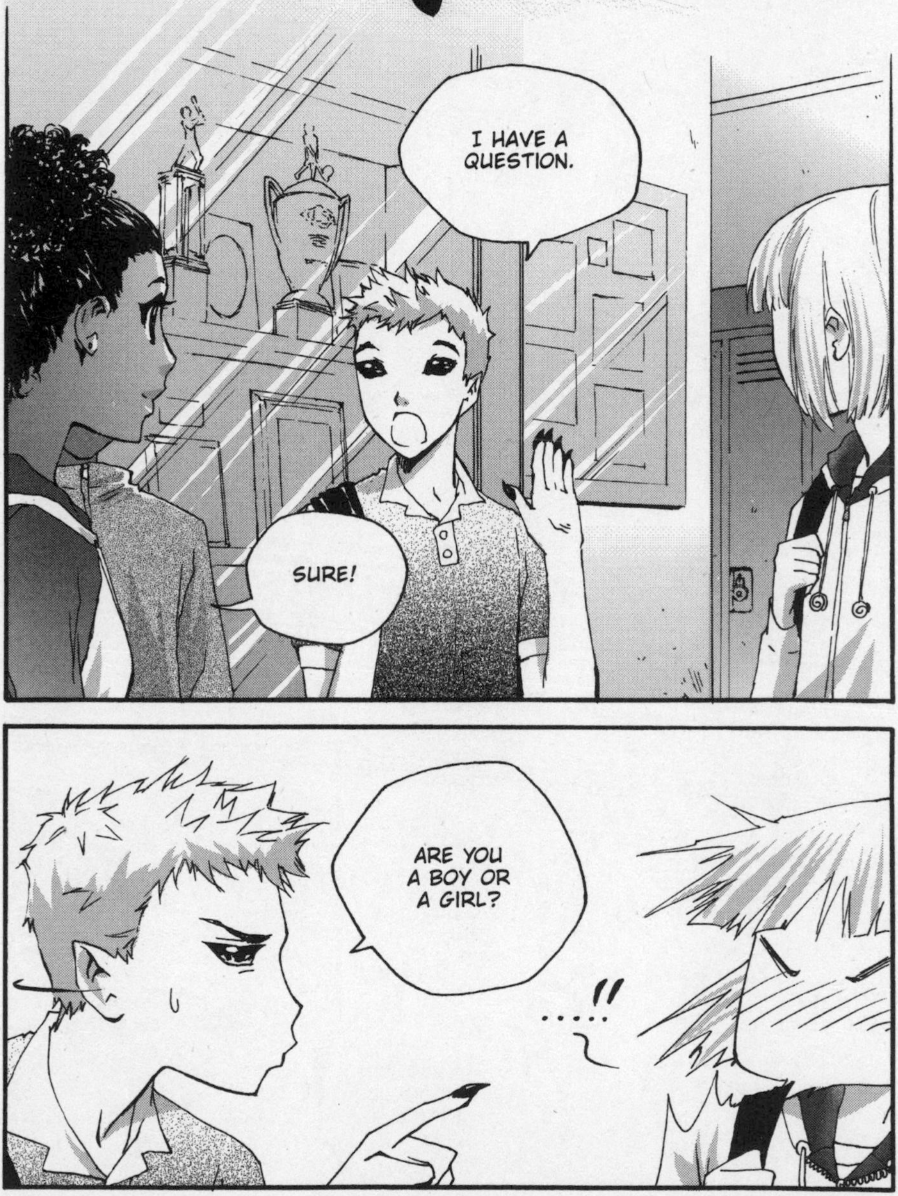
I HAVE A QUESTION.
SURE!
ARE YOU A BOY OR A GIRL?
.....!!

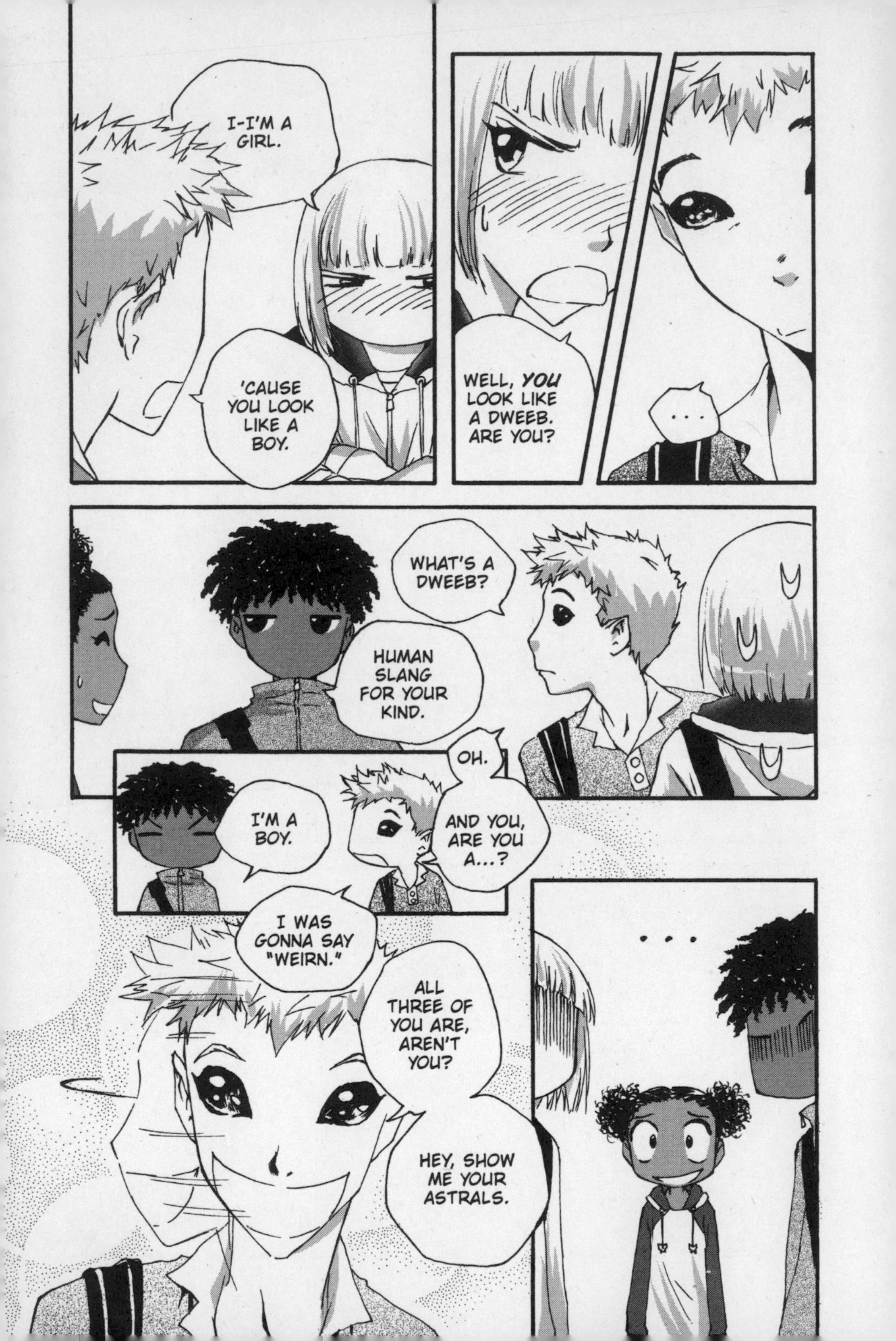

I-I'M A GIRL.
'CAUSE YOU LOOK LIKE A BOY.
WELL, *YOU* LOOK LIKE A DWEEB. ARE YOU?
...
WHAT'S A DWEEB?
HUMAN SLANG FOR YOUR KIND.
OH.
I'M A BOY.
AND YOU, ARE YOU A...?
I WAS GONNA SAY "WEIRN."
ALL THREE OF YOU ARE, AREN'T YOU?
HEY, SHOW ME YOUR ASTRALS.
...

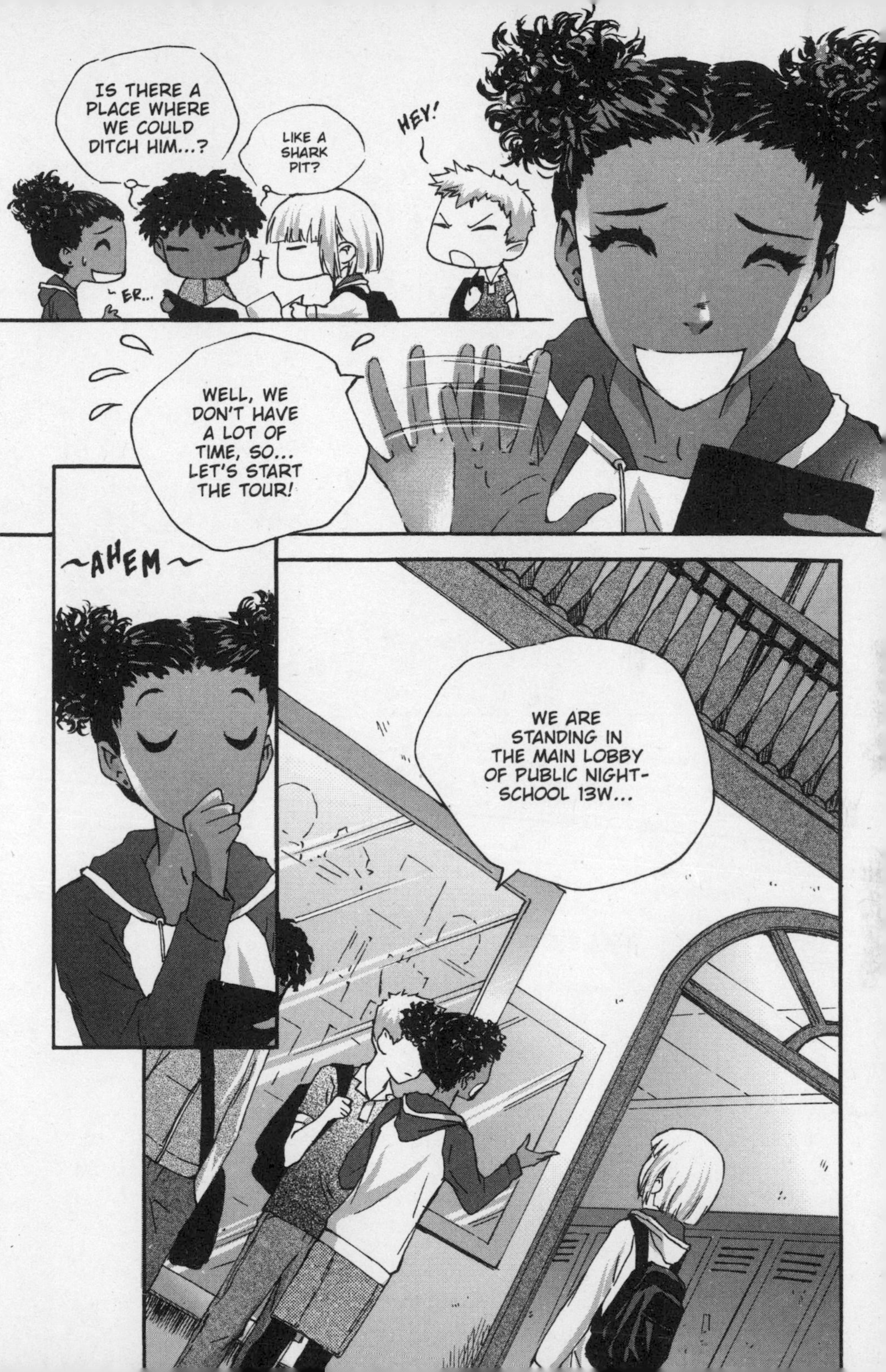
IS THERE A PLACE WHERE WE COULD DITCH HIM...?
LIKE A SHARK PIT?
ER...
HEY!
WELL, WE DON'T HAVE A LOT OF TIME, SO... LET'S START THE TOUR!
~AHEM~
WE ARE STANDING IN THE MAIN LOBBY OF PUBLIC NIGHT-SCHOOL 13W...

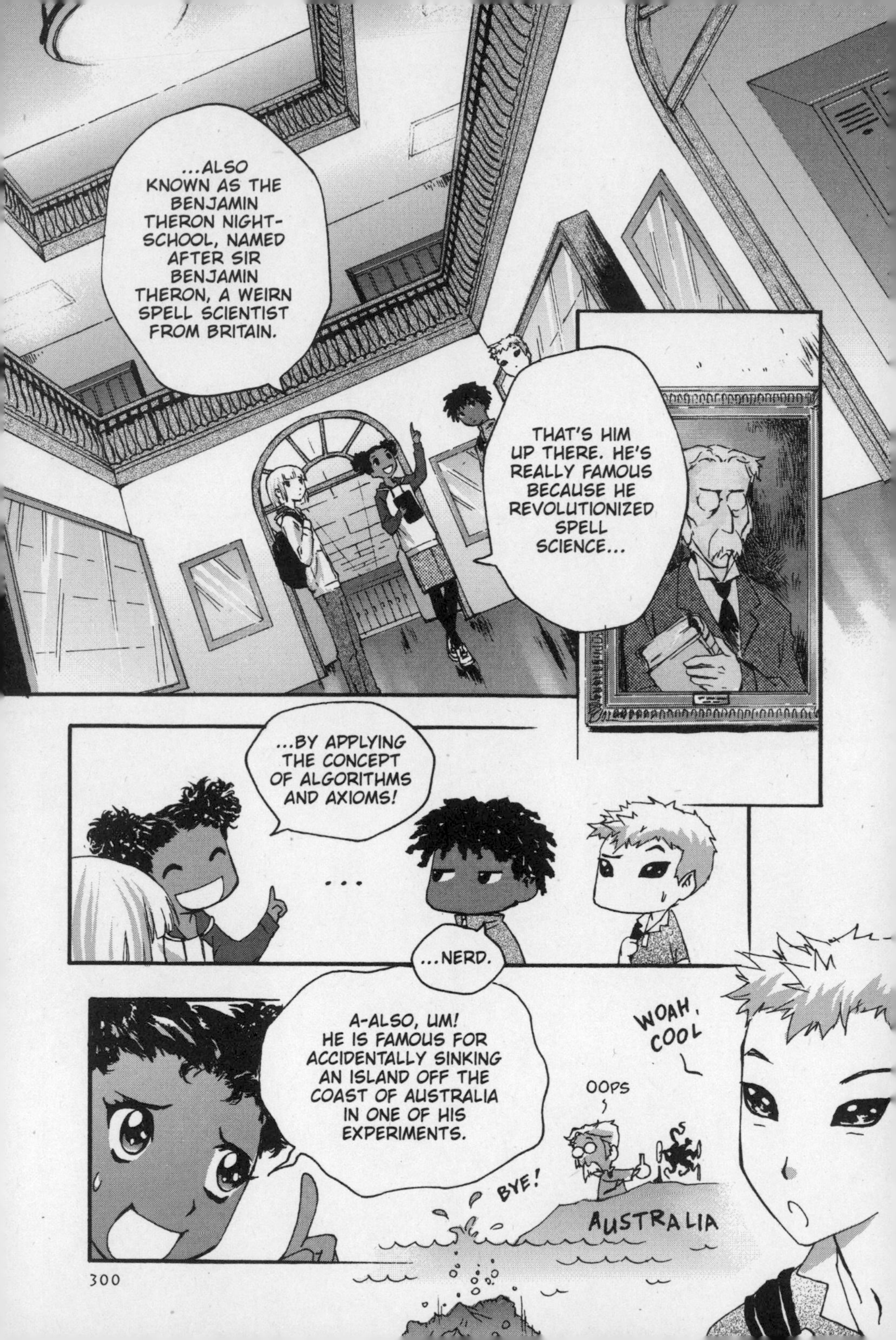
...ALSO KNOWN AS THE BENJAMIN THERON NIGHT-SCHOOL, NAMED AFTER SIR BENJAMIN THERON, A WEIRN SPELL SCIENTIST FROM BRITAIN.
THAT'S HIM UP THERE. HE'S REALLY FAMOUS BECAUSE HE REVOLUTIONIZED SPELL SCIENCE...
...BY APPLYING THE CONCEPT OF ALGORITHMS AND AXIOMS!
...
...NERD.
A-ALSO, UM! HE IS FAMOUS FOR ACCIDENTALLY SINKING AN ISLAND OFF THE COAST OF AUSTRALIA IN ONE OF HIS EXPERIMENTS.
WOAH, COOL
OOPS
BYE!
AUSTRALIA

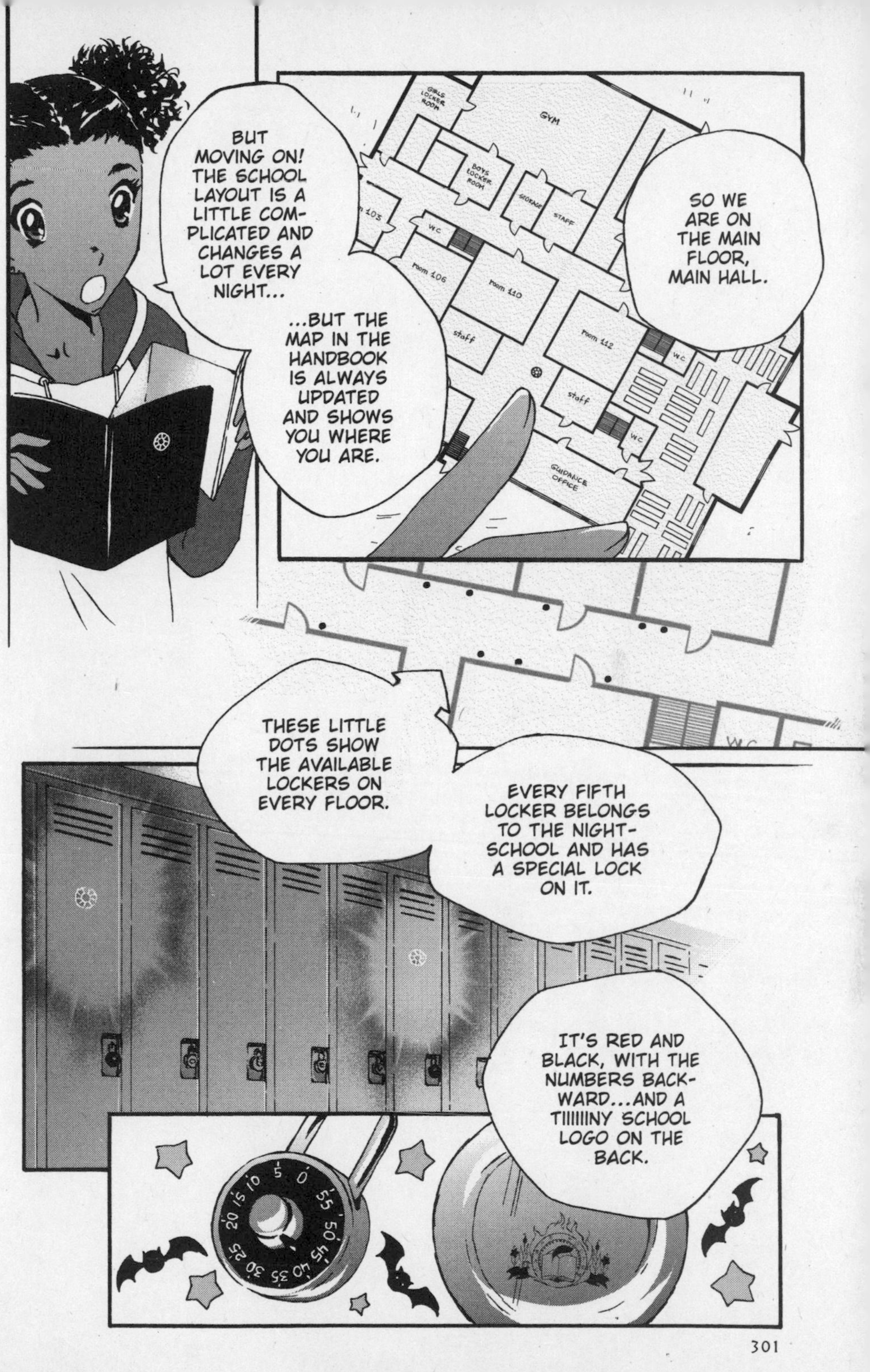
BUT MOVING ON! THE SCHOOL LAYOUT IS A LITTLE COMPLICATED AND CHANGES A LOT EVERY NIGHT...
...BUT THE MAP IN THE HANDBOOK IS ALWAYS UPDATED AND SHOWS YOU WHERE YOU ARE.
GIRLS LOCKER ROOM
GYM
BOYS LOCKER ROOM
STORAGE
STAFF
WC
room 106
room 110
staff
room 112
GUIDANCE OFFICE
SO WE ARE ON THE MAIN FLOOR, MAIN HALL.
THESE LITTLE DOTS SHOW THE AVAILABLE LOCKERS ON EVERY FLOOR.
EVERY FIFTH LOCKER BELONGS TO THE NIGHT-SCHOOL AND HAS A SPECIAL LOCK ON IT.
IT'S RED AND BLACK, WITH THE NUMBERS BACKWARD...AND A TIIIIINY SCHOOL LOGO ON THE BACK.

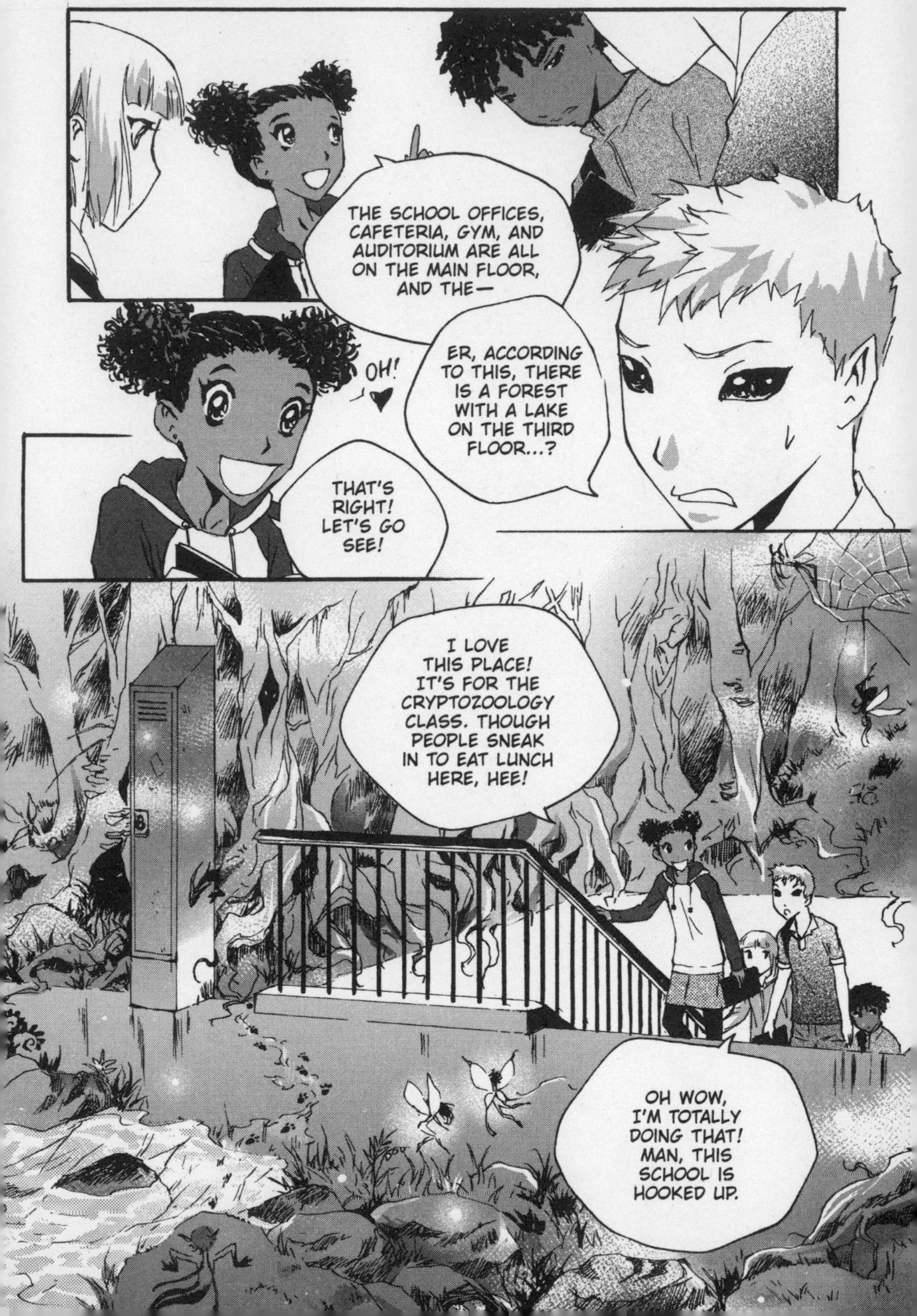
THE SCHOOL OFFICES, CAFETERIA, GYM, AND AUDITORIUM ARE ALL ON THE MAIN FLOOR, AND THE—
OH!
ER, ACCORDING TO THIS, THERE IS A FOREST WITH A LAKE ON THE THIRD FLOOR...?
THAT'S RIGHT! LET'S GO SEE!
I LOVE THIS PLACE! IT'S FOR THE CRYPTOZOOLOGY CLASS. THOUGH PEOPLE SNEAK IN TO EAT LUNCH HERE, HEE!
OH WOW, I'M TOTALLY DOING THAT! MAN, THIS SCHOOL IS HOOKED UP.

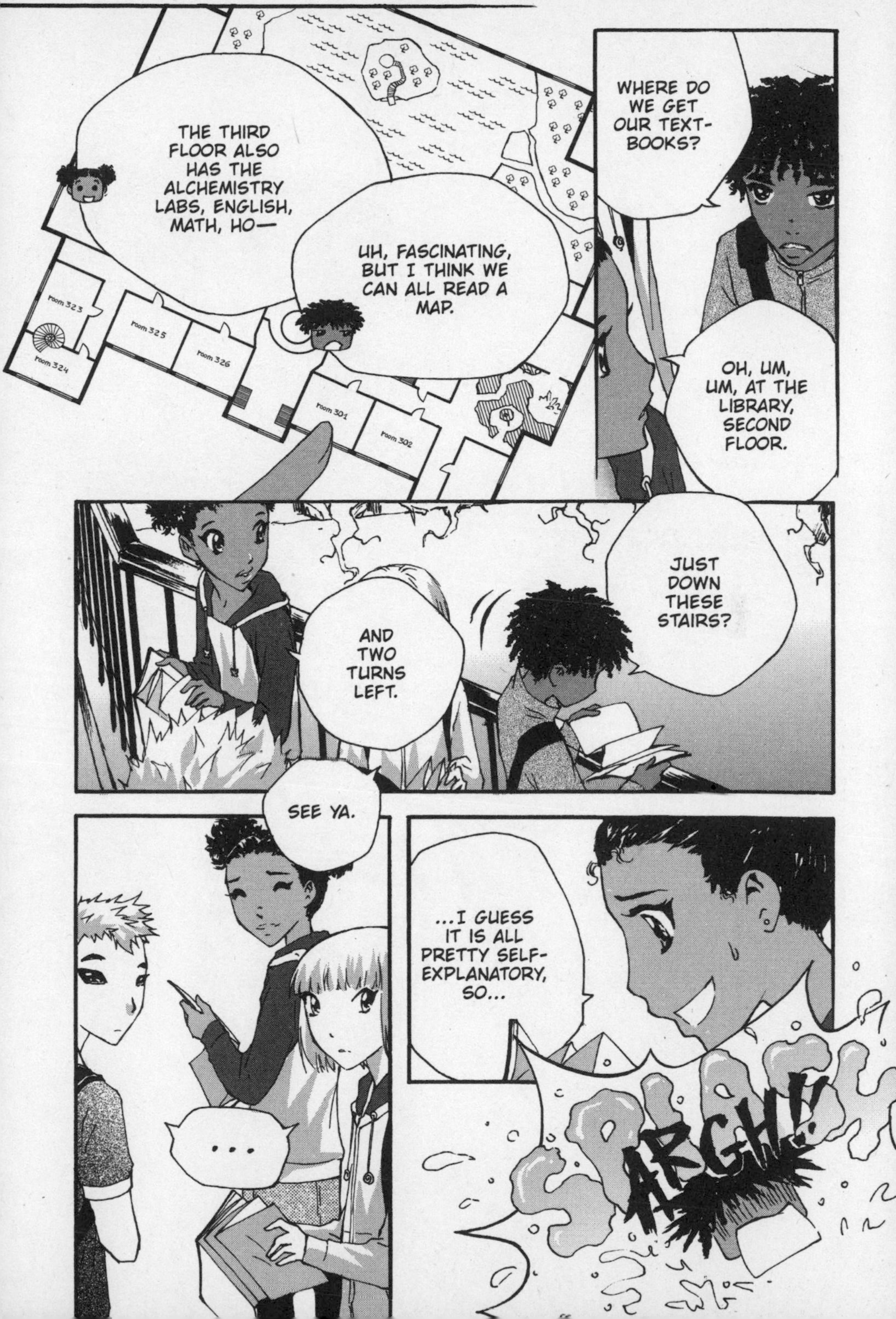
THE THIRD FLOOR ALSO HAS THE ALCHEMISTRY LABS, ENGLISH, MATH, HO—
UH, FASCINATING, BUT I THINK WE CAN ALL READ A MAP.
room 323
room 324
room 325
room 326
room 301
room 302
WHERE DO WE GET OUR TEXT-BOOKS?
OH, UM, UM, AT THE LIBRARY, SECOND FLOOR.
JUST DOWN THESE STAIRS?
AND TWO TURNS LEFT.
SEE YA.
...
...I GUESS IT IS ALL PRETTY SELF-EXPLANATORY, SO...
ARGH!!

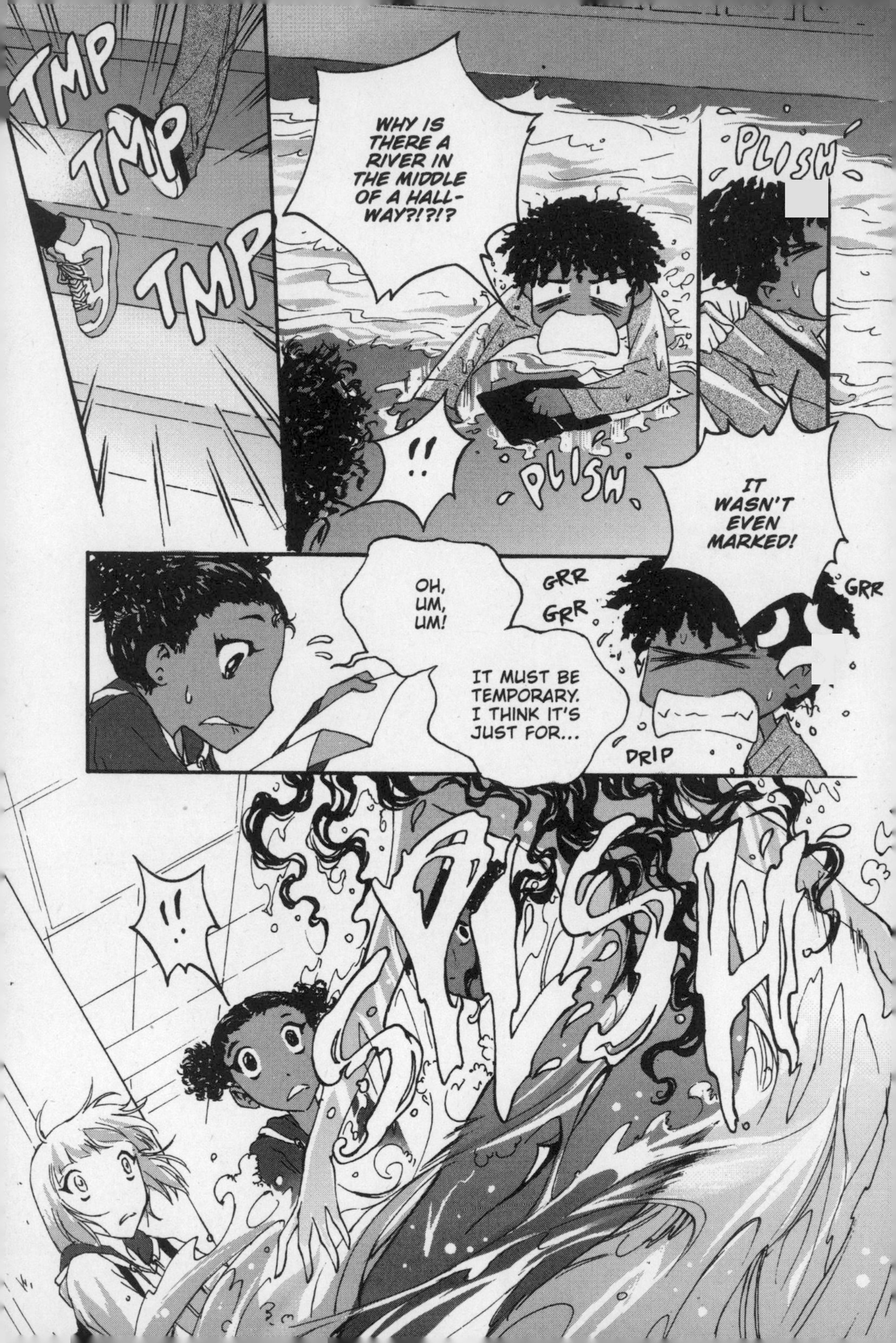
TMP
TMP
TMP
WHY IS THERE A RIVER IN THE MIDDLE OF A HALL-WAY?!?!?
!!
PLISH
PLISH
IT WASN'T EVEN MARKED!
OH, UM, UM!
GRR
GRR
IT MUST BE TEMPORARY. I THINK IT'S JUST FOR...
GRR
DRIP
!!

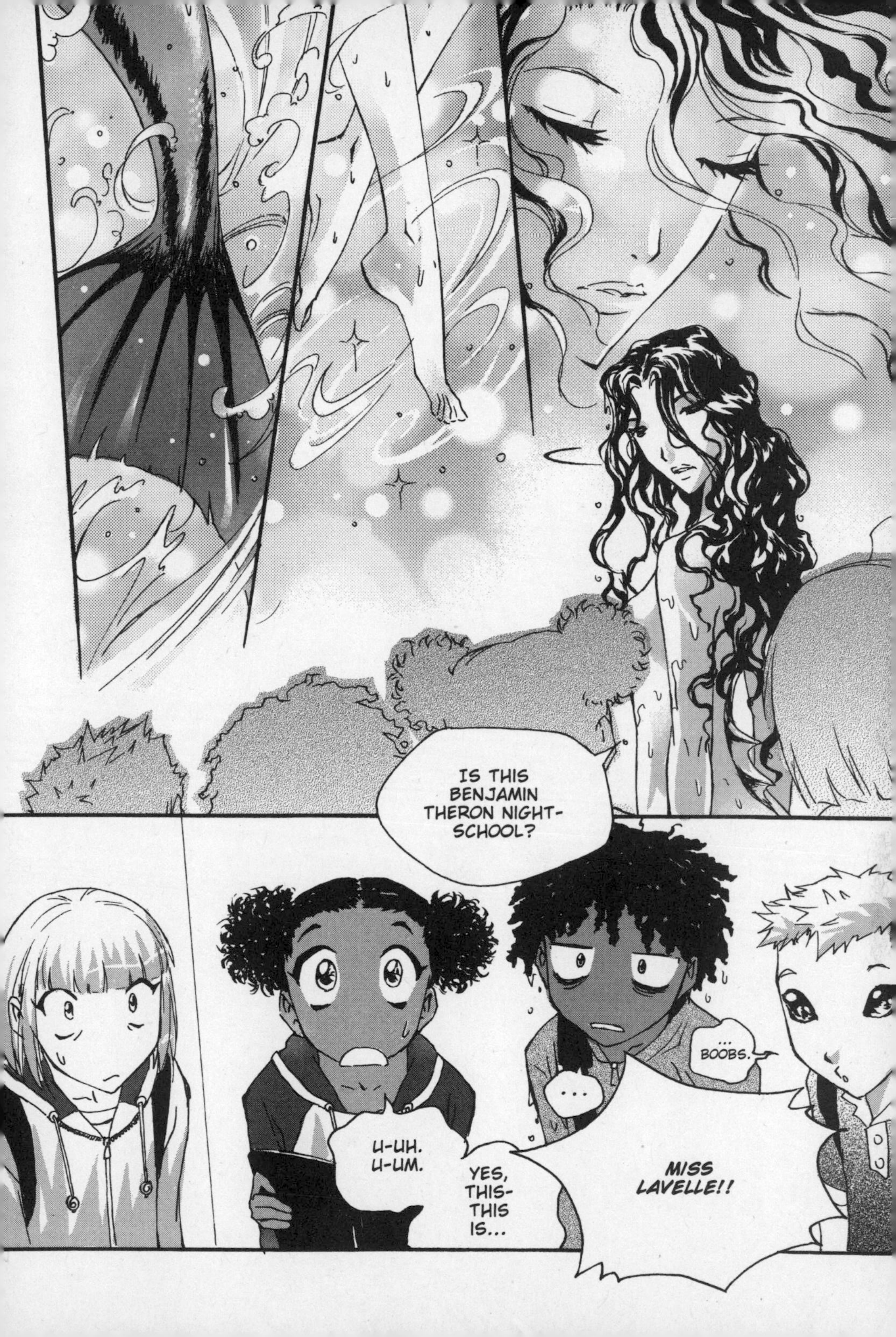
IS THIS BENJAMIN THERON NIGHT-SCHOOL?
U-UH. U-UM.
YES, THIS-THIS IS...
...
...BOOBS.
MISS LAVELLE!!

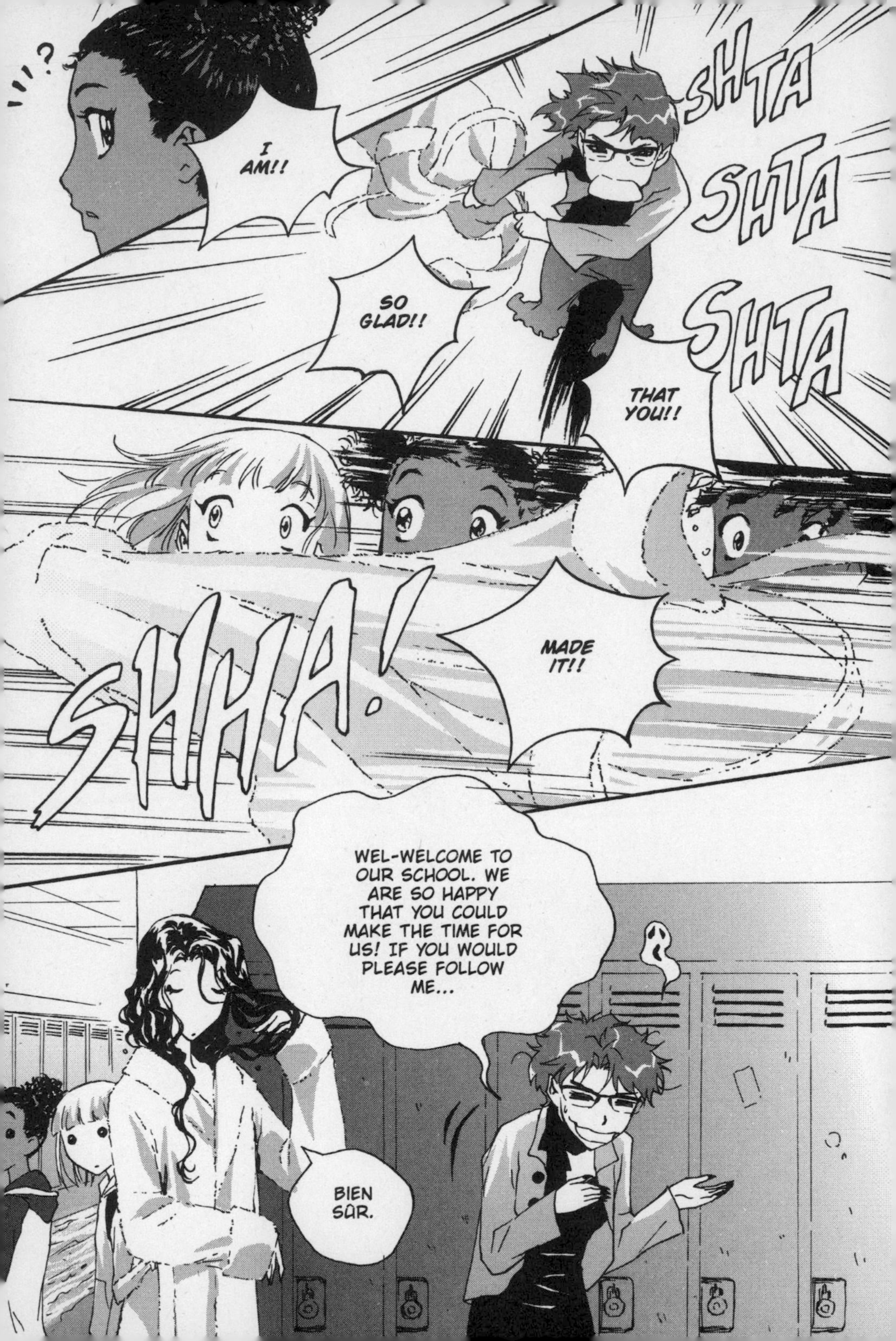

?
I AM!!
SHTA
SHTA
SO GLAD!!
SHTA
THAT YOU!!
SHHA!
MADE IT!!
WEL-WELCOME TO OUR SCHOOL. WE ARE SO HAPPY THAT YOU COULD MAKE THE TIME FOR US! IF YOU WOULD PLEASE FOLLOW ME...
BIEN SÛR.

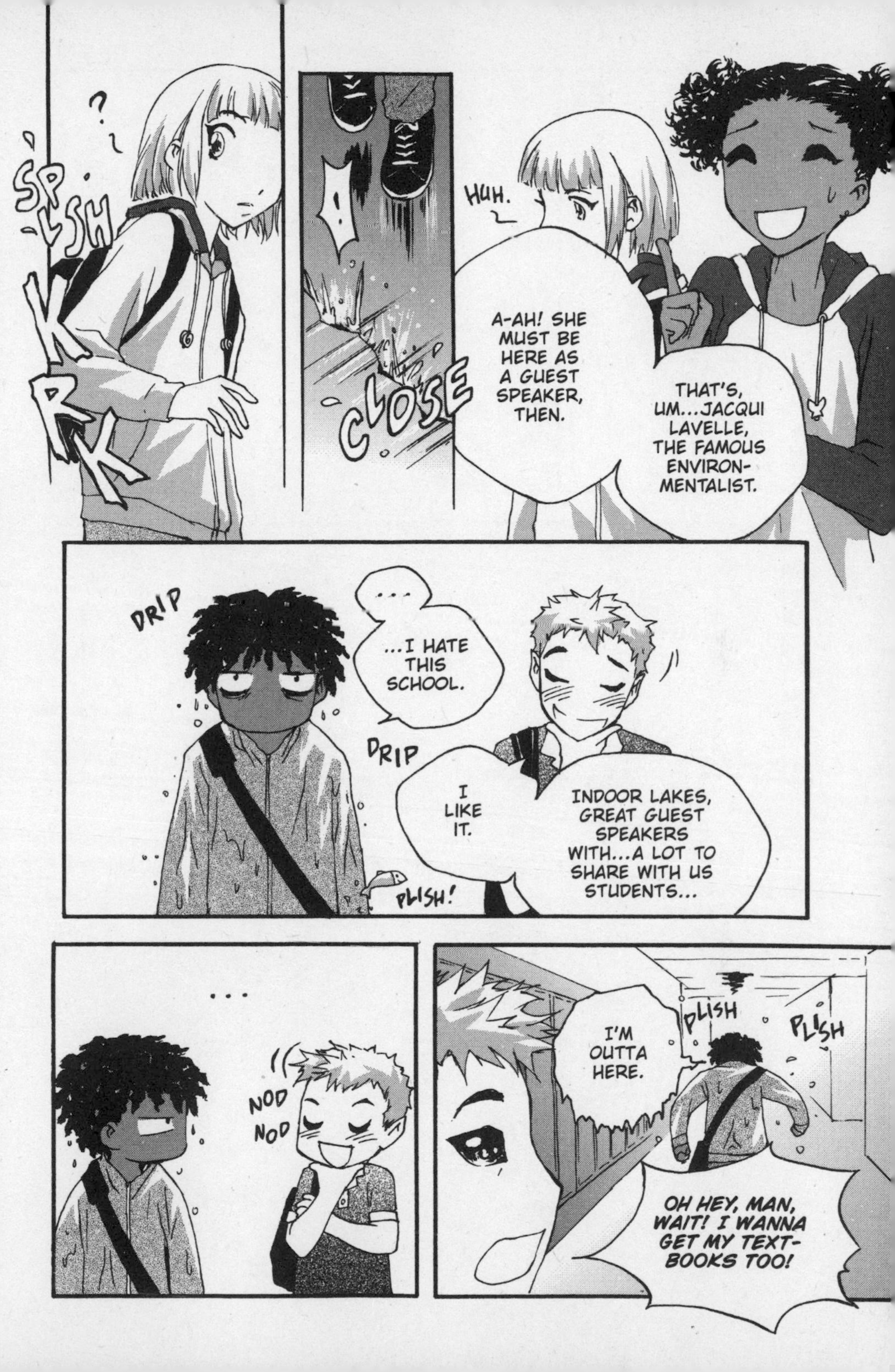
?
SPLSH
KRK
!
CLOSE
HUH.
A-AH! SHE MUST BE HERE AS A GUEST SPEAKER, THEN.
THAT'S, UM...JACQUI LAVELLE, THE FAMOUS ENVIRON-MENTALIST.
DRIP
...
...I HATE THIS SCHOOL.
DRIP
I LIKE IT.
INDOOR LAKES, GREAT GUEST SPEAKERS WITH...A LOT TO SHARE WITH US STUDENTS...
PLISH!
...
NOD NOD
I'M OUTTA HERE.
PLISH
PLISH
OH HEY, MAN, WAIT! I WANNA GET MY TEXT-BOOKS TOO!

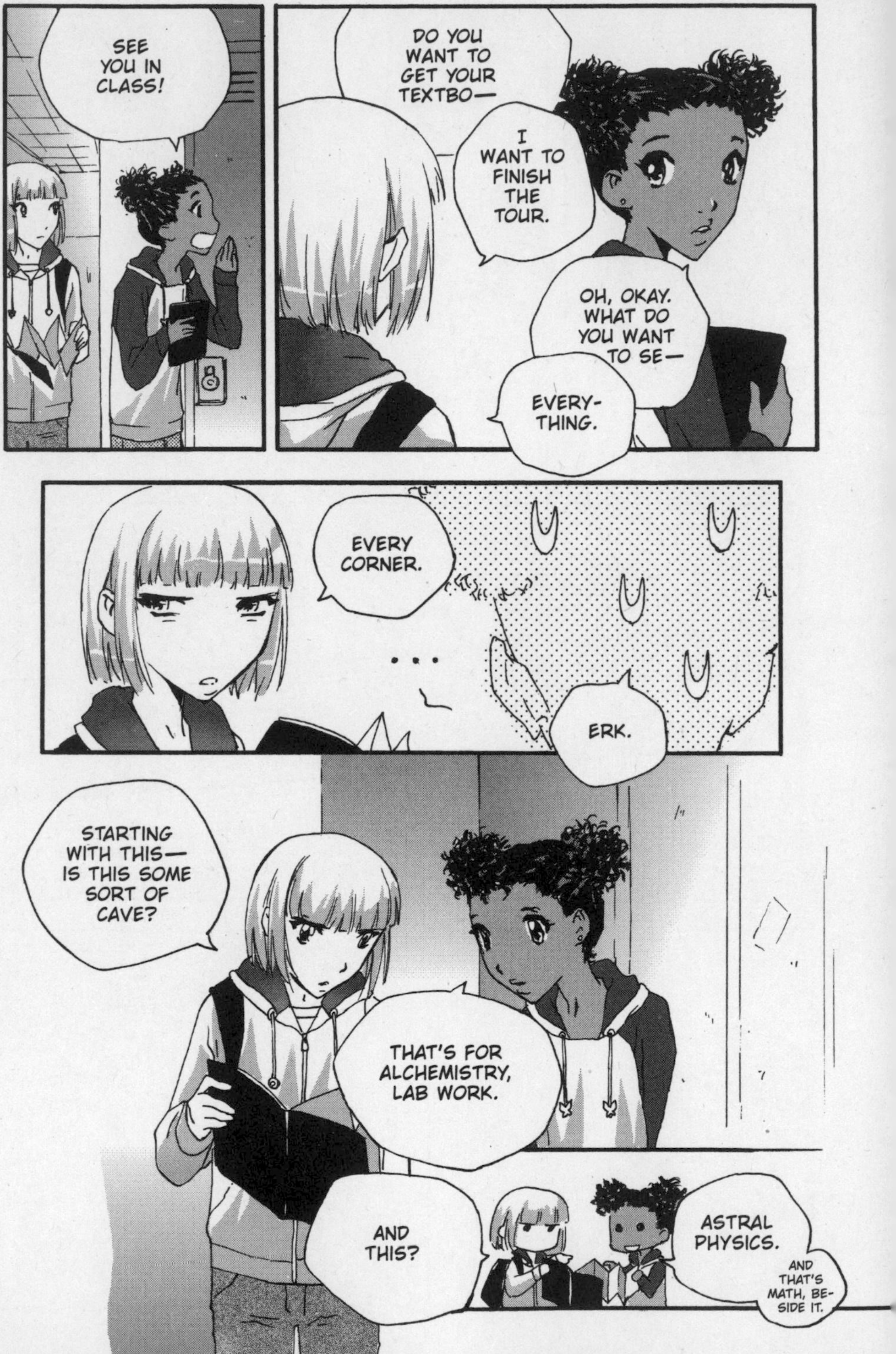
SEE YOU IN CLASS!
DO YOU WANT TO GET YOUR TEXTBO—
I WANT TO FINISH THE TOUR.
OH, OKAY. WHAT DO YOU WANT TO SE—
EVERY-THING.
EVERY CORNER.
...
ERK.
STARTING WITH THIS— IS THIS SOME SORT OF CAVE?
THAT'S FOR ALCHEMISTRY, LAB WORK.
AND THIS?
ASTRAL PHYSICS.
AND THAT'S MATH, BE-SIDE IT.

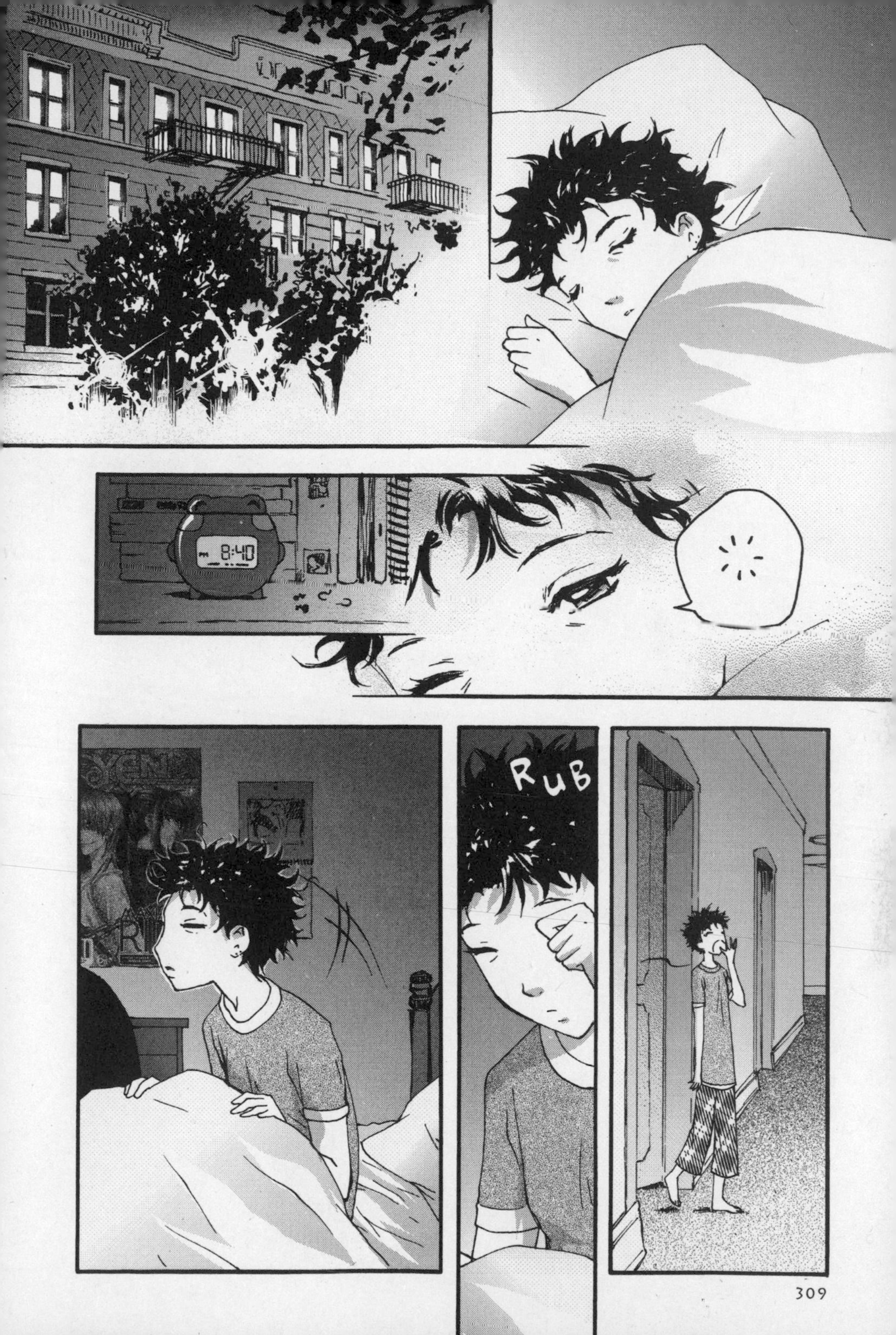
8:40
RUB

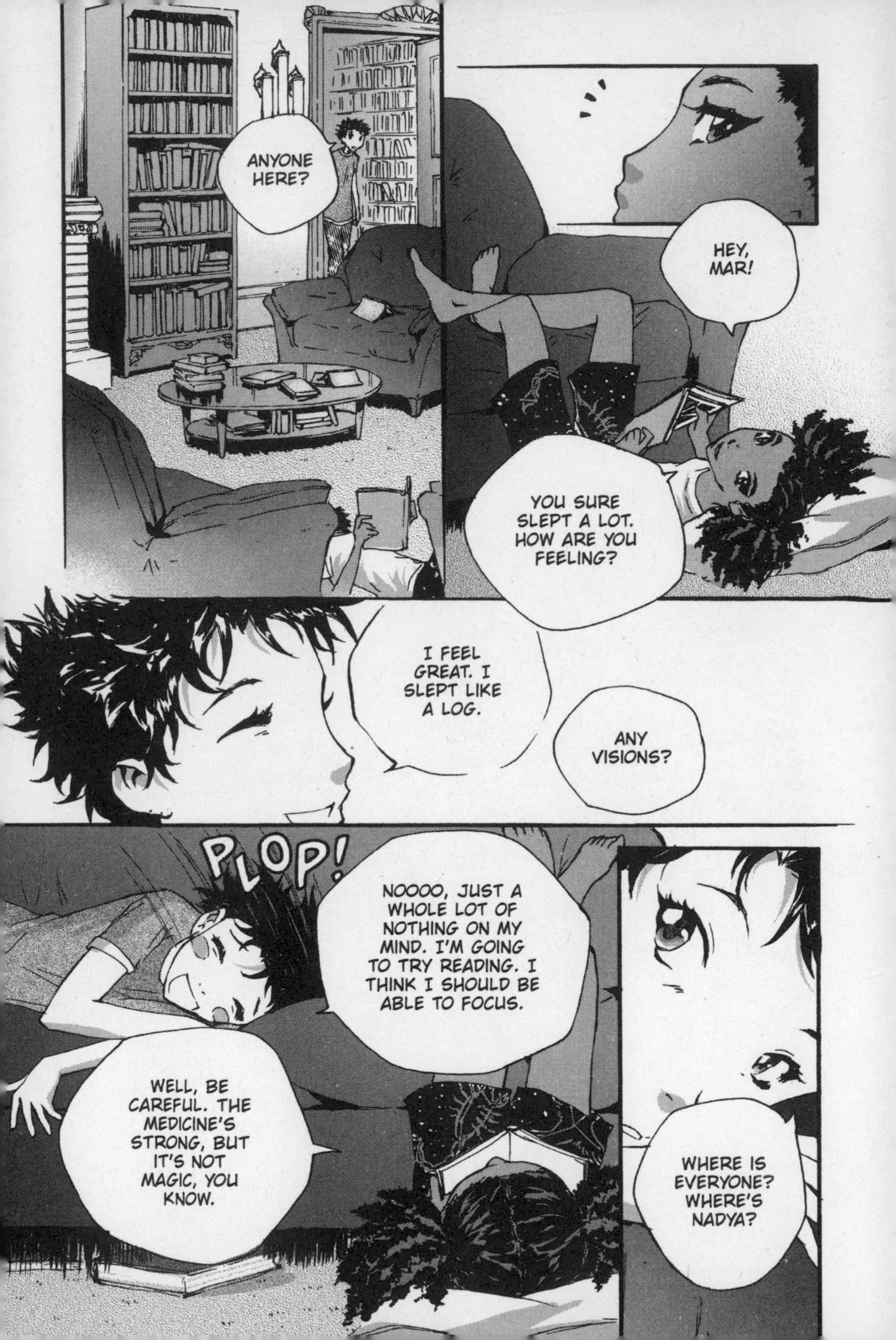
ANYONE HERE?
HEY, MAR!
YOU SURE SLEPT A LOT. HOW ARE YOU FEELING?
I FEEL GREAT. I SLEPT LIKE A LOG.
ANY VISIONS?
PLOP!
NOOOO, JUST A WHOLE LOT OF NOTHING ON MY MIND. I'M GOING TO TRY READING. I THINK I SHOULD BE ABLE TO FOCUS.
WELL, BE CAREFUL. THE MEDICINE'S STRONG, BUT IT'S NOT MAGIC, YOU KNOW.
WHERE IS EVERYONE? WHERE'S NADYA?

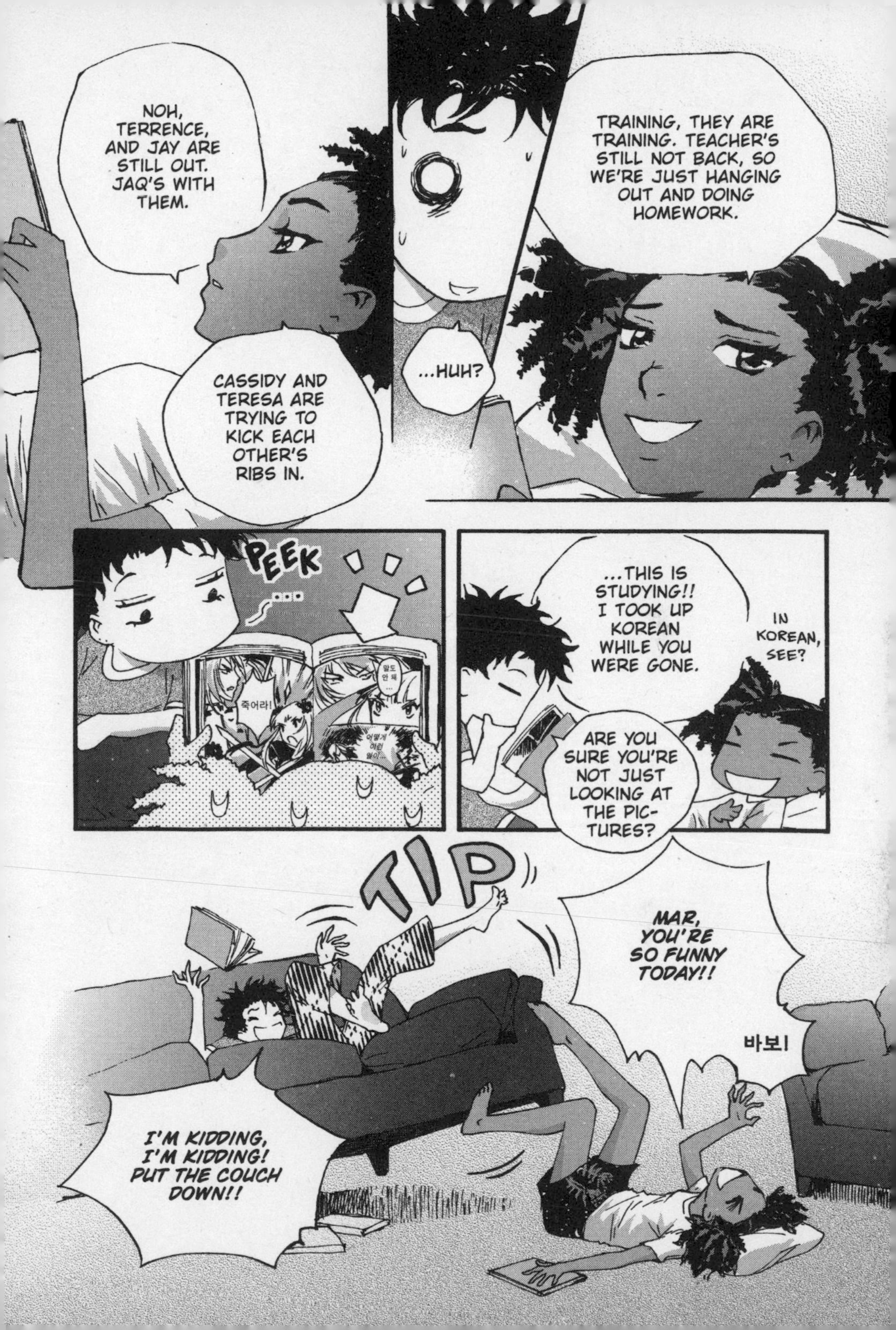
NOH, TERRENCE, AND JAY ARE STILL OUT. JAQ'S WITH THEM.
CASSIDY AND TERESA ARE TRYING TO KICK EACH OTHER'S RIBS IN.
...HUH?
TRAINING, THEY ARE TRAINING. TEACHER'S STILL NOT BACK, SO WE'RE JUST HANGING OUT AND DOING HOMEWORK.
PEEK
...
죽어라!
...THIS IS STUDYING!! I TOOK UP KOREAN WHILE YOU WERE GONE.
IN KOREAN, SEE?
ARE YOU SURE YOU'RE NOT JUST LOOKING AT THE PIC-TURES?
TIP
MAR, YOU'RE SO FUNNY TODAY!!
바보!
I'M KIDDING, I'M KIDDING! PUT THE COUCH DOWN!!

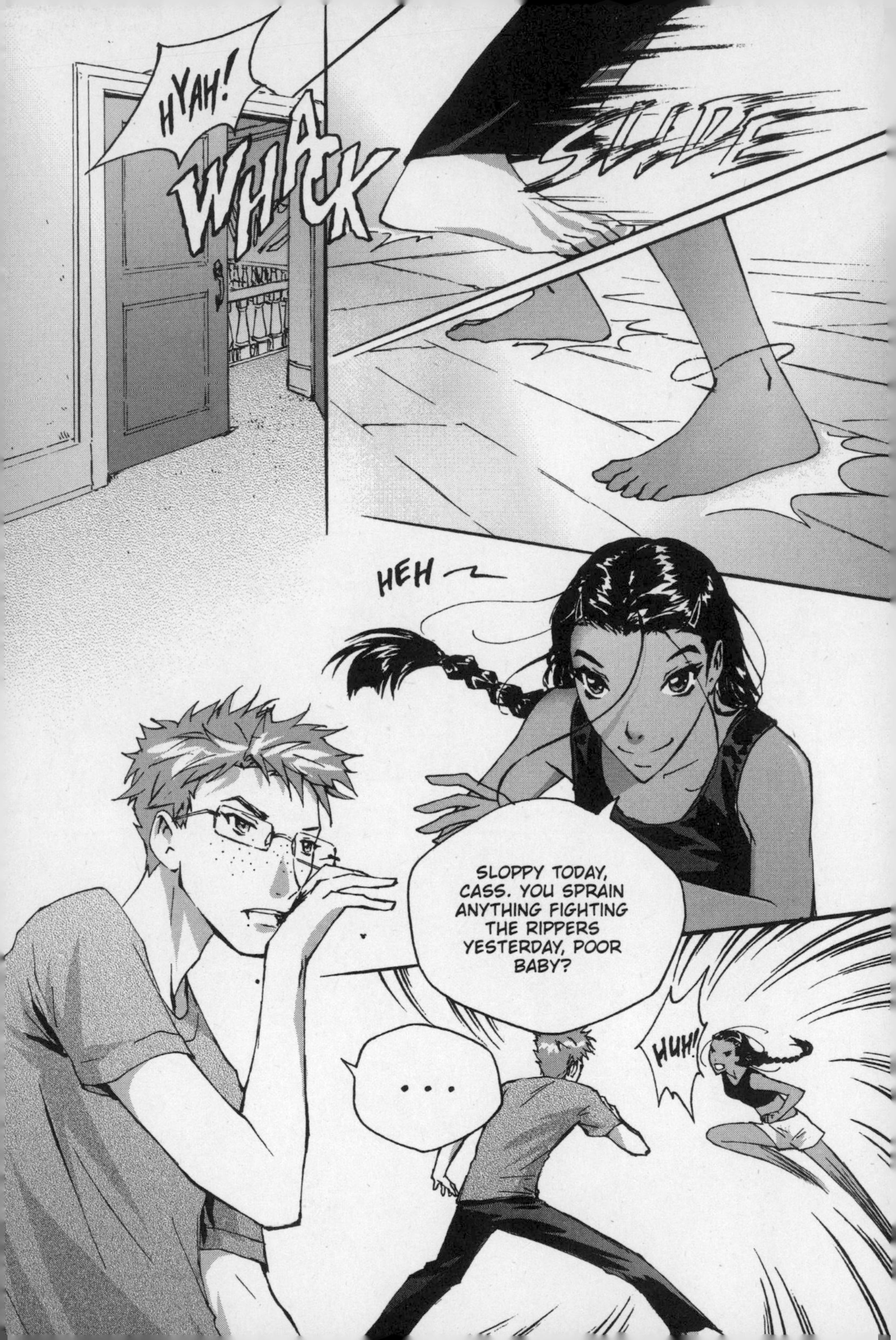
HYAH!
WHACK
SLIDE
HEH~
SLOPPY TODAY, CASS. YOU SPRAIN ANYTHING FIGHTING THE RIPPERS YESTERDAY, POOR BABY?
...
HUH!

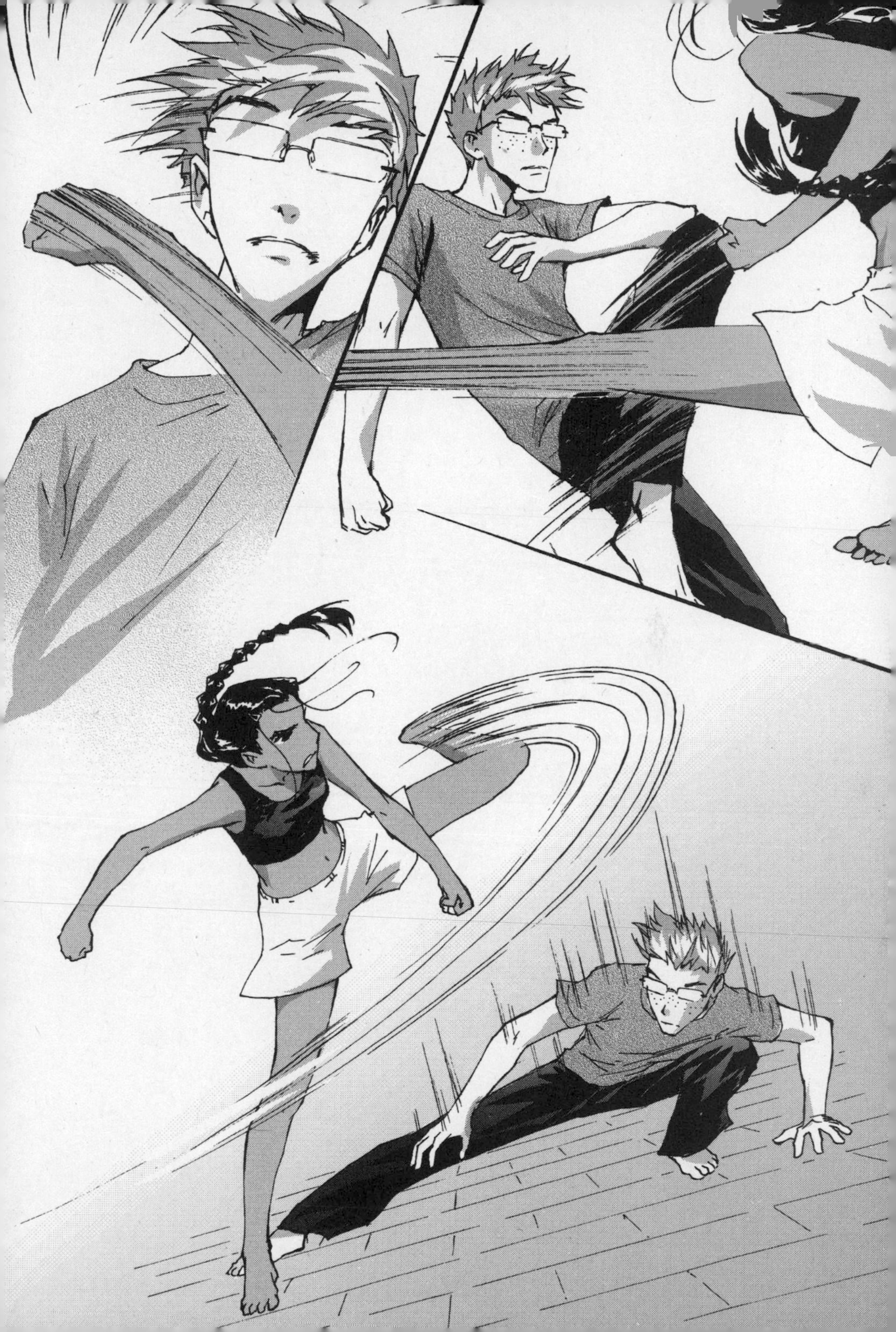

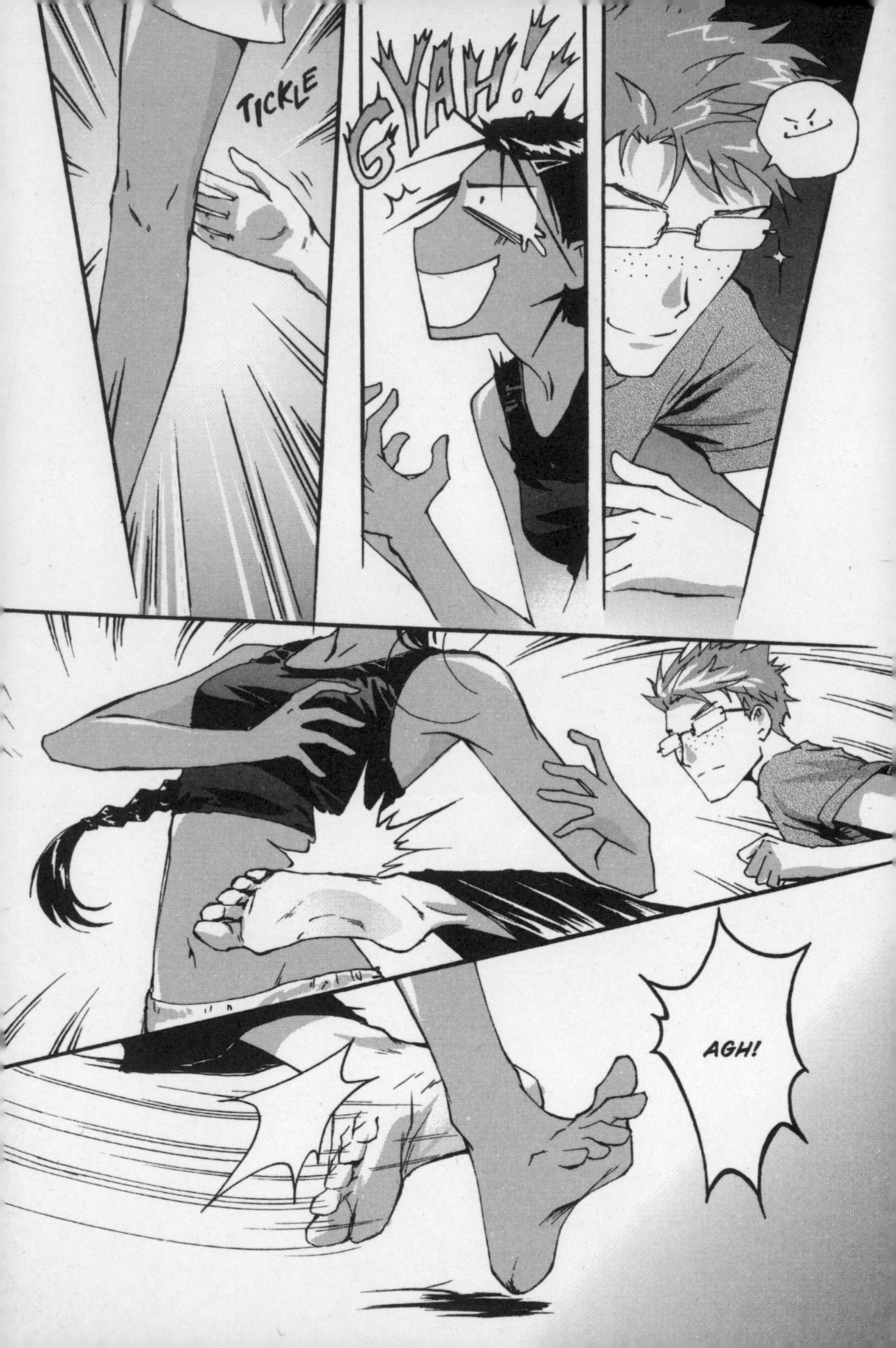
TICKLE
GYAH!!
AGH!

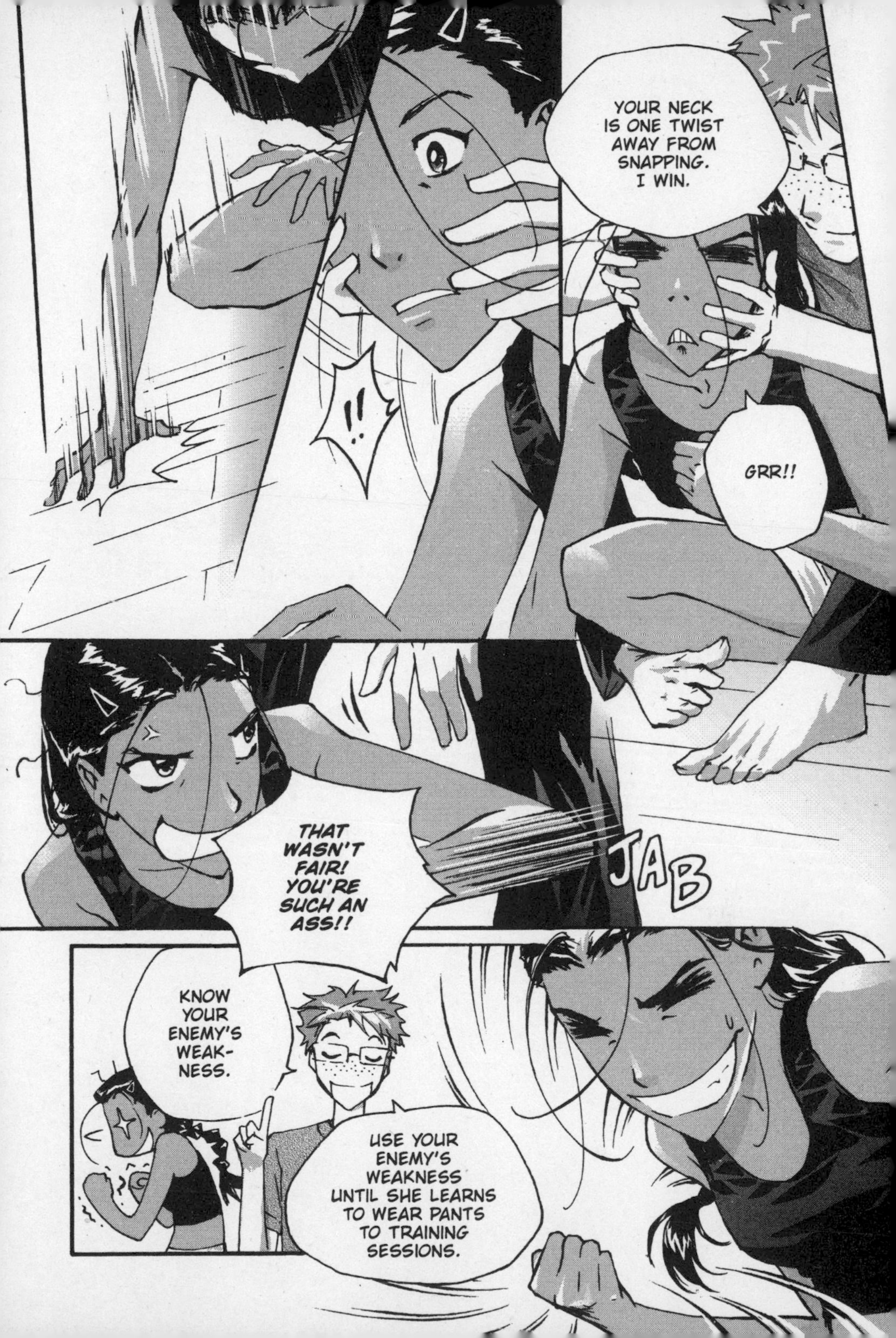
!!
YOUR NECK IS ONE TWIST AWAY FROM SNAPPING. I WIN.
GRR!!
THAT WASN'T FAIR! YOU'RE SUCH AN ASS!!
JAB
KNOW YOUR ENEMY'S WEAK-NESS.
USE YOUR ENEMY'S WEAKNESS UNTIL SHE LEARNS TO WEAR PANTS TO TRAINING SESSIONS.

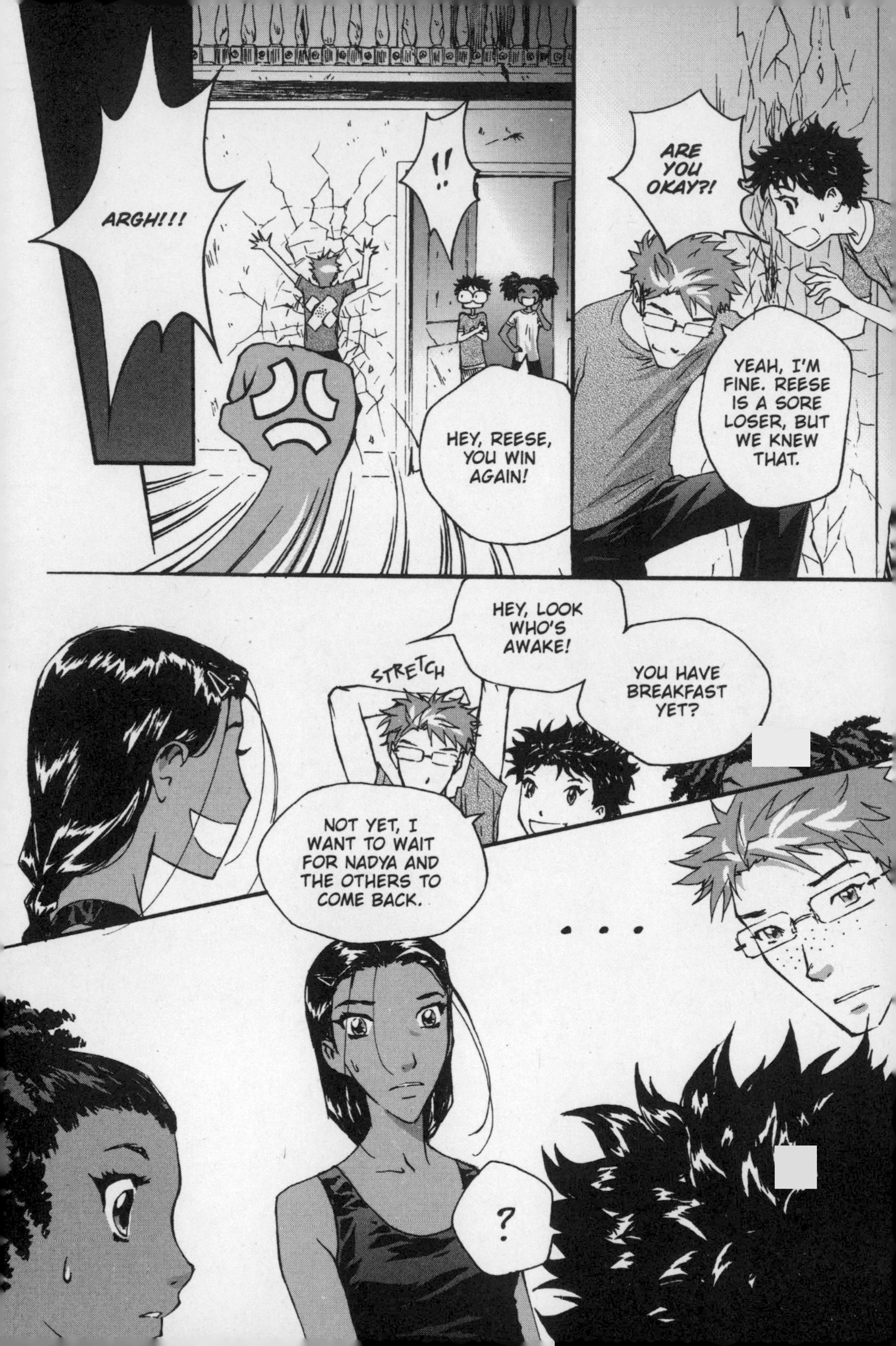
ARGH!!!
!!
HEY, REESE, YOU WIN AGAIN!
ARE YOU OKAY?!
YEAH, I'M FINE. REESE IS A SORE LOSER, BUT WE KNEW THAT.
HEY, LOOK WHO'S AWAKE!
STRETCH
YOU HAVE BREAKFAST YET?
NOT YET, I WANT TO WAIT FOR NADYA AND THE OTHERS TO COME BACK.
...
?

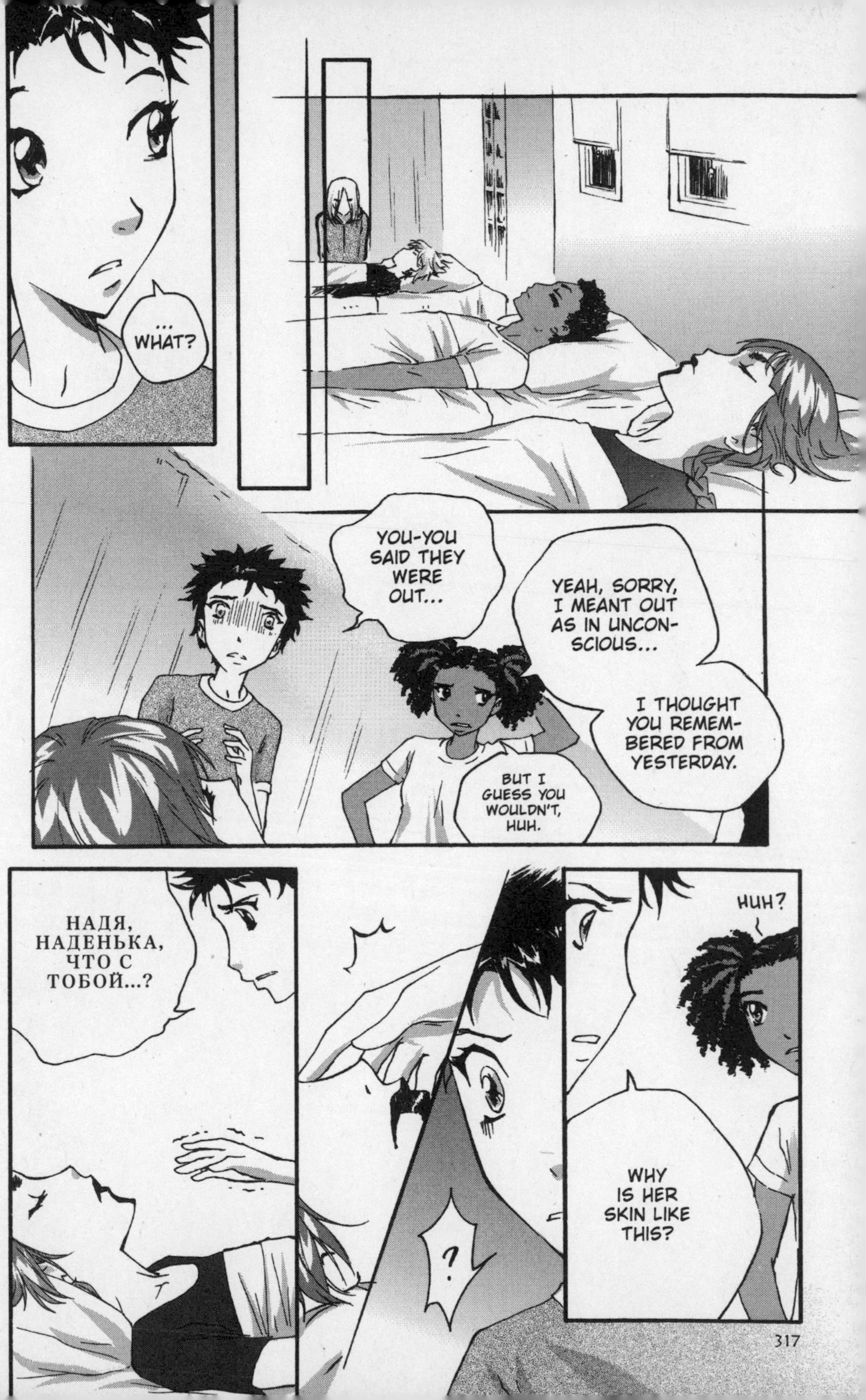

... WHAT?
YOU-YOU SAID THEY WERE OUT...
YEAH, SORRY, I MEANT OUT AS IN UNCON-SCIOUS...
I THOUGHT YOU REMEM-BERED FROM YESTERDAY.
BUT I GUESS YOU WOULDN'T, HUH.
НАДЯ, НАДЕНЬКА, ЧТО С ТОБОЙ...?
?
HUH?
WHY IS HER SKIN LIKE THIS?

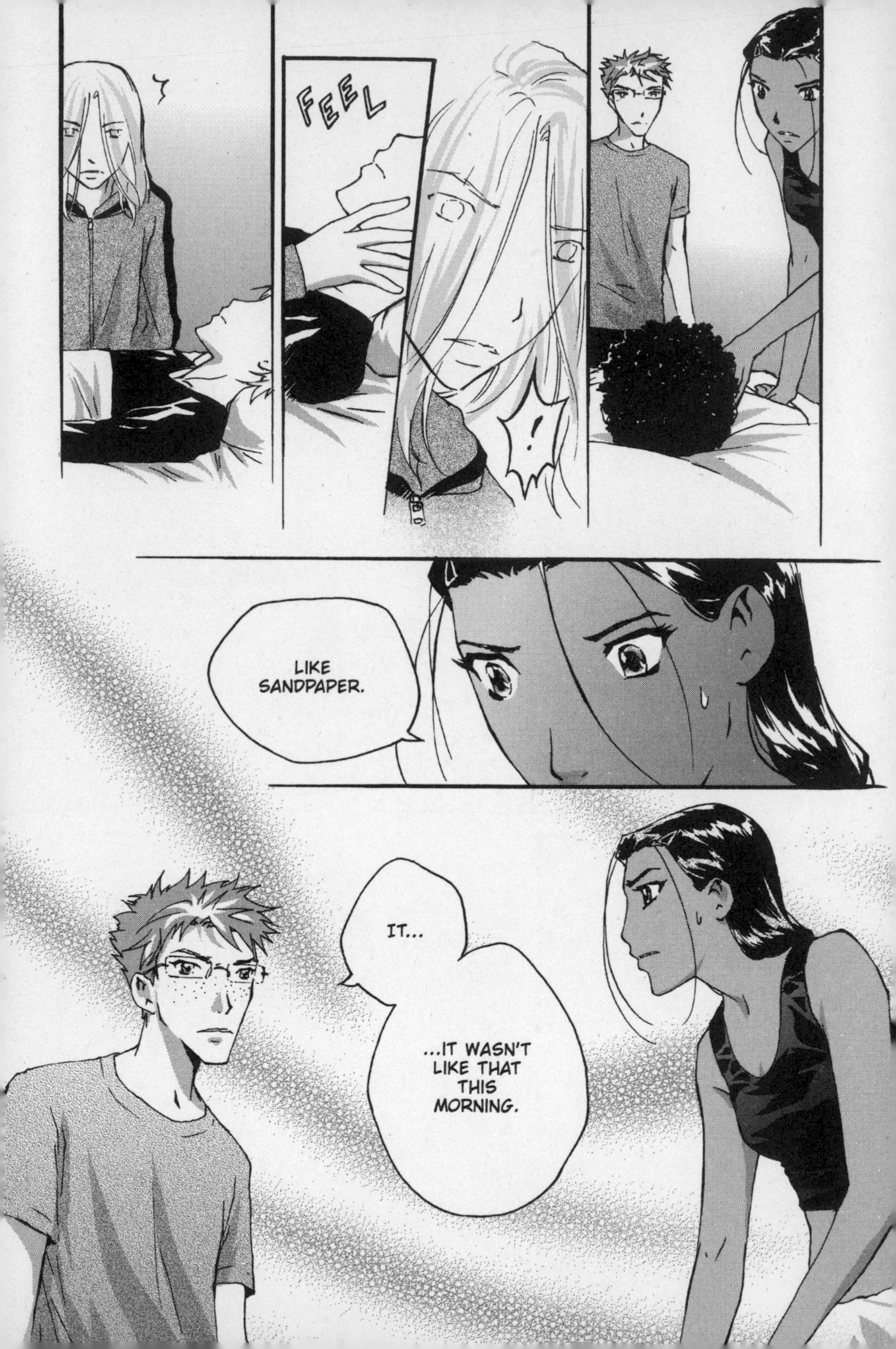
FEEL
!
LIKE SANDPAPER.
IT...
...IT WASN'T LIKE THAT THIS MORNING.

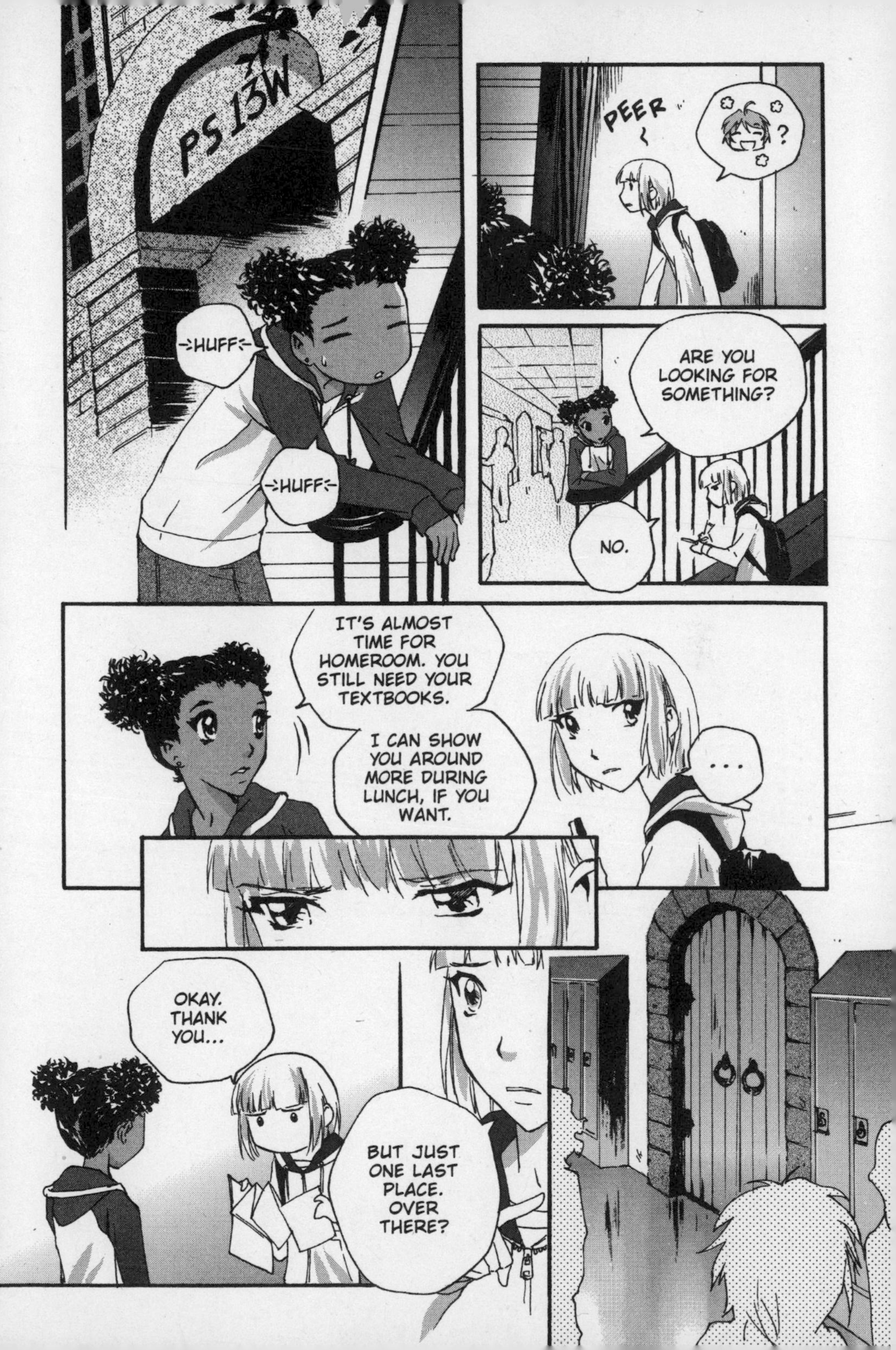
PS 13W
HUFF
HUFF
PEER
?
ARE YOU LOOKING FOR SOMETHING?
NO.
IT'S ALMOST TIME FOR HOMEROOM. YOU STILL NEED YOUR TEXTBOOKS.
I CAN SHOW YOU AROUND MORE DURING LUNCH, IF YOU WANT.
...
OKAY. THANK YOU...
BUT JUST ONE LAST PLACE. OVER THERE?

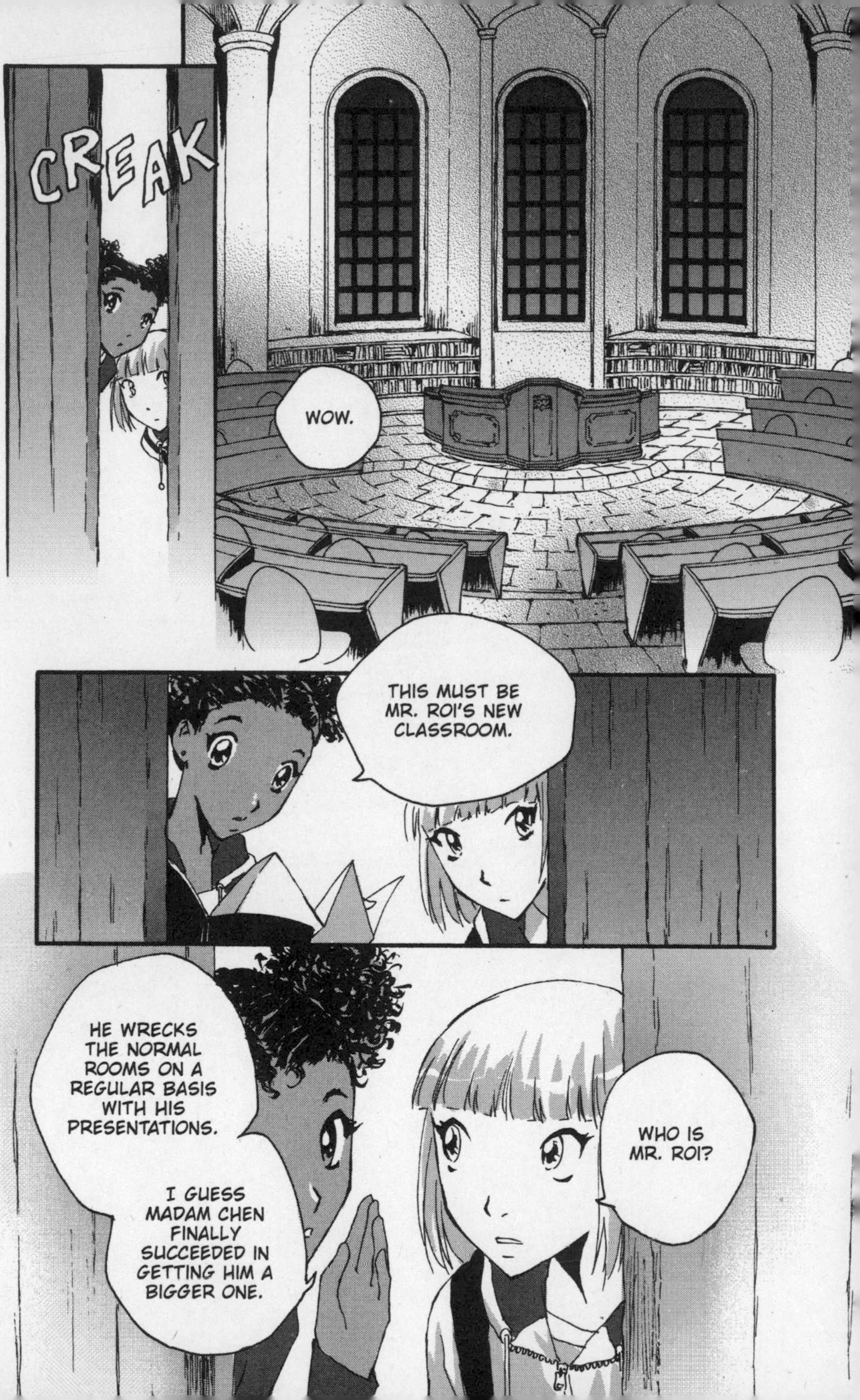
CREAK
WOW.
THIS MUST BE MR. ROI'S NEW CLASSROOM.
HE WRECKS THE NORMAL ROOMS ON A REGULAR BASIS WITH HIS PRESENTATIONS.
I GUESS MADAM CHEN FINALLY SUCCEEDED IN GETTING HIM A BIGGER ONE.
WHO IS MR. ROI?

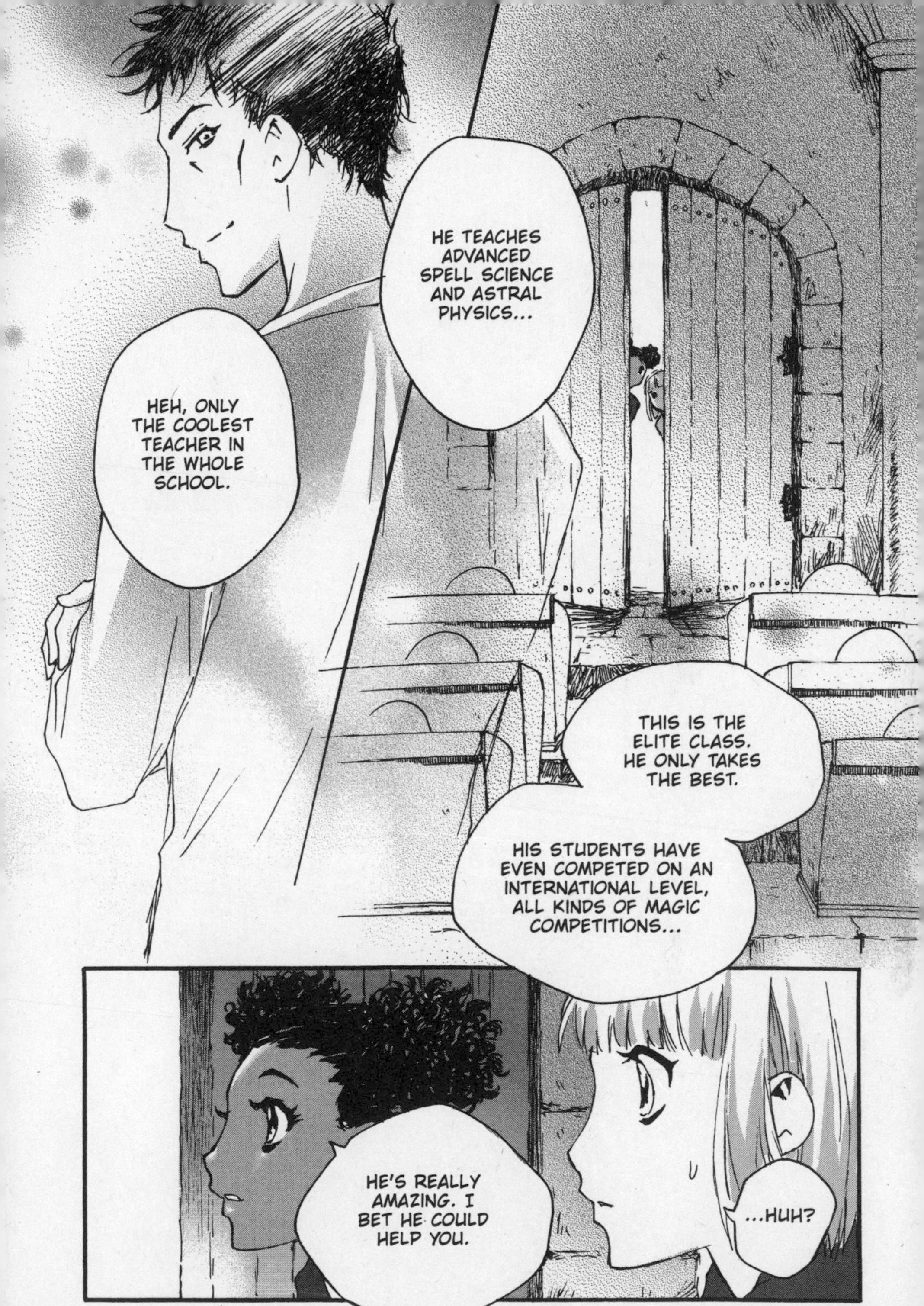
HEH, ONLY THE COOLEST TEACHER IN THE WHOLE SCHOOL.
HE TEACHES ADVANCED SPELL SCIENCE AND ASTRAL PHYSICS...
THIS IS THE ELITE CLASS. HE ONLY TAKES THE BEST.
HIS STUDENTS HAVE EVEN COMPETED ON AN INTERNATIONAL LEVEL, ALL KINDS OF MAGIC COMPETITIONS...
HE'S REALLY AMAZING. I BET HE COULD HELP YOU.
...HUH?

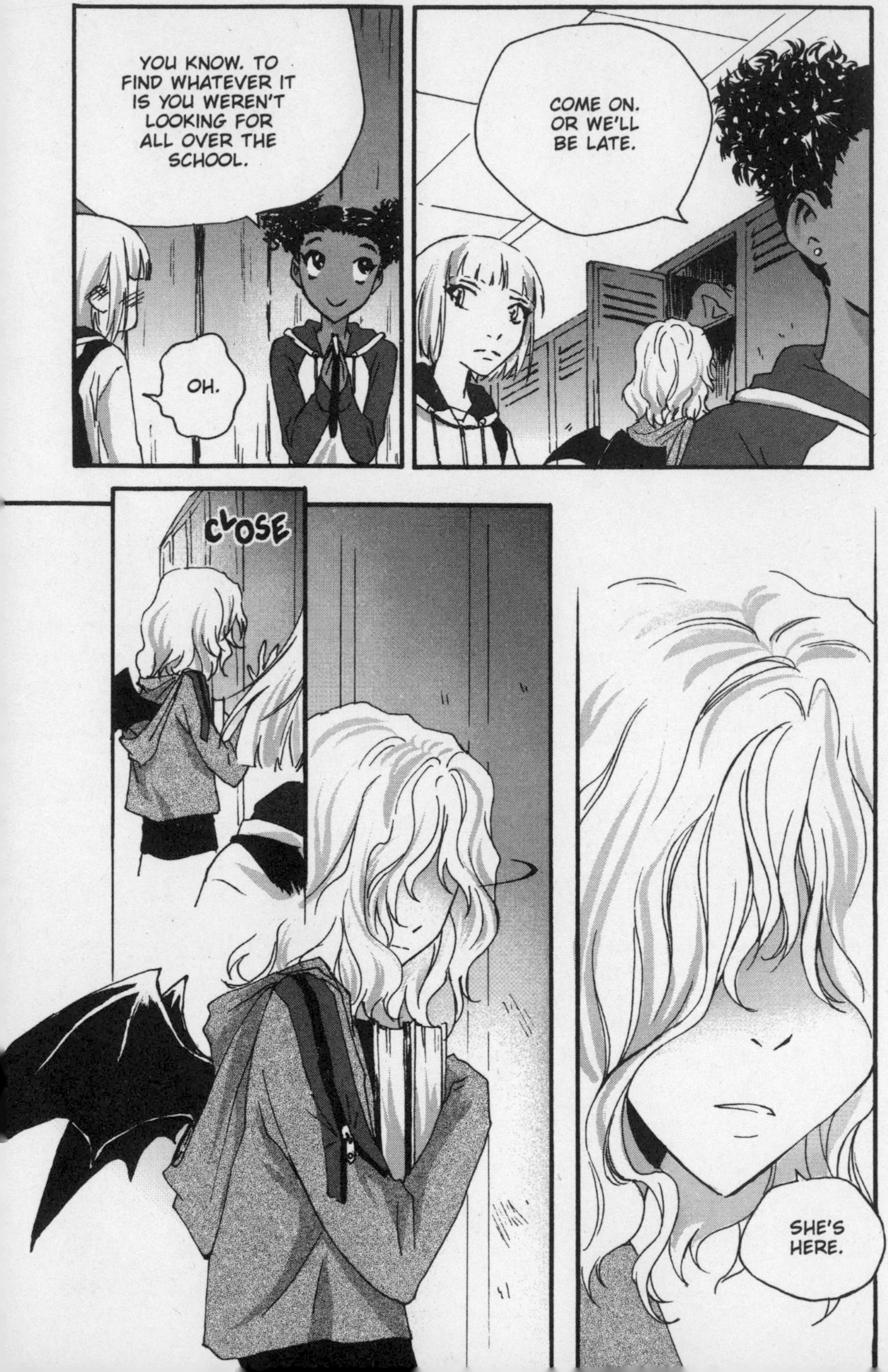
YOU KNOW. TO FIND WHATEVER IT IS YOU WEREN'T LOOKING FOR ALL OVER THE SCHOOL.
OH.
COME ON. OR WE'LL BE LATE.
CLOSE
SHE'S HERE.

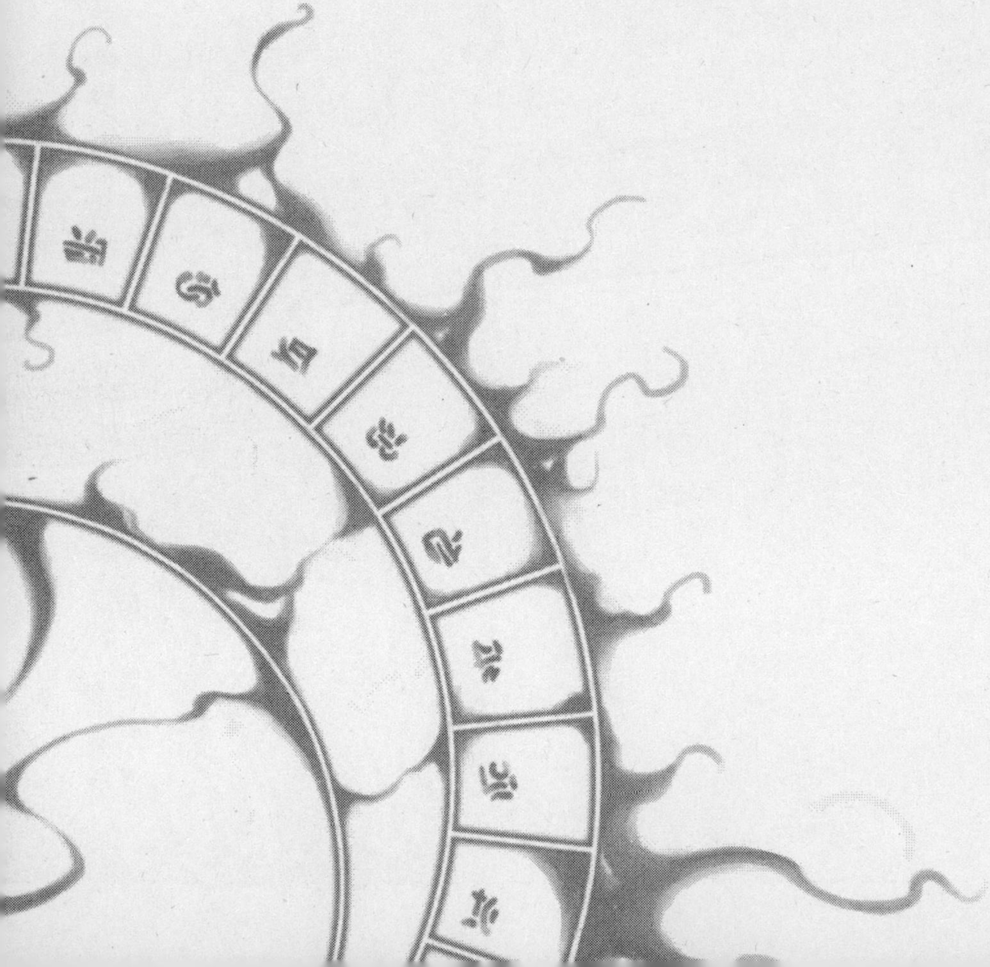

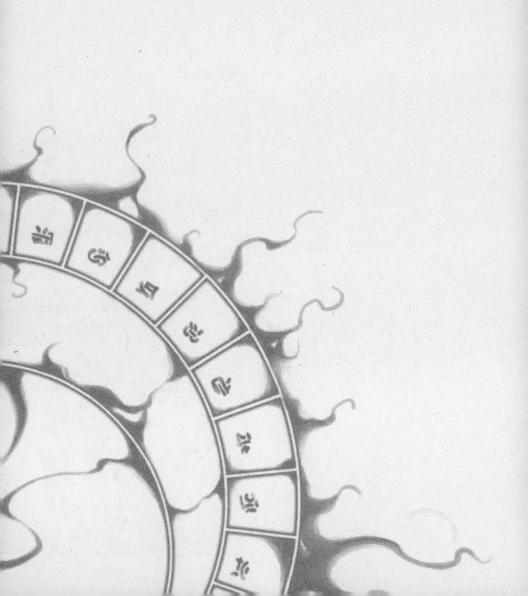

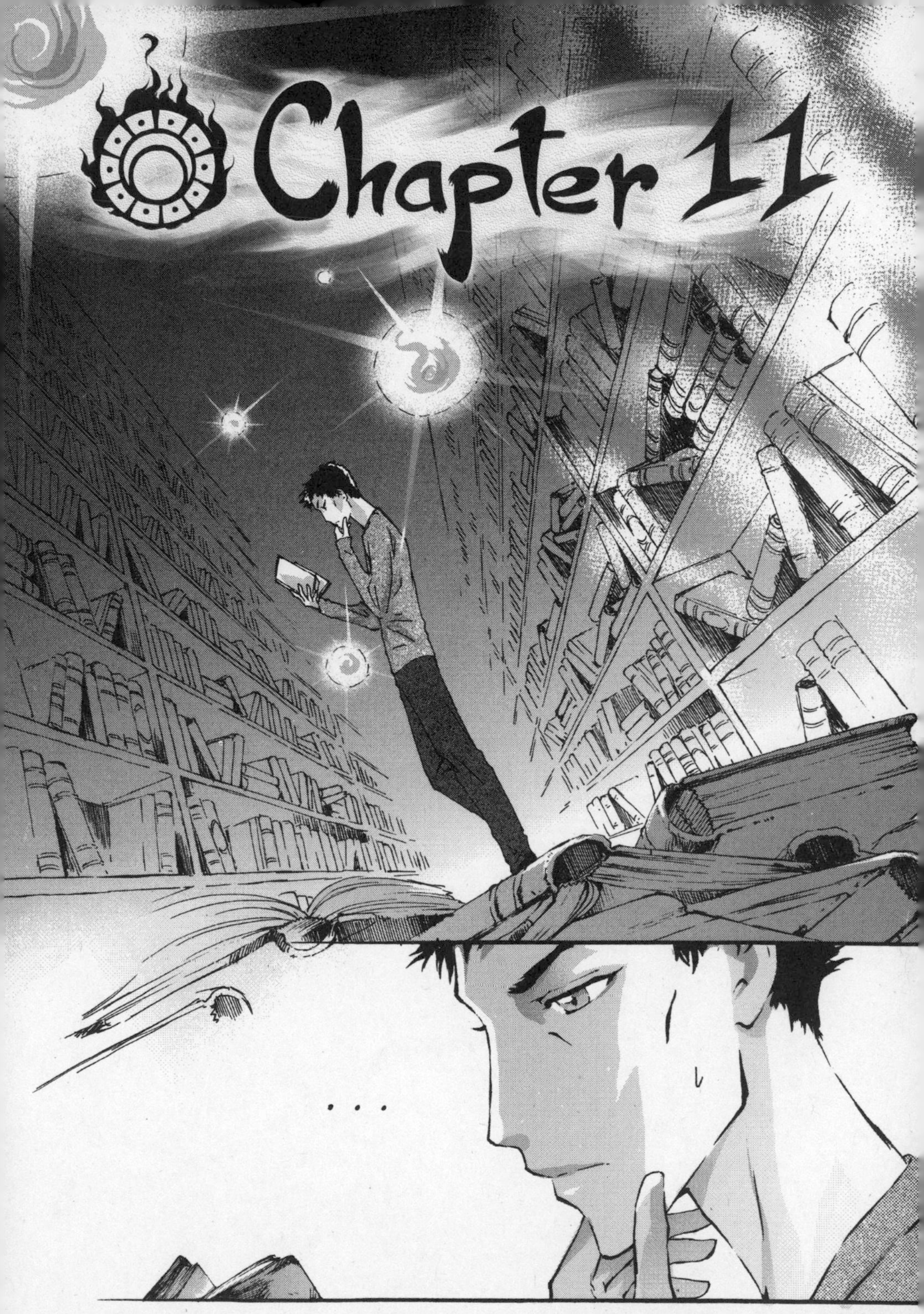
Chapter 11
...

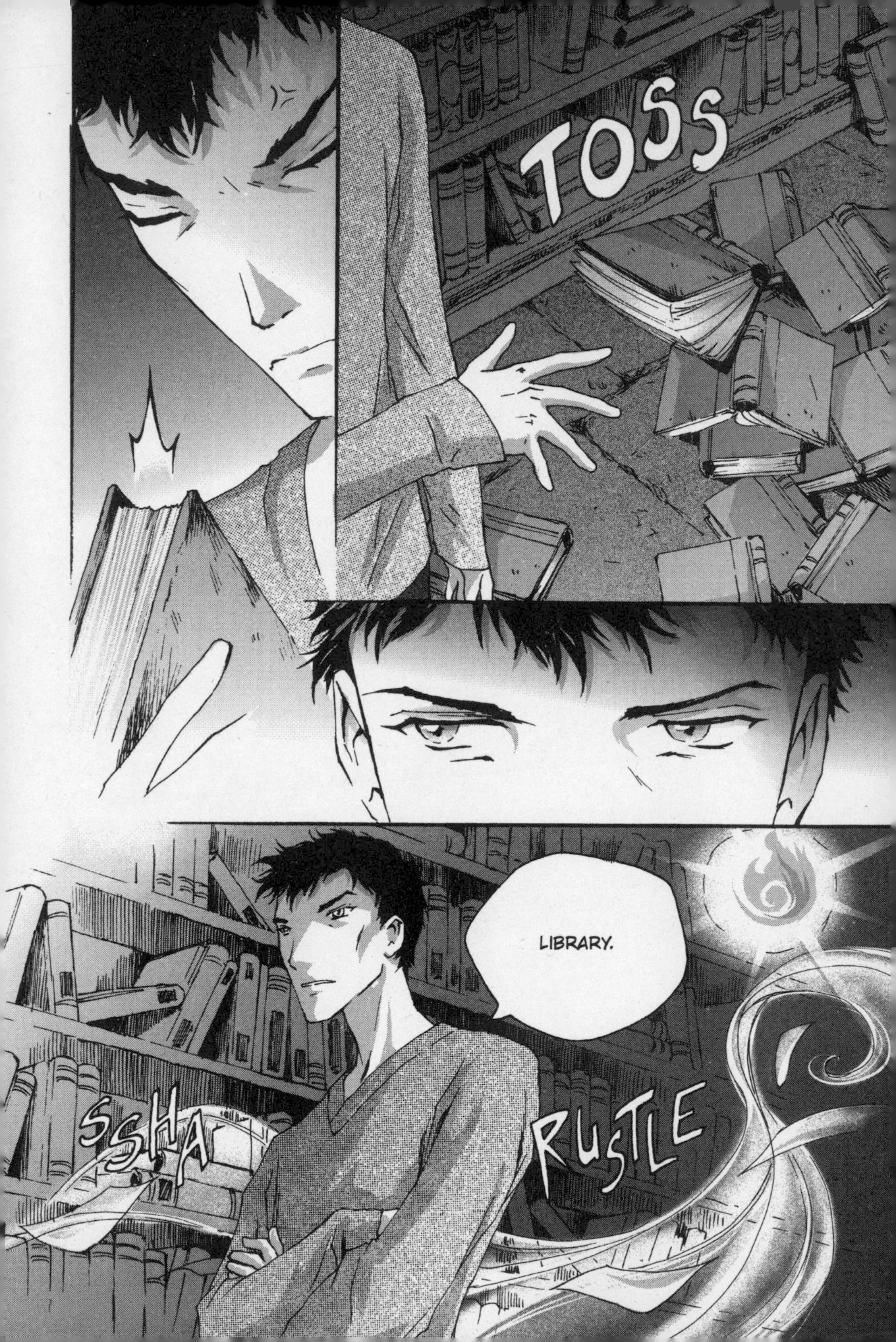
TOSS
LIBRARY.
SSHA
RUSTLE

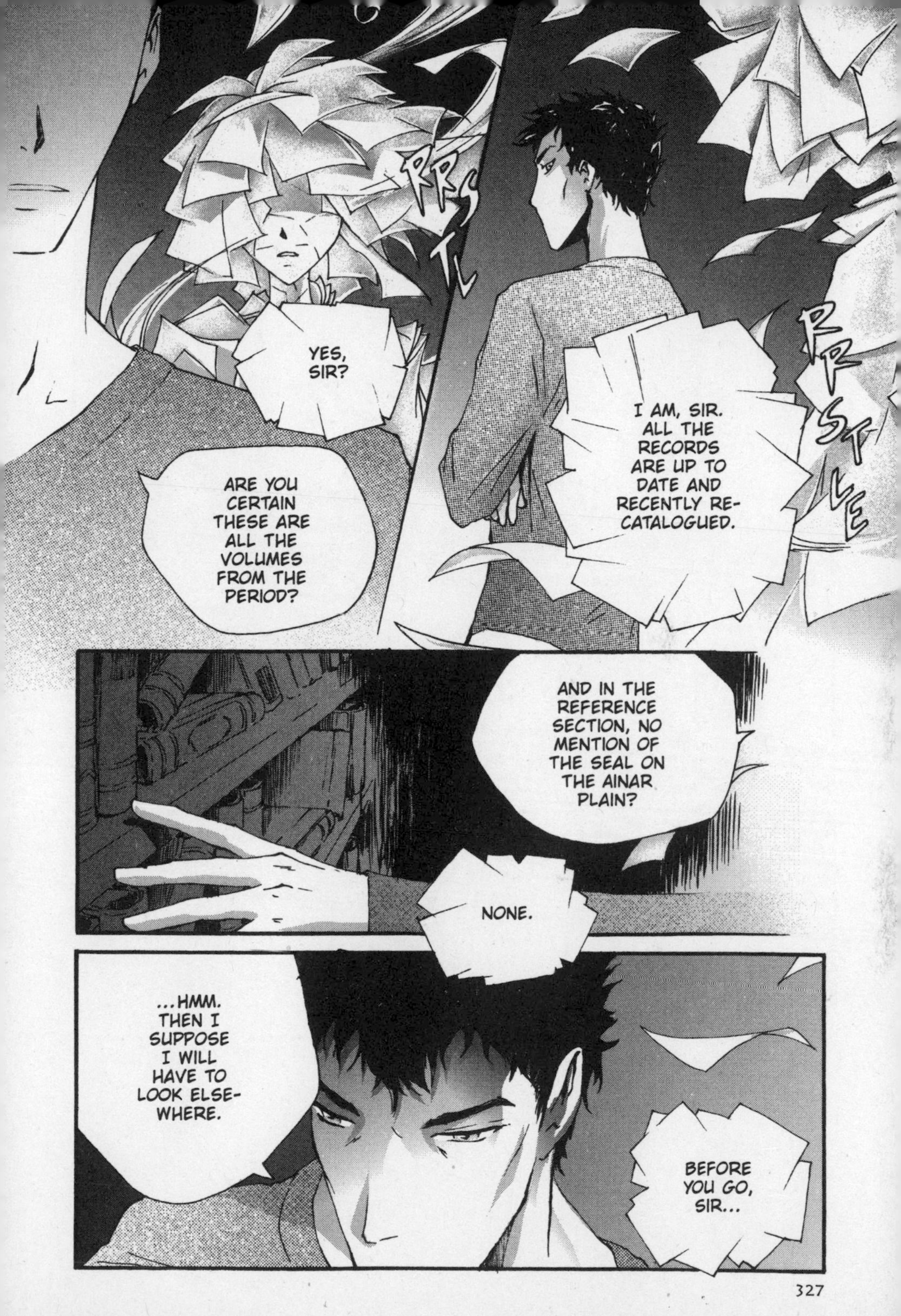
RRSTL
YES, SIR?
ARE YOU CERTAIN THESE ARE ALL THE VOLUMES FROM THE PERIOD?
I AM, SIR. ALL THE RECORDS ARE UP TO DATE AND RECENTLY RE-CATALOGUED.
RRSTLE
AND IN THE REFERENCE SECTION, NO MENTION OF THE SEAL ON THE AINAR PLAIN?
NONE.
...HMM. THEN I SUPPOSE I WILL HAVE TO LOOK ELSE-WHERE.
BEFORE YOU GO, SIR...

...YOU WISHED TO BE REMINDED OF YOUR CLASS. IT IS AT MIDNIGHT.

AH, THAT'S RIGHT. THANK YOU.

IS THE HUNTER STILL AROUND?

MR. DAEMON HAS BEEN GONE FOR SOME TIME. HE LEFT A MESSAGE REQUESTING SPEED IN YOUR INVESTIGATION.

I'M SURE HE DID.

THERE IS ALSO A LEYNET MESSAGE FROM MADAM CHEN, SAYING THERE IS A PLEASANT SURPRISE WAITING FOR YOU AT THE SCHOOL.

...OH?

WELL, SOME GOOD NEWS IS DEFINITELY WELCOME TONIGHT.

OH, AND BY THE WAY, THESE ARE FOR YOU.

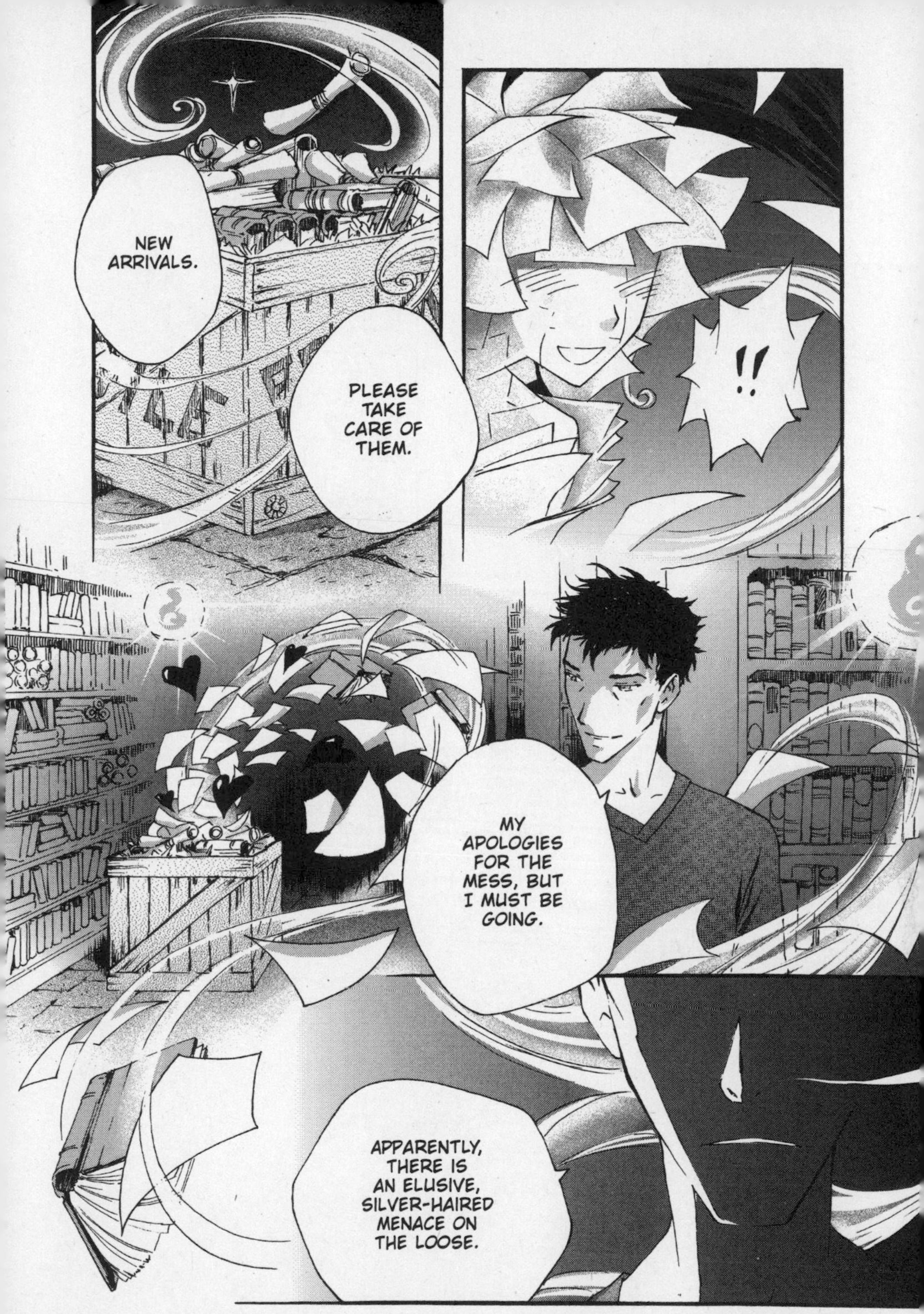
NEW ARRIVALS.
PLEASE TAKE CARE OF THEM.
!!
MY APOLOGIES FOR THE MESS, BUT I MUST BE GOING.
APPARENTLY, THERE IS AN ELUSIVE, SILVER-HAIRED MENACE ON THE LOOSE.

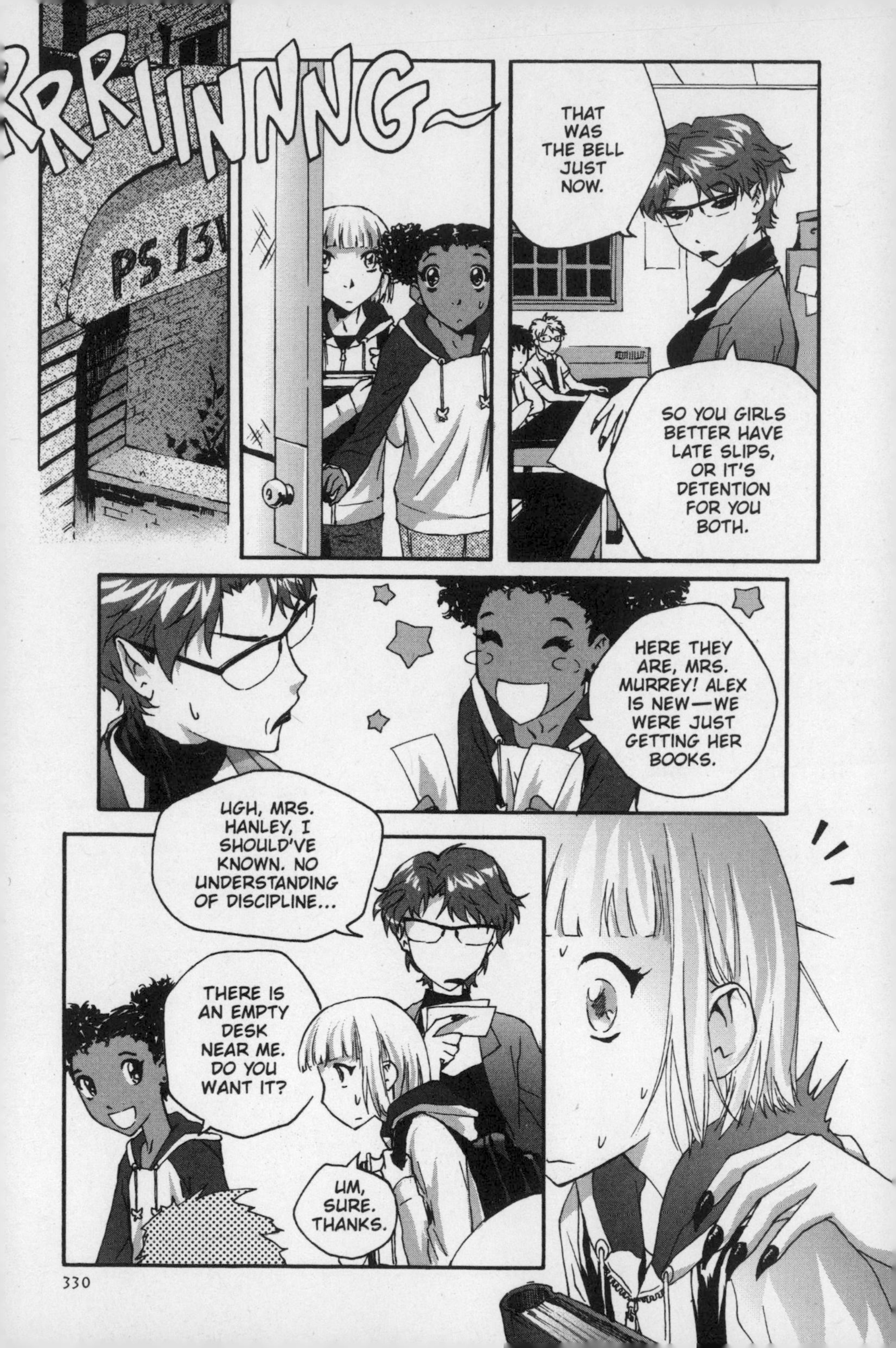
RRRIINNNG~
PS 13
THAT WAS THE BELL JUST NOW.
SO YOU GIRLS BETTER HAVE LATE SLIPS, OR IT'S DETENTION FOR YOU BOTH.
HERE THEY ARE, MRS. MURREY! ALEX IS NEW—WE WERE JUST GETTING HER BOOKS.
UGH, MRS. HANLEY, I SHOULD'VE KNOWN. NO UNDERSTANDING OF DISCIPLINE...
THERE IS AN EMPTY DESK NEAR ME. DO YOU WANT IT?
UM, SURE. THANKS.

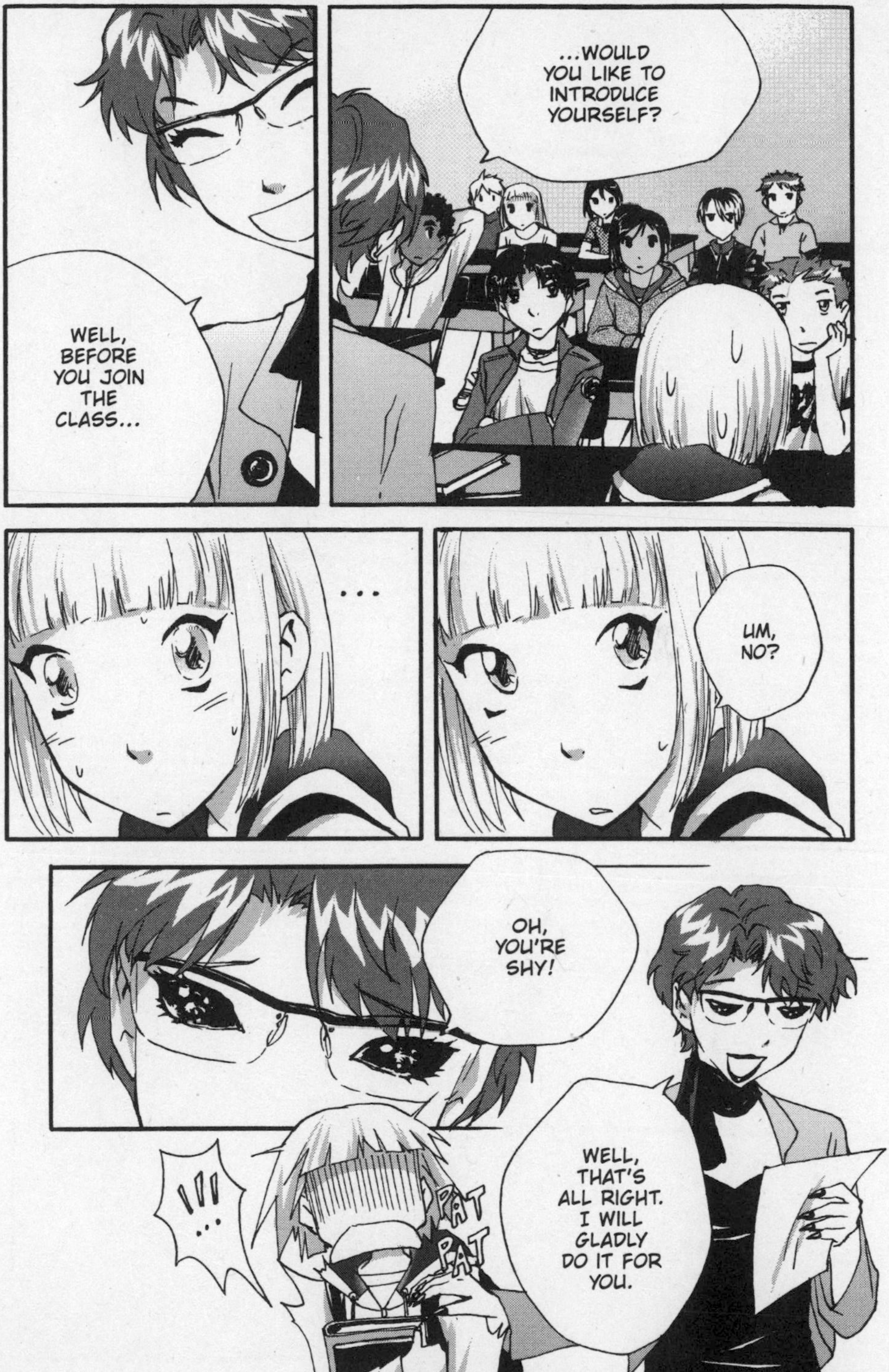
WELL, BEFORE YOU JOIN THE CLASS...
...WOULD YOU LIKE TO INTRODUCE YOURSELF?
...
UM, NO?
OH, YOU'RE SHY!
WELL, THAT'S ALL RIGHT. I WILL GLADLY DO IT FOR YOU.
!!! ...
PAT PAT

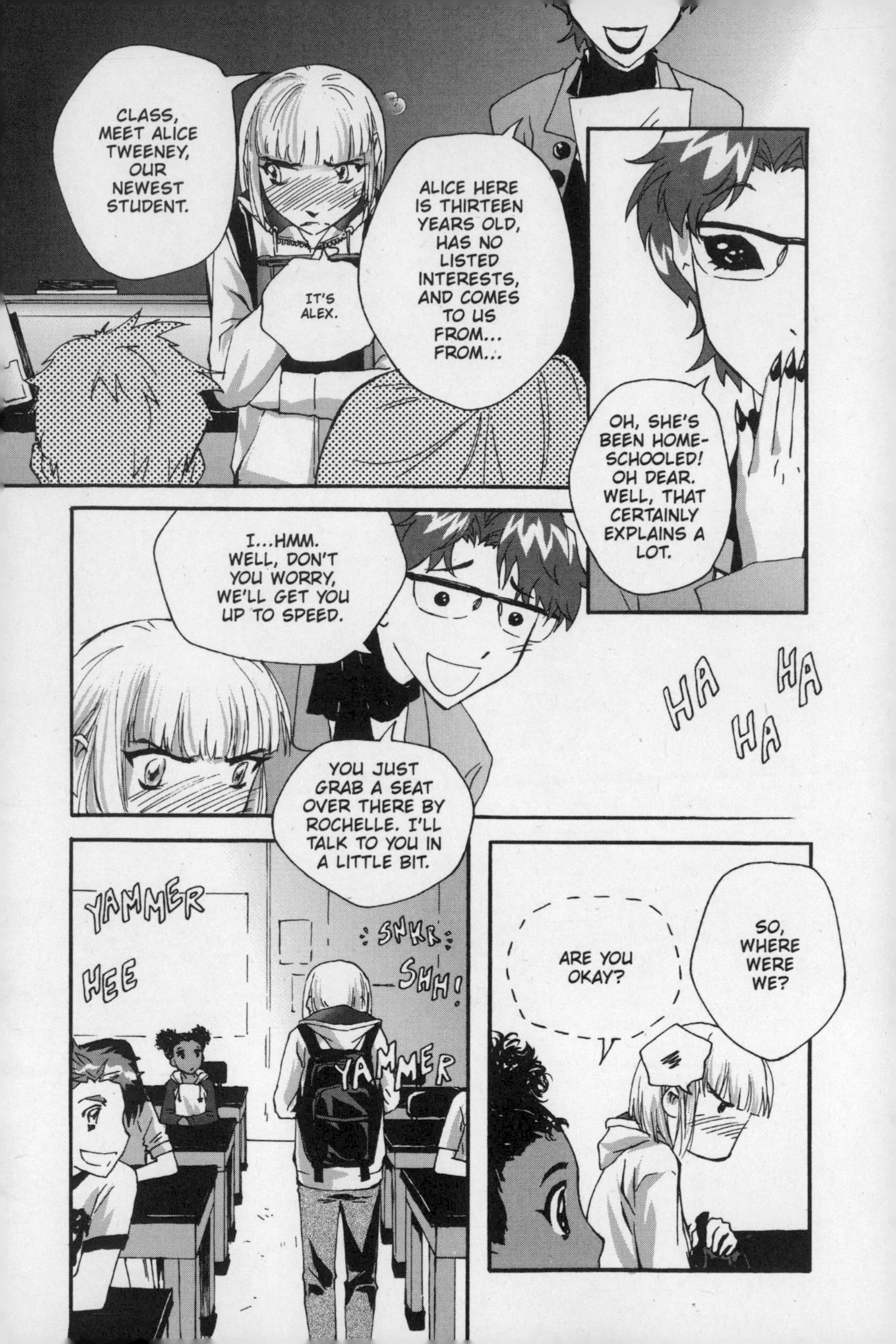
CLASS, MEET ALICE TWEENEY, OUR NEWEST STUDENT.
IT'S ALEX.
ALICE HERE IS THIRTEEN YEARS OLD, HAS NO LISTED INTERESTS, AND COMES TO US FROM... FROM...
OH, SHE'S BEEN HOME-SCHOOLED! OH DEAR. WELL, THAT CERTAINLY EXPLAINS A LOT.
I...HMM. WELL, DON'T YOU WORRY, WE'LL GET YOU UP TO SPEED.
YOU JUST GRAB A SEAT OVER THERE BY ROCHELLE. I'LL TALK TO YOU IN A LITTLE BIT.
HA HA HA
YAMMER
HEE
SNKR
SHH!
YAMMER
ARE YOU OKAY?
SO, WHERE WERE WE?

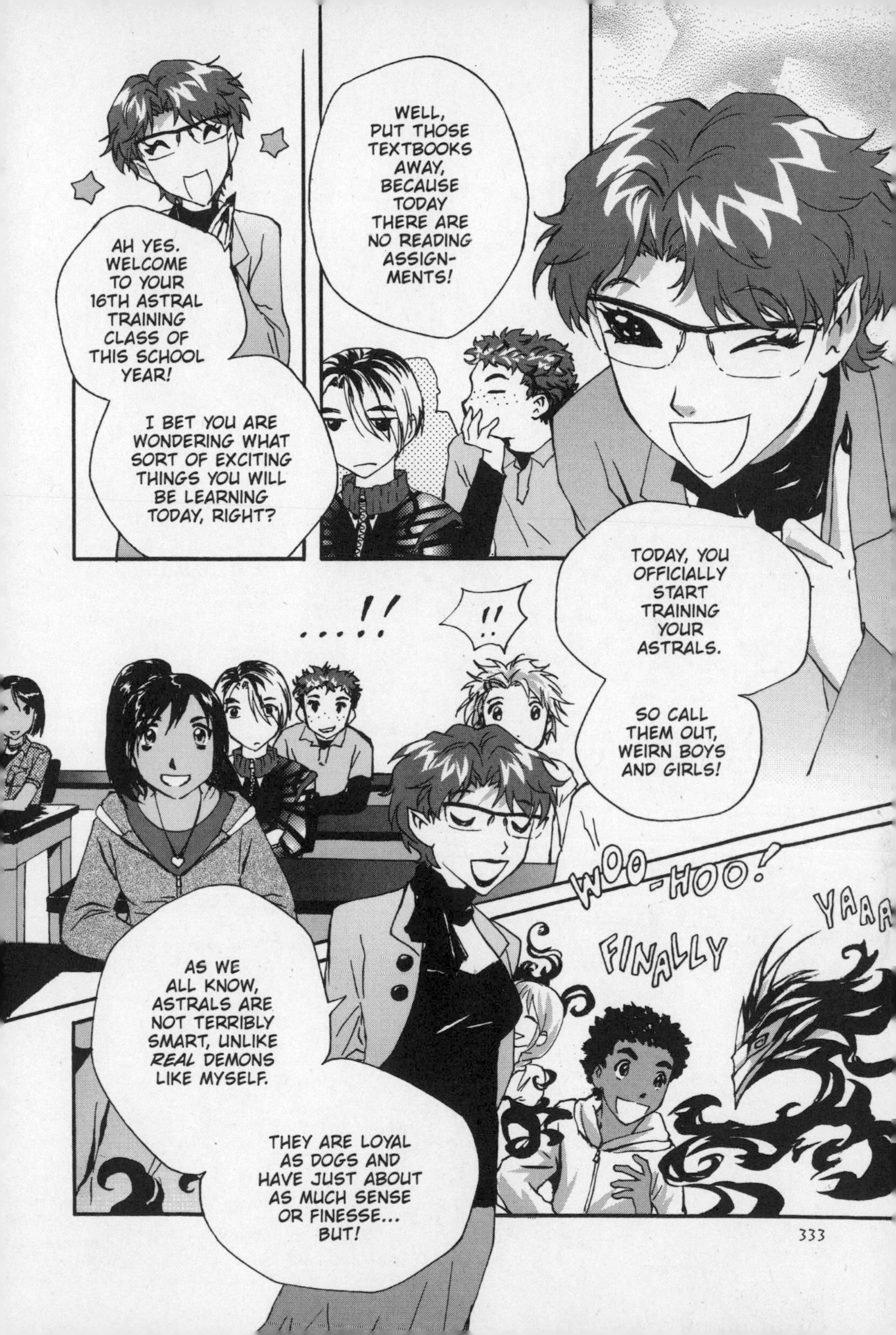
AH YES. WELCOME TO YOUR 16TH ASTRAL TRAINING CLASS OF THIS SCHOOL YEAR!
I BET YOU ARE WONDERING WHAT SORT OF EXCITING THINGS YOU WILL BE LEARNING TODAY, RIGHT?
WELL, PUT THOSE TEXTBOOKS AWAY, BECAUSE TODAY THERE ARE NO READING ASSIGN-MENTS!
TODAY, YOU OFFICIALLY START TRAINING YOUR ASTRALS.
SO CALL THEM OUT, WEIRN BOYS AND GIRLS!
...!!
!!
WOO-HOO!
YAAA
FINALLY
AS WE ALL KNOW, ASTRALS ARE NOT TERRIBLY SMART, UNLIKE *REAL* DEMONS LIKE MYSELF.
THEY ARE LOYAL AS DOGS AND HAVE JUST ABOUT AS MUCH SENSE OR FINESSE... BUT!

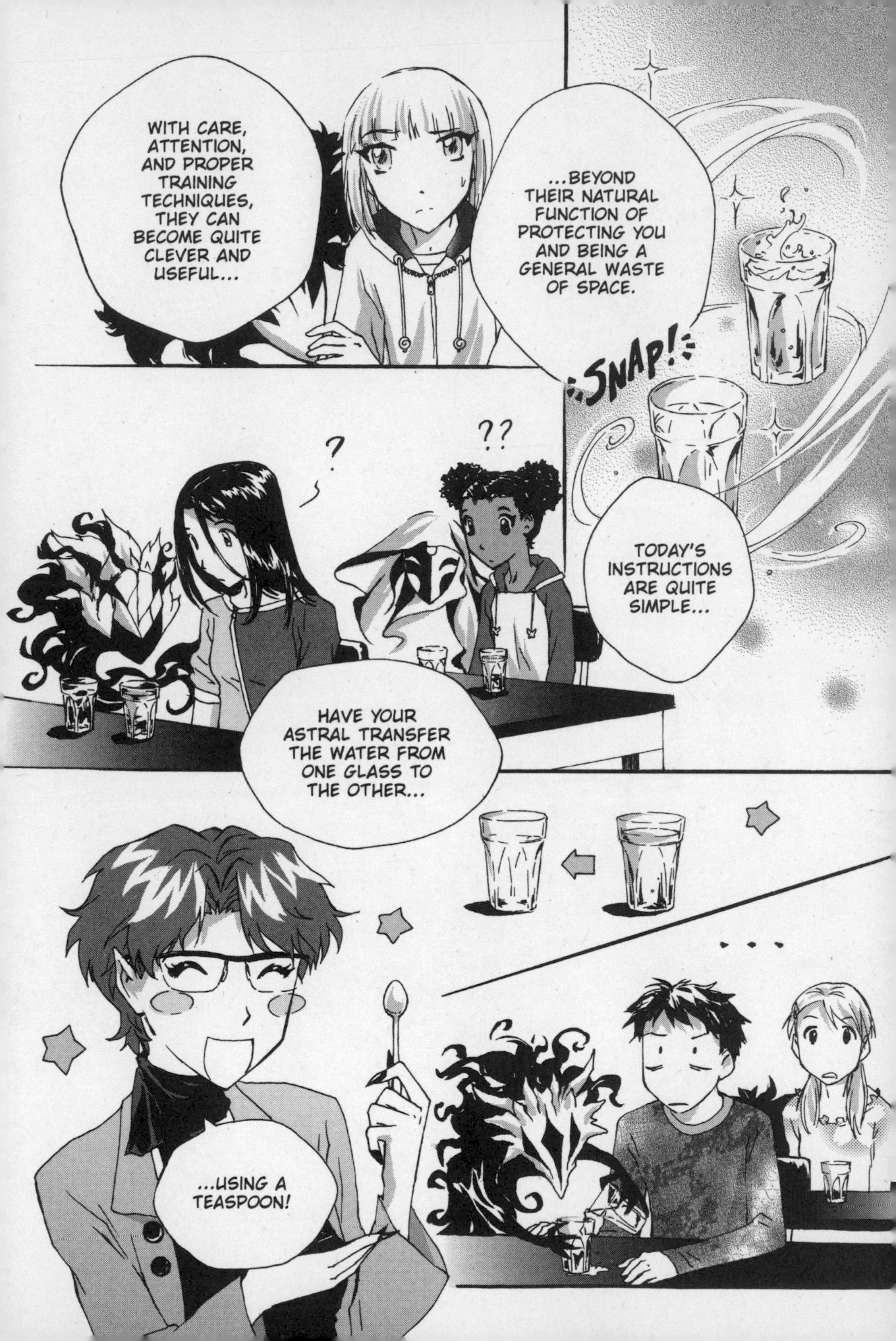
WITH CARE, ATTENTION, AND PROPER TRAINING TECHNIQUES, THEY CAN BECOME QUITE CLEVER AND USEFUL...
...BEYOND THEIR NATURAL FUNCTION OF PROTECTING YOU AND BEING A GENERAL WASTE OF SPACE.
SNAP!
?
??
TODAY'S INSTRUCTIONS ARE QUITE SIMPLE...
HAVE YOUR ASTRAL TRANSFER THE WATER FROM ONE GLASS TO THE OTHER...
...USING A TEASPOON!
...

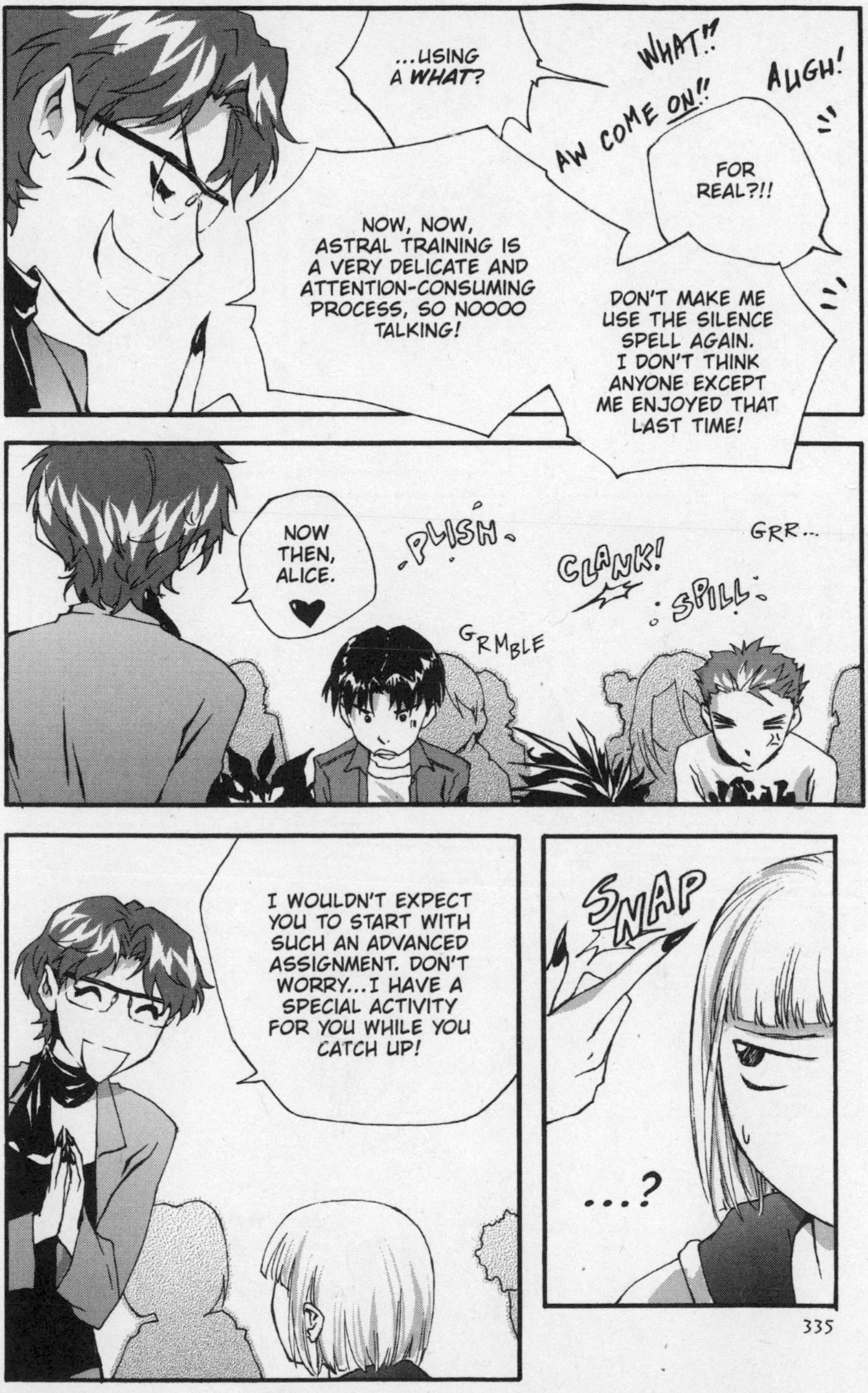
...USING A WHAT?
WHAT!!
AUGH!
AW COME ON!!
FOR REAL?!!
NOW, NOW, ASTRAL TRAINING IS A VERY DELICATE AND ATTENTION-CONSUMING PROCESS, SO NOOOO TALKING!
DON'T MAKE ME USE THE SILENCE SPELL AGAIN. I DON'T THINK ANYONE EXCEPT ME ENJOYED THAT LAST TIME!
NOW THEN, ALICE.
PLISH
CLANK!
GRR...
SPILL
GRMBLE
I WOULDN'T EXPECT YOU TO START WITH SUCH AN ADVANCED ASSIGNMENT. DON'T WORRY...I HAVE A SPECIAL ACTIVITY FOR YOU WHILE YOU CATCH UP!
SNAP
...?

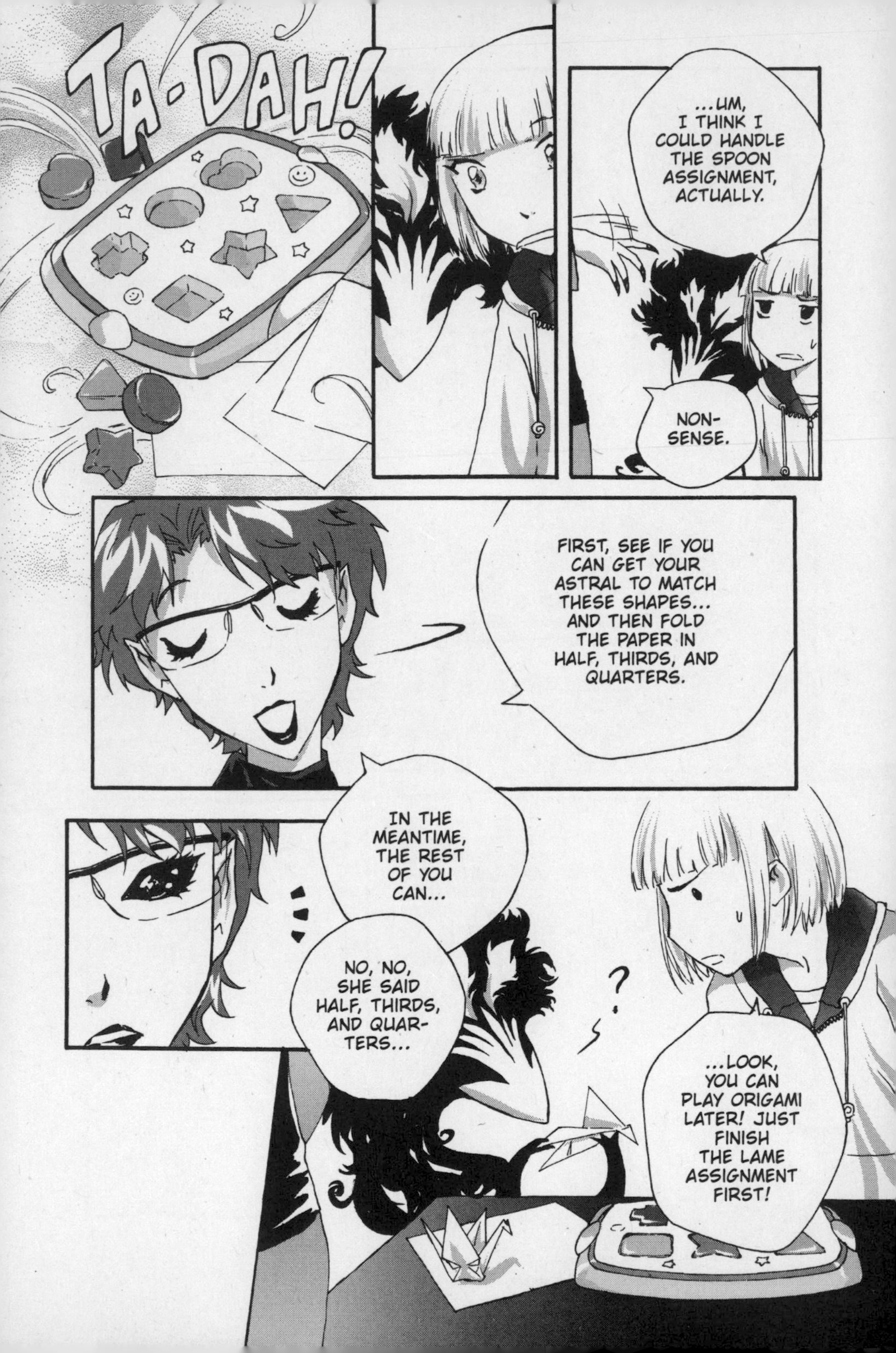
TA-DAH!
...UM, I THINK I COULD HANDLE THE SPOON ASSIGNMENT, ACTUALLY.
NON-SENSE.
FIRST, SEE IF YOU CAN GET YOUR ASTRAL TO MATCH THESE SHAPES... AND THEN FOLD THE PAPER IN HALF, THIRDS, AND QUARTERS.
IN THE MEANTIME, THE REST OF YOU CAN...
NO, NO, SHE SAID HALF, THIRDS, AND QUAR-TERS...
?
...LOOK, YOU CAN PLAY ORIGAMI LATER! JUST FINISH THE LAME ASSIGNMENT FIRST!

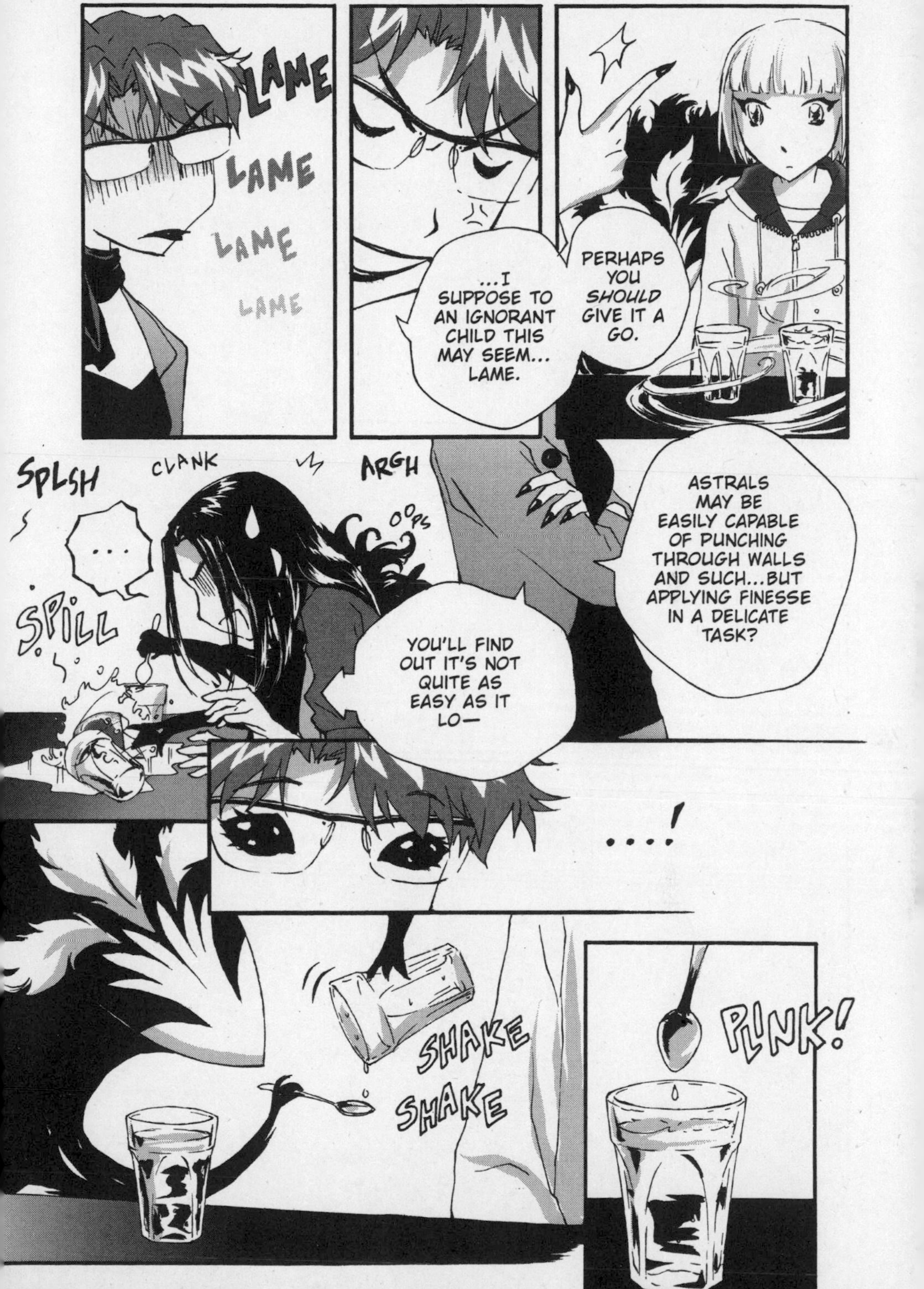
LAME
LAME
LAME
LAME
...I SUPPOSE TO AN IGNORANT CHILD THIS MAY SEEM... LAME.
PERHAPS YOU *SHOULD* GIVE IT A GO.
SPLSH
CLANK
ARGH
...
OOPS
SPILL
ASTRALS MAY BE EASILY CAPABLE OF PUNCHING THROUGH WALLS AND SUCH...BUT APPLYING FINESSE IN A DELICATE TASK?
YOU'LL FIND OUT IT'S NOT QUITE AS EASY AS IT LO—
...!
SHAKE
SHAKE
PLINK!

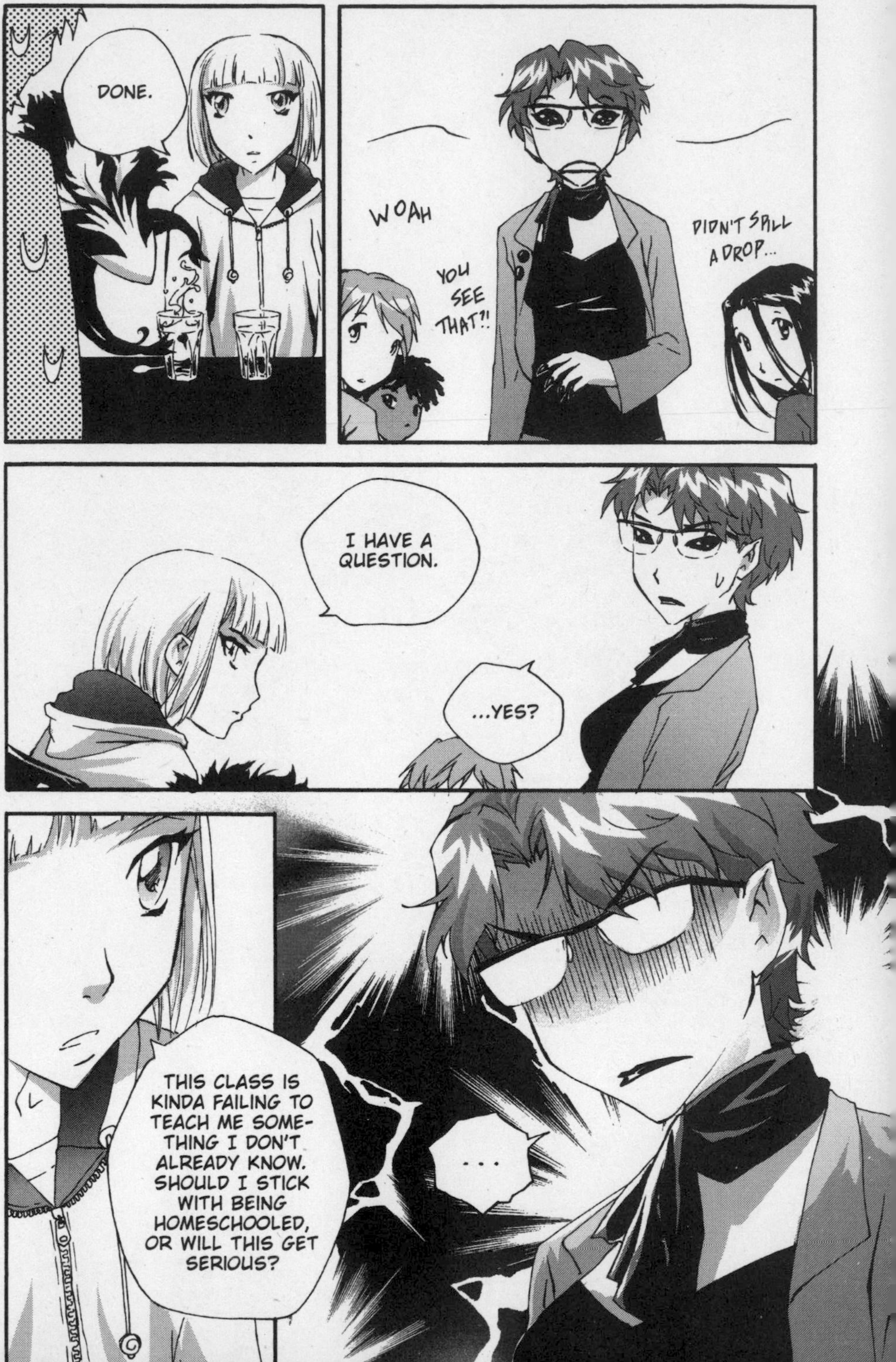
DONE.
WOAH
YOU SEE THAT?!
DIDN'T SPILL A DROP...
I HAVE A QUESTION.
...YES?
THIS CLASS IS KINDA FAILING TO TEACH ME SOMETHING I DON'T ALREADY KNOW. SHOULD I STICK WITH BEING HOMESCHOOLED, OR WILL THIS GET SERIOUS?
...

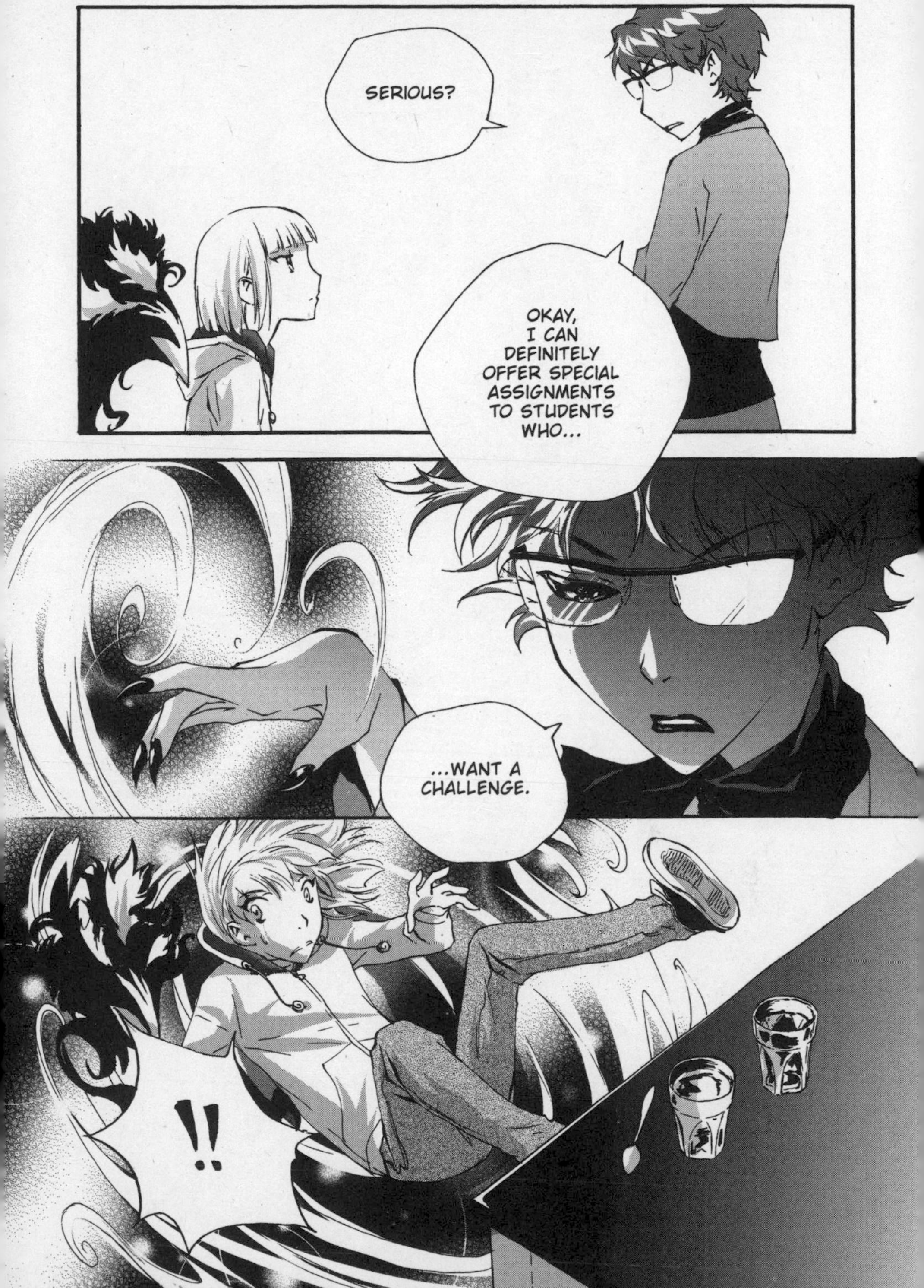
SERIOUS?
OKAY, I CAN DEFINITELY OFFER SPECIAL ASSIGNMENTS TO STUDENTS WHO...
...WANT A CHALLENGE.
!!

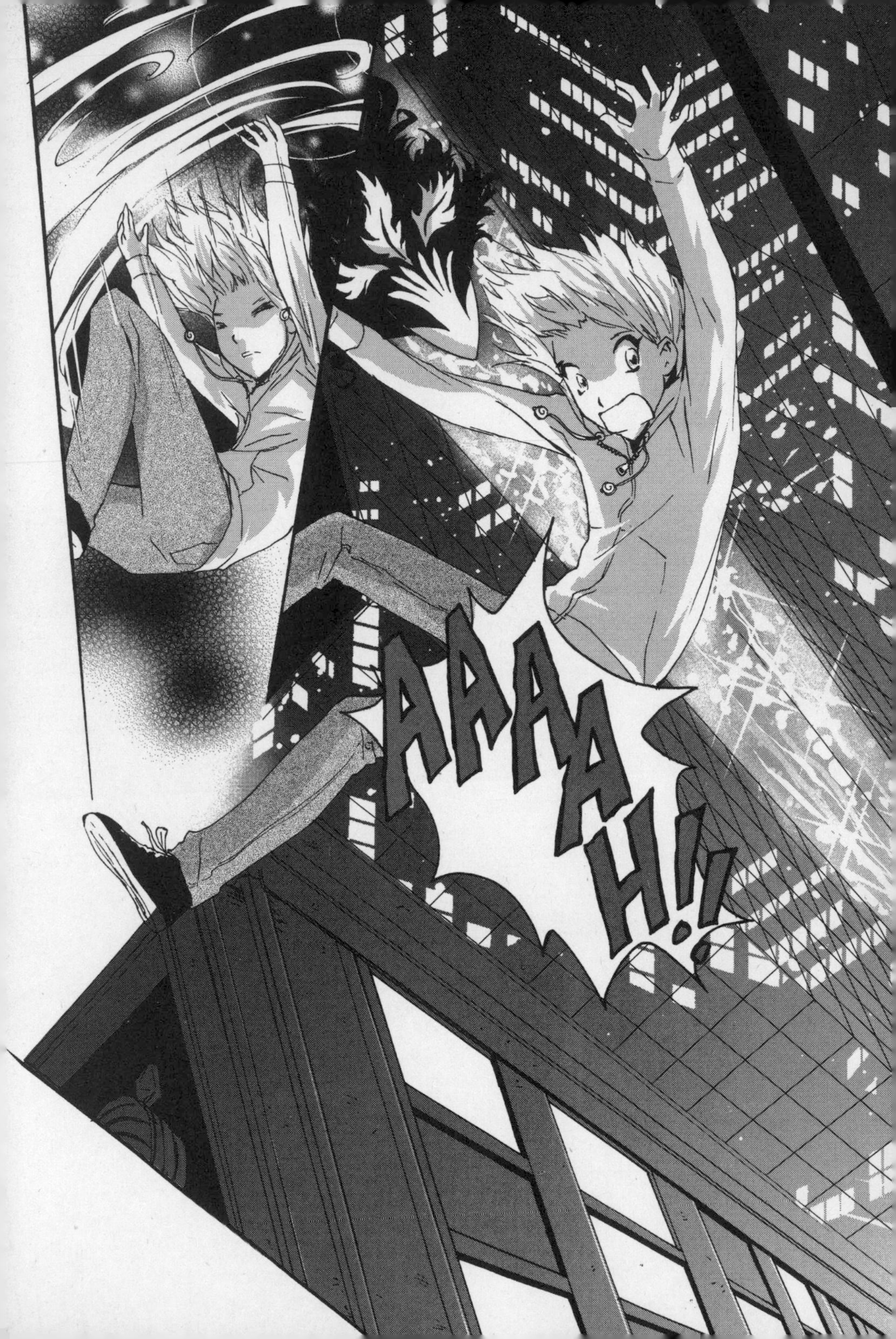
AAAAH!!

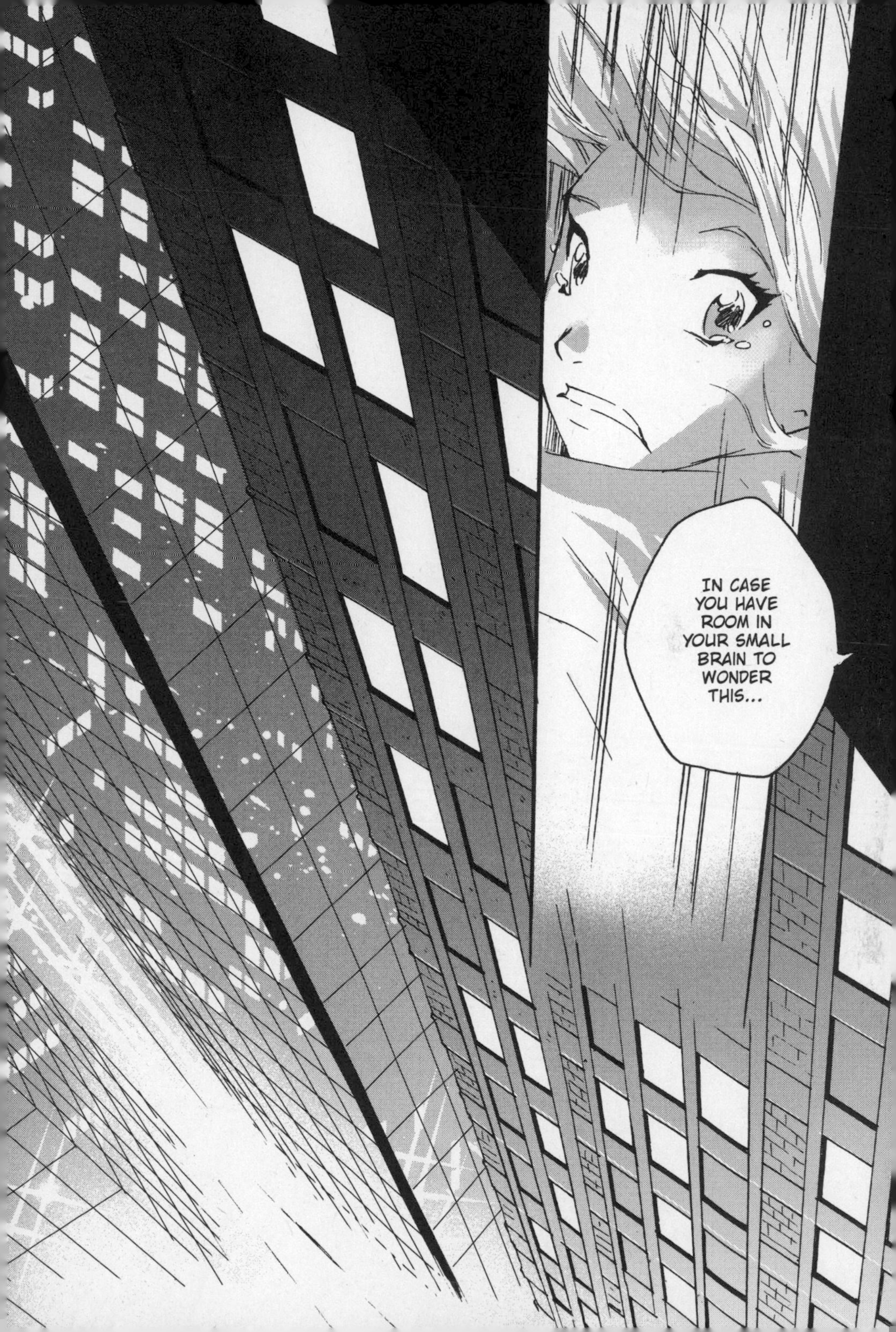
IN CASE YOU HAVE ROOM IN YOUR SMALL BRAIN TO WONDER THIS...

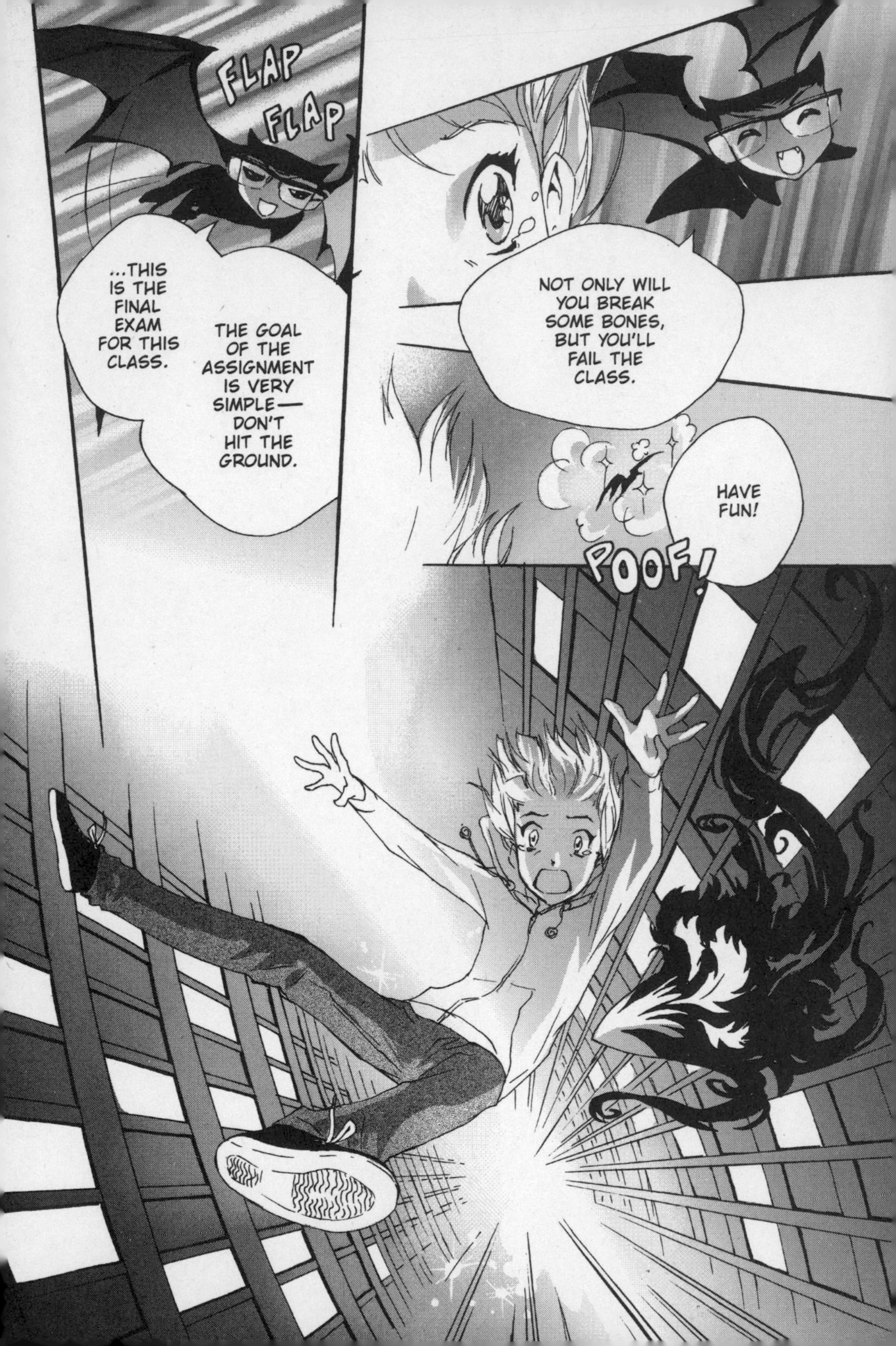
FLAP
FLAP
...THIS IS THE FINAL EXAM FOR THIS CLASS.
THE GOAL OF THE ASSIGNMENT IS VERY SIMPLE— DON'T HIT THE GROUND.
NOT ONLY WILL YOU BREAK SOME BONES, BUT YOU'LL FAIL THE CLASS.
HAVE FUN!
POOF!

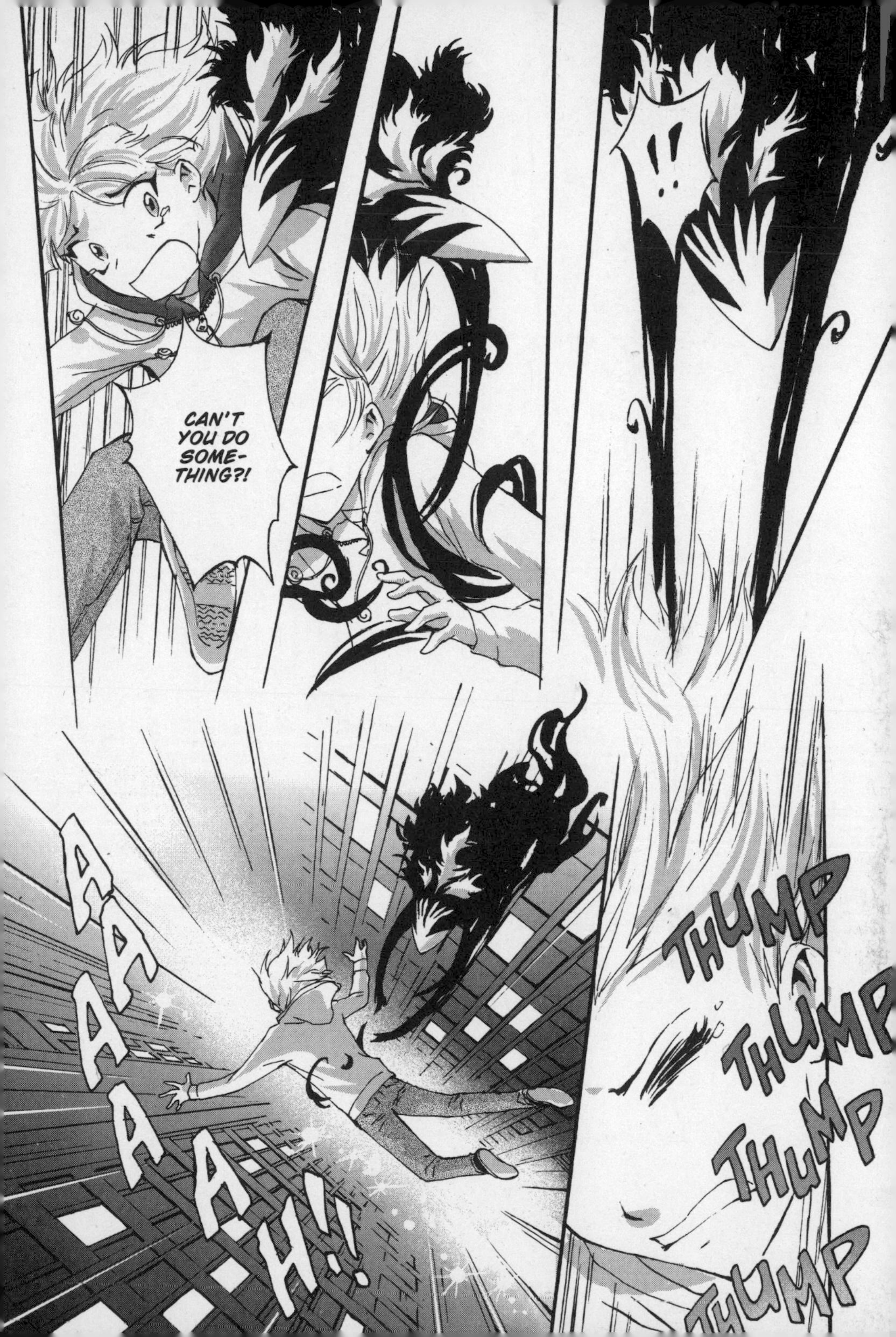
CAN'T YOU DO SOME-THING?!
!!
AAAAAH!!
THUMP THUMP THUMP THUMP

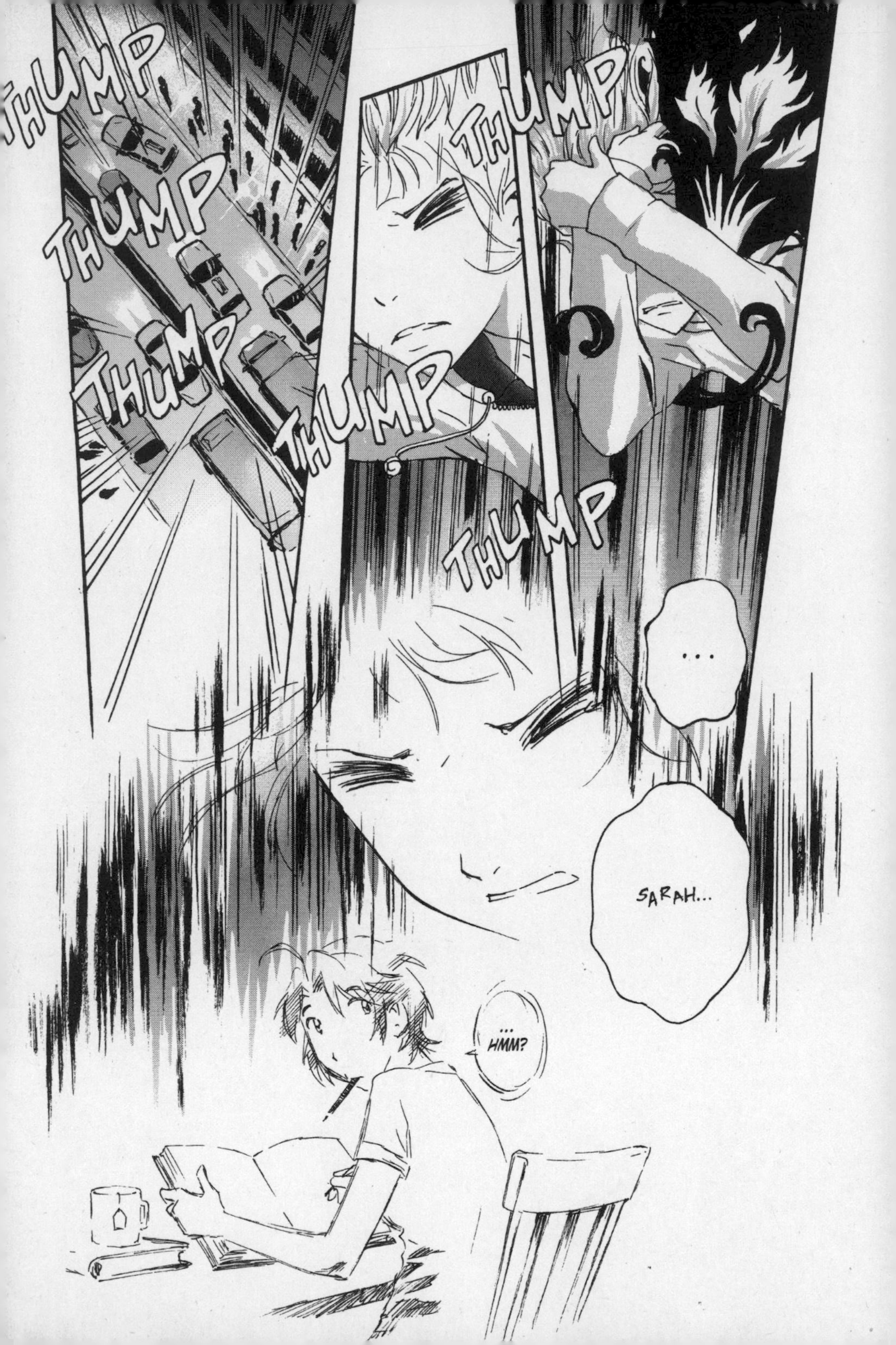
THUMP
THUMP
THUMP
THUMP
THUMP
THUMP
...
SARAH...
... HMM?

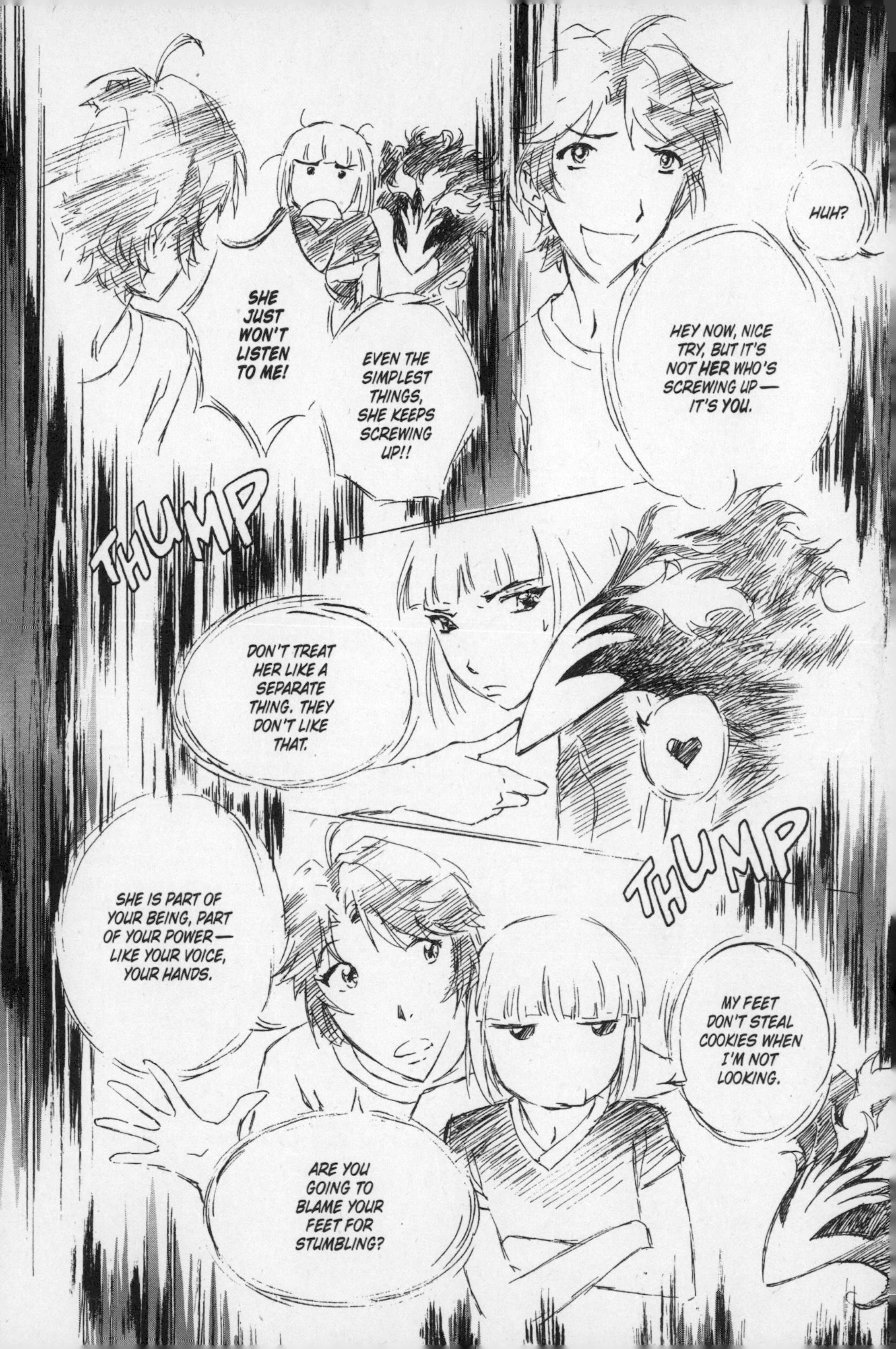
SHE JUST WON'T LISTEN TO ME!
EVEN THE SIMPLEST THINGS, SHE KEEPS SCREWING UP!!
HUH?
HEY NOW, NICE TRY, BUT IT'S NOT HER WHO'S SCREWING UP— IT'S YOU.
THUMP
DON'T TREAT HER LIKE A SEPARATE THING. THEY DON'T LIKE THAT.
THUMP
SHE IS PART OF YOUR BEING, PART OF YOUR POWER— LIKE YOUR VOICE, YOUR HANDS.
ARE YOU GOING TO BLAME YOUR FEET FOR STUMBLING?
MY FEET DON'T STEAL COOKIES WHEN I'M NOT LOOKING.

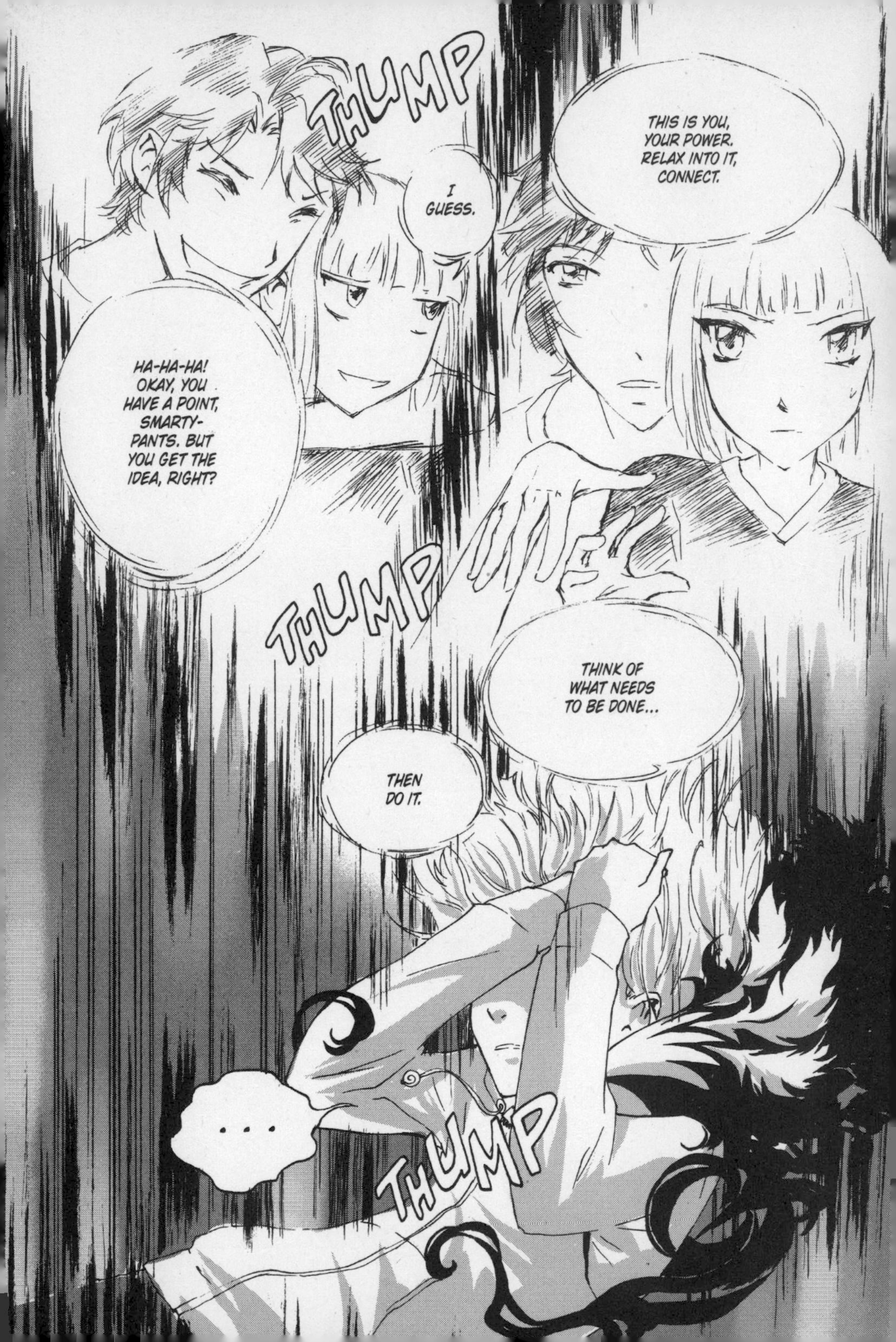
THUMP
I GUESS.
THIS IS YOU, YOUR POWER. RELAX INTO IT, CONNECT.
HA-HA-HA! OKAY, YOU HAVE A POINT, SMARTY-PANTS. BUT YOU GET THE IDEA, RIGHT?
THUMP
THINK OF WHAT NEEDS TO BE DONE...
THEN DO IT.
. . .
THUMP

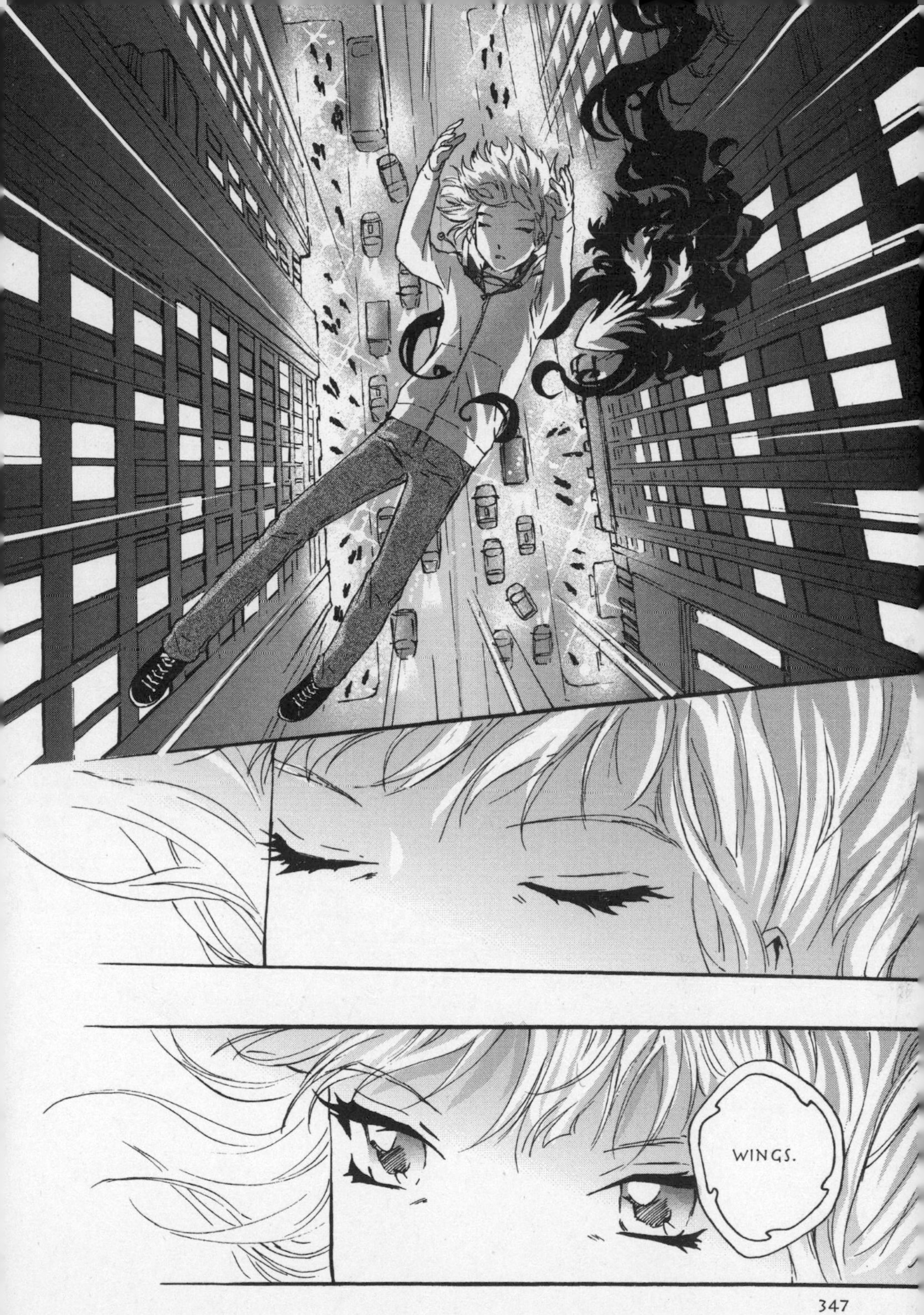
WINGS.

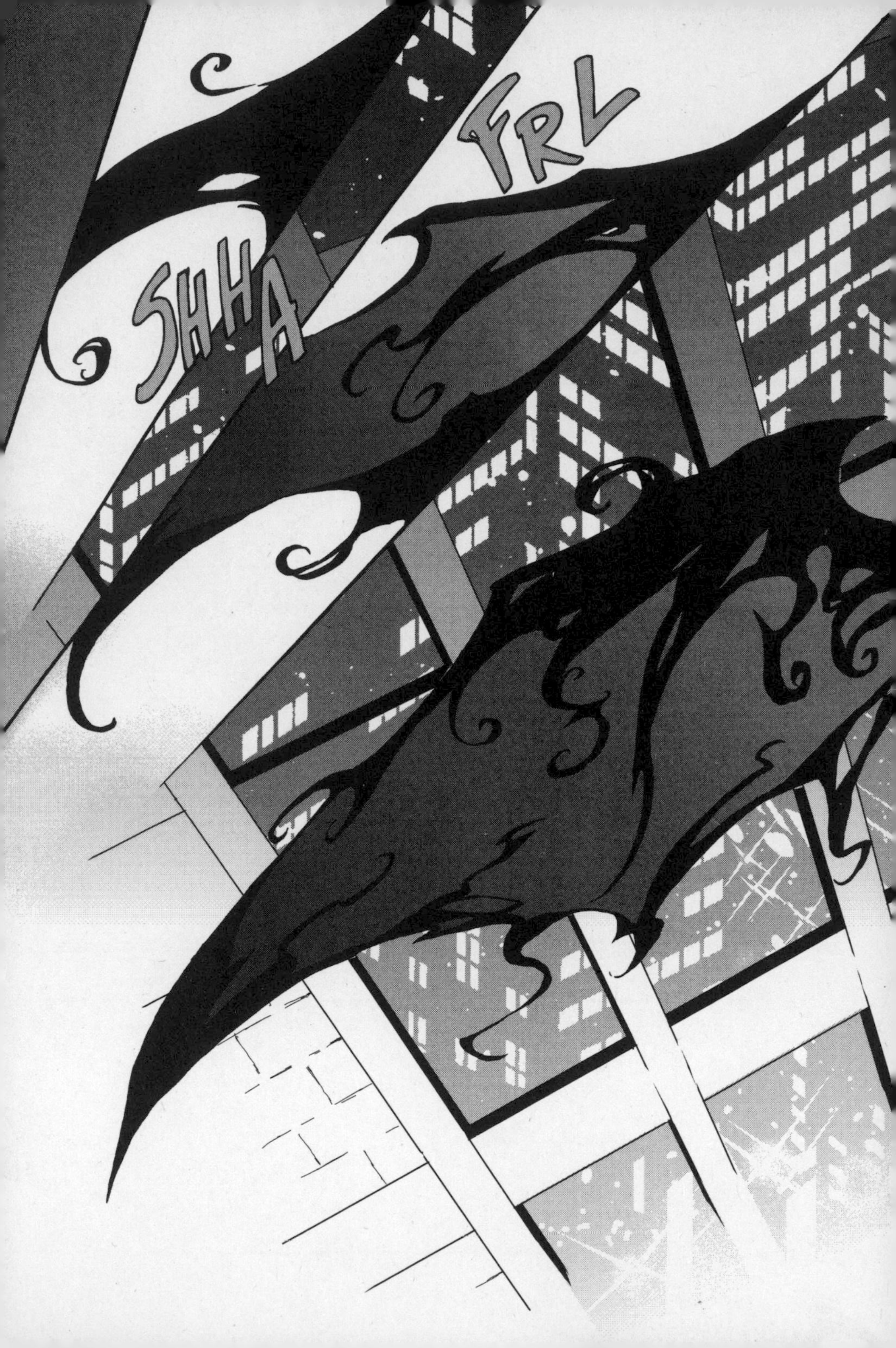
SHHA
FRL

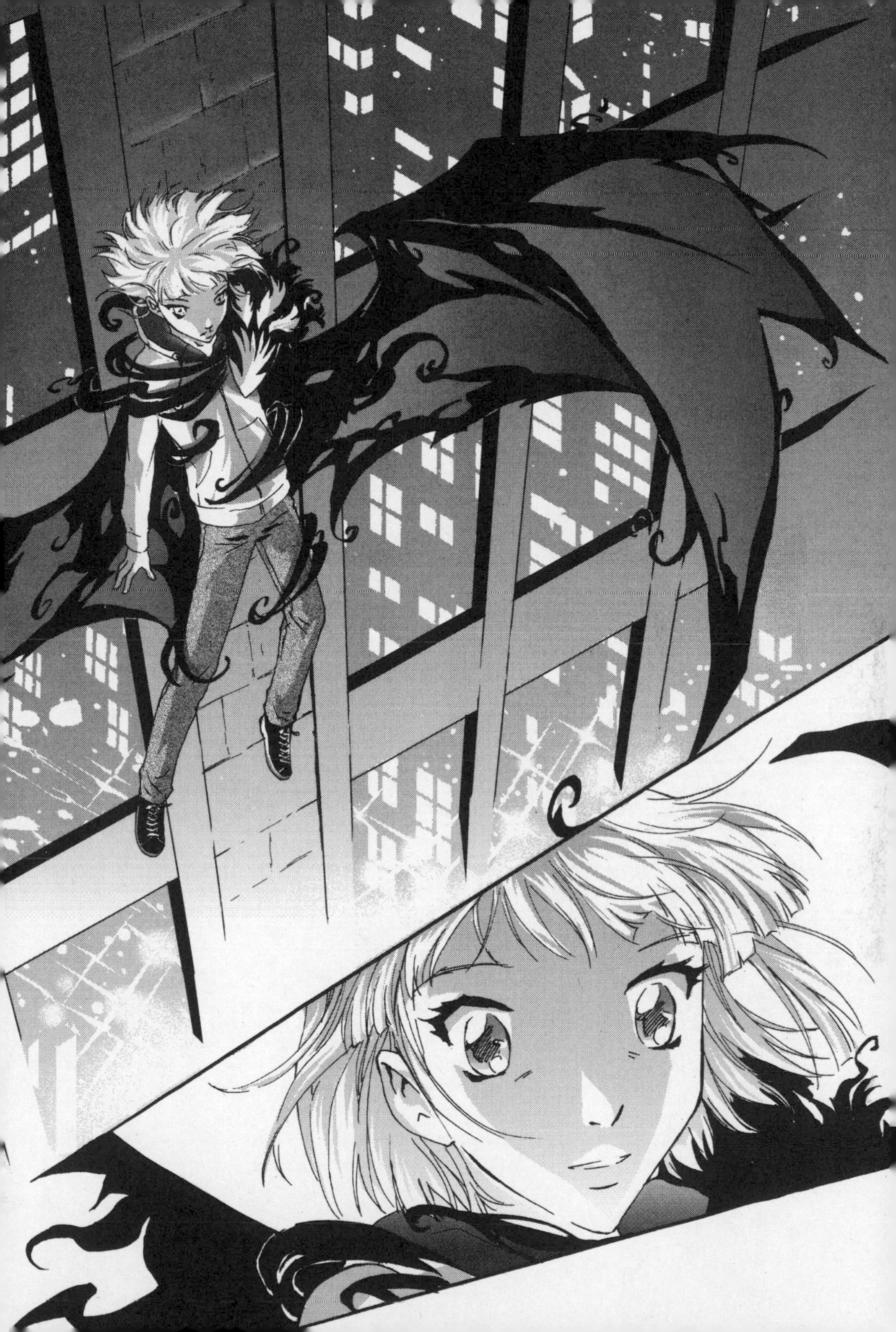

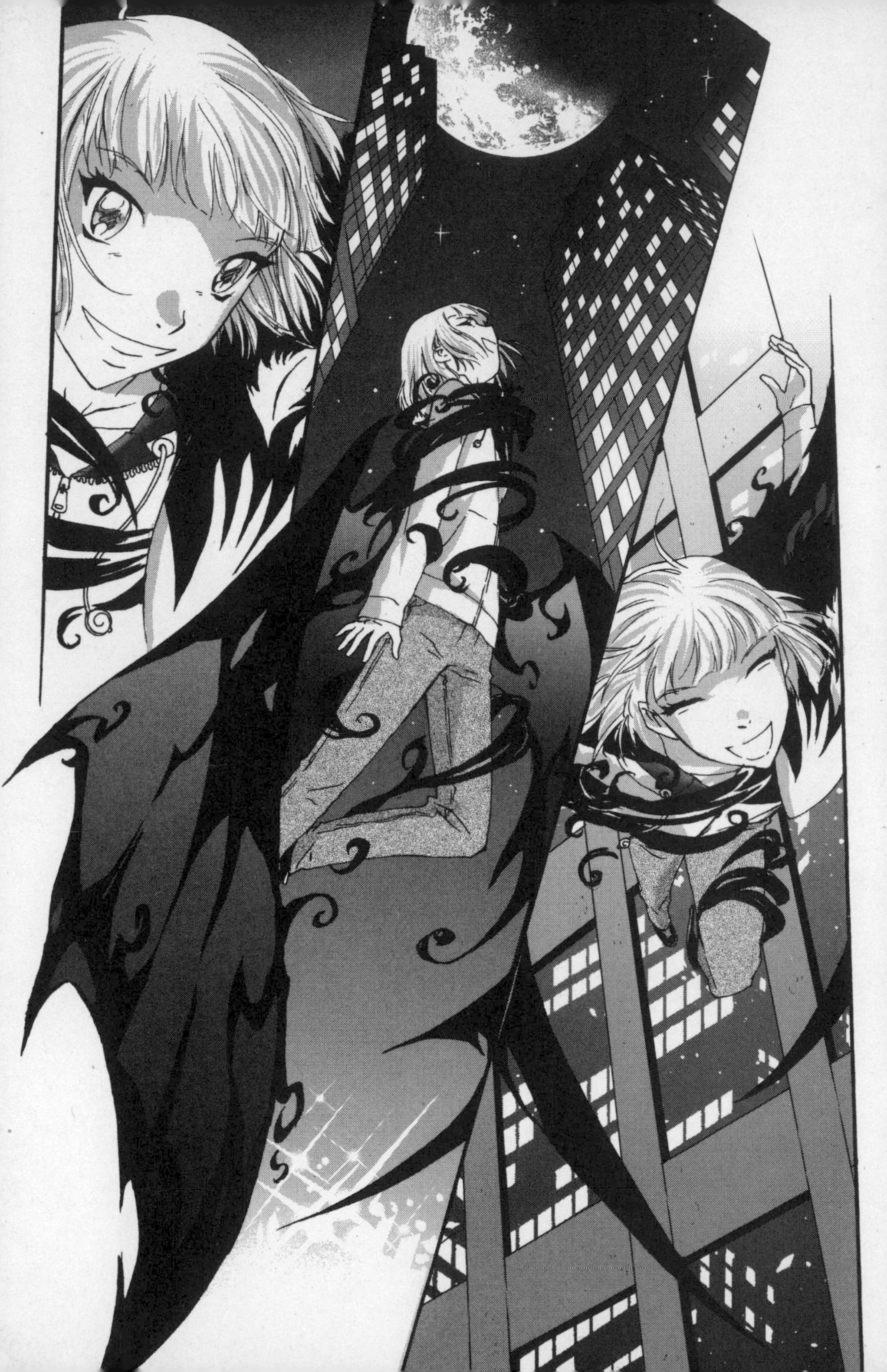

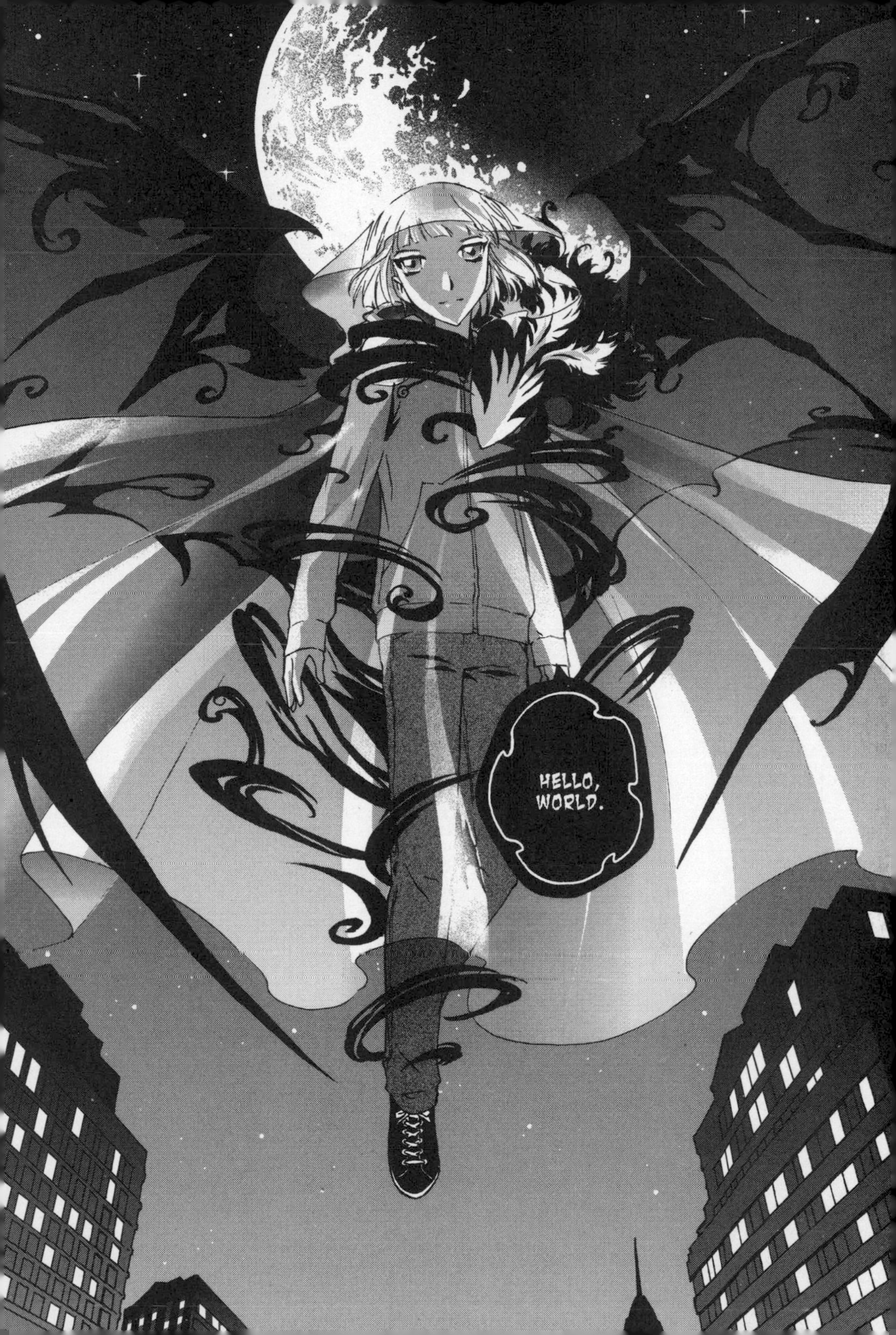
HELLO, WORLD.

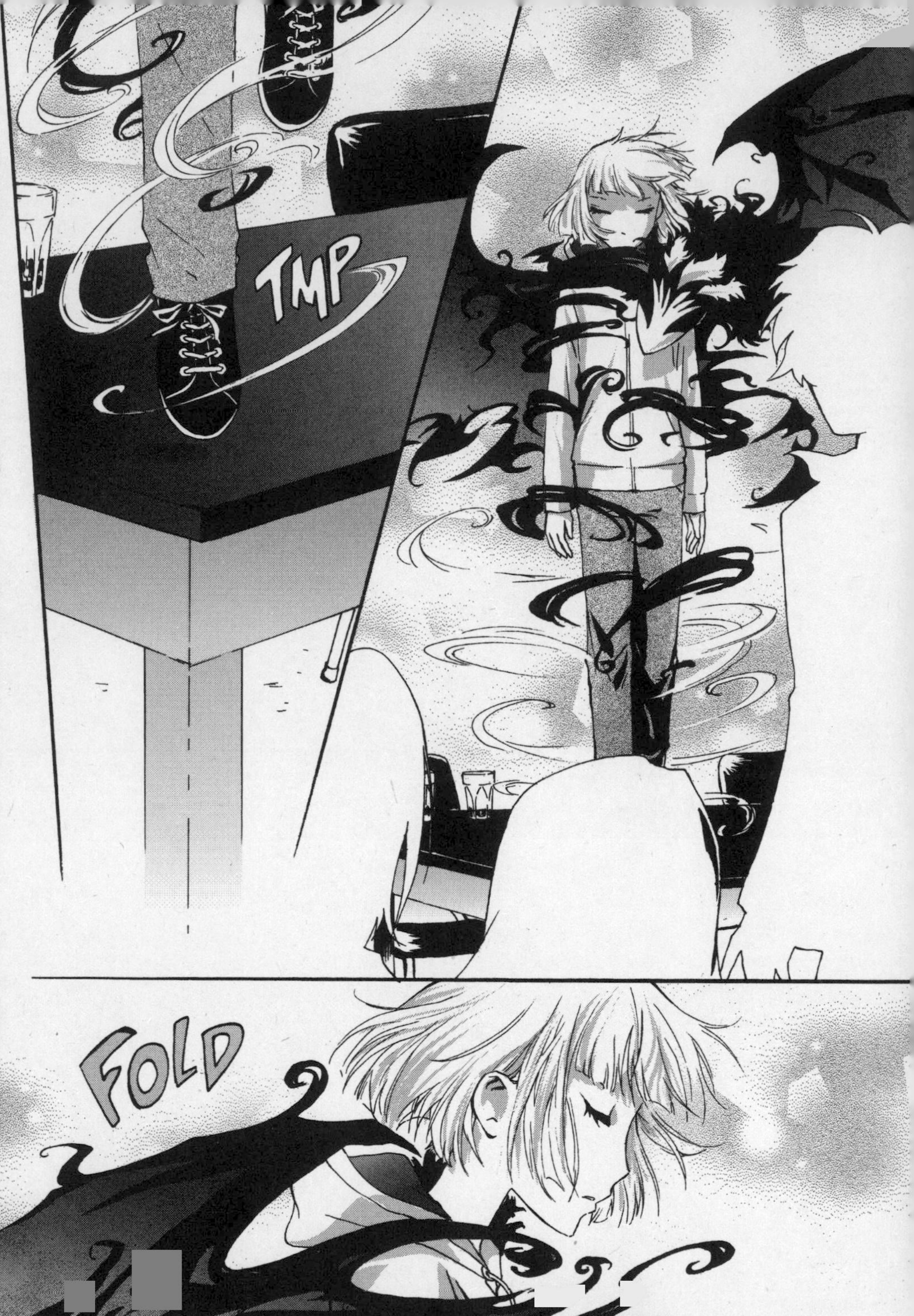
TMP
FOLD

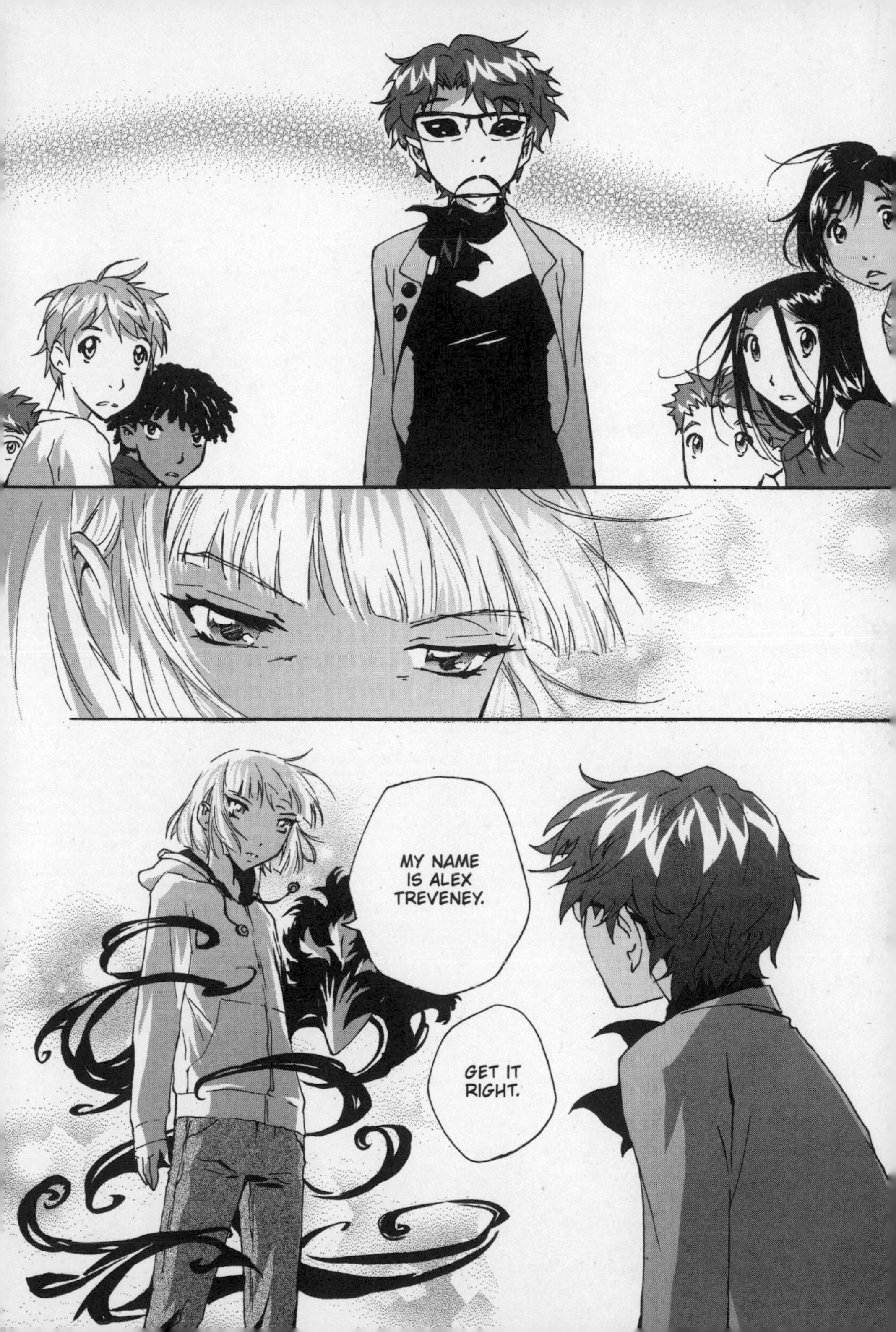
MY NAME IS ALEX TREVENEY.
GET IT RIGHT.

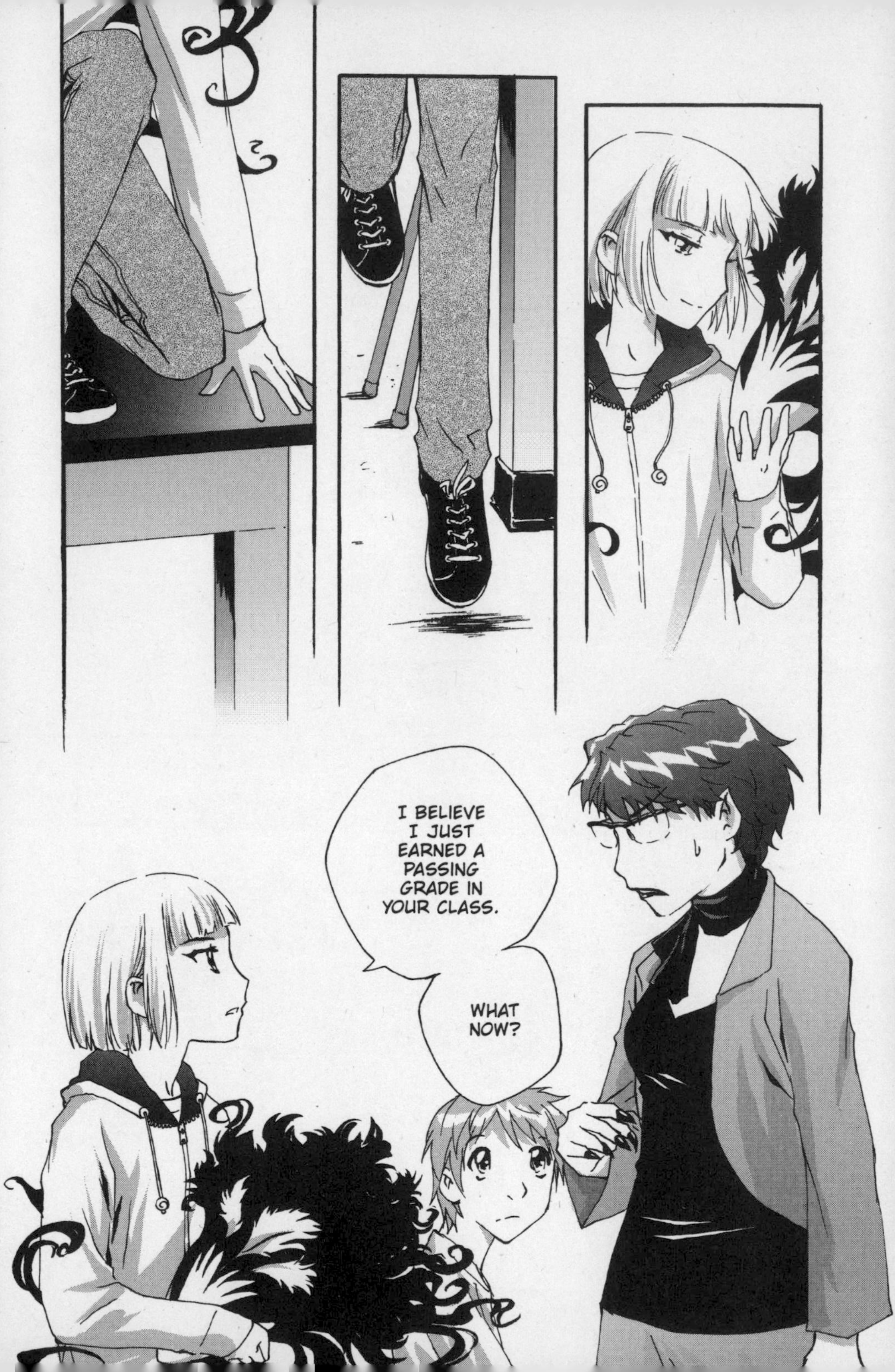
I BELIEVE I JUST EARNED A PASSING GRADE IN YOUR CLASS.
WHAT NOW?

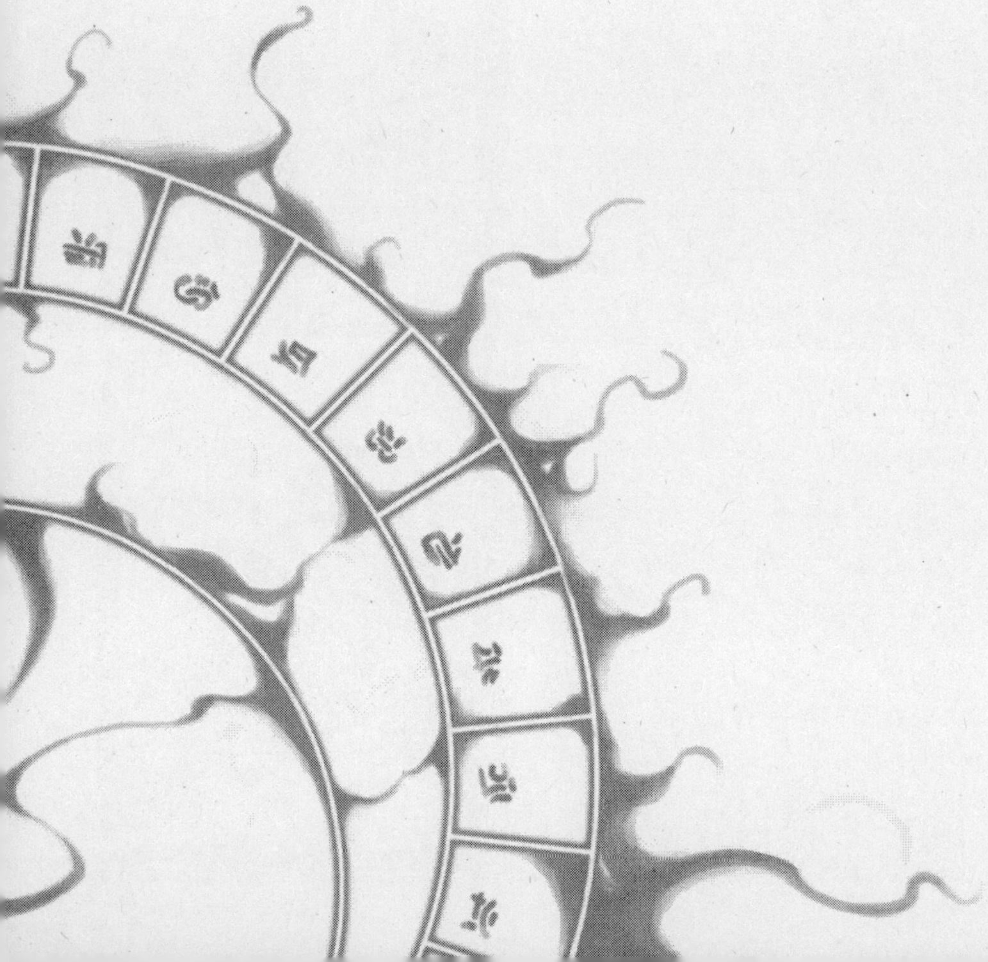

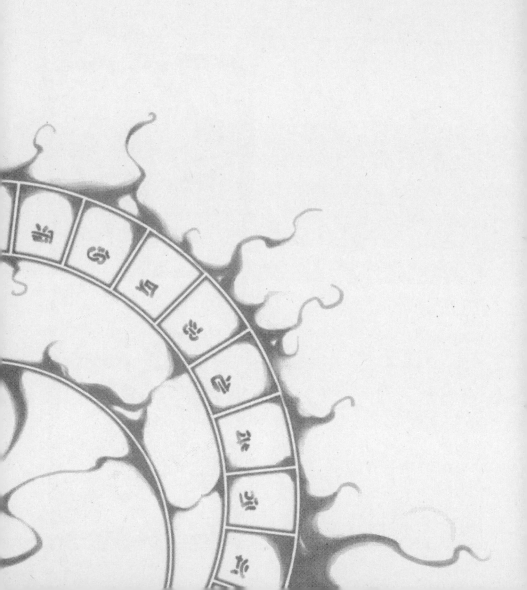

Chapter 12

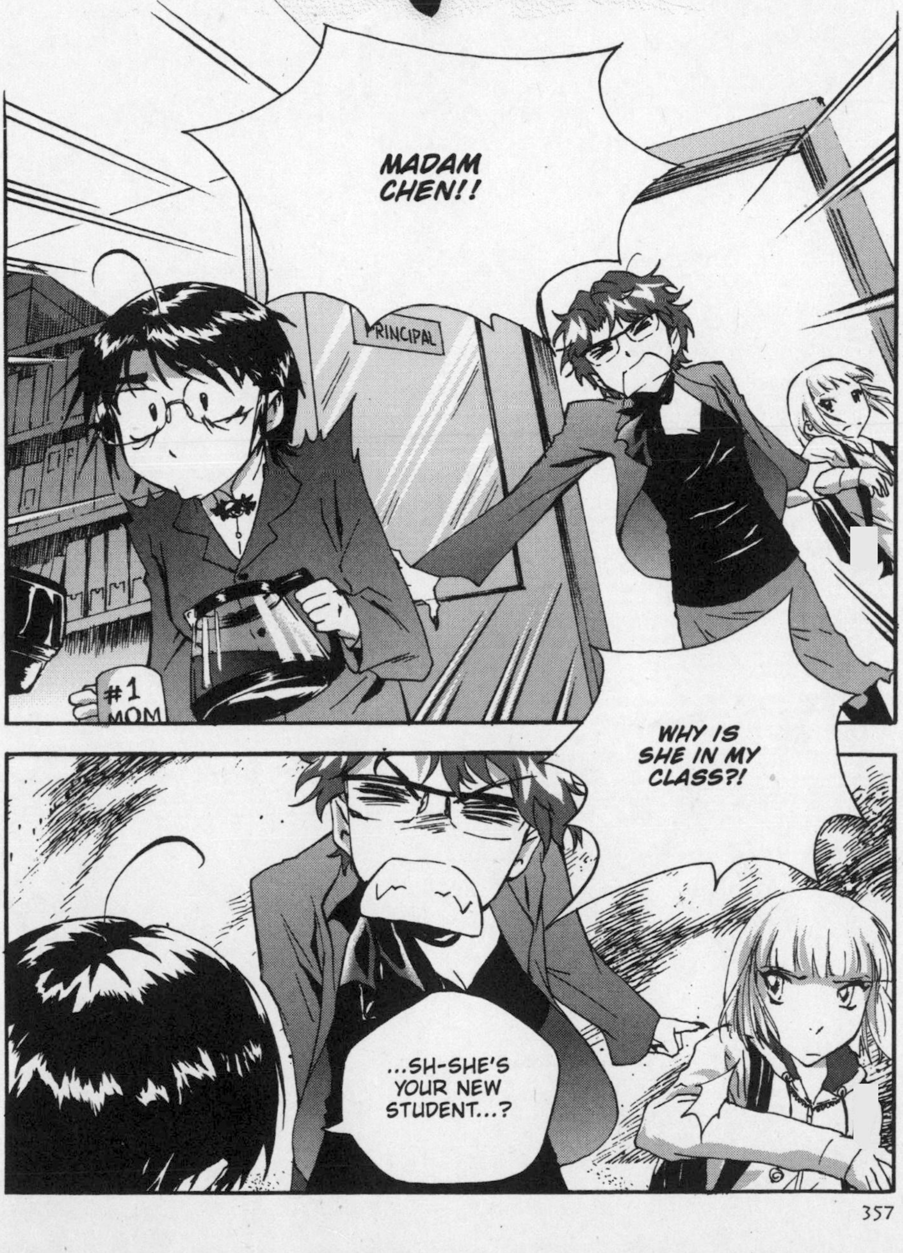
MADAM CHEN!!
PRINCIPAL
#1 MOM
WHY IS SHE IN MY CLASS?!
...SH-SHE'S YOUR NEW STUDENT...?

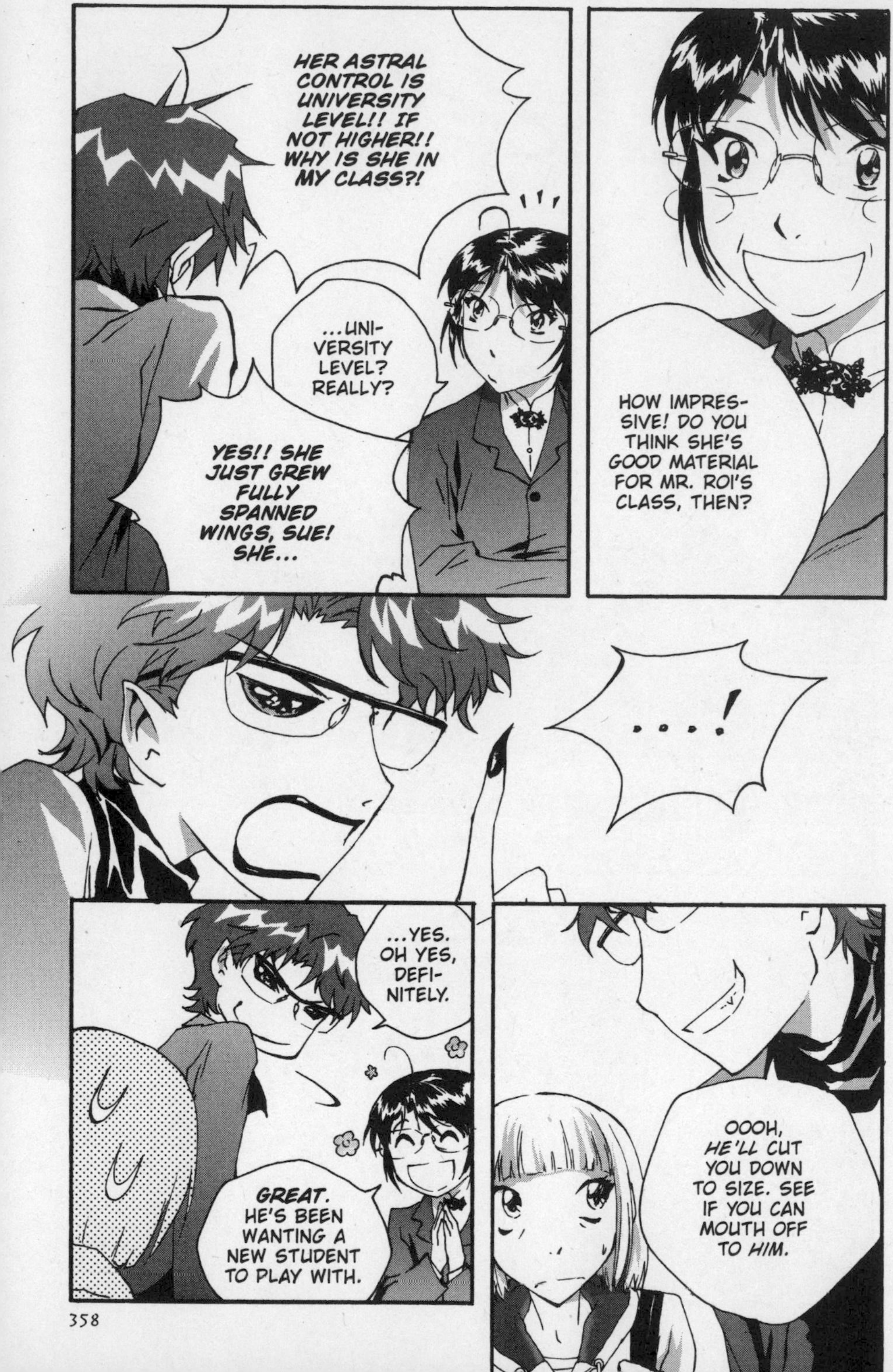
HER ASTRAL CONTROL IS UNIVERSITY LEVEL!! IF NOT HIGHER!! WHY IS SHE IN MY CLASS?!
...UNIVERSITY LEVEL? REALLY?
YES!! SHE JUST GREW FULLY SPANNED WINGS, SUE! SHE...
HOW IMPRESSIVE! DO YOU THINK SHE'S GOOD MATERIAL FOR MR. ROI'S CLASS, THEN?
...!
...YES. OH YES, DEFINITELY.
GREAT. HE'S BEEN WANTING A NEW STUDENT TO PLAY WITH.
OOOH, HE'LL CUT YOU DOWN TO SIZE. SEE IF YOU CAN MOUTH OFF TO HIM.

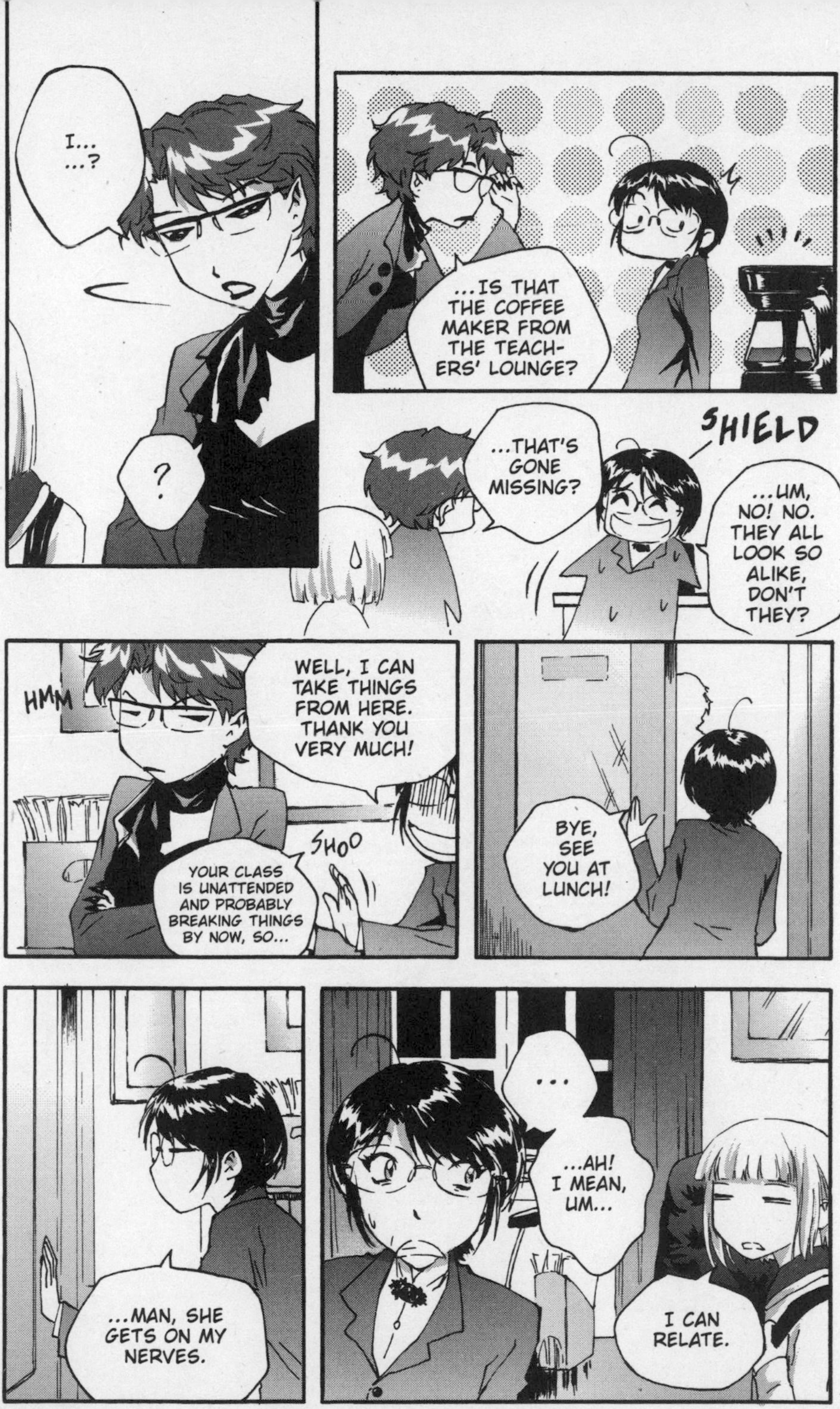

I...
...?
?
...IS THAT THE COFFEE MAKER FROM THE TEACHERS' LOUNGE?
...THAT'S GONE MISSING?
SHIELD
...UM, NO! NO. THEY ALL LOOK SO ALIKE, DON'T THEY?
HMM
WELL, I CAN TAKE THINGS FROM HERE. THANK YOU VERY MUCH!
SHOO
YOUR CLASS IS UNATTENDED AND PROBABLY BREAKING THINGS BY NOW, SO...
BYE, SEE YOU AT LUNCH!
...MAN, SHE GETS ON MY NERVES.
...
...AH! I MEAN, UM...
I CAN RELATE.

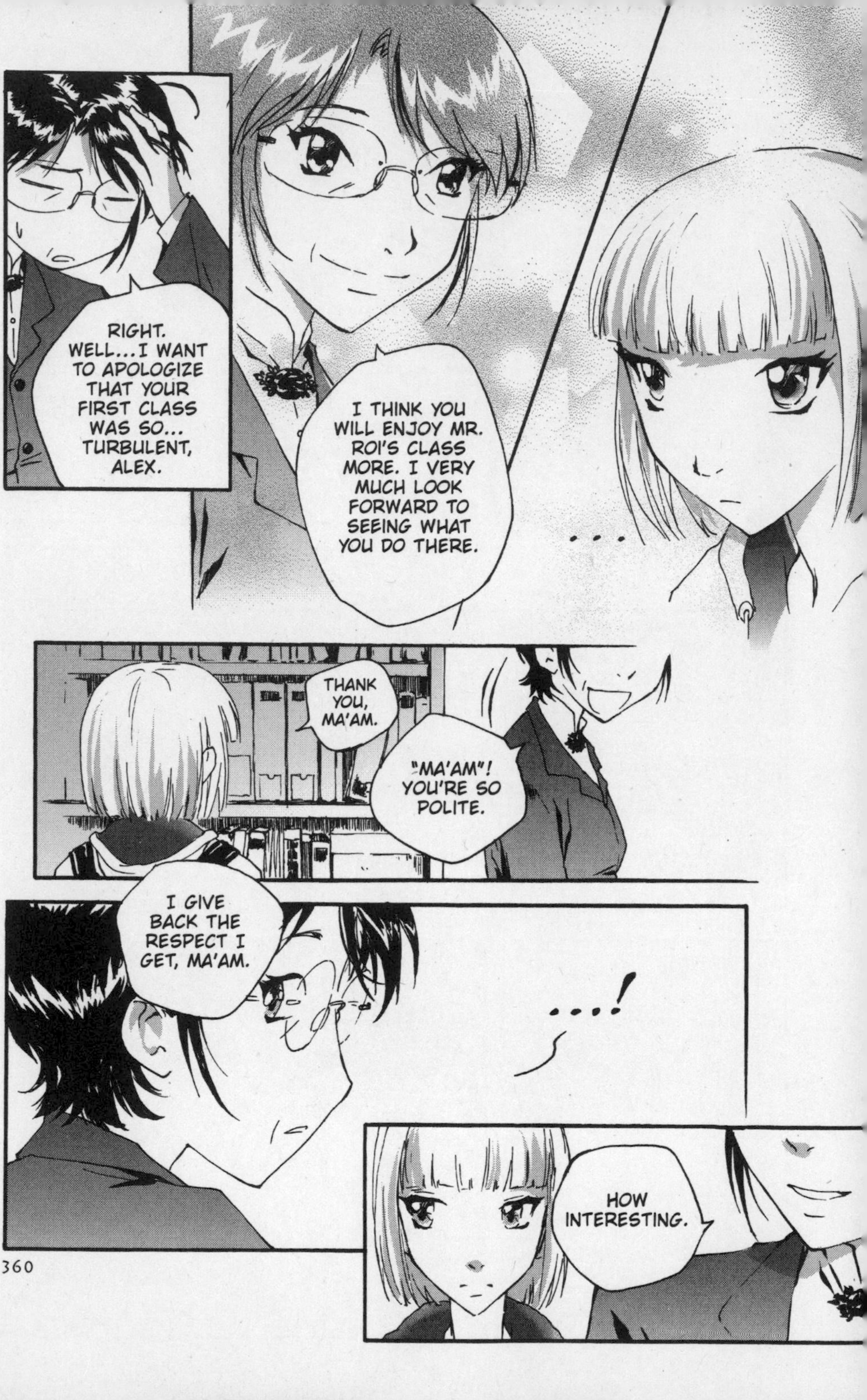
RIGHT. WELL…I WANT TO APOLOGIZE THAT YOUR FIRST CLASS WAS SO… TURBULENT, ALEX.
I THINK YOU WILL ENJOY MR. ROI'S CLASS MORE. I VERY MUCH LOOK FORWARD TO SEEING WHAT YOU DO THERE.
…
THANK YOU, MA'AM.
"MA'AM"! YOU'RE SO POLITE.
I GIVE BACK THE RESPECT I GET, MA'AM.
…!
HOW INTERESTING.

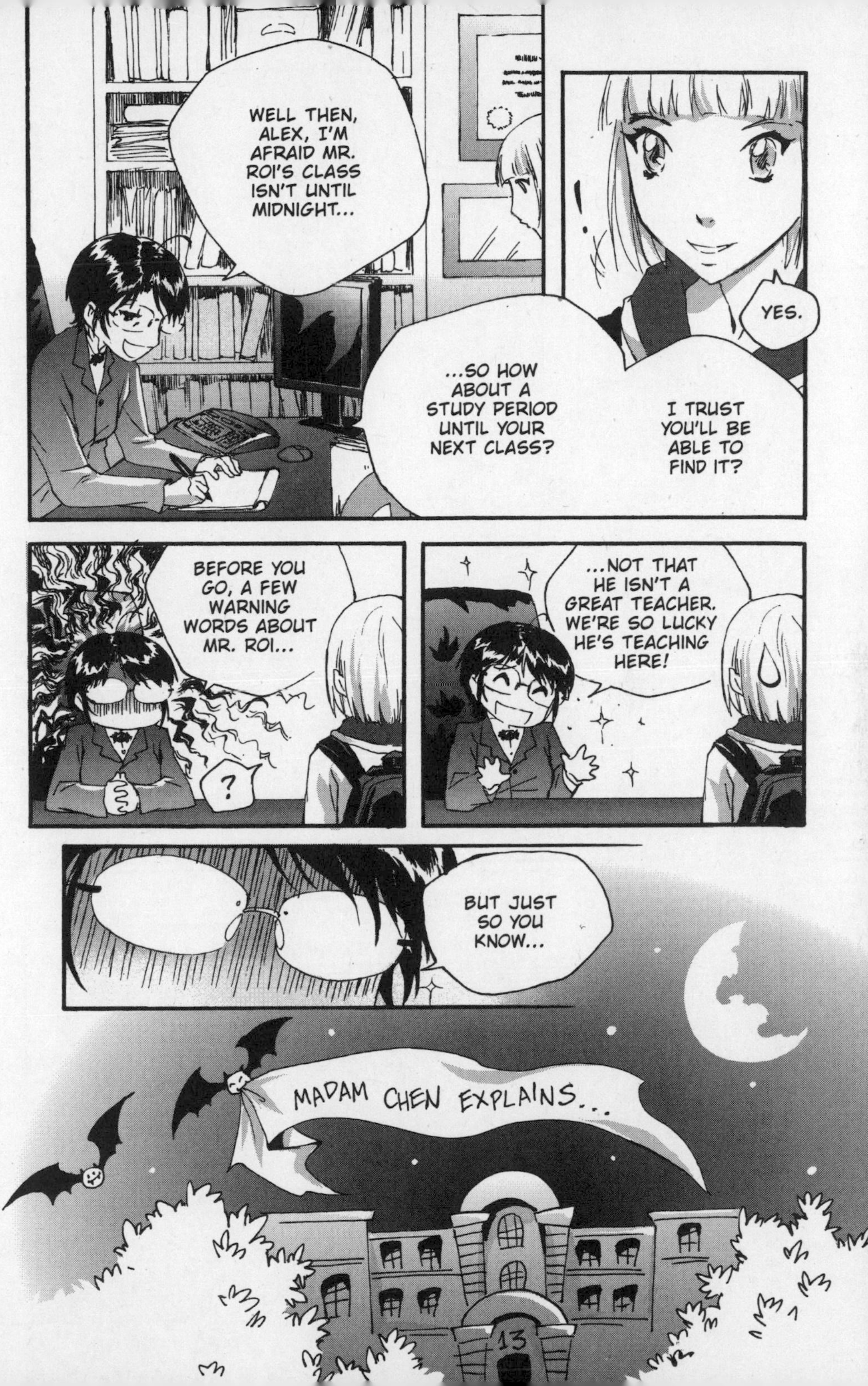
WELL THEN, ALEX, I'M AFRAID MR. ROI'S CLASS ISN'T UNTIL MIDNIGHT...
YES.
...SO HOW ABOUT A STUDY PERIOD UNTIL YOUR NEXT CLASS?
I TRUST YOU'LL BE ABLE TO FIND IT?
BEFORE YOU GO, A FEW WARNING WORDS ABOUT MR. ROI...
?
...NOT THAT HE ISN'T A GREAT TEACHER. WE'RE SO LUCKY HE'S TEACHING HERE!
BUT JUST SO YOU KNOW...
MADAM CHEN EXPLAINS...
13

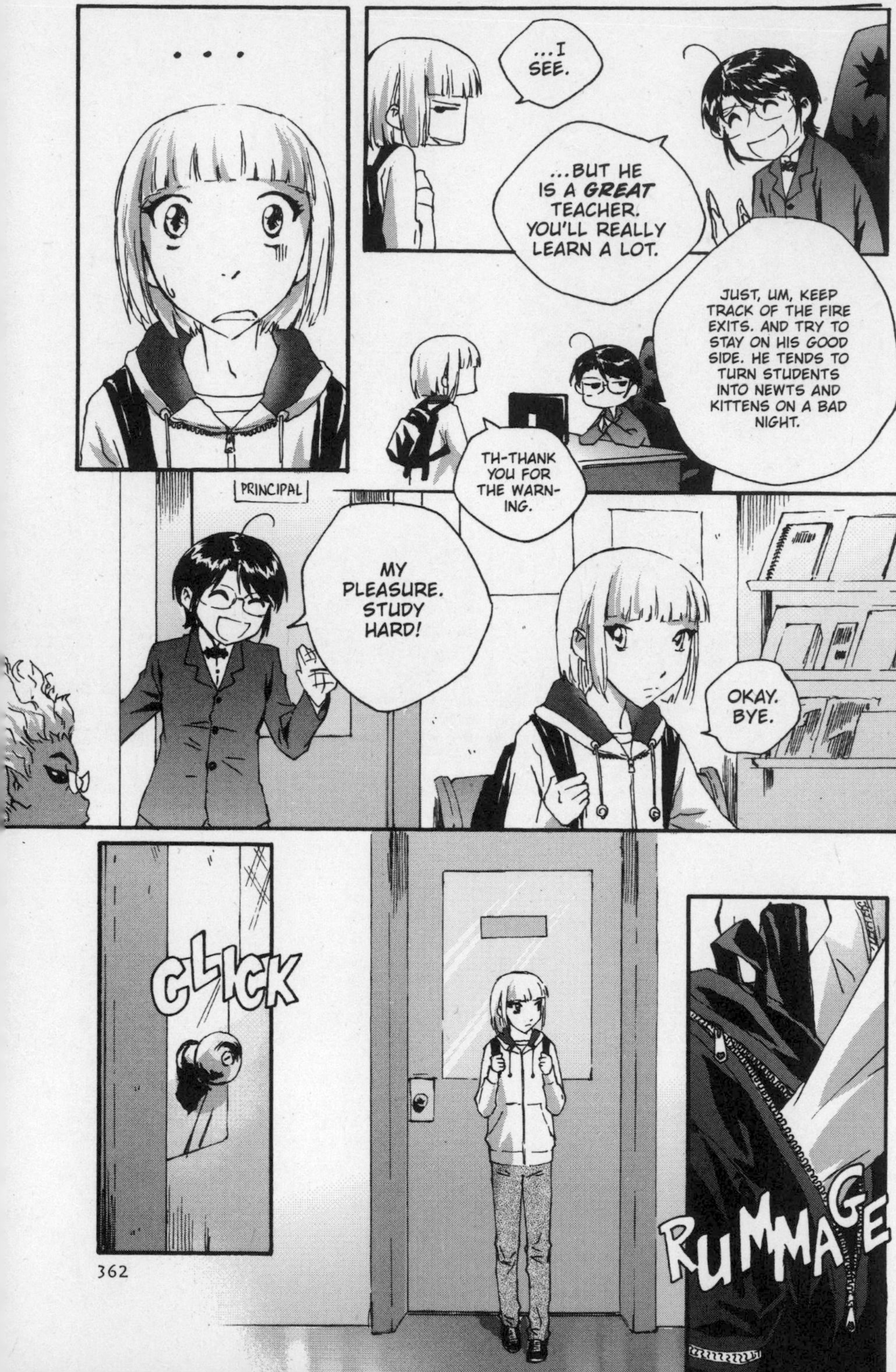

. . .
...I SEE.
...BUT HE IS A GREAT TEACHER. YOU'LL REALLY LEARN A LOT.
JUST, UM, KEEP TRACK OF THE FIRE EXITS. AND TRY TO STAY ON HIS GOOD SIDE. HE TENDS TO TURN STUDENTS INTO NEWTS AND KITTENS ON A BAD NIGHT.
TH-THANK YOU FOR THE WARN-ING.
PRINCIPAL
MY PLEASURE. STUDY HARD!
OKAY. BYE.
CLICK
RUMMAGE

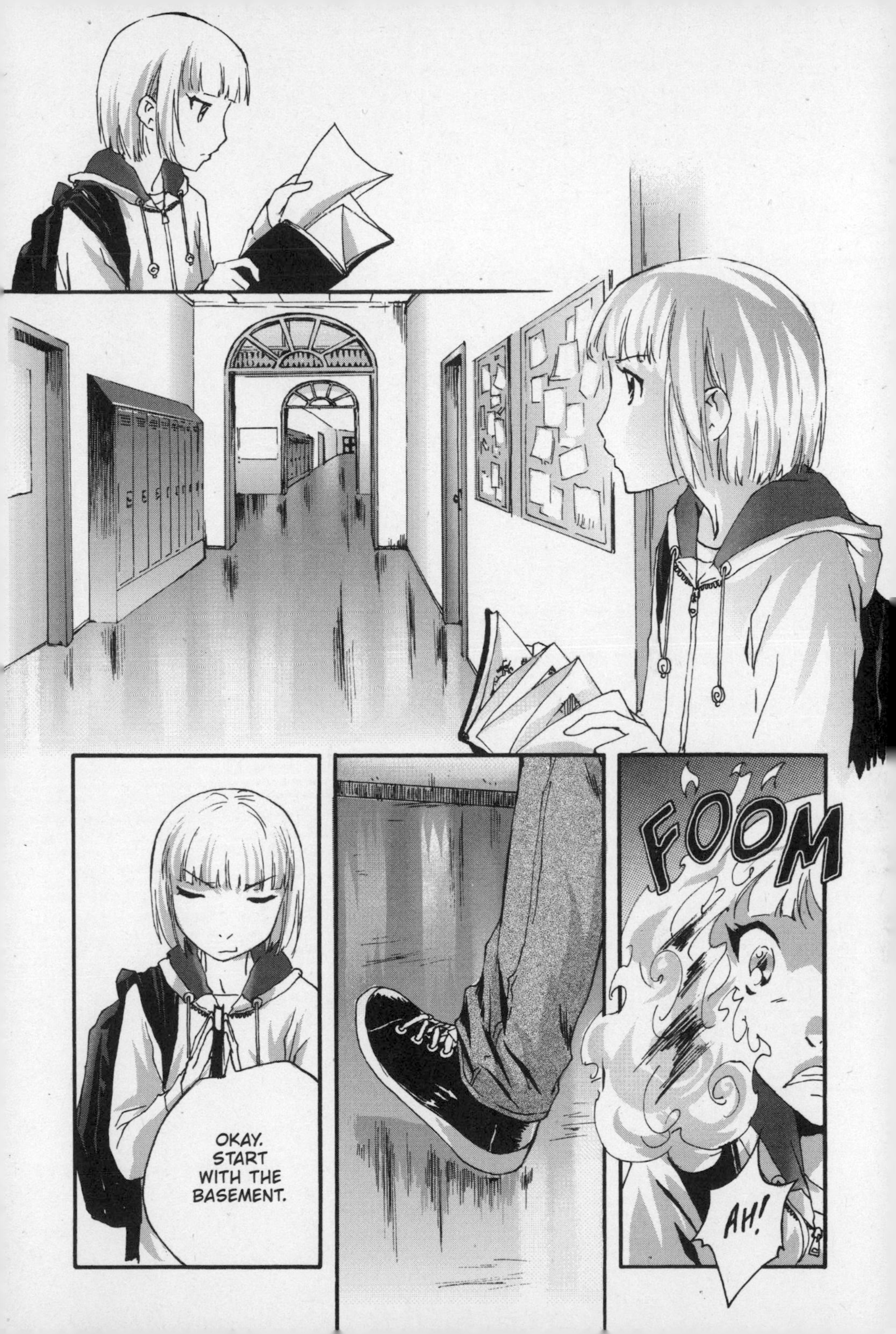
OKAY. START WITH THE BASEMENT.
FOOM
AH!

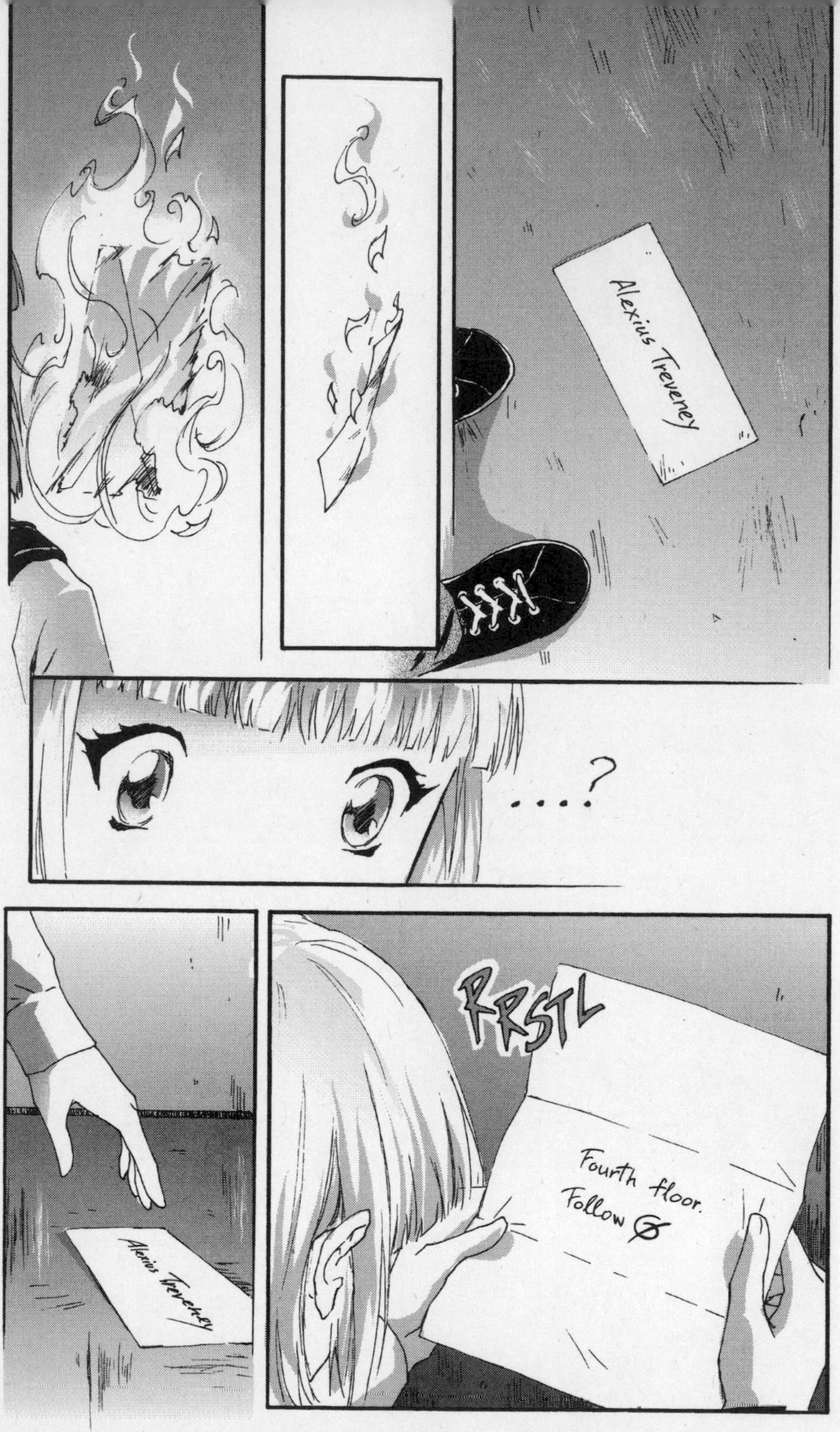

Alexius Treveney
...?
Alexius Treveney
RRSTL
Fourth floor.
Follow

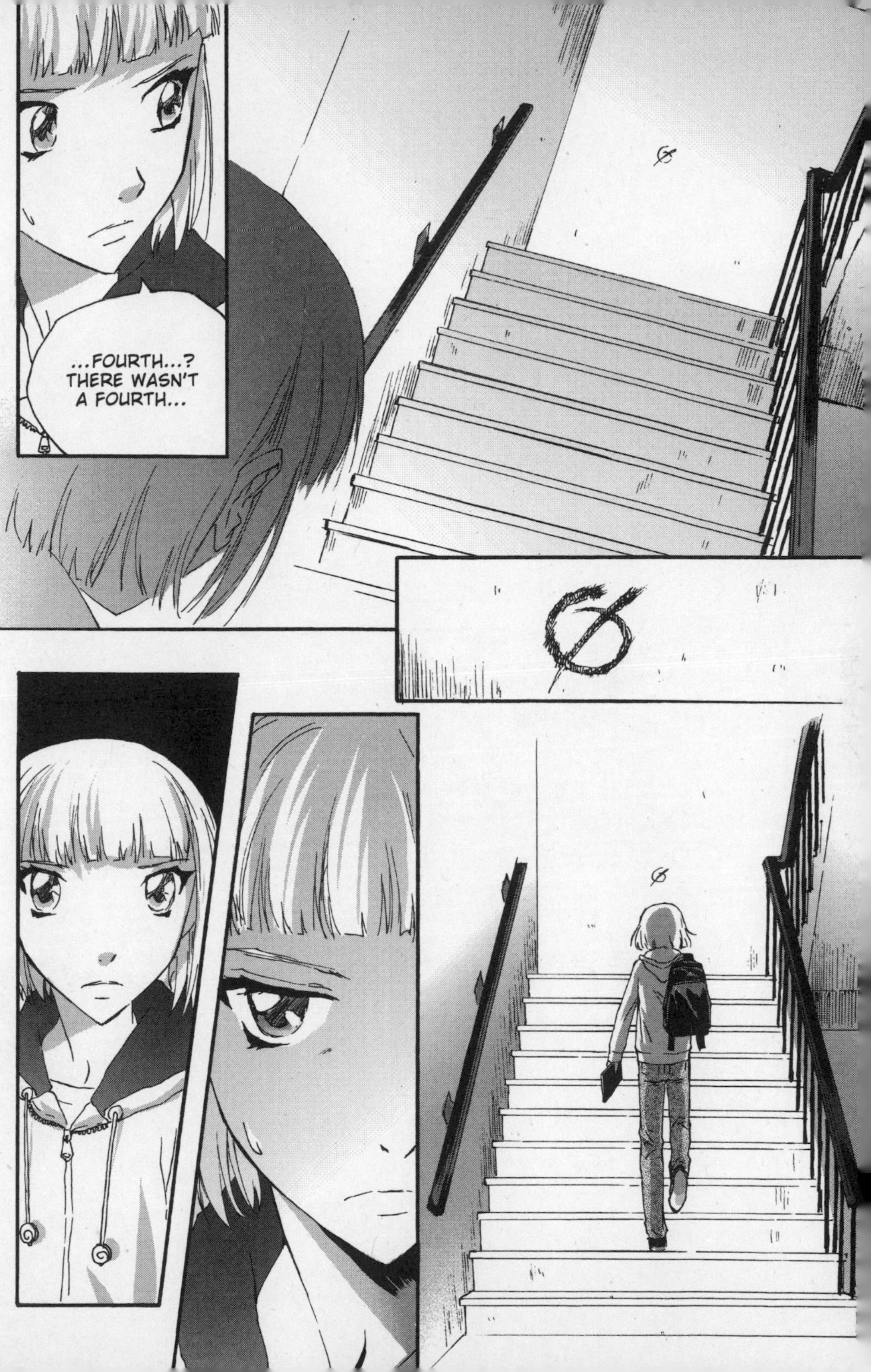
...FOURTH...? THERE WASN'T A FOURTH...

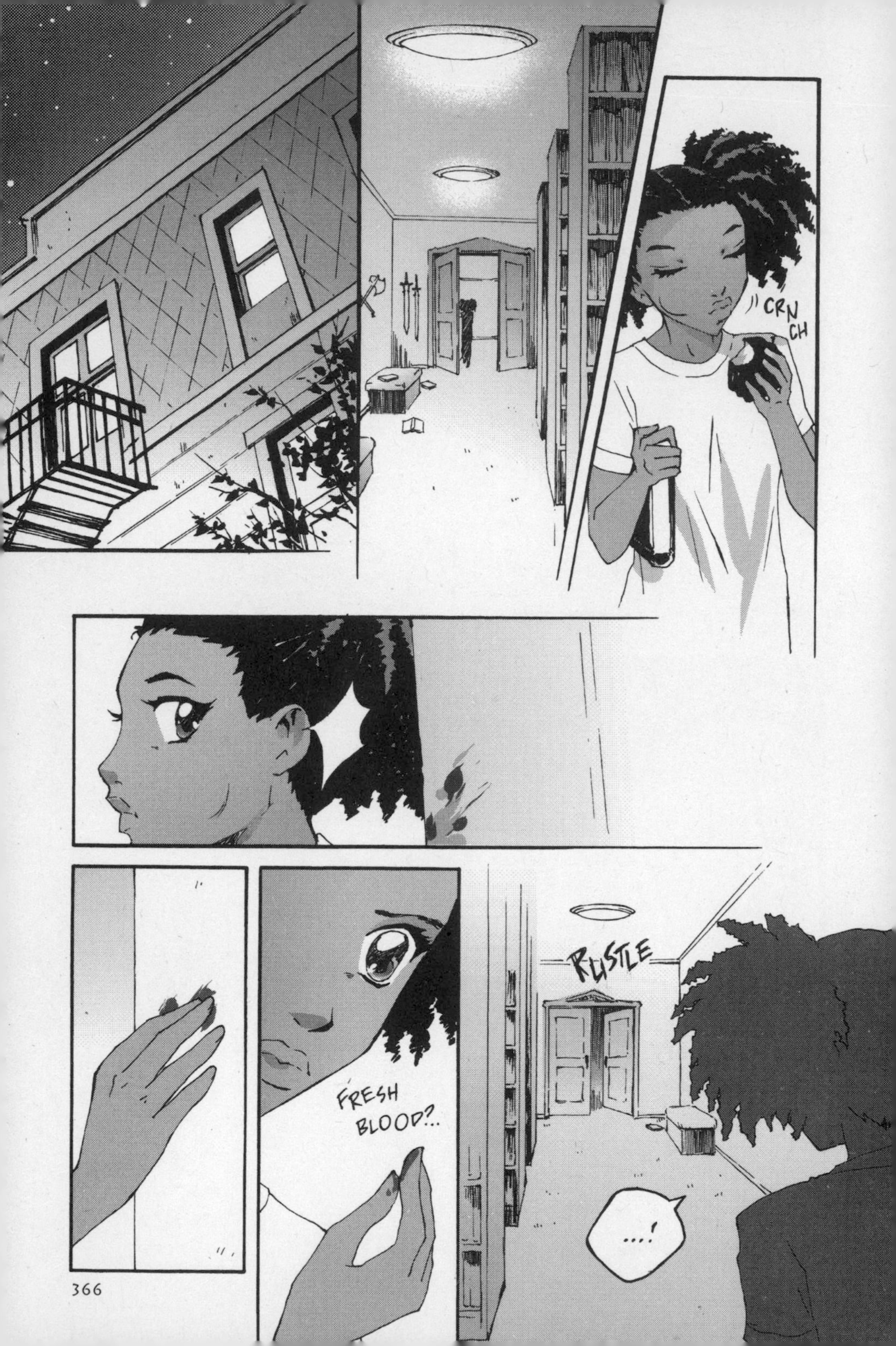
CRNCH
RUSTLE
FRESH BLOOD?...
...!

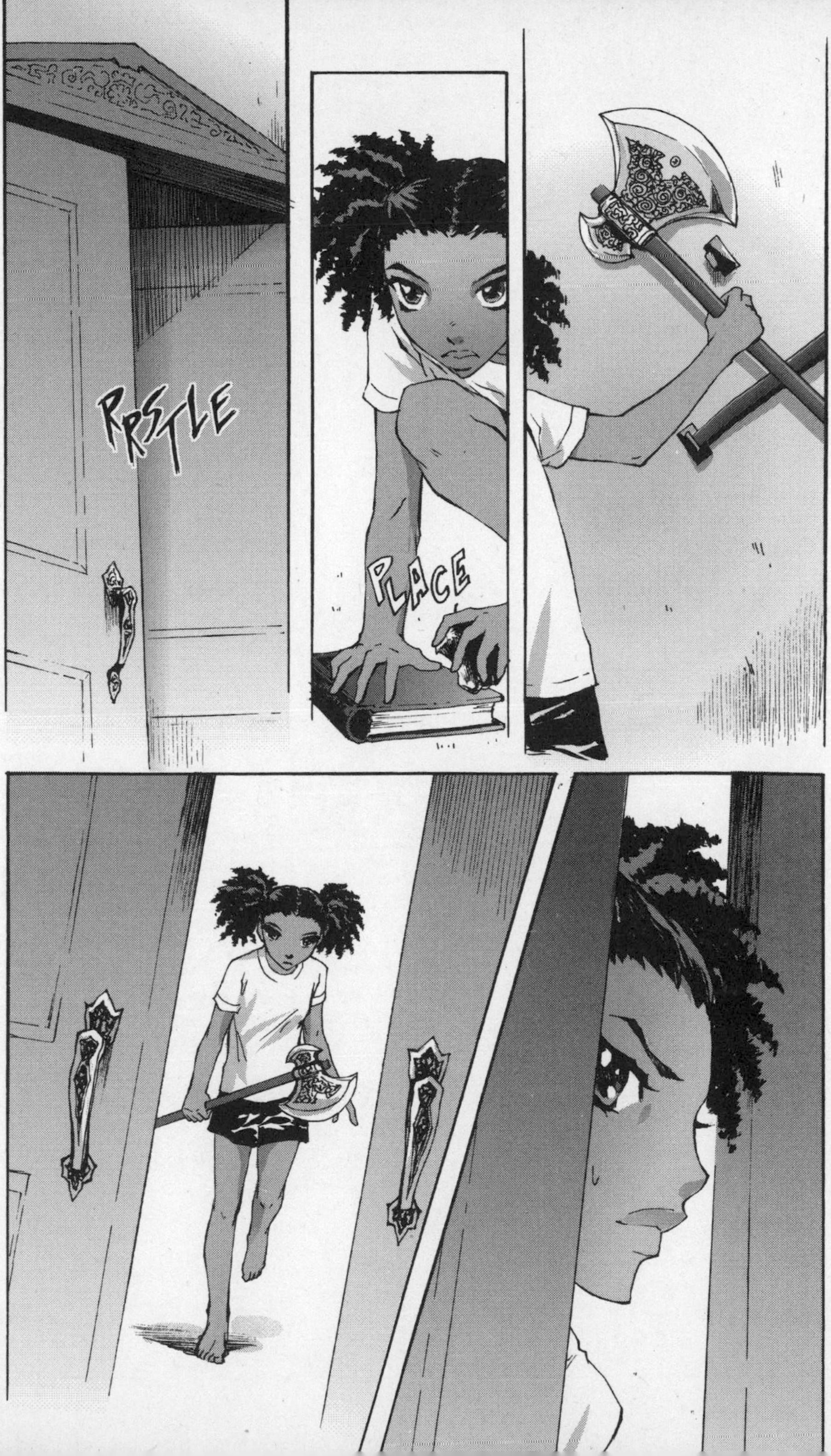
RRSTLE
PLACE

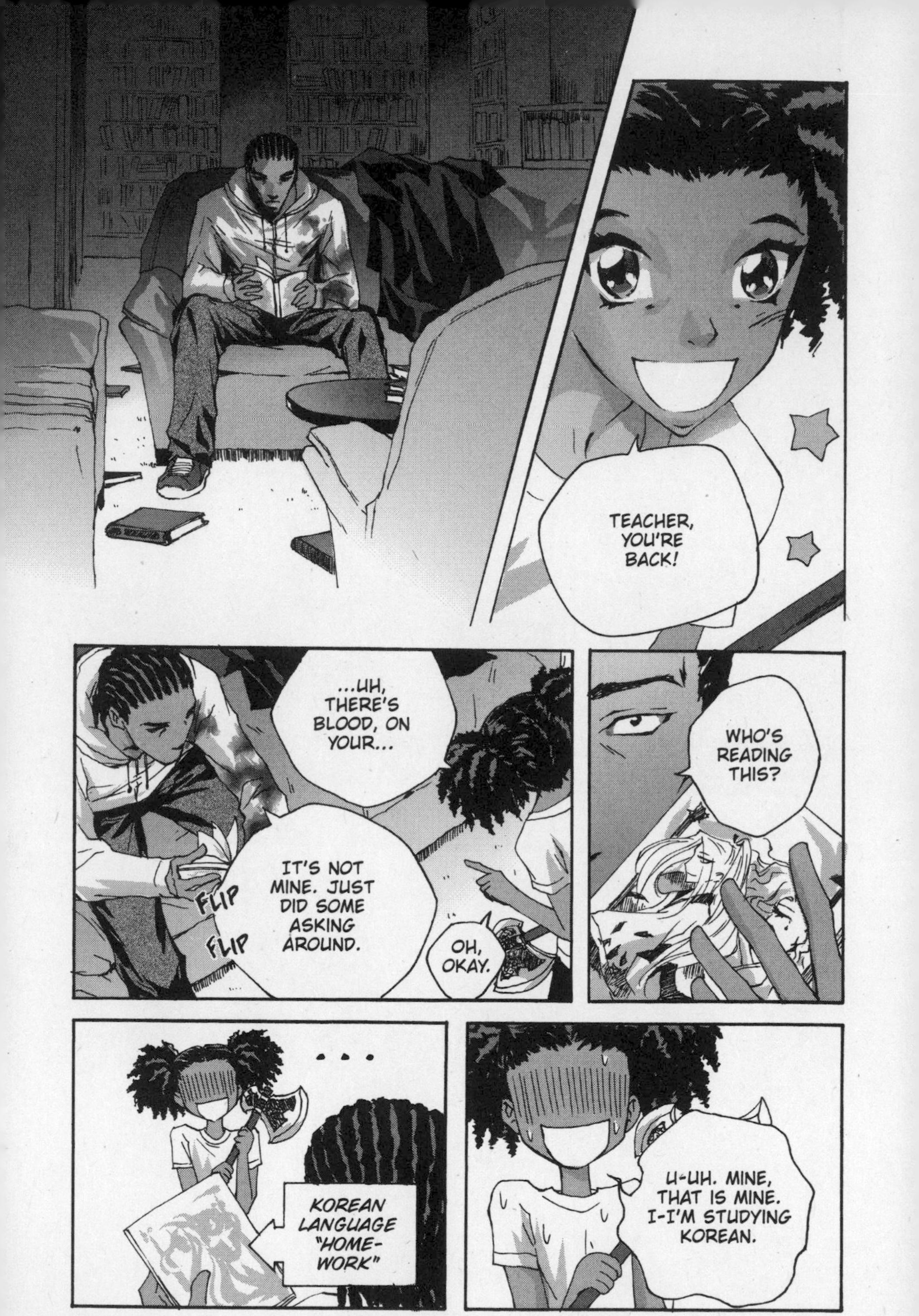
TEACHER, YOU'RE BACK!
...UH, THERE'S BLOOD, ON YOUR...
FLIP
FLIP
IT'S NOT MINE. JUST DID SOME ASKING AROUND.
OH, OKAY.
WHO'S READING THIS?
...
KOREAN LANGUAGE "HOME-WORK"
U-UH. MINE, THAT IS MINE. I-I'M STUDYING KOREAN.

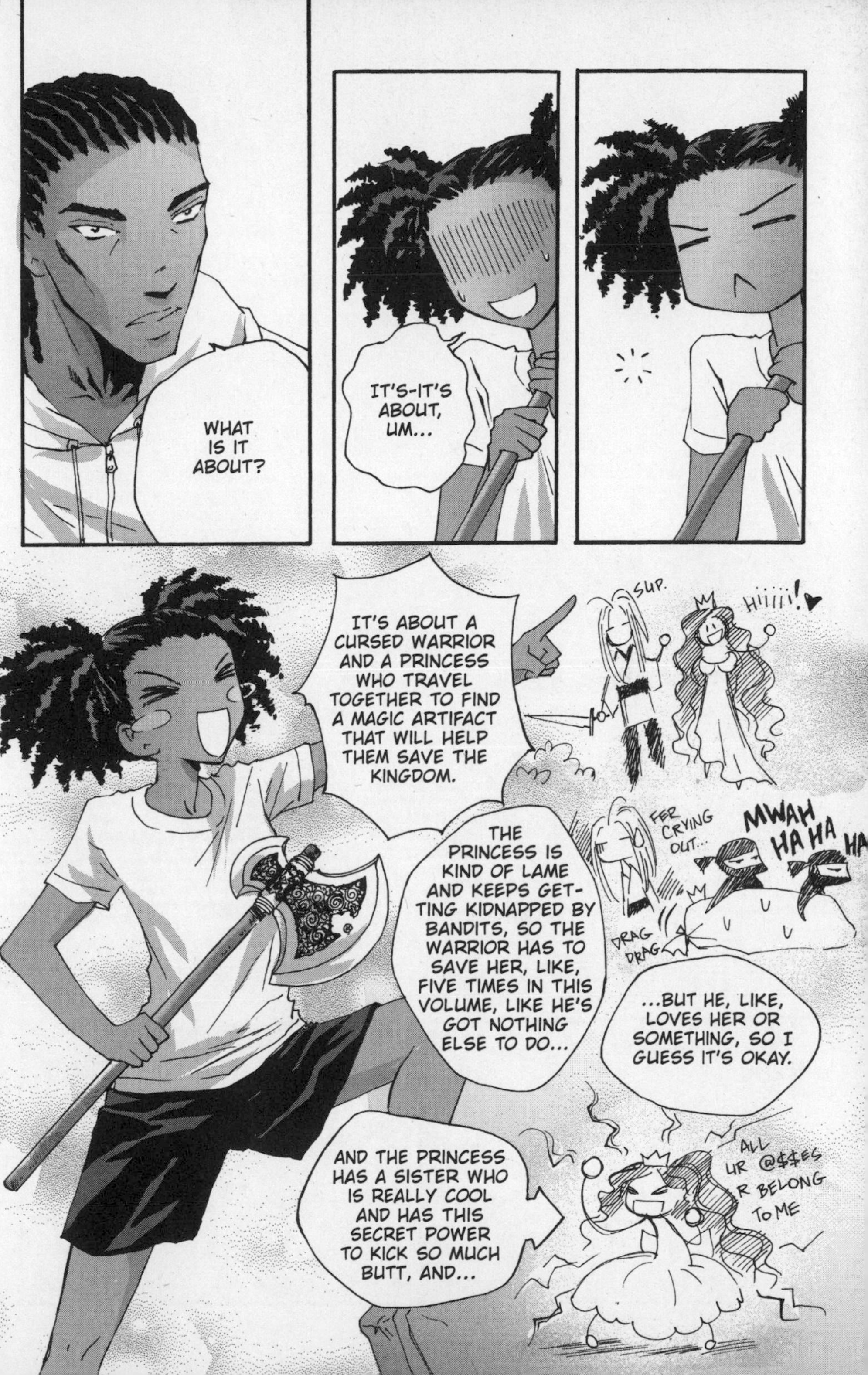
WHAT IS IT ABOUT?
IT'S-IT'S ABOUT, UM...
IT'S ABOUT A CURSED WARRIOR AND A PRINCESS WHO TRAVEL TOGETHER TO FIND A MAGIC ARTIFACT THAT WILL HELP THEM SAVE THE KINGDOM.
SUP.
HIIIII!
THE PRINCESS IS KIND OF LAME AND KEEPS GETTING KIDNAPPED BY BANDITS, SO THE WARRIOR HAS TO SAVE HER, LIKE, FIVE TIMES IN THIS VOLUME, LIKE HE'S GOT NOTHING ELSE TO DO...
FER CRYING OUT...
MWAH HA HA
DRAG DRAG
...BUT HE, LIKE, LOVES HER OR SOMETHING, SO I GUESS IT'S OKAY.
AND THE PRINCESS HAS A SISTER WHO IS REALLY COOL AND HAS THIS SECRET POWER TO KICK SO MUCH BUTT, AND...
ALL UR @$$ES R BELONG TO ME

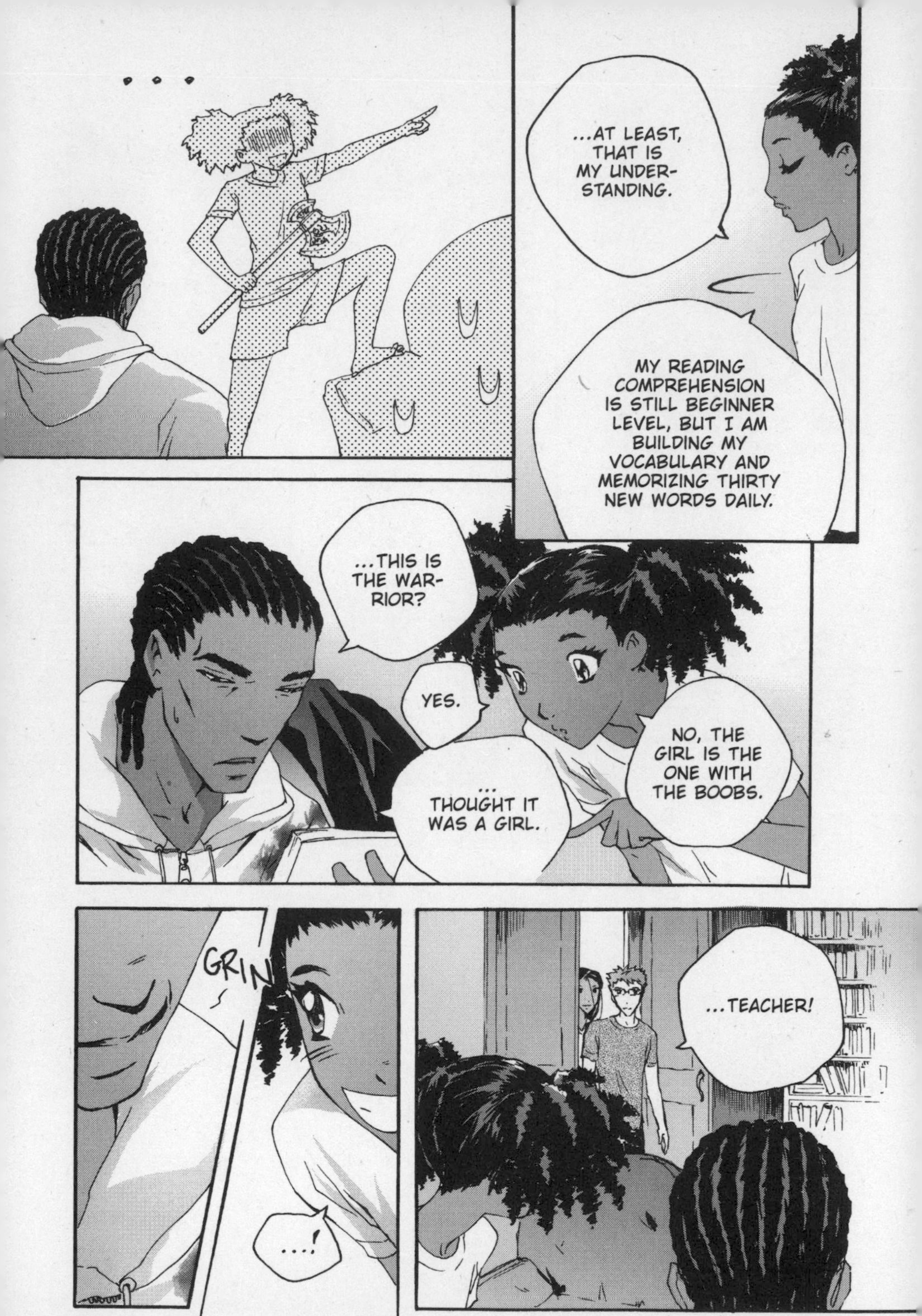
...
...AT LEAST, THAT IS MY UNDER-STANDING.
MY READING COMPREHENSION IS STILL BEGINNER LEVEL, BUT I AM BUILDING MY VOCABULARY AND MEMORIZING THIRTY NEW WORDS DAILY.
...THIS IS THE WAR-RIOR?
YES.
... THOUGHT IT WAS A GIRL.
NO, THE GIRL IS THE ONE WITH THE BOOBS.
GRIN
...!
...TEACHER!

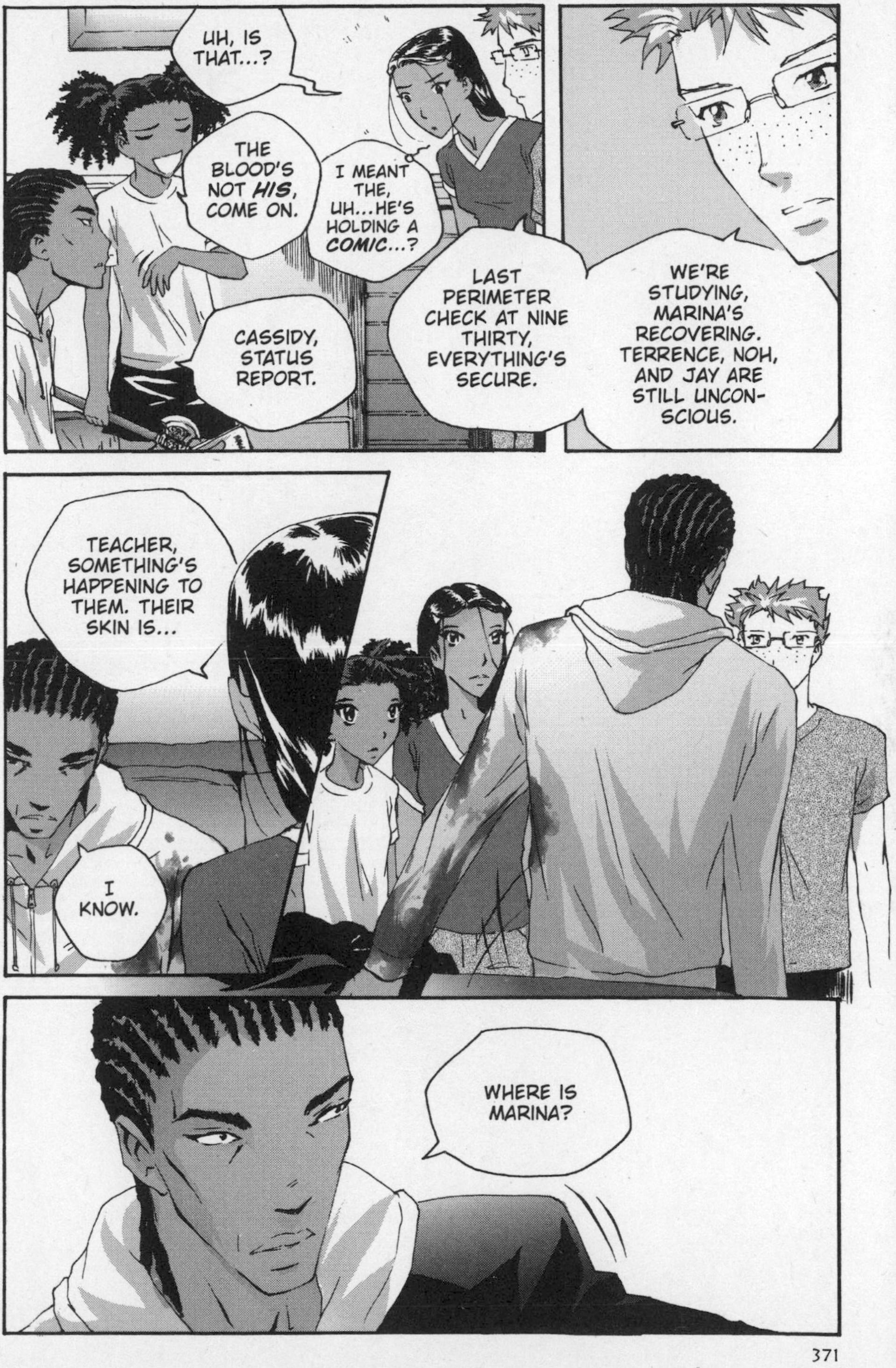
UH, IS THAT...?
THE BLOOD'S NOT *HIS*, COME ON.
I MEANT THE, UH...HE'S HOLDING A *COMIC*...?
CASSIDY, STATUS REPORT.
LAST PERIMETER CHECK AT NINE THIRTY, EVERYTHING'S SECURE.
WE'RE STUDYING, MARINA'S RECOVERING. TERRENCE, NOH, AND JAY ARE STILL UNCON-SCIOUS.
TEACHER, SOMETHING'S HAPPENING TO THEM. THEIR SKIN IS...
I KNOW.
WHERE IS MARINA?

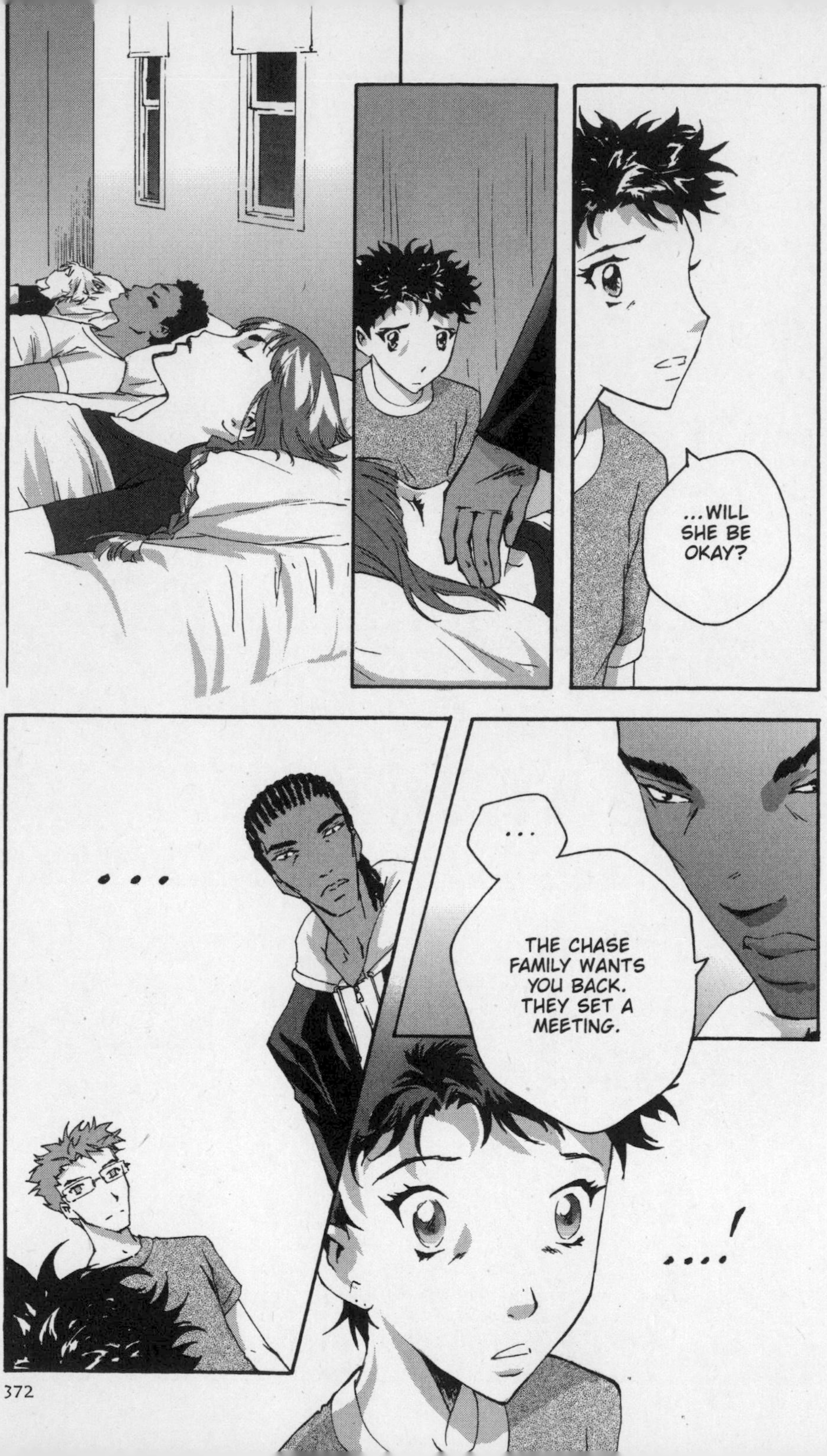

...WILL SHE BE OKAY?
...
...
THE CHASE FAMILY WANTS YOU BACK. THEY SET A MEETING.
...!

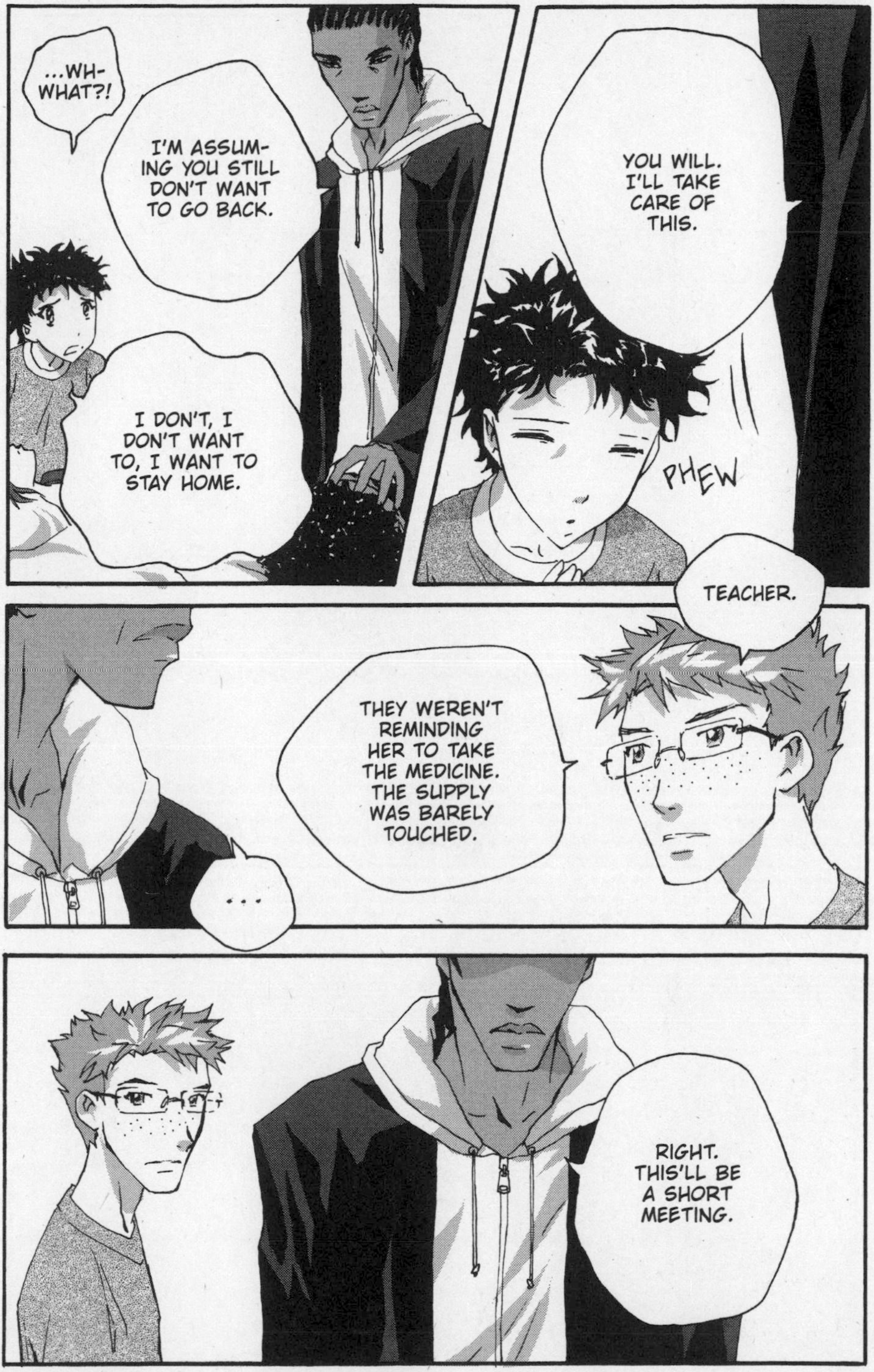
...WH-
WHAT?!
I'M ASSUMING YOU STILL DON'T WANT TO GO BACK.
I DON'T, I DON'T WANT TO, I WANT TO STAY HOME.
YOU WILL. I'LL TAKE CARE OF THIS.
PHEW
TEACHER.
THEY WEREN'T REMINDING HER TO TAKE THE MEDICINE. THE SUPPLY WAS BARELY TOUCHED.
...
RIGHT. THIS'LL BE A SHORT MEETING.

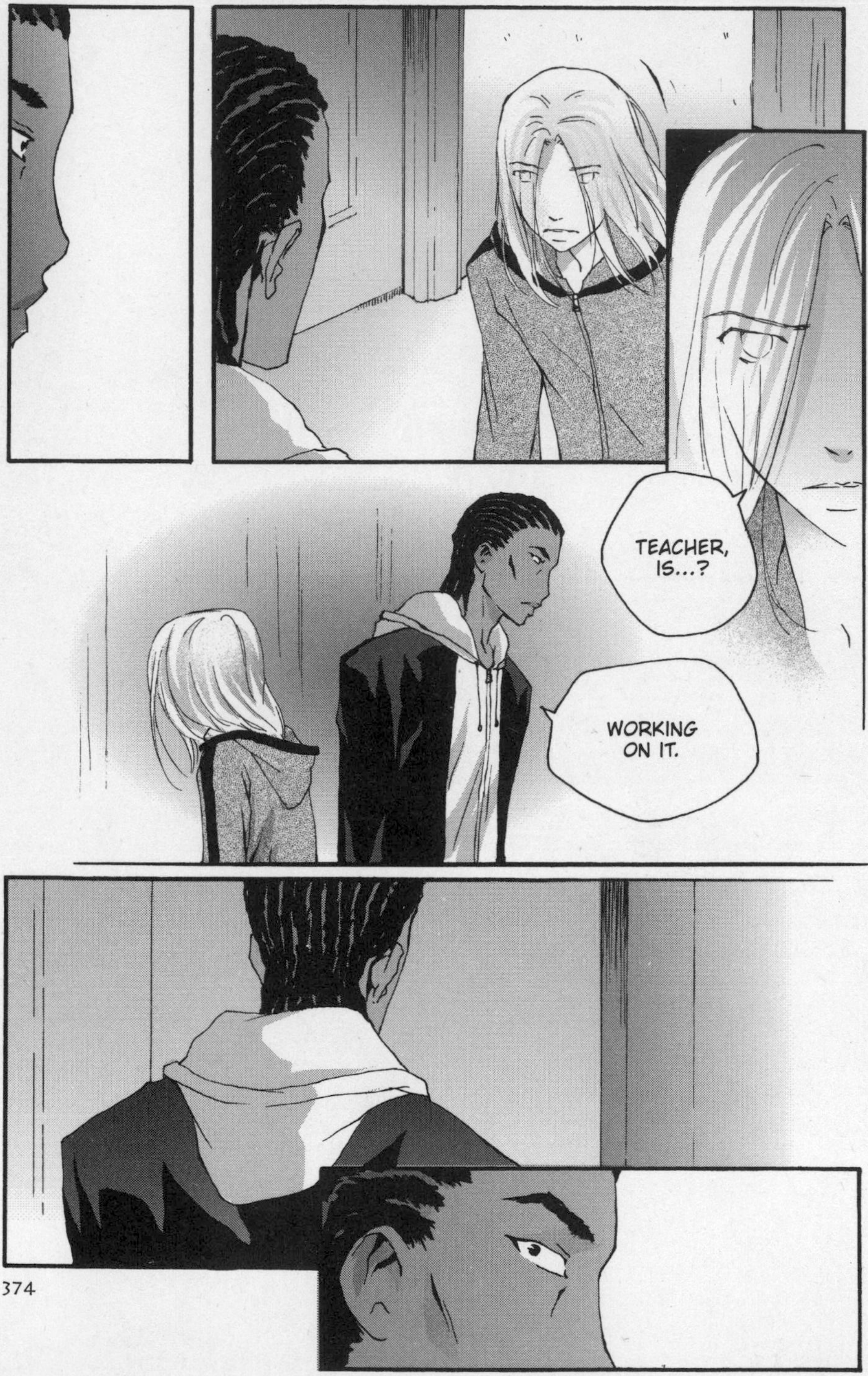
TEACHER, IS...?
WORKING ON IT.

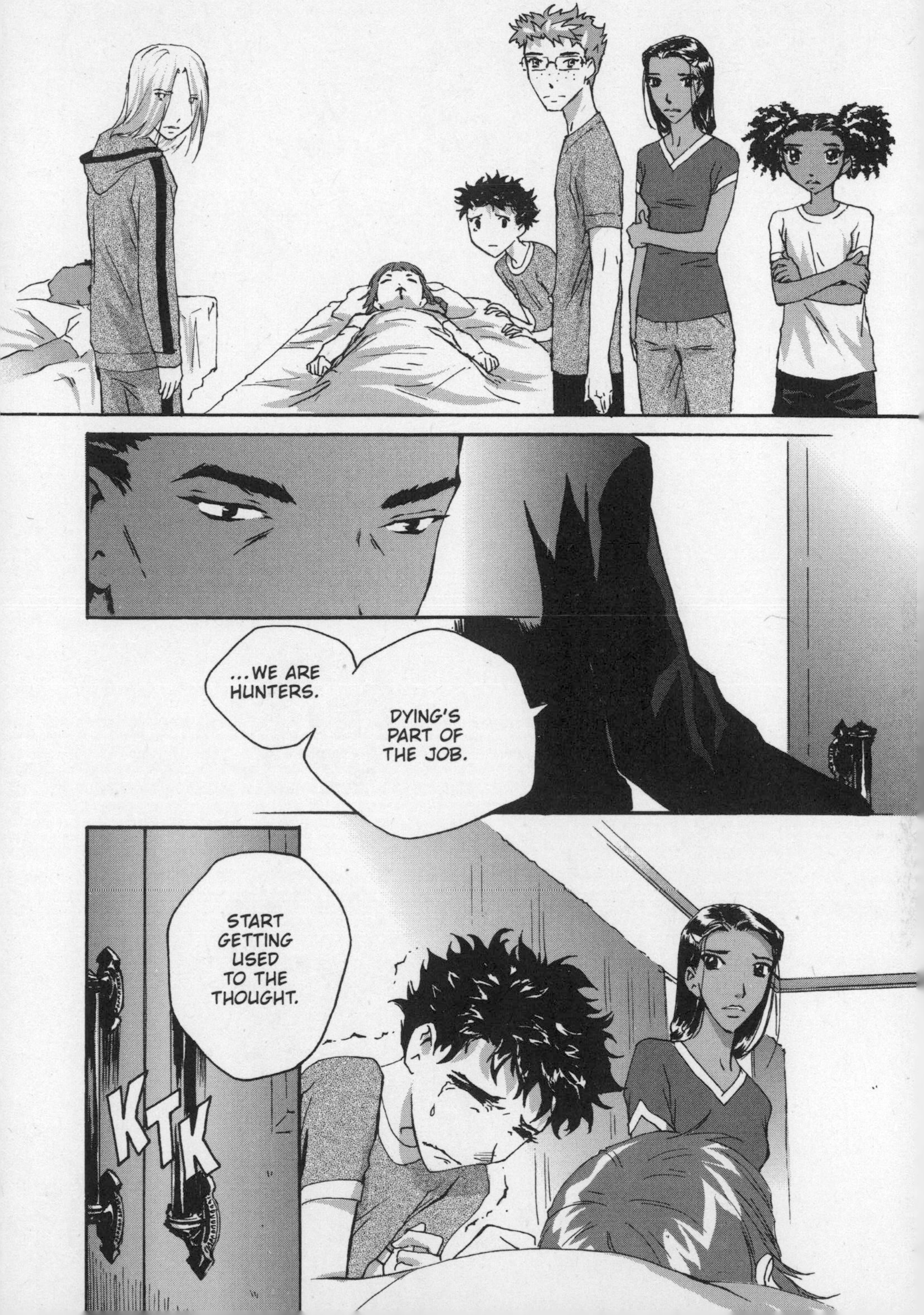
...WE ARE HUNTERS.
DYING'S PART OF THE JOB.
START GETTING USED TO THE THOUGHT.
KTK

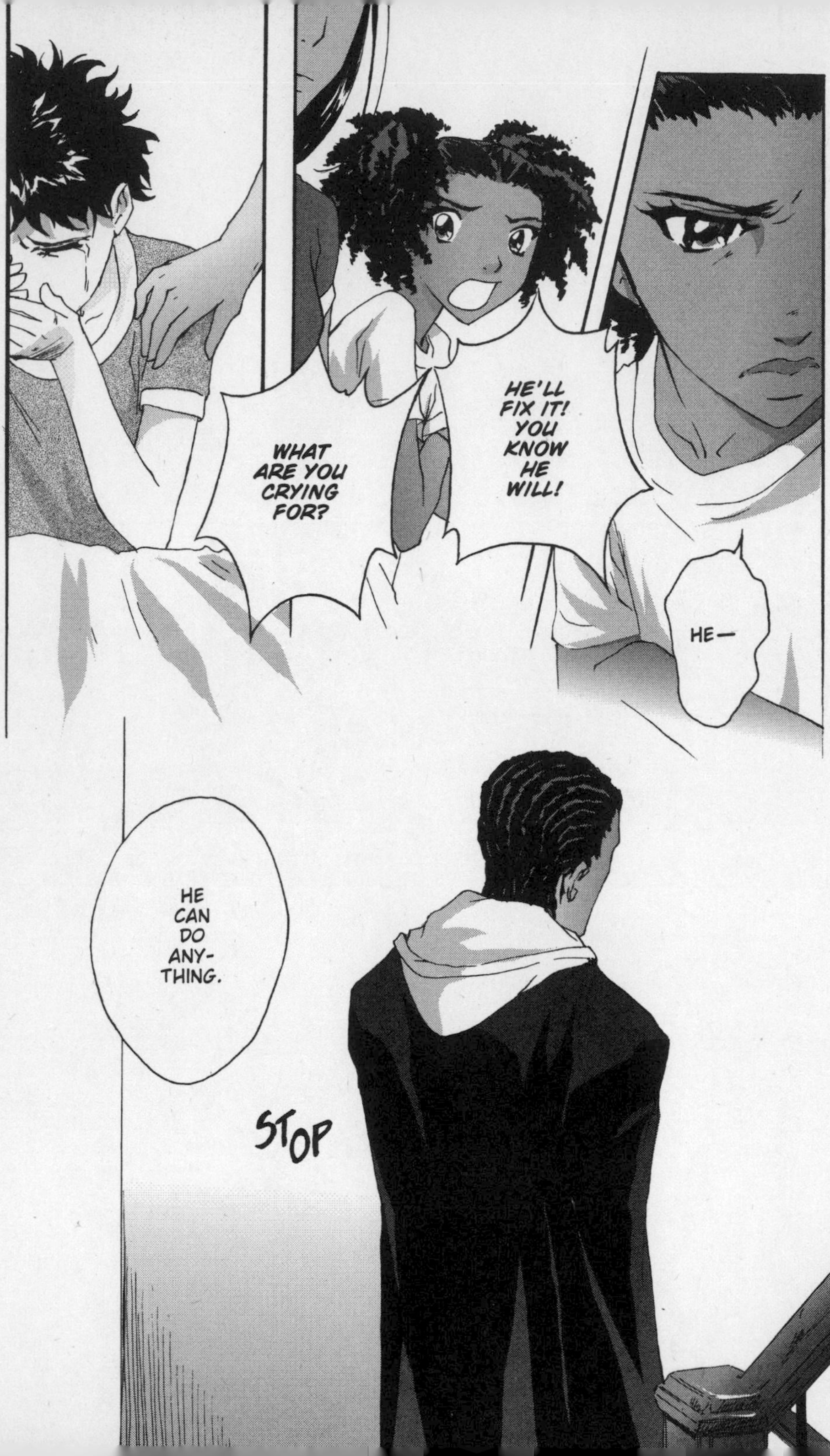
WHAT ARE YOU CRYING FOR?
HE'LL FIX IT! YOU KNOW HE WILL!
HE—
HE CAN DO ANY-THING.
STOP

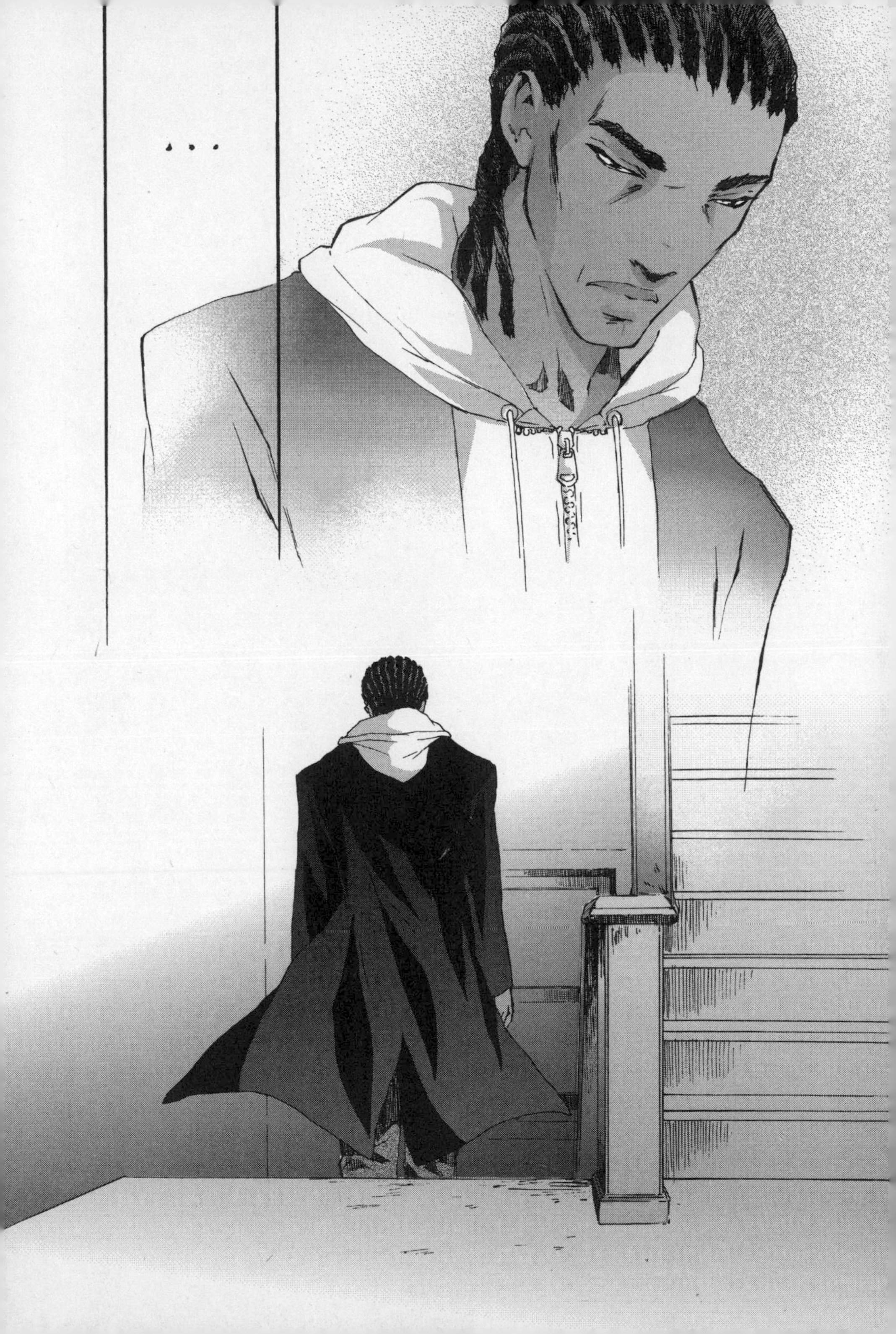
...

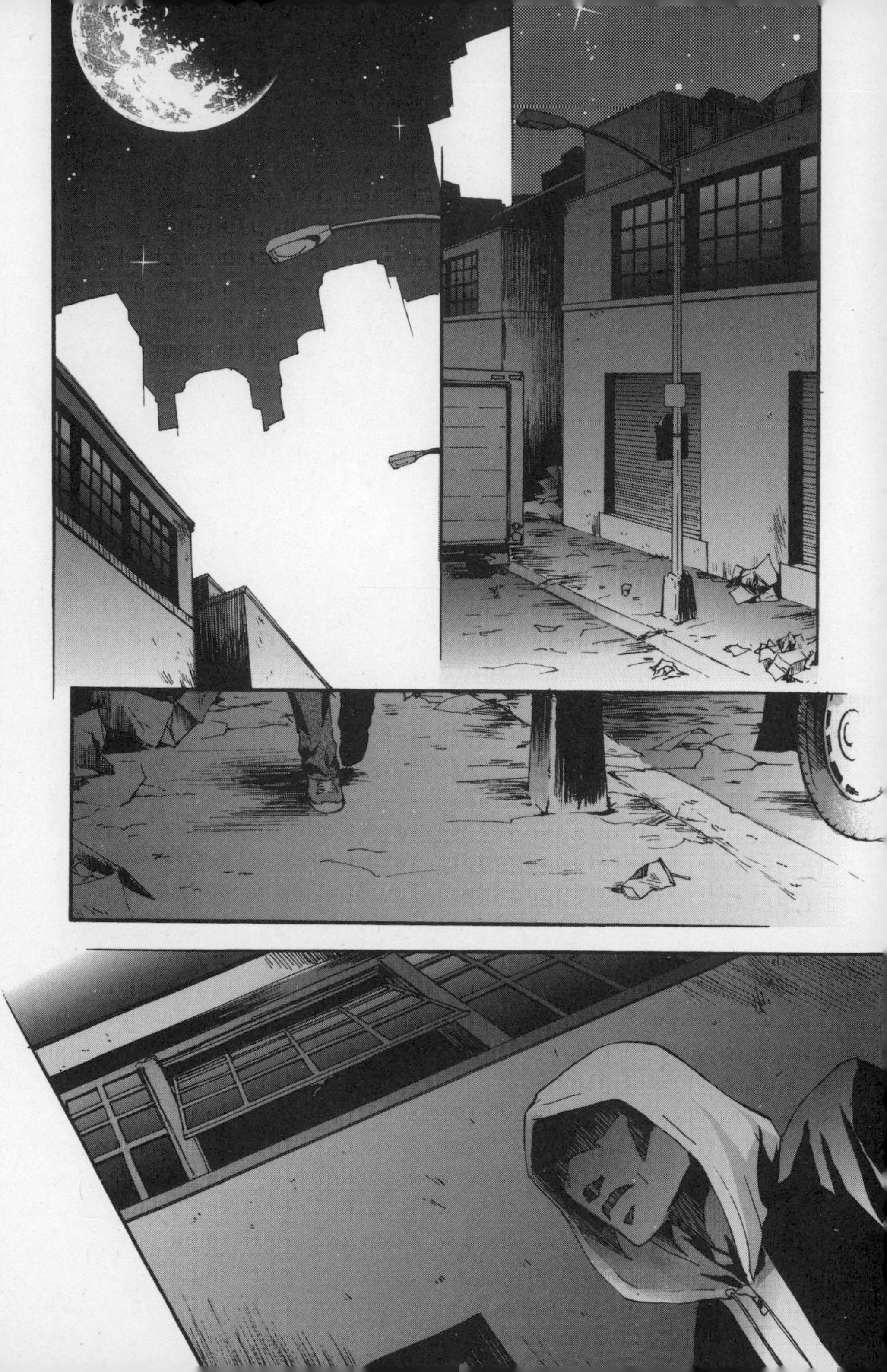

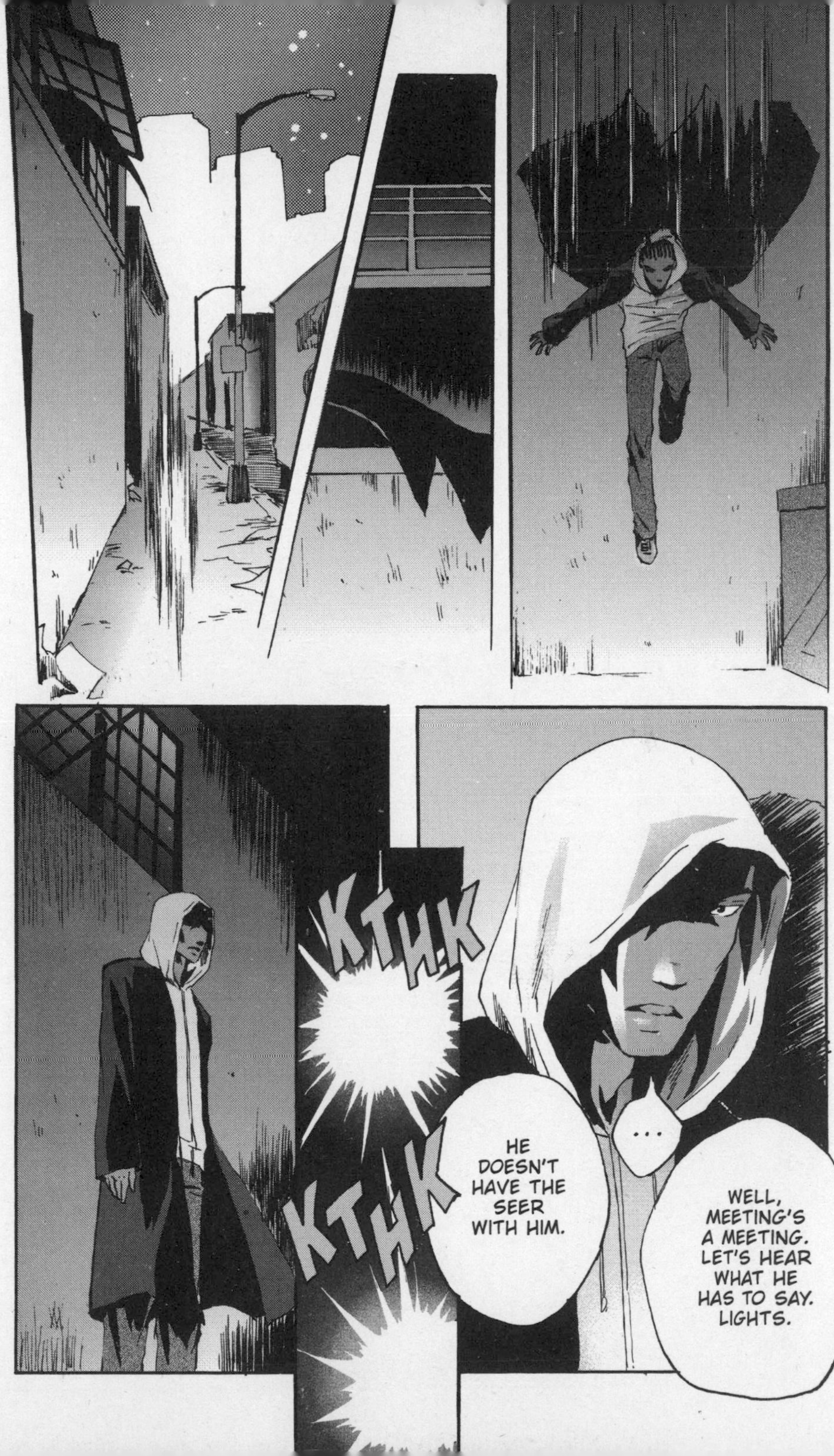
KTHK
KTHK
HE DOESN'T HAVE THE SEER WITH HIM.
...
WELL, MEETING'S A MEETING. LET'S HEAR WHAT HE HAS TO SAY. LIGHTS.

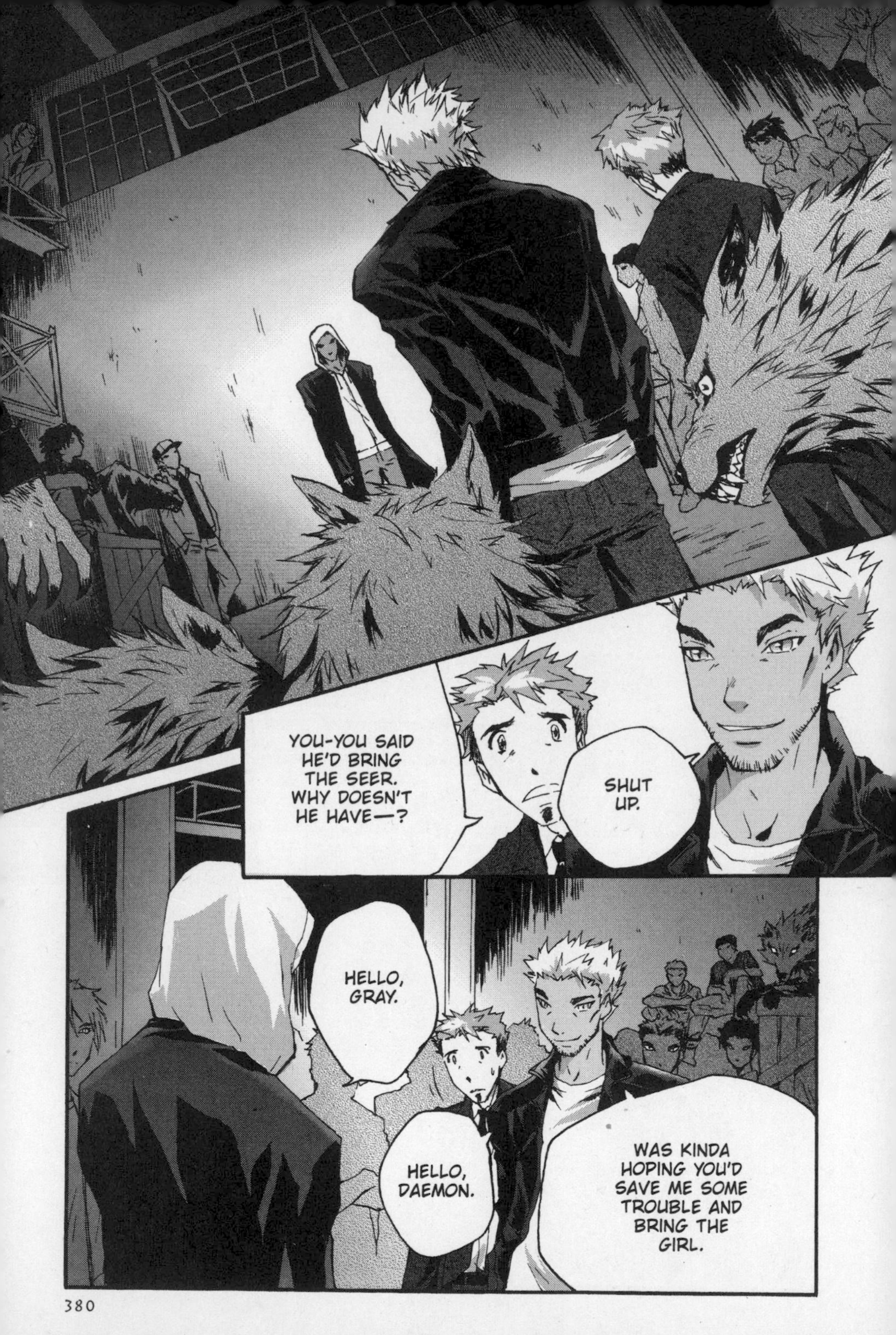
YOU-YOU SAID HE'D BRING THE SEER. WHY DOESN'T HE HAVE—?
SHUT UP.
HELLO, GRAY.
HELLO, DAEMON.
WAS KINDA HOPING YOU'D SAVE ME SOME TROUBLE AND BRING THE GIRL.

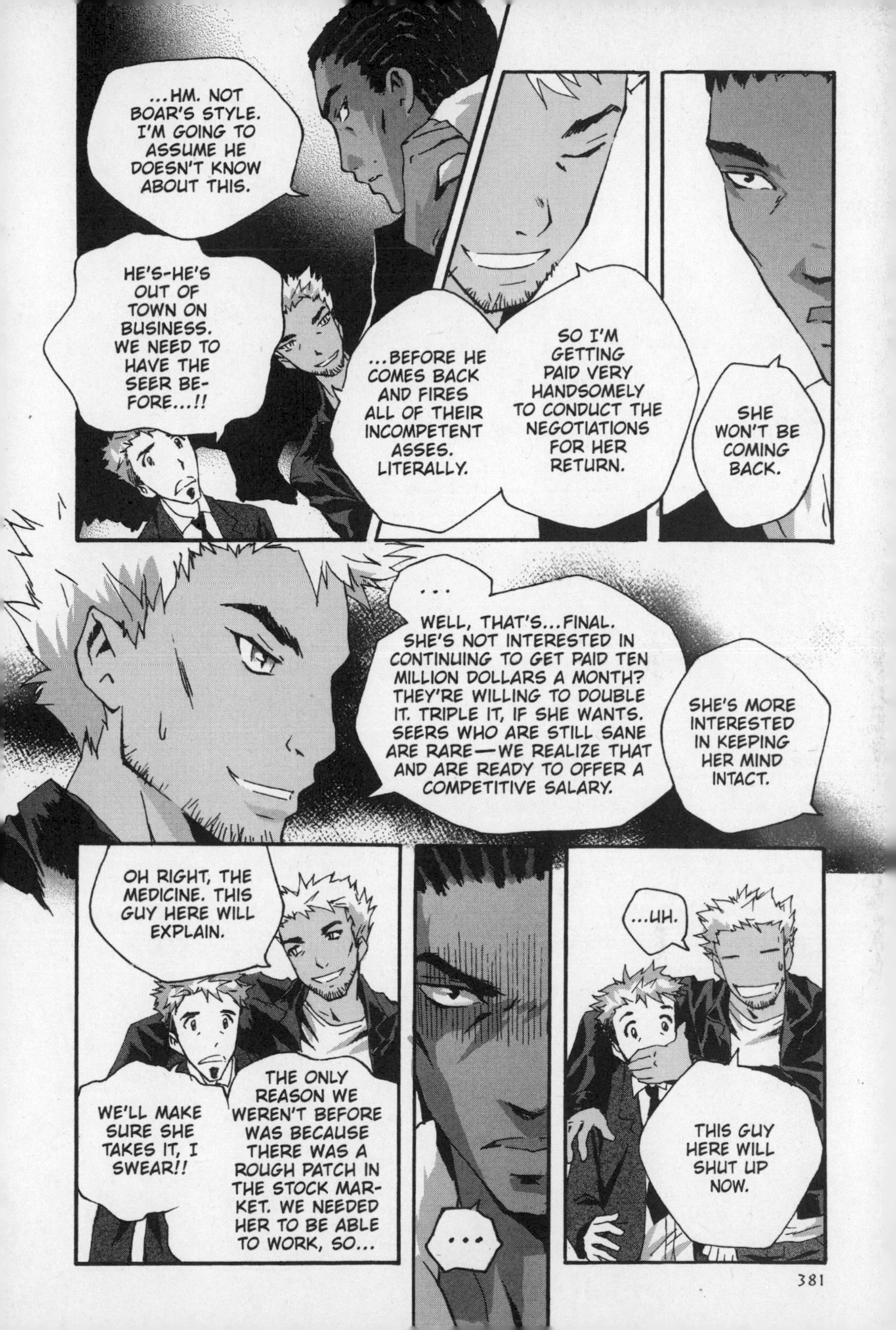
...HM. NOT BOAR'S STYLE. I'M GOING TO ASSUME HE DOESN'T KNOW ABOUT THIS.
HE'S-HE'S OUT OF TOWN ON BUSINESS. WE NEED TO HAVE THE SEER BE-FORE...!!
...BEFORE HE COMES BACK AND FIRES ALL OF THEIR INCOMPETENT ASSES. LITERALLY.
SO I'M GETTING PAID VERY HANDSOMELY TO CONDUCT THE NEGOTIATIONS FOR HER RETURN.
SHE WON'T BE COMING BACK.
...
WELL, THAT'S...FINAL. SHE'S NOT INTERESTED IN CONTINUING TO GET PAID TEN MILLION DOLLARS A MONTH? THEY'RE WILLING TO DOUBLE IT. TRIPLE IT, IF SHE WANTS. SEERS WHO ARE STILL SANE ARE RARE—WE REALIZE THAT AND ARE READY TO OFFER A COMPETITIVE SALARY.
SHE'S MORE INTERESTED IN KEEPING HER MIND INTACT.
OH RIGHT, THE MEDICINE. THIS GUY HERE WILL EXPLAIN.
WE'LL MAKE SURE SHE TAKES IT, I SWEAR!!
THE ONLY REASON WE WEREN'T BEFORE WAS BECAUSE THERE WAS A ROUGH PATCH IN THE STOCK MAR-KET. WE NEEDED HER TO BE ABLE TO WORK, SO...
...
...UH.
THIS GUY HERE WILL SHUT UP NOW.

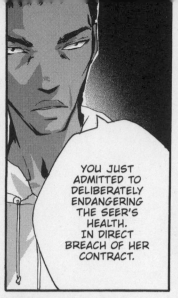

YOU JUST ADMITTED TO DELIBERATELY ENDANGERING THE SEER'S HEALTH. IN DIRECT BREACH OF HER CONTRACT.

THIS MEETING'S DONE.

WHOA, HEY! WAIT!

COME ON, MAN, HEAR ME OUT! I STILL GOT IMPORTANT THINGS...

KCHK

...TO SAY.

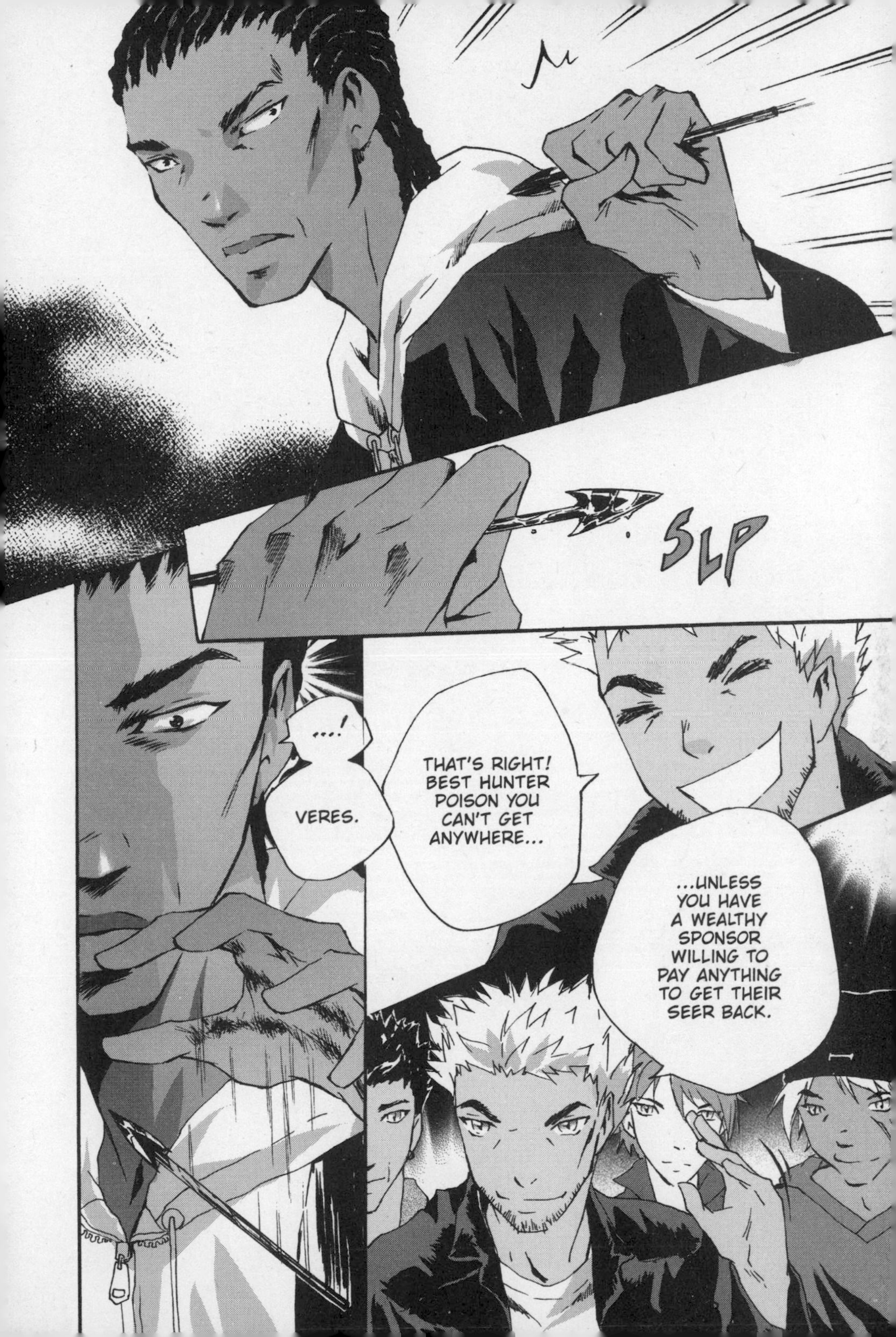
SLP
...!
VERES.
THAT'S RIGHT! BEST HUNTER POISON YOU CAN'T GET ANYWHERE...
...UNLESS YOU HAVE A WEALTHY SPONSOR WILLING TO PAY ANYTHING TO GET THEIR SEER BACK.

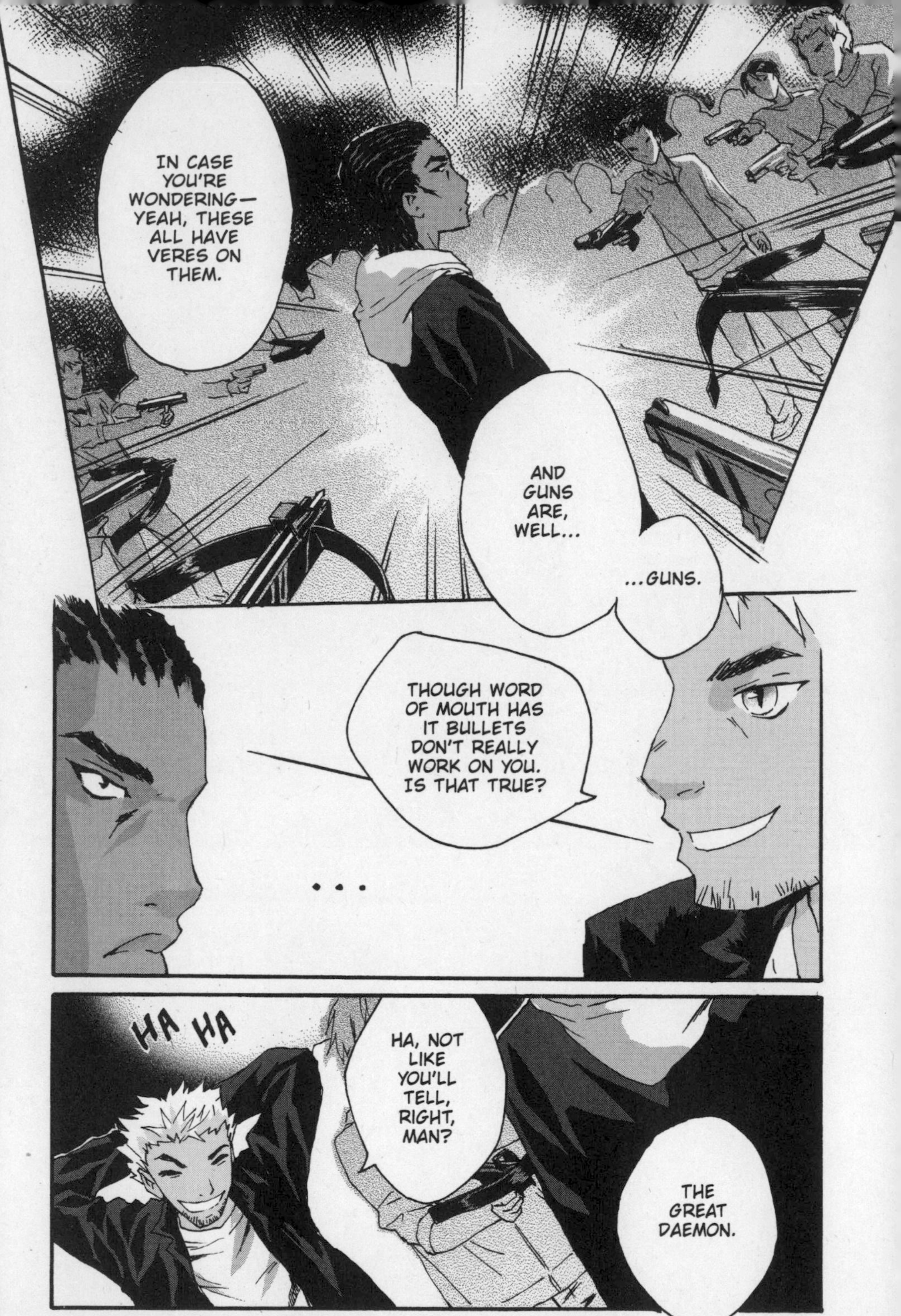
IN CASE YOU'RE WONDERING—YEAH, THESE ALL HAVE VERES ON THEM.
AND GUNS ARE, WELL...
...GUNS.
THOUGH WORD OF MOUTH HAS IT BULLETS DON'T REALLY WORK ON YOU. IS THAT TRUE?
...
HA HA
HA, NOT LIKE YOU'LL TELL, RIGHT, MAN?
THE GREAT DAEMON.

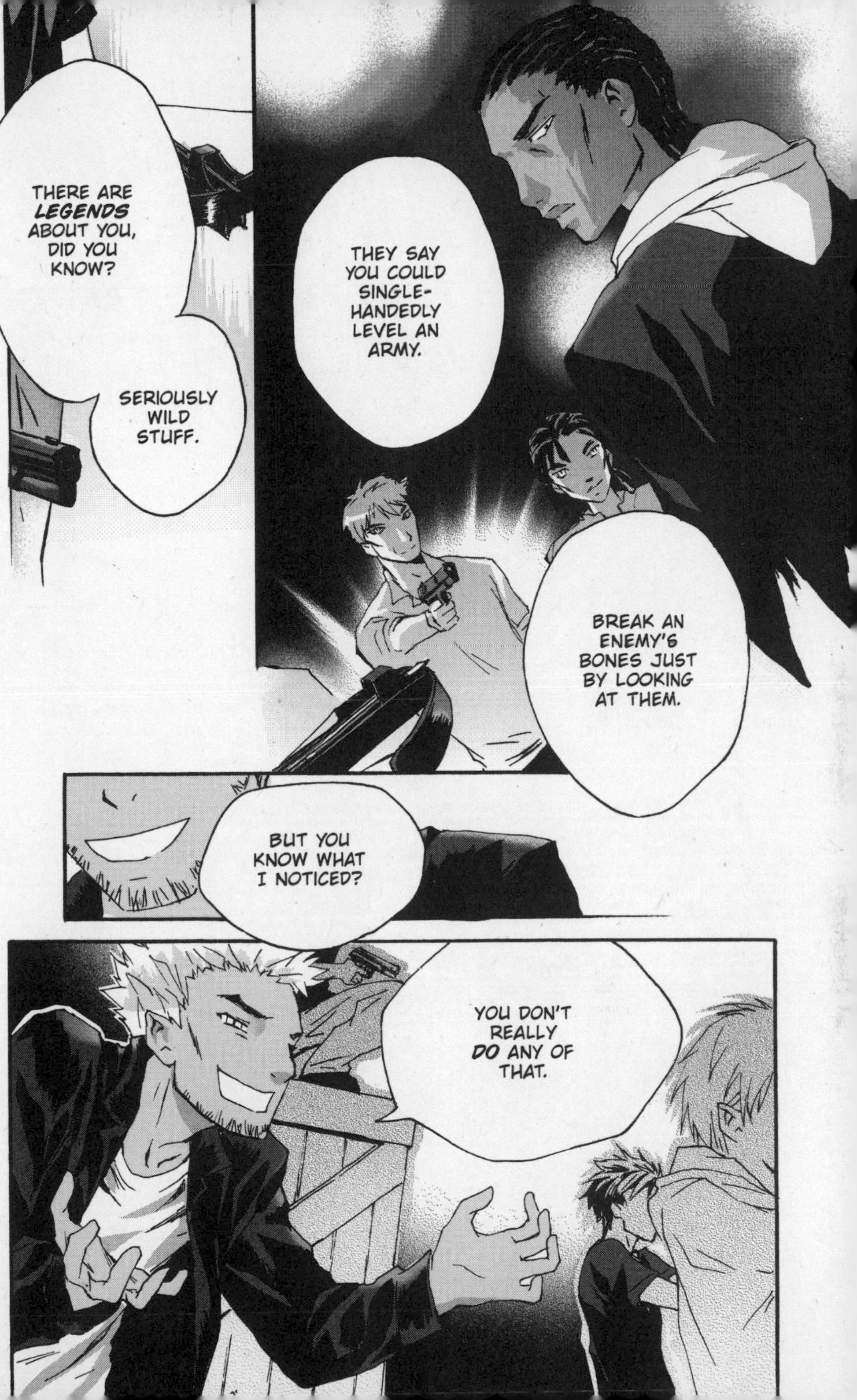
THERE ARE *LEGENDS* ABOUT YOU, DID YOU KNOW?
SERIOUSLY WILD STUFF.
THEY SAY YOU COULD SINGLE-HANDEDLY LEVEL AN ARMY.
BREAK AN ENEMY'S BONES JUST BY LOOKING AT THEM.
BUT YOU KNOW WHAT I NOTICED?
YOU DON'T REALLY *DO* ANY OF THAT.

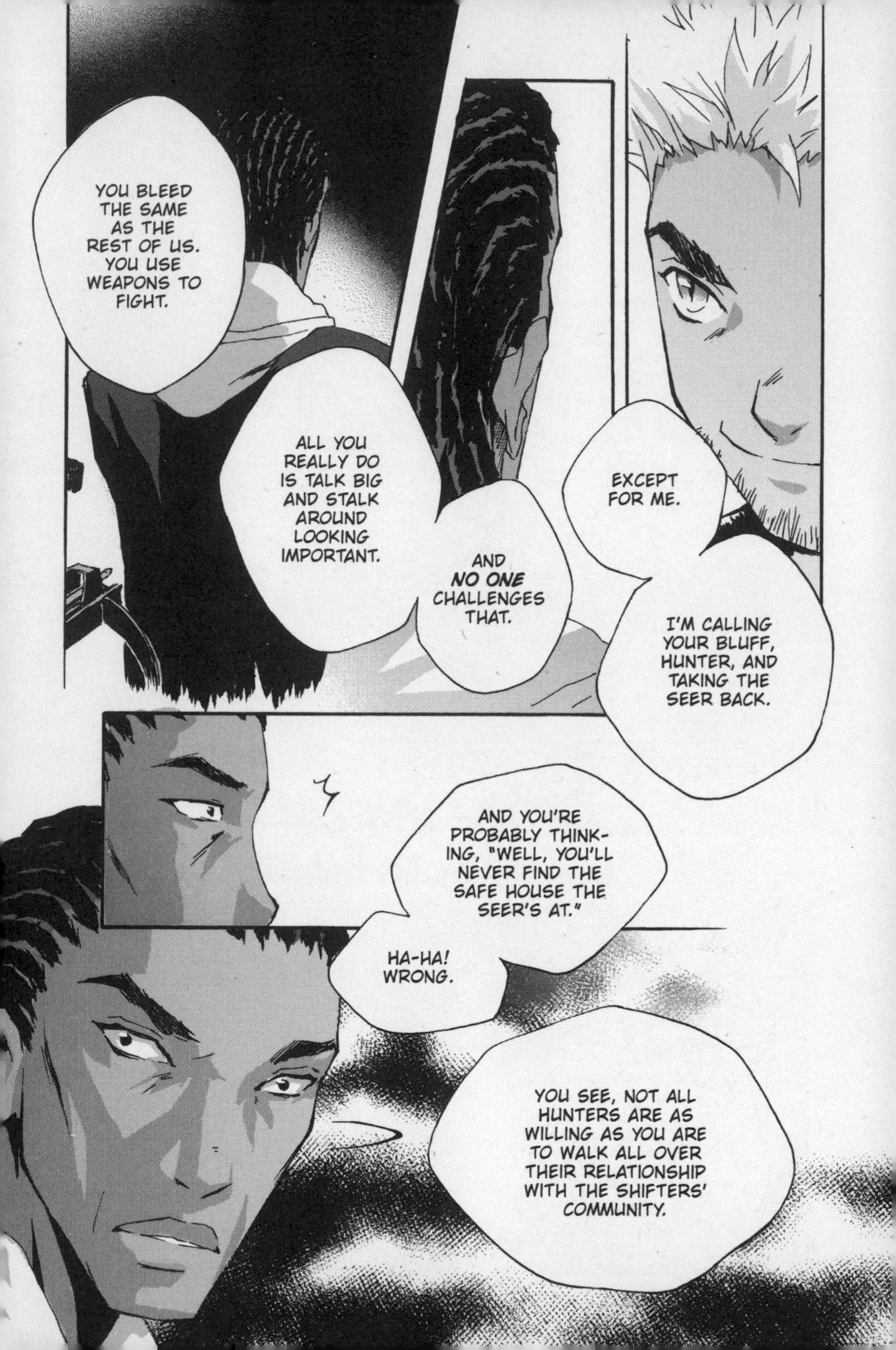
YOU BLEED THE SAME AS THE REST OF US. YOU USE WEAPONS TO FIGHT.
ALL YOU REALLY DO IS TALK BIG AND STALK AROUND LOOKING IMPORTANT.
AND *NO ONE* CHALLENGES THAT.
EXCEPT FOR ME.
I'M CALLING YOUR BLUFF, HUNTER, AND TAKING THE SEER BACK.
AND YOU'RE PROBABLY THINKING, "WELL, YOU'LL NEVER FIND THE SAFE HOUSE THE SEER'S AT."
HA-HA! WRONG.
YOU SEE, NOT ALL HUNTERS ARE AS WILLING AS YOU ARE TO WALK ALL OVER THEIR RELATIONSHIP WITH THE SHIFTERS' COMMUNITY.

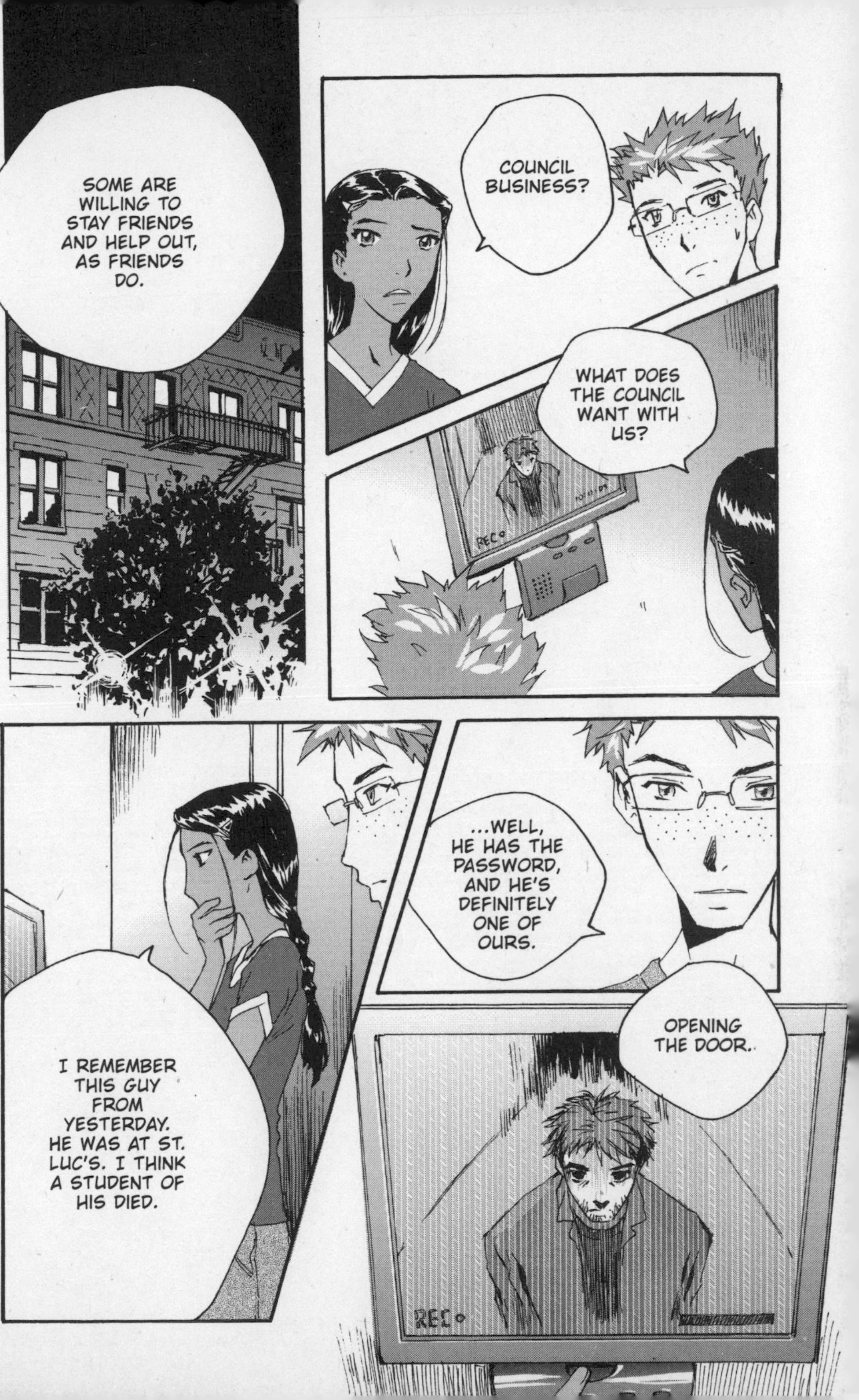
SOME ARE WILLING TO STAY FRIENDS AND HELP OUT, AS FRIENDS DO.
COUNCIL BUSINESS?
WHAT DOES THE COUNCIL WANT WITH US?
I REMEMBER THIS GUY FROM YESTERDAY. HE WAS AT ST. LUC'S. I THINK A STUDENT OF HIS DIED.
...WELL, HE HAS THE PASSWORD, AND HE'S DEFINITELY ONE OF OURS.
OPENING THE DOOR.

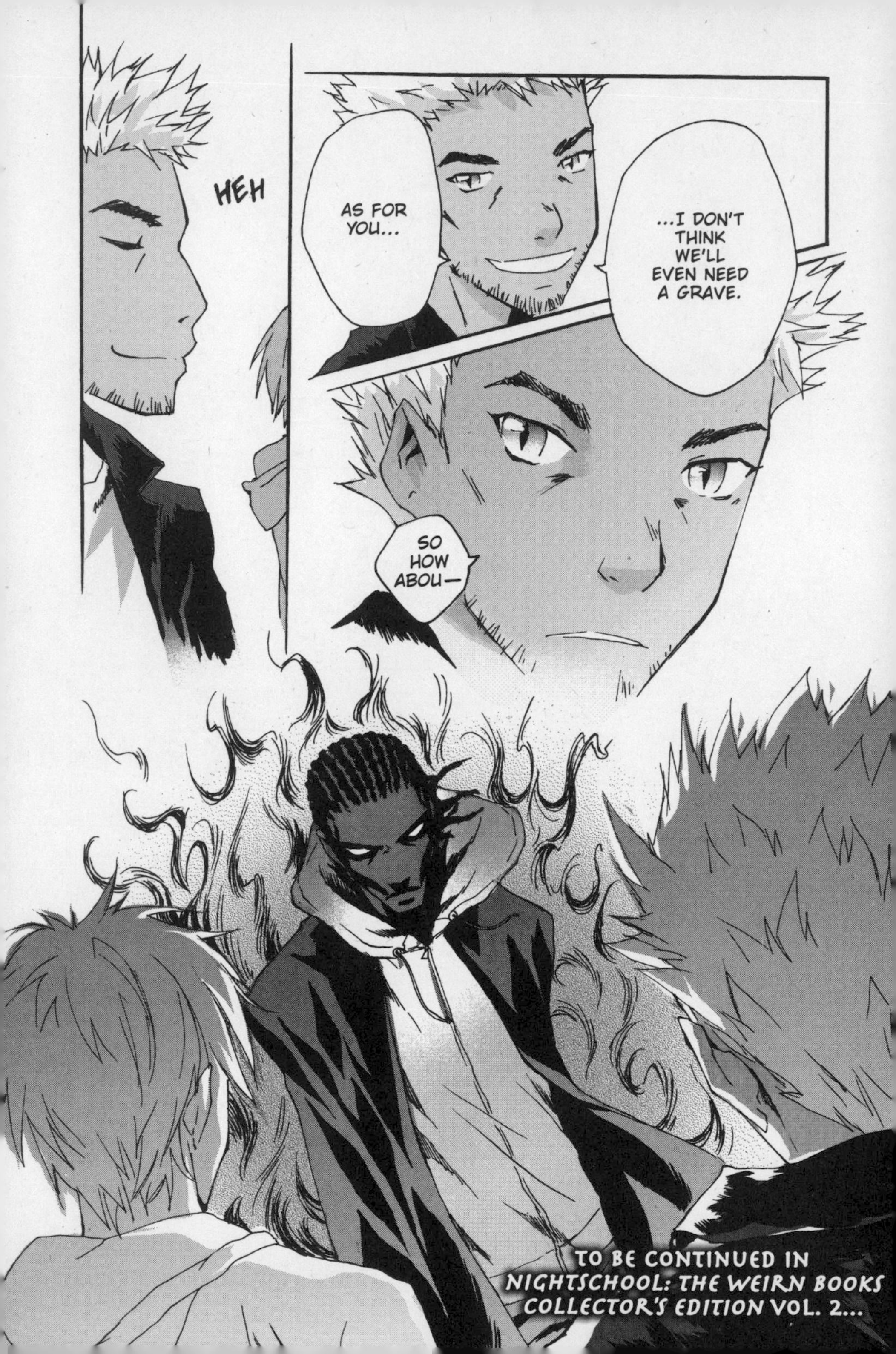
HEH
AS FOR YOU...
...I DON'T THINK WE'LL EVEN NEED A GRAVE.
SO HOW ABOU—
TO BE CONTINUED IN NIGHTSCHOOL: THE WEIRN BOOKS COLLECTOR'S EDITION VOL. 2...

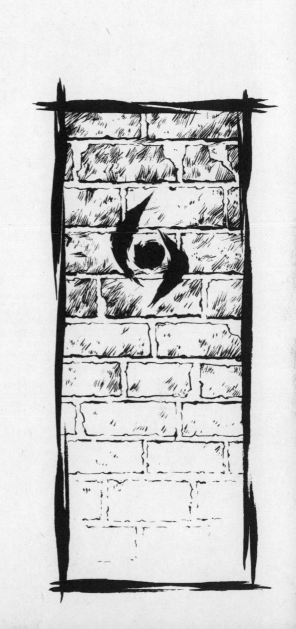

END OF VOLUME 2!

HOORAY!! (PLEASE DON'T HIT ME FOR THE CLIFFHANGER; I BRUISE EASILY AND CRY LIKE A GIRL...)
ON TO THE BONUS COMIC! NOW, I WAS GOING TO VOLUNTEER MY CHARACTERS FOR THIS AGAIN...

...BUT THEY WERE TOO SMART FOR THAT.

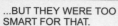
ON VACATION!
(look it up)
DICTIONARY

SO I AM GOING TO DISTRACT YOU WITH A STORY WHILE I PLOT MY REVE... I MEAN, THE THIRD VOLUME.

RECENTLY, I GAVE MYSELF A VERY SHORT HAIRCUT.

SNIP SNIP
←12"!

IT WAS PRETTY FUNNY.

HEY, SIS.

AAAA

I HAD TO GO TO A STYLIST TO FIX IT.

WITH MY NEWLY BUTCHERED HAIR, I WAS OFF ON A WHIRLWIND TRIP TO DO PANELS AND SIGNINGS AT...

TEXAS LIBRARY ASSOCIATION CONFERENCE!
→ HOUSTON, TX
ROCHESTER TEEN BOOK FESTIVAL!
FAIRPORT, NY ←

BOTH WERE AMAZING EVENTS, SO MANY COOL PEOPLE AND AWESOME FANS!! THANK YOU!!

...BUT THE TRAVEL IN BETWEEN WAS FULL OF MISHAPS AND DISASTERS:

MY PLANE TO ROCHESTER WAS CANCELED

THE NEXT FLIGHT IS WHEN?! ...BUT I'LL MISS ALL MY PANELS!!

THE AIRLINE MISPLACED MY LUGGAGE
...a towel is almost like pjs...

...erk, cel battery is almost dead...

I FORGOT MY COAT IN SUNNY HOUSTON AND SHIVERED BACK UP NORTH...

BRR!

AND THAT'S WHEN IT HAPPENED... WAY AFTER MIDNIGHT ON A RAINY FRIDAY NIGHT.

I CHECKED INTO A TEMPORARY HOTEL AFTER WE SOMEWHAT SALVAGED THE TRAVEL PLANS FOR THE NEXT DAY (THANK YOU, KATE!!).

TIRED AND COLD, I GOT INTO AN EMPTY ELEVATOR, WHEN SUDDENLY!

WAIT, EXCUSE ME!

SHE INTRODUCED HERSELF AS THE NIGHT MANAGER AND SAID MY ROOM WAS ON A NEW FLOOR.
THE WAY TO GET THERE WAS TRICKY, SO SHE WOULD SHOW ME.

SHE LOOKED DIRECTLY AT ME AS SHE SPOKE, SMILING; AND ALL I COULD DO WAS STARE, BECAUSE...

...HER EYES WERE BRIGHT YELLOW, WITH TINY HINTS OF ORANGE.
SHE TOOK ME UP TO THE TOP FLOOR... WHERE THERE WAS ANOTHER ELEVATOR, OFF TO THE SIDE.
VNNN
IT ONLY WENT UP ONE FLOOR (THOUGH IT FELT LIKE IT PASSED SEVERAL).
...IT OPENED ON THE WRONG SIDE.
FSSS
!
SHE UNLOCKED MY ROOM WITH HER MASTER KEY, AND I REALIZED THAT THE ROOM WAS...
...IN THE ATTIC.
DARKNESS AND RAIN WERE SCRAPING AT THE SLANTED WINDOWS.
THE NIGHT MANAGER LOOKED AT ME WITH HER YELLOW EYES, SMILING, FRIENDLY.
I'M JUST DOWNSTAIRS IF THERE ARE PROBLEMS.
ENJOY YOUR STAY.
CLICK
...
THERE WERE NO VAMPIRES HIDING IN THIS STRANGE ROOM (ALAS... I CHECKED), AND I DIDN'T SEE HER AGAIN THE NEXT MORNING.
WOW.
BUT THE SURREAL MAGIC OF THOSE FEW MINUTES STAYED WITH ME FOR MONTHS AFTER.
I WONDER IF THEY KNOW I'M MAKING A BOOK ABOUT THEM...
HEE.
I FELT LIKE I BRUSHED AGAINST THE VERY WORLD I WAS WRITING ABOUT.

Now, without further ado, I will introduce the awesomeness that is the next two pages!! Many *Nightschool* readers are also talented artists, so we ran a **Fan Art Contest** to show you what they can do. It was incredibly difficult to pick only eight from all the great art we received, so we ended up with several runners-up:

Emily Adams **Julien Faille** **Kaitlin Gagnon** **Sarah Miller** **Karen Yen**

Thank you!! We hope you enjoy your prizes :).

And finally... *drumroll* The contest winners are...!

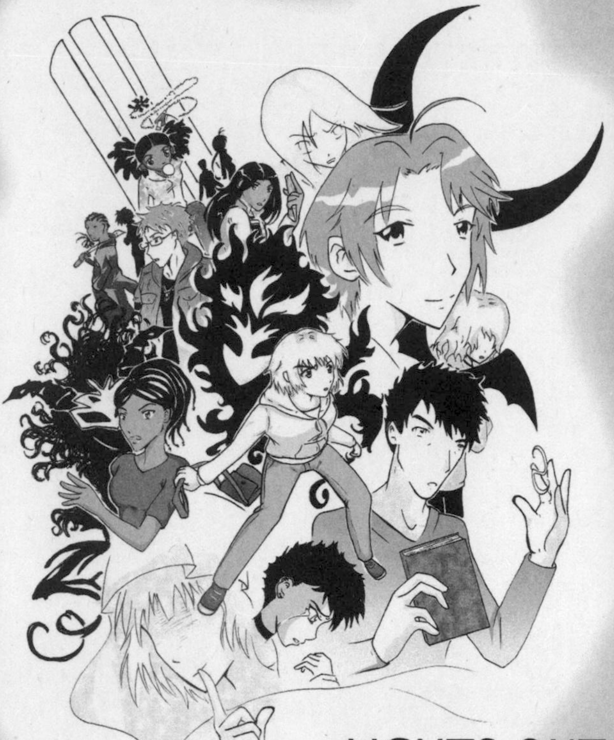

LIGHTS OUT
by ***Alcina Wong***
(I-I think half the characters are here... IMPRESSIVE)

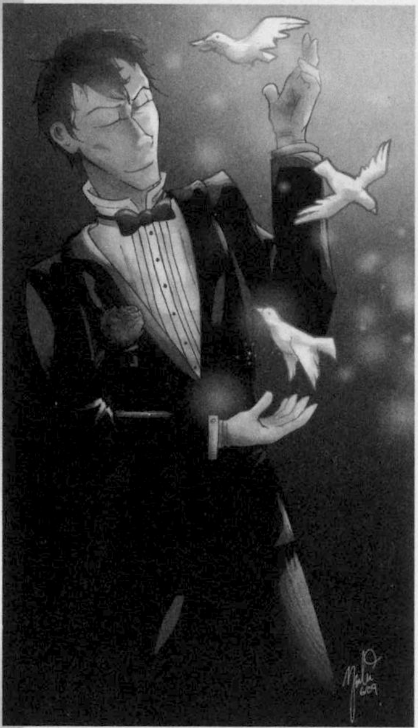

by ***Morgan Zamboni***
(Yay, Mr. Roi, looking sharp in a suit!!)

by ***Omnaya Omar***
(The rose in the original is a beautiful blue)

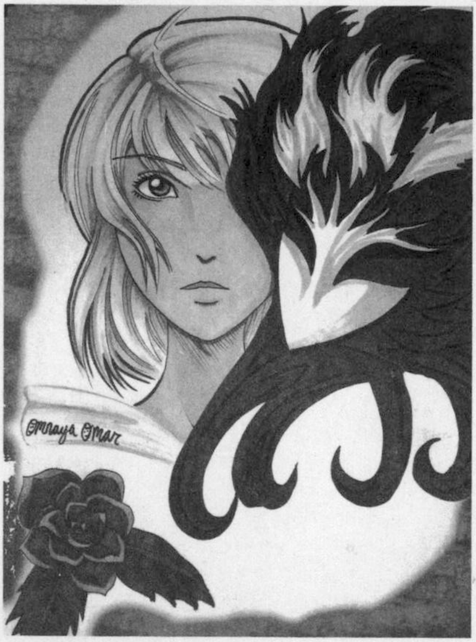
Omnaya Omar

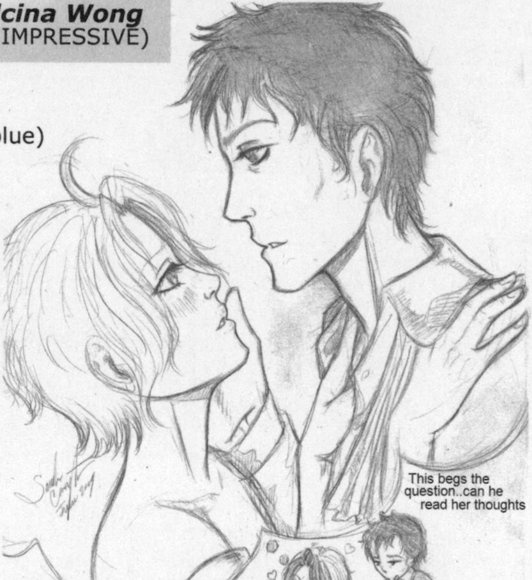
This begs the question..can he read her thoughts
Work place dating may = can of worms
Workplace Fanatasies are an entirely different matter

by ***Sarah Covington***
(Wakey wakey, Sarah :D)

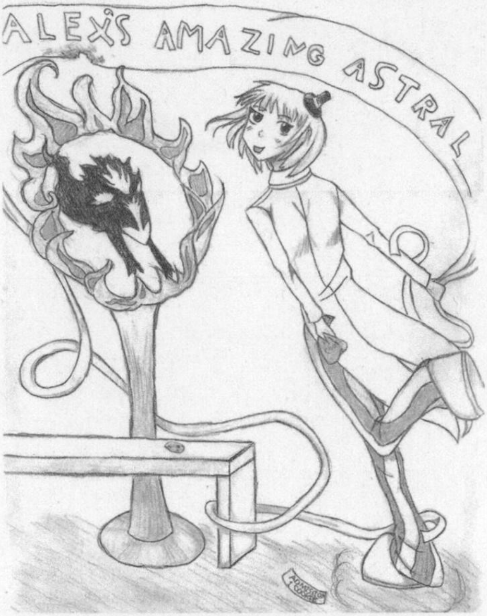
ALEX'S AMAZING ASTRAL

by ***Merritt Zamboni***
(Alex's Amazing Astral!! Too right! <3)

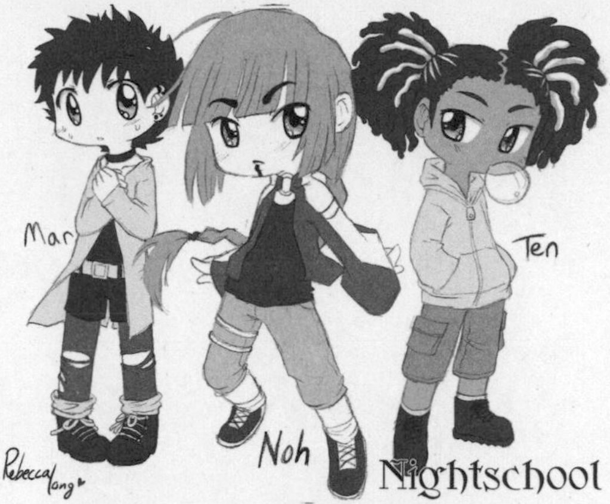
Mar
Ten
Noh
Nightschool
Rebecca Long

by ***Rebecca Long***
(SO. CUTE.)

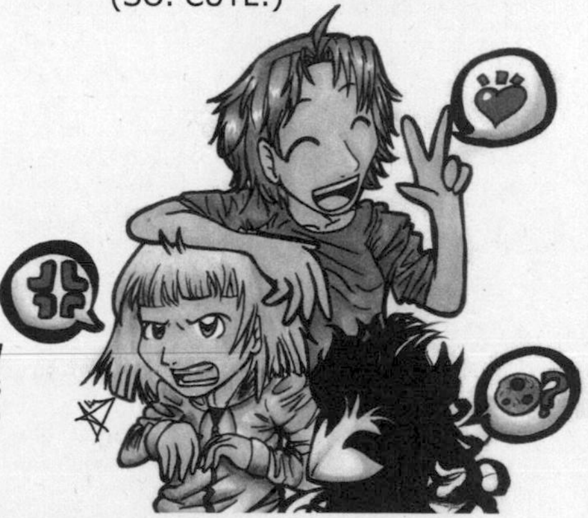

by ***Starlia Prichard***
(The family! Personalities captured *perfectly*.)

by ***Kaia Dumoulin***
(Originally in color, and SO beautiful...)

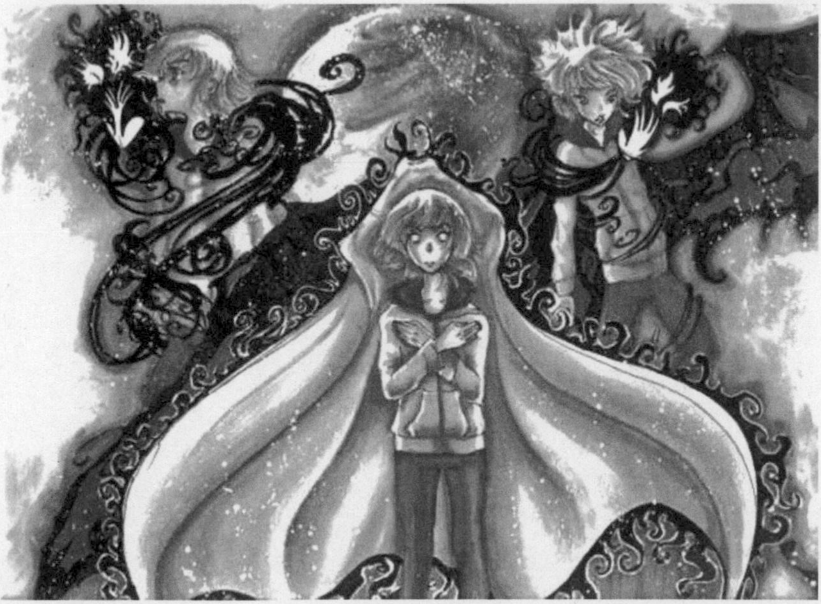

Nightschool
The Weirn Books
Collector's Edition 1

SVETLANA CHMAKOVA

Toning Artist: Dee DuPuy

Lettering: JuYoun Lee

This book is a work of fiction. Names, characters, places, and incidents are the product of the author's imagination or are used fictitiously. Any resemblance to actual events, locales, or persons, living or dead, is coincidental.

Yen Press
150 West 30th Street, 19th Floor
New York, NY 10001

Visit us at yenpress.com
facebook.com/yenpress
twitter.com/yenpress
yenpress.tumblr.com
instagram.com/yenpress

First Yen Press Edition: May 2020

Yen Press is an imprint of Yen Press, LLC.
The Yen Press name and logo are trademarks of Yen Press, LLC.

The publisher is not responsible for websites (or their content) that are not owned by the publisher.

Library of Congress Control Number: 2020935039

ISBN: 978-1-9753-1289-3

10 9 8 7 6 5 4 3 2 1

WOR

Printed in the United States of America